INCA MOON

Qori Qoyllur is the daughter of a humble fisherman. She doesn't know the beaches she calls home are part of the mighty Inca Empire. Innocence is shattered when an assassin finds her father, and a terrible secret is revealed. Summoned by mysterious nobles who claim friendship, and beset by unknown enemies, Qori goes to the holy city of Cuzco in search of vengeance. Thus begins a journey into the secret heart of a vast land where demigods rule millions in one of the most majestic, brutal, and tragic empires of the ancient world.

Inca Moon is a tale of courage and intrigue, ruthless ambition, and devotion betrayed. With Qori we travel through deserts, mountains, and jungles, face armies and assassins, experience the pomp and rituals of a vanished world. We follow her through tangled loves and loyalties, share emotions and personal tragedies, see her rise to become an Inca healer and, covertly, a special agent to the emperor. On this journey we meet great lords and ladies, heroes and scoundrels:

Reclusive Lord Atoq is an elegant man who directs the imperial spy web from his country estate. With the old emperor on his deathbed and conspiracy threatening to plunge the empire into civil war, Lord Atoq must send his elite agents into peril. Qori loves him like a father, but what secrets is he holding back?

Lady Sisa is breathtakingly beautiful. Men want her; women envy her. Why is she so feared?

Tanta Karwa is a healer to nobility and Qori's beloved mother-in-law. She knows the truth but cannot speak it.

He who rules the jungle, Condin Savana, Wizard of the East, sees Qori's destiny. He will arm her, but he will not interfere with fate.

These and other vivid characters inhabit the world of Qori Qoyllur. Based on old Spanish accounts and modern findings, this novel brings the Inca Empire alive with gripping authenticity.

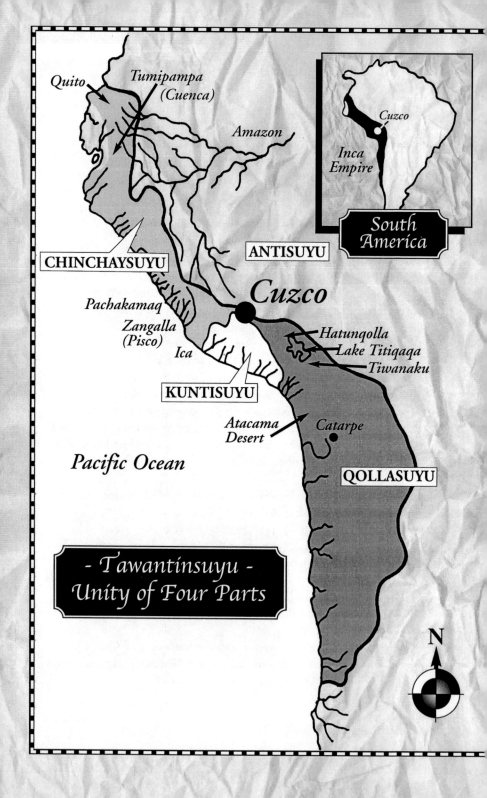

Quito

Tumipampa
(Cuenca)

Amazon

CHINCHAYSUYU

Pachakamaq

Zangalla
(Pisco)

Ica

KUNTISUYU

Pacific Ocean

Atacama
Desert

ANTISUYU

Cuzco

Hatunqolla
Lake Titiqaqa
Tiwanaku

Catarpe

QOLLASUYU

Cuzco

Inca
Empire

South
America

- Tawantinsuyu -
Unity of Four Parts

N

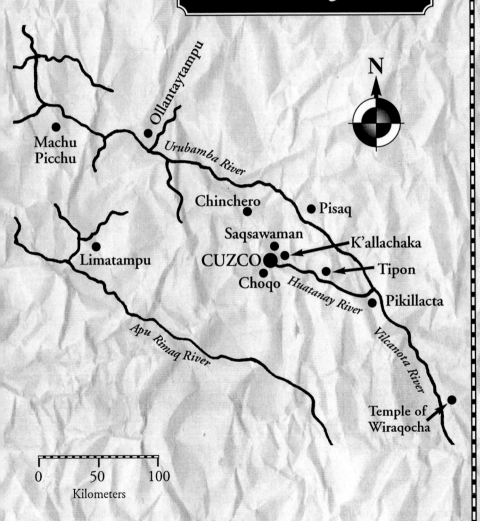

Map of the
Cuzco Region

N

Machu
Picchu

Ollantaytampu

Urubamba River

Chinchero

Pisaq

Saqsawaman

K'allachaka

CUZCO

Tipon

Limatampu

Choqo

Huatanay River

Pikillacta

Apu Rimaq River

Vilcanota River

Temple of
Wiraqocha

0   50   100
Kilometers

© Copyright 2001 Patrick Carmichael. All rights reserved.

No part of this publication may be reproduced, stored in a retrieval system, or transmitted, in any form or by any means, electronic, mechanical, photocopying, recording, or otherwise, without the written prior permission of the author.

Printed in Victoria, Canada

Cover illustration: Adapted from a 17th century drawing by Felipe Guamán Poma de Ayala

Cover design and layout: Scott Mushens

Back cover photograph of author: William Evans

National Library of Canada Cataloguing in Publication Data

Carmichael, Patrick Henry, 1952-
  Inca moon
  ISBN 1-55212-833-4
  I. Title.
PS8555.A752I52 2001   C813'.6   C2001-911017-0
PR9199.4.C37I52 2001

TRAFFORD

This book was published *on-demand* in cooperation with Trafford Publishing.
On-demand publishing is a unique process and service of making a book available for retail sale to the public taking advantage of on-demand manufacturing and Internet marketing.
On-demand publishing includes promotions, retail sales, manufacturing, order fulfilment, accounting and collecting royalties on behalf of the author.

Suite 6E, 2333 Government St., Victoria, B.C. V8T 4P4, CANADA

Phone	250-383-6864	Toll-free	1-888-232-4444 (Canada & US)
Fax	250-383-6804	E-mail	sales@trafford.com

Web site   www.trafford.com   TRAFFORD PUBLISHING IS A DIVISION OF TRAFFORD HOLDINGS LTD.
Trafford Catalogue #01-0233   www.trafford.com/robots/01-0233.html

10   9   8   7   6   5

For Elizabeth Anne

INCA MOON

translated from the original

Crónica de la India Qori Qoyllur

Archivo Nacional
Section: Viceroyalty of Peru
Document: #31/R17/210
Author: Oral Testimony of an Indian Woman
Scribe: Doña Catalina de Quintana

Note to Readers

The events in this book took place when the Inca Empire was vast and outwardly secure, the old emperor rested on his laurels, and the future Spanish invasion of 1532 was an undreamt nightmare. To Doña Catalina de Quintana we owe an enormous debt for painstakingly recording this account, though her chapter headings reveal she was horrified by many deeds candidly described herein, and felt obliged to warn Christian readers of exotic pagan rituals and intimate sins of the flesh. Nonetheless, she faithfully took dictation from its author, the Inca woman Qori Qoyllur, whose life in a world strange yet familiar is told in her own words. Of all the millions whose bones fill the Andean soil, the voice of Qori Qoyllur travels alone through time to tell a personal story, a story revealing the raw truth of a life in a world now vanished.

Pronunciations

For those who wish, the following examples will help approximate the sounds of foreign words in Inca Moon. Do not be thrown off by word appearance; if you sound it out you will come close. Generally, X's and J's are sounded h; I is ee; LL is ya; Q's are similar to hard K's; U is oo; and an apostrophe in a word is a glottal stop like that hidden in 'bottle' (bot'tle).

Achachi (a-cha-chee)	Illap'a (ee-yap a)	Q'enti (k en-tee)
akllawasi (ak-ya-wa-see)	Killa (kee-ya)	Qhari (kar-ee)
Aquixe (a-kee-hay)	khipu (kee-poo)	Qori (kor-ee)
ayllu (eye-yoo)	Oqllo (ok-yo)	Qoyllur (koy-yur)
Choque (cho-kay)	Pacaje (pa-ca-hay)	runa (roo-na)
Cuzco (cooz-co)	Pachakuti (Pa-cha-koo-tee)	siki (see-kee)
Ica (ee-ca)	puma (poo-ma)	Sisa (see-sa)
Illampu (ee-yam-poo)	Qolla (koy-ya)	ushnu (oosh-noo)

TABLE OF CONTENTS

I

In which the Events that begin this account Commence without hesitation.

The south wind drove us before white-fringed waves. Cold spray lashed my face. Another echoing boom of thunder rolled across the lake taking my breath with it. Now just four lengths behind us the lead boat swooped in like an eagle. Its flankers, slipping from sight and then rising on the crests, gained steadily. Lightning laced the darkness. I huddled in the stern of our reed boat watching the great sail of our pursuer coming up on the right. They're going to take us broadside, I thought. Capture is inevitable. Better to die by my own hand.

When the rain hit I looked back at the island of Taquile, only to see it vanish behind the gray-black veil racing toward us. I pulled my cloak tighter and drew my knees under my dress. Something whizzed past my ear. A shout jerked my head to the bow. The bowman gestured wildly over the side. He was alone, his mate gone. A second volley of sling stones whistled by, one catching the helmsman in the thigh, but he held on. The eagle boat, now two lengths out to our right, began closing. Pitching and rolling in their craft, the spearmen poised and the slingers reloaded.

I heard them shouting. They were Aymara speakers, but at first I couldn't tell from which nation. Qolla? I wondered, or Pacaje? No, Lupaqa. It doesn't matter; they're all against us. I slipped a hand under my shawl seeking Eagle Woman - my spirit-sister, and gripped the reassuring outline of her wooden tube. She lay snug against my breast, suspended from a cord at my neck. Her deadly secret can save me from the dishonor of capture, I thought. Be brave and unsheathe her now.

The squall hit with a blast that snapped our lines leaving the square reed sail flapping helplessly, pinned only to the top of the mast. The bowman leapt to catch a trailing rope, but the boat pitched sending him over the side. I grabbed a pole and held it out to the flailing arms in the water, struggling to keep my balance while the boat heaved and rolled sideways against the wind. The eagle boat fared little better, but her sail was intact and her crew worked frantically to lower it while the warriors huddled together. The wind threw a cold, cutting rain in my face, which then became a sheet-downpour of such intensity that the eagle boat turned to a shadowy blur, its flankers lost to sight.

"Take the steering oar," the helmsman shouted.

"I can't let go of this pole," I called back.

The rain bounced off the water blinding me. The man alongside tugged frantically, almost pulling me overboard. The stern swung out leaving us broadside to the wind, near capsizing. Suddenly the pole went slack. Nothing. He'd lost his grip. The lake was his bed now.

I lunged for the stern and took hold of the steering oar. "To the left," the helmsman shouted in my ear, "try to turn the bow." He scrambled to the mast, fighting to bring the sail under control.

The rain turned to stinging, bouncing hail, and in moments the craft filled with frozen pellets. The eagle boat slammed against us but no one tried to board, all hands there occupied bailing hailstones. I crouched over the oar, chin on my breast against the pounding, biting ice stones, unable to see more than arm's length. The helmsman appeared on his knees in front of me, frantically casting handfuls of ice over the side, but we sank lower under the weight while the waves rose around us.

An avalanche of water crashed over me tearing the oar from my grasp. The boat rolled, floundering sideways. Then a second wave hit and in a blink I found myself in the water, thrashing to reach the surface.

Reed boats float, at least until they become too sodden, and when I poked gasping to the surface I glimpsed the long bottom of our craft bobbing nearby. Beyond it the mast of the eagle boat wavered, and then above the din came shouts and the mast vanished. All this in an instant for the hail bounced off the water into my face, and then another wave plunged me under. Fighting hard I surfaced once more, but I could no longer see our boat or knew in which direction I faced. A hand thrust up beside me. I grabbed. My helmsman came up, sputtering and swallowing as much water as air.

"Kick your legs. Keep your head up," I shouted. He clung to me in terror pulling me down. "Your tunic," I yelled, "take it off." But he ignored me, eyes wild with fear. My wool clothes weren't made for swimming, and their weight alone was enough to drag me under. I took a deep breath and let my head sink, pulling the tupu pins and shaking loose from my heavy cloak and dress. Sandals, shoulder bag and bonnet went with them until I was naked, except for Eagle Woman who remained on a cord at my neck. When the weight of my clothes passed from me, so did the helmsman's grip. I surfaced gulping air, and for an instant I saw him clutching my empty dress. Then a wave passed over and he surfaced no more. I drifted alone with the night and the storm.

They can't swim, at least none I've ever seen. Though the people of Lake Titiqaqa pass their lives beside it and on it, the waters are too cold for play. Since I was raised on the shores of the ocean I could swim as well as a seal, though it was years since I'd done so, but once learned it's not forgotten. Now free and alone I floated easily on the swells. No cries for help, no wreckage, no sign of other survivors. The pursuit boats had met the same fate and vanished with their crews. The hail turned back to rain and slackened, but continued in a steady downpour. The worst of the squall passed but the night remained black.

Drift with the wind, I thought, and eventually you'll reach the north shore. But how long can I last in these frigid waters? My teeth chattered and I could no longer feel the water against my skin. I pressed my fingers together but felt nothing.

Swim! I ordered myself. Keep moving. You're the only one who knows the plans of the Aymara lords. The Emperor depends on you.

Even while forcing my limbs to move I knew I'd never reach shore. But there were reed banks at the shallow north end of the lake, and, it was said, even floating islands.

I had heard of the curious floating islands on the journey to Lake Titiqaqa. They are the domains of the Uru people, a nasty, brutish lot by all accounts, many of who hire themselves out as laborers on the mainland, though they stay apart and are despised by everyone. They speak an incomprehensible language, quite unrelated to any of the civilized dialects of the region, and no one knows where they came from, though they claim to have been there since creation.

Were the floating islands somewhere ahead, or was I in the wrong part of the lake?

For an eternity I thrashed in the icy water until my arms became too heavy to lift. I rolled on my back and tried kicking my feet, but they hardly responded. I wasn't even sure I was headed in the right direction. Only the rain and the swells and the blackness witnessed my struggle, and they didn't care. I envisioned myself as a tiny lamp flickering in a cold, black, cavernous room, and sputtering into blissful sleep. The face of my brother Qhari floated beside me. He held out his arms, beckoning me to rest. . . and drift with him. . . forever.

Something. . . something pressing against me. I was with Qhari now and didn't want to leave, warm and sliding off to sleep. I moved a hand to brush the thing away. It wouldn't leave. My eyelids fluttered open. Reeds? I floated over a bed of them, rising and falling with the swells. I clutched a handful and rolled over. A dense mass lay just ahead. With numb hands I pulled my way toward it, and with the last of my strength heaved my arms over the bank. Pressing my face against the spongy mass, I let my legs float free. The bank itself moved with the swells. I realized I had reached one of the floating islands, land of the despised Uru.

"Well, well, look at the garbage the lake washed up." The hostile voice spoke in the Lupaqa dialect. I looked up wearily. He towered over me, hands on his hips, legs set apart against the roll of the island.

There were other survivors, after all.

"There weren't any women in our boats," he said, "so you must have been in the one we chased. I thought I saw a woman just before we went over."

"Please," I said in Lupaqa, reaching a hand to him.

"Do you know how many men died trying to stop you? No, you evil bitch, there were no orders about taking prisoners."

He knelt over me and unfastened the mace hanging at his side. I dug my toes into the bank below water and slipped numb hands to my breast. Eagle Woman hung there, but I could scarcely move my fingers to unlock her stinger.

He raised his mace. "Now, this little fish goes back in the lake, forever."

Eagle Woman came apart, and with newfound strength I lunged upward, driving the stinger into his thigh. He yelled in surprise, covering the wound with his left hand, his right still raised and holding the mace. His eyes bulged, looking at me curiously, then his mouth fell open, tongue out, croaking for breath. Eyelids fluttering, the mace fell from his hand, his raised arm flopped at his side and his chin slumped. Still kneeling upright, all movement ceased.

I dragged myself out of the water and lay panting beside him, feeling the roll of the island beneath me. Overhead the sky remained dark and the wind blew, but the rain tapered to a drizzle. I was on land, or a sort of land, and alive.

I had been told the Uru live in small groups on some forty of these floating islands - their undisputed homelands, for none but they can live in such places. They build their islands by harvesting reeds and heaping them waist high, where they rot, providing the spongy ground on which they live.

"Look, there's someone over there. Isn't that. . .?" The voice trailed off. I found myself staring up at two more Lupaqa warriors, eyes fixed on their motionless comrade.

There wasn't time to replace Eagle Woman's stinger, even if I had the strength to raise my head, which I didn't. I lay on my back and stared up at them like a cornered doe. They peered down at me warily. One of them shook the kneeling man. The body fell sideways.

"Not a mark on him. What did you do to him? Who are you? Speak."

"Uru," I replied weakly.

"Uru? Uru women don't lie naked out in a storm. No, you're off that boat we chased. What did you do to him?" he asked gesturing at the fallen man.

"I found him so. Please, cover me. Help me."

The two exchanged looks. Their faces remained hard.

"Should we kill her now, or take her back for 'questioning'?" the short one wondered aloud.

"Why bother?" his companion replied. "I'm cold and wet. Let's tie her hands and roll her into the lake."

"Wait." I heaved myself up on one elbow. "I'm worth a hundred llamas."

"You? Why?"

"Reward. Your lord wants me alive."

They looked at each other again. The short one shrugged. "She's probably lying, but - "

The pole caught him full on the back of his head laying him flat, face down. The other whirled but took a pole butt in the stomach. A second blow laid him beside his companion. The Uru emerged from the night - short, stocky men, their only weapons the long raft poles they held upright like spears. One placed the end of his pole against my forehead, taking aim.

"Thank you for killing our enemies," I said in Runasimi, the Inca tongue. The man lifted his pole from my head and looked at the others. A babble began, of which I didn't understand a word. He turned back to me and raised his pole again.

I looked up at him. "Those filthy Lupaqa should sleep well tonight, and all the others I sent to a watery rest," I continued in Runasimi. He paused again, uncertain. Suddenly a woman pushed her way through the crowd and shoved my captor aside, shouting angrily at him. He shrank, showing deference. She knelt and removed her cloak, covering me while muttering in that strange language.

"Thank you," I said with relief.

She spoke to me in Runasimi then, or an accented, broken version of it, which I won't attempt to imitate, but the sense of it was this: "You speak the Inca language? I thought so. I was in service at an Inca garrison once. Here, cover yourself." She wrapped her cloak around me, and I was so relieved I paid no heed to her next remarks. "You're not much to look at, but it's not good for our men to see women naked, even skinny ones. Are those breasts? Well, at least you've got proud nipples."

Male nakedness didn't trouble her. When the men finished stripping the three Lupaqa and began arguing over the spoils she spoke sharply to them. Reluctantly, a cloak and tunic were handed over. She pulled me to my feet and retrieved her own cloak from around my shoulders, spreading it wide to shield me from the others. "Now put those on," she said nodding at the pile of sodden clothes. "I know they're wet but you'll soon warm up, and you won't be needing them for long anyway."

It was embarrassing having to put on men's clothes, and three sizes too big, but what troubled me more was the way she suggested I wouldn't be needing them for long.

One of the Lupaqa groaned, and promptly had his head smashed in. The same treatment befell his companion, and even the one I killed received several whacks, because they couldn't find a fatal-looking wound and wanted to make sure. They rolled the bodies into the water and pushed them down with the poles, maneuvering them under the bank. None reappeared. I imagined them floating against the spongy underside of the reed mass. A practical means of disposal, I thought, and a useful addition to their floating island. My hostess grinned. "There will be good fishing here for a while."

"Did any boats land?" I asked, wondering if there were more of my pursuers about.

"One overturned vessel washed up with a few half-drowned Pacaje clinging to it, but they didn't last long," she said, nodding to where the Lupaqa had vanished. "My husband is busy searching for others. We found many drowned bodies in the weeds. The fish will have a feast. No craft could survive that storm, unless, of course, it was manned by Uru."

"Thank you for saving me," I said, but she cut me short with a look.

"You treat us like animals on the mainland, but this is our land," she said pointing at the undulating ground. "Here you are at our mercy, and mercy is something our neighbors never show. Why should we? No, Inca, I covered you out of decency, but don't expect mercy. You'll join your friends - "

"My friends? I hardly speak their barbarous tongue. They were trying to kill me."

"Kill you? But you were among them."

"No, I was trying to escape in another boat. They would have caught me had it not been for the storm."

"Is it true?"

"Have you found other Incas? No, you haven't, because I'm the only one. Like you I hate the Aymara."

The Uru village clustered on a rise at the other side of the island, a collection of huts hardly more than a sling throw from where I'd crawled ashore. But in the darkness and storm the huts were invisible, being made of the same reeds as the boats and the island itself, and the Uru were snug in their dwellings while the storm blew over, unaware at first that strangers washed up nearby. Upon discovery their reaction was swift.

The rain ceased and the wind died to a breeze as we entered the village. The night sky brightened with stars again. My hostess wasn't convinced by my story, but thought her husband, the headman, might be amused by it, and decided to let him pronounce whether or not I would live to see the dawn.

A girl added rushes to the fire. Everything around me was made from those plants: rope, baskets, sleeping mats, hats, cloaks, door, walls, and roof, and a handful of green shoots even simmered in a pot by the hearth. The Uru, I realized, literally lived on reeds, and whatever else the lake provided.

The headman peered suspiciously at me across the fire. "Why were they chasing you?" he asked through his wife, who appeared to be the only one with a few words of Runasimi on the island. Most of the others - at least the men - seemed to have knowledge of the Aymara dialects, but I thought it best to insist on Runasimi. Awkward though the translation was, it set me apart from their hated masters who, I gathered, were exploiting them long before the Incas came.

"They were trying to kill me because I discovered their secret."

"What secret?"

The truth would mean nothing to them, so I tried to think of something they would understand. "They've been stealing llamas from the Incas - the Qolla, Lupaqa, Pacaje, all of them, thieves!"

When the woman translated the people crowding the hut laughed and the headman said, "You've only just discovered they're all thieves? Tell us something we don't know." When the laughter died again he leaned forward and fixed his eyes on me. "What makes you any different, Inca?"

I knew my answer would determine whether I lived or died. As a people the Uru were less than minor players in the great game of empire, and cared nothing for who succeeded to the Royal Fringe in Cuzco, but they hated the Aymara even more than the Incas. How to turn this to my advantage? Silence fell on the room, all ears waiting to hear me defend Inca rule.

"You know the Inca are more powerful than all the Aymara combined. If I can get word of this thievery to my master, they'll be punished. Imagine a row of poles topped with the heads of Aymara lords. Would you like to see that? And, the Incas will reward you with one hundred llamas."

The translation met with a round of approving murmurs. An elder stood and babbled to the assembly, and then another and another, each accompanied by much nodding. The headman seemed content with the collective decision and all eyes settled on me again, this time with a measure of respect, I imagined.

The headman's wife turned to me smiling. "You're going to make us rich," she said.

"Indeed, Mother, a hundred llamas is a fortune."

"Llamas? What would we do with llamas? Do you think we have room on our island to graze a herd? No, no, my dear, if the Incas will pay that much for your news, then the Aymara will give us anything we ask to keep you silent." She smiled sweetly. "We're going to sell you to them."

The Uru bound me with reed twine and shoved me into a storage hut, fastening the door behind them. At least they allowed me to keep the Lupaqa tunic and cloak which, though still wet, kept me warm. Eagle Woman remained with me, for the Uru recognized her as a charm and wouldn't risk running afoul of a spirit guardian, but with my hands tied at my back she was useless to me now. I stared into the darkness, weary beyond sleep.

It's hopeless, I thought. There is no escape from this floating prison - the Uru know their lake too well - and soon the Aymara will come for me. Will it be a quick death? No, they'll torture me first to be certain of how much I know, and then they'll entertain themselves with what's left of me.

I should have used Eagle Woman on myself when I was still able.

That's what I was trained to do - an imperial agent is never taken alive. I've failed my emperor, and all those who had faith in me when others declared women unfit for this work.

Does it all end here on this cold lake, so far from home, alone with no one to know the truth? Has it been for nothing - the years of hiding my family secret, so many times missing death by a whisper, and all those throughout my life who died defending me?

I cast my eyes inward across the years, summoning the faces and events that led me to this floating island. So many faces, and so few of them still alive. It began when I was a girl in the first blush of woman-hood on those long-ago ocean beaches.

I imagined myself in the hills behind those beaches looking down on a hut. I saw a family - a man and a woman, and their two children. They were the only people in the world. It was a world of sand and rock, sun and wind, and the eternal pulse of Mama Qocha, Mother of All Waters, incessantly washing the beach in front of their home. They awoke to Her rhythm each morning, and when Inti set the sky ablaze seeking rest beyond the horizon, they cuddled together and fell asleep to Her whispering sighs. The people were happy.

I could see those shores now, stretching on and on under a warm, hazy sun - the rocky headlands thrusting into the blue swells of Mama Qocha, hear the sea birds crying overhead, smell the tang of seaweed and salt air, grip the sand with my toes.

This was my world, until the strangers came. . . .

They came out of the eastern desert. Two figures pressed in the shimmering band where earth meets sky. Hardly more than wavering specks at first, momentarily slipping from sight amid the dunes, they came on.

"He might send soldiers to make a formal arrest," father had said, "but I doubt it. It's not a public spectacle he seeks. . . no, not retribution, only my silence - assassins more likely. Expect them at any time, from anywhere."

Closer, two men covering ground at a determined pace. I squinted and shaded my eyes, peering cautiously from the hills separating the

"They'll try to force me to betray the others first," he had said, "but I swore with them never to be taken alive. For myself I'm not concerned. I've had more than my count of years. My fear is for you. If they discover you're my children. . . expect no mercy."

I dropped to my knees. Had they seen me? Were these the assassins, or simply lost travelers? I raised my head and watched them disappear behind another dune. Soon they would be close enough to see clearly. Somewhere behind me father gathered birds' eggs along the sea cliffs. Where was he?

I crept back to scan the shores. Far down the beach smoke curled from the village at the mouth of the River Ica. The beach was empty - no danger from that direction. The strangers hadn't yet crested the dune. Looking up the coastline, I searched the barren, gray-brown hills and rocky headlands. Nothing moved but the wind and sand. Qhari was posted somewhere farther along. He must have seen the strangers too, if he wasn't fishing or caught up in one of his games. Had he already warned father? Should I hide, or call out? If mother were alive she would have known what to do. She lived long enough to see me through my first month of womanhood, and then she was gone, consumed by her illness.

I had never asked why we lived a solitary life by the sea cliffs, far up the beach from the village, or why we spoke one language with the villagers and another at home - a secret language Qhari and I were forbidden to use around our village friends - and our parents had never offered, or mentioned a world beyond our shores. And this we accepted like fish accept water. A child's world simply is.

The strangers came in view again, making straight for the hills above the cliffs - much closer now, moving with purpose. Both carried spears. One had long hair, but the other wore his short - very short. The danger was upon us.

Crouching low, I darted between the hills and down their seaward side toward the nesting crags, frantically searching for father. There was little time. The strangers would soon clear the hills.

Still no sign of Qhari. Was father's fate in my hands alone? I unwound the sling that held my hair against the wind, and snapped it taut. If I had to, I would face them alone.

Where the sand gave way to rock I climbed a promontory and saw father standing at the edge of a headland in the distance, resting his weight on his good leg. I shouted and waved but the wind blew my words behind me, and he was distracted by the angry gulls swooping and crying around him. A surf-washed bay lay between us. The strangers had not yet appeared.

I lost sight of him when I scrambled down and ran as fast as I could across the bay, slipping on rocks and nearly being swept away as waves stole my footing. And in the eternity it took to cross that bay and climb the opposite cliff, father's words came back to me.

"Know then, my children, that we are Incas from the village of Choqo near the sacred city of Cuzco. Our ayllu, which is to say our lineage, is called Añawarqe. We are nobles of second rank, related by marriage to Iñaca Panaqa, the royal household of the old emperor, Pachakuti."

Thus spoke father on the day Qhari returned from the village with news that Inca inspectors would soon arrive to take a census, and thus ended our life of innocence.

Father smiled at our astonishment. "I know; your mother and I kept this from you for your own safety while we sought refuge here on the edge of the world. But now the world has found us, and it's time for you to know all. Here is the mark that proves your birthright." He wore his hair long like the men of Ica, but with a flourish he now drew it back and for the first time we saw his ears clearly. The lobes drooped low and each was perforated by a large hole.

"That must have hurt," I said, hand at my mouth.

Qhari frowned and fingered his own lobes. "Father, why do you have holes in your ears?"

Father chuckled. "It's the sign of manhood. At the end of the initiation every young man has this done so he can wear earspools, the mark of an Inca warrior. And, unlike other nations, we have the honor of wearing our hair short, which also shows our earspools to best advantage."

Qhari and I sat entranced while father explained our true place in the world. It wasn't real to us then, no more than an exciting story, but we were swept along by the pride in his voice. Our people were the Children of the Sun, divinely ordained to bring light and order from chaos. Accordingly, our emperors forged an empire from many nations and now ruled the world, even to the sun-drenched lands of Ica - still independent when father arrived, now but one province among many.

And the cause of his flight? No, not our people he insisted, or the Emperor or gods - one man; one man with the power to reach out and destroy others to hide his crimes - crimes that father and his comrades had unknowingly witnessed, and nearly paid for with their lives before they guessed the truth and fled beyond the Empire's boundaries. But now those boundaries had expanded and there was no place left to hide.

Father sighed and replied to Qhari's protest, "Plead with Emperor Thupa Inka? You don't understand. One does not simply pay a visit to the Son of the Sun. We were soldiers on campaign and there is a chain of command. The murderer stands between us and the Emperor's justice."

At last I reached the final shelf and poked my head above the cliff edge, only to have the wind throw a blast of sand in my face. But it also carried voices.

"Don't bother lying. That scar on your forehead betrays you. You're Sayri. Admit it."

These words were spoken in Runasimi, father's language, but he replied in the Ica tongue, "Lord, I do not understand what you say. I'm but a simple fisherman of these shores."

My eyes cleared. I saw them standing in profile just ten paces away. The strangers pointed their spears at father, their cloaks snapping in the wind. Father wore only his loincloth and a gathering bag at his side. The splinter of whalebone he used for a walking stick supported his bent leg. He stood with head bowed, his back to the precipice.

"What did he say?" the tall one asked his companion.

"He said he's just a local fisherman," the man replied in Runasimi, "but he speaks our language with an accent." His long hair and the narrow bands of embroidery on his tunic marked him as a man of Ica.

"Shall I kill him now?"

"You were detailed to guide and interpret," the tall man answered. "If there is to be any killing, especially of Incas, it will be by my hand."

He turned to father and shook his head, his wobbling earspools exaggerating the motion. "It's no use, Sayri. You've aged, but you match the description perfectly. You are Sayri of Choqo. Now come, no more games. Where is your brother? Tell me that and I'll let you and your children live."

"My children," father shouted in Runasimi. The ruse was over. He pulled himself up to full stature and stared the assassin in the eye. "How did you know about them?"

"That's better, Sayri," the tall man said with a smirk. "Your children? Oh, your friends in the village were most helpful once the inspectors posed the right questions. They simply asked if there were any strangers in the region. It's a standard inquiry, especially when a new census is taken. The report that reached us was that two foreigners, a man named Tobacco and a woman called Silver Moon, came here years ago. The woman gave birth to twins - a boy, Valiant Cougar, and a girl, Golden Star, who come to get water and play with the children at the river mouth. The villagers themselves remarked that these are strange names, quite unlike those of Ica. But they made sense to us when translated into Runasimi; Sayri and Qolqe Killa, Qhari Puma and Qori Qoyllur - all good Inca names." He looked pleased with himself.

Father sighed. "Was it really that easy?"

"Yes, it was," he replied, gloating. Father's shoulders sagged. The man's eyes narrowed with interest. "I'm told you took elaborate precautions to sham your death and vanish, yet you overlooked this simple detail: You left your people but you couldn't leave your name." He clicked his tongue and shook his head again. "If a proper census had been taken when we first conquered this land we would have had you then."

Father shifted letting his bent leg dangle free, and stared over the man's shoulder as if digesting this news. But when I followed his gaze I saw what he was already aware of - Qhari, moving on his belly like a lizard, slowly creeping up behind the strangers. He, too, wore only his loincloth, but he dragged his casting net. Father's gaze flickered back to the men as he continued to stall.

"Who sent you?"

"Who? What does it matter? Your crime has found you out."

"What is my crime supposed to be?"

"Rape, murder, and desertion."

Again father measured Qhari's progress. He was close now. I flexed my sling.

Father held the man's eyes. "So it's being blamed on us. Did it ever occur to you that someone else murdered those women?"

The tall man balked. "A desperate ploy, Sayri. They warned me of your tricks, but we know the truth about you."

While the man spoke father kept his gaze level, but gestured with his left hand toward the guide. Qhari bobbed his head in understanding. I opened my pouch and withdrew the largest stone.

Father said, "Yet you offer to let me live if I tell you where the others are?"

"I'll be honest. You're a dead man. The villagers said your wife died a while ago, but if you cooperate I'll spare your children, and give you a swift end."

The wind gusted furiously now, and the men held their spears loosely in one hand while they wiped grit from their eyes. Father remained silent, hanging his head as if accepting defeat.

Qhari rose and circled the net above his head. I tensed.

The tall man shifted impatiently. "Well, Sayri, I can't stand here forever. What's it to be? Your children's lives. . . or death for all?"

Father lifted his head and glared at the assassin. "What's it to be? You rush me. I was trying to decide whether to kill you slowly or give you a swift end," he said snapping his left hand closed.

In that instant Qhari's net flew through the air. I leapt over the top in time to see it cloak the guide from head to waist. Father's stick had already bloodied the assassin's nose, and the two were locked in a struggle for the spear. Father's bent leg, the assassin now learned, wasn't so badly crippled. I took aim and threw hard at the assassin. The stone smacked father's ribs.

"Thank you, Qori," he managed between clenched teeth, "now go and help your brother."

Qhari charged the guide as soon as the net was thrown, catching him at the waist and tumbling him to the ground. The man tried to rise but Qhari remained glued to his back, keeping the net over him.

"Get his spear, Qori," he yelled.

I snatched it up and threw it to father, who broke from the assassin and dove to the side, coming up with the weapon in hand. The two faced each other, spears leveled.

The netted man stopped struggling for a moment. Qhari looked up at me calmly. "That was very clever, Qori. But now, what are we supposed to use? Do you think you might have given this one a poke first, or do you plan to tickle him to death?"

Suddenly the man came up on his knees with a roar, sending Qhari sprawling behind him. I grabbed a rock, straining to lift it chest high. The guide struggled to free himself of the net. I heaved the stone at his head. He slumped with a groan. The second blow laid him on his side . . . with the fifth his skull exploded like a ripe squash.

Qhari appeared at my side. "Well done, Qori! Now you're thinking. Quick, help me get the net so we can snag the other one."

If he hadn't pried the rock from my hands I would have kept dropping it on the oozing mass that was once a head. I trembled, looking down at the red and gray slime splattered on my legs. "Is he. . . is he dead?"

"Very. Now hurry. We must get this net off him."

We pulled at the net and rolled the body. I tried not to look at his shattered skull, while Qhari muttered something about how interesting it was to see the inside of a head. I looked over my shoulder at father. He was in a crouch with his back to me, maneuvering the assassin to the precipice with the tip of his spear. The assassin no longer smiled; his left hand covered a gushing wound in his side. Father was unmarked.

Qhari had the net free and gathered it for a final throw. I turned to watch the duel.

"Now speak, you worthless piece of shit," father said. "Who sent you?"

The assassin's heels found the cliff edge. He fell forward on his knees. "Spare me," he said, his voice catching in a whine.

"Drop your spear."

The man laid his weapon at his side and raised his hands to beg. Father stood over him with spear poised.

"Mercy, and I'll reveal everything. I'm sorry my guide killed your daughter."

"What?" Father's head jerked toward us.

"No, father!" I screamed.

As if in a dream I saw the assassin's eyes narrow, his right hand retrieve his spear, and the long blade vanish in father's stomach.

II

In which is told a Woeful Tale of circumstance and Murder Foul.

The winds ceased leaving the beach in calm to catch the last rays of the sun. I lit a fire by the windbreak in front of our hut. With the first curls of smoke the birds stopped their gliding and swooped down, hopping awkwardly toward me in hope of a handout. I threw sand at them, sending them squawking and flapping, but they soon edged forward again. Three days had passed since the assassin speared father.

Why bother with this daily ritual? I wondered as I set the pot to boil and added more dried seaweed to the flames. Who can eat?

Still, it was what mother taught me, and there is solace in routine.

I wore her garments now, the short, wrap-around skirt and loose, circular top of a fisherwoman, too large for a girl my age, but comforting.

I sensed a change in the air. The time of storms was coming, and with it heavy fog - the only moisture these shores receive - bringing shrubs and grasses to life for a few months.

The tides rose and fell, the winds blew, the birds still glided above, and even the seasons were deaf to our grief. How could the world continue?

I looked at our home, a low, one-room hut fashioned from arching whale ribs and reed matting. Mother traded dearly for that matting. Reeds grow along the river, the only fresh water on that coast, and the villagers always exacted a high price for our needs. It occurred to me that our hut, with the longest rib framing the entrance and the shortest at the rear, resembled a half cone resting on the sand above the high tide mark, like a great fish washed up on shore. I never thought to describe it so before, or any way at all. It was simply home, the only home I'd ever known, and the sole structure interrupting that long stretch of beach.

It was father who made me see our life with new eyes. His words had shown me another world, a world of green hills and forested valleys, snow-capped mountains, lakes, rivers, and rain that soaked lush pastures. "That's where we belong," he had said. "It's your true home."

Qhari came out of the hut, eyes red with sleeplessness. His lower lip trembled when he spoke. "Father wants to come out now," he said in a whisper. Our eyes met. We both knew what that meant.

For three days father suffered in the hut, taking no food or water. "Not much blood for a gut wound," he had said with a thin smile, "but this kind never heals. I may last a few days, but when my time comes I want to see the sky."

I nodded to Qhari. "If that's what he wants. . . ."

When the assassin speared him, father managed one glancing blow in return before collapsing, but it was enough to send the man tumbling backward over the cliff, his scream silenced by the jagged rocks below. Under father's direction Qhari and I threw the guide's body over the precipice also, and watched the remainder of it smashed before it, too, disappeared in a surge of swirling foam. Their spears followed, and then nothing remained to mark their passage except father's horrible wound. Somehow Qhari and I managed to get him back to the hut, but that took the last of his strength and he hadn't moved since.

"There, much better, thank you," he said, as we arranged him on the slope of the beach. His face was pale and taut. I patted the sweat from his brow. "Perhaps something behind my head so I can see better. Good. Yes, now I can look up and down the shores." He strained a smile. "The waters are calm this evening. Not much haze. Do you see that cloud out there? It looks like that big fish Qhari caught. Remember that one, Qhari?" We both turned our heads so he wouldn't see our eyes fill.

Qhari cleared his throat. "Tell us again, father. Tell us how it happened."

"Yes, you must remember my exact words if you're ever to regain your rightful place in this world. Very well, I'll tell it one last time." I ducked my head and stroked at the pain welling in my throat.

"Two years before your birth, when Thupa Inka became Emperor, the Qolla people and their allies around Lake Titiqaqa rebelled against us. My brother Maita and I followed Kontor, our ayllu war leader, and together we served in the imperial army when it fought its way south to the rebel capital of Hatunqolla. There were many Incas of noble birth in that city when the revolt began, and among them was Princess Sisa, a young half-sister of the Emperor. Thupa Inka promised her to the officer who found her alive. Although this was great incentive for our commanders the Qolla fought like demons, and it was several days before we penetrated the city.

"It happened at the akllawasi - house of the chosen women," he recalled with a frown. "Our troop was the first to reach it, well ahead of the main force, while swarms of Qolla still fought street by street around us. When we banged on the door and shouted an old priestess peered out in relief. She said there were two women with her, all the others having fled to the temple when the rebellion began. The three hid in brewing urns when the rebels came. After looting what was at hand, and afraid to be in that place of Inca holy women, the Qolla left quickly, sealing the entrance behind them. Since then the women had lit no fires and lived on dried fish.

"Then a second woman appeared at the door, a beautiful young woman wearing the courtly dress of a lady-in-waiting. When she saw our silver earspools she sneered, saying men who didn't wear the gold of royalty wouldn't rescue her. She demanded a warlord. Imagine! But the city wasn't yet safe, and over her protests Kontor insisted on entering to make sure all was secure. It was a bold move, for no man save the Emperor is allowed inside those sacred precincts. Yet, with fighting still raging all around, it seemed the prudent course. Kontor was gone a long time while the rest of us stood guard at the entrance. Then more of our forces arrived, driving the Qolla from nearby streets.

"Kontor returned alone and said he hadn't seen the third woman, but neither had he seen any Qolla. With that sector now safe we rejoined the battle. Kontor went to report the women to our commander, Lord Achachi, and then returned to lead us in the final charge that swept the city.

"It was a great rout, with tens of thousands surging southward. Here and there bands of Qolla paused to fight rear guard actions while their forces tried to regroup, but we gave them no rest, and by nightfall we stood on the shores of Lake Titiqaqa. Over the following weeks our advance continued relentlessly, and each day our troop was at the fore of the battles. Other units were granted rest when fresh companies arrived,

but our privilege was always to be in the most dangerous positions, leading charges or acting as decoys to draw the enemy out. When our ranks
were decimated they sent us reinforcements, but those of us from the
original troop were kept on duty at the front.

"Many times Kontor sought out Lord Achachi requesting rest for our
company, but the reply was always the same; Achachi didn't understand
the orders either, they came from above him, but our duty was to fight,
and if necessary, to die with honor in the service of the Emperor. That
we would have done had it not been that one morning we found our sentries strangled, even though they were posted inside the perimeter, and
those ahead of them were untouched. It was as if we weren't dying fast
enough on the battlefield.

"Kontor went to report these deaths, but Lord Achachi had been
recalled to fight against the jungle peoples who were also rebelling at that
time. Kontor said our new commander showed little interest in our plight.
But while Kontor was away tales of the aftermath at Hatunqolla finally
reached us. Princess Sisa was found hiding in the akllawasi, but two
women were found dead in another part of the complex; the younger one
raped and mutilated, a foul deed blamed on the fleeing Qolla. Yet with
our own eyes we saw those women alive after that sector was liberated.

"It became clear to us then. Someone must have slipped into the
akllawasi after we left, and before the rescuers arrived. With confusion
still reigning in the city, and unaware the princess hid nearby, he
assumed he was the first on the scene and seized the moment to indulge
his twisted passion. Somehow he learned we were there ahead of him,
perhaps from one of the dying women. Because we were the only ones
who knew it wasn't the Qolla, he arranged our end. Clearly it was a person of highest rank, one with the authority to command Lord Achachi."

"That's when you planned your escape," Qhari said.

"Yes. Maita said it was the only hope of seeing justice done, and
after much argument Kontor finally agreed. Perhaps Lord Achachi was-
n't aware of the murders, but he knew who issued the orders that doomed
us. We had to convince him of the truth but there was no way of finding
him then, not with thousands of men in the field and battles everywhere.

Only Kontor, Maita, me and our standard bearer were left from our original troop of fifty. We had to hide until peace returned, and then find Lord Achachi.

"It was Maita's idea to behead those dead Qolla and change clothing. Kontor thought we should stay together, but Maita convinced us it was too dangerous. We chose different routes, without telling one another of our destinations lest one of us be caught and forced to betray the others. But we planned to meet again. Since Hatunqolla was liberated on the holiest day in the festival of Wiraqocha, we decided that seven years hence to the day we would gather at the Temple of Wiraqocha, a two-day journey south of Cuzco, and thereafter to meet every five years until all were accounted for and justice done.

"I attended that first meeting, traveling at night through the high country and avoiding all roads and villages, until I found a band of pilgrims to fall in with."

Qhari and I nodded, vaguely remembering when father was away for a long time.

"I arrived late. The crowds were dispersing, but I searched among the thousands still gathering their belongings. It was Maita who found me, and words cannot express the joy I felt at embracing my brother once again. He, too, had come late, but he glimpsed Kontor at a distance passing a checkpoint that morning. We searched, but Kontor had already left. Still, at least we knew our captain was alive. Not so the standard bearer. Maita saw him captured by one of our patrols the day after we parted. Although we all swore never to be taken alive, he was, and he must have talked before he died because Maita twice eluded spies seeking him by name. The murderer knew about us, and his agents sought us everywhere."

"And you learned nothing about Lord Achachi?" Qhari asked.

"Maita heard that Lord Achachi was then serving on the northern frontier beyond Quito. It might be years before he returned to Cuzco."

"Is he there now?"

"He could be, Qhari, I don't know. It's been seven years since Maita told me about him. I missed our last meeting because of this," he gestured at his twisted leg, broken while fishing from the crags. "The next meeting is in three years' time." Then a spasm wracked his body, leaving him gray-faced and gasping. Qhari and I sat helplessly beside him, holding his burning hands.

"You should know the rest," he said in a whisper, hurrying to finish. "The night before we fled I arranged for a message to be sent to your mother in the event of my death. At the end of the mourning period she was to make a pilgrimage in my memory to Pachakamaq, a great shrine on the shores of Mama Qocha to the north of here. The route down from the highlands is by way of the Zangalla Valley, which at that time was beyond the Empire's borders. That's where I waited, and that's where we were finally reunited. My one sorrow was that she didn't bring our son. The child injured himself shortly before she set out. He was only three years old then. It delayed her departure, and in the end she left him with the ayllu. We grieved for him, but your mother refused to risk losing me again, and so she stayed. The gods took pity. You were born early, just seven months after she arrived, and we were a family again."

He had never mentioned a son before. Startled, I asked, "What is our brother's name?"

"His name? We called him wawa - mother's child, like all those of his age. He wasn't old enough to have a name of his own."

Children are given names at their first hair cutting, about age four or five, and receive a different permanent name when they reach adulthood. This comes for girls when they began their moon times, and a few years later for boys, though Qhari was given his name at the same time as me because mother was very ill and wanted us named together.

I met Qhari's eyes again. Somewhere we had an uncle Maita, and a brother - a family.

Father coughed and squeezed our hands. "When you're grown you know what you must do," he said in a voice so low we had to bend close to hear. "Look for Maita and Kontor at the Temple of Wiraqocha, and find Lord Achachi. Whether or not Achachi realizes it, he knows who the murderer is - the one who ordered us to certain death. This demon must be exposed. It's the only hope for you to regain our family honor and claim your rightful place. I'll not rest peacefully until those long-ago murders, and my own death, are avenged."

We each still held one of his hands, and we clasped our free hands over him. "I promise, father, you will be avenged," Qhari vowed.

"And I promise, too," I said, the tears spilling down my cheeks.

Qhari furrowed his brow. "How will we recognize - " but father started coughing again.

Father's lips moved with hardly a sound. "There's no more time. Qhari, go and catch me a gull."

"That's a child's game, father, I - "

"Yes, but you used to do it for me when you were small. I want to see you run on the beach again. That's what you do best." He turned his head to me. "Qori, go and count the sand crabs for your old father. How many do you think are on the beach this evening? You used to tell me there were more than all the fingers and toes in the world could count. Are there still that many?"

These were the tasks he busied us with while mother prepared the meal, and he sat by the water mending his nets as the sun went down. The sun was now an orange ball a finger's breadth from the sea.

"I want to watch you out there until the sun sets. When you return, pull the blanket over my head. I'll sleep out here tonight."

I threw myself across him, sobbing. He stroked my hair.

"Qhari, tomorrow you must dig a deep hole beside your mother's grave. Take me there, but do not mark my resting place. You know how everything is preserved in these sands. Tell them I slipped from the cliffs and was washed out to sea. Without my body they cannot be sure of my identity, and that is safer for you. Deny any knowledge of my past. Speak only the Ica tongue and pretend to learn Runasimi. As for the assassin and his guide, you never saw them, do you understand? Good. Now, take your sister to the water's edge, and let me watch you run."

III

Of how the Twins were Summoned, and of that which befell them in the Desert Wastes.

The sun hammered the gravel plain. It was only midmorning but already the soldiers sweated, heads drooping, spears balanced on their shoulders, each captive to his daydreams while the line straggled onward.

Qhari nudged me. "Over there," he whispered, nodding at the rolling hills to our right. "Something moved."

I searched. Foxes hunt at night, and even snakes and lizards stay out of the desert sun. Only vultures and people are foolish enough to travel the wastelands in the heat of day. Then a dark spot poked from behind a distant rise, paused, vanished. A moment later it scurried behind the next hill. I wondered if our escorts, all highlanders unaccustomed to desertscapes, knew we were being spied upon.

As if hearing my thoughts one spoke up. "Did you see him, Captain?"

"You think me blind? Of course I saw him. . . and his friends. They've been following us since dawn." The captain squinted into the sun, surveying the hills. The two men spoke in Runasimi, which Qhari and I still pretended barely to understand. Concern creased the soldiers' faces.

The captain beckoned our guide, a local man, and demanded, "Who are they?"

The guide shrugged. "Most likely renegades and thieves, Lord."

"The Emperor doesn't allow brigands."

The guide made a show of shared indignation. "Quite right, Lord. You should go out there and remind them of that."

The captain, a scarred veteran with a hard, swarthy face and body to match, sighed heavily. "Can't you manage your own people?"

"Within our province certainly, Lord, but we're in the desert lands between Ica and Zangalla. No one rules here save the gods ... and the Emperor, of course," he added quickly.

"What do they want?"

Again he shrugged. "Perhaps nothing. Sometimes bandits fall on unwary travelers, but I've never heard of them attacking imperial guards. Don't trouble yourself, Lord. They'll leave us soon. Come. We'll have to hurry to reach Zangalla by nightfall."

When the guide took up the lead again the captain motioned his second aside. Qhari and I edged closer. The captain pointed ahead with his mace to slopes studded with gnarled huarango trees. "Do you see those hills? That's where they'll hit us, where the cover is best."

"Do you think they'll attack?" the man asked.

"I don't know. The guide doesn't think so, but I haven't survived this long by taking chances. Besides, this is no ordinary patrol. The governor announced we'd be departing at midmorning on the royal road, then called me from my bed with orders to leave in the middle of the night, and take this back trail to Zangalla. Why the secrecy? I've no idea what's so important about these children, but it's our duty to deliver them safely. So keep the men together and your eyes open."

Our little column started forward again with Qhari and me in the middle. The soldiers moved warily, keeping one eye on the hills ahead and the other on the eastern horizon. I imagined I was one of them, and father led us.

The day after we buried father a party from the village came searching for the two strangers, and upon learning of father's "fatal fall from the cliffs," as Qhari put it, insisted on taking us back with them. The village at the mouth of the River Ica is a cluster of cane huts scattered over two dunes, which grow annually from the shells and garbage heaped beside the dwellings. There was a squabble over who would take in the orphans, and the fishing gear, blankets, clothing, pots, and all that our parents had accumulated over the years. It was settled when the headman eyed the pile and decided it was his duty to look after us. And there we thought we would stay, safe in that little village on the shores of Mama Qocha, until we were old enough to search for Lord Achachi and make our own pilgrimage to the Temple of Wiraqocha. But two ten-day weeks later a messenger arrived, summoning us to the court of Lord Aquixe.

"He's the native lord of all Ica," the headman explained, as surprised as we were at this summons, "what the Incas call a Hatun Kuraka. His father ruled before the Incas came, and now he presides over all the chiefs of Ica, although they say there is also an Inca governor at his court. Our village is subject to Lord Ullujaya, who is subject to Lord Ocucaje, and above Lord Ocucaje is our young Lord Aquixe who dwells in the great Ica Valley, a two-day journey inland. But why does he want you? How does he even know your names?"

Those questions dogged our steps the next day as the messenger led us along a line of branches and stones that marked the path through the desert sands. Gone were the cool salt breezes, replaced by a still, morning sky, and the fiery blast of afternoon winds. It was the first time Qhari and I were away from the shores, but whatever uncertainty lay ahead we were together, and every turn presented new discoveries. The narrow, winding channel of the River Ica is choked with bushes, so travel is far easier on the plains above. But occasionally the steep margins retreat, leaving low basins of green shining in a sea of sand. To our delight, these oases are filled with huarango and lucuma trees - the first trees Qhari and I ever saw - and fields of maize, beans, quinoa, squash, hot peppers, gourds, cotton, and all manner of useful plants, the produce of which we knew but the vegetation we had never seen. And the villages bursting with people - so many people! And so many unfriendly dogs coming out to growl and snap at us.

At last we entered the great Valley of Ica, a green and fertile place, full of fields and orchards with towns scattered among them. The messenger told us the valley is two day's walk in length, and a half-day wide. We proceeded along a broad, straight road lined with ancient huarango trees, and between their low, writhing branches we glimpsed temples and palaces of mud brick rising like brown hills from the level valley floor. They stand singly, or in clusters of three or four, and while some are barely taller than a man others are many times that height. Then I spied yet greater mounds beyond the trees ahead. As we drew closer they filled the landscape.

The messenger turned to us, grinning at our wide-eyed stares. "Welcome to the Court of Ica."

I knew what Qhari was thinking. The realization gradually built in me, too, as our journey progressed. The village at the river mouth, that metropolis of our innocence, was nothing more than a distant hamlet on the fringe of power, a power proclaimed by the massive hills of brick that rose around us. Yet father had said Ica was but one province among many in the Empire. How great the Empire.

Lord Aquixe's palace was a wide mound with three ascending platforms, each boasting a fresh coat of white plaster. Lines of workmen busily extended one side by dumping baskets of rubble behind a thick wall of rammed earth. The upper levels were like a village, covered with wattle-and-daub huts, and buzzing with servants. But this we only saw from below. An elderly retainer dismissed our messenger and took us around to the back of the palace mound, where sentries guarded the entrance to a small, square compound of mud brick - the Inca governor's abode.

"Lord Aquixe is at his residence in Cuzco," the man said, "but his chief counselor is with the governor, and will receive you here."

Qhari and I looked at each other. It was not Lord Aquixe who summoned us.

The Inca governor, a man of years, sat on a low stool regarding us gravely, his thin, lined face framed by huge golden earspools and a tuft of parrot feathers crafted like a flower on his brow. The feather flower rose from a gold plaque that bore the image of a serpent with heads at both ends. A local noble sat on a still lower stool at the governor's side, acting as translator. The servants and guards were dismissed. Qhari and I knelt, awed and terrified.

"What are your names?" the governor asked in Runasimi with a grandfatherly smile. It seemed an odd question for the messenger had sought us by name. The translator repeated his words in the Ica tongue.

"I am Valiant Cougar, Lord," Qhari replied in the coastal dialect, "and this is my sister Golden Star." The noble translated.

"Qhari Puma and Qori Qoyllur, good," the governor said. "And you are twins?"

We waited for the translation and then nodded.

"Who were your parents?"

"Tobacco and Silver Moon, Lord," I said feeling bolder.

"And where did they come from?"

Qhari looked at me and shrugged. "From their parents, Lord?" he ventured.

The governor smirked even before the translation came. "I mean, before they lived in Ica," he said gently.

Qhari's bottom lip rose. "They always lived here, Lord."

"Did your father ever mention his service in the Emperor's army?"

Qhari looked confused. "Army? No, Lord. Perhaps you have mistaken him for someone else. Our father was always a fisherman."

"Where is he now?"

Before the noble could translate I rushed to answer. "Dead, Lord, fallen from the crags and washed out to sea. There is no body." Qhari pinched me. The governor peered into my face while he waited for the translation, but he had understood me. He spoke the Ica language. I shrank.

The governor dismissed the translator with a wave. The man protested, "But Lord, these little ones don't speak your tongue."

"Thank you," the governor said with finality, eyes narrowing. The man departed shaking his head.

The governor stood and clasped his hands behind his back, regarding us intently. Silence. My stomach turned. Suddenly he bellowed, "Guard." Instantly a man appeared at the door. Speaking in a torrent of Runasimi the governor shouted, "Take these two little dung-eating vultures outside and gut them."

I sucked in my breath, covering my mouth with my hand. Qhari drained of color, eyes wide.

The governor grinned, dismissing the guard with a wave. "I thought so," he said. "You speak Runasimi as well as I do, don't you?"

I sank with a sigh. Qhari lowered his head, running his hand through his hair.

The governor chuckled. "Your performance was good, but you'll have to do better from now on."

We gaped at him.

"Don't worry," he said, "you have powerful friends." Then a shadow crossed his face and he muttered, "Almost as powerful as your enemies."

I exchanged a glance with Qhari. His eyes spoke caution. Was this a trap?

The governor looked at us again. "Quite right," he said as if hearing our thoughts, "trust no one. I don't know the full story, and I don't need to know. My part is to get you safely to Cuzco. Others will take over from there. You don't realize what's at stake, do you? No, I thought not. It doesn't matter. One day you will, and the Empire will be grateful to you. . . if we can keep you alive."

What was he talking about? Qhari placed his hand on my arm and shook his head, urging silence. The governor nodded to himself. "I'll assign a servant, one of the locals, to 'teach' you Runasimi. Study her accent and mistakes. Learn to speak like her. This will help with your disguise. If your enemies discover that you were raised with Runasimi they'll know for certain who your father was, and assume you know about his past. Right now they can only suspect; don't give them any more clues. In the meantime I'll let your friends in Cuzco know you're safe. When they're ready I'll send you there under escort. But keep your silence, always," he said slamming a fist into his palm. "Approach no one on your own, and never, ever, repeat what I've told you. Yours are not the only necks stretched on the log," he said stroking his throat. Then, fixing us with his eyes again, he asked, "Is your father really dead?"

We nodded. Truthfully.

"Hmmm. . . I believe you. Then you really are our only hope."

What did he mean by "our only hope?" I pondered yet again as our escort led us across the desert. What is it they want from us, and for what purpose? The faces of the soldiers around me held no answers.

The captain raised his hand to signal a halt where the plain gave way to hills. Inti was directly overhead. All eyes searched the tree-scattered slopes. The guide returned from his forward position. "This is where we need to be cautious, Lord," he said to the captain. "I don't think they'll give us any trouble, but, to be safe, why not send a few men out on the flanks?"

The captain scratched his chin and looked at the sky, then turned to his men. There were nine, all dressed like him in black and white checkered tunics, red cloaks tied about their waists, and domed wicker helmets with a standing red fringe running from ear to ear. I thought them magnificent. Each carried a thrusting spear and a small, square shield covered in a hanging cloth painted with emblems. I felt safe. Why the hesitation?

"You two," the captain shouted at a pair of soldiers, "take the flanks. Stay on the high ground ahead of us. You three, break out your slings. I want two forward and one at the rear. The rest of you shield the children. Tight formation. Now move."

Qhari's eyes sparkled. "Golden Star, get some stones," he said using the Ica tongue. All morning he'd been imitating the soldiers, and probably fancied himself one of them preparing for battle. I drew my sling from my shoulder bag and joined in the gathering, much to the soldiers' amusement.

I missed the freedom of my peasant clothes. The governor had supplied us with garments befitting the court of Ica. Qhari wore a cloak and tunic cut in the Inca fashion, but with bands of embroidered fish and birds in the Ica style. I wore a calf-length, white cotton dress and a wide belt of colored yarns, with a shawl that reached to my ankles. I thought myself quite the lady at Ica, but now felt encumbered.

I tied the shawl around my waist like the men, and shifted the little obsidian knife hidden beneath my belt. Qhari carried one also, tucked at the back of his loincloth under his tunic. The governor shrugged when he gave them to us, unsure himself what we would do with them, but wanting us armed however lightly. The brittle, black stone of the tiny blades was flaked to keen, serrated edges, but they were of little use for anything but cutting, which they did with remarkable efficiency.

I stretched my sling. "I doubt you'll need that," one of the men said with a grin. I ignored him.

"We may all need them," an older, stern-faced man told him.

"What do you mean?"

"This is your first tour on the coast, isn't it? Well here, my young friend, they use spear-throwers. Do you know what they can do? They'll ram a dart clean through a man from two hundred paces. If we're attacked you'll be lucky to get close enough to see their faces. In a skirmish like that you'll need your sling."

The spear-thrower is sometimes used by fisherman, too, and is indeed a powerful weapon, though innocent in appearance. It's simply a stick, no more than elbow to finger tip in length, with a hook at the end. The hollowed, fletched end of a dart - as long as a man and tipped with an obsidian point - is fitted into the hook, so the dart and throwing stick rest together. When the dart is launched only the stick is grasped, which acts like an extension of the arm, arching the dart high and propelling it with such force that. . . well, I didn't doubt the soldier's warning.

"Ready? Look. Now. Careful," Qhari said to me in heavily accented Runasimi, a mischievous smile on his face. He enjoyed mimicking our language teacher, a local woman whose Runasimi we could barely understand. But, as the governor predicted, she taught us to pronounce and confuse our words in a manner expected of two peasant children from a distant province. She also taught us what she could of the Empire, beginning with its name.

"It is called Tawantinsuyu - The Four Quarters." Qhari and I privately decided this was a reasonable translation, although Unity Of Four Parts, or, The Parts That In Their Fourness Make Up A Whole, came closer to the concept of the word. "The royal capital of Cuzco, where dwells Emperor Thupa Inka, is at the center of the world," she said. "Around it are the four divisions: to the east of the mountains is Antisuyu, to the south of Cuzco is Qollasuyu and to the north Chinchaysuyu, both of which are vast and extend from the sea to the mountains and jungle slopes. We dwell in Kuntisuyu, the western part. Each suyu has an overlord, who is a brother of the Emperor, and each is divided into provinces like Ica, ruled by its native lord with the assistance of an Inca governor."

From what we saw at Ica the Inca governor did more than assist. But, since orders always came from the local Hatun Kuraka's mouth, or his designates, the people felt they were only following the wishes of their native lord as they always had, and the Inca presence was not intrusive.

From her we also learned that, as was customary with all newly conquered lands, the current Hatun Kuraka of Ica, Lord Aquixe, was sent to live in Cuzco when still a boy. There they taught him to speak flawless Runasimi and govern wisely in the manner of the Incas. When his father died he returned to rule his people, and his son went to dwell in Cuzco. The most sacred objects of Ica, like the large, milky crystal upon which the well-being of the valley depended, also took turns dwelling in Cuzco, another being sent each year when the previous one returned home. While in the holy city, this wak'a resided in a temple where it conversed with the holy things of other provinces, and even with the Inca gods. All the provincial lords of the Empire had the privilege - indeed, were required - to maintain a household in Cuzco, where they lived for four months each year so they could visit their sons, worship the cult objects of their homelands, and consult with the Emperor. Even at our tender age we recognized the brilliance of this system. The word 'hostage' was never mentioned.

"They want you sent to Lord Aquixe's residence in Cuzco. You're to leave tomorrow," the Inca governor announced after we had passed only a week at Ica. Still not knowing how far away Cuzco lay, we didn't know enough to be impressed with the speed at which messages were exchanged.

"Lord, who are our 'friends' and what do they want with us?" I demanded, stamping my foot. He had told us nothing.

"They want you safe. That's all I can say. It's too dangerous for you to know names. They'll help you avenge your father. . . and set other matters right in the Empire."

"Then who are our enemies?" Qhari asked.

"Those names are even more dangerous. I've already told you enough to risk my head, don't ask me to gamble my family, too. Just follow along. You'll be given answers when you need them."

"If you know about us, then the Emperor must know, too," I said. "Won't He help us?"

"No, the Emperor knows none of this, and if He did He couldn't intervene if He wanted to. But if we're successful He will be grateful to you. Trust me."

He said we would depart the next day, but he woke us himself in the middle of the night and bundled us into his courtyard, where a messenger waited. He whispered to the man, who instantly set off at a run. Then the captain arrived, still yawning.

"A change of plan," the governor said. "I've received some unwelcome inquiries. I want you to leave with the twins immediately. Take my personal guards - they're the only ones I can trust - and follow the desert trail north to Zangalla where our people are expecting you. Once there you'll be safe. Arrangements have been made to slip you in with a caravan bound for Cuzco.

"I commend them to your care, Captain," the governor said pushing us forward. "On your honor as an imperial officer, and your personal oath to me, get them safely to Cuzco. Much depends on this," he said stroking his neck again.

The trail twisted around gravel-strewn slopes, hiding all vision of what lay ahead. The two flankers were out of sight for some time, and the captain looked worried. When he signaled a halt the men crowded around.

"It's too quiet," he said.

His second nodded. "Did you see that condor circling ahead of us? I don't like it. They bring death."

"True," said the guide looking concerned now, "they're carrion eaters, and this one has landed."

I searched the sky. The great bird had vanished.

"I thought you were sure there wouldn't be any trouble," the captain said, his tone chiding.

The guide studied his feet. "Maybe I was wrong. We should turn back."

His nervousness spread to the others. I looked from face to face. The soldiers shifted uneasily, avoiding one another's eyes.

The captain dismissed the guide's suggestion with a snort. "Imperial guards always complete their mission. But . . ." he paused, looking around, "where are those flankers? You and you," he pointed at two of his men, "run ahead and call for them. The rest of us will wait here."

The two trotted off but only reached the next bend when they stopped, rigid as stone. "Captain!"

We ran to their sides. Up ahead the condor flapped its huge black wings at us, guarding its feast - two fresh human heads set in the middle of the path. The flankers had been found.

"Quick," the captain shouted. "tight formation. Take the high - " his words caught. Warriors appeared on the ridges above us with slings and spear-throwers poised. We spun around, but the trap closed. We were surrounded.

A grim-faced man stepped from behind a tree near the heads. "No use, Captain," he said. "Drop your weapons."

The condor circled angrily above. The man calmly watched it with his good eye, the other closed by a scar running from forehead to cheek, and then he turned to us. "Unless you want to give that bird and its whole family a feast," he said pointing a finger skyward, "I suggest you drop your weapons. Now."

He spoke in accented Runasimi, but it wasn't the accent of Ica. His hair swept back over his shoulders like all men of the coastlands, but there were no markings on his clothing to distinguish his nation.

The captain planted his hands on his hips. "What do you want?"

"Just the twins. Then you can be on your way."

I huddled closer to Qhari and saw my questions in his eyes. Obviously they knew who we were, but what did they have planned for us? The soldiers backed close around us forming a tight circle, their spears lowered.

"We are an imperial escort," the captain shouted, "under official orders - "

The man balked. "Spare me. You're surrounded and outnumbered. Surrender."

"I didn't think that would work," the captain muttered calmly to the man beside him. "So. . . let's try this." He raised his voice again. "We have a hundred men following close behind. They'll arrive - "

"That's not what my runners tell me. Now drop your weapons."

The captain nudged the soldier on his other side and said, "That one never works either." The man's taut features broke into a grin. Keeping his voice low, the captain said over his shoulder, "Now for the serious negotiations." I held my breath wondering what he would come up with.

The captain shouted, "Very well, I'll make you a deal."

"A deal?"

"Yes. I'll let you have the boy and girl. . . in exchange for your weapons. . . and ten guinea pigs."

Qhari chuckled nervously with the soldiers. I missed the humor but saw they stood less rigidly now. Shaking his head sadly the captain reported in all seriousness, "I don't think they'll go for it. No guinea pigs for us tonight."

"Enough jesting, Captain. You're all dead men," the brigand shouted, raising his arm.

"Wait. Since this concerns my men I'll have to consult with them. We'll give you our answer in a moment."

Their leader looked confused, but, turning his head from side to side, he shrugged and waited.

The captain looked at his second. "Well, how many do you count?"

"Altogether, at least sixty of them, Captain."

"Let's see. . . that's sixty murdering renegades against eight imperial guards, a guide, and two children. Well," he said with a satisfied nod, "not very good odds for them."

The men on the hills must have wondered why our little group was laughing again. But the soldiers were relaxed now and ready to follow their leader to the death, which appeared imminent for all of us.

A short, thickset guard stepped forward, shifted his spear to his shield hand, and pushed his wicker helmet down firmly on his brow. "What's the plan, Captain?" he asked. I was wondering that myself.

"Spear-throwers and slings are less accurate against moving targets. Also, we have the element of surprise."

The guide looked puzzled. "Surprise, Lord? What do you plan to do, surround them?" The men found that humorous too, but the guide looked annoyed, and frightened.

"A good idea," the captain replied as if taking him seriously, "but I fear we lack one or two men for that. No, our surprise lies in the fact they think they have us."

"They don't?" I wondered aloud.

The captain patted my head. "Not yet, little one. Now listen, men. When I shout "Illap'a," scatter and charge that hill," he said nodding to the right. "Tumble and zigzag at first, and space yourselves well apart. That will confuse their aim. Before they have the second volley ready we should be at the top. There are no more than six or seven of them up there. You," he nodded at the guide, "take the girl, and you," he gestured to his second, "take the boy. Shield them with your bodies." He looked at the faces around him and hefted his weapon. "If anything happens to these children I'll ram this mace so far down your throat it'll come out your ass. Understand?"

I certainly did. I didn't like the image, and I didn't doubt he'd do it. The soldiers' faces showed they didn't doubt it either. At that moment facing a line of brigand spears seemed preferable, and less dangerous, than crossing the captain.

"When we reach the top, you two keep running with the twins. Don't stop until you're far from here. The rest of us will form a skirmish line and hold them off; no, better yet, we'll finish them all off, then meet you in Zangalla." He raised his brows and nodded encouragingly at his men, "Good plan, isn't it?"

Eyes rolled, but everyone nodded obediently.

"I know," he said modestly, "I always have the best plans. That's why I'm captain."

"Enough stalling," the brigand chief called from up the trail.

The captain faced him. "We've decided," he yelled back.

"And?"

"And we're going to accept your surrender."

Startled, the brigand chief looked away chuckling and shaking his head. That's when the order came, "Illap'a!"

In the next moment I found myself rolling over and over in the guide's arms. Men somersaulted and dived around us. All were up in an instant, running zigzag up the slope, shrieking their war cries. Stones and spears hit the sand around me. I caught a glimpse of Qhari with his guard hunched over him, already charging upward. Beside us a soldier went down with a scream, a fletched spear pinning his leg to the ground. In terror the guide dropped me and turned to run, but found himself facing the captain with his mace raised.

"To the top, dog turd, with the girl."

The guide dragged me upward, my feet barely touching the ground, while the captain charged at his heels. Another shower of stones and spears. Two more fell. Now near the summit. A final volley. Another casualty. Then, spear against spear, the remaining soldiers charged the crest. A stone sent Qhari to his knees. His guard stood over him fending off two brigands with his spear. I jerked away from the guide's grasp and jumped one of the brigands from behind, clawing at his face. Qhari's guard plunged his spear, gutting the lout with a single thrust. The captain's mace removed the back of the other attacker's head.

I threw my arms around Qhari. He clasped his hands to his breast and rocked back and forth, eyes watering. "Qhari, are you hit in the chest? Don't die on me!"

"No, stupid. It's my hand. Somebody hit me with a stone," he whined.

"Oh. The middle of a battle and some nasty man threw a stone at you. Shall I tell the captain on him?"

"Well it hurts," he said, and sniffed.

Just then a brigand stumbled backward over us and lay prone, his throat slashed. Qhari looked at him and sniffed again, protectively rubbing his hand. "Serves you right," he said to the body.

That was the last of the duels for the moment. Seven lay dead on the hilltop. One was another of ours.

"Right, that was easy enough," the captain said cheerfully, slapping one of his two remaining men on the back. He turned to Qhari's guard. "Get these children away from here. Head west until you're out of the hills, then north. You'll need the guide. We'll cover your rear. Now go before they surround us again. Quick! Move!"

Having broken through the encirclement we dashed headlong down the back slope to lower ground. The guide made for a gully offering cover. We followed, our guard behind us, urging us on while keeping watch over his shoulder. Twice I fell face down but Qhari had me up in an instant. There was no breath to speak with. We ran.

The last I saw of the captain he stood alone, staring down six attackers, but yielding no ground. The broken shaft of a spear protruded clean through his shoulder. His last words echoed over the hills, "Come on you motherless shit eaters, you can do better than that. Illap'a!" He charged.

Around hills and down slopes, turning this way and that, darting from one lonely tree to the next, our feet bruised by jagged stones, we stumbled on and on over sun-scorched rock. The howls of our pursuers faded as they fanned out to search for us, but the guide, who seemed to know those hills like a condor, kept us angling away from them. By late afternoon, just when I was too exhausted to go another step, our guard finally allowed us to collapse in the shade of a crouching tree.

"It's over," he said. "We've lost them." He collapsed beside us, wiping the sweat from his face with a bloody hand. I hadn't noticed his wound before.

"Where are we?" I asked. It seemed the ground hadn't changed since our flight began.

The guard looked around for the first time, trying to gather some sense of direction, which Qhari and I had long since lost. "I've no idea. Where's that guide we've been following?"

"Here I am," the guide called.

We looked up. He stood nearby with a crowd of renegades around him, grinning like a fox and gesturing over his shoulder. "There's a fine camp for you over here."

The one-eyed brigand chief turned to him. "You've done well. It went exactly as you said it would."

IV

Of the Micheq, and Perils faced in the Jaws of the Great Speaker.

The first spear tore through his throat. The second and third slammed into his chest before he hit the ground. He writhed and gurgled at our feet, then lay still. So died our protector, the last imperial guard of our ill-fated escort. We faced the brigand chief alone.

"Come, little ones," he said, his good eye burning like a coal, "there's someone here who wishes to meet you."

The brigand encampment lay in a gully behind the next ridge, a hasty affair with but one small tent. Everywhere men sprawled beside their equipment, nursing wounds. Qhari spit at the treacherous guide as we walked past. He smiled wickedly at us. Inside the tent a man waited, sitting cross-legged, his cloak drawn over his head. We were shoved to our knees facing him, our hands bound at our backs. The brigand chief dismissed his men, there being little room in the tiny cotton enclosure, and stood behind us. Qhari held my eyes, reminding me of the oath we'd sworn over father's grave - death before betrayal. Brave words for two orphans, but we had resolved that, since we were alone in the world, henceforth we must think and act for ourselves. That notion, too, was new to us, and thus far achieved with varying degrees of success, but at least we grasped the need for silence. What did we know that was of use to others? Very little, except where and when uncle Maita and Kontor met, but that was enough to seal their fate.

When we smoothed the sand over father's grave, Qhari spoke with a determination I'd never heard from him before. "Father was swept out to sea, Qori," he said flatly, rehearsing our story. "Without his body they can never be sure who he was. We know nothing about his past, we don't speak Runasimi, and we didn't see any strangers. That's all you have to remember."

The authority in his voice was reassuring, but he'd never spoken to me like this. We were twins. We had lived every day of our lives together, and though we fought as children do, our feelings were one. Often, words were not necessary between us; I knew his thoughts, and he mine, and they were the same.

Then he said, "Last night I worried about what might happen to us. I thought about dying, and I was afraid. But then I thought, If I die, what will happen? I'll be with mother and father again, that's all. Will I meet father with pride, or with shame? That depends on how bravely I meet death. If I'm afraid then I'll die badly. I imagined all the ways I might die and, yes, some were awful, but you saw how father bore his pain. I'd rather die quickly, if I must, and fighting like father. Then I pretended I was already dead, and suddenly there was nothing left to fear. I think. . . well, I can't say it right, but, if you're not afraid to die, what can they threaten you with? What's left to be afraid of?"

Yes, I thought, I, too, am marked for death - today, tomorrow, it doesn't matter. Accept it. There, that wasn't so bad. If I die it will be in a just cause . . . but I won't go without a fight.

With the freshly turned sand at our feet and gulls careening overhead we joined hands at father's graveside, just the two of us alone in the barren hills, looking down on the empty beach where once lived a family. In truth, the names and places - Lord Achachi, uncle Maita, Captain Kontor, the city of Hatunqolla, the Temple of Wiraqocha - had little meaning in our sheltered lives then, no more than a family honor and a place in a world we didn't know. But they were important to father, and so for his sake they would be for us, too. It was father's murder that fed the fires of revenge. That was real. It happened before our eyes. An unknown sender of murderers stole father's life, and with him all that was good and precious in ours. We resolved anew that no matter how long it took, no matter what dangers we faced, nothing would stop us from tracking this beast to his lair.

That resolve was now being tested.

"Where is he?" the seated man demanded in fluent Runasimi. It was an Inca speaking. Qhari and I remained silent.

"Which way did he go?" His tone was impatient. Qhari caught my eye - they thought father was alive.

With a wave he directed the brigand chief to put a knife to my throat.

"We know all about you," he continued, "and if you don't tell me where he's gone, you're both dead." The blade pressed. I nodded.

"That's better. Now speak."

"Lord," I said in the Ica tongue, "I don't understand. What do you want from us?" Qhari's eyes flashed a smile.

"You understand me," the man said, his voice a growl, "and so does the boy."

"Golden Star, what does he want?" Qhari asked.

"I don't understand him, Valiant Cougar. I think he's speaking the language they tried to teach us at Ica."

The Inca released an exasperated sigh, then repeated the questions in the Ica tongue, which he spoke tolerably well, adding the threat of cutting our throats if we didn't answer. Qhari and I held fast, our eyes on each other, as we told how father fell from a cliff and was washed out to sea.

"And the two men who came to find you?"

"We saw no one, Lord," Qhari replied.

"What did your father tell you about his brother?"

"We have no uncle, or any other family," I said, still trying to see his face. The cloak hung to the tip of his nose revealing only a thin, cruel mouth. "Our parents always lived by the sea. If we had relatives they would have told us. Now we're orphans, alone in the world. Have mercy." I began sobbing and Qhari followed my lead, his eyes grinning through the tears.

"Perhaps they're telling the truth," the brigand chief said in his accented Runasimi.

"Maybe. . . and maybe not. The governor at Ica thinks they know something, or he wouldn't have had them smuggled out in the middle of the night. If our spies hadn't been alert we would have missed our chance."

So that's what the governor was afraid of, I thought. Even in his own garrison he knew spies surrounded him.

The man drummed his fingers on his knee, watching us closely. "Let's be done with this. Cut their throats."

The governor had shown us that trick. I held my face impassive.

"But, Lord," the brigand protested after a pause, "they're only children." His words sounded rehearsed.

"I don't pay you to question my orders. But, perhaps you're right. No need to be hasty. They might still know something. Have your men prepare a fire. We'll see if these guinea pigs squeal when they're roasted."

The brigand stepped outside to shout orders. Qhari and I avoided each other's eyes so as not to give ourselves away, but I knew his insides, too, were quivering.

We sat in silence for an eternity while my mind raced. Eventually the brigand reappeared to report, "Lord, the wind has come up and we can't get a fire started."

I sighed inwardly.

"Incompetence! I'm surrounded by incompetence. Very well, break their legs. If they still won't talk, then cut their throats."

I decided I'd been silent long enough. "Father did tell us something that might help you," I said.

Qhari caught my eye. He knew I was stalling and joined the game. "These ropes are cutting my wrists," he said. "Please-please, Lord, untie me. My sister will tell you everything."

The interrogator shrugged and the brigand undid our bindings. Qhari rubbed his wrists, eyeing me, speculating on what story I would come up with. So was I. Qhari stretched, stroking the small of his back.

"My father gave me words in a strange tongue I don't understand, and said I could only whisper them in the ear of an Inca."

The man became attentive. "Come closer, little one," he said waving me forward. "Don't fear. I wasn't really going to hurt you. I'm Inca. Tell me the words your father spoke."

Qhari gave me a nod. He saw my plan.

Hesitantly, I knelt beside the Inca. He raised the cloak, turning his ear to me. I cupped my left hand and leaned forward to whisper, while sliding my right arm behind him. Qhari regarded the brigand chief with a look of innocence and said, "You're very ugly."

"What?"

That was the moment's distraction I needed. My right hand flashed around the Inca's shoulders, pressing the obsidian blade to his throat. The little knife had stayed tucked inside my belt, out of sight and forgotten, until Qhari rubbed his back reminding me of his hidden blade, and my own.

Qhari leapt to his feet and faced the brigand chief, knife in hand. The man snatched up a war club and went into a crouch. "Wait," the Inca said, cautiously raising a hand to the brigand. The man hesitated. Wetness seeped over my knife hand. In the excitement the blade had already cut deep. Any sudden move and his neck would open.

"Now don't get excited, young woman," the Inca said slowly, not moving. "Put the knife away. I won't hurt you."

"Tell this renegade to drop his club, and stay silent," I said, keeping my knife in place. The Inca complied. The man let his weapon fall, a look of resignation on his face. Qhari ordered him to kneel and stood behind him with his knife at his throat.

Qhari grinned at me. "Well done, Golden Star."

"And now?" the Inca asked, still frozen in place.

It was a good question. We could walk out of the camp with our hostages, but their spear-throwers would have easy targets as soon as we turned our backs.

Qhari stared coldly at my captive. "Let's see this Inca's face." The cloak still covered his eyes.

Suddenly a spear zipped through the tent wall. Screams and war cries filled the air. A brigand shouted at the entrance, "Lord, imperial troops," then fell into the tent with a spear in his back.

"What the - " the brigand chief started to say, but just then two men struggling outside tumbled against the tent, bringing it down around us. I thrashed about encased in billowy cotton, the Inca, Qhari, and the brigand chief lost to sight. Someone stepped on my back. Another stumbled over me and paused to kick the lumpy, wiggling shroud. I lay still, covering my head with my hands, expecting a spear to rip through me at any moment. The shouting continued all around.

When the noise of battle subsided I cut through the cotton shroud, emerging to a scene of devastation. Bodies sprawled everywhere, mostly brigands, and imperial guards strutted around finishing off the wounded. Qhari helped me up. My first thought was of the Inca and the brigand chief. I looked around. "Where have they gone?"

Qhari pointed across the gully. The brigand chief lay on his back, his good eye wide, his entrails beside him. A head rolled down the slope, coming to rest at our feet. It was the guide.

"And the Inca?" I asked.

"I saw him flee with some others," Qhari said. "They'll run him down soon."

A captain walked over to us. "Are you the twins?"

We nodded. I said, "But how did you know where to find us?"

"The governor at Ica sent a runner ahead to Zangalla. He wanted us to meet you part way, but when you didn't arrive we searched and found the ambush site. It was easy to trail them here. They weren't expecting us," he said waving his hand at the scene.

"Have you taken prisoners? Who are they?" I asked.

The captain looked surprised. "Prisoners? What for? No one attacks an imperial escort and lives."

"You can see for yourself it's badly in need of repair," the bridge keeper said, "and soon the afternoon winds will set it flapping like a strip of cloth. I wouldn't try it today. But, tempt the gods if you wish. It's your life."

The great suspension bridge stretched off across the chasm before us, its cables sagging low in the middle, the walkway on a tilt; and far, far below in a swirl of white the Apu Rimaq struggled between sheer cliffs, engulfing us in its deafening roar. Where the far end of the bridge met the opposite cliff tiny figures peered back from a platform.

The micheq surveyed the swinging structure. "This is the Emperor's bridge, and it's your responsibility to keep it in repair," he said, as if the bridge keeper should fix it while we watched.

The man lifted his nose. "I advise travelers and report its condition to the Inspector of Bridges in this province. Each year those cables are replaced. It takes seven villages to make them, and two hundred men on either side to set them. It's your luck my bridge is due for its annual repairs next week. Besides, there have been caravans crossing both ways each day for months. That's thousands of people and animals. And you wonder why my poor bridge is in such condition."

"We must cross, bridge keeper," the micheq replied.

The custodian held up his hands. "My bridge can hold you and your entire caravan if you're careful, but not today. Soon the winds will gust up the canyon, and you don't want to be out there when they hit. Go and rest your people on the plain above at Kurawasi, and return in the morning when it's calm."

"We can't wait," the micheq said when the man had gone. "They could be above us on the trail now, and if not, I'm certain they'll be here in the morning. We can't risk it. An armed escort awaits you on the other side at Limatampu. From there you'll be safe, but for now. . . we must cross this bridge."

The governor of Zangalla, following instructions from his counterpart in Ica, had arranged our journey to Cuzco. We met him only once, a nervous little man who wanted us away from him as soon as possible, and volunteered even less information than the governor at Ica, insisting only that, officially, we never met and he knew nothing about us. His concerns were justified when, a day later, word arrived that the governor of Ica was dead; something he ate which did not agree with him, it was said.

The following morning Qhari and I were assigned a guardian. He was an Inca wearing copper earspools - a small but solidly built man with a quiet, attentive manner, and though he spoke little no gesture or nuance escaped him. He had an enormous forehead, tiny eyes slanted downward, and no visible upper lip, though his bottom lip was full. I wondered what his wife looked like. He was a micheq, or shepherd, a minor official concerned with daily administrative matters, but his bearing and a certain deference accorded him by the governor suggested 'micheq' was only a non-military rank of convenience. When I asked him his name he replied, "Micheq," and that was the extent of our conversation.

That day we departed with a caravan bound for Cuzco, the micheq ostensibly going to deliver provincial accounts and Qhari and I attending as his servants, though the plan was still to deliver us to the residence of Lord Aquixe in the city.

The Zangalla governor was sure there were spies in his midst also, and thought it safer to send us secretly without an armed escort; the journey across the desert from Ica having shown that our enemies were not deterred by imperial guards. He also mentioned, hesitatingly, that uniformed soldiers are subject to the commands of those in higher authority, implying that our enemies had the power to countermand his orders. An unsettling thought. We would be safe in the hands of his trusted micheq, he said, giving the word a hollow ring, and if the micheq could not get us through then no one could. His last words to us were, "The Empire will be grateful to you. . . if you reach Cuzco alive."

The journey began slowly, or so it seemed to us, because llamas, especially those bearing cargo, are not swift animals, and often contrary. Two hundred of the long-necked beasts accompanied us, most carrying sacks of bird dung from the islands off the coast destined for highland fields, and with them forty drivers.

From Zangalla the road continued upwards, ever upwards as we ascended past villages of round, stone huts with conical roofs of grass, clustered on terraces along the narrowing valley margins. And then it rained - true rain, not the mist of the coast, but a torrent that fell like a river. Gray clouds hung low, hiding the mountaintops. For the first time we heard the sling of Illap'a crack thunder, and saw His brilliant garments flash lightning as He twirled to dip another jug from the Celestial River.

Rain was but the first of many marvels. The caravan soon reached the puna lands where chill winds sweep the grassy plains, and the sun shines with cold intensity from an impossibly blue sky. The puna is the land of sky, a vast dome over endless rolling pastures. The air is breathlessly thin and the mountains appear at your fingertips, yet retreat with every step.

Daily we passed llamas and alpacas in herds so vast they stretched to the horizon, some animals with solid coats of brown, black, gray, or white, others mottled, all with bright tassels marking ownership dangling from their tall ears; they made a splendid sight against the green hills with snow-capped peaks beyond. While llamas are found everywhere, being used as beasts of burden and occasionally for meat, alpacas were new to us. They look much like llamas, except the adults are smaller and have shorter necks, and their hair is much thicker, covering their heads and hanging low from their bellies. Their hair produces the finest wool for weaving and they are prized for this alone, being unsuited to carrying loads and far too valuable to eat.

Many mornings we awoke to find the ground stiff with frost, and several times, much to our delight, snow descended during the night from its mountaintop home to blanket the puna, only to vanish under the midday sun. This became a much-anticipated event after the drivers showed me how to pat the snow into balls suitable for pelting my brother.

Throughout our journey we traveled the qhapaqñan, or royal road. Where it ascends through the mountains the road is narrow, often clinging to slopes with stairways of stone positioned on the steep ascents. But once in the puna lands the qhapaqñan is ten paces wide and marked by low walls of rocks and bushes. The roadway is swept clean and maintained by workers from the local villages, and wherever possible it follows a straight line to the horizon. Along some stretches it even has flagstone paving.

Everywhere along the qhapaqñan are message runners stationed in huts spaced one long run apart. In this way communications are passed with utmost speed for the word is always in motion, day and night, through any weather. No one interferes with the Emperor's messengers, and we had to step aside often to let them pass.

At the end of each day's journey there is a tampu, a roadside lodging which also serves as a checkpoint. Depending on the needs of a region some are small, being little more than a cluster of buildings, while others are complexes with shrines and royal lodgings, great halls for feasting and billeting workers, and row upon row of storehouses filled with cloth, weapons, food, and all manner of necessities. Travelers are provisioned from these stores, as are the resident priests and administrators, but the storehouses are always maintained in fullness for the army, so it can march swiftly to any point and be supplied along the way.

During these travels Qhari and I pretended to continue our lessons in Runasimi with one of the Zangalla llama drivers, studying his coastal accent, and all were amazed at our rapid progress in this difficult language. After a time we no longer had to feign ignorance of Runasimi, unless it suited us, but when we spoke it we were careful to use a broken, accented version.

The micheq became friendly as the days passed, and though he never told us his name and remained guarded about his family, we discerned he'd seen much service with the army and traveled widely. In truth, he was quite good at making conversation that revealed absolutely nothing about himself, nor did he ask anything of us. If he knew who we were he never acknowledged it. It was clear his allegiance was to the governor of Zangalla, and Qhari and I were another assignment, a cargo to be delivered at all costs. Once it was established that nothing was to be asked or offered we settled into an amiable routine, and I think he became fond of us. We certainly felt safe with him.

The open puna once more gave way to jagged, crowded mountains with plunging ravines. Through these we descended to warm, sunny valleys patched with fields and forests, and thence upward again, but never so high as the snow line, though the night air was chill enough to see our breath. We reached Kurawasi without incident where a runner from the governor of Zangalla caught up with us. By some subterfuge our enemies had learned we were in a caravan headed for Cuzco, and they had dispatched men to overtake us. The message stressed that by the time this news reached us our pursuers would be less than a day behind, but the governor had a trusted friend at Limatampu and we would be safe there. What lay between haven and us was the mighty Apu Rimaq, and along this twisted, surging stretch there was but one crossing.

From the plain at Kurawasi the caravan descended down and down, the earth slipping away, a rumble building in our ears, until at last we glimpsed the fast-flowing river far below in a gigantic ravine closed in by sheer cliffs. From the heights above all that can be seen in the dark gulf is a string of white smashing over boulders, from which rises the vast roar that gives the river its name - Great Speaker; and swaying across this chasm like a thread is the famed hanging bridge over the Apu Rimaq.

The narrow trail down to the bridge restricts passage to one person at a time as it zigzags along the cliff face, a bare rock wall on one side and on the other abyss. No bush or blade of grass finds root among the shattered rocks in this sunless ravine, and as the canyon narrows the deep, hoarse roar of the Great Speaker vibrates in your bones. To see the caravan I had to look up or down, though I preferred up, where I could see five tiers in the line of llamas winding their way back and forth across the cliff, all with their ears bent forward, picking their way down steps cut in the living rock.

"We'll have to get the llamas turned around and start back up," the caravan leader said, shaking his head at the swinging bridge. "It's too late to cross today." As he spoke the turbulent air of the canyon stiffened setting the bridge swaying farther from side to side.

The bridge keeper, standing by his stone hut under an over-hang, nodded approval. "When you come back you'll have to unload the animals and lead them across two at a time; for a train your size that will take two mornings. The afternoons are impossible, as you can see," he said gesturing at the ravine, "but return at dawn and I'll get you started."

I stood at the edge of the precipice with Qhari, both of us staring down, mesmerized. Far below the Great Speaker leapt and bellowed over black rock, sweeping the canyon walls and daring us with its deep roar. On my right rose the stone piers to which the bridge is anchored. I studied the structure. Two braided cables as thick as a man arched downward across the gorge, and set over them crossways were narrow poles like the shafts of spears, tied at either end with rawhide for the walkway. Suspended above on each side hung two more massive ropes, one at waist height and the other well overhead, which, by a web of lesser cords, were connected to the floor cables. Of itself it looked solid, the great cables braided from many ropes of tough fiber, but the overhead tension on one side was greater, placing the walkway on a slant, and here and there cross-poles were missing where heavy feet broke through. The bridge was in need of repair, though still passable if not for the gusts that set it swinging nervously. Yet the great bridge was dwarfed in the canyon of the Apu Rimaq, no more than a cord precariously strung through the air between bare, vertical cliff faces with the awesome Great Speaker rumbling below.

The caravan leader gestured his insistence that the animals be turned, although on the narrow path this seemed near impossible. The micheq shook his head in resignation as if to say, 'It can't be done, not today,' when a commotion turned our heads to the trail above. Three strangers squeezed their way past the halted llamas, nearly pulling the beasts off the ledges as they grasped and pushed and clambered over and under them, ignoring the drivers who cursed them for madmen. "Sooner than expected," the micheq muttered. His eyes moved to the swaying bridge and then to us. "We have no choice now."

Qhari looked no more pleased at the prospect than me.

"We'll fight," I said for both of us.

The micheq smiled wearily, then jerked his head toward the descending pursuers. "I know their type. They're not ordinary men. I can handle one, perhaps two, but not three of them. I've sworn to lay down my life for you, but I'm not about to throw it away against impossible odds. Our only hope lies across this bridge."

It was like stepping into nothingness. With one foot on the solid rock ledge and the other on the shifting walkway I grasped a side rope to steady myself, but my fingers wouldn't let go of it. The first length of the bridge was steep, curving down and away from the cliff in a great arc. Qhari and the micheq already worked their way down the walkway, legs braced wide against the swaying motion, arms extended for balance. Qhari glanced back to see me frozen on the first step.

"Come on," he shouted. "Hurry!"

I tried, but the moment I set my weight forward and felt the sway underfoot my fist clenched on the rope again. The cables squeaked and groaned as the wind stiffened, swinging the bridge in a wider arc.

"I can't," I called back.

Qhari glanced at the micheq, who still faced ahead concentrating on his next step, and then nodded to himself. Like a lizard he threw himself flat on the walkway and wiggled back to me on fingers and toes.

"Now, let go of the rope and take my hand," he said, pulling himself up at my side.

"I can't."

Shouting erupted behind us as the three men arrived at the foot of the path, not twenty paces away. Their leader had a bandaged neck. The caravan drivers crowded angrily around them but they pushed their way through ignoring the insults. No one had yet noticed us attempting the bridge, but as the men strode forward all eyes turned on us and paused in wonder.

"What are they doing?" someone shouted. "You there, get off the bridge, it's not safe."

"Look, there's one already out there," another yelled, pointing at the micheq. He had finally paused and was beckoning us with his hands, eyes pleading.

"What are you doing here?" the caravan leader demanded of the strangers. In answer they pushed him aside and came at us. All were large men, and with the same determined eyes. They knew who they were looking for and their quarry perched before them.

A slap on my cheek made me release the rope and bring my hand to my face before I knew what I was doing, and having accomplished that Qhari grabbed me and fell back, rolling both of us down the walkway. He dragged me on my knees, lurching drunkenly from side to side as the bridge swayed under us. "Don't look down," he shouted. "And don't grab the ropes or you'll never let go. Come on, hurry."

Feeling the walkway sag and swing under me I wanted to drop on my belly and hang on forever, but I was on the bridge, finally, and Qhari tugged me forward. Looking back I saw the men crowded at the anchor tiers above, pointing at us with mouths moving, but their voices drifted away under the roar of the Great Speaker. Concentrating on Qhari's back, I advanced one shaking step at a time.

While the bridge swayed at either end it swung freely at the lowest point of its arc, which the three of us now approached apprehensively. What it is about such places I cannot say, but my eyes continually sought the tumbling water far below, staring at what they did not want to see, placing me where I did not want to be, drawing me into the dark gorge. "Don't look," Qhari kept shouting, as much to himself as to me.

My hair blew sideways and my cloak tore away, carried like a fluttering leaf down the yawning gloom of the canyon. The bridge lifted beneath us swinging far to the side. For an instant there was nothing under my feet, and then I lay tangled in the side ropes while the bridge swung back in the opposite direction, leaving my stomach behind. Qhari and the micheq struggled to their knees, Qhari glancing around nervously to make sure I was still there. His eyes fastened behind me. Amid a flurry of wildly gesticulating arms from the watching crowd, two of the strangers edged their way along the bridge after us. The man with the bandaged neck waved them on from where he waited by an anchor tier. Another blast of wind howled down the canyon.

On hands and knees we crawled forward. The bridge was a living thing, twisting and lurching and groaning beneath us as it swung like a great hammock, each cross-pole in the walkway shifting independently, and the engulfing roar of the Great Speaker making it impossible to hear our own thoughts. The feared midday gale now blew my hair straight out, forcing me to keep my head turned into the wind, and sudden blasts hit in succession leaving us paralyzed and clutching the walkway lest we be blown into the abyss. Yet still the strangers came on, now crawling on their hands and knees too, but never stopping, relentlessly scuttling like crabs toward us.

Afraid to move but too terrified to stay in this howling danger, I stretched out full and pulled myself forward one hand after the other, jamming my toes between the cross-poles and pushing ahead. Qhari and the micheq waited for me to reach them so we could stretch out side by side while we attempted the midpoint of the bridge, where it hung lowest and twisted most violently over the chasm.

We crept on, reaching the middle, and then a lull in the wind allowed us to our knees for a scramble forward before the next blast hit. But the wind was fickle. A gale came from below, lifting the bridge and then battering it from the side again, flipping us and shifting the structure away. I grabbed air, then flailed at the side ropes but fell through their web. There was only openness and the river surging below when a hand clamped my ankle, stopping the fall and holding me swinging over the torrent. Far below, white streaks smashing over jagged rock spun by as the bridge continued swaying in a huge arc.

With a lurch I dropped lower, but the fall was checked again. Straining my neck upward I saw the cause. It was Qhari who gripped my ankle with both hands, having caught me just as I slipped through the webbing, but he lost his balance too and the micheq now held him by his feet, leaving the two of us swinging free over the Apu Rimaq. The strangers were close.

The river swung by again and I let my arms dangle over my head, out-stretched, ready for the endless fall that must surely come. Qhari's face was taut, wide-eyed and determined. I knew he'd never let go of me and so we'd fall together, the two of us, together always. Then the tugging began, and little by little I felt myself being pulled upward. A glance showed the micheq on the edge of the bridge, knees up and feet pressed to the side ropes, hauling Qhari in hand over hand, his face set and muscles straining to the task. From my upside-down position I admired the under-side of the bridge, then felt a grip on my free leg. In a moment my hands grasped the ropes, but the strangers had theirs on the micheq.

I was vaguely aware of the struggle, but if there was shouting it was lost in the roar of the Great Speaker while I heaved myself through the side ropes and hugged the walkway, shaking and twisting though it was. Qhari pulled me to my knees and began dragging me ahead, but the incessant shifting of the bridge toppled him again. Our man shook off the attackers and placed himself between us and them, legs set wide, defying them with a knife that magically appeared in his hand. They both drew daggers. He turned and frantically waved us on, then whirled on his opponents. Qhari grabbed my hand again but the bridge twisted and jerked from under us, sending everyone sprawling into the webbing. This time I recovered first and helped Qhari onto the walkway, where we stayed on hands and knees scrabbling over the rippling cross-poles.

A huge hand closed around my foot, pulling me back. I turned on my side and kicked. The stranger stretched out full, one hand clamped on the bridge and the other dragging me back. Beyond, his companion sat atop the micheq ready to plunge his dagger. Qhari dove over me, and as my foot slipped free the stranger jerked to his knees holding a gash on his arm. Qhari lay on his back in front of the man threatening him with his tiny obsidian blade. In a fury the man pulled his dagger and raised it high. I lunged, piling into him as another blast slammed into the bridge, swinging it high and wide, and sending the three of us grabbing for the side ropes. Both Qhari and the stranger lost their weapons, needing both hands to hang on, but upon recovery I produced mine and slashed at the attacker's grip. I must have imagined his howl for I couldn't have heard anything above the roar of the Great Speaker, and then he had both hands on his chest, one protecting the other. Qhari lifted the man's legs and shoved him over backwards. He tumbled through the webbing but managed to grab a rope, his lower body swinging free.

We should have finished him but the more immediate danger was the wind and the twisting bridge. Somehow the micheq shook off his attacker and dragged himself over the walkway toward us. He left a smear of red behind him, and one leg was useless. He paused to raise his head and wave us on. Behind him his assailant edged forward again, both men now weaponless and clawing to get off the bridge. Qhari and I turned and scrambled ahead.

The bridge curved upward at a steep angle as the opposite cliff drew closer, and here the swaying wasn't as bad as in the middle, but gusts still threatened to tear us loose and we had to flatten against the walkway while they blew over. To our utter amazement the man we left swinging still hung on, and his partner now helped him back onto the bridge. Both crept forward at the heels of the micheq, who paused again to wave us on.

Then hands reached down to us, for several had gathered on this side to watch the performance; when they took hold of me I turned on my back and let them pull me up. The great arc of the bridge danced below, and on it three men still struggled onward, but the strangers had reached the micheq.

I found myself sitting beside Qhari, our legs on the shifting bridge but seated on solid rock, dizzy, my body still swaying and nausea building. The assailants grabbed the micheq. Weak, and knowing he couldn't fight both of them, he used the last of his strength to stand and seize one of the attackers. He glanced up to make sure we were safe, then, arms clasped around the man, he dove to the side forcing both of them through the webbing and into the abyss. The river swallowed them.

The remaining man watched them fall, then stared at us and set his jaw. Qhari and I looked at each other. My exhaustion was etched on his face. I felt as if I had no bones in me - a doughy lump with bruised and aching limbs, and barely enough strength to turn my head back to the bridge to watch the stranger draw closer. Those around us stood back in silence, realizing the drama was not done and wanting no part of it.

It came like rolling billows on the sea, starting at the far end and rippling down the length of the bridge, one mighty blast of wind whining through the canyon that lifted and snapped the bridge like a cord, sending the lone occupant high in the air. He seemed to hang there for an instant, then slowly tumbled head to toe like a diver, but never straightened before he vanished in the yawning mouth of the Great Speaker. On the far side the man with the bandaged neck shook his fist at us.

V

**In which Qori meets an Old Woman, Lord Achachi becomes
Suspect, Qhari is Strangled, and the Hatun Kuraka drinks maize
beer with the Apu Panaqa.**

The channels in the middle of the streets ran full before the downpour finally stopped. But even during the rain the bustle never ceased
beneath the thatch eaves jutting over the pavement, providing protection
for those intent on their errands. Massive walls of angular stones rose
around me, and again I paused in wonder to run my fingers over the joins
- no mortar was used, the blocks rested on their own weight; not even a
knife blade could be wedged between them. It seemed to me these great
walls stood like the Empire: immense, eternal, yet composed of many
intricately fitted parts; and here, in the ceremonial heart of Cuzco, they
silently reminded all that this was truly the center of the world.

From the corner of my eye I caught a glimpse of the blur again, this
time ducking into a side street. An uneasy feeling built each time I ventured outside our kancha. Something in the back of my mind, or just
beyond my vision, troubled me. Today I was certain. I was being followed. By whom? What did they want from me?

After saying a prayer for the soul of the micheq at the bridge, Qhari
and I stumbled on to Limatampu. We soon learned the kuraka of that
place was the friend of whom the Zangalla governor spoke. But he did-
n't want to hear our tale, and merely shrugged when we told him the
micheq was lost at the bridge. "You're safe, and that's what's important," he said. We spent the night under heavy guard, never told who
chased us, why men died for us, or what was required of us in Cuzco.
The next day found us back on the road for the holy city, but this time
surrounded by two squadrons of heavily armed troops.

The road continued through forested valleys and pastures sheltered by
rounded, grassy hills, with snow-capped mountains ever floating above
the horizon clouds, the air thin and cool but hardly noticed in the lush
green vistas. And it was in this setting that our journey ended when we

crested a ridge and looked down on the great bowl that is the head of the Huatanay Valley. Thousands of high, thatched roofs in an orderly grid marched across the valley below us - the sacred city of Cuzco.

On every road approaching the city there is a sentry post where all are routinely questioned and searched, and nearby is a shrine where travelers offer thanks to the gods for a safe journey and make offerings to Cuzco, for the city itself is a wak'a of highest order. Being in the company of an imperial escort, Qhari and I were ushered through these preliminaries. While an officer whispered with the guards we admired the fabled city of which we heard so much, and immediately saw that it was infinitely greater than all the tales combined.

Cuzco is said to symbolize a puma, the royal beast. The city is the puma's body, the Emperor represents the head, and the residents are its limbs. But with some imagination one can even see a puma's outline in the layout of the city. The great hill of Saqsawaman overlooking the city on the north is the puma's head, and from either side of Saqsawaman flow the Huatanay and Tullu rivers, which are channeled and seem to mark the puma's back and feet. The place where these rivers meet on the southern outskirts is called the Puma's Tail. The great square - five hundred paces long by four hundred wide - sits under the belly of the puma, and is framed on three sides by temples and palaces, and on the fourth by the Huatanay River. Four roads leading in from the four suyus converge on this center. Standing on the ridge that first day Qhari and I could plainly see that Cuzco was indeed the navel of the world.

No longer did we doubt the stories of treasures stored there, for even at a distance one could see the glint of the Qorikancha walls - the golden enclosure behind which all the major gods resided, encircled by a band of solid gold. Inside, temples sheathed in silver and gold reflected the afternoon sun. The wealth of the Empire flowed into Cuzco, and by law all sacred metals and fine cloth that entered the holy city could never leave.

On the hillsides around the city stood endless rows of storehouses from which all needs were met with regular dispersals of food, cloth, and everything the inhabitants desired. But the permanent dwellers were few for only royalty lived in the city, while the servants and craftsmen who maintained it walked in from nearby villages each day and departed at night.

Surrounding the royal core a series of lesser districts radiated out in neat blocks, their kanchas, or compounds, built of mud brick in place of the fine stonework in the city proper, but all sprouting steeply pitched thatch roofs. Here lived the provincial lords during their annual four-month residency, their kanchas located around the city according to their suyu and province. Since we came from Kuntisuyu, the western quarter of the Empire, and from the province of Ica within Kuntisuyu, the kancha of Lord Aquixe, Hatun Kuraka of Ica, was situated in the Qayawkachi district on the western outskirts, between the kanchas of the lords of Zangalla and Nazca, valleys that neighbor Ica to the north and south. Thus the layout of Cuzco mirrored the Empire.

For all the security that had surrounded us from Limatampu, upon arrival Qhari and I were unceremoniously deposited at our Hatun Kuraka's residence, and our escorts departed without a word. Lord Aquixe turned out to be a short, chinless young man with bulging eyes and a high, nervous voice. On the day we met he was resplendent in a feather tabard on which orange and green birds flew in a sky of yellow, and his arms were wreathed in gold and silver bands. I thought him an imposing figure in his finery, as long as he didn't speak. He was per-plexed when his steward presented us.

"Orphan twins from one of my fishing villages?" he squeaked. "The governor thinks I can use them here? For what?"

"Perhaps he thought they would be a novelty, Lord," the steward said. "Twins are blessed by the gods and reflect well on you."

"Well . . . I suppose. See if you can make them into decent servants or something."

Thereafter he ignored us, being much preoccupied with primping for parties around the city, attending them, and recovering. We were set to work as servants, though there were already enough of those in the crowded little compound, and wondered daily whether our unknown friends would contact us before our enemies discovered where we were.

The steward, a plump little man with the air of one accustomed to cringing before nobility and lording it over those under him, knew something about us. He alone was not surprised at our arrival, in fact, he seemed to have been expecting us, and even granted us a measure of civility as if we were guests and not servants. Our tasks were light, and he always kept track of our whereabouts.

The only rule governing our existence was that we were never to set foot outside the compound, and this the steward enforced most sharply. We longed to see the sights of the city and came to think of him as our jailer. Then, in the second week of our captivity, he was called away for a few days, and in spite of his warnings we seized the opportunity to run errands about the city. Though the Ica governor had cautioned us against trying to contact anyone, we saw no harm in attempting to ascertain the whereabouts of father's old commander, Lord Achachi. He knew who gave the orders that doomed father's troop, and was therefore the first link to the murderer. Since our 'friends' had delivered us to Cuzco, surely they wanted us to succeed.

"Stand aside, girl," a soldier barked.

Pressing myself to the wall I turned to see a lady and child approaching, the pair seated in a litter borne on the shoulders of eight men. An attendant hurried alongside holding a parasol of red and blue feathers above them. Soldiers in checkered tunics paraded ahead and behind. Such spectacles still left me breathless, awed by the majesty of those who ruled the world.

"Lady Sisa."

Startled, I turned to find an old woman at my elbow, bent nearly double with age and resting her weight on a staff. Wisps of gray hair fell from beneath the hood protecting her against the still sputtering rain.

"I said, that was Lady Sisa and her daughter," she repeated, nodding up the street where the litter still floated above the crowds.

Father's story came back in a rush. "Grandmother, is she the same Princess Sisa who was rescued at Hatunqolla during the Qolla rebellion?"

"You are a clever girl. That must have been before you were born, my child. You've learned your lessons well. She is indeed the same

Princess Sisa, now the wife of Lord Sapaca," she said in her throaty voice.

Emboldened by this chance meeting with one who knew the city, I rushed to the question foremost in mind. "Grandmother, is Lord Achachi in Cuzco?"

"Achachi? Lord Achachi? That's a common name, I - "

"He served at Hatunqolla when Princess Sisa was rescued," I said hoping to stir her memory.

"Oh, that Lord Achachi. The Achachi of Iñaca Panaqa," she replied, using the proper term 'panaqa' for a royal lineage. "He is Visitor-General of the Empire," she said lowering her voice reverently. "Some say he is on an inspection tour of Kuntisuyu now, but with officials you never know, they just turn up here and there. Why are you interested in him? And how is it you know so much about the Qolla rebellion?"

"Oh, a soldier who served with Lord Achachi told me all the stories. He said Lord Achachi was a man of great courage, and I always hoped one day I might see him."

"You are new to the city?" she asked. I nodded. "Yes, I see by your dress you're from Kuntisuyu. Those sea birds woven on your belt. . . from the province of Ica, perhaps?"

"It is so, grandmother. I serve the Hatun Kuraka of Ica, Lord Aquixe. My Lord wishes to visit the wak'a of our people, and I'm now returning from delivering his request to the temple."

"Then you're headed to the Qayawkachi district. I'm going in that direction, too. We can walk together and you can tell me of this land of Ica."

What she wanted was someone to lean on as she shuffled along, and an ear for her endless prattle. But it would have been discourteous to deny her either and I hoped to learn more.

The streets bustled with an array of costumes and coiffures from provinces throughout the Empire. As I learned on the journey to Cuzco, this was both a matter of pride and law, for all had the privilege, and obligation, of wearing the distinctive style of their homeland and no other, so they were instantly recognizable. At my urging the old woman happily pointed out the markings of each province, and I couldn't help but stare, quite rudely, at the passersby. There were light-skinned

Chachapoya and dark-skinned Chimu, Pinco, Wamali, Rucana, Charka, Quechua, Chincha, and many others - all the peoples of Tawantinsuyu. Here and there parrots from the jungles of Antisuyu paraded by, squawking on their perches, and one man even carried a monkey that, like the toucans, looked forlorn in the chill mountain air.

Many of the people we passed had molded heads, either flat with hardly a trace of forehead, or cone-shaped domes. This was not new to me because head shaping is common for boys and girls of many nations, and even practiced among the villagers of Ica, but I had never seen so many varieties in one place before. It's done with cloths and boards tied to a baby's head soon after it's born, so the soft bone grows into any desired shape. I've never known this to affect the intelligence of one so transformed. Those who had a board tied to their foreheads are called flat heads, while those whose skulls were bound with cloths to make them grow upward are called long heads. Both these shapes are widely seen, although one or the other is more prevalent in different areas, and applied with degrees of severity. It isn't an Inca custom, but is proudly displayed by many provincials. I suppose the mothers did this to make their children special.

We crossed a stone bridge over the Huatanay River, gushing with runoff through its narrow channel of stone blocks, and entered the outlying residential districts. Here the fine stonework gave way to walls of mud brick set on rough stone foundations, but still protected by the overhang of thatched roofs. I glanced at the kanchas, each representing a province of Kuntisuyu, and marveled again at the organization my people had brought to the world. The old woman leaned on my arm as she shuffled along, chattering away, until a long pause brought my attention back to her.

"I said, it's good to have rain so late in the season. The city is cleaner after a rain."

The city was always clean because scores of workers saw to that daily, and all refuse and night soil vanished in the many ducts running above and below ground that fed the rivers, while other channels were reserved for fresh water. But I allowed the comment, assuming she referred to the freshness that follows a rain.

"Yes, grandmother, the air is fresh - " I began, when Qhari stepped from a side street.

"You've found a friend, sister," Qhari said in the Ica tongue.

"Valiant Cougar," I replied self-consciously, suddenly aware I had been speaking perfect Runasimi with the old woman. "I was just helping this grandmother down the street. You've finished your errand, too?"

"You were speaking fluently in her tongue," Qhari said rapidly in a low voice, frowning at me.

"Eh? What are you saying?" the old woman asked, startled to hear the Ica language.

"He's my brother, grandmother," I replied in accented Runasimi. "I must go now. Stay well." I dropped her arm and hurried off with Qhari.

"That was stupid," Qhari whispered when we were away from the old woman. "That's how they'll catch us. If you must speak Runasimi always use the accent, and remember to jumble your words."

I hated it when he was right so I lifted my chin and sniffed. "She was just an old woman. She doesn't know or care who we are. Besides, they know we're here. I was followed today."

"Followed? By whom?"

"I didn't see who it was, but I saw Lady Sisa. Remember the princess father told us about? Well, she's here, and married to a lord named Sapaca. The old woman even knew of Lord Achachi. Qhari, these are real people!"

He looked at me in surprise. "Did you ever doubt it?"

"Well, no. . . but that old woman. . . ." I turned to where I left her. She had vanished.

"That old woman," Qhari finished, "could be anyone, or she may know someone, or she might just wander up and down the streets telling everyone about the interesting girl she met, and eventually her tale could reach the wrong ears."

Chastised now I walked quietly beside him, trying to think of some retort but knowing he was right. He turned to me. "Did you say Princess Sisa is married to Lord Sapaca?"

"That's what the old woman said."

Qhari looked thoughtful. "Father told us Thupa Inka promised Sisa to the officer who found her alive. This Sapaca must have been the one who rescued her."

"Yes, I suppose."

"But father also said his captain, Kontor, reported the women at the Hatunqolla akllawasi to their commander, Lord Achachi."

"Yes, well?"

"Then why didn't Achachi rescue the princess and marry her?"

"Maybe Sapaca got there first."

"Maybe. But the one who murdered those women arrived before the princess was found. Who else knew about them besides Achachi?"

"Qhari, you're not suggesting. . . ? Lord Achachi was their commander. . . . Father said the orders that doomed them came from above Achachi."

"That's what Achachi told Kontor. But. . . ?"

"You there, boy," a man's voice shouted from a doorway, "come and lend us a hand."

It was a newly built kancha. The walls were up but the roof poles awaited placement. Qhari looked at me and shrugged, then went to the door. I followed, curious to see what the workmen were doing inside. Qhari stopped at the threshold and questioned me with a look. "I don't talk Runasimi good," I assured him in my thickest accent. He smiled. We entered.

The compound looked empty. Stacks of mud bricks covered with straw sat in the middle of the patio, thatch occupied a corner, and roof poles leaned against the walls. There was no sign of the man who beckoned us.

"Over here," the voice called from a side room.

My stomach tightened. Something was wrong. "Valiant Cougar - " I began, but Qhari, fascinated with the construction, was already through the door and engulfed in shadows. Silence.

"Valiant Cougar," I called, sure now that something was amiss.

"He's here," the voice replied. "Come. We need you, too."

I glanced back through the kancha door to the street. There lay safety. Every part of me screamed run! run! But Qhari? He would never abandon me.

I reached for my knife. Gone. I'd left it in the kitchen that morning. Snatching up a brick I leapt into the room, landed in a crouch, and whirled to face the dark form lunging at me. Whack! My brick caught him full in the face. He howled, covering his nose with both hands. For an instant I saw blood spilling between his fingers. Then huge hands grabbed me from behind, pinning my arms to my sides and covering my mouth.

"You little bitch," a bloody face growled at me. "Let me have her."

"Cover yourself, fool," the voice that had beckoned us said. "She's not likely to recognize you with a face like that, but we're not taking any chances." The man pulled his cloak over his head and turned his back on me, muttering and spitting out a tooth. I saw enough to know he was Inca, and the man pinning me from behind spoke perfect Runasimi, also.

He spun me around. Two hooded men stood over Qhari, who knelt with a gag tied at his mouth. One of them wrenched Qhari's arms behind his back, twisting them up to his shoulders. The other had a cord around Qhari's neck.

"Now then, Qori Qoyllur," the voice breathed in my ear, "I know you're a brave girl and not afraid to die, so I won't threaten you with death." I recognized the voice now - the same man who questioned us in the desert. So, you escaped after all, I thought. I wondered if that was you with the bandaged neck at the bridge.

He squeezed me tighter. "Let me remind you I know who you are, and I know you understand me, so this time don't bother playing innocent. Where is your father? Has he gone to meet your uncle? Where are they hiding?"

When he eased his hand from my mouth I bit it. Smack! The slap set my ear ringing, but I heard him curse, "You little bitch!" He still held me fast with one arm. The bloody-faced man balked to hear his companion share his opinion of me. My captor stuffed a corner of his cloak in my mouth.

"Now then," he began again, trying to control his voice, "I'm not going to kill you. No, do not fear of that. But if you don't tell me what I need to know your brother is going to die."

I stiffened.

He jerked my head toward Qhari. "Yes, he's going to die slowly. It will be the last thing you ever see, because afterwards I'm going to gouge out your pretty eyes. What do you think of that, Qori Qoyllur? Not so brave now?"

My thoughts whirled. Not Qhari, never! I struggled to speak. He took the cloth from my mouth, keeping his hand away from my teeth.

"We're under the protection of Lord Aquixe," I said, trying to keep an Ica accent. "If you harm us he'll - "

My captor laughed. "Aquixe? He's the least of our concerns. Qhari Puma's body will go into the river and vanish in the night. As for you, who are you going to identify without eyes?"

He caught my neck in the crook of his arm and pulled me down, pushing my face close to Qhari's. Qhari winced as the man at his back twisted his arms higher, holding him firm. Qhari's eyes held no fear, only pain, and silent words that thundered in my head as if he shouted them aloud, 'Never tell, no matter what happens.'

"Now, Qori Qoyllur, speak now," the voice demanded.

The cord tightened around Qhari's throat and his eyes bulged.

"Speak or he's dead."

Qhari turned purple.

"Tell me. Where are they?"

A rasping sound torn from Qhari's throat burned in my ears.

"Save your brother."

My mouth tried to form words, but no sound came.

"Bitch!" was the last I heard. The arm squeezed my neck. The room went black.

When consciousness returned I lay on my back staring up at the darkened sky. The first evening star twinkled beyond the jutting silhouette of a roof pole. The slapping of sandals on cobblestones faded outside in the street. An earthy smell of fresh mortar hung in the damp air. Then I remembered where I was and - Qhari! Where's Qhari?

Jolting upright I swept the room with a glance. It was empty but for a dark form lying facedown on the floor nearby. I rolled him over and cradled him in my arms, rocking gently, my tears streaking the mud on his face. His eyelids fluttered and he stirred.

"Qhari, oh, Qhari, please stay with me. Don't die and leave me alone."

He coughed painfully, then his eyes opened and he looked up at me with curiosity. "Save that for my funeral," he said in a hoarse whisper, "I'm not done yet."

"I thought you were dead."

"Don't rush me. And stop squeezing me so hard."

"Well!" I dropped his head letting it thud on the floor. He groaned. "Then look after yourself," I said.

I rose and stood over him with hands on my hips. "You were the one who led us in here, Qhari Puma - yes, you - right into a trap."

Qhari sat up stroking the bruise at his neck. "It's true," he said, "but they won't harm us again."

"Why? What do you mean?"

"They're afraid of us. At least, they're afraid to kill us now. Someone wants us alive."

"Who? Why?"

He dismissed my questions with an impatient wave. "How should I know? But they threatened to kill us, and then left."

"They were going to gouge out my eyes," I reminded him, still trembling at the thought.

"Yes," he nodded thoughtfully, "they've tried everything now, and they know we won't talk." He looked up at me. "You were very brave, Qori."

I brushed my hair back and looked away. "Well, you were brave, too."

"Yes I was," he said, pleased with himself.

My hands returned to my hips. "Well, it wasn't your eyes they were going to gouge."

"No, but it was my neck." He held up his hands before I could say another word. "Anyway, I don't think they'll try that again. They know we're here, and they'll be watching us. We must be careful."

68

"And do what?"

That question was soon answered for both of us.

"My Lords, you honor my humble kancha," Lord Aquixe said to his visitors, "Please, come and sit."

"Thank you, Lord, but we'll not stay long. Our records show you brought two new servants into the city - twins, I believe. With your permission we'd like to see them."

I peeked from our room. Two Inca nobles stood in the patio. Friends or foes? What did they want with us?

The steward returned the day after our adventure, and upon learning we were going out in his absence he summoned us immediately. Far from sympathetic, when he saw the bruise on Qhari's neck he was furious with us. No explanation was asked. We had disobeyed. We had challenged his authority and placed him in an awkward position. We were ungrateful. We were foolish little brats, and on and on he raved while Qhari and I hung our heads. As much as I hated to admit it he was right. He might have at least listened to the superbly crafted story I prepared in which we were the innocent victims of a misunderstanding, but he would not. We had to remain in our room until he decided what to do with us. That was three days ago, and now, thoroughly chastised and repentant, we were more than ready to come out; but, to face what?

The Inca nobles looked about with unconcealed disdain while Aquixe summoned the steward, and ordered him to bring the twins and keros of aqha for his guests. We were served along with the tumblers of fermented maize drink.

Observing custom each man dipped a finger in his kero and flicked a drop in offering to Mama Pacha - Mother Earth, before taking a deep draught.

"Have they caused any trouble?" Aquixe asked in his squeaky voice. "If so I'll have them put to death immediately." From him it sounded more like a whine than a threat.

The men chuckled. One said, "Not at all, we're only interested in them because they're wak'a wacasqa - twins, born two of one belly - unusual and therefore special to the gods. Now, let's have a look at them."

Qhari and I stood with our heads respectfully bowed, examining our wiggling toes.

Aquixe pointed at Qhari. "This one is Valiant Cougar, and the girl is Golden Star."

"Interesting names, Lord," one said, "but what are they called in Runasimi?"

Aquixe looked embarrassed. "Forgive me. The boy is Qhari Puma and the girl is Qori Qoyllur."

"Do they speak a civilized tongue?"

The Hatun Kuraka ignored the slight and questioned the steward with a look. "They're learning Runasimi, Lord," the steward answered for him, "and are already quite intelligible."

"Their parents?"

Aquixe looked pleased to have the answer. "They're orphans from one of my fishing villages."

The visitors turned away sipping their aqha, and discussing us as if we weren't present. Lord Aquixe, much to his obvious annoyance, was left out of the conversation. I shifted closer to overhear.

"What do you think?"

"The girl looks like a boy."

I wanted to kick him.

"Most do at her age. Will the Esteemed Mothers have her?"

"I am Apu Panaqa. That is my decision."

"Indeed, brother, and was it your decision to come here?"

The Apu Panaqa frowned. "No more than it was yours."

"The boy has good limbs. If he has wind we can make him a message runner."

"I have other matters to attend. The directive was clear. Let's be done with this."

They turned. "Most Fortunate Lord," the Apu Panaqa said, "since the gods have favored you with these twins it's only fitting that we honor you also. Therefore, I'll enter the girl in the akllawasi and the boy will become a servant. Perhaps he'll even be made a messenger."

Qhari and I stared at each other. They were going to separate us!

Aquixe grinned. "My Lords, you do me great honor. I trust the Emperor will be pleased to learn of my offering?"

The Apu Panaqa rolled his eyes at his companion, but turned back with a smile. "Most certainly. I'll inform Him myself." Then he gave me a measuring look. "Girl, have you begun your moon times?"

I blushed as all male eyes turned on me. "Yes, Lord," I answered in a small voice.

"Are you chaste?"

"Lord?"

"Have you been with a man?"

"No, Lord." I wanted to be invisible.

"Well, the Esteemed Mothers will determine that for themselves." He looked at the Hatun Kuraka. "Clean them up and deliver the girl to the rear of the akllawasi at midday. A guard will call here for the boy."

VI

Of Qori's life in the Convent, the Foolish Tales these Indians tell of their Origins, the Solitary Sin, and of how word arrives from an unexpected quarter.

"What are you doing here?" a girl asked as I sat down in the back row. I sniffed and ignored her. Everyone turned to look and began whispering about me. This was a beginners' class. It was bad enough I had to sit with them for their afternoon lesson, but the reason for this punishment was none of their concern.

I stared at the outer wall, many times the height of a man, which blocked all view and sound from the busy streets of Cuzco. I knew those streets, though I hadn't seen them in three years. For all the news allowed from the outside world the akllawasi might as well have been on a distant mountaintop. But the sky was open and free. Lazy clouds drifted overhead. Was Qhari watching those same clouds?

I opened my bag and sorted through the colored yarn. Braiding a wristband, the simplest task, how demeaning. And being forced to do it with all these little girls and their wagging little tongues. True, the cloth panel I completed on my loom that morning had a few tiny errors - well, maybe more than a few - and I stitched it on backwards to its mate, but anyone could have made that mistake.

After the officials left Lord Aquixe's kancha Qhari and I begged not to be separated, but our pleas fell on ears of stone. "Children, you don't understand the honor granted you, and me, and all our people," Aquixe had said in his squeaky, nasal voice. "Besides, once chosen you belong to the Emperor. Your family and your lord have no further claim on you." Then he explained Qhari's position: he was to join the ranks of the yanakuna, or 'helpers,' who were retainers for life like permanent servants, though it was an honorable status with chance of advancement. He would be given to one of the noble houses and attached to a lord. Qhari might serve in Cuzco, or on a royal estate, or travel with his master throughout the Empire.

"And me?" I asked fearing the answer. I knew that one of the compounds on the great square was the akllawasi, house of the chosen women, but what was a chosen woman?

"Ah, yes, Golden Star. You're being sent to the akllawasi here in Cuzco - the most prestigious akllawasi in the Empire, I might add - where you'll be trained for a few years. Only the most beautiful girls from all parts of Tawantinsuyu are sent there." He paused, regarding me as if wondering why I was selected. "Yes . . . the most beautiful . . . anyway, there you'll be taught to cook and weave and all manner of virtuous things befitting a woman."

His words bore the weight of a mountain. I would have much preferred to join Qhari and see the Empire. "And after the training, Lord?"

"Afterward? Well, the akllas are distributed among the worthy men of the Empire as a special mark of favor from the Emperor," he replied as if my fate was of little consequence, "and others are married to the gods and spend the rest of their lives serving in temples." I wasn't sure which outcome sounded worse.

Even in our last moments together we planned. "I'll send word to you if I can," Qhari assured me, "and I'll listen for news of Lord Achachi. When you leave the akllawasi we'll go and confront him together."

I brushed a tear from my cheek. "Why are they doing this to us, Qhari?"

"You'll be safe inside the akllawasi, and I with my new master. This must be the doing of our friends, to protect us. . . at least, I hope it's their doing."

Those were his last words to me, for just then a guard appeared and took him away, refusing to tell their destination. And for three years I wondered if our fates were the choice of our friends or our enemies, and whether each knew the others' plans.

A commotion rose from the next courtyard, the last in a series dividing the length of the akllawasi. I strained to hear. A new group of girls was being admitted, and with them the hope of news from Qhari.

Three times each year tribute came to Cuzco, and along with it girls from all parts of the Empire. Most chosen women simply entered the akllawasi of their home province, but the fairest and those of highest birth were sent to Cuzco. These arrivals preceded major festivals during which the senior akllas were distributed, graduating to the roles of wives, concubines, or priestesses. Soon it would be my turn.

The younger girls were kept in the akllawasi for four years, but the older ones, like me, already in womanhood, were trained for three. In a few weeks I would line up with the other senior girls, parade in front of the crowds in the great square, and for the first time learn what fate was decided for me.

I imagined the new girls clustering inside the rear door. I saw it often enough. They were all ten to twelve years of age, some the daughters of nobles, others of commoners, each wearing the dress of her province, wide-eyed, frightened, and already homesick. The Apu Panaqa, the official who selects the girls, passed his khipu to the Most Esteemed Mother through the door, for even he was forbidden to enter this world of women. The Most Esteemed Mother handed the khipu to an assisting priestess who pulled the main cord tight between outstretched hands, letting the pendant cords dangle. Then the Most Esteemed Mother ran her hands down the cords, fingering each knot on the record, and checking the girls to make sure the knots tallied with the head count. The door closed, and our new sisters suddenly realized they now truly belonged to the Empire.

The Cuzco akllawasi is the only akllawasi I have ever known to have a rear door, or any other door besides the front entrance, which is guarded on the outside by old men day and night. Of course, having no comparisons at the time I thought nothing of it. It seemed no more than a convenience for the priestesses who walked to the Qorikancha each day, a block farther down the street. When the Apu Panaqa pushed me through this back entrance the Most Esteemed Mother protested loudly, for I arrived not with a group but alone, and unannounced.

"What is the meaning of this?" she had demanded. "Do you think you can come here whenever you choose and deposit one girl? This is not proper. How dare you disturb the sanctity of this house."

I had to conceal a smile. The Apu Panaqa shrank before her and stammered, "M-Most Esteemed M-Mother, p-please accept my humble apologies. I have come to deliver this girl to the Emperor's storehouse by special request. Please allow me to explain."

He leaned forward and whispered in her ear. The expression on her face changed from a scowl to a frown, then surprise.

"Very well," she said, "it shall be so. And, my Lord, please return my sincere wishes for good health," she added with a knowing look.

The Apu Panaqa smiled, bowed, and backed away with a sigh of relief. The door slid closed.

Though my entry was irregular what followed is customary, and awaited all the new girls now crowded in the rear courtyard. An old priestess led me to a small room where she seated herself on a blanket. Pulling her shawl over her head she beckoned me to kneel in front of her, then leaned forward to whisper, "Have you sinned, my child?"

Sinned? What was a sin? I shrugged. "No, Mother."

"Come, child, no one is without sin."

"Do you sin, Mother?"

"Impertinence! Pride! Disrespect for your elders! These are your first sins. Now, have you neglected to honor your ancestors, or broken the Emperor's laws? Have you blasphemed against the gods? No? So say you. Are you chaste? Yes? Have you let boys touch your private places? No? Are you sure? Very well. You are a wicked girl, but Mother Moon will forgive you if you truly repent. To show Her you are penitent, and to remind you of your sins, you will abstain from salt, meat, and peppers for a week, and suffer two blows of the stone."

I had no idea I was so sinful. A week is a long time to go without my favorite foods, but I was more concerned about the stone. What did she mean?

"Turn and face the door."

Still kneeling I complied hesitantly, afraid to turn my back on her. She produced a long, stone pestle from behind her. "Turn your head to the door."

Thud. The first blow knocked me forward on my hands.

"Sit up," she commanded.

Thud. Again the pestle fell, this time bruising my left side.

"Now, face me." She studied my teary eyes for a moment, and then said most pleasantly, "Good. You are forgiven."

Thereafter during weekly confessions I learned to admit minor sins, often made-up, to appease my confessor and avoid such stern penance. But all too frequently others implicated me in their confessions, and at meals I spent as much time in the mush line as in the stew line, and often went to bed with a sore back.

Confession was only the first ritual when I arrived at the akllawasi, and again I thought of the new girls waiting in the rear courtyard.

After my bruising the old priestess moved her shawl back to her shoulders, bid me rise with her, and said, "Now, remove your clothes."

I must have stared blankly at her for she spoke more briskly then. "Do as I say. Quickly, girl, out of your dress."

I did as commanded, standing naked before her with my dress at my feet and head lowered, feeling embarrassed and confused. Her first words did nothing to put me at ease. "You're a skinny little thing," she said as she turned me around, "and there are blemishes on your chin and shoulders, but that's common enough for one your age. They'll stop troubling you in a few years." Then she made a most thorough examination from the soles of my feet to the top of my head, so that when she was finished there was no part of me that hadn't been studied and poked.

"You're free of any permanent flaws," she said. "Now, lie on your back and bend your knees."

While I complied she dipped her middle finger in a jar and knelt beside me. "Open your legs. No, wider." When I felt her cold finger squeeze into my raka I gasped and closed my legs.

"Stop that," she commanded. "Don't be foolish, child. This isn't hurting you. It's only to make certain you're pure and worthy of being a chosen woman. Now, open and lie still."

I closed my eyes and held my breath until she finished. In truth, it took but a moment and didn't hurt, but it was a new sensation for me then, and one which left me pondering the possibilities.

76

Satisfied with what she had found, or not found, the priestess returned me to the Most Esteemed Mother and reported, "This one is flawless and chaste."

When the Apu Panaqa said he was delivering an aklla to the Emperor's storehouse I felt like a sack of maize. After my inspection I felt more like a chunk of meat, and not a very desirable cut when the Most Esteemed Mother took my chin in her hand, turned my head this way and that, and said, "Not the quality we're accustomed to in this akllawasi, but I suppose we'll have to take her."

Those poor girls now entering, I thought again. Perhaps it's better they don't know what's about to happen to them.

The priestess in charge of the afternoon's lesson arrived and seated herself against the wall. Although this was a class on religion we immediately bowed our heads and began braiding, for an Inca woman's hands, be she noble or commoner, are never idle.

"In the beginning Wiraqocha, The Creator, made the sky and the earth," the priestess began, "but all was in darkness."

Not this one again, I groaned inwardly. I could repeat the origin story word for word. But it was the first telling for the younger ones who came from distant provinces, and they sat alert.

"Then He made giants from stone and sent them to walk the earth. After a while these giants displeased Him, so He caused a great flood to destroy them, and others He turned back into stone. This is so, for there are many ancient places where you can see these stone giants still standing where Wiraqocha left them."

"But Esteemed Mother," a girl in the front spoke up, "were there not also people before the great flood? My mother said that when the flood came and all things perished, a woman and a man climbed into a drum and floated away. Later, when the water subsided, they came to rest at Tiwanaku, and they are our ancestors."

"Not our people," another said. "My mother told me that a month before the flood all the llamas became sad and stopped eating, and they stared constantly at the sky. When a herder asked them what they were doing, they showed him a group of stars that had come together to dis-

cuss the coming deluge. This herder took his six children, along with
some food and llamas, to the top of a hill. When the waters rose so did
the hill, and when the waters receded the hill returned to normal size.
The children of this herder are the ancestors of my people."

The priestess, who listened patiently, held up her hand for silence.
"What your mothers have told you they believe to be true, and for them
it is so. I'm sure others among you can add your own stories, but if
you'll be patient I shall tell you what was revealed to our Emperor, the
Son of the Sun, and the high priests; and if you doubt what I say, how
then do you account for the ancient stone statues found in so many
places?" As this wisdom took hold a respectful silence settled on the
gathering.

The priestess continued with the story of how Wiraqocha decided to
bring light into the world, and so He caused Inti and Mama Killa - Father
Sun and Mother Moon - and all the stars to rise from an island in Lake
Titiqaqa. Then He made people His own size from clay, and painted
clothes on them to represent different tribes. He gave them life, and to
each tribe its own language, songs, customs, and foods, ordering them to
travel under the earth and emerge from lakes, hills, or caves in the region
they were to settle.

"Among these first people," she said, "were the Incas, led by four
brothers and four sisters. When they were ready to leave Inti called
them to Him, saying, "It is given to you and your descendants to rule
over all nations. Always remember to venerate me, and think of me
as your father, for you are my blessed children." Then He gave them
the imperial emblems: a war club and scepter of gold, a royal standard, and a tasseled headband that only the emperor may wear, the
Royal Fringe. Thus the Incas, Children of the Sun, were divinely
chosen at creation to rule the world.

"These ancestors emerged from caves at Pacariqtampu, a place south
of Cuzco. This is so, for you can see those caves today. Inti gave them
a rod of gold and told them to cast it into the ground as they traveled.
Where the rod disappeared the Incas would found their capital. On their
journey one of the brothers threw his sling with such force that ravines

opened along the sides of the Huatanay Valley. This is so, for you can see those ravines today. This troublesome brother was lured back to the origin caves and sealed inside. At the hill called Huanacauri another brother devised the Inca manhood rites, and then turned himself into stone. This is so, for those rites are still performed in the same way at Huanacauri each year, and all can see the stone that was this brother. When the Incas reached the fertile land at the head of the Huatanay Valley the golden rod disappeared in the earth, and the Incas built their first houses where the Qorikancha now stands. A third brother also turned himself into stone, so he could be the wak'a that guards the fields. This is so, for you can see that boulder, which is still worshipped today.

"But some savages who lived in the valley did not know who the Incas were and tried to drive them away. Among the Inca sisters was Mama Huaco. She slew one of these savages and tore out his heart and lungs, carrying them dangling from Her mouth when She attacked the others. They were so terrified by this fierce woman they fled. Thus it was that Mama Huaco won the valley for the Incas."

It always pleased me to think that one of our first ancestors was a conquering warrior-woman, however gruesome Her manner may have been.

The priestess took a deep breath and continued with the story as if chanting a prayer. "The remaining brother married one of His sisters, and they became the rulers of the Incas, founding Chima Panaqa, the first royal lineage. This is so, for their descendants still live in Cuzco today. They called the savages back from the hills and showed them how to irrigate and work the fields, how to sow and harvest, spin and weave, and make clothes. Thus, these natives, who were little more than naked animals when the Incas arrived, became civilized. And in the sacred field of Sausero, Mama Huaco planted the first maize, bringing one of the greatest gifts to all people. This is so, for the sacred field is still sown and harvested by Inca nobles, and each year cobs are sent to temples throughout the Empire."

At this point in the story another buzz of confusion rippled among the girls. One from a distant province spoke up. "Mother, my people also have a maize goddess, but she is not called Mama Huaco. She is a daughter of Mama Pacha, the Earth Mother." Heads bobbed around her.

The priestess smiled patiently. "It is so. All things of the earth come from the regenerative powers of Mama Pacha. She has many daughters who are rightfully worshipped for the bounty they provide. The Axomamas give us potatoes, the Coyamamas provide metals, and potters who work the clay of the earth worship the Sañumamas. These and others are the daughters of Mama Pacha, and among them are the Saramamas, the goddesses of maize and fertility. You may know them by different names in your home provinces, but are they not all daughters of Mother Earth?" Heads nodded. "Very well, then there is no conflict in our teachings. It is just that Mama Huaco is first among Saramamas, and She shares Her bounty with all other maize goddesses."

This always seemed fair and reasonable to me, as it did to the girls seated around me that day. It did not deny any provincial beliefs, it only blended Inca and local traditions, adding a higher level of Inca prestige.

When the lesson ended I hurried to the rear courtyard to look over the new arrivals. Some were still emerging teary eyed and stunned from their confessions and inspections, but the first through already stood about awkwardly in their new clothes. I felt the mournful looks on their faces, remembering my own first weeks when such a terrible longing seized me I couldn't eat or sleep. But longing, although never entirely gone, faded with time.

The akllawasi covers an entire city block; albeit a long, narrow block. What at first seemed an endless maze of passageways, courtyards, storehouses, open-fronted buildings, dormitories, and little shrines soon became all too familiar. The new girls, too, would soon settle into the busy routine that continued from dawn until evening devotions.

The girls in each dormitory worked as a team to maintain the akllawasi, and the duties rotated. One week we worked in the kitchens, either cooking, serving, or cleaning up, and the next sweeping out the courtyards and shrines, or polishing the temple vessels, delivering fuel, brewing aqha, and serving the priestesses. When not at our chores we were at our lessons: weaving, cooking, dancing, etiquette, languages, religion, and law and governance.

Being composed of so many disparate peoples, numerous languages were spoken throughout Tawantinsuyu, but the Inca tongue, Runasimi, meaning Human Speech, was the official language of government, and all kurakas and aspiring provincials learned it. Naturally akllas, regardless of origin, were expected to be fluent by the end of their training, and the Esteemed Mothers were greatly impressed with my proficiency in mastering Runasimi. We also learned the courtly Pacaje dialect of Aymara - the mother tongue of the Lake Titiqaqa region in northern Qollasuyu, that being one of the most populous and important regions of the Empire - and a few languages from the provinces of the Chinchaysuyu quarter, while those from Chinchaysuyu learned dialects of Kuntisuyu and Antisuyu. Of my many talents I must confess that I truly excel at languages, and was fluent in no less than five by the end of my third year.

An army of officials presided over the orderly administration of Tawantinsuyu. The Emperor directed the overlords of the four suyus who passed his commands to their governors. Below each provincial governor there was one man in charge of every ten thousand families, and another for each five thousand, one thousand, five hundred, one hundred, fifty, and finally every ten families. Thus the word of the Emperor reached the most humble dwelling with lightning speed. In addition, a host of traveling inspectors crisscrossed the Empire.

Throughout Tawantinsuyu people paid their taxes in labor - the mit'a system - except for nobility who were tax exempt. In every province certain lands were set-aside for the Emperor, being used to support His administrators and the affairs of state, and other lands were given to support Inca temples. The amount of land devoted to the Emperor and the temples varied according to the size and needs of each province, and the remainder was left to the local lord and his subjects. The people paid their taxes by taking turns working the Inca fields: cultivating, planting, irrigating, harvesting, and delivering the produce to storehouses. This supported the temples and administrators, and left a surplus should the imperial army pass through. During droughts the storehouses were opened to feed the people, and the stores repaid in times of plenty.

Others served their mit'a by maintaining nearby roads and bridges, or making weapons, sandals, clothing, and all manner of things destined for the Emperor's stores. But the raw materials were provided from Inca lands, so the people contributed only their labor. And this was done in turns so no family was unduly burdened. The people had most of the year to look after their own sustenance, and pay a similar tribute to their native lord.

The men also fulfilled their mit'a obligation by serving in the army when required, for all men are warriors. But even then no more than one in ten was called, unless the need was great, and all his clothing, weapons and food were provided from the imperial stores.

Law was largely a matter of agreed custom, and the rules were few enough that even a peasant could carry them in her head, never having recourse to plead ignorance. The ancient customs of each province were tolerated, provided they didn't jeopardize the imperial peace. Laws were merciful, and justice swift. For example, travelers who pilfered from roadside fields out of hunger were not punished, and the local poor received only a reprimand, but the thief who did so out of greed was publicly given many blows of the stone, and after the second offence put to death. So it was with property theft, the station and need of the culprit being taken into account, and persons who 'found' stolen property could not be accused of stealing it. But theft from the Emperor or one of the gods was another matter - regardless of circumstance death was immediate.

A number of laws were enforced to preserve the sanctity and safety of holy Cuzco. Crumbling walls and old roofs had to be replaced, and all canals kept clean. The threat of fire spreading through the city was always present, because of the thatch roofs in densely packed areas. Therefore it was only right that arson was punished by death, and if a house caught fire because of its owner's negligence those who helped put out the fire could divide the property among themselves.

Overseeing all Cuzco regulations was a force of twelve lords and twelve hundred men. The lords took turns patrolling the streets, one each month with his hundred men, and if anyone was found breaking the law - even sleeping with his wife during a fast when such contacts were prohibited - an object was taken from him. At the end of the year he was brought to judgment with his confiscated possession serving as evidence.

Modesty, honesty, and perpetual industry are the aspired virtues of all Inca women, as the Esteemed Mothers reminded us daily, and the same can be said for men. These qualities are taught from infancy, and in Cuzco instilled with the phrase used for greetings and farewells throughout the city; Ama llulla, ama sua, ama kella - Don't lie, don't steal, don't be lazy. Cleanliness is also a virtue, although peasants are less prone to observe it. By Cuzco law anyone found serving food or drink with dirty hands, regardless of their station, was forced to wash in public and drink the filthy water. In the akllawasi we bathed daily and washed our hair each week.

Sin is held to be the cause of disease, infirmities, and misfortune. As the Esteemed Mothers taught, "Who is without sin? Who is without calamities? Is it not so that one causes the other?" Wisely, I never argued with them, but what has always troubled me is what constitutes a sin. I've never met a priest who didn't delight in expounding at great length on this, but the difference between divine will and priestly will hasn't always been clear to me. Still, at the tender age of which I speak, the Esteemed Mothers' threats of eternal damnation in the underworld - that terrifying place where souls are tormented by demons and forced to eat charcoal, snakes, and toads, and drink muddy water - kept me fearful, if not always obedient. Royalty, I might add, always go to the upper world regardless of their behavior, where they enjoy perpetual bliss with Father Sun in places of great delight, feasting from the offerings made by their descendants on this earth.

Chores, lessons and devotions kept us busy from dawn to dusk, and our only free time came at night in the dormitories. Then the sisters of my chunka, or group of ten, sat up talking in the privacy of our room, sharing secrets and wallowing in all-out gossip sessions. Even after the wick of our single lamp was snuffed the visiting continued between pairs of girls snuggled together, giggling in the dark.

A favorite topic was boys. Since we entered the akllawasi just at the time we were beginning to take an interest our discussions were limited, being mostly derived from what older sisters had reported. In our innocence Qhari and I often examined my raka and his pesqo, but eventually we tired of the game. In those long-ago days his pesqo hadn't yet learned to grow and stiffen, as some of the girls claimed to have seen. So the mystery of what was under a man's loincloth was still a matter of urgent speculation for me.

One of our chunka sisters was from the land of Chimor on the north coast of Chinchaysuyu. Whether her stories were real or made up I couldn't then decide, but I always listened intently when she described religious festivals where everybody seemed to be doing everything with anybody in front of everyone. Women even took men's pesqos in their mouths! Some of our sisters found this repulsive, indeed, sinful, but I was fascinated. The Chimu girl always told the best stories, leaving me burning with curiosity.

Eventually I discovered how to pleasure my raka. At first I was embarrassed to think that others might hear me, so I held my breath when my fingers began to roam, coughing gently to hide the gasping between breaths, and biting the blanket when release came. But there was much coughing in our dormitory, and rustling of maize husk pallets. I came to realize that nobody was concerned about the origin of these night sounds, which everyone contributed to and no one mentioned the next day.

Of those in my chunka, Sumaq T'ika - Beautiful Flower, became my closest friend. Her name suited her, for she was indeed the prettiest girl in the akllawasi. Why she took an interest in me I cannot say, but I was greatly flattered that one of her beauty and noble birth chose me as her partner for the morning chores. We were of an age, but she treated me like an elder, and I warmed to the pleasure of having someone to care for. In the evenings when our chunka gathered around the lamp she cuddled beside me while I stroked her hair and repeated the day's lessons. Sumaq T'ika wasn't slow, on the contrary, she was exceedingly clever. I think she made me recount the teachings just to hear my voice.

"Qori Qoyllur," a priestess called, "help me move these new girls over to the kitchens. Few of them speak a civilized tongue yet."

I approached a girl standing alone and confused in the middle of the courtyard, fumbling with the tupu pins on her new dress. After confession and inspection, the third formality of entry was issue of new clothing produced from the akllawasi looms. Now divested of her native costume, the last vestige of her homeland, it was impossible to tell where she was from.

"Let me help you, sister," I said. She shook her head numbly. Poor thing, I thought, it's not only the language you don't understand.

"Like this," I said adjusting her tupus. She was now clothed like the rest of us in the style of Inca women. The garments had confused me at first, too. The ankle-length dress is a single piece of cloth like a blanket, wound around the body under the arms, with the back edges pulled forward over the shoulders where they are fastened with two tupu pins at the front, leaving the arms bare. Even though the dress overlaps down one side, it can be arranged so that when a woman walks the edges open to expose her leg, which is more daring and allows greater freedom of movement. But the side fold usually remains closed for modesty and warmth. A wool belt, which is a hand span in width, encircles the waist, and is tied by strings at the back. This middle binding is intricately woven in many colors, and greatly flatters a woman's natural form. Over the dress a cloak is worn that hangs to the knees in back, and is pinned with a third tupu at the breast. But these garments were too large for the new girl, who couldn't have been more than ten, and it took some arranging before she could even walk properly. With a smile and a nod I directed her to the nearest kitchen.

"I heard that priestess call you Qori Qoyllur," a girl said from behind. I turned to find one of the new arrivals looking at me curiously.

"I am of Iñaca Panaqa," she said lifting her chin.

That explained the ease with which she wore her new clothes, and her fluent Runasimi; she was Inca, a daughter of the royal lineage of Pachakuti. The strange old woman who walked with me in the streets long ago said Lord Achachi was also of Iñaca Panaqa, the ninth royal house. My heart quickened. "Yes?" I encouraged her.

She looked around once to make sure no one was listening. "Your brother is watched over. Stay silent, and stay safe."

"Where is my brother? Who sends this message?"

"That's all I can say. I really don't know anything more, and I'll never speak to you again so stay away from me." She hurried off.

Is this reassurance, or a thinly veiled threat? I wondered. 'I have your brother. If you remain quiet I'll leave him alone.' Who? Who is 'watching over' Qhari? Achachi? Maybe Qhari is right about him. Kontor reported the women at the Hatunqolla akllawasi to Achachi, which gave Achachi the chance to carry out the foul deed, and he had the authority to order Kontor and his men to their deaths to cover himself. But is Achachi even in Cuzco?

I had to be sure. A plan began to form.

'

VII

In which Qori has Dance Lessons, is saved by a most Outrageous Lie, eats Roast Guinea Pig with peanut sauce, and Lies again.

Our entire line of dancers tumbled sideways in a heap. It wasn't my fault. . . not exactly. We all held hands with me at the end when I stumbled pulling the next girl down who in turn pulled her neighbor, and so on until the whole troupe lay tangled.

Tanta Karwa laughed. "Everyone up and try it again." She clapped her hands for attention. "Qori, take the same position but lift your feet."

Tanta Karwa was our favorite, always quick to laugh yet somehow keeping order and taking us through the lessons without a sharp word. Our usual dance mistress was away, and Tanta Karwa, though not an Esteemed Mother, was a frequent visitor who assisted with the lessons and running of things. She was of middle years, ancient as far as we were concerned, though her hair was as full and black as mine, and the approaching lines of age only added a kindly grace. Her clothes were in rich but subdued colors, and of such fineness that only the absence of gold jewelry distinguished her from a royal lady; a large silver tupu fastened her cloak, and she wore three more pinned down the front.

The elderly Esteemed Mother who kept time on the drum during rehearsals was secretly nicknamed Cormorant. She reminded us of that dark, crotchety old bird with its hook-tipped bill, which aptly described her and her nose. She was also our Chunka Mother. One priestess was assigned as general guardian to each group of ten girls, although she taught her specialty to all the girls of the akllawasi, be it dance, drumming, weaving, cooking, or whatever, and each gave religious instruction on the deity she served. But as chunka guardian she was also mentor, example, and confidante, and stayed informed of each girl's progress in the various skills. At least, that's how it was supposed to be. Old Cormorant was none of those things to us, and though she was all sunshine in front of the other Mothers, in private she cuffed us into silence so we wouldn't bother her.

All the Esteemed Mothers married a deity, either Inti, Illap'a, or one of the lesser male gods, and remained virgins in their husbands' service throughout their lives. And each attended a goddess, her husband's female counterpart. Thus, only the wives of Inti fed, dressed, and carried the statue of Mama Killa, Inti's celestial wife, and those married to Illap'a tended Mama Pacha, because His rain makes Her fertile.

Only Wiraqocha stands alone for He is The Creator, The Beginning, Ancient Foundation, Instructor Of The World, Maker Of All Things, Father Of The Sun And Moon. Referring to Him as male is a matter of convenience, because Wiraqocha was before all others and therefore neither strictly male nor female. There were many temples dedicated to Wiraqocha, as there were to all the major gods, but the most famous, and the one I longed to see, was the great Temple of Wiraqocha near the town of Raqch'i. But alas, the last meeting of father's comrades came and went four months earlier, while I stared at the inside walls of the akllawasi. The next meeting wasn't for another five years. By then, twenty-two years would have passed since the murders at the Hatunqolla akllawasi. Would uncle Maita and Kontor still be alive?

"Now, back in line," Tanta Karwa said trying to sound firm, "and remember, eyes forward, three steps to the right, one to the left, two right, four left - three, one, two, four. After every third sequence drop hands, clap, and twirl to change places with the girl on your left. Ready?"

This was only one of many steps. We always danced in lines, usually two lines facing each other, with hands or arms linked, and clapping the rhythm when we parted to twirl and dip. The lines surged toward each other, then back, then forward again until the dancers changed position with those opposite. In one of the more intricate steps each line curved around to form a circle, and the two circles passed through each other to change sides. In the middle of a dance we often paused to sing the praises of the gods or the Emperor in a chorus of high, shrill voices, this being the preferred voice of song for girls and women alike.

"Much better, Qori," Tanta Karwa called when we finished the sequence. "That's all for today. We'll meet again tomorrow. Remember, your presentation is only a week away, and then you'll be dancing for the Emperor and Empress in the great square."

As we turned to leave Tanta Karwa came up to me and said softly, "Qori, after the evening meal it would be a good idea for you to visit the shrine of Mama Killa, alone."

It was Tanta Karwa's way to suggest, never order. If I didn't go she wouldn't say anything, but I often found it wise to follow her advice. What did she want? Dread filled me. I sensed the answer to that question but wouldn't allow myself to make it real by putting it into words. Yes, I decided, I'll meet you at the shrine of Mother Moon. Perhaps you don't know. Perhaps this is about something else. Perhaps . . . .

Tanta Karwa was the only outsider allowed to pass a few nights in the akllawasi, which she did regularly. She said the akllawasi was her haven, and though she maintained that she came to replenish her soul I think she equally enjoyed the time away from her other life. We knew little about her, for her visits were always on condition that she not speak of the outside world. Anything that might distract us from our lessons, such as news of our families and friends, was thought disruptive, and since we belonged to the Emperor there was nothing we needed to know except His will for us, which would be revealed in the fullness of time.

But from hints dropped in passing or overheard, we knew Tanta Karwa was a village confessor of women, and assisted in rural ceremonies. But more important, and no doubt the reason she was granted the singular privilege of visiting the akllawasi at will, she was a physician, a healer of first order, said to be consulted by royalty. She treated illness in the akllawasi too, and though the Esteemed Mothers insisted that prayer and a pure heart were better cures than her herbs, we knew they quietly sought her remedies, and then loudly credited the gods with their recovery.

Of Tanta Karwa's personal life we knew only that she was a widow, she had a son, and, most significantly for me, she was from the village of Choqo near Cuzco. Choqo was my parents' home - my true home - and I often wondered if she had known them. But when I tried to lead her into conversation, hoping at least to know what Choqo looked like, she became a clam and shook her head sadly, keeping her vow of silence on all worldly matters.

As usual, Cormorant stared at me disapprovingly.

"Don't pay any attention to old Cormorant, Qori," Sumaq T'ika said, taking my hand as we walked together. "Tanta Karwa will be proud of you when you dance for the Empress."

Fortunately she mistook the cause of my distress. I played along. "I wish I had your grace," I said, head down.

"But you do. You're a beautiful dancer. I'll be right next to you when we enter the square." She squeezed my hand.

Until now, there was a silent agreement between us not to mention the coming presentation. We had been through too much together, and grown too close, to even imagine the inevitable parting that soon would be upon us. The selections were made according to beauty, rank and skill. Of course, since everyone believed I was a commoner I had no rank, and only Sumaq knew I had beauty and skill. Aside from Tanta Karwa, the Esteemed Mothers continually overlooked my qualities.

After entering the akllawasi I came to understand the true destiny of akllas. Some were given as ladies-in-waiting or governesses to royal families. Others were chosen to be priestesses and serve in the temples of the Empire, teaching new generations of akllas. And many were given as wives, consorts or concubines to the Emperor's favorites - men who distinguished themselves in His service. Both noblemen and commoners were honored in this way. One or two akllas might even become concubines of the Emperor Himself, though rumor said He already had more than He could bed in a year. And me? What fate awaited me? Every aklla asked herself that question a hundred times a day as our presentation drew near, but it remained unspoken, and unanswered. We would be told, Tanta Karwa assured us, when the selections were completed.

Sumaq T'ika listened to the silence that came upon me. "Don't look so sad," she said, "or the sorceress will come for you." We looked at each other and burst out laughing. An Esteemed Mother paused to frown at us, then hurried by muttering and shaking her head.

My thoughts flew back to another dance lesson an eternity ago, and once again I heard Tanta Karwa shouting, "No-No-No! You stupid hook-nosed old potato! You call yourself a drummer? Can't you keep the simplest beat? It's one, two, three, four-five. Do you think you can remember that?" Cormorant dropped her drum and ran sobbing from the dance court. This was so unlike either of them that the rest of us hung our heads and searched the ground. Sumaq T'ika looked calmly at her hands, clenching and unclenching them, then with a shrug she remarked, "Fat fingers."

My body, too, felt bloated. Then I remembered my moon time was due. Not long after my arrival I slipped into the rhythm shared by all women of the akllawasi. Eventually I came to understand the signs in myself and those around me. For me it began in the week prior to the onset. First came the insatiable hunger for a particular food. One month it was fish, another peanuts, or honey, popped maize, hot peppers, even quinoa gruel, and I couldn't get enough of it. Soon followed a more bothersome craving - that of my raka, which sent me into such flights of fantasy I could scarcely concentrate on the task before me.

These urges became as regular as the moon. Don't misunderstand me. I'm not an intemperate woman. Well. . . perhaps I have been from time to time, but only when an opportunity presented itself, or could be easily manufactured. In the absence of opportunity, contrived or otherwise, I'm usually able to control these monthly passions. But I've always been thankful those around me can't hear my thoughts. During my youth in the akllawasi I was only beginning to understand the rhythm of these urges, and I confess that, in those days, I was wont to indulge them.

It began with sneaking extra peppers at the evening meal, and developed into carefully planned night raids on the storehouses. Stealing food is no small sin, it's a serious offense against the gods and the Emperor, which made the purloined fare even more delicious. All the girls in our chunka were in on it, at least for the planning stages. When it came time for action somehow it was always Sumaq T'ika and I who were elected to slip out of the dormitory, and while she kept watch it was always I who entered the storehouse most likely to hold the items of that night's desires. Since each girl had her own craving they gave me a list as if sending me to a village market. In truth, I came to pride myself on filling that list, and temporarily winning the undying gratitude of every chunka sister. And I wasn't unaffected by their admiration of my daring, or displeased when Sumaq and I were treated as unofficial leaders, for who doesn't relish the admiration of others?

It was the honey that did it. It wasn't even for me. My craving was fish that month. One of our chunka sisters was caught with honeycomb on a day it wasn't being served. Under questioning she broke down and confessed the source. Sumaq T'ika and I promptly found ourselves facing the Most Esteemed Mother.

She sat in her room, which, aside from having a floor of white plaster and being her private domain, varied little from our dormitory. Three tiny lamps flickered shadows on the windowless walls. When we entered she put something away in a jar and hastily licked her fingers.

"Is it true?" she asked in a level voice. We knelt before her, heads bowed, and timidly nodded. Fear twisted my belly. The only solace I could find was knowing that whatever terrible fate awaited us, Sumaq and I would face it together.

"Sumaq T'ika, how could you?" she scolded. "You are royalty, yet you let Qori Qoyllur, a commoner, lead you astray."

"Most Esteemed Mother," Sumaq pleaded, "it's not her fault. I forced her to stand watch. It was I who entered the storehouse, and it is I alone who deserves punishment."

It was a brave lie. I loved her for it.

The Mother turned to me. "Is this so?"

Dilemma. If I allowed Sumaq to sacrifice herself I'd be sending her to an uncertain fate alone, and if I told the truth about leading those thieving expeditions I'd condemn her more by revealing her lie.

"Mother," I said respectfully, "it was the sorceress who caused Sumaq to believe this." The Most Esteemed Mother's eyes opened wide. Sumaq turned to gape at me. "Yes," I continued earnestly, "this sorceress made me believe the same about Sumaq, and she turned us into thieves with her magic."

The Most Esteemed Mother stared at me a moment, then rolled her eyes and cleared her throat. "What sorceress is this?"

Even Sumaq looked at me expectantly, intrigued to hear what I would come up with. I narrowed my eyes and grimaced as if repelled at the memory, then slowly raised my palms to frame my face and began in what I imagined to be a most eerie voice. "She comes on the night wind, creeping over walls and around corners like mist. She can make herself tall - taller than a tree, or as small as a mouse. Her clothes are black - blacker than the blackest night, and her passing leaves the air cold as ice. Slowly she comes, searching for victims on which to work her magic, and when she finds some poor, innocent girls. . . " I spread my fingers wide for emphasis, "she casts a spell on them and forces them to do her evil bidding." I settled back with a solemn nod.

In the pale glow of the lamps I could see Sumaq was mesmerized by the tale, her hand at her mouth as she envisioned this evil sorceress, quite forgetting I was making it up. But the Most Esteemed Mother pursed her lips, trying, I suspect, to stifle a smile. "And just how does this sorceress cast her spell on innocent girls like you?" she asked.

I had to think fast. I once heard of a sorcerer who worked magic with bad air, or some such thing, and without due consideration the next words leapt from my mouth.

"She farts on them."

The Most Esteemed Mother leaned forward as if she hadn't heard me correctly. "She does what?"

It wasn't what I'd meant to say, but having said it I had to stick with my story. I stared back at her earnestly, my face a mask of sincerity. "She lifts her dress and farts all over them. She blows magic farts. . . really."

There was a momentary pause while the Most Esteemed Mother and Sumaq looked at each other, and then back at me. Suddenly the room filled with hysterical laughter. The Most Esteemed Mother clasped her stomach and rolled on her side, pounding her fist on the floor. Sumaq simply collapsed on her back and roared at the ceiling. I was indignant. I admit it wasn't one of my better stories, but it was the best I could do at the moment.

The Most Esteemed Mother had tears rolling down her cheeks when she raised herself on one elbow to ask, "Re. . . really?"

When I responded with a solemn, "Yes, really," she was gone again, head beneath a blanket, kicking, both fists pounding the floor. I wondered if she was having a seizure. What was so funny about a sorceress who blew magic farts?

Sumaq finally sat up, gasping for breath; and the Most Esteemed Mother found the strength to raise herself while she wiped tears from her cheeks. "I have never. . . " she panted, "ever, in my lifetime of service . . . heard the story of the. . . the far. . . the farting sorceress." And then she and Sumaq collapsed once more in silent, heaving spasms. Eventually, completely spent, they both sat up and the Mother continued, "Neither have I ever laughed so hard." She wiped her cheeks and brow. "Well, my daughters, you have been very wicked and should be cast from the akllawasi, or worse. But at least you can still make an old woman laugh. Perhaps we'll keep you. But you must do penance. Your chunka will have two months without meat, salt, and peppers; and you will have six . . . no, four months of the same. I'll spare the stone this time."

She looked at me and shook her head in disbelief. "Your penance will begin as soon as you leave this room, but as long as you're here," she lifted the lid from the jar beside her, "would you care for some honey?"

It's amazing how quickly those who are popular fall from grace when an indiscretion is revealed. The entire akllawasi buzzed with news of our misdeeds. Our chunka, once the envy of all, was shunned. Whenever one of us approached a circle of girls in conversation they fell silent, while the bolder ones offered cold, sarcastic greetings before turning away with a snicker. Others simply sat and stared at us over their food bowls, nudging and whispering to one another. I stuck my tongue out at them.

The worst came a week later when those of our own chunka turned against Sumaq T'ika and me. They were tired of the bland food and tired of being shunned and gossiped about. Some we had considered dear friends even proclaimed they never wanted anything to do with the escapade, and now we had shamed all of them. I don't recall any of them hesitating to share in the excitement of the planning, or to place their orders and gobble up the rewards. But memory is often a matter of convenience. Sumaq and I now found ourselves shunned even by our own chunka sisters. We became our own group of two, thankful we at least had each other to share this misery, and through it all we grew closer still.

With the passing of another season our penance came to an end, and once more Sumaq and I joined the regular food line. By this time our deeds were old gossip and the girls began to accept us among them again. We even attained a degree of popularity, or notoriety. Some, having tired of wagging their heads and tongues, privately maintained they were never really among those who turned against us. To prove their loyalty they pointed out the girls who were most vicious in their attacks. We found this amusing, but allowed them to flutter around us and boast they were friends with the two most daring girls in the akllawasi.

In truth, there were a few whose friendship was genuine, and we enjoyed their company, but we had learned how quickly friends could turn, and we never again shared any real secrets with them. Besides, not even those we liked ever passed the 'test of the oath of secrecy,' a new game of our devising. Sumaq and I would make up some outrageous story and solemnly confide it to one of the girls, making her swear never, ever, to tell anyone. Then we'd bet on how long it would take before the 'secret' buzzed up and down the meal lines. Our stories were innocent enough, such as what the Esteemed Mothers really ate when no one was around - honey-coated llama shit. But, whispered in the strictest confidence under a solemn oath of secrecy, such fibs seemed plausible to our gullible sisters. It's truly astounding what people will believe when they want too.

In this way we came to know those who couldn't hold their tongues for a day, those who might last a week, and a few who could go a whole month before confiding the secret to a best friend, who told her best friend, who told her chunka, and the news sailed, spreading so rapidly the source was seldom discovered. Even when confronted we always claimed to have heard it from someone else. And it was amazing how our original ideas grew in the minds of others, until, when finally repeated back to us, we scarcely recognized them.

This exercise left me with a healthy skepticism of gossip, and was a good lesson on the importance of keeping my own counsel. But it also showed me how easily people are led, and how words can be planted to bear whatever fruit is desired.

"Will your family be at the presentation?" I asked Sumaq as we walked to the kitchens.

"They'll probably be in the crowds, but it doesn't matter. I belong to the Emperor, not them." I recognized the edge in her voice and shrank from the topic. Sumaq was of Apu Mayta Panaqa, the fifth royal house, but she never spoke of her family or position. At their mention, especially of her mother, some bitter memory clouded her eyes, something so hurtful she couldn't even confide it to me. I respected her silence for I had my own secrets, and of my family she never asked more than I volunteered, which wasn't much. I trusted Sumaq T'ika as I trusted my brother, yet all who knew the true story were in danger, and I loved Sumaq too much to place her in jeopardy.

Sumaq stopped suddenly, her hand on my arm. I followed her stare. The new aklla who brought me the message walked by. Twice since her arrival I stood behind her in the meal line, desperate for further word of Qhari, but she pretended not to notice me. It's true, I decided, she's only the messenger and knows nothing about me. Then who prompted her? 'Your brother is watched over. Stay silent and stay safe.' I decided it was indeed a veiled threat. Whoever sent it wants me to know that Qhari is in his power, and our well-being depends on my silence. Is Lord Achachi behind this?

I said nothing to Sumaq about the message, and now she studied my face. "I've seen you looking at that girl, Qori. What is it about her?"

It wasn't like Sumaq to ask what I didn't offer, but the jealousy in her voice was unmistakable. "It's nothing," I replied, "I only thought I'd seen her somewhere."

"I remember seeing her years ago, but I forget her name. She's of Iñaca Panaqa. Do you know anyone from that royal house?"

Only Lord Achachi, I thought. "No, of course not," I said.

"Then you're mistaken?"

"Yes."

Sumaq nodded. The matter was closed. There was no need for me to notice the new girl anymore.

Sumaq looked at me intently. "Tanta Karwa asked me to polish serving trays for the Qorikancha tonight. Did she ask you?"

"She said nothing about it to me."

So, Tanta Karwa has made certain she and I will be alone at the shrine of Mama Killa tonight, I thought.

"Do you want to come anyway?" Sumaq asked, urging me to agree with raised brows and a nod.

"I think not. You go." She looked away as if I'd slapped her. I felt like a traitor. My dearest friend, I thought, and she knows I'm hiding something from her. Oh, what a twisted mess this has become.

Dark clouds brought a pattering of rain from the evening sky. We sat with our food bowls beneath the eaves framing the kitchen courtyard. The rainy season began well. Soon the longest day of the year would be upon us. The month-long festival of Capac Raymi was underway. I took no pleasure in the special delicacies served that evening to mark the festival, though roast guinea pig in tangy peanut sauce is the most delicious repast ever devised. Sumaq T'ika spoke with everyone around her, except me, whom she pointedly ignored. Her indifference cut me like a knife. Everything, I would have told her everything, if only to have her smile on me again. . . but first I had to face Tanta Karwa.

Then I spied my messenger sitting across the courtyard with the new girls. It was impressed upon her that, with the message delivered, she must have nothing more to do with me. Very well, I thought, it is time to plant the seeds.

My gaze settled on another girl, one who proved through the 'test of the oath of secrecy' that she couldn't hold her tongue for a day. I went over and sat beside her.

"Have you heard there's great sorrow among those of Iñaca Panaqa?" I asked.

"Really? Why?"

I almost rolled my eyes. This was too easy. News of any royal person is always gulped and spewed forth with amazing speed, especially if disgrace is involved.

"It's probably not true," I cautioned her, "but it's being said that Lord Achachi failed in a battle against the savages of the north, during which he lost an arm, and has now returned home to Cuzco to die in disgrace."

This wasn't really a lie. I warned her it wasn't true, and, in fact, it was being said because I was saying it. The response was boringly predictable.

"Say you so? Oh, the poor man. But what a dishonor for his family!"

Nothing more was required. Before long the story would reach my messenger. She would surely defend the honor of her panaqa, and hopefully provide the correct information on Lord Achachi's whereabouts. This would also make the rounds and come back to me. If Achachi is in Cuzco, I reasoned, then I have tracked the threat to its source, and Qhari will be nearby.

In the gathering shadows I made my way to the shrine of Mama Killa. Tanta Karwa had to be faced. But I resolved to say nothing unless confronted, even though I desperately wanted the answer.

VIII

In which Unspeakable Sins are confessed, of which Maidens and Youths must not read.

The shrines of the akllawasi stood in a row against a wall of the central courtyard, flanked at the far end by confessionals and at the other by a room where the temple vestments and service were brought for cleaning. My reluctant feet now took me to Mama Killa's shrine where Tanta Karwa waited. It stood beside the shrine of Inti in the center of this grouping, and as I passed the vestment room I saw Sumaq T'ika glance out the doorway at me, then quickly look away. She sat on the floor polishing a golden serving tray. Guilt seized me again. I passed by without a word.

I paused at the open door of Mama Killa's shrine, a small room lit only by the brazier set on a tripod before the image. The dried llama dung that fed the brazier burned like coals, casting a soft glow upward. Mama Killa stood in a niche against the back wall, Her image that of a woman, though no more than arm's length in height. The upper part of Her body was gold, the lower half silver, and She wore miniature garments that Her attendants changed daily.

Tanta Karwa sat alone by the brazier, deep in thought. Sensing a presence, she lifted her head with a start. When she saw me in the doorway she turned to the goddess and bowed with a smile as if some prayer had been answered, then rose and motioned me to her side. We faced Mama Killa and performed the much'a gesture of reverence, bowing low from the waist with outstretched arms held level with our heads, palms open and upward. Then we brought our fingertips to our lips and kissed them toward Her.

Tanta Karwa intoned, "Mama Oqllo, watch over Qori Qoyllur, who is your servant, and guide her in all things." She turned to me and smiled encouragingly. "You may ask or say anything in front of Her, for She knows all the secrets of your heart."

That wasn't a comforting thought just then. I dodged.

"Why do you call Her Mama Oqllo?"

Tanta Karwa smiled patiently. "Mama Oqllo is the name of our Empress, who is the daughter and earthly representative of Mama Killa. It's customary to call Mama Killa by the Empress's name, for they are almost one in the same, and we thereby honor both. Do you have any other questions?"

I thought quickly. "Silver is the metal of Mama Killa, and gold is for Inti, yet this statue," I pointed to the image, "is half gold and half silver. Why? And why do the second rank nobility, like you, wear silver only?"

She smiled and nodded. "Good. These are good questions, and they bear on matters you should understand before you go forth in the world. First, it's said that gold is the sweat of the Sun, and silver the tears of the Moon, for They toil and weep on our behalf. Gold and silver are sacred metals and, like Inti and Mama Killa, or husband and wife, they are equal. Among the royals men and women have the right to wear gold and silver, but those of us in the lower nobility wear only silver. This doesn't make silver less sacred, or imply that female is less than male, it's simply a convenient way of distinguishing the grades of nobility. Besides, Mama Killa weeps greatly for the sins of Her children, and silver is more plentiful.

"Some images of Mama Killa are pure silver, like the great disc bearing Her face in the Qorikancha, but this statue is half silver and half gold to remind us of our two natures. All women are part male, and all men part female. True, there are behaviors, manners, and customs deemed most appropriate for each, but within each there is an element of the other. If this were not so how could a person be whole?"

I must have looked puzzled for she went on, "Consider, Qori, do you not have right and left legs, right and left arms, right and left eyes? If you lost a leg, or an arm, or an eye, would you be whole? Every complete thing has two opposite but complementary parts. Neither part, be it right or left, male or female, day or night, is more important than the other. Both are equal and necessary for harmony."

In my face she saw the wisdom of this teaching take hold, and she warmed further to the subject. "Even the holy city of Cuzco is divided into two parts, or sayas, Hanancuzco - upper, and Hurincuzco - lower. You must not think that hanan is greater than hurin, they are simply areas within the city, complementary opposites. The royal households of our first five emperors belong to Hurincuzco, and those of the last five to Hanancuzco." She studied my face a moment. "Imagine a circle with a line down the middle, or tilted to one side. Neither half is greater or lesser than the other, neither is complete without the other, and together they balance each other. These are the sayas. The divided circle could also represent male and female. . . or the union of any two people," she added with a meaningful glance, which I pretended not to notice.

Thus was my first lesson on the duality of our natures, which is even reflected among the gods, among our rulers, and in the organization of the holy city. But Tanta Karwa's last words touched on another question, one I had barely begun to formulate, yet troubled me greatly. But Tanta Karwa knew, even before I did.

I can't say exactly when it began with Sumaq T'ika and me. She later said it was the first day we met. For me it came gradually as our friendship deepened. All that we shared drew us ever closer - the secrets, the night raids on the storehouses, the esteem of others, even our disgrace and shunning. Eventually our friendship became love and was consummated.

It started with fumbling beneath the blankets at night. At first I was surprised when Sumaq T'ika, who slept on the pallet beside me, reached out in the dark and laid her hand on my arm. That night I was lying on my back trying to satisfy my raka as quietly as possible, and at her touch felt embarrassed that she knew what I was doing. But her fingers were as wet as mine, and I did not, indeed, I could not stop them from gliding down my belly and searching for the place that made me gasp and open my legs. When release came I buried my face in her shoulder to stifle the moans, and she held me close until the last shudders left my body limp. Then she cradled me and whispered sweetness until I fell asleep in her arms.

Thus passed many nights. I became as curious and eager to please her body as she mine. And when she whispered, "I love you, Qori," I didn't hesitate to reply, "And I you, Beautiful Flower."

There are those who never experience another of the same sex, and among the women of the akllawasi most were so, as far as I'm aware. Some girls played with each other beneath the blankets, but eventually tired of the game. I think it might have been this way for me had it not been that Sumaq T'ika was of another sort - one who truly loved women. She was so skillful and confident in her attentions I might have guessed it wasn't her first time. But it never occurred to me then. What happened seemed to come naturally, and was yet another adventure we shared together.

The day came when Sumaq looked into my eyes and whispered, "I love you so. I want to do everything with you." I took this to be another of her endearments and assured her I felt the same. That evening when I slipped away from devotions to meet her in the rear courtyard, I learned what she meant by 'everything.'

I found her waiting for me by an open-fronted building where sacks of quinoa were stored out of the rain. Silently she took my hand and led me to where a blanket lay in the corner.

Sweet murmurs, that's what I remember of what followed, that and tickling eyelashes, smooth brown skin, long black hair brushing over me, gentle caresses, gliding fingertips, and a fluttering pink tongue that searched every part of me. Sumaq guided me through this love-making, and I, full of curiosity, attempted to please her in the same ways. Unembarrassed, she whispered her desires, urging me to take the lead. Thus she instructed me and I was grateful, for I wanted to please her, too. In doing so, I learned that one of the greatest satisfactions is satisfying another.

That was the first of many uninhibited encounters. With each I became more skilled and learned to whisper my special wants, to which she eagerly complied. And I learned that when two embrace so, there is a time for loving stares and earnest endearments, a time for closed-eyed abandon, a time for tickles and laughing together, and a time for cuddling.

But doubts assailed me. Was our love a sin? An aklla is supposed to be chaste - was I still chaste? If an aklla is discovered with a man the two are buried alive. What would happen if Sumaq and I were found together? I couldn't bring myself to voice these apprehensions to her. We were too close. But a lingering guilt plagued me. I needed to hear it from another, yet feared the answers.

Tanta Karwa's voice brought me back to the shrine of Mama Killa. "I have been thinking of you, Qori. We should talk."

"Of what do you wish to speak?"

"What would you like to talk about?"

Was my guilty conscience that obvious? I began to search for some topic, anything but what was truly in my thoughts. Tanta Karwa saw the evasion coming and spoke again. "Qori, before you divert me with another question I have something to ask you."

She knows! I thought. But how could she? I want to tell someone, someone like her, but will she understand?

"Are you happy, Qori? Is there something that troubles you? Please tell me."

I knew I couldn't hold back any longer. I was desperate for advice, guidance, understanding. But had I committed a terrible sin? Would I be buried alive and damned to the underworld forever? "I seek confession," I said in a small voice.

Tanta Karwa smiled gently. "There's a time for confession, and a time for confiding in friends. Sometimes it helps when we share our burdens with someone a little older. Let's go for a walk, I know a quiet corner in the front courtyard, and then if you still want confession we can do that, too."

The front courtyard was out of bounds to akllas, being reserved for the priestesses, and was known to me only from those times I was called before the Most Esteemed Mother. Stacks of blankets and clothing occupied an open-fronted building, the produce of the akllawasi looms ready for distribution to worthy persons during the forthcoming ceremonies. Tanta Karwa led me to a pile as high as my shoulders. She gave me a conspiratorial wink and pulled herself up to sit with her legs dangling over the edge.

Well, I thought, I'm with Tanta Karwa, and not even the Most

Esteemed Mother can rebuke me for this bit of fun.

It was late. Dusk had given way to darkness. High on our perch, we were alone in the gathering stillness as the akllawasi settled down for the night. There was no more evasive chatter from me, or prompting from Tanta Karwa. She sat quietly beside me staring out at the darkened courtyard, and when I began to speak she pressed my hand to let me know she was listening, but her eyes remained straight ahead. Once having found my voice I talked, and talked, and talked. She didn't interrupt. I told her of Sumaq T'ika, of the love I had found in her eyes and in her arms. When I ended with the question, "Have I sinned?" she turned to me with a reassuring smile.

"No, Qori, you haven't sinned. The world needs more love in it. Wiraqocha gave us these bodies to love with, and Mama Killa understands the special love you and Sumaq T'ika share. But tell me this, do you and Sumaq use anything that resembles a man's pesqo?" When I shook my head she looked relieved and said, "Good. That is the one thing a chosen woman must not do."

"You knew about us?" I asked.

A smile flickered on her lips. "Anyone who understands these things need only see the two of you together, and I noticed both of you missing evening devotions a few times," she added with a sideways glance. I hung my head but no rebuke followed.

"But many do not understand," she continued. "It's not in their nature to see the harmony in two who are the same. You're familiar with the Emperor's concern that all those of marriageable age should be married, for our wealth is in our numbers. This is true for the Empire, and for each ayllu, and for couples who need children to care for them in their old age. Because of this, those who aren't married are not only thought unfortunate, they're considered unnatural. It's forbidden for two Inca men to lie together, although it's said some of our subject peoples indulge this practice. In those provinces it's unofficially tolerated because it's an ancient custom, and even part of some religions. Of two women I can't say, for it's never spoken of, yet you and I know such love exists." I blushed deeply.

Tanta Karwa sighed and pushed back her hair. "I'm telling you this because you should know how it is in the world beyond these walls. Soon you and Sumaq T'ika will be leaving here and you will be parted. That's the one inevitable sadness of your love."

"Will we be given to men?" I asked.

"Perhaps. Only the gods know for sure. For Sumaq T'ika's sake I hope she's made a priestess, for I feel she's one of those who can only love women. As for you, you may find that men are not disagreeable. Sometimes our preferences change with time and place. Only remember this, never use your affections, whether toward man or woman, for selfish ambition. This is a terrible abuse of Mama Killa's gift, and She punishes those who misuse it."

These last words, sternly spoken, hinted she had more to say, and invited my question, "Do people pretend affection to deceive?"

"Oh, my little one, you have much to learn about the world. Yes, they do. And in so doing they hurt others most cruelly. It happened to me."

I sat back prepared to listen, pleased that Tanta Karwa wanted to share a confidence with me, and already commiserating with her.

"My first love was a girl named Ronto," she said. I glanced at her in surprise, suddenly grasping her understanding of Sumaq T'ika and me. "I was about your age when I was sent to wait on the ladies of Iñaca Panaqa for a season. Ronto was a peasant from a distant village who, it was whispered, had secured her place in the household kitchen by using her charms on men. She wasn't much older than me in years, but much wiser in the ways of the world. Of her beauty, what can I say? She shone like an emerald in a pool of crystals. Though she could have any soldier or servant in the kancha, she turned her attentions on me. I too was far from home and eager for a friend, and Ronto was full of flattery and made me feel special. I helped her rise from the scullery to become a maid, and our friendship grew to love. It was she who introduced me to the carnal pleasures, and I believed her when she told me she loved me more than life itself." Tanta Karwa's eyes misted over and she bowed her head in silence.

"But Ronto was false!" She spat the words and narrowed her eyes at the memory. "She didn't love me. She only used me to get close to my mistress, a widow who arranged matches among royalty. That was Ronto's ambition - to marry a nobleman, and she stopped at nothing to achieve that end. Once she caught my mistress's eye she seduced her too, for Ronto had the power of beauty and sheer force of presence to manipulate those around her; and she abandoned me, simply turning to ice one day without explanation. She tore my heart out!

"Years later I learned what happened, and what her fate was. In exchange for her favors, Ronto made our mistress promise to arrange a marriage for her to a nobleman. When one of Emperor Pachakuti's concubines died leaving her only child, a princess, orphaned at court, He sought a suitable governess, and our mistress, who had begun to fear Ronto's impatience and threats of exposure, recommended her. I imagine Ronto was furious at first, but, being the governess of a princess, at least she traveled in royal company. She might have convinced the princess to arrange the marriage she wanted, but the gods interceded to punish her for all her wickedness."

"What happened to her?" I asked, eager to know the outcome of this tragic tale.

"Ronto was with the princess, one called Sisa, at Hatunqolla when the Qolla rebellion began. That was long before your time. Perhaps you've heard of it?" I bobbed my head. "Well, Ronto and the princess hid in the akllawasi with a priestess for many days. Lord Sapaca eventually rescued the princess, but just before our armies broke through the Qolla returned and found the other two. Both were killed, Ronto in a most foul way."

"What happened to them?"

"The priestess died defending Ronto, I imagine. It's said Ronto was raped, her tongue cut out, and then they strangled her. Our old mistress told all this to me years later. In truth, it was more of a confession she made to me, having realized both she and I had been used.

"Now, that's a secret I've shared with you. I know you'll keep it safe. You see, Qori, I do understand how you and Sumaq T'ika feel about each other, and I don't want either of you hurt. But your parting is inevitable. Do you understand?"

I nodded shakily.

"No love is a sin within these precincts, Qori, but the world beyond is less understanding. And remember, whatever paths your future brings beware of guile, and always remain true to yourself. Now, do you still want confession? No? Well, perhaps you wish to offer Mama Killa special prayers for guidance. . . and acceptance. The aklla selections begin tomorrow. In a few days you'll know what your future holds."

IX

In which Qori is judged before the great Ladies of the Empire, and of how the Devil caused these Indians to make Despicable Sacrifices in their Heathen Temples.

"Do you think they will listen to us this time?" the priestess standing beside Cormorant asked.

"All we can do is recommend," Cormorant replied, "the final decisions are theirs. They know the needs of the Empire."

I slipped closer behind Cormorant. She and the other priestess stood looking from the second courtyard into the first, where a royal delegation arrived. The Most Esteemed Mother, dressed in her shimmering vestments as High Priestess of the Sun, greeted the noblewomen. Female attendants hovered behind their mistresses holding parasols of bright feathers.

"Have you heard of the recent trouble in Iñaca Panaqa?" the priestess asked Cormorant. "It's said Lord Achachi returned home legless, and in disgrace."

My ears pricked up. No! I wanted to shout, he only lost an arm. I should know. It was my story to begin with.

"Don't believe everything you hear, sister," Cormorant said. "One of our new girls is his granddaughter, and she saw him but a month ago, with body and honor intact. He's been in the city for several weeks."

"Oh," came the disappointed response.

That's all I need, I thought. Achachi is in Cuzco. Qhari's suspicions about him are well founded. He even used his own granddaughter to pass on his warning. But he won't harm us, I reminded myself, at least not yet. As long as the possibility remains that father might be alive Achachi wants us safe, if not for information, which we've proven we won't provide, then to bargain with. At least now I know the enemy. I'll have to decide how to deal with him after . . . after whatever fate awaits me when the aklla selections take place.

I edged away from Cormorant when I spotted Tanta Karwa lingering nearby. At our urging she extended her visit to be with us during the selections. Though she had no voice in the outcome of these matters it was comforting for the senior akllas to have her present, the only one who showed sympathy for our fears and expectations.

Tanta Karwa turned with a smile. "Qori, I didn't see you there. Have you come to spy on our first ladies, too?"

All were clad in soft garments, rich in color and weave, and all wore the head cloth of married royal women - a long piece folded twice inward so it's no more than a palm in width, which is draped over the head and part way down the back, leaving the tresses uncovered on either side.

"They're our first ladies?"

"Yes," she said turning to the delegation, "each is first lady of a royal house, and together they'll decide your place in the world. The one dressed in silver is Mama Oqllo, our Empress."

I gaped at this semi-divinity, Daughter of the Moon, Empress of Tawantinsuyu, and the most powerful woman in the world. Yet, aside from being very short - no taller than me - there was little to set Her apart from the others. Her face was friendly rather than beautiful, and my esti-mate of Her age changed with the light and Her expressions. All this surprised me, never having seen an empress before, but what did I expect - that She would be more than all other women? By title, yes, but in presence She reminded me more of somebody's mother.

Beside Mama Oqllo stood a noblewoman holding the hand of a girl who, in face and dress, was the doll image of her elder. After the Empress, this pair received the Most Esteemed Mother's warmest greet-ing. The woman seemed familiar. I asked Tanta Karwa.

"That's Lady Sisa and her daughter. The two are never apart. Don't they look charming together? Lady Sisa is First Lady of Chima Panaqa, and female Speaker of Hurincuzco."

I remembered the old woman pointing Sisa out to me in the streets long ago.

"She's also Speaker of Hurincuzco?"

"Of course. Chima Panaqa is the royal lineage founded by our first ancestors, the oldest and most venerated house. The couple that lead it represent all five households of Hurincuzco at court. The Emperor confers with Lady Sisa's husband, Lord Sapaca, on all major decisions, as does the Empress with Lady Sisa. In truth, the title of Speaker used to rotate annually between the panaqa leaders of Hurincuzco, and still could, I suppose, but it stays with Lord Sapaca and Lady Sisa by unanimous consent, so skilled are they at representing the concerns of their entire saya."

Once my eyes came to rest on Sisa I could scarcely look elsewhere. It wasn't her beauty - although every female charm conspired to create perfection, the effect somehow magnified by the small reflection at her side - it was her presence. Even beside the Empress, Sisa filled the courtyard. Here stood the last fruit of the old emperor's loins, born of a minor concubine, but a princess nonetheless. Orphaned at a tender age like me, and almost lost in a rebellion, she rose by marriage to become one of the most powerful women in the Empire. If only she knew my story, I wondered, would she help this orphan make a good marriage?

Sumaq T'ika appeared beside me and quietly slipped her hand in mine. After my talk with Tanta Karwa I returned to our darkened dormitory and showed Sumaq how much I cared for her. Later, as I held her close, I confessed there were secrets about my past I kept from her, and everyone, but they didn't lessen my feelings for her. Perhaps it was unnecessary. I was already forgiven. But I needed to know that all was right between us in our last days together.

Sumaq lifted her chin at the first ladies. "So they've come," she said. Being the daughter of a royal house she knew the first ladies, and named all but one.

"And who is that?" I nodded toward the woman she'd missed, who remained steadfast at Lady Sisa's side.

Sumaq sneered. "Oh, that hook-nosed old bitch is Lady Hilpay, First Lady of Apu Mayta Panaqa, and my dear, sweet, loving mother."

I inquired no further.

Old Cormorant went forward unbidden to hover beside Lady Hilpay with a proprietary air, grinning as if she was part of the reception.

"Sister," Cormorant exclaimed loudly, glancing around to make sure the other priestesses saw her with the First Lady of Apu Mayta Panaqa, "how good of you to come and see me again." A hug of greeting might have been expected to follow such a welcome, but all Lady Hilpay offered was an uncertain half-smile and an embarrassed glance at Lady Sisa, who rolled her eyes and looked away.

Cormorant was also of Apu Mayta Panaqa, which she never tired of pointing out to all within hearing, but Sumaq explained to me long ago that Cormorant was no more than a distant panaqa sister to her family, having come from a minor, impoverished branch of the lineage. Sumaq's grandmother arranged for Cormorant to enter the akllawasi, and after she died Cormorant regarded Hilpay as her benefactress, constantly petitioning her for promotion within the temple ranks. When Sumaq walked through the akllawasi door she was assigned to Cormorant's chunka, where Cormorant fussed over her and reminded her daily that she and her mother were the best of friends. It was the wrong thing to say to Sumaq, who knew her mother barely tolerated Cormorant anyway, and she responded with a cold indifference that marked their relationship to this day. But Sumaq was also convinced that Cormorant reported her every move to her mother, for Cormorant would do anything to please the First Lady of Apu Mayta Panaqa.

Watching Cormorant fawning over Hilpay would have been humorous if it hadn't been so pathetic. Cormorant was old, and in all her years of service she never rose beyond minor priestess rank. The royal ladies looked uncomfortable, Lady Hilpay most of all. Not wanting to mar the welcome but wishing to be rid of the obsequious Cormorant, the Most Esteemed Mother took Cormorant's elbow and suggested she have the honor of serving aqha to the Empress and first ladies, then ushered the women forward with a deep bow.

Watching the first ladies filing behind the Empress I suddenly realized that, although akllas belonged to the Emperor, He was a figurehead for the realm. We really belonged to Tawantinsuyu, and it was the royal women balancing the needs of the temples and government with those of each panaqa who decided our final destinations. The distribution of akllas was surely a matter of delicate negotiation among them. What would they decide for me?

"She looks plain," one said.

"Yes, but at least she smiles. Some of the others looked like they were in mourning."

"That's natural," another said. "They're nervous. This one seems confident, perhaps too confident."

While this appraisal of me continued I knelt with my head respectfully lowered, struggling to maintain dignity and the trace of a smile, while my insides quivered. I felt like leftover food at a banquet that some guests, already gorged, were idly considering.

Sumaq T'ika was called before the delegation on the first day of the aklla selections, along with others considered the prime of the akllawasi. After the second day the Empress and Lady Sisa didn't bother to return, and the number of first ladies in attendance also shrank. This was the fourth day. Only a few of us remained. Tanta Karwa knelt silently to one side twisting a corner of her cloak, while old Cormorant stared at me coldly, willing me not to disgrace her in front of the noblewomen. The four ladies delegated to complete the task - Sumaq's mother among them - lounged on cushions before us, their maids holding the ever-present feather parasols above them like banners. The debate continued as if I weren't present.

"She has a small mouth. Her lips aren't full."

"She's skinny. There isn't much under that dress. And she's shorter than most."

"But her hair is a rich, full black."

"True, and her eyes. . . what is it about her eyes?"

"They're large and match her hair. They suit her face."

"Interesting face, neither round or long, more . . . what would you say . . . oval?

"Yes, and she has high cheekbones. But her nose is small, almost upturned. I prefer a long nose with a proper tip." It was Lady Hilpay speaking. I was glad Sumaq didn't look like her mother.

"Well, her skin is a light copper and free of blemishes. That much can be said for her."

"She's still plain."

"Perhaps she doesn't meet our usual standards, but there's something about her."

"I agree. I thought of dismissing her at first, but the closer I look, well. . . yes, there is something about her."

"It's a wonder they allowed her to enter the akllawasi. I see nothing special. She's plain."

One of the ladies turned to Cormorant. "What's her name?"

This was the point at which Cormorant recited a girl's lineage and her abilities. I wondered what she would say about me.

"Qori Qoyllur," Cormorant said bluntly.

Lady Hilpay stiffened and whispered to the woman beside her, who passed the comment along. My stomach knotted. Why has my name caused such a stir, I wondered? What does she know of me, and from whom? Is it because of Sumaq, or does it concern Qhari and me?

"Of her talents," Cormorant said slowly, "she has promise in - " But Lady Hilpay held up her hand for silence. All four ladies looked at one another and nodded.

"That's all," Hilpay said. "Bring the next girl."

"But. . . my Lady, please," Tanta Karwa protested from the side, earning herself a line of scowls, "just let it be said on the girl's behalf - "

Hilpay cut her off. "I said, that's all. Now, may we proceed?"

Cormorant dismissed me with a jerk of her head, and lifted her nose to Tanta Karwa, then hurried off to fetch the last of her charges. I bowed to the examiners and moved away, etiquette demanding that I not turn my back on those of rank until I was some distance from them. Then I went looking for Sumaq.

"So, the old bitch examined you, too." Sumaq spat the words. "Did I tell you she had the nerve to smile at me?" She was referring to her own evaluation, of which she had told me nothing, but I felt her humiliation, and rage, at having been judged by her own mother in front of others. Sumaq didn't wait for my response. "What did she say about you?"

"She didn't like my nose." We looked at each other and laughed, the first laugher I'd heard from Sumaq in days. "But I'm sure she could teach old Cormorant a few things on the drum," I added. "Do you think they practice with their noses?" Sumaq burst into giggles and I gave her no rest, bobbing my head into my hands as if beating a drum. Qhari would have been pleased.

Later, I wondered aloud whether Lady Hilpay recognized my name. Sumaq shrugged and shook her head. There was no reason she could think of why her mother would have heard of me. At the first opportunity I put the same question to Tanta Karwa. She looked worried.

"Yes, it seemed that way," she said. "I was hoping you could tell me why."

"Was it because of Sumaq and me?"

"No, Qori. That secret has not, and will never, pass my lips." I looked in her eyes and knew she spoke the truth.

That left two possibilities. Either Sumaq's mother was directed by my friends, or by my enemies. Which? And what fate had been arranged for me?

When the aklla selections began, so did our public dancing. Each afternoon the front door of the akllawasi opened and we stepped from those shadowy walls into the dazzling light of the great square. The days were clear and overpowering in their sudden openness. We hadn't seen the city in years, or its crowds that now strained to catch a glimpse, pointing and shouting while the chosen women were paraded for all to see, and soldiers held their spears sideways to keep the throngs back.

Looking above the crowds and thatched roofs, my eyes feasted on green hills, pleased to find them as remembered. And on ridges set against the horizon the sun pillars still marked the seasons, pointing like tiny fingers at an immense blue sky, waiting for Inti to rise and set each day.

Two structures broke the expanse of the great square. In the southwest corner a round tower of handsome stone marked the place where the four directions meet, and from which the four roads leading to the four suyus radiate outward. From this tower the priests had a clear view of the sun pillars and stars. In front of the akllawasi, and closer to the center of the square, stood the ushnu - the platform from which the court reviewed ceremonies, parades and festivities. Beside the ushnu was a boulder with a gold-sheathed basin cut into it, from which a drain led to an underground channel so libations could be offered to the gods and ancestors.

All the emperors and empresses came to our first performance. Each pair were carried on a litter with great pomp by their panaqa, and arranged so they could visit among themselves while being served the choicest food and drink. Since Thupa Inka and Mama Oqllo were the tenth emperor and empress, there were nine pairs of richly attired mummies - five being the ancestors of Hurincuzco, and four the ancestors of Hanancuzco. It was the old empress Mama Añawarqe who fascinated me most. Añawarqe was the name of my parents' ayllu - my ayllu - and father said we were related to Her.

Beside Mama Añawarqe, and no more animated, sat Her husband the great Pachakuti, founder of Iñaca Panaqa, and truly the founder of Tawantinsuyu. Before His time, Tanta Karwa had confided, the rulers were little more than warlords who raided but never conquered beyond the Huatanay Valley. Even so, Pachakuti granted them emperor status because they were, after all, His ancestors. Through military and diplomatic genius, Pachakuti was the first to permanently subjugate new lands, pushing the Inca boundaries ever farther. Thupa Inka, who inherited His father's talents, completed the conquest of the world, or all the world worth having.

But while Thupa Inka inherited His father's brilliance, and the power that comes with the Royal Fringe, He inherited no riches of His own. Such is the law of succession, which requires each ruler to found his own lineage and create new wealth, thus insuring imperial growth. His brothers and sisters stay in their father's panaqa, and maintain his treasure and lands so that his cult is perpetuated. The royal lineages are, of course, exempt from taxation, but from their ranks come the top military leaders, diplomats, priests, governors and administrators needed to rule Tawantinsuyu.

Since each panaqa is independent, and each has its own founder who was once emperor, all claim a voice at court. At the time of which I speak, I could only imagine the delicate and endless negotiations that took place between the ruling couple and the various panaqas so that none felt slighted, and alliances against imperial decisions avoided. But according to Tanta Karwa the greatest concern was insuring unity between the royal houses of Hanancuzco and Hurincuzco, for factional disputes at this level could shatter the Empire. While there were thousands of Inca nobles, Tawantinsuyu had millions of subjects from many nations, and some with beastly natures given to revolt. A flash of discord in Cuzco could ignite distant rebel armies, waiting only for the merest hint of weakness among their rulers. Harmony between the sayas - hanan and hurin - had to be kept at all costs, for what is one half without the other?

To the music of drums, flutes, and panpipes we danced before the ushnu, its summit now crowded with nobles in all their finery, among them the Empress and Emperor. Mama Oqllo presided over the dancing, but of the Emperor I saw nothing but a heap of brilliant cloth capped by huge gold earspools and a tasseled red fringe. Thupa Inka never rose, or showed any movement at all. Is this royal protocol, I wondered, or is he still ill?

We learned of the Emperor's sickness a few months earlier. Sumaq and I were preparing aqha with some other girls when the news reached us. We stood in a circle, chewing maize kernels and spitting them into an urn of warm water to ferment, for such is the brewing of aqha, when old Cormorant came hurrying by. Concern creased her face and she spoke in an urgent, hushed voice.

"A sickness has befallen the Emperor, my daughters. Do not linger here. Finish your task quickly and go to the shrines to pray for His recovery. There will be no classes until this crisis is passed. A special confession will begin soon."

I should have realized the gravity of this news, but at mention of another confession I groaned. "But we just had confession two days ago."

"Yes, and you'll have it again today," she said, "and every day thereafter if necessary. Have I not just told you the Son of the Sun is ill? Do you imagine it's His fault? No! He suffers because His people are wicked. We must all cleanse our hearts, especially you, Qori Qoyllur."

As much as I hated to admit it I deserved this rebuke, and I resolved the Emperor would not die because of my sins, even though the truth would undoubtedly earn me severe punishment.

I shouldn't have feared being alone in doing penance. Everyone, including the Esteemed Mothers, was on a diet of unsalted maize gruel for the next two weeks, and many had sore backs. Cormorant assured us these measures included not only the people of Cuzco, but everyone throughout the Empire. In every temple bales of the finest cloth were burned, and hundreds of animals sacrificed. The offerings also included the most precious gifts of all - children . . . and akllas. One day a girl from our chunka answered a summons from the Most Esteemed Mother, and never returned. Girls from other chunkas followed her each day for an entire week.

"They were chosen for this honor when they entered the akllawasi," Cormorant explained, "and waited only to fulfill their destiny. When all is well, many years may pass before this greatest sacrifice is required."

"Where are they now?" I asked.

"They've gone to a life of ease and pleasure in the upper world with Father Sun and Mother Moon. There, they wear beautiful clothes and feast on the finest food and drink. The Celestial Couple smile on them because they offered themselves that Their son might live on to guide His people."

I wondered whether they really 'offered' themselves, but Cormorant's eyes said the subject wasn't open to discussion.

A cloud of gray smoke from the sacrifices at the Qorikancha hung over the akllawasi, blotting out the sun, but still the temple fires continued day and night, and the ceaseless wails and lamentations from the city pierced the high walls of our sanctuary.

At last the offerings and prayers worked. Inti took pity on His son and relief swept the city with an audible sigh. The Emperor, it was said, had not only recovered but again enjoyed the health of a young man.

That's what was said. But now, seeing that heap of cloth atop the ushnu, I began to wonder, as I'm sure many did, especially the

Emperor's heirs.

Sumaq T'ika stayed at my side throughout the dancing. For these performances every girl wore a dress of her own making to show her skills, except for me, because I always had a poor loom on which to work, so my clothes were issued from the akllawasi stores. They gave us sandals of the usual design - toeless, and fastened from heel to instep with thick cords of alpaca - which made dancing on the pebble pavement of the great square much easier. Tiny bells around our wrists and ankles jingled merrily as our lines dipped, twirled, and wound across the square. I didn't stumble once. . . well, perhaps once or twice, but Sumaq always caught me and no one noticed.

The surface of the great square was never even, because pilgrims to the holy city were forever turning the pavement to carry away handfuls of earth - sacred soil from the center of the world - and even the nobles were fond of burying gold and silver figurines there as offerings. Though it was a constant annoyance to the city officials, who can decry a devout act?

At first we danced only for the Incas of Cuzco, for all provincials had to leave the city at the beginning of the festival while the tribute flowed in, and the Inca rites of manhood performed. Several hundred boys from the royal houses completed their training with the final ordeals and races, and were declared warriors. They now lined the square, each proudly holding the weapons provided by his uncles, and trying not to finger his first earspools, which drooped from freshly opened and still bloody lobes, the permanent mark of an Inca warrior. Although warriors they now were, they wouldn't be considered adults until marriage, and the posturing between these youths and the maidens in the crowd provided a show of its own.

On the last two days of the festival, when the gift giving began, the provincials were allowed to return and participate that all might see the Emperor's generosity, and pledge themselves anew.

On all the days we danced I searched the crowds for Qhari. . . in vain. A forest of jostling faces surrounded the great square, but only on the last day did I recognize one. It was Lord Aquixe standing proudly in the front row wearing his splendid feather tabard and every scrap of gold he owned. He showed no sign of recognition. I was, no doubt, a detail long forgotten. Did the Emperor reward you for offering twins, I wondered? Does the Emperor even know that Qhari and I exist? Not likely, I decided. Yet somewhere in that swirl of faces were poised friends. . . and enemies.

"Sumaq? Sumaq T'ika? There you are. I've been looking all over for you," Tanta Karwa called hurrying toward us. Sumaq and I sat alone in a quiet corner, sharing the silence, and wondering. Our presentations would begin on the morrow, yet still we received no word of the fates chosen for us by the first ladies. We rose as Tanta Karwa approached.

"I've just spoken with the Most Esteemed Mother," Tanta Karwa said breathless with excitement, "and Sumaq . . . you're to be married to Illap'a - a wife of Thunder, a priestess!"

Eyes brimming, Tanta Karwa cupped Sumaq's face in her hands. "Oh, Sumaq, I'm so happy for you. My prayers have been answered." She clasped Sumaq to her breast and looked up at the crescent moon. "Thank you, Mother, thank you, thank you."

I stood to one side, my hand at my mouth. It was the best that could happen to Sumaq. The thought of her being given to a man terrified me, and Tanta Karwa, but for Sumaq the prospect was a living nightmare. Now she was safe forever behind the temple walls, beyond the reach of men and a world that could not accept her true self.

Tears of relief rolled down Sumaq's cheeks. "Oh thank you, Tanta Karwa, thank you!"

"It's Mama Killa you have to thank for your good fortune," Tanta Karwa replied, eyes dancing. "And there's more news. You'll not be sent to the provinces. You'll stay here in the holy city with us." Sumaq hugged her again, releasing a sob of joy.

I cleared my throat. Tanta Karwa smiled at me absently, and then caught herself. "Qori. . . yes, I didn't mean to forget you. The Most Esteemed Mother said you're to be given a husband also. . . a mortal husband."

"Married? To whom?"

"She didn't say, but I'm sure the first ladies arranged a fitting match.

You'll be presented to your new husband in the great square tomorrow." She placed her hand on my shoulder. "I did what I could, Qori." I nodded, knowing she had, and knowing that others determined my future in spite of what Tanta Karwa might have said had she been given the chance.

"I've arranged for both of you to be excused from devotions this evening," Tanta Karwa said, "and you may stay out as late as you wish."

"Qori," Sumaq whispered, resting her head on my shoulder, "I'm sorry you're leaving. I'll miss you." She raised herself to look into my eyes.

"And I'll miss you," I replied, stroking her hair. "But at least I know where you'll be." I pulled her back to my shoulder before those big, beautiful eyes of hers found the truth in mine. The truth was, I would miss her, but I was eager for the outside world, to find Qhari, to confront Lord Achachi, and, yes, to have a man and finally see what made their loincloths bulge so.

Sumaq sighed happily. "Yes, you know where to find me. You need only visit the Qorikancha. I'll be watching for you."

The question was, where would I be? What if I was given to some provincial and had to live far from the capital?

At least I was to be married, and since by law a man is allowed only one wife there was consolation in knowing I'd be principal woman of the household. An aklla given to a man who already has a wife becomes either a consort or a lesser concubine. These are honorable positions. Their children are recognized and fully legitimate, although they aren't ranked as highly as those of the wife.

The Emperor Himself had but one wife, the Empress, His sister. In imitation of our first ancestors, Thupa Inka, perhaps at his father's insistence, revived the custom of marrying His full sister, so the bloodline would be pure. But full brother-sister marriage was forbidden on pain of death to all save the royal couple. After the Empress, He had several consorts who were half-sisters or cousins, and then a host of concubines, the daughters of powerful kurakas exchanged for political alliances, and girls selected for their beauty from every akllawasi in the Empire. The children of all these women were called princes and princesses. The number of royal persons in Cuzco with these titles was enormous. They were subtly ranked according to their mothers' lineage, but to non-royals the distinctions were meaningless. They were all lords and ladies of highest nobility, and destined for positions of authority in the Empire.

The status of akllas given to kurakas, and those who distinguished themselves in some way, depended on the men. A girl might find herself the prize of some first- or second-rank Inca nobleman, or a provincial lord, or even a common soldier who won his honors on the battlefield. Only through a gift from the Emperor could a man add more women to his household, and since this was a singular mark of royal favor, akllas were highly honored and welcomed into their new homes. At least, that's what we were told.

I puzzled over the significance of this for my future. It was also the law that once a woman was widowed she couldn't marry again, unless she was inherited by her husband's brother, but a widowed man could take a new wife. His concubines, if he had any, couldn't fulfill this role, thereby reducing the possibility of intrigue. In such a case the new wife became the first woman of the household. I therefore reasoned that either I was to be married to a widower or to a young man who hadn't yet taken a wife. Which would it be?

Sumaq T'ika snuggled against me. No more words broke the silence. All that needed to be said, or could be said, was in her eyes. We spent that last night together simply holding each other.

X

**In which a New Life begins, the Dead Feast Together, and too
much maize beer is drunk.**

"You there, what's your name? Oh, yes. You stand behind this girl.
And you? No, you're three places forward. Where is Qori Qoyllur? Ah,
there you are. Your place is over here." The Most Esteemed Mother
continued arranging us in the front courtyard until she had all the brides
in a line. "Now, don't move from your place, do you understand? This
is the exact order you must keep when you enter the square. I'll lead
you. Your husbands are being lined up in the same way right now."

Each girl carried the tunic, black headband, and shoulder bag she wove
for her husband - an exhibition of her proficiency - and these we bundled
in our shawls and tied at our backs. But the weaving mistress gave me
inferior wool to spin, so my creations weren't ready. Once again they
issued clothing to me from the general stores. We each received a small,
bronze tumi knife to slip in our wide belts, another traditional wedding gift
for our husbands. While we waited I held the tumi by its semi-lunar blade,
and idly stroked the handle rising from the middle of its straight side. It
ended in a llama head with the two ears standing straight up, and a tiny
half-ring at the back for fastening to a cord. This is a male llama, I decided, a virile symbol worthy of a man. But what man?

Cormorant eyed me coldly. Defiantly I returned her stare without
blinking. For three years I'd endured her sourness, and in all that time I
couldn't recall a kind word ever passing her lips. She didn't like any of us,
that was true, but her strongest displeasure fell on me. Now she came to
gloat over my leaving, and I was impatient to see the last of her, too.

"Go and enjoy your husband, Qori Qoyllur," Cormorant said. The
sarcasm in her voice made it sound as if I was about to receive some ill-
gotten gain. In that instant I almost felt sorry for her. It was spite and
envy she hurled at me. Yes, envy, I was sure of it - envy of me and every
girl who walked out that door for the last time. In those scowling, wrin-
kled features I caught a glimpse of a girl full of hope, a girl escaping

humble beginnings to become a chosen woman with the expectation of marrying a rich lord. And then crushing disappointment - made a priestess to spend the rest of her life behind temple walls, forever denied men and children. Bitterness watching generation after generation of akllas granted all she dreamed of, while her only rewards were the lines of jealousy etched ever deeper on her face.

Promotion within the temple was all the social standing Cormorant could hope for, yet even this eluded her, her acolytes becoming her mistresses and then being replaced by still younger women. True, she was inept at whatever she undertook; that was evident to everyone, except her. She probably still harbored dreams of becoming a high priestess one day. Poor Cormorant, I thought, I see you clearly now, and even so, I still don't like you.

Whatever Cormorant saw in my gaze angered her further. Her eyes flared. "Nothing good will come of you, Qori Qoyllur." She turned and stalked away.

Tanta Karwa brought Sumaq T'ika to see me out. They stood to one side watching the preparations, sadly shaking their heads as they watched Cormorant bid me farewell. Sumaq had paraded in the square with the other new priestesses earlier that morning. Her ordeal was over now. She was forever safe in the sacred precincts. Tanta Karwa came forward and placed her hand on my head, invoking a blessing from Mama Killa. When she finished I met her eyes. For all I knew this might be the last time I'd see her. "I won't forget you," I said.

"I know," she replied, looking away as if all her girls said the same thing. They probably did, but each meant it, and Tanta Karwa's bored response was her way of hiding the tears that edged her eyes. She swallowed hard, brushed my cheek, and stepped back.

Sumaq grasped my hands. I stared into her eyes, remembering our years together. "You know where I am," she said earnestly.

"I'll come when I can," I promised.

Tanta Karwa gently drew her away. I looked at Beautiful Flower one last time as our outstretched hands parted. 'Friends, always,' she mouthed the words. I nodded. Always.

"Straighten your backs," the Most Esteemed Mother ordered. "Remember, keep your heads up and your eyes lowered. Walk slowly, and with dignity. Stay two paces behind the girl in front of you. When the line stops you may turn and face your new husband." She hurried to the front and adjusted her vestments, then nodded and the door slid aside.

In a trance I walked through the front door of the akllawasi for the last time, hardly aware of the stately drum and flute music accompanying our entrance into the great square, or of the crowds that waited in hushed silence. Eyes down, I followed the girl in front of me, vaguely aware of the ushnu rising on my left, and a row of men waiting in front of it. The line stopped with a final thud of the drums. Silence descended on the square. We turned in unison. I couldn't lift my eyes.

Mama Oqllo's voice came from the top of the ushnu, speaking of duty, service and reward, directing Her words to include the grooms and the akllas and the crowds beyond. This was the moment for all the people to see that even common men and women, loyal servants of the Empire, could receive the highest honors. While she spoke I finally found the courage to raise my eyes.

He stood before me grinning wide, devouring me. I was flattered. A pleasant looking man a few years older than me and a head taller, slim and well muscled. The thick, black hair cut straight across his forehead hung to the tops of small, silver earspools. Young, Inca, and minor nobility - yes, I decided, you'll do very well.

While the Empress continued her speech his eyes darted over the girls on either side. He was comparing me. I knew what he was thinking. Slim like a boy, Cormorant once said of me. Well, whether you like it or not, I thought, it's my body and it holds all the passions of any woman. And you, husband-to-be, aren't the most handsome man I've ever seen, either.

When the Empress ended her speech the high priest of the Sun stood between our lines and signaled the Most Esteemed Mother. She, dressed as high priestess of the Sun, walked at his side down the lines carrying a golden tray. The tray held sacred bread made of maize flour mixed with the blood of sacrificed llamas. The priest blessed the bread and placed small pieces in our mouths. Then he raised his voice for all to hear, declaring this a gift of the Sun, which would remain in our bodies to bear witness against us should we ever speak ill of the Sun or the Emperor. We replied that never in our lives would we do such a thing. Everyone in Cuzco had already eaten of the sacred bread and made the same vow in shrines throughout the city.

This ceremony completed, Mama Oqllo spoke again, asking if we were prepared to enter into marriage. In response, our men took a step toward us and turned to face the ushnu, each one placing his bride behind him. This gesture didn't put man before woman, for both are equal in marriage, it simply meant the man was prepared to defend and care for his woman. I found myself admiring broad shoulders and a well-formed male siki.

Mama Oqllo looked to her husband, and when an arm rose feebly from beneath that pile of cloth, she turned back and gave the official blessing to our marriages.

The musicians began a joyful clamor and a roar of approval echoed from the spectators. Each man took his bride's hand and led her toward the waiting crowds. We were not yet married. This was only the public betrothal and imperial blessing. The marriage ceremonies would be completed with the men's families later that day.

Through all of this my groom and I hadn't spoken a word to each other, and I still had no idea whom I walked beside. He seemed intent on leading me straight into the crush, but as we approached the crowd I jerked his hand impatiently. "Who are you?" I asked.

He paused and drew himself up. "I am T'ito, Imperial Khipu Kamayoq," he said looking down his nose at me, as if I should have been cowering in awe of him.

A khipu specialist? I thought. A knot counter. I am marrying a knot counter? Why not a gallant soldier, or a builder, or someone who does more than sit all day fingering knotted cords and muttering over the records. He is young, so 'Imperial Khipu Kamayoq' must be a recent title, and I am evidently his reward for having done something of merit, but what a knot counter might do to earn such favor I can't imagine. I wondered whether he was my reward, or my punishment. Either way, I wasn't about to be intimidated.

"I am Qori Qoyllur, from the court of Lord Aquixe, Hatun Kuraka of Ica," I replied, matching his boast. It wasn't exactly a lie. I had passed through the court of Ica.

"The daughter of a Hatun Kuraka? The Emperor has blessed me."

"I said, I came from his court," I corrected him.

He shrugged as if this was a minor point. He seemed more pleased with himself than with me anyway, and if he chose to elevate my status beyond that of a peasant I wouldn't complain. Secretly I knew myself to be his equal.

"Ica is a province in Kuntisuyu," he said as if instructing me. "That is also my suyu. I'm from the village of Choqo, just outside of the city. My mother is the healer Tanta Karwa."

He said this proudly in a matter-of-fact tone, assuming I'd never heard of Choqo or his mother. Tanta Karwa, I thought, she knew all along! She picked me for her son! It was too much to grasp in the instant. In the akllawasi I'd always wanted to call her mother, and though she was ever kind I had no idea she was selecting a daughter-in-law. Even after she knew the truth about Sumaq and me she chose me. Why? It doesn't matter right now, I told myself, still gaping at T'ito. He gave no indication of being aware that I was even acquainted with his mother. Obviously Tanta Karwa hadn't shared her deliberations with her son. Amused, I resolved to keep it our secret.

Ideally a woman is married to a man of her own ayllu, but there would be several ayllus in Choqo. I never learned the name of Tanta Karwa's lineage. Was it too much to hope that just possibly. . . ?

"What is your ayllu?" I asked, almost afraid of the answer.

He threw back his shoulders and replied, "Añawarqe."

What forces are at work, I wondered, that of all the men in Tawantinsuyu I should be married to one from my own ancestral ayllu? This has to be the doing of my unknown friends, enacted through Tanta Karwa and Lady Hilpay. Whatever Sumaq holds against her mother, I bless her name.

I thought of father, whose fondest wish always was to return to his home one day. And I thought, I have returned for you, father. Surely this is a sign that you are forgiven.

Pleasantly lost in these revelations, I allowed T'ito to pull me into the crowd. Many from Choqo were there to congratulate him. The men jostled around, clasping his forearm and slapping his back, while granting me only an appraising nod. In truth, this is the polite way for men to behave toward women they don't know, but it left me feeling very much the trophy, especially since T'ito was so busy with their attentions he didn't think to introduce me.

The women were more attentive. They introduced themselves and inquired about my lineage, and when I told them I came from the court of the Hatun Kuraka of Ica a buzz of excitement swirled around me. When they fingered my clothing, remarking on the fine weave and colors, I remained modestly silent, allowing them to assume I'd made them. This was my moment too, and I saw no point in tarnishing first impressions with unsolicited confessions. Besides, I would have worn an exquisite outfit of my own making like the other brides, but someone spilled aqha on it the day before, and so I wore clean apparel from the akllawasi stores.

A man wearing the livery of a royal messenger appeared at T'ito's side. The Choqo people nodded respectfully and moved back, clearing a space around us. The man looked solemn. He lowered his voice and leaned toward T'ito. "I bring a message from your mother. She saw your presentation and is very proud, but her services are required elsewhere now." He cast a meaningful glance at the empty ushnu. Ours being the last ceremony of the day, the nobles had already left the square and the crowds were dispersing.

T'ito frowned. "You mean the - "

The man put a finger to his lips and mouthed, 'The Emperor.' He raised his voice to a whisper, "All is well, but He has presided since dawn. Tanta Karwa is summoned to help Him rest. You won't mention this to anyone, of course?"

I glanced at the sky. Everyone rose before dawn and it was only mid-morning, an odd time to rest.

"Of course, I understand. But will my mother be at the wedding this afternoon?"

"I'm afraid she may be needed for some days. But she asked me to say how proud she is of you. Your relatives will present the bride at the ceremony, and Tanta Karwa will meet you at Tipón soon. I'm sorry, but you know she's needed."

"Yes, I understand," T'ito replied glumly. "Thank you for the message."

With a look of sympathy for T'ito, and an appraising glance at me, the man moved off. T'ito turned to the others. "Mother has been called to tend . . . to tend a noble," he announced. "We must continue without her."

The news elicited much head shaking and tongue clicking, but the ayllu closed around us again and soon the festive mood returned. A man playing a joyful flute started down the streets and the Choqo celebrants followed, T'ito moving me along with one arm while he talked to everyone but me.

T'ito and I walked together in the center of the procession as we entered the open countryside. The air, heavy and moist, promised rain from gray-tinged clouds. Green shoots poked from red fields, birds flittered among the trees, and llamas sprinkled the hillsides. With the city pavement far behind, the simple joy of walking on Mama Pacha came back to me. I began to feel a part of Her again. Is this a dream? I wondered. Am I really free? A raindrop brushed my cheek, telling me it was so. I couldn't stop grinning.

"Your mother tends the Emperor?" I asked T'ito in a whisper.

"Yes she does," he said, chin high but keeping his voice low. "She's one of many who attend Him, but she's a kamasqa, one who heals with plants, and her powers are sought by all the royal houses. The people know she tends nobles, but they don't know about the Emperor." He looked at me sternly. "That must be left unsaid."

I nodded. The need for secrecy was obvious. The defense and orderly conduct of Tawantinsuyu depended on the Emperor. Rumors of lingering ill health would only cause concern, and discord. I changed subjects.

"You haven't mentioned your father."

"Oh, he died long ago."

"I'm sorry. I know what it's like to lose a father."

He shrugged. "He died an honorable death when I was a child. I don't even remember him."

"Do you have brothers and sisters?"

"No. There's just my mother and me."

I thought he might inquire about my family but he showed no interest.

"Where did you train to become a khipu kamayoq?" I asked, intent on learning what I could.

Again his chin lifted. "At the House of the Imperial Khipu Kamayoqs in Cuzco."

"In Cuzco? You were taught with the royals?"

"Uncommon, it's true, but my patron Lord Atoq recognized my uncommon abilities," he said casually, glancing sideways to see if I was sufficiently impressed with the name of his patron, of whom I had never heard. I was more curious than awed. He elaborated for me.

"Lord Atoq is the Emperor's nephew, and among his most trusted advisors. He bears no official titles by choice, but he oversees the imperial khipu kamayoqs, and the administrators of the qhapaqñan, including its bridges, tampus and messenger stations."

"And one such as this is your patron? How did it come to be?"

"You mean because I'm not a royal?" he said defensively. "All worthy men may rise in station. The Emperor rewards those with vision and talent."

I allowed him this self-descriptive boast, but pressed, "And Lord Atoq?"

He shrugged, trying to look modest. He didn't succeed. "I've always been good with numbers and remembering things. I suppose he heard about me from the elders of Choqo. Lord Atoq is always looking for those with my abilities. Because I'm exceptional, he ordered me apprenticed to the khipu masters in Cuzco. After my training I became an assistant, but a few months ago I found a discrepancy in the khipu records from the province of Wanaku. It was an extremely clever deception. Not even my master noticed it."

"The numbers didn't tally," I suggested.

"Oh, the numbers were fine, it was the tying of a certain khipu that was odd. The imperial khipus are similar in their method of recording, but each khipu kamayoq has his own peculiarities when twining the cords and tying the knots. To your eyes they'd all look the same, but to those of us skilled in these matters there are tiny differences in quality. When I examined the Wanaku khipus I could see they were all made by the same person. . . all that is, except the one recording the Emperor's herds. A different hand tied it. I checked earlier Wanaku khipus and found the royal herds had been declining for three years, which is when these odd khipus began to appear. I reported this, and the Emperor's inspectors did the rest."

"What happened?" I asked, genuinely curious, and begrudgingly starting to admire his cleverness.

"They investigated. It was found the governor himself substituted the herd records, and used the surplus to enrich himself. He repented and begged. The Emperor showed mercy, only confiscating his wealth and demoting him to captain of a small garrison on the Chiriguano border, for life."

"And you were rewarded."

"Of course. I was promoted to full Imperial Khipu Kamayoq, and given an aklla for a bride."

And I was given a clever knot counter, I thought, and a pompous one at that. Still, he's probably the envy of every khipu kamayoq in Cuzco, and, after all, he is Tanta Karwa's son, and from my own ancestral ayllu. This has gone well, and I'm grateful.

"We're meeting your mother at Tipón? Where is it?"

I accepted another of his superior looks. "It's on a hillside farther down the Huatanay Valley, no more than a half-day walk from Choqo. Lord Atoq invited us to pass a few days there among the gardens. Would you like to meet him?"

"I would be honored." I ignored his look that said, 'Yes, you will be.' "And your mother, Tanta Karwa, she's been invited also?"

"Oh yes. She goes there often. Mother cured Lord Atoq of a fever years ago, and he was so grateful he recommended her to other royals. She still tends him when he needs her."

It was unkind, but I couldn't help thinking that perhaps Lord Atoq's interest in T'ito was due to his mother's skills as healer, or diplomat, or both.

Rounded, grassy slopes closed in, marking the entrance to a side valley. We entered, crossing a stream and passing below the town of Qhachuna. Farther along the land rose to a tiny valley, steep-sided and cut deep by a fast stream, where a scattering of single-room houses marked the village of Choqo. T'ito paused at a dwelling on the outskirts and presented it with a flourish, "My mother's house, and yours," he said, "until I can build one for us."

I wasn't overly impressed at first sight, but then my eyes were still full of the city. The house varied little from its neighbors - somewhat longer than wide, built of mud brick on a foundation of fieldstone, with a high, thatched roof, and a small patio in front framed by storage huts. But it had a certain charm and prosperity about it. It was the first dwelling at the entrance to the valley, and had ample space around it. The grounds were well kept and sprouted a variety of trees and bushes. A stack of firewood leaned against one of the outbuildings. Three llamas grazed near a tidy herb garden, straining their tethers. Yes, I decided, it will do nicely.

"Most beautiful grandfather, honored ancestors, we present this woman from a distant land, a gift from the Emperor, and seek your council. Shall we adopt her into Ayllu Añawarqe? Will you bless her marriage to the man T'ito?" The priest crouched beside the central figure and listened intently, turning his head to include the other bundles in this consultation.

We knelt in a crowded hut occupying the middle of the village plaza - a narrow, grassy patch which is the only flat ground in the valley. I was told it belonged to the ancient founder of Choqo and was therefore a wak'a, venerated by all. T'ito fidgeted at my side. The most important men and women of Choqo peered through the doorway behind us.

The ancient founder sat before us with the other ancestral ayllu leaders grouped around him. Pots of food and aqha lay in front of them. They were feasting together.

Of course, there was no question about my acceptance; a gift from the Emperor is never refused, and my presence brought honor to the whole village. But seeking the guidance and blessing of the ancestors is an indispensable ritual for any matter affecting the community.

They sat motionless, each wrapped in layers of fine clothing embroidered with the designs of Choqo. The outer garments looked new, but beneath them I glimpsed older weavings, some probably as old as their wearers. Exposed areas of their faces and hands showed brittle, dark brown patches of dried skin stretched over bone. Most had been dead longer than living memory. At least, their bodies were dead, but the parched husks still housed the part of their spirits that remained behind to watch over their descendants.

The priest muttered now, conferring with the mummies. Everyone waited, a hush settling over those outside.

Before entering the hut T'ito explained the ancestors were brought down from their home at Llipiquiliscacho - the communal tomb on the hillside above, also revered as a wak'a of Choqo - especially to meet me and be among their people again. I felt truly honored. Their presence bestowed great moment on my wedding.

The priest picked up his rattle and began a chant praising the ancestors. The close air inside the cramped hut held a heavy, musty smell from the bundles. The priest paused to flick a fly away from the ancient founder, He from whom all the ayllus of Choqo descended. The mummy's hollow eyes stared back at me.

The founder, T'ito had said, was descended from the wak'a Cumpi Huanacauri, which consisted of ten stones on a nearby hilltop. These stones were in turn descended from the sacred boulder on the hill of Huanacauri where the Inca youths' initiation rites are held, and was, I recalled from the origin story, really one of the brothers who accompanied the first Incas on their journey to the Huatanay Valley. Thus, through ancestors and shrines, all the people of Choqo were related to the royal dynasties of Cuzco.

The priest's chanting ended with a furious shake of his rattle. Silence filled the room, broken only by a sharp intake of breath behind me. The priest placed his ear to the founder's mouth, and then moved to each of the ancestors in turn.

"It is well," he announced. "The woman Qori Qoyllur is welcome in Ayllu Añawarqe and the community of Choqo. The marriage of T'ito is blessed." As this news passed a sigh rose from the crowd waiting in the plaza.

Since I was an outsider and had no kin present, or so it was assumed by all, one of T'ito's relations took me to her home where she and her husband played the role of ritual parents. I wondered if I was indeed related to them. There, other women of the ayllu pressed around me and kept my kero full, each insisting on welcoming me with her own toast, to which I drank deeply. My stomach tightened when an old woman remarked that I reminded her of someone she knew long ago, and other elders, peering closely at me, agreed. Did they see my mother sitting before them again? I returned their scrutiny with innocent surprise. No, they decided, I was from Ica and the resemblance must be coincidence. The person they knew disappeared long ago.

I wanted to tell them what had happened to their friend, that her daughter had returned, but I dared not break my oath to father. He was right. If one question led to another, and the whole truth became known, only disgrace could follow. What right did I have to burden others with such a truth; and if I did, would they still want me among them? No, I decided, I must wait until father's name is cleared of all wrongdoing. It's enough that I've come to be among my parents' ayllu again. If Qhari could only be with me now . . . .

The elder women huddled around me to formalize my adoption. Keros brimmed again. The woman who shared the title of ayllu leader with her husband explained that Choqo had seven ayllus, four of hurin-saya, and three of hanansaya. Each ayllu had its own name, and each contributed labor to communal tasks: maintaining the plaza, local paths, and community shrines, keeping irrigation canals open, and, in turn, sponsoring village festivals.

Within the sayas the lineages were ranked, with the oldest having the greatest status. Ayllu Añawarqe is an exception, she said. It is the youngest ayllu of hanansaya, but has enormous prestige because it is the only ayllu of Choqo recognized as minor nobility, at least in name if not in circumstance. This came about when the old emperor Pachakuti married a woman of Choqo named Añawarqe, who then became Mama Añawarqe, Empress of Tawantinsuyu. Her kin quickly formed a new ayllu in Her honor, whose members had the right to wear silver and the privilege of being called Khaka Cuzcos - Uncles of Cuzco. They were treated, I was assured, with respect by the Cuzco royalty, and naturally had a special relationship with Pachakuti's lineage, Iñaca Panaqa.

Like all ayllus, Ayllu Añawarqe held lands that were redistributed among its families each year, as the number of households, and the number of people in each, increased or declined. Neighbors help one another sow and harvest their crops. A herd of llamas and alpacas is tended in common, but each family owns a few of these animals, and, within reason, can increase its own wealth. Guinea pigs and ducks are also family wealth, carefully husbanded and traded for the silver tupus and earspools. The younger women present all wore at least one silver tupu, but the elders each displayed several, some quite large, handed down from their mothers' mothers.

The recital ended and we stood. The headwoman spoke formally, "Are you, Qori Qoyllur, prepared to share in the common duties of Ayllu Añawarqe, acknowledge its leadership, and abide by its customs?" My enthusiastic "Yes" met with cries of "Welcome, sister!" A new kero full of aqha appeared - a slim-waisted tumbler of black wood, lacquered green, red, and yellow, showing women offering libations in the field. It passed from hand to hand, each woman performing the finger dip to Mama Pacha by shaking a drop on the packed earth floor before taking a sip. The last swallow was mine, and then they presented the kero to me as a permanent record and proof of this event. Later I put it to good use toasting the men of the ayllu and, eventually, the entire community.

The kero of Qori Qoyllur was seen and approved by all.

At midafternoon T'ito arrived at the door accompanied by a crowd of relatives. My ritual parents presented me, and to show his acceptance T'ito placed a woolen sandal on my right foot. Then our party proceeded to Tanta Karwa's house where I showed my acceptance by presenting T'ito with the clothing issued to me at the akllawasi, and the bronze tumi knife. He immediately donned the clothes while women giggled and made lewd comments as they tried to catch a glimpse, and slipped the knife into his shoulder bag. Following this, my ritual mother lectured me on my duties to my new husband and the ayllu, and an older male relative of T'ito's did the same for him. The kin presented us with gifts, and with these formalities concluded, food and aqha appeared along with musicians. The serious festivities began.

Although she was not present, Tanta Karwa provided amply for her son's wedding. Huge jars of aqha kept the celebration flowing throughout the remainder of the day. The toasting was endless. Etiquette required us to return each toast with deep draughts, and our tumblers were instantly refilled when another well-wisher stepped forward to congratulate the bride and groom. I excused myself as often as possible, feigning interest in cooking and trying to keep my hands defensively occupied with a food bowl, but the women were as adamant as the men that I should never be thirsty, and a refusal, however polite, could be taken as an insult.

Brief showers pattered the ground, but a downpour, as much as I would have welcomed the interruption, did not follow. As the sun waned, men and women staggered, dancers stumbled, and quarrels erupted. The aqha achieved its desired effect, placing the guests in another world, closer to the wak'a of the ayllu. My own moods passed from elation to pleasant intoxication, followed by slack-jawed drunkenness, and finally sullen withdrawal. Fortunately, by the time I reached this last stage everyone was too preoccupied to notice. T'ito downed kero after kero and stood upright only because another man, who was in little better condition, held him up.

Finally an old woman shouted orders that, surprisingly enough, the other women obeyed. They separated T'ito from the men and aqha, and poured several bowls of thick potato soup into him. Drawing me aside, the elder served me the same and whispered, "We'll leave you with your husband now. Don't worry. It might hurt at first, and there may be some blood, but after a while you'll come to want it as much as he does."

The last ritual of marriage was about to take place, the great mystery unfold, the stuff of my fantasies realized, and all I could think of was keeping my stomach down.

XI

**Concerning the Wedding Night, of which only Married
Persons may read, and then of the Hidden Valley,
where is met Lord Achachi.**

Our guests escorted us to the door of Tanta Karwa's cottage amid
much backslapping and bawdy comment. I felt better, and T'ito, though
unsteady, could at least stand. The clamor of the celebrants faded as they
gathered the remains of the feast and stumbled off to finish the evening
in a stupor. T'ito slid the wicker door shut and leered at me, or tried to,
the result being a foolish gape. I lowered my eyes demurely when he
removed his aqha-stained tunic and leaned against the wall to steady
himself, clad only in his loincloth. A lamp on the floor cast the only light
in the room, illuminating his legs and torso.

At last, a male body stripped and waiting for me, I thought. But what
am I supposed to do? What's expected of me? I waited for him to say
something, to lead me, show me. But he remained silent, his face
masked in shadow.

Well, I thought, clothing must be removed, that much I know, and if he
doesn't wish to undress me then I will. I pulled the tupu from my cloak and
let it fall. He didn't move. My belt followed. Still no sign. Moving slowly, I raised my hands to the tupus at my shoulders and paused, allowing him
a moment of anticipation before all was revealed. Then, jerking the tupus,
I shook my dress to the floor, standing naked before my husband for the
first time. But still he didn't speak or move from the wall.

I can't see his eyes. Is he watching my performance? What am I
supposed to do next?

The Chimu girl's stories in the akllawasi returned to me. I knelt to
untie his loincloth - that very male garment with its enticing pouch. How
often in my fantasies had I done this? Savoring the moment, I trailed my
fingertips up his thighs and cupped the pouch, squeezing gently. It filled
my hand. What marvelous things were hidden behind that bit of cloth?
Urgently I untied the knot, jerking his loincloth aside. His pesqo dangled

before my hungry eyes. But wasn't it supposed to stand up? I knew what to do; at least I thought I did. Gently, I lifted his pesqo to my mouth.

Smack! The blow stung my cheek, knocking me backwards.

"You dirty provincial bitch," he slurred. "I've been warned of those filthy Chimu habits. Our people aren't so debased. How dare you."

He took another drunken swing at me, missed, and fell sideways on the straw. In moments his snoring filled the room.

What had I done? No one told me how to act, or what was expected. How was I supposed to know? I longed for the whispering guidance Sumaq T'ika had shown me. Why couldn't he do the same? My wedding night ended with me sitting alone in the dark until I cried myself to sleep.

The next morning I rose early and prepared my husband's breakfast while he slept on. I stoked the fire through the opening at the front of the clay oven, and covered the three holes on top with pots for boiling potatoes, quinoa porridge, and soup. Any one of these would have sufficed for the morning meal, but I was determined to show him I wasn't deficient in all ways. How could I face him? I wished he would sleep forever.

When he finally woke I was outside kneeling at the grinding stone, preparing a sauce of hot peppers to go with the potatoes. I worked the big, smooth rocker stone from side to side, smashing the peppers beneath to a pulp. I imagined his pesqo there, too. It would serve him right. He came to the door. Without looking at me he went to a jar of water and splashed his face, then drank deeply and held his head in both hands. After a time he noticed me, but said nothing and went back inside to sit and hold his head some more. Good. I hoped he suffered all he deserved.

I entered the cottage and quietly set the food bowls in front of him. He sat for a while in silence, peeling the boiled potatoes and dipping them in spicy sauce. Without looking up he said, "The potatoes are raw. My mother will teach you how to boil them properly."

Boil potatoes? I fumed inwardly. Of course I know how to boil potatoes! I excel at cooking. The wood is damp, that's the problem.

He spoke again, still without meeting my eyes. "There's no need to mention last night to anyone. I'll do it properly tonight."

I nodded and returned to the hearth. Does he even remember what happened? I wondered. Is this his way of admitting he didn't do his part? Is he feeling guilty too? I wanted to talk but he remained withdrawn.

When next he spoke it was of small matters about the house, showing me where things were stored, muttering about laying new thatch and needing fresh bedstraw. Was there enough food and firewood? From the way he spoke I gathered his mother's patients provided most of the household needs in exchange for her healing powers.

His relatives left us alone that day, no doubt recovering from their own excesses. By midafternoon his spirits lifted and he was once again boasting about his work and the people he knew. I sat and listened appreciatively. There were no questions about me, but at least he was talking to me, and I resigned myself to the role of adoring audience. Whenever he spoke of khipus his eyes shone, and it was easy to be carried along with his excitement, even though I had no idea what he was talking about.

While I cleared the supper bowls he stretched and yawned loudly. It was early and he didn't look tired. I couldn't capture my enthusiasm of the night before, but I was still curious, and eager, to get it over with. While he knelt to straighten our blankets on the straw in the corner I reached for my dress pins.

"What are you doing?" he demanded.

"Removing my tupus?" I replied hesitantly, fearful of doing something to upset him again.

"Why? Are you changing your dress?"

"No. I just thought. . . thought I should."

"I don't know the customs of your people, but here everyone sleeps in their clothes. You can remove your belt, of course."

"But last night you shed your tunic, and I thought. . . ."

"Oh, did I? Well, someone must have spilled aqha on it. I was probably just changing." Then a thought came to him and he muttered to himself, "That explains why I awoke without it this morning."

"T'ito," I asked, "do you remember what happened after?"

"Of course. I went to sleep. I was tired. Do you have to bring that up again?"

"No, of course not. It's not important," I replied quickly.

So, I thought, the lout was dozing against the wall. He didn't see me undress. He doesn't even remember hitting me! I would have been angry if I hadn't been so relieved. What I did, or tried to do, was lost to him, and I had my first harsh lesson in Inca sexual mores without anyone knowing. Or does he remember and is just pretending forgetfulness? I wondered. Whichever, I won't chance trying to please him again, or myself, until I know what he expects. Tonight I'll be a rag doll and force him to show me.

I lay rigid beside him with my arms at my sides. . . waiting. Eventually, with the blanket over his shoulders, he turned and briefly pressed his lips to mine. It wasn't a kiss; it was a stiff pressing of lips. His hand kneaded my breast, then disappeared below to untie his loincloth. He tugged at the fold of my dress. I raised my hips to help him pull it open. He moved on top of me and I opened my legs to him. He fumbled above me, forcing his pesqo against my thighs and belly, everywhere but where it was supposed to go. I wanted to guide him but dared not interfere. With an exasperated groan he finally took it in hand and pushed against my raka, but still several tries followed before he found the entrance.

I wasn't wet enough to receive him, but I doubt that even occurred to him. He pushed harder. Tightness. Pressure. Intrusion. That's what I remember of my first coupling with a man. It was over in a moment. He rolled off, leaving me sore and sticky. This was the great mystery, the great event?

I glanced over at him. His eyes were closed but he smiled. Whatever just happened evidently pleased him. Why didn't I feel pleasure? I wondered. Is this really what women giggle about? Was there something I should have done, or is there something wrong with me? These thoughts were only slightly tempered with a certain relief at no longer being a virgin. I am a woman, I thought with satisfaction, and my marriage is consummated.

We reached the last guard post shortly before midday. Still puffing from the steep climb, I hardly noticed Inti poking through the shroud of drizzle that followed us down valley all morning. The rain tapered to a sputter. Looking back, the Huatanay River was a string of blue amid checkered fields. Below me at the valley's edge wisps of smoke rose through the treetops marking the town of Qispikancha where our climb began. While T'ito exchanged greetings with the sentries I turned to look at the royal estate of Tipón.

Tipón is nestled in a high valley, so well hidden behind the folds of rising hills that it's all but invisible from the Huatanay far below. The scene before me stole my breath. Broad, ascending terraces filled with pleasure gardens swept the valley floor, and on the far side overlooking the gardens stood a palace complex - the abode of Lord Atoq.

When the messenger arrived in Choqo asking T'ito and me to meet Tanta Karwa at Tipón, he added, "And Lord Atoq is hoping you won't mind looking at some Chinchaysuyu khipus for him. Lord Achachi is bringing them."

T'ito had puffed out his chest and glanced sideways at me. I nodded eagerly, but my excitement wasn't for him.

After the messenger left I asked T'ito about Lord Achachi. "Yes, Lord Achachi is of Iñaca Panaqa," he replied. "He was probably at Hatunqolla. I don't know. He's one of the Empire's most celebrated warlords, Conqueror of Antisuyu, and another of the Emperor's many half-brothers. He's also Visitor-General of Tawantinsuyu. I met him once when those strange khipus from Wanaku started arriving. In truth, he delivered last year's records to Cuzco himself, and suggested I take a closer look at the one counting herds. I think he suspected the governor, too." Self-absorbed as usual, he didn't bother asking why I was inter-ested in Achachi, but simply concluded, "It will be good to see him again," as if they were old friends.

Yes, I thought, it will be good to meet you at last, Lord Achachi, and find out what you've done with my brother. Not even a warlord, even if he is Visitor-General and the Emperor's half-brother, will keep me from my sworn revenge.

I checked my bundle to make sure our fine garments had stayed clean and dry. T'ito joked with a guard and gestured toward me. The man leered at me as he waved us on, shouting more congratulations to T'ito. Another messenger dashed by, the fourth to pass us since we started the climb from Qispikancha.

We descended into the elegant, sculptured valley of Tipón, crossing a terrace lined with all manner of trees and bushes on the approach to the palace. Tiny birds flittered and called among the greenery. The path lay heavy with the color and scent of every flower in the highlands, now glinting crystal droplets in the sunshine that suddenly bathed the valley. Everywhere stone channels sent water cascading down fountains and gurgling along open conduits, following the terrace lines back and forth across the valley. The sound of rushing water is the music of that enchanted place.

Another guard greeted T'ito when we arrived at the great stone stairway leading to the palace above. While they spoke I admired the fountain that emerged from nowhere beside the stairs, rushing down cut rock to the channels below. We stood aside as another messenger rushed by. Grudgingly, I felt impressed by T'ito's familiarity with this place and its guardians. Still, it is a half-day's journey from Cuzco, or a full day at the nobles' leisurely pace. Why did a powerful man like Lord Atoq dwell so far from the center of power?

"Because it's his way," T'ito said as he dismissed the maid who settled us in a small room of our own.

"But I thought the imperial administrators were all directed from Cuzco. How does he watch over them from here?"

"He doesn't need to go to Cuzco," T'ito said giving me a sly look, "they all report to him here. Didn't you see the runners coming and going? They're on the road day and night between Tipón and Cuzco. A message can be delivered and returned in a morning."

"Does he ever go to Cuzco?"

T'ito thought a moment and shrugged. "He hasn't since I've known him. He doesn't like crowds. People come when they're summoned. None dare refuse him. Few have actually met him, usually only the highest officials, and they're mostly relatives."

"But isn't he overseer of the khipu kamayoqs and the royal road?"

"Unofficially. I told you, he refuses all titles. He's a modest man. Yet at mention of his name you should see those haughty lords of Cuzco scurry to do his bidding. His duty is to watch over the affairs of the Empire. He once told me he likes to do this at a distance. It helps him see better." The laugh that followed was of one who shared a joke he didn't understand.

I couldn't find the humor either, and was wondering what it meant when he became serious. "Remember, it's a great honor to be a guest here. These are the rules: Never wander about unless invited. You may go down to the gardens when you wish, but you must never go into the hills around here. And when you see people come and go, never ask their names or their business. If they want to tell you they will, otherwise, forget whomever you happen to see." I heard another's voice in these instructions, one who spoke them many times - Tanta Karwa? Lord Atoq?

We just finished changing from our wet traveling clothes when a servant appeared at the door. "Lord Atoq will see you now."

T'ito looked at her in surprise. "So soon? This is an honor! Hurry, Qori."

"It didn't take long for word of our arrival to reach him," I said.

T'ito looked at me with disdain. "He knew we were coming as soon as we arrived at the town below, perhaps before. Lord Atoq knows everything."

I was beginning to believe him.

The servant led us to an open-fronted building in a rear courtyard where attendants moved straw mats, cushions and blankets out into the sun. I was prepared to be awed by the great Lord Atoq, but when I looked about no one met my expectations. Several men standing in a circle holding khipus wore fine tunics and modest gold earspools, but the ostentatious jewelry and plumes I had come to expect of royalty were absent. Perhaps Lord Atoq had not arrived?

While T'ito and I waited to be noticed the group parted, all bowing low and backing away from one man who handed a large khipu to an assistant with instructions. This is Lord Atoq? I wondered. His tunic was of fine, dark red cloth, but plain, and the black cloak, headband, and sandals did little to enliven his appearance. The required gold earspools dangled beneath his short hair, but aside from these no sacred metals or jewels adorned his person. It was a costume of simple, confident elegance.

I judged Atoq to be Tanta Karwa's age. His silver-streaked hair suggested a still older man, but it made him look wise and distinguished. He was handsome, lean, and taller than most men. The lines creasing the corners of his eyes and mouth suited him.

"T'ito," he called, "welcome to Tipón. It's good to have you with us again." He dismissed his aid, and while the man bowed and backed away Atoq strode toward us. We bowed from the waist.

"And this is your bride," he said. I kept my eyes respectfully lowered. "An aklla no less. She's beautiful. You've done well."

Atoq was the first man ever to call me beautiful. I liked him immediately.

"Only through my Lord's good graces," T'ito replied with uncharacteristic modesty.

"Not at all. You deserve this honor. The Emperor rewards those who serve him well. Come and sit with me."

The servants placed his carved ceremonial stool in the sunshine. He bade them depart with a wave, and pushing the stool aside sat on three folded blankets. Still, the servants fussed around him and, bemused, he finally clapped his hands. "Enough, thank you. I'm quite comfortable. Now please leave me with my guests. Very well, some aqha to welcome them. No, I don't need the parasol. I want to dry out these old bones!" The attendants laughed and departed.

Atoq was the first lord I knew who thanked his servants, and allowed them to laugh with him.

"And you, Captain," he said to a hulking soldier, "take your good men elsewhere for a time. I'm sure T'ito will protect me." T'ito shared a chuckle with the guards as they filed past.

Atoq gestured to the mat before him. "Now please, sit." Of course I didn't take him literally and knelt as etiquette required, but he corrected me with a smile. "No, young woman. You only kneel in a formal audience. Here you may sit."

I glanced at T'ito for reassurance. He nodded vigorously and sat cross-legged himself. I tucked my knees to the side and modestly pulled my dress fold closed. Cupping my hands in my lap, I kept my head bowed.

"Young woman, this is not a formal audience," Atoq said, directing my gaze to the empty stool beside him. It was three hands high and the black wood was beautifully inlaid with turquoise and red shell. The blankets on which he sat still elevated him above us so a trace of decorum was preserved.

"You may raise your eyes," he said to me. Stunned, I lifted my head. He smiled casually, but I sensed him taking my measure. For an instant I looked into his eyes. One was slightly clouded, but the other pierced me. Now I understood why he needed no outward shows of authority, for here his true power revealed itself. At that moment his eyes showed only avuncular interest. His gaze shifted to T'ito. A long pause followed before T'ito realized Atoq waited for an introduction.

"Her name is Qori Qoyllur," he said. "Qori, this is my patron, Lord Atoq."

A man of Atoq's standing need not have waited for this polite formality, or even acknowledged me, but he did, and I warmed to him further. A maid handed us keros of aqha, then vanished as quietly as she appeared. Following Atoq's lead I dipped a finger and flicked a drop to Mama Pacha, then drank deeply.

"From where do you come, Qori Qoyllur?" That was the only direct question he asked me. I told him I came from the court of Ica, and hoped he wouldn't press. He didn't, but I soon found myself drawn into an easy conversation, comparing coastal and highland climates and customs that, I realized later, revealed a great deal about me.

Eventually Atoq turned the conversation to T'ito, and listened with approval to all the news from the House of the Imperial Khipu Kamayoqs in Cuzco, especially concerning T'ito's fellow officials. Then Atoq referred to the recent ceremonies in Cuzco, setting T'ito on a new course. From time to time Atoq blinked, always once and very rapidly. I thought nothing of it until I realized that each blink corresponded to a name mentioned in passing, as if he instantly searched a record and made an entry. Perhaps this wasn't a formal audience as Atoq insisted, but a great deal of information was processed and stored behind those blinking eyes.

A soldier approached and whispered in Atoq's ear. Atoq stiffened. "You will excuse me now," he said to us. "There are matters that require my attention."

T'ito bolted to his feet pulling me with him. "Of course, Lord. It has been an honor." He held a low bow and backed away. I fumbled my own bow and followed. It was clear that when Atoq granted leave it was taken immediately. A sweating messenger pushed by as we left the courtyard.

Back in our room I pondered how I might turn this acquaintance with the powerful Lord Atoq to my advantage. On the journey to Tipón T'ito explained that Atoq belonged to a branch lineage of Capac Panaqa - Emperor Thupa Inka's line - because his father, Tupac Amaru, was the Emperor's elder brother. Prince Tupac Amaru was originally favored to be the next emperor, but their father, the old emperor Pachakuti, decided on Thupa Inka in the end. Tupac Amaru took this displacement graciously and pledged his allegiance to his younger brother. In return, Pachakuti granted him the unprecedented honor of joining Thupa Inka's new panaqa as a branch lineage, and gave him several estates. This arrangement once again proved Pachakuti's wisdom, for although Tupac Amaru distinguished himself in his father's armies, his real talent was diplomacy and administration, while Thupa Inka inherited his father's military genius.

Prince Tupac Amaru ruled over Cuzco when Thupa Inka was away campaigning for years at a time, thus freeing the Emperor to enlarge the Empire. Of course, Tupac Amaru also shared handsomely in the spoils of conquest. The two always worked in harmony, and Tupac Amaru loyally guarded his brother's position.

Once, a powerful half-brother of theirs plotted to seize the Royal Fringe, and he had many followers in the provinces. But Tupac Amaru learned of this treachery, for he kept eyes and ears everywhere, and arranged for the pretender to be killed along with his supporters. Now Tupac Amaru was old and lived quietly at his estate of K'allachaka outside

Cuzco, no longer troubling with the daily affairs of the Empire - those duties and the power that went with them having passed to his eldest son, Lord Atoq.

Atoq can be a powerful ally in my search for justice, I thought, controlling as he does all the imperial records, as well as the royal road and its messenger stations throughout the Empire. But Achachi also holds immeasurable authority as Visitor-General. I must move cautiously. Solid evidence against Achachi is needed before I approach Atoq with the full story. First, I will confront Achachi and learn what I can, for he still has Qhari hidden away somewhere. In the meantime, perhaps the best way to Atoq is through his wife. I asked T'ito about her.

"His wife? Lord Atoq's wife died long ago, and he's never taken another. He doesn't have consorts or concubines that I know of, although I'm sure his uncle would give him the pick of the Empire. He chooses to live a simple life without women, but I doubt he lacks female company when he wishes." He said this last with a wink.

"And children of his own?"

T'ito laughed. "There are probably many in the villages on this estate who call him father, but none are officially recognized." His face became serious. "I'm like a son to him, you know."

T'ito seemed to believe this, certainly wanted to, and there may have been an element of truth in it, but I assumed what he meant was that Atoq was like a father to him. I envied that. There was alluring danger about Atoq, an enticing aura of power, understated and genteel, but nonetheless absolute. It drew me.

I saw Atoq the next afternoon, but he didn't see me, not at first. Achachi was expected that evening, and a servant relayed Atoq's wish that T'ito examine some old Chinchaysuyu khipus in preparation for his arrival. I went to wander the gardens.

The air lay heavy and moist among the greenery, and the canals gurgled happily. I followed one along the foot of a high terrace when I heard Atoq's voice on the path nearby. A wall of dripping bushes separated us, and at his first words I peered through the branches in excitement.

"Tanta Karwa," Atoq said, "such a pleasure to see you again."

"My Lord does me great honor. How pleasant to find you in your gardens."

"Is that not what you prescribed," he said holding up his hands, "and don't I always follow your advice?"

She laughed and then scolded him. "Not as often as my Lord should. Has your cook been brewing the herbs for your stomach?"

"Yes," he replied, hesitating like a boy with a secret.

"And have you been drinking it?"

He made a face. "It doesn't taste very good, but she forces it on me when she can."

Tanta Karwa wore her hair in a braid coiled to the back of her head, exposing a long, delicate neck graced by a necklace of red shell beads with an emerald pendant. The touches of make-up at her eyes and mouth, though imperceptible to a man, made her look younger. Her clothes shone in the sunlight, a yellow dress with red and purple trim, and a red shawl with a stripe of yellow, all clean and unwrinkled and no doubt freshly donned to meet Atoq. Tanta Karwa's appearance in the akllawasi, though always neat, was far more subdued. It surprised me to see her now as a woman, looking younger, and blushing under Atoq's gaze.

She raised herself on her toes to look into Atoq's clouded eye. "I've brought some tobacco for that. As soon as you have time I'll boil it in aqha, add salt and sweet root, and wash your eye. That should help." She ignored his grimace. "And I'll have your chamberlain tie a packet of tobacco to your head tonight. It will help you sleep."

He gave her a resigned nod, then stepped closer and lowered his voice. "How is my uncle?" he asked, referring to the Emperor.

"I'm afraid He isn't well, Lord. He doesn't have the strength for long ceremonies anymore. The left side of His body remains paralyzed. He's still in Cuzco, but in a few days He will return to His estate at Chinchero. Rest is the best thing for Him. I've done what I can."

"And what do the others say?"

She sighed. "The priests pray and the sorcerers wail and babble. Some claim He will recover."

"Will He?"

She looked him full in the face. "I fear Inti will call Him home soon. If He stays at Chinchero and the administrators stop pestering Him, He may be with us for another year or two, but I've never known one in His condition to recover."

"Thank you, Tanta Karwa. As always I appreciate your honesty. What are people saying about His heir?"

She shook her head. "Mama Oqllo assumes it will be Her son Titu Cusi. Why else would the Emperor keep him secluded below Tipón at Qispikancha?"

"Why indeed? He's safe in my care, but. . . ." He arched an eyebrow at her.

She gave a resigned nod. "But. . . Lady Chuqui is boasting as always that her son is favored."

Atoq stroked his chin. "Mama Oqllo is the Empress, and as full-sister and wife it's Her son who should follow. But, Lady Chuqui is also a sister and Principal Royal Consort, and it's always the most capable, not necessarily the first in line, who wears the Royal Fringe. We must watch Lady Chuqui carefully."

He took her arm and together they walked down the path, she gliding softly. As they left my hearing Tanta Karwa listed the names of those tending Thupa Inka, and those who entertained this Lady Chuqui, while Atoq blinked rapidly.

I hadn't meant to eavesdrop and exhaled with relief when they moved from sight. It wouldn't have impressed either of them to find me spying. But now I was eager to greet Tanta Karwa, woman to woman, one free soul to another, and thank her for arranging my marriage. My husband wasn't the stuff of dreams, but my mother-in-law was a blessing. I followed up the path, intent on being unaware they were ahead of me. As I approached from behind Tanta Karwa paused and lifted her face to Atoq.

"It will be a chilly night. Does my Lord wish company?"

Her voice was full of expectation, and her disappointment evident when he replied, "You know nothing would give me greater pleasure, but

I'm afraid some important messages are expected tonight."

"Only for a short while," she urged.

He looked on her with sad eyes. "Perhaps next time."

I was shocked! Did people their age still do it? Apparently so, and Tanta Karwa's hopes, though unfulfilled, left no doubt Atoq could do it better than T'ito. T'ito was right, Atoq didn't want for female company, but did he know about his own mother? I wasn't sure I approved, but then I seldom approve of those who have something denied me. Yet I liked them both. It was the dilemma of a child catching her parents lovemaking.

To break the moment I announced myself by scraping my foot on the path and shouting "Ouch," too loudly. They looked up as I bent to examine my toes. I pretended suddenly to notice them.

"Lord Atoq, forgive me, I didn't see you," I said bowing. Then to Tanta Karwa I bowed deeply and came up grinning with arms outstretched. She hesitated, her smile thin and creases returning to age her eyes, and then she met my arms in an uncertain hug. What was wrong?

"I see you two have met," Atoq said.

"In the akllawasi," Tanta Karwa replied flatly, releasing me with a questioning look.

"Ah, yes, I forgot you go there," Atoq said to her. "You must know all the akllas. Well, I trust you approve of the wife chosen for your son."

Tanta Karwa's eyes became huge. She responded without enthusiasm, "Oh yes, I'm sure Qori will be a fine wife for my T'ito."

"Yes. . . well," Atoq said, aware of Tanta Karwa's hesitation, "there are a few things I must tend to now. I'll leave you two to get better acquainted. Please join me for the evening meal," he said to both of us, then departed.

"Qori. . . please forgive me," Tanta Karwa said, shaking her head as if to clear it. She placed an arm around my shoulders. "I didn't mean to be rude just now, but I had no idea you were the one chosen for T'ito."

"You didn't? But I thought you arranged it?"

"Not me, Qori. I mean. . . of course I'm pleased it's you, but. . . ."

When I first glimpsed her with Atoq on the path I felt full to bursting like an inflated sealskin, but now the plug was yanked and I withered before her eyes, wishing there was a hole in the ground to crawl into.

"Qori, I'm sorry," she said, seeing the effect of her words. "I'm surprised, that's all. I was busy with. . . with an important patient, and I didn't see who was presented to T'ito, and no one could tell me and then I rushed straight here and - oh Qori, I didn't know it was you."

I knew what she was thinking - Sumaq T'ika. "The marriage is consummated," I said bluntly, not knowing how else to say it. "And I'm like other women. I like men." For her benefit I sounded more confident than I felt.

She looked flustered but relieved. "Yes, well I was a little concerned about your friend in the akllawasi, but I always felt you'd find other interests. No, that's not why I was surprised."

Pride flared within me. "I came from the Court of Ica," I said, thinking she was concerned about my lineage. If she only knew the truth. I didn't like any of this and felt terrible inside.

"Yes, I know. I'm sure you have honorable ancestors. It's just that . . ."

"What?"

She dipped her head. "I feel foolish saying this, but ever since we first met I've had the strangest feeling about you. You remind me of someone I knew once. She was also from Choqo, but she disappeared long ago. It's not your face - no, something else - the way you carry yourself, the way you speak."

So, you knew my mother, too, I thought. Father always joked that Qhari and I didn't look like either he nor mother, and since it's said that twins are the children of Illap'a mother must have lain with the god of thunder. But Tanta Karwa sees beyond my features and still recognizes my mother in me. Oh, if only I could tell her the truth.

"A coincidence, I'm sure," Tanta Karwa said, "yet how odd you should be the one to join my family. It's almost as if she had come back.

"But no. You're Qori Qoyllur, and if I had any influence over choosing an aklla for T'ito - which I assure you, I did not - I would have chosen you."

She smiled warmly then and held her arms wide to me, and as I met her embrace I couldn't help muttering, "I have come home to you, mother."

After an awkward meal during which Tanta Karwa hardly moved her eyes from me, Atoq dismissed the two of us but asked T'ito to stay. When T'ito returned to our room he said Lord Achachi arrived, but the meeting was private and Achachi would be leaving at dawn. Claiming sleeplessness, I went out to look at the sky, and position myself in ambush. I didn't have to wait long.

"Lord Achachi? I am Qori Qoyllur."

He spun to face me in the shadows. A new moon floated behind the clouds. No guards were in sight. He looked nervous.

"Who? Well . . . what is that to me?" he said.

"I received the message from your granddaughter; 'Your brother is watched over. Stay silent and stay safe.'" I searched his face. It remained impassive except for his eyes.

"What are you talking about? Who are you? Does Lord Atoq know you're here?" He did it well, but his eyes gave him away. He knew who I was.

He was shorter than I had imagined, and much older - gray-haired, scarred, and thickset, but he still had a commanding presence. With a blanket wrapped around him leaving only his head exposed he looked like a stump of timber. I almost wanted to like him. Father knew him and trusted him. Why? Surely he had to be the one who slipped into the Hatunqolla akllawasi and. . . I imagined the governess Ronto, ravished and mutilated. Beast! And now he has Qhari.

"Of course Lord Atoq knows I'm here. He's a friend of mine." The boast was meant to sound like a threat. It worked. His broad face twitched.

"It's true I'm honored to have a granddaughter in the Cuzco akllawasi. That's common knowledge. But I don't know anything about a message, and I don't know you. Now go away."

He turned to leave but I caught his arm. "Where's my brother?" I tried to sound firm but it came out like a whine.

He exhaled heavily. "Young woman, you may think we're meeting in secret, but there are no secrets at Tipón. These walls have ears." He tapped the stones. "I don't know what you're talking about, but perhaps you had best heed this message of yours and stay silent."

"I'll tell Lord Atoq about you."

"Tell Atoq what? If your brother is missing then you're afraid he might stay missing, permanently. Besides, I've known Atoq all his life. What are you going to tell him about me?"

There was only one thing I could threaten him with, hollow though it was, but he couldn't know that. "When I see my friends in the akllawasi, I'll ask them to make sure your granddaughter stays in good health."

He shoved his face in mine. "Thank you," he hissed between clenched teeth, "and I hope your brother stays in good health. If you come near me again, perhaps I'll find him for you, and you won't like it."

XII

In which Qori meets the Empress, Sorcerers Perform, a Disgusting Addiction is spoken of, an old wound is healed, and Horrible Truths are revealed.

We bowed low, holding our arms outstretched above our heads, palms up, and performed the much'a to the Empress, kissing our finger-tips toward Her. I could scarcely believe I was attending an audience with the Daughter of the Moon.

"Thank you for coming, Tanta Karwa," She said looking up from Her embroidery. "I see you've brought an assistant."

"She is Qori Qoyllur, Highness."

"A pretty name. Welcome to my court, Qori Qoyllur."

I bowed low again, heart pounding.

We removed our sandals before coming into the presence of the Empress, and as we approached Her a servant relieved us of our wild-flower bouquets, for one never appeared before the Empress or Emperor without a token gift. Now, having been acknowledged, we crawled forward with heads lowered and kissed Her feet. My lips burned from touching divine flesh.

We retreated to a kneeling position several paces back. Mama Oqllo said, "I trust you'll not mind waiting while I finish with the auguries." She motioned to a man kneeling to one side, an earlier arrival. "I want my daughters to visit their brother at Qispikancha tomorrow, and thus far the omens are good."

She turned Her attention to the diviner again, who cut open a bird and removed the entrails. Mind waiting? I thought. Is that really a question?

Late afternoon sun streamed into the courtyard illuminating the gray wall of fitted stone behind the Empress, Her short frame seated on a dais of blankets and cushions. A maid shaded Her with a feather parasol. She added a few more stitches to Her work while She awaited the diviner's results.

The man examined the entrails, muttering to himself. He smiled. The omen was good.

Months had passed since my visit to Tipón. In that time much had happened - and not happened. T'ito's long absences made me almost a widow. He spent most nights at the House of the Imperial Khipu Kamayoqs in Cuzco, returning home but once a week. This troubled Tanta Karwa, for the distance from Cuzco to Choqo is easily traversed daily. She thought he should be spending more time with me. His excuses made it sound as if the Empire would fall apart without his vigilance, but it was clear he preferred the city and company of nobles to the countryside. For my mother-in-law's sake I pretended to be hurt, but in truth I didn't miss his boasting or tedious fumbling beneath the blankets.

Tanta Karwa allowed me to accompany her on healing missions throughout the valley, and even to attend royalty in the city. I felt the exultation of a dove freed from its cage to glide the fields at will. Commoners needed permission from their kurakas to walk from one village to the next, and even the nobles had to state their reasons for travel at guard stations along the major roads. The Cuzco sentries were especially strict, keeping a record of all who entered and departed the city daily. But as a healer of renown Tanta Karwa needed no leave. All the guards knew her and merely waved us on with a courteous bow. To prevent gossip no inquiries were made of healers and seers known to attend the royal houses.

On these outings I slung the strap of her healing bag over my shoulder and walked proudly beside her. She was never without her bag. It was her badge of station, known almost as widely as her name. Lines of red llamas marched across the bright yellow surface, and red tassels dangled below. It held bundles of dried leaves, bark, roots, herbs, a sack of pebbles, and all the mysterious needs of her profession.

Tanta Karwa always wore her necklace of red shell beads with its small emerald. The tiny beads were drilled from thorny oyster, the sacred shell that comes from the far northern seas. It is also used for offerings and even powdered into medicine. The emerald, too, came from the distant north. The sacred value of the stone and beads was enormous, but to Tanta Karwa their worth was inestimable because the stone was her spirit guardian - her sister, and helped with her healing. Its name was Añawarqe.

"It belonged to my mother's mother," she said, when I inquired about the stone's name, "and was a gift from her sister, one called Mama Añawarqe. I think you've heard of Her."

The only other items we carried on these ventures were the little ceremonial bundles tied at our backs, and our drop-spindles and wool. The bundles contained only rags, but were necessary because all those entering Cuzco had to carry a symbolic burden as a sign of humility, honoring the holy city and its royal couple. No one, neither man nor woman, peasant or noble, was allowed entrance without observing this ritual. The wool and spindles kept our hands busy spinning yarn. A proper Inca woman of any class is always productive.

Tanta Karwa was so proficient at spinning she could do it while she strolled, dropping the spindle and setting it twirling with a flick of her fingers to produce a fine, continuous strand. But then, her wool was of much better quality than mine, which was so coarse it caused my yarn to break frequently.

We talked of many things while we walked, and eventually I couldn't help mentioning Qhari and wondering aloud where he was. She raised her eyebrows when I explained. "Your twin?" she said. "You are wak'a wacasqa? We are indeed honored. And you don't know where he is? I'll ask Lord Atoq to make inquiries for you." Before I could reply she hurried on, "A twin, and you never mentioned it. You are a humble person, Qori Qoyllur. It's a good quality. I'm proud to have you for a daughter. . . that is, daughter-in-law." She took my arm and held her head high.

Humility isn't among my many qualities, but I wasn't about to break the moment. Daughter - she called me daughter. I pulled her close and lifted my chin to the passersby.

Another diviner knelt before the Empress. Like the others he dressed oddly and wore his hair long, for such is the prerogative of those who consult the spirits. He produced a bag of coca leaves, stuffed several into his mouth to form a quid between teeth and cheek, and mixed others with

llama fat to make a cone. Then he asked for a brand from a nearby brazier and touched it to the cone.

Tanta Karwa carried coca leaves in her healing bag, but it wasn't her
custom to chew them, although many of the nobles are addicted to the
habit. As she explained when I first commented on this, coca grows only
in the hot lands. Because it's a sacred leaf and a precious import to the
mountains, its use is generally restricted to the nobles, priests, seers, and
healers. Every chewer carries a small gourd bottle of lime, with a long
pin attached to the underside of the stopper, so when the top is removed
the lime-covered pin can be inserted into the quid. It's said the lime
releases the power of the leaf, which produces a feeling of well-being,
and reduces thirst and weariness. But the habitual users have green
slime at the corners of their mouths, their lips and teeth are tinged green,
and their breath is musty. It's not a custom I'm fond of, although many
at court practice it.

"Highness," the coca man said gesturing to the smoldering remains
of the cone, "it does not burn well."

The Empress leaned forward to look. "It burned well enough,"
She said.

"True, but there's one leaf that wasn't consumed by the flame."

Mama Oqllo sighed. "What does it mean?"

The coca man thought for a moment. "It means the weather will be
good for a journey, but there's something that keeps you here."

"Nonsense. The other auguries were all good." She held Her chin
skyward while the fingers of Her right hand drummed Her thigh.
"Well," She finally said, "should I stay or go?"

The coca man held his hand downward with the two longest fingers
extended, then spat in his palm and watched the green juice run down his
fingers.

"You can see it doesn't cover both fingers equally," he said. "Your
Highness shouldn't go."

The Empress turned away with a sniff. Clearly this was not the outcome She wanted.

The bird man spoke up. "My Lady, it's well known coca is the least trustworthy of the auguries."

The Empress rewarded him with a nod, but still She was hesitant. Looking about, Her eyes settled on us.

"Tanta Karwa, you have knowledge of the stones. Let us hear their counsel."

Tanta Karwa took the little sack of pebbles from her healing bag and knelt before the Empress, offering it to Her. Thrice the Empress withdrew a handful and dropped them in front of Tanta Karwa. Each time Tanta Karwa counted the stones before returning them to the bag for the next throw.

The stones weren't part of her usual healing methods. She seldom used them. The secret, she confided, is that all answers are to be found on the patient's face. The stones merely brought out the secret hopes and worries hidden there, which sometimes caused illness. She rarely employed them to predict events as others did, for she wasn't a seer, but she couldn't refuse the Empress. It mattered not. We already saw the hope and hesitancy on the Empress's face.

"Highness," she said after the third throw, "the stones agree with the coca leaves."

The bird man snorted. "The stones are no more trustworthy than the leaves."

The Empress exhaled heavily and waved the seers away, then turned to Tanta Karwa. "It's my daughter, Koka. The girl can't sleep, and she hardly eats or speaks. It must be she of whom the leaves and stones speak. That's why I summoned you. I want her fit to travel tomorrow."

"My Lady, when did this begin?" Tanta Karwa asked softly.

"Four days ago."

"And when did you decide to visit Qispikancha?"

The Empress shrugged. "I suppose it was four or five days ago."

"Forgive me, Highness, but is there any reason why Princess Koka might not wish to visit Qispikancha?"

The Empress looked indignant. "Of course not. Since her father went to rest at Chinchero, as you advised, I've been busy tending affairs in the city. The children have been shut away here in the palace. They love to visit our country estates and see their brother, the Heir. No, Koka wants to come, but some demon has overtaken her."

"May I see the princess?"

With a wave Mama Oqllo summoned a maid to lead us to the princess's room.

Royalty, I discovered as we were led through the palace, live little differently from the rest of the people, which is mostly outside. Their rooms, too, are small, being used only for sleeping. There are no furnishings beyond rush mats on the floor, and maize husk pallets with alpaca blankets and pillows. The walls are windowless but lined with niches, and in these are kept lamps - small bowls of llama fat with wicks - and assorted personal items. Wicker panels stand ready to slide across the doorways for privacy. Were it not for the richness of the cloths, blankets, and ornaments in these compartments none would be greatly different from our little house in Choqo. It was such a room that we now entered.

The maid announced us at the threshold and introduced us to the girls within. Princess Koka, a young woman of about fourteen years, sat huddled in a blanket on her pallet, eyes red-rimmed, staring blankly. Her younger sister Kusi Rimaq sat beside her holding her hands.

When the maid left Kusi Rimaq spoke first. "The others did nothing," she said, revealing that Tanta Karwa wasn't the first healer summoned. "Please, please help her. I can't bear to see her so." Tears filled her eyes. "I pray it's not q'aqcha."

Tanta Karwa stiffened at the suggestion. Q'aqcha - the theft of one's soul by an evil spirit or sorcerer - is among the most difficult and dangerous ailments to cure. Tanta Karwa was an expert at treating q'aqcha, which required powers beyond those of most healers. According to her it is largely a matter of reuniting the mind and life force with the body. The Empress must have shared Kusi Rimaq's concern, and that's why She summoned Tanta Karwa.

"I'll do all I can," Tanta Karwa said. "Please leave us now."

With one last sorrowful look at her sister the princess left quietly, sliding the door closed behind her. Tanta Karwa set to work. Gently, soothingly, she asked questions while she looked in the girl's mouth and eyes, and tested the warmth of her cheeks. Princess Koka muttered her responses, which was a good sign; at least she could still speak. No, she replied, she hadn't received a sudden fright recently, or wandered near lakes or mountains or tombs where spirits dwell, or dreamed of such places. No, there was no vomiting or diarrhea, and she wasn't thirsty.

At last Tanta Karwa motioned me into the corridor where she whispered, "She has some symptoms of q'aqcha, but others are lacking. I think the problem lies elsewhere. We'll know in the morning. I'll leave you some herbs for brewing - "

"Me?" Tanta Karwa had never involved me in her healing before.

She leaned closer. "I'll arrange for you to stay with the princess tonight - alone. The herbs will calm her, but I suspect sometime tonight she'll tell you what the real problem is. You're closer to her age and a stranger to this house. She'll confide in you and you'll know what to do."

"But I'm not a healer. How will I know what needs to be done?"

"You will," Tanta Karwa said with confidence, "and you'll tell me when I return in the morning. You needn't explain it to me if you don't wish. The trust between a patient and her healer is sacred. I'll follow your counsel whatever it is, and tell the Empress it's my decision."

She left before I could protest further. Kusi Rimaq moved elsewhere that night. I sat alone with Princess Koka by a single, flickering lamp, with the door to the little room closed. For a long time we sat quietly, Koka staring at the walls and me still awed to be sharing a room with a princess; but eventually I became bored. Koka, far from aloof royalty, was behaving like a sulking child, and a stubbornly silent one at that. How was I to know what to do if she refused to speak? What would Tanta Karwa do? My thoughts drifted back to the events of that morning; my first visit with Sumaq since leaving the akllawasi.

"Qori!" Sumaq's hand flew to her mouth, her eyes wide and fixed on mine. In an instant we locked in an embrace. A sob of joy escaped her.

Tanta Karwa was busy ministering elsewhere in the city. I greatly anticipated this reunion, although, I confess I had motives other than simply visiting my dear friend.

We stood in the golden garden of the Qorikancha, where Sumaq supervised the placement of life-size people and animals and plants, all of pure gold, being set out for a special ceremony. The nine old empresses, each represented by a full-size golden statue dressed in exquisite robes, watched a life-like shepherd lead a herd of llamas past a field of gold and silver maize plants, where perched emerald-eyed birds.

Sumaq stood back, holding my hands, giving me that adoring smile. "I knew you'd come," she said. A nearby priest reminded us with a frown that we stood on holy ground. Sumaq released my hands and lowered her eyes. "Come with me," she whispered.

With head bowed I walked a pace behind her as she led me to a secluded alcove used as a confessional. Decorum must be maintained, I reminded myself, for Sumaq T'ika is now a priestess, and this is sacred ground.

On entering the Qorikancha garden I passed her mother and paused to greet her. She swept by me, beak held high, without a nod of acknowledgement. But she was smiling. What puzzled me now was that Sumaq, too, was smiling when I came upon her, even before she saw me. Surely mother and daughter had seen each other. Why the smiles?

"All is well between us now," Sumaq said when I mentioned seeing her mother. She sat before me with her shawl over her head. I knelt in front as if offering confession. We spoke in whispers. My marriage, of which I related only the formal details, and her new life as a priestess had been discussed already.

"How did this come to pass?"

"Tanta Karwa."

"Tanta Karwa?"

"Yes, you know how she is. I don't know what she said to my mother, but one day when I was alone in my husband's temple she brought her to me. The three of us talked about nothing, and then Tanta Karwa left us. That's when my mother told me the terrible secret of our panaqa."

"The terrible secret?"

"Well, not entirely a secret. The elders of all the royal houses know, but nobody mentions it."

"And?"

"You are of my heart, Qori. I know you won't tell anyone about this."

I nodded.

Sumaq took a deep breath. "It happened in the reign of my ancestor, Capac Yupanqui, who founded Apu Mayta Panaqa, the fifth royal house of Hurincuzco. When he was made emperor he took for his wife a woman named Chinbo Mama Caua. It's said she was very beautiful and of a good heart. But later a madness came upon her. Three times each day she fell to the floor screaming, tearing at her face and hair, and none could stop her. Finally, one day, the servants were drawn to the kitchen by a child's screams."

Sumaq faltered. I placed my hand on hers. She looked away. "If it's too painful. . . . " I said.

She fixed me with hollow eyes. "The madness caused her to roast her own infant son, whom she planned to eat."

Silence engulfed us. I knew not where to look.

"Do you hate me now?" she asked in a tiny voice.

"I love you, Sumaq. The sins of your ancestors aren't yours." She grasped my hand, and then let it fall when a shadow moved by. We resumed our confessional postures.

"That's what my mother told me," she said in a whisper, "but there's always gossip and suspicion. Capac Yupanqui remarried, but the shame of madness in his line remains. A royal house must never be disgraced. There can't be any hint of scandal - ever. Since that time the women of our panaqa are most strict in their conduct so the deeds of the past will be forgotten. And that's why my mother was. . ." she paused and swallowed hard, "was so angry when. . . when she found me with my chambermaid."

My hand found hers again.

"No, please. . . I must tell all. It wasn't the maid who started it, not really. She wasn't much older than me. She even tried to say 'no,' but I insisted. After my mother found us the girl disappeared. Then there was another who. . . well, I thought she wanted me to touch her, but she didn't, and she told everyone about me. That's when my mother screamed at me in front of my father, my brothers, even the servants. I thought I would die of shame. But I never knew about. . . about the panaqa secret."

I lowered my head. The painful truth was out. What could I say?

Sumaq spoke as if hearing my thoughts. "There's nothing to be said, Qori. That you have heard me is enough. The burden is lighter already."

I nodded.

"I can't change who I am, Qori. I thought my mother didn't understand, but she does. It was because our panaqa must avoid. . . 'unseemly behavior,'" she made a face, "that she was cruel when. . . when she learned about me. She thought she could change me. But when she realized she couldn't she used her influence to have me enter the akllawasi and become a priestess, thus saving me from the marriage my father planned. I thought she was only getting rid of me. I didn't know about the arranged marriage, or the mad empress. I suppose I never really considered what I was doing, or how it would affect the panaqa. I only thought of myself. But now I know my mother acted for everyone's benefit. We've made our peace."

I wanted to hug her but a shadow passed by the alcove again. "And now you are friends," I said with a sigh.

Sumaq hesitated. "Well, at least we're not enemies. As Tanta Karwa says, that's a start. Anyway, mother is still worried Lady Sisa will find out about my. . . my preferences."

"What does Lady Sisa have to do with it?"

Sumaq pursed her lips reflectively. "She's Lady Speaker of Hurincuzco. You've seen how the other first ladies fawn over her, and my mother is no exception. One word from Lady Sisa, even a hint of disapproval, and reputations can be ruined, whole families shunned. As long as mother stays in Lady Sisa's good graces our mad ancestress will remain forgotten, but if Sisa should hear of new improprieties . . . ." Sumaq let the emphasis on this last word fade, its meaning clear.

"Lady Sisa would hold this over your mother?"

"Not just over my mother, Qori, over our whole panaqa."

This didn't match with the outward charms of the Lady Sisa I saw arriving for the aklla selections, and I wondered if Hilpay contrived this threat to cover her own shame over her daughter's nature. Perhaps it's so, I mused, but that's not a question to trouble Sumaq with now that she's finally reached a truce with her mother. Whatever Hilpay's feelings are toward Sumaq, she's still done me a great service.

"I think your mother arranged my marriage," I said, hoping to set the conversation in a new direction.

"What?"

"Yes. I didn't mention it before because, well, you weren't getting along then."

"What makes you think it was her doing?"

"Don't worry. It has nothing to do with you and me. It's just that when old Cormorant said my name during the selection your mother acted as though she'd heard of me. I think someone asked her to watch for Qori Qoyllur. As I said, I was given a good match. I want to thank her. And I'm grateful to whoever asked her to do this for me. Who do you suppose it was?"

Sumaq jerked her head in surprise. "I have no idea."

"My benefactor may wish to remain anonymous, but I'm curious. Aren't you?"

Those who were supposed to be my 'friends' in the city had still not revealed themselves, though surely they knew where I was, and daily I wondered who they were and what they were waiting for.

"Yes, but - "

"Will you try to find out for me?"

"Of course."

Another shadow glided past the alcove, reminding us that we had been talking for some time. "It must seem to those waiting I have a lifetime of sins to confess," I said. Sumaq laughed.

We stood. It was time to ask the favor that took me to the Qorikancha that day, although I hated to involve Sumaq in my schemes. Still, I wanted to be certain about Achachi. A tiny shadow of doubt remained. During our brief exchange at Tipón I saw in Achachi's eyes that he knew my name, but he hadn't admitted it was he who gave the message about Qhari to his granddaughter.

"Sumaq, do you remember that girl who entered with the other new akllas just before I left, the one I thought I knew, but was mistaken?"

She lifted her brows at the memory. "Yes."

"When you see her next, whisper that her grandfather is pleased she delivered his message to Qori Qoyllur. I want to know what her reaction will be."

This, I decided, would positively confirm that Achachi held Qhari. His granddaughter was guileless. Her face would tell Sumaq everything I needed to know.

"But - "

"Please, Sumaq. I promise to explain everything on my next visit."

"But it's not possible, Qori. She's no longer with us."

"What do you mean?"

Sumaq cupped her hand around my ear and whispered, "The Emperor is still sick and the priests said Inti needed more strength to heal His son, so they made sacrifices to Him here in the temple at dawn yesterday. The girl offered herself."

"She offered herself?"

Sumaq shrugged. "Well, that's what is said. It was a closed ceremony because they don't want rumors about the Emperor's health flying around the city, and only a few priests attended."

The need for the sacrifice, and secrecy, was obvious, and akllas were carefully chosen for the honor, but why this aklla? A cold terror seized me. I hinted to Achachi that his granddaughter was in my power. It was an idle threat but now she was dead, a glorious death to be sure, but nonetheless dead. I shuddered. Will Achachi blame me? Will he take his revenge on Qhari?

"Sumaq, when will the girl's sacrifice be announced to her family?"

"When the Emperor is better, I suppose."

"And if He doesn't recover?"

"Well, she was of a royal house. . . perhaps soon."

"Where is Lord Achachi?"

Sumaq looked startled as if I had suddenly changed subjects. "The Visitor-General? Who knows? The lords don't make their schedules public, but why are you interested - oh yes, the girl was Lord Achachi's granddaughter. Well, I'm sure he'll be proud when he learns of her supreme offering."

Or furious, I thought. Find Qhari before Achachi learns about his granddaughter. That could be any day. Where is Qhari being held? I've seen enough of Cuzco to know he isn't here. Achachi's panaqa has many country estates. Yes, that's where they'll keep him, but at which one? Where does Achachi spend his time when he's not traveling?

The alcove had been shadowed so many times I was surprised not to find a line waiting when we emerged. The only person in sight was dear old Cormorant the drummer, lurking near a doorway. I smiled at her. She scowled and disappeared.

At two hundred paces from the Qorikancha, where a street crosses the main avenues leading to the golden enclosure, I paused to put my sandals back on, for this street marks the boundary where footwear must be removed before approaching the holy sanctuary. And here I met Tanta Karwa who had come looking for me. I asked how she managed to reconcile Sumaq T'ika with her mother.

"It wasn't my doing," she replied with her usual modesty. "They both wanted it. I merely provided the opportunity by inviting Sumaq's mother to join me at the temple for prayers." She looked at me for a moment and then explained, "A healing matter." I nodded. One doesn't question a healer about her patients, and prayer is an expected part of any cure.

"But, mother, how did you get them talking?"

Tanta Karwa gave me the fond smile she used whenever I called her 'mother' and, looking down, fingered the tupu at her breast. "Well, Sumaq once confided to me that there was trouble between her and her mother. I suspect you know about it?"

I nodded. Sumaq never told me she spoke to Tanta Karwa about her mother, but then, I never told her the secrets I shared with Tanta Karwa, either. .

"I felt the time was right to offer a cure," Tanta Karwa said, "so when I had them in the same room I spoke first, about nothing really, just talk of forthcoming festivals and a bit of innocent gossip. Eventually each began commenting on what I said, not to each other, not directly, but they drifted into a conversation through me. That was the first step, to get them talking in front of each other, and about nothing of concern.

People want to talk, Qori, especially when they're hurting. But sometimes they're stubborn and know not where to begin. Provide them a chance to speak, and once they start they won't stop until the pain of their hearts is laid forth. So it was with mother and daughter. Once they found their voices, and without realizing it, they began speaking to each other about small matters. That's when I left. They did the rest."

To my next question Tanta Karwa had no more idea than Sumaq. "Lord Achachi? If he's not in the city, or off on one of his tours, he could be at Pisaq or Ollantaytampu, or perhaps at the new estate his panaqa is building at Machu Picchu." She looked at me curiously as if about to ask why I was interested, but then a more pressing concern crossed her mind. "I came to find you because the Empress has summoned me. We must go to the palace immediately."

Princess Koka cleared her throat and sighed heavily, bringing me back to her room. So, I thought, she's beginning to bore even herself. I spoke about the great desert and the green Valley of Ica, mostly to amuse myself and pass the time, and eventually I caught her attention. She started asking questions, and then a conversation began. She seemed eager to hear about my life in the akllawasi, and in her excitement soon forgot herself. When I told her the story of the farting sorceress she collapsed in fits.

I'm not sure which of us began eating first from the fruit bowls set about the room, but it was only after we consumed everything that I realized Koka's appetite was as voracious as mine. She seemed as surprised as I was when the bowls were empty, and asked what I would like to eat next. My time of moon was coming, and with it all the usual urges. Just then the taste of popped maize, nicely salted, appealed to me. Koka thought this an excellent idea. She went to the door, called out, and although it was the middle of the night a maid appeared instantly, then hurried off to fulfill the princess's wishes. Soon we munched contentedly.

Koka told me about the life of a princess, which sounded almost as confining as that of an aklla. The princes, she complained, were given mistresses and allowed to bed the chambermaids, but a princess could not lie with a man until she was married, and it wasn't fair. She was as curious as the next girl, and several handsome guards excited her interest.

At her urging I told her what I knew about men, which wasn't much, but for her amusement I wove a tale of passion, telling my fantasies as if they were real and almost believing them myself. Being that moon time when anything in a loincloth interested me, my descriptions became most heated. What she pictured I can't say, but to me my fantasy lover was always decidedly male, and faceless. But when Koka alluded to my husband with a shy grin, probably assuming it was he of whom I spoke, I could only think of T'ito with disappointment. She must have seen this, for she quickly declared that some men are disgusting. That's not a word I would have chosen, but she said it so vehemently I knew more was to follow. Dawn was close, and in the next moments the truth came tumbling out.

"My brother is disgusting."

"The Heir? You mean Titu Cusi, the one your mother is taking you to visit at Qispikancha?"

"He says he's the Heir, but father hasn't publicly declared it yet."

"And he's disgusting?"

"He is. He's a year younger than me, but he's always trying to. . . to touch me."

I laid my hand on hers and looked away, waiting for her to continue.

"He says he will be the next Emperor, and that means I'll be his wife. Then he can. . . can touch me all he wants. He says it's his right so I might as well get used to it now. . . and let him do what he wants."

"Does your mother know?" I asked gently.

"I tried to tell Her, but She said it's the way of boys, and She wouldn't let me say anything more. She gives Titu Cusi everything he wants!"

I pulled her head to my shoulder in sympathy. Tanta Karwa was right, I knew what to do.

XIII

Of the Sacred Paths, and a Pagan Rite of womanhood where Qori lies, drinks too much, and deceives Lord Sapaca.

"And that's what you think best?"

"Yes," I said.

Tanta Karwa waited for me to explain, but then nodded approval at my silence. She had said I might not want to tell her. In truth, I knew Tanta Karwa would understand, but I didn't want to betray Koka's confidence.

The Empress drummed Her fingers on Her thigh when we told Her. "Well, at least it's not q'aqcha."

"Mother Moon be praised," Kusi Rimaq shouted.

Mama Oqllo frowned at her. "Oh, hush up." The princess shrank back to her kneeling position.

"I can't put this journey off another day," the Empress said, palms open. "With my husband resting at Chinchero there are many matters of state that require my attention. As it is, we'll only be able to pass one night with Titu Cusi before returning. But. . . " She paused and sighed heavily, "if that's what Koka needs then the poor girl will have to stay behind. I'll order an escort for you."

Mama Oqllo leaned back and stroked Her chin, pondering the sky. "Since Koka must remain here, she might as well represent me at the quicuchicuy ceremony in Hurincuzco today. I suppose it's the least we can do to keep Lady Sisa and Lord Sapaca happy."

From the Qorikancha there radiates a series of ritual paths called zeq'e along which numerous shrines are located. These are divided among the four suyus, and extend well into the countryside beyond the city. The paths are not straight or always marked, but one can follow them by proceeding from one shrine to the next. They vary in length and the number of wak'a along each, but all are within sight of Cuzco, a half-day walk in any direction. Since there are over forty zeq'e paths there are hundreds of shrines. Some are hills, springs, ravines, flat places, or boulders, and others are houses, plazas, temples, fields, or ancestral tombs. Different lineages are responsible for the maintenance and regular offerings made to the shrines along each path: sea shells, llamas, guinea pigs, miniature garments and figurines being common, but the nobles also offered sacred metals and coca leaves, and on special occasions even child sacrifices depending on the prestige of the wak'a.

Many shrines are only of importance to local groups, but some are attended by all, such as Mascata Urco, Yancaycalla, and Urcoscalla, where one first gains or loses sight of holy Cuzco, and Ñan, who is prayed to for safe roads. On one of the zeq'e paths in the Chinchaysuyu quarter is the wak'a Puñui, who grants untroubled sleep. Following the 'remedy' I proposed to Tanta Karwa, who in turn convinced Mama Oqllo, it was to Puñui that Koka and I directed our steps that morning, along with a maidservant and six guards. Tanta Karwa returned to Choqo, and the Empress took Princess Kusi Rimaq to Qispikancha.

The wak'a Puñui is a patch of flat ground within the city proper. It would have taken little time to visit had I not prescribed walking a complete circuit around the outskirts of the city in homage to the shrine, ending with a second visitation to leave offerings, thus consuming the morning. Princess Koka, elated at avoiding her brother, skipped from the palace into the open countryside.

Being the month called Cawawarkis - the time when fields are turned in preparation for planting - the air lay heavy with the smell of fresh earth. Everywhere men worked the soil with footplows. These are short poles with a narrow bronze blade attached to one end. Above the blade a crosspiece projects from one side, which acts as a footrest. A man grasps the pole, jumps up, and with his left foot on the crosspiece drives the blade into the ground, pulling the pole back to turn the earth. The plowmen work in pairs, and kneeling before each pair is a third man breaking the clods with a stone club. Whoever owns the field provides aqha for the thirsty workers, so the toil is accompanied by much song and gaiety.

Upon returning to Puñui the princess buried a bag of coca leaves as an offering to the wak'a, and we both made fervent prayers giving a fine performance for the maid who would report back to the Empress. Of course Puñui received credit for curing the princess, and Tanta Karwa received a new dress from the Empress. But I received the greatest reward of all, and one I can say in all honesty I hadn't anticipated, for I acted out of compassion. That was the gratitude and friendship of Princess Koka.

After the prayers I motioned to take my leave, but Koka, now in high spirits, insisted I accompany her to the quicuchicuy ceremony at the kancha of Chima Panaqa, where Lady Sisa and Lord Sapaca were hosting the royal houses. Of course I welcomed the invitation, indeed, I'd been hinting at it ever since the Empress mentioned the ceremony that morning, but I didn't want to appear too eager.

Lord Sapaca, I reflected, rescued Princess Sisa from the Hatunqolla akllawasi, so he must have arrived soon after Ronto and the priestess were murdered. Can Sapaca verify that Achachi was nearby, perhaps even still at the akllawasi when he arrived? Surely Lord Sapaca, Speaker of Hurincuzco, knows where Achachi is spending his time, and therefore the likely place of Qhari's confinement.

When we arrived at the kancha the guards left us, and the maid waited outside in the street.

"Princess Koka, we are honored," Lady Sisa said placing an arm around Koka. "It's unfortunate your mother couldn't attend also, but we know how busy She is at court, and my daughter understands. She'll be presented just as soon as I can separate her father from his aqha."

Lady Sisa turned her radiance on me while Koka made the introductions. "Any friend of Princess Koka's is welcome in our kancha," she said taking my hand in both of hers. "We're pleased you can join our celebration. Thank you for coming." From nowhere a servant appeared with keros. Lady Sisa offered these with her own hands, taking one for herself, and joined us in the finger dip to Mama Pacha and the first swallow. Then, seeing others arrive behind us, she excused herself and went to greet them, passing her tumbler to the maid who trailed behind.

I was speechless. The Lady Speaker of Hurincuzco actually drank with me, after serving me from her own hand!

Koka turned to me with a grin. "What do you think? Is she not beautiful?"

When I saw Lady Sisa at a distance during the selections at the akllawasi I thought her stunning. Now, with her scent still lingering, I had to confess she took my breath away. It wasn't the exquisite garments and jewelry adorning a well-endowed female form, or the touches of makeup outlining her huge, liquid eyes and blushing her cheeks, it was all of this, but more. She radiated sensuality, unaffected and proper, but complete. I watched while she greeted new arrivals, placing them at ease and making each feel the most important person present. There was a confidence that left no doubt she was in control of everything and everyone around her. All eyes followed her. The men wanted her. The women wanted to be her.

Koka led me through the crowded courtyard, nodding to those we passed who raised their keros to her. I stayed close, feeling lost and underdressed in this crush of royalty, and afraid someone would mistake me for a maid.

Koka gestured with her kero to a knot of women occupying a corner. "Of course, that old potato would be here," she said.

I followed her gaze to the central figure, a short, ample woman dressed like Koka in red and black. "Lady Chuqui," Koka said, "one of my father's sisters, and His principal consort. She thinks her son should be the next Emperor. Naturally she's here to curry support from the households of Hurincuzco. See how they fawn over her? My mother will hear of this."

I recognized the hooked nose next to Lady Chuqui - Sumaq T'ika's mother, Lady Hilpay. While a maid stepped forward unbidden to fill our keros, I wondered how I might approach her. She arranged my marriage to T'ito, or knew who had, and this seemed a good opportunity to contact my unknown friends. That T'ito was a disaster as a husband was not their fault. At least they managed to have me married into my own ancestral ayllu.

Koka tugged me along, circling the courtyard. The guests spilled into side patios, and from one of these came a burst of male laughter. We paused to look inside. A group of noblemen gathered around a big man who attempted to put a gold bracelet on another's wrist. Koka snickered.

"Lord Sapaca tries to give everything away," she said shaking her head.

Before I could comment Lord Sapaca completed his task amid much hilarity, retrieved a two-handed kero, which he somehow managed in one hand, and took a draught big enough to drown in. Then he turned slightly from his circle of admirers, reached under the front of his tunic, let out a mighty blast of gut wind, and pissed against the wall! Those around him paid no attention, continuing their conversation as if nothing untoward took place. I said, "That is the great Lord Sapaca, Speaker of Hurincuzco?"

"I know," Koka said turning away with a grimace, "he's as crude as a peasant. But he's the head of Chima Panaqa, and represents all the households of Hurincuzco at court. Father says he's the shrewdest bargainer He's ever known."

Nonetheless, Lord Sapaca was such a complete opposite from his wife I couldn't help but wonder aloud, "How can Lady Sisa stand him?"

"She can't, but you'd never know it to see her with him. She's too much the lady to notice his ways. Besides, she's married to him. Lady Sisa is one of father's half-sisters, although her mother was only a minor concubine to my grandfather. I suppose that makes Sisa my aunt, like Lady Chuqui, but I have so many aunts," she said with a shrug. "Anyway, the story is that father married Sisa to Sapaca because Sapaca rescued her in some battle."

I knew the tale well but made no comment, deciding to wait for a more opportune moment to approach Sapaca.

We continued meandering through the crowd. When Koka stopped to speak with someone I stepped aside to let another pass, and found myself alone surrounded by strangers' backs. Edging forward nervously, I smiled at those backs, trying to appear as if I belonged and was on my way somewhere, but in the process I became hopelessly separated from Koka.

When I finally emerged on the fringe of the crush I was surprised to see a familiar face, and almost rushed straight to him in a burst of nostalgia, eager to have someone to stand beside. Fortunately I stopped short before embarrassing myself. He won't remember me, I thought, even if he were sober, which he most certainly is not. Still, I lingered watching surreptitiously from nearby.

Lord Aquixe was a short, slight man to begin with, but he was dwarfed beside his burly companions. The Inca lords continued their visiting over his head, ignoring him completely, while Aquixe nodded up at them, turning from one to the other as if he were part of the conversation. His headdress accentuated his massive forehead, and his frog-eyes bulged over a sharp nosed, thin lipped, chinless countenance. No feather tabard today, instead he wore a pectoral of red shell beads. It was too big for him, quite awkward on such a small man, but he probably thought it made him look larger, and it certainly blared his wealth. His clothing, I noticed, was in pure Inca style, with only the mandatory trim of bird and fish designs to mark his provincial origin.

"Your crop yields are down?" Aquixe interjected in the men's discussion, his words coming in a slurred squeak. "Then I'll send you a few loads of bird manure from my coastal islands. No, please, I insist. It's nothing."

The lords only paused while Aquixe spoke, none looking at him, and when he finished they resumed their conversation as if he'd said nothing. Considering the encrusted laborers who harvested that bird dung, and the sweating drivers who delivered it into the mountains on Aquixe's behalf, I shook my head and thought, Is this what becomes of your people's wealth, Aquixe, passed out with a wave of your hand to curry favor from those you worship, and who will never accept you among them?

The men replenished their keros while Aquixe gulped his aqha trying to catch up with them, dribbling much down his front in the effort. Being smaller of stature he couldn't match the drinking pace, though he seemed determined to do so. He looked unsteady on his feet already, and the festivities were just beginning. Wryly amused I hovered, keeping watch on Aquixe, but before long someone shouted, "It's time, they're bringing her out."

Koka was nowhere in sight, so I squeezed to the front of the crescent forming at the far end of the courtyard, having my kero filled yet again in the process. Lady Sisa stood expectantly in the open space, and Lord Sapaca, remarkably steady on his feet for a man who must have already drunk a vat of aqha, proudly emerged from a doorway leading his daughter. A gasp of approval swept the crowd. "Beautiful, just beautiful," they murmured. She was.

Sisa's daughter, who looked to be in her twelfth year, wore an outfit matching her mother's in every detail, and she inherited all her mother's charms. Sapaca led her to Sisa's side, and with the girl between, all three bowed to the cheering onlookers. Lord Sapaca was visibly moved, but Lady Sisa and her daughter retained calm, dignified expressions, as if untouched by the adulation.

Although my womanhood rites were, of course, far less elaborate, and Qhari was my only audience, nonetheless my parents insisted on observing proper Inca ritual. I knew what the girl had been through, and what was about to happen. When her first moon time arrived she fasted for three days in seclusion, being fed only a little raw maize on the third day. This being her fourth day, early this morning her mother washed her, with special attention to the combing and braiding of her hair, and presented her with the new clothes and white alpaca sandals she now wore. Next, she would be lectured by an elder female relative on how a woman behaves, and how she must always obey her parents, and then her most important uncle would give her the adult name she'd carry for the rest of her life. In the absence of kin, my own parents assumed those roles themselves. But here there was no shortage of relatives.

When the lecture on womanly conduct began it amused me that Lady Chuqui, not about to miss an opportunity to appear before an audience, maneuvered herself into this role, even though she was not of Chima Panaqa or even Hurincuzco. Of course, lineage and saya aside, had the Empress been present She would have been asked to do this as a sign of special favor. Lady Chuqui cleverly took the Empress's place.

The lecture over, Lady Chuqui reluctantly returned to the front of the crowd, and one of Sapaca's brothers stepped forward to bestow the girl's adult name. He was another giant of a man, with Sapaca's thick lips and heavy brow; and like most of the men present he wore a broad collar of round feathers, the emblem of Chima Panaqa.

The man raised his voice. "Young woman, because you are as beautiful as a hummingbird, I name you. . . Q'enti. Q'enti of Chima Panaqa!"

he shouted, standing behind her with arms raised. The crowd roared its approval.

Q'enti walked to the banquet laid on mats along one side of the courtyard, where she began serving her guests, starting with her most important relatives. That would have put me at the end of the line, but just then Koka reappeared and insisted I stand next to her. I didn't argue. The sun dipped low. My stomach growled. Koka was full of whispers about some boys she'd met, and I gave her what attention I could while eyeing the sumptuous feast.

The food won the attention contest. Looking down rows of heaped bowls I saw that my craving for popped maize would be satisfied again today, but first I had to pass platters of roast llama, fish, duck, several varieties of boiled maize, potatoes, hot pepper sauces, stews of squash, beans and quinoa, and fruit trays laden with pacae, guava, lucuma, avocado and pineapple imported for the occasion from the lowlands. I sampled each dish thoroughly.

Delighted with the freedom of being on her own at an adult gathering, Koka again drifted away after the meal, joining some girls and, I suspected, boys in an adjoining patio. Thirsty from having stuffed so much popped maize into my mouth I allowed my kero to be filled again, and again, until I felt bold enough to wander the crowds on my own.

"In truth, She didn't think the quicuchicuy of Lady Sisa's daughter important enough to interrupt Her leisure in the countryside," Lady Chuqui announced to her flock of admirers, referring to the Empress. I paused nearby in the shadows.

"She's gone to Qispikancha to see that son of hers. . .the one born in the far north at Tumipampa. . . such a backward corner of the realm." Lady Chuqui left a pause for everyone to remember that her son was born in Cuzco. Then her voice dripped honey. "I do hope the boy is all right. They keep him so far from the city. He never appears.at court, you know. Do you think something is wrong with him, perhaps some infirmity of the mind?"

I knew well the sowing of a rumor when I heard one, having sown more than a few myself, and I knew before the festivities ended it would be repeated as solemn truth.

"Excuse me, my Ladies," I said, "but I attended the Empress this morning before She left. Of course, She said nothing to me, but. . ." I paused to look around secretively, then lowered my voice, "it's being whispered that Her son Titu Cusi enjoys virile health, and as for Her journey to Qispikancha, well, you know what lies above that town, and who lives there."

I thought 'virile health' was a tactful description of Titu Cusi's behavior toward Koka, and as for the rest, well, it was being whispered because I was whispering it. Besides, I only implied the obvious; Qispikancha was the entrance to Tipón where Lord Atoq lived. If they wished to find greater meaning behind my words, which they did judging by the looks on their faces, that was up to them.

"Who are you?" Lady Chuqui demanded coldly, squinting her tiny, near-sighted eyes at me.

"Only a humble servant of the Empire, my Lady, who accompanies Princess Koka to this celebration," I replied with a bow. Before more questions could be asked I bowed to them all with a polite, "My Ladies," and faded back into the crowds.

Pleased with my newfound boldness I allowed my kero to be filled again as I went in search of other adventures. I didn't have to look far.

"Excuse me, my Lady, but I just wanted to thank you for arranging such a fine marriage for me."

Sumaq's mother looked down her hooked nose at me. "And who are you?"

"Qori Qoyllur. I'm Sumaq T'ika's friend from the akllawasi."

She blinked and shook her head with a start. "I don't know you," she said as if answering an accusation, then added quickly, "and my daughter has nothing to do with this."

"She has nothing to do with what?"

Hilpay looked flustered. "With you, whom I don't even know."

This floundering denial took me aback. "Well, please express my gratitude to our 'friend,'" I said.

She looked puzzled. "Young woman, I don't know who you are

or what you're talking about." With that she turned her back and strode away.

While I pondered this rebuff over a fresh kero, a commotion by the entrance caught my attention. Drawing closer, I saw Lord Aquixe in a drunken stupor being carried out between two stout servants. The men each grasped an arm, holding him upright to preserve the illusion he was walking, but his feet dangled off the ground and his head rolled on his shoulders. A group of soldiers and noblemen clustered nearby shaking their heads.

"Farewell to the mighty Hatun Kuraka of Ica," one sneered. "What was he doing here anyway? I suppose he invited himself again." The others nodded his sentiments.

The voice sounded familiar. Where have I heard it? I wondered. No, not recently, long ago. Images of Qhari kneeling beside me in the dark came back. That's it! The man who threatened us in the desert and in Cuzco. A sobering chill ran through me. My enemies are close. Have they seen me? I looked up trying to put a face to the voice, but the men turned their backs and drifted away.

"Qori, there you are," Koka said appearing at my side. "I know it's late, and my maid has been waiting all this time in the street, but couldn't we stay just a short while longer? Please-please-please!"

Having realized my old enemies were about I wanted to flee immediately, but Koka thrust me into the role of chaperon, placing her happiness in my hands. Behind her I noticed a boy posing against a wall, trying to appear grown-up and casual, while casting furtive glances at Koka.

"For a short while," I said. The two vanished in an instant.

Moonlight filled the courtyard, its corners and side buildings pools of shadow. Guests took their leave but others lingered, and the aqha continued flowing. I shielded my kero when a maid tipped an urn my way. Drifting by a group of women I heard one say, "Did you hear the news? The Empress went to Qispikancha because Her son is fathering too many bastard children there." Although she tried to sound disapproving her voice held a note of admiration.

How interesting, I thought. News travels faster here than it does in the akllawasi. All I said was Titu Cusi enjoys virile health, and already they have him siring his own lineage. But potency is an admirable trait for a future Emperor, so I let the remark pass.

"That may be," the woman beside her replied, "but I heard Qispikancha is only an excuse. The Empress really went to confer with. . ." she looked around, "the Lord of Tipón."

"Is there trouble in one of the royal houses?" another asked, and then added quickly, "I wonder which one?"

"That's not it at all," another said. "I heard the Emperor is about to proclaim Titu Cusi as His heir. The Empress went to inform him and discuss the confirmation with. . . " she too looked over her shoulder before finishing in a whisper, "he who dwells above Qispikancha."

Why don't they call Atoq by his name, I wondered? Don't they know it, or are they afraid to say it? But it pleased me to know my 'suggestions' not only circulated, they grew beyond all expectation. I continued wandering the courtyard hoping to find Lord Sapaca in a sodden and talkative state. Music drifted on the night, and beyond the snaking, sometimes staggering lines of dancers I spotted Sapaca making his way toward another group of revelers. Here is my opportunity, I thought. Lord Sapaca, where is Achachi holding Qhari? Did you see Achachi at the Hatunqolla akllawasi when you rescued Sisa? Can you place him there? No-no, I cautioned myself, don't rush. Be subtle with him.

"Lord Sapaca, how good to see you again," I said. Sapaca looked down at me bleary eyed, a half smile playing on his thick lips, struggling to recognize me. "Don't you remember me?" I said feigning hurt. I patted his arm. "Of course you do. I certainly remember your company."

Earlier I overheard that Sapaca enjoyed every woman in Cuzco who would have him, and half of those who wouldn't. No maid or common woman was safe in his presence. If there's a kernel of truth in this, I reasoned, he won't remember every tryst of his career, especially if he's aqha-soaked most nights.

"Why yes. . . of course. . . I, uh. . . . "

"Yes, my Lord," I said wickedly, leaning my head back to look up at his face, and wondering fearfully if all of him was the same size, but hurrying on without pause, "I believe Lord Achachi introduced us, didn't he? Is he still at Ollantaytampu?"

Sapaca tried hard to remember me through his aqha haze, and, intent on being polite, answered distractedly, "Achachi? Ollantaytampu? No, he was at Pisaq, but now he's inspecting some provinces in Kuntisuyu, I think."

"Of course, Pisaq, how foolish of me."

Thank you, Lord Sapaca, I thought. That answers one question. At least Achachi is away from Cuzco and may not hear about his granddaughter for some time. I wonder if he has Qhari with him, or hidden at Pisaq?

"You fought in the Qolla rebellion, Lord, have you ever heard of the brave men of Choqo?"

Sapaca looked thrown by this change of direction. "Men of Choqo?"

"Oh yes," I replied quickly to keep him off balance, "the heroes of Choqo. Their names were Sayri, Maita, and Kontor."

Father had given us mother's account of how, after he and the others were believed dead, a bard came to Choqo to gather descriptions of the fallen warriors so they could be presented in song. I didn't really expect Sapaca to have heard of them, my intent being to introduce the subject of the Qolla rebellion. But when I said those names a sobering shadow passed over Sapaca's face. In the pause that followed I saw in his eyes memories clawing their way back to consciousness - troubling memories. "I've never heard of them," he stated.

"They served under Lord Achachi," I said, "and were at the Hatunqolla akllawasi where you rescued Lady Sisa. Did you see Lord Achachi at the akllawasi?"

Sapaca sobered. "Yes," he answered tersely.

"Perhaps Lord Achachi was already there when you arrived," I suggested.

"No, definitely not. He came later."

"But surely he was there before you?"

"I see where this is leading," he said, now sober and nodding to himself. "Someone has started a rumor that I wasn't the first to reach the akllawasi. Malicious gossip! Who started it, Achachi? Well, I can tell you that I found Sisa - me, Sapaca. And as for Achachi, he was nowhere near the Hatunqolla akllawasi until after Sisa was saved."

XIV

In which a Strange Battle takes place according to the customs of these Indians, and Startling Revelations are laid forth.

"Qori, look out!"

A stone zipped passed my ear, missing by a fingerbreadth. The volley thudded into our ranks, but in the next instant those around me whirled their slings. With each stone returned by another the hail began and both lines moved back, leaving the more daring alone on the field to duel.

I was ready. Dropping my cloak I scanned the opposing side for a woman my age. My quarry sighted, I advanced with sling circling. She came toward me, stopping twice to throw, but I didn't pause or flinch when her stones flew by. Close enough now to see her fear, I let fly. She went down with a shriek, her legs buckling beneath her. Two of her comrades ran forward to pull her back. My stones hit both of them before they dragged her ten paces. I advanced to the middle of the field and held my ground. Three opponents prepared to face me.

Though it was the heart of the rainy season Inti shone from a clear morning sky. The earth was wet and warm, and the early crops ripe for harvest. This season is called Pacha Phukuy - Blowing Offerings to the Earth. It's a time for festivals and sacrifices, and it was a blood sacrifice I now sought on the field of honor.

T'ito arrived the day before. "My dove, how good to see you," he had said, planting a kiss on my cheek. "Are you not with child yet?" I tried to smile while shaking my head, thinking it a foolish question. He was so seldom home. He wobbled his earspools and clicked his tongue as if it were my problem. More than a year had passed since our marriage, yet still his seed wouldn't sprout; and he hadn't found time to build our own house as is customary for newlyweds. He simply left me with his mother and visited when it suited him.

"I've been extremely busy in the city with matters of utmost importance," he said, "but I insisted on taking time to be with my ayllu for the tinku this year."

Not with me, with the ayllu, I thought. How impressive. "I'm sure the people will be pleased."

"Yes, they do fuss over me." He tried to sound like Lord Atoq. "Is mother in her herb garden?" I directed him to the plot behind the house.

A child of my own? I thought. I dream of a tiny bundle in my arms, my daughter, kicking and gurgling, needing me. Each time I see the village women with their infants the longing comes over me. It's love I have to give, and no one to give it to. T'ito as the father of my baby? No, he has no place in my world of daydreams.

I had tried to make a marriage with T'ito but he never let me get close to him, never shared his feelings or the secrets of his heart. I can't love one who doesn't share. The face he showed me was the same face he showed the world. From the start our marriage was little more than a habit. We never made love, we had sex; or rather, T'ito had sex, I endured. Am I fated to spend the rest of my life with this stone? I wondered. Can I ever learn to love him?

My conversation with Lord Sapaca about Achachi had ended abruptly when he stomped away, leaving me in stunned silence. I flushed Princess Koka and her young man from a storage hut, both red-faced, and promptly marched her back to the palace where she, mistaking my silence for anger, made me promise not to tell her mother about the boy, and to come visit her soon. But I was in such a state of bewilderment I hardly remember our parting. Since the day Qhari and I were separated I believed Lord Achachi was the fiend at the Hatunqolla akllawasi. But Sapaca was adamant - Achachi wasn't at the akllawasi until after Sisa was rescued.

Achachi can't be the murderer, I thought over and over, yet he knows something. He recognized my name at Tipón; of that I'm certain. What does he know? He knows who commanded him to send Kontor's troop into battle until death, father said, and the purpose of that was to eliminate witnesses. The order must have come from the murderer himself. Is Achachi aware that Ronto and the priestess were murdered, or does he believe the official story that the Qolla slaughtered them? Surely he must suspect something. Then why won't he help me? He claimed not to know me, and he threatened Qhari if I approach him again. And now his granddaughter is dead. That's no coincidence. Will he take revenge on Qhari, or me, or on both of us?

Tanta Karwa and T'ito came around from the back of the house, he gesturing wildly as he described some new khipu of his making, and she listening with an indulgent smile.

T'ito glanced my way. "Oh, Qori, I hope there will be sweet potatoes for supper tonight. Now I must go into Choqo to see my friends."

Obviously I wasn't among his friends.

The tinku of the previous year found T'ito too busy to attend, and me with Tanta Karwa on a healing mission to a nearby village. Though she refused to leave her patient she kept fretting about missing the annual tinku. At first I had no idea what she was talking about, for in daily speech tinku refers to blending ingredients for cooking or medicine.

"That is so," she replied when I asked, "it's a mixing of elements that brings something new into existence. When two rivers converge in swirling foam to make a single flow they are also said to tinku. Such places are powerful and dangerous, full of uncontrolled forces," she cautioned. "When people tinku the word means encounter, but it's a swirling, violent encounter like the meeting of rivers. Two forces unite and shed their blood, thereby feeding the weather spirits of the mountains and Mother Earth, and blending themselves in renewed union. In most towns the ayllus of hurinsaya tinku with those of hanansaya, but our custom is to tinku with the people of Qhachuna," she said, referring to the next village down valley.

"But they're our neighbors. Why do we fight them?"

"Because it's necessary to lose life's blood in order to perpetuate life. Does life not feed on death? Consider the herds and plants of the field. They are born and die that we may live. It's Mama Pacha and the mountain spirits who give us life. Would you offend them by not returning what is so freely given? The village of Qhachuna is our paired opposite - our equal. Its founder is also descended from the ten stones of wak'a Cumpi Huanacauri, so we're related. By merging in tinku both our communities are renewed and we are made whole again. The place of this encounter, the field of Kotakota Pampa, is a shrine on a zeq'e path that lies on the boundary between our lands. It's a fitting place to renew ourselves and proclaim our ancestral rights."

"Do people die?"

. "If it's a good tinku one or two are slain, but at the very least blood must flow to feed the earth. Slings are usually the only weapons allowed, but sometimes the young men use staffs."

"And women fight too?"

"Certainly. But it's the men, and especially the younger boys, who do most of the strutting around. Sometimes girls are captured and taken as brides, though there is usually some agreement beforehand on who is going to catch whom."

"Next year I'll help Choqo win the field," I replied solemnly.

"Win? There is no winning or losing. No land is gained or lost. That's not the purpose."

"Then I'll slay a man of Qhachuna for Choqo."

She smiled at the boast. "Man, woman, child, it matters not who, or from which side, just as long as a sacrifice is made."

"I'll vanquish our enemies," I said, working myself into righteous anger.

"Enemies? Qori, you haven't been listening. Those of Qhachuna are our sisters and brothers. That's why we tinku with them. The tinku only happens by mutual agreement on the field of Kotakota Pampa. There are no hostilities beyond that."

Thereafter I practiced at every opportunity. The sling felt more comfortable in my hand than spindle or loom. Tanta Karwa's squashes and gourds, skillfully stalked, fell victim to my aim like so many Qhachuna heads.

Another stone whizzed by. They wanted my blood now. I stood firm and dared them. One by one the three Qhachuna women ran forward to face me. The first took my stone on her shoulder, the second on her breast, and the third straight in the mouth. When the last one fled, having left her teeth on the field, a line of five Qhachuna women formed in front of me.

My pouch was empty and I stooped to pick stones off the field. Their volley came. I somersaulted, but still took a solid hit on the thigh. Pain ripped my leg, but it didn't stop me. When I regained my feet four Choqo women appeared at my side, screaming at our opponents that five against one upset the balance. The Qhachuna women looked uncertain. I sensed a rout at hand. With my sling once again circling I called on my sisters to advance. They followed, and at our first volley the Qhachuna women fled.

It seemed natural for me to give that command, and only natural the others should follow. But I was told later it was unprecedented behavior for women on the field of Kotakota Pampa. Having chased our opponents away, my ayllu sisters embraced me and pulled me back to our lines.

"Save your strength, Qori. The day is young. Did you see them run?"

"We did it," another shouted, "We pushed them back."

"Did you see Qori out there alone? She hit four of them before we even got there."

In truth, I hit six, but after the story passed around the number grew to ten, which I, of course, modestly denied, pretending not to have kept count.

Tanta Karwa applied bandages and poultices at the rear of the Choqo lines. She glanced at my thigh, already sprouting a purple welt. "That's a good one," she remarked casually. "You'd better keep moving or it will stiffen and we'll have to carry you home. Now excuse me, I have more serious wounds to attend."

Indeed she did. Several people lay around her, peering back at me through swollen, blackened eyes. Some held cloths to bleeding faces, two looked unconscious, one cradled a broken arm, and another rocked back and forth holding his knee. I wandered over to the aqha urns.

The festivals of Pacha Phukuy began a week earlier. A tree was erected in the plaza around which much dancing, feasting, and drinking began. The tree and its festival were provided by a couple from one of the hanansaya ayllus, who derived great honor from hosting the event. At the end of the celebration another couple from a different hanansaya ayllu claimed the privilege of sponsorship for the following year. It would take that long for them and their kin to prepare. Two days later another tree appeared and the festival repeated, this time hosted by a couple from a hurinsaya ayllu. Those of hurinsaya tried hard to out-dance and out-drink us. Both trees were called mallki - ancestor, but the hanansaya tree was considered female and the hurinsaya tree male, for it takes a man and a woman to form a household, and two sayas to make a community.

A few days later after everyone recovered from the celebrations, which occurred in the same way at Qhachuna, the tinku began at dawn. With both sides impatient to begin the kuraka of Qhachuna stepped onto the field with his wife and other ayllu heads, to be met midway by the kuraka of Choqo with his wife and our ayllu leaders. Each person held a kero, and upon meeting their opposite offered greetings and exchanged toasts. They said prayers, and each side contributed something to an offering that was buried in place. With these polite formalities conclud-ed they agreed the tinku would begin, and the parties returned to their respective sides.

The shouting started, ascending gradually from a murmur of playful taunts to a roar of insults accompanied by rude gestures. Both sides worked themselves into frenzied anger. When I heard what they shout-ed at us I too became caught up in the rising emotions, and called back as good as they gave. Two Qhachuna boys ran forward, turned, and pulled up their tunics to show us their backsides. Two boys from our side responded in like fashion. Then individual men began stepping for-ward, shaking their fists and yelling obscenities. Whenever one advanced, a man of the same age and saya from the other side came toward him. A few women joined in to be met by their opposites, and soon the two sides were within sling range.

I stood beside T'ito and withdrew a new sling from my bag. "For you, my husband. May it serve you well."

He gave me a genuine smile. "Thank you, Qori." He pulled it tight, admiring the checkered pattern woven into the cords. In truth, I had asked another to make it for me, there being no decent yarn available to me at the time, but I saw no need to correct his assumption that it was fashioned by my hand. After all, I had ordered it for him myself.

"I'll hurl some stones for you, too," he said. "Now don't get too close to the front line. Stay back here and be careful."

Stay back? I thought. Hardly. But at least he's showing concern for me. I smiled sweetly and watched him swagger to the front. Then I pulled out my own sling and found a place in the women's line farther along. A moment later the first volley struck.

Now, standing beside the aqha urns, flushed with success and the admiration of those around me, I watched the men's lines dueling. Earlier, individuals ran forward, threw, and quickly retreated, but now more and more of our men tried holding positions in the middle of the field, taunting their foes. This being my first tinku, I was unaware that such prolonged exposure to danger is uncustomary. At close range the slings are deadly. Serious casualties ran high on both sides. I finally caught a glimpse of T'ito. He was not among those holding ground at the center.

Screams jolted my attention to another part of the field, where a Qhachuna youth dragged away a Choqo girl. Several of our sisters came to her defense, pulling her back and beating the boy with their fists. He was persistent. I was about to join them when I remembered Tanta Karwa's words about 'prearranged captures.' Looking closer, I recognized the girl. She had been living in sirvinakuy - trial marriage. It's a widespread custom. By mutual consent the relationship is either severed or formalized in marriage at the end of a year, or after the first child is born. The girl gave birth a few months earlier, thereby proving her fertility and making herself more desirable, but rumor said she was disenchanted with her man and already enjoyed a lover. As I watched it became evident the shrieking and struggling was all for show. She was a willing captive. Her lover claimed her, honorably. A short while later a Qhachuna girl was similarly 'captured,' thus obviating the rules requiring people to marry within their ayllu, and bringing another outsider into the Choqo fold.

I made two more forays onto the field that day. Each time I walked to the middle and dared all comers, but those who came against me did so only to save face for Qhachuna, and quickly retreated.

The tinku ended in midafternoon when Tanta Karwa announced that one of ours, a man whose temple was caved in by a rock, had died. The kurakas of both towns, now limping and accompanied by their wives and attendant couples, met in the middle of the field. They agreed enough blood had been shed to placate Mama Pacha and the weather spirits. We buried the dead man on the field as a final offering. Two days later a boy of Choqo also died of his wounds and was buried nearby.

The people of Qhachuna and Choqo had met in violent encounter to provide a single river of blood for the benefit of all. The gods received their blood offering, land boundaries were again proclaimed, individuals proved their bravery, wives were captured, and whatever private tensions existed beforehand were directed to the field and spent. The tinku was successful, as attested later by a bountiful harvest.

The day was a personal victory for me. Previously, my status in Choqo came from others: a woman from the court of Lord Aquixe of Ica; one of the Emperor's chosen women; wife of T'ito the Imperial Khipu Kamayoq; daughter-in-law of Tanta Karwa the Healer. Now they valued me not as an appendage to another, but in my own right as a fierce fighter. In truth, I didn't set out that day to prove any such thing. What happened on the field of Kotakota Pampa came naturally and surprised even me, at least it surprised me later when I thought about it, for at the time I didn't think; I acted. We limped back to Choqo. I felt exhausted but strangely at peace with myself, fulfilled and cleansed.

I hardly saw T'ito during the day. On the homeward journey he walked ahead, silent and aloof. I turned to Tanta Karwa. "Why isn't T'ito talking to me? What have I done now?"

"The talk is all about you for a change, not him. You may have won honor in the eyes of the people, but you've done nothing to draw him closer to you."

"Was I wrong to fight for Choqo?"

"No, it was expected of you. But you didn't have to do it so vigorously."

"Does he hate me now?"

"His pride is hurt. Even the men are talking about you. They're calling you Chañan Qori Koka."

"Who?"

"Chañan Qori Koka. She was a warrior-woman who ruled both Choqo and Qhachuna in the time of my grandmother. She led her people against an invading Chanka army and destroyed it, thereby saving

188

Cuzco. You're the first to be so called in my lifetime. It's a great honor."

"But I didn't even take a life."

Tanta Karwa gave me a sideways glance. "You didn't take life, but you urged others to offer theirs. Perhaps you didn't notice, but many emulated your stance in the middle of the field. That's how our man died."

"Am I responsible for the actions of others?"

Tanta Karwa arched her brows and shrugged. "You set an example they were shamed into following. But, it's the gods who decide who will live and who will die, and someone had to make the sacrifice or it wouldn't have been a proper tinku. I suppose the gods decided it was his time. I heard you organized a line of women and ordered a charge. Did you really give orders?"

"It didn't happen quite like that. Our advantage was clear and I only spoke the obvious."

She looked at me curiously. "Why did you stand in the middle of the field?"

The answer leapt from my mouth. "Why does one stand on the edge of a cliff and stare down?"

She nodded thoughtfully. "You tempt death."

"I don't tempt it. But I'm not afraid of it either. I stare it in the face, and strangely enough it makes me feel alive."

Tanta Karwa thought on this for a moment. "I think we're both discovering a new side of you," she said quietly.

Somehow I always knew this part of me existed, ever since the day Qhari and I resolved that once one lost the fear of death there was nothing left to fear. But it was not until the tinku, and not until those words of explanation sprang from my mouth, that I began to accept this side of my nature. I felt drawn to the thrill of danger, the challenge and elation of death, and I knew I could strike without hesitation. A pity there were no longer any warrior-women.

"Impossible, is he not?" Tanta Karwa stood beside me at the door watching T'ito's figure retreat down the path to Cuzco. The dawn came with a light drizzle, a good sign that the mountain spirits were pleased with the previous day's sacrifice. T'ito departed with hardly a nod in my direction.

"It's difficult, mother," I admitted.

"I know. I can see it in both of you. Do you know why he's so uncomfortable around you? No? I think it's because he doesn't know how to act, although his pride will never let him admit it."

She placed her arm around my shoulders.

"Remember, his father died when he was young, and I've often been away. He didn't have a set of parents to watch when he was growing up. Did he ever tell you about his leg? He broke it when he was small and limped for a long time afterwards. He still does if you look closely. The other children teased him mercilessly. Children are like that. He never told me. Perhaps he barely remembers it now. I only learned of it later from an ayllu sister. She said he also boasted about me constantly, and that didn't make him popular with the other children. But he kept their taunts out by building a wall around himself. By the time I realized it the years had passed and the mortar set, so now not even I am allowed inside."

It was my turn to put my arm around her.

"Where do the years go, Qori? He loves me, and he's proud of me, perhaps too proud. When I was away he boasted to comfort himself, and that boasting became a habit of arrogance. You see, we want for nothing. Those whom I cure provide for all our needs. T'ito didn't have to learn the ways of the fields and herds. I took him with me when I could, to spend more time with him. He made friends among the children of the noble houses I served. At first I was pleased, but it was a mixed blessing. He began to affect their ways, and that did nothing to teach him humility. Then, after his manhood rites, Lord Atoq took an interest in him. Of course I'm grateful and deeply flattered, but that too has been a mixed blessing. Sometimes I look at him and I still see that lonely little boy waiting for me by the door. He hides those feelings behind that wall of vain superiority. That's why he never married before you. He fears intimacy, as if it will somehow make him weak."

"Then it's not my fault?"

"No, never think such a thing. The problem is his."

190

"But what am I supposed to do? How is a wife to act?"

"Men are strange creatures, Qori. We women like to talk about things and share, but that's difficult for most men. I can't say why. Perhaps the Creator made them so to teach us patience, like the biting insects. For some men sharing isn't talking, it's simply being together. Others will talk, but not just anywhere at anytime. You have to learn when your husband is open to conversation. Discover when he's most relaxed, perhaps when you're alone together after the evening meal, or in bed. And never criticize or contradict him in public."

"But mother, I've never contradicted him, and he's never home long enough for me to learn his moods. We've been married over a year and I hardly know him."

She hugged me. "I know. That was general advice. I forgot we were talking about T'ito. I suppose he's the same beneath the blankets?" My blushing silence answered her and she sighed heavily. "I thought so. You two must spend more time together. He won't listen to me, but he will listen to Lord Atoq. Leave this to me. But remember, if something can be arranged you must be patient and bring him along slowly. Be careful not to question him or demand anything. Whatever he offers let him do so of his own accord."

"But how will I get him to talk?"

"You'll know when the moment is right. Begin with some casual words about your day and how you're feeling, and then share a confidence with him. He may not respond at first, but be patient. Eventually that wall of his will come down, even if it's only one stone at a time. Once there's some trust between you what happens under the blankets will also improve."

"Thank you, mother." She hugged me back.

Many months had passed since Tanta Karwa asked Atoq to find Qhari for me, and as yet there was no reply. I decided to approach the subject gently, hoping to remind her.

"T'ito said you met Lord Atoq when you cured him of a fever," I said.

"Well, in truth I met him a few months before," she admitted with a girlish grin that hinted at a story.

I raised my brows. "Say you so?"

She needed no more urging. This was a day for sharing.

"It happened like this," she said. "My husband went to serve in Thupa Inka's army when the Qolla rebellion started. That was before your time, but I know you've heard of it." Indeed, I thought. "He went with his brother, and both of them died on the same day."

"What was your husband's name?" I asked. No one had told me, and I hadn't inquired. The names of the dead aren't spoken lightly.

"What? Oh, his name was Maita."

Maita? I thought. That's the name of father's brother. How many men named Maita from Choqo died in the Qolla rebellion? Could it be this is the same Maita, my uncle, whom father said is still alive?

Tanta Karwa was looking at me. Catching myself I said, "I'm sorry. I was thinking how sad it must be to lose a husband."

"Yes it is, but that was long ago. They say he died bravely beside his brother, my sister's husband, and some other men of Choqo. They were declared heroes, and a bard even came to Choqo to gather their descriptions so he could present them in words when he told the story.

"Well," the enthusiasm in her voice picked up, "some months later we widows were invited to a feast at Tipón. Lord Atoq arranged this for us to honor the memory of our husbands. He also served in that same war and commiserated greatly with our loss. The feast was most lavish, such as we had never seen before, and we were so honored to be hosted at a royal estate. In truth, the festivities went on for three days."

"For three days?"

"Yes, and four nights," she said blushing.

"Do you mean. . . ?"

"Well. . . you must understand that we were all young women, and it was almost a year since our husbands marched off. The dreary mourning rituals went on endlessly, and this was the first chance we had to be away from the ever-watchful eyes of our kin. We were flattered by all the attention, and surrounded by handsome courtiers who kept our keros full." She smiled at the memory. "Perhaps we can be forgiven if some of us took solace in the arms of those young men. I know I wasn't the only one to lie with Atoq himself."

Perhaps I shouldn't have been surprised. From what I'd seen in the garden at Tipón she still went to him eagerly. And who could blame her? Even at his age Atoq was a handsome man. In his younger years he must have been irresistible. I began to wonder if Atoq really was T'ito's father.

"You won't tell anyone, especially not T'ito, will you?" she asked earnestly. I assured her the secret was safe with me.

"It was a few months later that Lord Atoq summoned me to cure him of a fever. You see those lloque shrubs over there? A brew of their leaves and bitter bark cures most fevers. That's what I gave him. It was a minor thing, but he was so grateful he recommended me to his relatives. Now all the royal households summon me. Of course, all manner of wizards and oracles are consulted too, but my herbs are usually accepted as part of the cure," she said, pride edging her voice.

Remembering her report to Atoq on the Emperor's health, I asked, "And you also keep Lord Atoq apprised of what you see and hear on these visits to royalty?"

"He has eyes and ears everywhere, of which I am the least," she replied as if to a compliment.

It seemed the lives of those around me were inextricably linked to Lord Atoq, patron of all and faithful guardian of the peace. I hoped some day I could serve the Emperor through him, too.

Some parts of Tanta Karwa's story still troubled me. Her husband Maita died with his brother, who was married to her sister. Could it possibly be. . . ? Trying to sound casual I said, "I have not met your sister."

"Oh, she disappeared years ago while on a pilgrimage to Pachakamaq. She's the one I mentioned to you at Tipón, the one of whom you remind me. They say those of the Cavina nation believe a soul doesn't stay in the upper world but is born again here on this earth. It's a ridiculous notion, of course, which our religion frowns on. But looking at you I could almost believe it so. Is something wrong?"

I can only imagine the shock on my face. "This sister of whom I remind you, what was her name?" I managed in a weak voice.

"Qolqe Killa," came the reply.

When she said my mother's name I almost collapsed. My thoughts raced. Tanta Karwa is my aunt, my own true flesh and blood! No wonder I'm drawn to her like a daughter. And her 'dead' husband Maita is indeed my fugitive uncle. That makes T'ito my first cousin, a bit close, but first cousin marriage is allowed among royalty, and since we're secondary nobility an exception might be made for us.

Tanta Karwa looked at me with concern and placed her hands on my shoulders, searching my face. "Qori, what is it?"

"Oh, nothing." I tried to recover while saying to myself, You promised father. You must never tell. "I'm just curious about my new relatives."

Fate, or some guiding hand, not only returned me to my parent's ayllu but into the bosom of my family. But there was still one more to be accounted for, one I waited patiently to meet by chance since arriving in Choqo - my elder brother, the one who injured himself before mother left for Pachakamaq. Father said he was left with the ayllu. I wondered how to raise the question without being too obvious when Tanta Karwa spoke again.

"You might as well know all. There's another reason for the wall T'ito has built around himself. Try as I might, I have never been able to relieve him of a pain, a fear he carries. Ever since he was small and hurt his leg he's felt abandoned, because soon after it happened my sister left on her pilgrimage and never returned. You see, I never had children of my own. T'ito is her child. I adopted him."

XV

**In which the Hapless Couple is summoned, a Perilous Mission into
Lands Unknown is assigned, and the old Warlord laughs.**

The maqana is a vicious weapon. It is like a two-handed sword that
stands to the height of a man's chest. The thick blade is of hard black
wood, pointed, with sharp edges. But it's not a weapon for stabbing or
slashing. Its great weight makes it more efficient as a club for hacking
and crushing. The soldiers fondle them lovingly, calling them 'Head
Splitter' or 'Arm Smasher' or 'Rib Crusher' with all the warmth usually
reserved for a lover. But it wasn't until this day that I saw what a maqana
could do in the hands of an expert.

The man knelt, hands tied at his back, ropes fastened at his neck and
wrists pulled taut by guards in front and behind. The executioner stood to
the side, absently stroking his maqana while he measured his target.

T'ito gave me his 'None of our affair' look and hurried me past. No
one paid attention to us. I paused to look back.

It was a deft blow. A single, lightning arc bringing the blade down on
the man's neck. Workers paused when the sharp crack! sounded through
the valley. The body collapsed as if there were not a bone in it. The executioner nodded to himself, pleased with his work, then produced a long
obsidian knife and finished severing the neck with a few quick strokes. An
attendant appeared with a basket to carry the head away.

The summons to Tipón had come with urgency. T'ito and I were
required, now. It reached him first in Cuzco. He collected me at Choqo
and we hurried down valley, full of speculation. But the execution that
greeted us on the garden terrace dampened his enthusiasm, and increased
my fear to panic.

Barely a week had passed since I learned the truth. Tanta Karwa and
T'ito were still unaware of it. There was no need to burden them. The
unforgivable sin had been slipped on me like a noose - married to my
own brother.

Whoever arranged this needs no further hold over me, I realized.

Threats against Qhari and me failed, but now T'ito's life is also at the whim of our unknown enemy. And, worse yet, Tanta Karwa's honor and the honor of Ayllu Añawarqe are dangling. Tanta Karwa will never survive the disgrace. Sumaq's mother, Lady Hilpay, is part of this. She knows who arranged it. And to think I even tried to thank her! She will suffer for her role, oh, how she will suffer. And what if I find the one who directed her, what good will it do? Even if someone as powerful as Atoq believes me innocent he can't undo what's already been done.

Whether by mortal design or by the will of the gods, it mattered not. For everyone, except our semi-divine rulers, the law was clear on incest, the punishment final. Can this be why Atoq summoned us? I agonized through the night, waiting for our audience the next morning.

"Don't thank me. You've earned it," Atoq replied. T'ito straightened his back, grinning broadly. I was still breathless with relief. "The old khipu master won't be leaving his post for another six months," Atoq said, "but then it's yours. Acarí is a small province, just a tiny coastal valley with a tampu station, but do well and in time there will be more important positions for you. I promise."

It was a huge promotion for T'ito, being made Chief Imperial Khipu Kamayoq of an entire province. I was pleased for him, and for myself. I saw Tanta Karwa's hand in this, although I'd never tell T'ito. She promised to have Atoq arrange for us to be together, and this posting was clearly the solution; and just then, being away from Cuzco appealed to me greatly.

This time our meeting wasn't in the open courtyard. We were taken to one of the palace's inner rooms restricted for Atoq's personal use. No servants or guards attended. The door was shut against the morning sun. Lamps flickered in niches, providing the only light. Two grim-looking men stood with folded arms behind Atoq, who sat on his ceremonial stool. We knelt before him. This is a formal meeting, I realized. Why the secrecy?

Atoq picked at an imaginary spot on his tunic. "But while you're waiting for this new post, there's something I'd like you to do for me."

He let the words hang in the air while he glanced over his shoulder at the men behind him. They remained like statues, staring straight ahead. He turned back to us and cleared his throat.

"From time to time situations develop. . . delicate situations that threaten the Emperor's peace." Atoq paused again, fixing us with a stare. We waited.

"It grieves me to tell you this, but a matter has come to my attention that requires immediate redress, a difficult matter concerning an offense committed by a member of our own nobility. It occurs to me that you, T'ito, and your wife, can help the Emperor set matters right."

"I'm always at my Lord's command," T'ito said.

"Good. And you understand that nothing can ever be said about this beyond these walls?"

"Of course, Lord. Your trust is safe with me."

"And you, Qori?"

"Yes, Lord."

"You understand that you'll be carrying out the Emperor's wishes, and I'm sure He will be most grateful."

The Emperor! I wanted to shout. Consider it done. T'ito and I simply nodded in unison.

Atoq sighed as if reluctant to continue. "Very well, then. A member of a royal house used poison to remove a rival." We gasped. "I know," Atoq said, "poisoning is one of the worst crimes imaginable, and by law the poisoner and his family are put to death. It's unthinkable that a noble would ever do such a thing, but, alas, the unthinkable has happened. Of course, the Emperor won't order the execution of an entire royal lineage. That would cause too much dissension, especially since the criminal is of Hurincuzco. Besides, such an elimination could never be kept secret from the commoners, and it wouldn't be proper for them to know one of their nobles committed such an evil deed. But justice must visit the culprit. We tried to remove him quietly but he eluded us and fled into the jungles of Antisuyu. Whenever our soldiers come close to catching him, he escapes again. I suspect his kinsmen warn him."

Atoq paused and sighed again. T'ito and I glanced at each other out of the corners of our eyes. What did this have to do with us?

Atoq continued, "Since this criminal is too crafty for our regular forces we must resort to other means. My spies have located him again, but they're not trained in the art of. . . shall we say, 'removal.' Besides, this man is too dangerous. He's killed others since his escape, and he's said to be a sorcerer. What's needed to trap him is a team of experts."

T'ito looked up. "Experts, Lord?"

"Yes, experts at the art of removal, such as these." He waved at the men behind him without taking his eyes off us. Both continued to stare straight ahead.

Atoq shifted on his stool and stretched his legs. "My spies tell me this poisoner, who now calls himself Chani, is living among the Chuncho beyond the eastern frontier of the Empire. Since he's outside our borders we can't send soldiers after him, and the Chuncho have never been cooperative. Therefore I'm sending these men," again he waved over his shoulder, "and a few others disguised as traders. But Chani has proven to be cautious, and devious. He may suspect a group of men. I think this plan has a better chance of succeeding if they appear as mere bearers led by a young couple."

Atoq looked at us expectantly. T'ito's brows lifted. "You mean. . . you mean us, Lord?"

"It's good of you to offer," Atoq replied. "I know the Emperor will be grateful."

"But Lord," T'ito sputtered, "I know nothing of. . . of 'removal' or jungles or trading."

Atoq waved his objections aside. "Not important. My men will do everything. Your only duty is to act as the leader of this expedition, and with your wife at your side no one will suspect otherwise. You and Qori will divert attention and my men will seem no more than part of your baggage. The Chuncho use Chani as their translator because they don't speak a civilized tongue in those forests. Once Chani is located you need do nothing more. My men will take over from there."

While T'ito looked about in bewilderment trying to absorb this, I could barely contain myself. Travel, a hunt, the Emperor's favor, I thought, I'm ready to leave now. Surely this isn't what Tanta Karwa had in mind for us, but the prospect is far more exciting than a sleepy coastal valley.

"Now remember," Atoq said, "this Chani is a clever and dangerous sorcerer. They say he appears like an old man to gain the confidence of his victims. Never forget he's a vicious killer: Don't attempt anything on your own. You're not trained in the arts of removal. You're only decoys to draw his attention away from my men. They're the experts. And remember, they're in charge of everything, including you."

Without taking his eyes from us Atoq said, "This is Tintaya, Inspector of the Qhapaqñan. . . among other things." The tall man behind him with the cruel mouth and cold, arrogant eyes looked directly at us. He nodded curtly. "He's the leader," Atoq said. "You'll obey him at all times. And this is Zapana, Steward of K'allachaka, my father's estate, and also Tintaya's second in command." The other bobbed his head but kept his eyes level. "Zapana has traveled the jungle trails of Antisuyu before," Atoq said giving him a fond look. "Four of their men will join you. They'll carry salt and cloth to trade for macaw feathers with the Chuncho."

My eyes remained on Zapana. It was he who wielded the maqana on the terrace the previous day, and when I saw him calmly sizing up his target I thought he looked familiar. Now, seeing him at attention behind Atoq, the resemblance was unmistakable. He was a shorter and younger version of Atoq himself, and every bit as handsome. Of medium height, perhaps a head taller than me, I judged, with a finely featured yet manly countenance, and eyes that could be serene or stern, but at the moment were evasively noncommittal. I thought, Even if Atoq doesn't officially recognize his children, as T'ito maintains, he certainly looks after them. Steward of a royal estate is no small title. It's surely a cover for his real duties, like Tintaya's Inspector of the Qhapaqñan. Having this younger Atoq for a traveling companion is a pleasing prospect, indeed.

As I admired Zapana's broad shoulders a servant called from beyond the door, "Lord, your uncle has arrived."

"Excellent," Atoq called back. "Please show Lord Achachi in, immediately."

"Nephew. A pleasure to see you again." The voice was cordial but reserved.

T'ito and I leapt to our feet when the door slid open, bowing from the waist, as did the two 'experts.' Atoq himself rose and momentarily held a half bow.

"And you, uncle. I'm pleased to see you're in good health as always."

T'ito and I backed against the wall to make space in the tiny room.

Achachi chuckled. "As good as can be expected. At my age every day is a blessing."

"Not at all, uncle. The gods are with you. You honor me with this visit." A stool appeared where T'ito and I had knelt.

I breathed raggedly, stomach flipping, and thought, Achachi! Back from his inspection tour. He must know about his granddaughter. Does he know T'ito and I are brother and sister? Is that why he's here, to expose us?

Atoq gestured in our direction. "These are two young friends of mine, T'ito and his wife Qori Qoyllur." T'ito and I bowed even lower until I stared at my knees. "You may kneel," Atoq said to us. We complied, straightening our backs against the wall, heads lowered, but my peripheral sight quickly settled on Lord Achachi.

To my utter relief Achachi ignored us as if we were part of the furnishings. No flicker of surprise or recognition. Good, I thought, I'm happy never to have seen you, either. You're not the Hatunqolla murderer, Achachi, but are you friend or foe? This isn't the time to find out. I'll play your game until I know Qhari is safe.

Achachi seated himself on his stool, which was just as elaborate but slightly higher than Atoq's, and casually stretched his short legs in front of him. They were like tree trunks, matching the rest of his stocky, solid frame, and the head that spouted directly from his shoulders. He wore a jaguar pelt instead of a cloak, and a gold plaque in the shape of a two-headed serpent glinted on his chest, the emblem of Pachakuti's lineage, Iñaca Panaqa. Scars, some long, some folded, some star-shaped puckers, covered every exposed part. Surely a story and a victory went with each. As I stared at a thin white line on his cheek he chuckled again.

"Just an old veteran's souvenirs from a few skirmishes," he said and winked at me.

Ashamed at having been caught staring, and relieved he chose to appear friendly, I lowered my eyes immediately. T'ito gave me a disapproving glance.

Atoq laughed. "A few skirmishes, indeed. My young friends," he said to us, "you're in the presence of our greatest warlord, and Visitor-General of Tawantinsuyu."

Achachi waved off the titles. "Just a humble soldier. Please be seated, nephew." Atoq sat facing his uncle.

"Now then, nephew, as you well know I've been relieved of my duties as Visitor-General." Atoq lifted his brows in surprise. Achachi's booming laugh filled the room. "Please, nephew, don't jest with me. That happened some days ago, and you probably knew about it before I did. I'm too old to be marching all over the realm. My brother the Emperor has finally seen fit to let me settle down. I'm now Overlord of Chinchaysuyu - as you know - but thank you for allowing me to make the announcement."

Atoq held up his hands and shrugged his innocence.

Achachi continued, "Your father tells me the recent counts from Chinchaysuyu are temporarily in your keeping, is this not so?" Atoq nodded. "Which explains why I'm here," Achachi said, folding his legs against his stool and leaning forward, fists on his thighs, "but doesn't explain why I'm here now. Your father, that great knot counter Tupac Amaru," he paused to chuckle again, "only saw fit to tell me where the Chinchaysuyu khipus were a few days ago, and suggested they'd be ready for my viewing today at Tipón. You've summoned me. Why?"

"Uncle, please," Atoq protested, "I would never dream of summoning you."

"Of course not," Achachi replied, "but you desire my presence here for some reason other than the khipus. They could have been sent to Cuzco. Now, let's stop sparring and start talking. What do you want?"

Atoq made no further pretense. "I'm sending these people into Antisuyu on a matter of security," he said. "They'll be traveling beyond the Paytiti River."

Achachi's eyes widened. "Beyond the Paytiti?"

Atoq ignored his surprise. "Since you're well acquainted with the native ruler of those lands, I was hoping you might prevail upon him to grant them safe passage."

Achachi straightened his back and thought a moment. "First you must understand that Condin Savana is the Wizard of the East. He rules those jungle lands by magic. There are many tribes. He is chief of none, yet he is supreme, feared and respected by all. They seek his counsel, and none - not the Opatari, the Mañari, or the Chuncho - would dare defy him."

"But he's their representative to the Empire, is he not?" Atoq asked.

"Those of the jungles aren't like civilized mountain people. Each village stands alone, and they often fight against their kinsmen in the next village. Even when they unite there's never one warlord to command them. Their alliances are temporary, and each headman makes his own war and peace. But yes, to answer your question, he counsels the tribes on their dealings with the Empire, and none dare disobey Condin Savana."

While Achachi spoke his eyes went several times to Tintaya, but he ignored Zapana - studiously.

"You conquered him," Atoq said.

"Conquered Condin Savana? No, nephew. When my brother became emperor those of Antisuyu refused to send their annual tribute of chonta wood spears. I marched with Him to put down that revolt. There were a few setbacks at first, minor skirmishes really, but word reached the Qolla we had been defeated. Thinking us weak the Qolla rebelled, and I went with Thupa Inka to deal with them. After Hatunqolla they sent me back to continue the Antisuyu campaign. I fought in those jungles for three years, and in the end Condin Savana prevailed upon all the chiefs of all the tribes to make peace. He allowed me to place the Empire's boundary pillars along the Paytiti River, but on condition we keep no permanent garrisons there. We never really conquered them. Beyond our coca fields on the mountain slopes we rule in name only. As long as they pay tribute, and provide archers for our armies when needed, we leave them alone and they don't bother us."

"Can this wizard grant my people safe passage through those lands?" Atoq asked.

Achachi sighed. "Yes, he's the only one who could. . . if it pleases him. But you're sending them beyond the Paytiti, beyond the agreed boundary?"

"It's necessary."

"Why?"

"As I said, a matter of security."

Achachi stared at him intently. "Yes, I suppose that's all I need to know, or will be told. Very well. I'll send messengers and provide you with men."

"You're very kind, uncle, but neither is necessary. It would be unwise to send word ahead lest this mission be jeopardized. As for men, I already have enough."

"But you've no idea what those jungles are like, or its peoples. It would be suicide."

"Thank you for your concern." He directed Achachi's gaze toward T'ito and me with a nod. "If you'll just provide them with a petition to Condin Savana asking only safe passage and cooperation, I'm sure they'll be fine." Atoq fingered his mantle knot, and then looked up. "He will honor your request?"

Achachi shrugged. "Perhaps. We've learned to respect each other, and he's never crossed me, nor I him. It's because of this trust our nations remain at peace."

"Good. Then it's settled. My people leave at dawn tomorrow."

T'ito and I stared at each other. Tomorrow?

"No," Achachi said firmly, "not tomorrow."

Atoq drummed his fingers on his thigh. "And why not, my Lord?"

"Because I must send gifts. These can be brought from Cuzco while I compose a proper message. It will take only a few days."

"Unfortunately we don't have a few days. As for gifts, I'll open the storehouses here. Choose whatever you wish."

"You're most kind, nephew. But Condin Savana doesn't want cloth or any of the usual things. Crystals, turquoise and emeralds please him most, also charms and medicines. These must be personal gifts from me to him."

Atoq thought this over. "Very well, I'll provide the sacred stones myself, and this woman," he pointed at me, "will prepare samples of our medicines and whatever charms you wish."

Evidently I was to play healer as well.

"That's most generous, but please don't trouble yourself. I'll send one of my runners to Cuzco immediately and have the items here by dawn tomorrow."

Atoq countered again. "That won't be necessary. Please, I insist. Everything you could need is right here. Besides, I'm sure you'll want to examine the Chinchaysuyu khipus, and that will take several days. This other matter need not concern you further."

The finality in Atoq's voice signaled an end to the conversation. I admired his skill at politely out-maneuvering one of the greatest lords in the Empire, one he clearly didn't trust. Achachi and his people would be detained with administrative matters until our mission was well on its way. This time there would be no advance warnings.

Achachi planted his huge hands on his knees and ponderously raised himself with a sigh. He was old, but he was also playing the part. His muscles still bulged. Atoq rose with him. The two clasped forearms, but Achachi held the grip a moment longer.

"There's one question you haven't asked, nephew."

"And that is. . . ?"

"Where to find Condin Savana."

"At his capital, I presume."

Achachi's rumbling laughter filled the room again. "You really don't understand, do you?" We all waited to hear what might follow.

"The Wizard of the East has no capital. The jungle is his home. He could be anywhere, in or out of his body." Atoq sucked in his breath. "Yes, nephew, he has the power to change shapes. Sometimes he appears as a harpy eagle, or a great snake, or a jaguar. They say he can become mist if he chooses. He'll see your people coming long before they enter his lands. For their sakes I hope he allows them to meet him in human form. Then again, he may decide to let the Chuncho deal with them. I'm not sure which would be worse."

XVI

Of a journey through the clouds to a Forbidding Land,
where Death stalks the hunters.

I felt the arrow tip pressing my breast before I saw anything. Frozen in mid-stride, I followed the long, serrated point to the shaft, which continued into the dense green beside the path. My sight adjusted to the filtered light. There, scarcely four paces away, a shape took form - a short brown man hidden by the leaves and mottled shadows of the forest. He stood inert, his bowstring taut.

We walked right into it. They blended with the bushes along both sides of the narrow trail and merely waited for us to stumble into their trap. No one moved. Heart pounding, I slowly turned my gaze up the trail. T'ito stood rigid, arrows pressed against his back and chest. Beyond him Tintaya and the guide were also immobile and threatened from all sides. I didn't have to turn to see how the others fared.

"Speak to them," Tintaya ordered the guide.

The guide didn't move but replied in a frantic whisper, "Don't say anything. They don't know your language and it will frighten them."

"If they wanted us dead we would have been so long ago," Tintaya said. He was right. I had to admire his calm. "Tell them we bear a message for Condin Savana."

At mention of Condin Savana, the only words our captors understood, a murmur swept the bushes. Our guide, Eaten, remained motionless. "Don't move," he said, "and don't look them in the eye or they'll think you're challenging them." Then he raised his face to the sky and spoke the Chuncho tongue in a trembling voice.

We waited, motionless. Sweat dripped from my nose and chin. I forced my mind elsewhere, back to the coolness of the upper cloud forest. That was a sight. We stood on the ridge under a blue sky looking east, a solid floor of cloud waiting below. It took an entire day to descend through that tangle of trees, roots, bushes, and spongy moss. Permanently shrouded in heavy mist, one can never see more than a few paces ahead. No animals or birds trouble that unearthly place. There is only silence and cold fog. Once, I stepped off the path to relieve myself, squatting between snarled roots on a carpet of moss. Suddenly my foot broke through. I peered down. The forest floor lay far below.

That was the day I asked Zapana if he thought we'd succeed in our mission. He didn't answer immediately, and when he did his words were measured.

"Tintaya is a more determined man than the inspector who preceded him."

"There was another?"

"Yes. I was his second, too. We came close to catching Chani in the Yanasimi lands, but eventually we had to turn back."

"What happened to your leader?"

"I believe you saw him being separated from his head," he said dryly.

"The one you executed on the terrace at Tipón? What did he do?"

"It's what he didn't do. He failed to catch Chani. Lord Atoq doesn't like failure."

No wonder Tintaya is determined, I thought. Then, pursuing the moment I said, "Lord Atoq is your father."

Zapana looked amused. "You're not the first to notice that. My mother came from Lake Titiqaqa in Qollasuyu. She was an aklla and later became lady-in-waiting to Lord Atoq's wife. If she had survived my birth he would have made her a concubine, but. . . . "

"You mean he hasn't adopted you? You're not recognized as his legitimate son?"

"You ask too many things," Zapana said turning away, but his curt reply answered my question.

Angry voices brought me back to the trail. Questions were shouted at Eaten. He swallowed hard, sweat trickling from his fingers, his answers directed to the sky again. He was of the Mañari tribe, assigned to us at the last garrison beneath the great cloud forests of the eastern slopes. Having served as a bowman in one of the provincial regiments he spoke passable Runasimi, and was familiar with many of the Antisuyu dialects. Yet in any language his words were slurred for he suffered from the wasting uta disease, which ate away his nose and parts of his lips. Since we couldn't pronounce his real name we called him Eaten. He swore a sorcerer placed the uta curse on him, but Tintaya suspected he committed a sin and the gods were punishing him. That wasn't my concern. Just then I was more interested in knowing whether he could talk the Chuncho out of making us the village feast.

A babble rose from the bushes as our captors called back and forth to one another. I heard Condin Savana's name mentioned frequently. Eventually Eaten sighed with relief and turned to us. "They've agreed to take us to their village and let their headman decide our fate."

"Good," Tintaya said, "now let's be on our way."

"Move slowly," Eaten cautioned, "and don't make any sudden moves. The danger hasn't passed. They could change their minds at any moment. Avoid speaking, but if you must, do it quietly."

The long arrows remained pointed at us while several men stepped warily from the bushes and prodded us forward. One came up to T'ito and shouted in his face. Another feinted toward Tintaya, jumping back at the last moment. Tintaya didn't flinch.

T'ito looked shaken. "Why did he shout at me? What are they so angry about?"

Eaten said, "Because, Inca, this is their land. You're strangers here, not lords, and you had best remember that. They shout because they're afraid of us."

Tintaya nodded approvingly. "Good."

Eaten made the grimace that was his smile. "Not good, Inca. When they're afraid they're just as likely to fill you full of arrows."

After crossing the Empire's boundary on the Paytiti River the previous day Eaten became surly. He no longer referred to T'ito and me as Lord and Lady, or called the men by their names. To him we were now all just 'Inca.'

When T'ito presented the banded stick of authority at the garrison and asked for a guide, the commander summoned Eaten from the coca fields. "This one will do," the commander said. "Besides, I can't stand to look at him anymore. He's a small loss. Do you really think you're going to come back from those jungles alive?"

The same question showed in Eaten's eyes. He protested, claiming to lack knowledge of the distant forests. "He lies," the commander said. "He's guided our patrols all the way to the Paytiti. We always lose a few to the jungle, but the Mañari should give you no trouble. Now, the Chuncho on this side of the Paytiti, watch those motherless vipers. As for their cousins on the far bank, who knows? Worse probably. It's said they eat their victims."

"Say you so?" T'ito's voice held his disgust.

"No one has ever returned to claim otherwise," the commander said. "Why you want to trade with them escapes me. At least let me send an escort with you as far as the Paytiti. No? Then I suggest you make offerings to your ancestors. You'll be meeting them soon."

Tintaya eyed the cringing guide. "Commander, may I humbly ask if this Mañari is worthy of my master's trust?" Tintaya was very good at playing lead porter to his young lord.

"Probably. He speaks the languages well enough and has never given my men trouble. He's afraid because his people and the Chuncho raid each other. We've tried to put a stop to that, but by the time we arrive the Chuncho have long since faded into the jungle again. And I know the Mañari mount revenge raids on Chuncho villages, though they won't admit it." He looked sternly at Eaten, who hung his head and looked away.

The paths were little more than game trails, crisscrossing, starting and ending abruptly. Eaten frequently climbed tall trees to search for smoke on the horizon, directing us to the next village. We left the hilly country of the high jungle and entered the lowlands. Eaten walked ahead, followed by Tintaya, then T'ito, me, four more of Atoq's men, and Zapana at the rear.

T'ito and I wore light cotton garments, but the others were stripped to their loincloths as they struggled under their packs in the suffocating heat of the great forest. I had never seen so much naked male flesh openly flaunted, and for the first few days, until I got used to it, was exceedingly glad no one could hear my thoughts. But they had their look, too.

My dress, sticky with sweat, clung to me, leaving little to the imagination. The men did their best not to notice, but invariably ended up talking to my breasts. Tintaya was more obvious, openly leering each time he glanced my way. To my relief T'ito kept his distance. I wasn't sure what I'd do when my husband - my brother - demanded his conjugal rights. The thought made me cringe. But T'ito, still unaware, hadn't troubled me since before the tinku. Just as well. But one day he would. What to do then?

The commander was right about the perils of the jungle. We set out as a party of nine. On the third night we awoke to screams. Tiny gray spiders had somehow found their way into a porter's hammock. He might have survived the bites given time to recover, but Tintaya would not spare the time, or leave him alone in the jungle. He slit his throat. Two days later the man in front of Zapana fell off the path into a nest of vipers. He didn't howl long. In the moments it took for the rest of us to arrive he was already silent, eyes frozen open in terror, a fat serpent coiling on his chest, another darting its forked tongue over his face.

The remaining seven of us now approached the Chuncho village, surrounded by hordes of our shouting 'hosts.' Naked children and bare-breasted women lined our arrival, adding their voices to the screech of insults and accusations discernable by tone and gesture in any language. Passing through the outer ring of round huts, we entered the circular plaza.

The thudding of drums almost drowned out the shouting. Three lines of warriors with bows drawn charged toward us, then veered to the side and ran full circle around the plaza. Others crowded close to menace us with stone axes. A woman ran up and spit on me. I clung to the last words Eaten spoke before we entered the village, "If you show any fear, they will kill you."

The drums stopped with a deafening thud. The warriors ceased their circling and the crowd backed away. A stocky young man strode confidently toward us. Eaten stepped forward and spoke to him, gesturing at our party. Their chief? No one bowed at his approach but all stepped aside deferentially. He appeared no different from the other men. His hair hung like an inverted bowl, shaved above the ears. Feather ornaments dangled from his lower lip, ears, and armbands, and a bone ring pierced his nose. Rows of black and red dots covered his entire body, the only modesty being a narrow strip of cloth passing between his legs, held in place by a string about his waist. His eyes calmly moved over us, but, politely, held no one's gaze.

Several of the warriors started shouting and threatening us again. The man silenced them with a look and turned back to Eaten, listening intently, asking a few questions. Eventually Eaten announced, "This headman is called Vinchin. He says he'll receive us and discuss trade." There was a sigh of relief in Eaten's voice. "He says Condin Savana is in the forest. I asked him to send messengers to the wizard, but he said Condin Savana knows we're here and will appear if he chooses."

"And if the wizard doesn't come?" T'ito asked.

Eaten shrugged. "The only reason we're still alive is because they're afraid of Condin Savana. If he doesn't appear they'll probably kill us."

We sat beneath the thatched roof of the headman's hut, sipping manioc aqha from large bowls. Half of the hut was enclosed where the family's hammocks hung, the other part open and crowded with curious villagers. Clearly privacy was not an issue with these people. Dusty, naked children with runny noses trotted among the seated adults, who indulged them absently as they climbed on and off laps, toyed with feather ornaments, and interrupted with chasing games. T'ito and I faced the headman and a group of elders. Eaten sat to one side and translated while Tintaya, Zapana, and our two remaining porters squatted behind. Excited babbling arose when T'ito opened our bags displaying their wealth of salt and cotton cloth.

"What's he saying now?" Tintaya asked in a whisper. "T'ito, take control of this." T'ito was gawking about and now shook himself, concentrating on playing the role of trader, about which he knew nothing. As he spoke Eaten translated. The headman said something. Eaten shuddered, his voice wavering again. "Vinchin wants to know why he should trade with us. He says he could kill us now and take our goods for trespassing on his people's land."

Shaken, T'ito fell silent. I raised my voice. "He should trade with us because of this." I threw the small bag of gifts from Achachi to Condin Savana at the headman's feet.

The bundle was sealed with the sign of the two-headed serpent. Atoq and Tintaya had searched through it carefully, while Achachi made T'ito and me memorize a long speech of greeting. Satisfied there were no secret messages hidden among the contents, or in the greeting, at least none that could be detected, Atoq allowed the bag sealed along with the herbal medicines I gathered from the Tipón terraces. This was our first opportunity to present the package. At every village we passed our inquires about Condin Savana were met with the same reply, "He is in the forest."

"This bag contains magic sent from our grand wizard to Condin Savana, along with a message that only we can deliver," I declared. "If you treat us badly Condin Savana will be furious with you." Tintaya pressed my back to show his approval.

Eaten translated but the headman ignored him, turning to scan the faces behind him. He passed the bag to a man huddled inconspicuously in the back row. The two exchanged words at length. Vinchin nodded and handed the bag back to me with a few words. Eaten began to say, "He says he will trade - " but I had already spotted the target.

"Father," I addressed the headman directly, cutting off Eaten's words, "we don't trust our translator. He does poorly." Eaten stared at me slack-jawed. "You have one who speaks our language much better. Let him help us, and you can be assured that everything we say is true."

The headman glanced at Eaten's expression and again turned to the man in the back row, who lowered his head behind his hands. A sharp exchange followed. I glanced over my shoulder at Tintaya and Zapana. Their eyes told me they saw him also. T'ito looked confused.

It became obvious once Achachi's bag was passed to him. Even though his hair, ornaments and body paint were the same as the other men, his skin tone was different and his features that of a highland man, especially the beaked nose. There was something else about him that bothered me at first glance. Then it became clear. His earlobes were missing. An Inca man always has large, drooping lobes to hold his earspools. There's no hiding those marks of manhood, unless they're removed. No mistake, I gloated, this is Chani the poisoner.

After more sharp words from Vinchin the man reluctantly came forward to sit in the front row, still keeping his head down, rubbing his brow. Tintaya whispered behind me, "Don't say anything to startle him. We need to get him alone. Just talk of trade."

Eaten shrank into sullen silence. T'ito, having heard Tintaya, waved at me in resignation. The negotiations were now mine.

I looked at the headman. "How shall I call your translator?"

"Just 'translator,'" the man replied quickly, but Vinchin made him repeat this exchange, and laughed. "Chani," he said. I pretended indifference at the name and turned my attention to Vinchin.

"Macaw feathers," I said, "blue, red, yellow, green - all colors." Chani translated simultaneously. "We'll trade a bag of salt for six bundles." I arched my hands to indicate bundles the thickness of a man's thigh.

"Nonsense," the headman replied through Chani. "I'll give three, and only two if they're red feathers." Thus began the bargaining. All the while I thought, It will take time, perhaps days to get Chani alone. That's Tintaya's problem. Mine is to drag out this haggling so he can find his opportunity. Certainly nothing can happen with the entire village gathered. And if Condin Savana doesn't come, what then?

I had enough experience with village trade to know the tricks of bargaining. Before long I had Vinchin and his men laughing with me. Good. With everyone staring at me, Tintaya had time to plan his moves. Even Chani seemed more relaxed, chuckling with the rest. At times I caught him staring at me from the corners of his eyes, and flattered myself I had enchanted him, too. But I never forgot Atoq's caution - Chani ingratiated himself with his victims, he was a cunning sorcerer, a viper never to turn one's back on.

What followed happened quickly, and not as I might have planned. It began with what I thought was an innocent request to see the quality of their feathers, another ploy to gain time. The headman pointed at Chani, who translated his exact words, "This one keeps count of our feathers. He'll go and fetch a few bundles." Chani rose. Tintaya urgently pressed my back. We couldn't let Chani out of our sight or he might flee into the jungle.

"Excellent," I replied, keeping Chani standing there to translate. "Let me send my porters to help him."

"That's not necessary," Chani said quickly, then translated his words into Chuncho. Before the headman could answer I continued, "It's no trouble, please, I insist as a matter of courtesy."

"Why?" the headman demanded.

"Please, Lady, allow me," Tintaya said already rising. But Zapana leapt to his feet and placed a hand on Tintaya's shoulder, motioning him to sit.

"Don't trouble yourself," Zapana said. "I'll be pleased to assist." He nodded at Chani. "Shall we?"

I followed their lead in ignoring the headman's question, and quickly unfolded a length of cloth to distract attention. It caught Vinchin's eye and he absently waved Chani off, no longer concerned about who went with him or why. Zapana tapped one of our men on the shoulder as he left. The man immediately rose and followed. No one seemed to notice.

They were gone a long time - too long. I pressed Eaten back into service while I extolled the quality and bright colors of the trade cloth, but I was running out of words. I could feel Tintaya's tension mounting as time slipped by. The headman lost interest and looked about for Chani.

Tintaya rose and announced he would go and help the others. Without waiting for comment he turned and pushed his way through the crowd. Vinchin frowned and stood. I had to hold him. I jumped up and draped a cloth around myself, modeling it like a dress, and began a hopping dance. Pulling a Chuncho woman to her feet for my partner, I led her round and round the headman. His laughter caught, and the crowd began to pound the rhythm. That's when I saw Tintaya half carrying Zapana toward us.

"Quick," Tintaya shouted, "he's escaped." Everyone was on their feet in an instant. With one arm still around Tintaya for support and the other covering a gash on his head Zapana blurted, "I'm sorry, it was my fault. He was too fast for us."

"And our other man?" I asked.

"Dead," Zapana replied, but he was more concerned with Chani. "We must give chase immediately. He already has a good start on us."

Eaten tried to relate these events to the Chuncho headman, who looked like he might strike us at any moment. "He wants to know why," Eaten said. "Why did this happen? What did we do to cause it?"

"Tell him we did nothing," Tintaya answered tersely. "There's no time to explain. We demand revenge and we must take it ourselves."

"Then tell me why," Eaten said planting his hands on his hips. "I never believed this was just a trading venture. What's going on?"

"That's not your concern and you'll follow my orders like everyone else," Tintaya shouted back. Eaten looked at T'ito, who nodded that Tintaya spoke the truth.

The smiling faces that surrounded me moments earlier now threatened violence. The Chuncho didn't understand what was being said, but there was clearly a change of leadership among our party. In the confusion several men picked up stone axes and pressed closer. Vinchin shouted at Eaten.

Zapana now stood on his own, partially recovered. Tintaya pushed his way to Eaten's side. "Tell this headman we know Chani isn't one of his people. He's Inca. And since he killed one of our men it's our right to avenge the death. If any harm comes to us, or if anyone tries to stop us, Condin Savana will destroy this village."

This caused enough uncertainty for Vinchin to wave his men back.

"There's no more time for discussion," Tintaya said to Eaten. "We leave immediately. Tell this headman we'll return soon and give him all the salt and cloth."

Eaten translated and turned back to Tintaya. "Vinchin wants to know why he should trust you about Condin Savana."

Tintaya let out an exasperated sigh. "We don't have time for this. T'ito, you and Eaten will join us. I need every man." He looked at me and then at Vinchin. "Tell him we'll leave the woman here as a hostage."

214

XVII

In which Qori meets the Wizard of the East, and is taken to the Spirit World where she is beset by Demons.

"I said, if you want to live another day, give it to me now." The voice came loud with the words enunciated slowly, as if to a dull child.

It wasn't the threat that caused my mouth to fall open; it was the words, pronounced in perfect Runasimi, and their speaker, a tiny old man seated across the hearth from me, naked but for the strip of cloth between his legs.

Three days had passed since the men dashed into the forest after Chani. Without Eaten to translate the Chuncho and I were reduced to communication by gestures. Theirs were few and always unfriendly. Only two things were clear: if I set foot outside Vinchin's hut the villagers would kill me, and if the men didn't return soon, or Condin Savana failed to appear, I was dead anyway.

The old man must have come while I pondered these outcomes. I didn't notice him until he spoke, and such was my surprise I merely gaped, forcing him to repeat himself.

"I bear a message and gifts for Condin Savana," I said. "But they're for him alone. If you try to harm me he'll punish you horribly."

The old man chuckled. "Will he?" He spat into the fire. A sharp crack! followed and sparks flew up.

"Your cheek will get sore if you don't take that other exploding nut from your mouth," I replied calmly, pleased that Eaten showed me the trick one night on our travels.

He let out a hollow laugh. "So, no amusements for this little Inca," he said with a sneer. His tongue worked in his mouth. He spat something over his shoulder.

"Who are you?" I asked.

"Condin Savana," he said.

"And I am Qori Qoyllur, Queen of the Incas," I responded lightly.

His expression froze. Clearly he wasn't accustomed to being disbelieved, or trifled with. My impudence startled him, and in his hesitation

I saw that neither was he accustomed to being startled. This reaction, more than any words, established that he was indeed Condin Savana. I knew then I sparred with the Wizard of the East, a dangerous game. My stomach knotted but I refused to let the fear show on my face. I had made my move. Now he would either respect me, or kill me.

"No one but a fool, or a very strong spirit, dares speak to me in such a manner," he said. "Which are you?"

"That's for you to decide."

He inclined his head and smiled. "You hold your face well, but I see in your eyes you now know who I am. And you cleverly confirmed that by tricking me into showing my face. Very good. I'll hear you."

I had pushed far enough. The banter was over, ending in a respectable standoff. Now it was time to see whether Lord Achachi's petition would get us out of the jungle alive.

"We're a trading party - "

"Stop. I know what you and your friends are pretending to be, and whence you come. I've been following your progress since you entered my forest." He smirked at my expression. "I saw your party the day I snatched that monkey from the tree."

It was true. Shortly after leaving the garrison a huge harpy eagle swooped a screaming monkey from a high branch above us. Was he really that eagle? Eaten told the story in the next village. Condin Savana might have heard it there, or perhaps Lord Achachi was right, the wizard was a shape changer.

"If you knew we were looking for you why didn't you appear?" I said quickly to hide my uncertainty.

"I just told you, I did. And did you not hear me stalking your camp at night?"

Several times we heard coughing sounds, which Eaten identified as a jaguar hunting the night forest. Yet Eaten assured us they were common. Anyone might have guessed we would hear some on our long trek, but. . . .

"Anyway, I was only waiting to see what you really wanted," he said. "And now your true intentions are revealed. Why are you seeking the one called Chani?"

To deflect the question I stood and formally recited the long message of greeting from Lord Achachi, emphasizing the part about granting us protection. He listened intently. I handed him the bag sealed with the sign of the double-headed serpent, which he opened, carefully examining the contents. He seemed more interested in numbers and colors than the objects themselves.

"What are these plants?"

When I explained the healing powers of the herbs gathered from Atoq's terraces he raised his brows.

"You're a healer?"

"I'm learning." Until that moment I never thought of myself as a healer, but I had learned a great deal from Tanta Karwa, and now the notion appealed to me.

He pursed his lips and took my measure with new respect. Then he made me repeat Achachi's message twice more while he fingered the crystals and charms. At last he sat back and stared at me in silence for a long while.

Women appeared and handed us bowls of stew, then quickly retreated. I looked at my bowl in horror. A child's hand floated on the surface!

Condin Savana gave me a questioning look.

"It. . . it. . . it's true," I sputtered. "They eat people."

Condin Savana laughed. "That's a monkey's paw. The Incas like to say we forest people eat each other, and it's a story we don't discourage. It keeps them away. But we don't really eat people, aside from the occasional Inca." He winked and laughed again.

I set the bowl aside, my appetite suddenly gone, and tried not to watch him eat what looked like a child's foot.

Finally satiated, he wiped his greasy hands on his belly and smacked his lips. "Very well," he said abruptly, "I'll help you."

"You'll help the men find Chani?"

"Chani? They'll never catch him. No, Achachi asked me to prepare the bearer of his message. He's the only Inca I trust. I'll honor his request. When the others return - if they return - they can leave here in safety with you. That's all."

Some code must have been used as Atoq feared, for there was nothing in the message about 'preparing' anyone, least of all me. And for what? Besides, it was intended that T'ito deliver the message. But events had taken a new twist. I decided to play along. Our lives depended on it.

"And how will my 'preparation' begin?"

"Tonight you will die, and be born again."

"What is it?" I asked.

Condin Savana handed me a bowl of thick, evil-smelling liquid. "Ayawaska, the dead man's vine."

I turned my face aside and grimaced.

"Drink deep," he ordered.

Still I hesitated. "Why must I drink this foul concoction?"

"It will cleanse you, and through it you will pass into the spirit world. There you will see many things, including those who wish you harm. I'll be with you, and I'll interpret your visions. With this insight I'll know how best to prepare you against the dangers of this world. If you're strong a protective spirit will come, and this spirit will guide you throughout your life."

He went on to describe what I might see, including the creatures of the forest, and people from my past and future life. Most terrifying to me, although he cautioned not to show fear if it came, was the mother spirit of the drug, a brightly colored snake, which might appear in that form or as a beautiful woman and teach me its song. If it came as a snake it might enter me. Above all, he said, no matter what I saw I must never lose myself in fear. I must be strong and keep control, otherwise I'd stay in the spirit world forever. "Now, drink and be reborn," he said.

I exhaled and lifted the bowl to my lips, taking the brew straight down to avoid the bitter taste. The last drop gone, I set the bowl in my lap and struggled to keep my stomach down. Condin Savana looked surprised.

"I didn't mean for you to drink it all," he said. "This is an especial-ly potent batch. But don't fear, I'll go with you."

He filled the bowl and quickly drank an equal amount.

The jungle drowses in the midday heat, but it's teeming at night.

When we entered the clearing at dusk, night birds began their discordant clamor of whistles and high-pitched songs. Condin Savana said the penetrating shrieks were the calls of the recent dead who still roamed the earth. Spirits or not, the dim curtain of green around us was alive - rustling, flittering, scampering, crawling, slithering - and shivers ran down my spine.

"Don't look at it," he said waving at the jungle behind him, "look into it. Only then will you see the countless entities, dead and alive, that make the great forest a living thing where life thrives on death in the eternal cycle. Tonight you will become one with it."

After announcing in the village that he would 'prepare' me, Condin Savana went into the jungle and returned with several lengths of vine. He had these boiled for a long time, until dusk began to settle, and then led me to the clearing. Vinchin and three women from the village attended as helpers, but they didn't drink the ayawaska. Condin Savana arranged us in a circle to keep evil spirits away.

Again my stomach heaved and a rancid taste entered my throat. Condin Savana watched me closely.

"Keep it down as long as you can. That will make your visions stronger." He stood and shuffled back and forth in front of me, shaking his rattle and whistling.

Nausea and dizziness built until I could contain it no longer. I barely managed to crawl to the edge of the clearing before the vomiting began, and to my greater mortification I voided my bowels, again and again and again, between vomiting episodes. And when there couldn't possibly have been anything left, I continued heaving and spewing from both ends. How long this lasted I can't say. It seemed endless, but at some point I vaguely remember being dragged back to the circle, weak and shaking. That's when the spirit world blew open before my eyes.

The darkness vanished. The forest became a vibrating green blur, then sharpened to intense clarity. I saw each tree, each bush, and each leaf, all pulsating in unison like the beating of one heart. An ant walked heavily across the back of my hand, then paused to smile up at me. My chest and head pounded in rhythm with the forest. I became one with it.

All sense of tiredness and discomfort left me.

A great tapestry hung before me like a panel full of visions - a deer, tapir, caiman, harpy eagle, viper, macaw, ocelot, centipede - all the creatures of the jungle I saw on the journey. People gradually replaced the animals. Father pulled his net and gave me a worried look, mother kindled a fire at sunset, Qhari grinned and raised his hand in greeting, Tanta Karwa sat in a beautiful garden, Sumaq T'ika knelt before an altar, Lady Hilpay turned her back and walked away, old Cormorant followed her, Lord Atoq's face was expressionless, Tintaya leered, T'ito appeared terrified, Chani looked at me curiously.

The tapestry vanished. I became aware that Condin Savana questioned me, but what he asked and what I answered, if anything, I can't remember. Then I saw the great constrictor, shimmering in glowing colors. It wound its way toward me. "Courage," I heard Condin Savana shout. I struggled to hold myself. If I was ever to return from the spirit world I knew I must accept and not struggle against the visions. The great snake coiled in front of me and lifted its head to the level of my eyes, hovering no more than a hand span from my face. I sensed a slimy wetness on my legs beneath my dress - I had befouled myself yet again - but I summoned courage and didn't let my eyes waver from the creature. A sweet song as from the lips of a woman came to my ears. I must have been sitting slack-jawed, for suddenly the serpent plunged its head into my mouth! I felt its long coils slither through me.

I saw myself alone in the mountains. A bird-headed woman walked toward me. She had a great, curved beak, and a disc of feathers around her face like an owl. Three long feathers rose fan-like from the top of her head, and her feet were talons. She placed a protective arm around me and guided me up a stony path.

I drifted over the night jungle, floating above a circle of people in a clearing. I saw myself kneeling there. Far, far away a light flickered in the forest. Wind swept my hair. I hovered over the light, a small fire where two desperate men huddled.

I walked down a long path. Far ahead a shining figure beckoned me onward. Another hurried just in front of me, laughing scornfully over its shoulder. I couldn't see their faces. Dark things fluttered around me. On either side of the trail were souls like wisps of smoke. They held out their hands and called pitifully, begging me to pull them back on the path. My heart ached for them. I wanted to help, but I knew if I did they would become people again, and I would be forced to follow them away from the shining figure.

I lay on the grass in the clearing, too weary to raise my head. Dawn streaked the sky. Condin Savana bent over me, a concerned look etching his face.

"You've returned safely from the spirit world," he said. "You died, but you've been reborn in this world with new powers. You'll need them. Danger surrounds you. The outcome is uncertain."

Three days later I sat with Condin Savana by the hearth in Vinchin's hut. It took that long for me to recover from my night in the spirit world. For most of that time I lay in a hammock, sleeping, and being fed copious amounts of rich soup in my few wakeful moments. Today I began eating solid food again.

Condin Savana had waited for me to recuperate, saying nothing of our night in the clearing. Now he leaned toward me, his face grave.

"The spirits showed me that you are burdened with a destiny. What that is I cannot say, but there is a purpose to your being. It may take a lifetime to unfold, if you live that long."

I blinked and waited for him to continue.

"You seek danger and it seeks you. Are you strong enough to survive and fulfill your destiny? Perhaps. But many around you will die, and many others will try to destroy you."

"Who was the shining figure?" I asked.

Condin Savana inclined his head and stared at me. "I think you know."

I had to approach this carefully. I remembered him asking questions while I was in the power of the ayawaska, but I couldn't remember my answers. How much had I revealed about myself and our mission to catch Chani? Why had Lord Achachi sent a secret message requesting that I, or T'ito, be prepared - and prepared for what? I thought the shining figure must have been Father, but I dared not mention him so I stared back at Condin Savana in innocence.

He studied my face and sighed. "Very well. It was you."

"Me?"

"Or more precisely, that which dwells within you - the spirit that guides your quest. You and it are one."

There was no longer any point in pretending we were a party of traders. He'd seen through that even before the night of the spirits.

"My quest? You mean Chani?" I asked hopefully.

He waved his hand in exasperation. "Don't play with me. I've been to the spirit world with you. You know what I'm speaking of. You're searching for someone - someone who fears you, or should. That was the person with the mocking laugh who ran ahead of you on the spirit path. You chase, and in so doing you're led. This person has probably already interfered in your life in unseen ways, and if threatened will kill you."

"Who is this person?"

"You don't know? Then it's for you to discover. But Achachi wants you to succeed."

"Why?"

"You don't know that either? Then it's for him to tell you, when and if he chooses. This much is clear, he doesn't trust whoever sent you here; otherwise he wouldn't have used the code we agreed upon long ago. I advise you not to tell your master about Achachi's hand in this. You are but a leaf between two strong winds. If either feels threatened you will be blown away. Your life depends upon silence."

"What am I to do?"

"Nothing, and everything. When you leave here continue as before. Bend with the wind. And be patient. Follow the Shining One and do what you must."

"And that is?"

He sighed again and leaned back on his hands, contemplating the fire. "Many will die. Some by your hand, some by the hands of others. Those were the souls you passed on the spirit road. If you waver from the path, even though some whom you love are in danger, you won't succeed. And if you hesitate to strike when the time comes, you'll die."

I held my face impassive but quivered inwardly.

"If you're to live," he said, "you must be prepared against the powers that conspire against you. You must be strong. You must fight! It's not by accident that you came to me. You came for a purpose, and my purpose is to help you as I can."

"And what is my purpose?"

"You are an active element. Your purpose is not just to witness, but to shape events."

My thoughts turned to immediate problems. "What of Chani?"

"You keep asking about him," Condin Savana replied peevishly. "Achachi said nothing in his message other than you were to find him. I don't know what he means to either of you, and it's not my concern. As I told you before, once Chani takes to the forest he'll never be found. Your friends will not be successful. Besides, there are only two of them left."

"Just two? Which ones? What happened?"

Although Condin Savana had time to learn their fate while I recuperated, once again he returned to my visions on the night of the spirits. "The two we saw sitting by the fire far off in the jungle. They're lost now, but they may yet find their way back here. I don't know which two, but I suspect either Chani or the Chuncho from another village killed the other three."

I felt nothing for Atoq's men, although I would have liked to see the leer wiped from Tintaya's face, but T'ito, what of him?

"I hope one of them is my husband," I said, "because it is he who was supposed to deliver Lord Achachi's message, and therefore he who should have accompanied you to the spirit world." I thought this would shock him, but he laughed.

"You may think that, and Achachi may think it, too, but not me. Perhaps your plans didn't go as you intended, but all has unfolded as it was meant to be. Of this I am certain. No one has ever traveled the spirit world with me as you have, or dealt with such powerful visions so bravely. Did the mother spirit of the ayawaska not come to you? Did she not honor you with her song? Did you not allow her to enter you without fear?"

"It is so, but I was terrified."

"Yet you mastered your fear. This has given you great power over yourself, and because of it power over others. What can possibly frighten you now? You are in control. Besides, you have a spirit guardian."

"The bird-woman?"

"Of course. She is Eagle Woman, a female harpy eagle. They're bigger than the males and the greatest raptors of the forest, with talons longer than jaguar claws. They're also more patient, sitting high on a limb without moving a feather all day, until they sight their prey whose end comes swift and silent. She'll watch over you. She's a powerful force. Look, I've made this for you."

He passed me a charm. The core appeared to be a solid, round length of chonta wood, slightly longer than my palm, carved and painted with symbols. An eagle feather covered one side, and on the other several painted quills were attached.

"Its name is Eagle Woman," he said as I turned it in my hand. "She's your spirit guardian - your sister. You must carry her with you always." I thought of Tanta Karwa's spirit guardian, the green stone named Añawarqe.

He allowed me to admire it a moment longer, then said, "You're a healer. Every healer has a spirit helper. People will think you carry it for that purpose alone."

"But I'm only learning."

He held up his hand. "And I will teach you more. You must have the power to save life as well as take it. Eagle Woman will help you do both."

"How?"

"Her spirit will help you divine your patients' needs, and protect you from the evil of others. But, her force alone may not always be enough to deflect danger. Therefore she carries other powers. Deadly secrets."

He grinned at the question on my face. "Look at those hollow quills on the back. They're painted so no one will notice they're not empty. If you break off the ends a powder will spill out. When mixed with food or drink your enemy will die vomiting blood."

"Poison? But that's the worst crime. If I'm found with this I'll be executed, and my family with me. You can't mean - "

His raised hand silenced me again. "If you're caught, but you won't be. You're too clever for that. And only you and I know the secret."

"But what if it's examined?"

"Let them look at it. Wear it in front of everyone. Show it to people if you wish. Few will dare touch a healer's spirit guardian, and even so, none will take it apart."

He turned it over and brushed the eagle feather aside, revealing a tiny paw mark burned into the wood. "Do you see this? It's my mark, the six-toed jaguar." He directed my eyes to his right foot. He had six toes. "Any wizard, seer or sorcerer of real power will recognize this symbol. It tells them I made Eagle Woman, and the one who carries her is under my protection. Once this is known no one will bother you or Eagle Woman."

"But what if they think I stole Eagle Woman from you?"

His head went back in hearty laughter. "Nobody steals from the Wizard of the East. Nobody."

I thought of the poison again and shuddered. "But to kill by such vile means?"

He waved this aside. "Killing is killing. When your life depends on it the means do not matter. Remember, if you don't act you're dead."

I made no reply. The truth of his words took hold. If I had to kill I knew I could, and the method was of no concern. The means of death were now in my hands.

"You may not always have the time or opportunity to employ this powder," Condin Savana said, "but don't worry, Eagle Woman has another secret."

He took the charm from me and held it upright. It appeared to be a solid wooden cylinder, but with a quick twist and a jerk the lower section came off. He held it up for my inspection. A thin, barbed blade of palm wood protruded from the loosened section, which now formed a handle. The point and barbs were needle sharp, but a thick coating of dark resin covered the blade.

"Of itself it's a tiny weapon," he said, "but observe the resin." He drew his finger along it. "You see? Harmless to touch, unless you have a sore or open wound. But it's lethal when jabbed into an enemy."

"Another of your poisons?" I asked, taking it from him for closer examination.

"Like the powder, it's not of my making. No, these came to me through those who dwell in the great forest far to the north, and they're said to originate still farther north. The resin is made in different strengths. They tip their arrows with the weaker varieties to bring down monkeys and deer. But this. . . " he pointed at the coating on the wicked little blade, "this is of the purest, most concentrated potency. Put that stinger in a man and he'll die before your eyes."

I picked up Eagle Woman and examined the hollow upper half. Several more coated stingers were fastened to the inside. The two parts of Eagle Woman fitted so tightly when pushed together only a fine seam was visible, and this easily covered with a band of fresh paint.

Condin Savana took it from me and once again withdrew the stinger. "Notice the base of the blade is notched. You can't cut or slash with this. It's made to go straight in, and once in, the stinger will snap off and remain embedded. The barbs make it impossible to pull out. If you do it properly it won't even leave an obvious wound. Any fleshy part of the body is a good target, but the stomach and neck are especially suitable for quick effect."

His words were so dispassionate he might have been giving me advice on deer hunting. Still daunted by the lethal charm, I said, "I didn't think the Wizard of the East needed such things."

He smiled. "I don't. That's why I'm giving them to you."

A week passed and still the men didn't return. Now under Condin Savana's protection, I had freedom of the village and surrounding forest. Even so, I felt more confident with Eagle Woman dangling from a cord around my neck. She went with me everywhere, even to my hammock at night. I would have felt naked without her reassuring presence.

The Chuncho left me alone and even made gestures of deference in my presence, for I was now the wizard's apprentice. Condin Savana taught me the healing powers of many plants, and gave me samples of those that could be dried and kept for future use. Among these was a powder that brought sleep. I tried it on myself one afternoon, mixing a pinch in a bowl of manioc aqha, and the next thing I knew they were shaking me awake for the evening meal.

"I must leave," Condin Savana announced one night.

"Where are you going?"

He looked at me as if it was a stupid question. "Into the forest," he replied.

"What of my husband and the others?"

"They'll arrive the day after tomorrow."

I knew better than to press him on this. Every time I mentioned them he silenced me with a stern look. They were captives of their fate, he said, and he wouldn't interfere.

"What will happen to us after you leave?"

"Don't fear the Chuncho. They and the other forest peoples know you're under my protection, and you protect those who walk with you. If there's any question you need only show them my mark on Eagle Woman. You're safe under the sign of the six-toed jaguar."

"You've done much for me. What can I do for you?"

He thought a moment, then gave me a message for Lord Achachi. I repeated it until firmly committed to memory. Like the message I brought it consisted of a simple greeting, but I knew it was a code.

"Does he still wear the jaguar skin I gave him?" Condin Savana asked.

In my mind's eye I saw Achachi's squat form hunched on his stool, the jaguar pelt draped over his shoulders. "He does."

"Good. He needs my protection, too."

Condin Savana stood and stretched. Such a skinny little old man, I thought, but with such power.

"I've grown rather fond of you, young woman. You are a force. Good hunting, Qori Qoyllur - Queen of the Incas." His laughter echoed in the night.

I lowered my eyes respectfully. "You've given me much wisdom."

"I've given you some knowledge. Knowledge is the knowing of things. Wisdom is understanding how knowledge should be used, and that you must discover on your own. I have given you the means to shape your fate. Whether or not you succeed in your quest is up to you. Many unseen forces will oppose you in this, but remember, hesitate and you are lost."

The shriek of a night bird caused me to turn and stare into the dark. When I looked back Condin Savana had vanished. Somewhere close by a jaguar growled.

XVIII

In which Eagle Woman claims her first Victim, the Savage Chief glares, a vile soldiers' oath is spoken, Carnal Temptations descend in the night, Qori lies - which she does so often this scribe will no longer remark upon it - and Lord Atoq gambles.

The village wakened before I did. Vinchin and his family were moving back into the hut, temporarily abandoned during Condin Savana's stay, and the smell of roasting meat reached me in my hammock. I rose and followed the scent. The sinuous form of a small constrictor hung on a wooden grill above the fire. Fresh birds' eggs had been gathered at dawn. My mouth watered. I sat down to a hearty breakfast of snake and eggs.

Later, I left the village and wandered alone to the garden clearings where the women went to harvest manioc. Suddenly I saw him. He seemed not at all surprised to see me, barely pausing in stride to lift his hand in greeting as he came along the path toward me. I froze, my hand clutching Eagle Woman. There's no place to run, I thought. Condin Savana is gone, and what remains of our party has not returned. I'm alone with Chani.

He came on with an odd smile, the inviting grin of a viper, I imagined. Has he returned to kill me? I wondered. Well, the target comes to me, and where the others failed I must not. Condin Savana counseled me to continue in my master's service, and Atoq wants this man destroyed. It's up to me.

Pretending not to recognize him, I returned his wave and went forward, forcing a smile. Condin Savana's words echoed in my head, "Hesitate and you are lost." The distance between us narrowed and my stomach tightened, but I held my outward composure. Chani stopped as if suddenly unsure of himself, or sensing danger. Was I too obvious? Would he run, or attack?

He waited while I walked up to him, stopping less than an arm span away. I could smell him. Whatever his plan was, mine was already in motion. He opened his mouth to speak, but before the first word came out I looked over his shoulder and gasped. His head jerked following my startled gaze - at nothing. Such a simple trick. In the same instant Eagle Woman's stinger vanished in his neck. His hands flew to the wound and he staggered backward. I remained still, waiting to see what would happen. The stinger broke from the handle as Condin Savana said it would. I had done as instructed. If the poison didn't work and Chani recovered, I was dead anyway.

He fell against a tree, eyes wide, his mouth working like a fish. Then his eyelids closed and his mouth went slack. He gurgled, but couldn't swallow. A bluish tinge crept over his face and his head slumped on his chest. He collapsed and lay still. The effect took only moments.

I went to my knees in front of him, all strength suddenly drained, shaking, unable to catch my breath. Tears came. I wanted to brush them away but I couldn't raise my hands. I slumped back on my heels, my face to the sky, a terrible pain in my throat, and when the sobbing started it came in waves enough to fill the ocean. Father, I never emptied myself of grief at your death, as if denying it somehow kept you close. Qhari, my brother, my heart, torn from me. Have I ever truly wept for you? No, I stayed strong for you, as if you'd return any day. But you never did, never will. I am alone - me, Qori Qoyllur, alone and hollow - sobbing my heart to the forest, and the man dead by my hand.

A macaw swooped above in a flash of color, landing on a branch overhead. It edged closer, cocking its head in short, jerky motions, curious to see the earth-bound creature who poured her soul to the heavens. Striking blue and yellow, more like turquoise and gold with tinges of green, it perched like a rainbow, twitching its long tail feathers. Another macaw landed, hopped toward the first, and tapped its curved beak against its partner's. The pair began preening each other. Eaten said macaws mate for life.

I used the hem of my dress to wipe my eyes, and then my gaze settled on Chani once more. I did what men failed to do, I thought. I faced the villain alone. I am alive and he is not. I won! Something new filled the emptiness inside me, something I had sensed before, but never truly known. A feeling of detached curiosity came over me. I leaned forward to examine the wound. Only a small spot of blood marked the entry. Calmly, I sat beside the body and fitted Eagle Woman with a new stinger.

The survivors stumbled into the village the next day. There were only two, as foretold, both covered in scratches, emaciated, and feverish. Their story unfolded between bowls of stew and manioc cakes. They didn't even glimpse Chani after his escape from the village. On the third day, my night of the spirits, the party was ambushed. They never saw the attackers, only arrows flying from the bushes. Their fletching marked them as Chuncho, but from another village. The two survivors fled and became lost in the jungle. It took them a week to find their way back.

My news that Condin Savana had come and granted us safe passage home was met with relief. Of course, I didn't mention Achachi's coded message, or Condin Savana's deadly gift. These had to remain secret. But I proudly announced I'd dealt with Chani.

"You did what?" Zapana said.

"I killed him. . . yesterday. Isn't that what we were sent to do? He must have thought you dead, and came back to finish me. But I was faster."

Tintaya looked skeptical. "You killed him? Are you sure you didn't have some help from Vinchin and his men?"

Their surprise and then disbelief irritated me. If I were a man they wouldn't have questioned my word.

"Would you rather I'd died so you brave warriors could stumble back here to avenge me? I killed Chani with one of Vinchin's arrows, and I did it alone. The village doesn't even know about it."

"Show us the body," Tintaya demanded.

It was true the village didn't know about Chani's death. I saw no reason to upset Vinchin by announcing I'd deprived him of his translator. And I was pleased that I thought to return later with one of his arrows to plunge into the wound, erasing all trace of Eagle Woman's stinger. Her secrets were mine alone.

I led them off the path to where I'd hidden the body under some bushes. Although only a day old it was already white and crawling with insects. Any meat that doesn't move soon disappears in the great forest.

But the features were still recognizable and Vinchin's arrow was in place. When I pulled the bushes aside both men jumped back, the flies and stench assailing them. They glanced quickly at the face and the arrow, then retreated.

"Well?" I asked after we returned to the trail.

Zapana turned to Tintaya and shrugged. "Well, it's Chani. Vinchin doesn't appear any more hostile than usual, so he must not know about it. I suppose we'll have to believe her. She killed Chani."

"And saved your head," I said, reminding Tintaya of his unsuccessful predecessor's fate.

Tintaya rolled his eyes and nodded with a heavy sigh. It delighted me to see male pride so wounded.

As Eaten feared, he met his end in the Chuncho lands. I wondered if his face would be restored in the afterlife. The last of our four porters also died.

And T'ito? Tintaya and Zapana hadn't actually seen his body, for he became separated from the others when the attack began, and later they dared not go back to look for him, but he couldn't have survived on his own. "He's gone, Qori," Zapana said placing his arm around my shoulders. I feigned sorrow, but in truth I felt relief.

T'ito, my brother - my husband, I thought. I never really knew you. You allowed no one that measure of closeness, which makes your death easier to take. We were a tragic pair trapped in a loveless, incestuous marriage. Now we're both free, you to walk in peace with our ancestors, and me to avenge father's death.

I am a widow, I reflected. The law forbids women to marry a second time, and there is no brother-in-law to inherit me, so I'm free of men. Others can feel sorry for me, I only see possibilities.

We prepared to leave the village a few days later, after Tintaya and Zapana recovered. Vinchin provided a guide as far as the Mañari lands where, he indicated by gestures, we would find another to take us into Opatari country and back to the garrison. From there the road was safe and well marked into the mountains.

When we gathered our few belongings Vinchin surprised us with two large bales of macaw feathers. Condin Savana must have ordered this before he left. Our salt and trade cloth was long since distributed around the village. The feathers pleased me greatly. Not only was our mission successful, but even the trading cover turned a handsome profit. Lord Atoq would be pleased.

While handing over the bales in stony-faced silence, Vinchin deliberately extracted a handful of feathers and glared at me. In exchange for his missing arrow, I assumed. I shrugged. Feathers well spent.

Tintaya and Zapana were less pleased with the treasured feathers. They had to carry the bales on their backs like porters, while I walked ahead as the leader of the expedition. This was only reasonable, I assured them, to maintain our disguise as traders on the return trip. It was clear neither liked playing the lowly porter of a woman. I enjoyed their discomfort immensely. They grudgingly followed, even granting me an undertone of respect because of Eagle Woman, who hung proudly at my breast. At first they were incredulous when I told them she was a gift from Condin Savana, and I went to the spirit world and learned healing from the Wizard of the East, but when they saw the mark of the six-toed jaguar disbelief became sullen regard.

Though both men stripped to their loincloths and struggled under bales of equal size, Tintaya still asserted his position over Zapana in a host of petty, annoying ways. He insisted on walking in front and making Zapana carry the hammocks, food, and cook-pot, and whenever we stopped he shouted at Zapana to make the fire and prepare his food and bed. On the journey out their men took care of these duties, but now there were no men left to command. Zapana accepted all this quietly, his eyes veiled of response, which seemed to make Tintaya goad him all the more. I could see this wasn't about rank, it was personal, and Tintaya looked for an excuse that Zapana wasn't about to provide. I tried sympathizing with Zapana but he didn't want my pity, simply dismissing the matter with a curt, "Tintaya is in command."

The garrison commander looked astounded to see us.

"By the golden balls of Illap'a!" he exclaimed, invoking that popular oath of soldiery, "I never thought I'd see you again. Don't tell me you crossed the Paytiti. You did? Incredible. The first to see those lands and return. You lost a few, I see. Well, that happens. Thank you for getting rid of that uta-eaten wretch of a guide. Couldn't stand to look at him. And your husband, Lady? I'm sorry. May he rest peacefully with his ancestors."

At Tintaya's urging I asked the commander to send a runner ahead to announce our successful return. The message was directed to one of Tintaya's men in Cuzco, the supposed sponsor of our expedition, who would pass it on to Lord Atoq long before our arrival. That night, while Tintaya sat tight-lipped and Zapana regaled a gathering with tales of the Chuncho lands, I noticed a man slip away from the fire and disappear up the road to the mountains. Another messenger? I wondered. For whom?

As we ascended once more through the silent mists of the cloud forest my gaze settled on Zapana's broad shoulders. He stole into my thoughts more and more frequently in disturbingly pleasant ways. I chided myself for entertaining such fantasies so soon after my husband's death. My husband? No, just T'ito, and try as I might I couldn't force myself to miss him. In life he'd given me too much familiarity with his absence.

Since leaving Tipón we kept a watch nightly, even while we were still inside the Empire's boundaries. This seemed odd to me but was explained as a precaution. A precaution against what? I wondered. Whom does Tintaya fear in Inca lands? The question was never answered, but even now on our homeward journey Tintaya and Zapana took turns standing guard. The night we arrived at the tampu above the cloud forest Zapana had second watch.

The night was still, and chilly. Even the tampu dogs, usually snarling and snapping over scraps, settled down for the night. While most travelers slept in a common room, a long building like a great hall, we were granted a stone cottage of our own. Tintaya returned from his watch and, wrapping himself in his blankets, stretched out on the earthen floor. He soon snored softly. Unable to sleep I rose and went into the night.

Stars crowded the cloudless heavens. The Celestial River shone like a band of white dust across a black cover, and within it were the Yana Phuyu, the dark cloud animals, blacker than the night sky. Though the dry season would begin soon the outline of the Llama could still be seen; as could the Uñallamacha - the suckling baby llama below it, and Atoq - the Fox, Hanp' tu - the Toad, and Yutu - the partridge-like bird. The slow, stupid Yutu never catches the Toad in their nightly race. Mach' cauy - the Serpent, was hardly visible, for it was time for Him to go below ground, and with Him the rainbow-serpents vanished for a season.

"In the field behind us," Zapana said, assuming I came out to relieve myself. He stood wrapped in a blanket with his back against the wall a few paces away.

"I only came to see the sky," I said.

"Look at the stars of Qollqa - the Storehouse," he said. "See how brightly they shine? It will be a good planting season. But you can see them better in the open behind the cottage. Go around and stand by the corral."

The llamas bunched together for warmth, legs folded under, and a few long necks turned to focus huge liquid eyes on me. The little ones, born but a few months earlier, rested their fuzzy heads on their mothers' flanks. The seven stars of the Qollqa twinkled above.

Zapana's voice came softly from behind, "You were very brave to face Chani alone, Qori." I hadn't heard him approach, but I wasn't averse to sharing the night sky.

"I did what I had to."

"Did he say anything before. . . ."

"I didn't give him a chance."

I felt him nod to himself in the pause that followed, then he said, "You're a rare woman." His voice was low and husky, and his praise genuine. He wanted me. Not because I was a woman but because I was me. I turned my head slightly, suddenly aware of his maleness, and stepping back found myself leaning against his warmth.

He was older than me by several years, and experienced. I knew he was married, but that only made him safe, and deliciously forbidden. The arrogant Tintaya wasn't to my taste. Zapana at least had a human side, and he was as handsome as his father. I had no girlish thoughts of romance. He was a man; I was a woman; the night had no eyes.

Zapana remained motionless, allowing me to rest against him. Go ahead, I urged in my mind, put your hands on me, caress me where you wish. I trembled and my heart pounded. I never felt this way with T'ito. It was right, the time was right for me and I had to possess this man, this beautiful man in the night.

Still he hesitated. I shifted slowly, pressing back against him, responding to his warmth. When his hands gripped my shoulders I sucked in my breath. His fingers pressed but he held me stiffly, hesitating as if in an agony of indecision.

Now, I thought, take me now. Anything you want. Only do it!

"Qori. . . I had best return to my post." His hands fell away and before I could turn he walked off, leaving me alone and shaking.

The next morning Zapana gave no sign of what had passed, or almost passed in the night. He was no more or less attentive to me, or I to him. Nothing was said. Yet each time I looked his way I couldn't help imagining what might have been, the two of us frantic beneath the stars with the llamas placidly looking on. I felt foolish having offered myself so brazenly, and then being denied. Doesn't he want me? I wondered. No, I can feel that he does, there's something else. His wife? Perhaps. I tucked these thoughts away in a private place, determining one day I would have him to my satisfaction. The challenge made him all the more attractive.

Eventually we reached Yuncaycalla, the gateway shrine where travelers catch their first glimpse of Cuzco and make offerings, and where guards search all those who come and go. No one dared touch Eagle Woman as Condin Savana predicted, and we were waved through with deference. Eight of us entered the jungle. Only three returned. I paused at the shrine to offer a few feathers in thanks. I survived, I thought. I am reborn. I am strong.

"Qori!"

The shout came from behind, a familiar voice I hadn't heard in years. I hardly dared believe what I knew instantly to be true. Could it really be. . . ? I turned slowly. "Qhari?"

"There's no time to explain everything," Qhari whispered, drawing me aside. "When you went to the akllawasi I became a servant to Pachakuti's heirs, Iñaca Panaqa, and served as a messenger between their estates. A few nights ago Lord Achachi came to me. He told me about you and said he knows what happened to father, and he'll help us if I follow his instructions. Then he gave me a message for you. The next day they assigned me to the Pisaq road - "

"Wait, Qhari, is it really you?"

His words had come in a torrent and I was too shaken to make sense of them. He stopped himself, and placing his hands on my shoulders looked into my face. "Yes, it's me, sister. Look at you. You're a woman now."

I held him at arm's length, still not believing the young man he had become, and handsome, yes, very handsome, and with the lean, hard body of a runner. Even a sister couldn't help noticing that. He blushed under my open appraisal, and self-consciously pushed his hair back over his shoulders, revealing the shell earrings marking his provincial origins. He served, but unlike me he wasn't adopted back into Inca society.

A pain welled in my throat. "You look well, brother," was all I could manage before crushing him to me. When he finally broke the embrace his cheeks were wet, too.

"Qori," he began again urgently, "did you hear me? Achachi wants to help."

"I thought Achachi was the murderer," I said dully, knowing now that he wasn't. "You said so before you left."

"Well, it was a good guess, but I was wrong. There's no time now. I'll explain what I can later. This is what you must do. Tell your lord that you met me here by chance, and ask him to have me transferred closer to you."

"That's all?"

"That's all for now. Achachi said we're not to seek him. He was very stern about that. He'll contact us when the time comes."

Tintaya walked over. "My Lady has found an acquaintance?" he asked giving Qhari a suspicious look.

"Yes," I replied pleasantly, "this is my brother, Qhari Puma. We haven't seen each other for years. What a happy coincidence. Qhari, this is my head porter, Tintaya."

Both played their roles. Tintaya bowed as a porter should, and Qhari acknowledged him with a polite nod.

I gave Qhari a look. "Well, I hope to see you again, brother." He held my eyes, catching the implied danger.

"And you, sister. I hope it will be soon."

"If the gods so desire," I said, while thinking to myself, Or if Lord Atoq will grant it.

"But that's impossible," Lord Achachi exclaimed.

Atoq grinned at his uncle. "I concede it's irregular, but not impossible for the Overlord of Chinchaysuyu. I'm sure you can prevail upon your panaqa to grant this favor."

"Yanakuna are servants for life. We don't trade them like llamas," Achachi said, setting his jaw.

"No, my Lord, of course not, you're right. But as I explained, I merely wish to reward this young woman for her excellent service. She only wants to see her brother more often, and it's little enough to ask. Consider that she's lost her husband. Widowed so young. . . ." He clicked his tongue and looked at me sitting by the bales of feathers. Tintaya and Zapana sat behind me in the Tipón courtyard.

Achachi said, "You sent her, and the cargo is for your panaqa, not mine."

"Did she not bring you greetings from Condin Savana?"

"Yes, and I thank her for that." He nodded at me without recognition. "But I'm not beholden to her, or you, nephew. It was only because of my personal request to the Wizard of the East that she returned at all. You still haven't told me what the real purpose of their mission was."

Atoq brushed the question aside. "A matter of security. Now come, uncle, surely you'll not deny this small favor?"

"I can, and I will. The man Qhari stays in service to my panaqa." He lifted his chin and looked away.

Atoq appeared unperturbed. "I believe you're fond of gambling, uncle. May I suggest a game of fives with unusual stakes?"

"Such as?" Achachi said, trying not to show interest.

"If I win you arrange for this Qhari to be sent to my father at

K'allachaka." Achachi raised his brow and made a face. "And if you win, uncle, you may keep the bales of feathers."

"Those are high stakes," Achachi said, stroking his chin and eyeing the bales.

Without waiting for further discussion Atoq turned to a maid who hovered nearby. "Please bring aqha and the fives board." His look told her to hurry before Achachi changed his mind. She produced the requirements in moments, and the two men were soon lost in the game.

What's Achachi doing? I wondered. Is he truly one of the 'friends' I've waited patiently to meet? He once threatened to harm Qhari, but now he claims to be helping us. Surely he's heard about his granddaughter. And T'ito? Does Achachi know who T'ito really was? Why did he send us to Condin Savana to be 'prepared'? And why is he concealing all this from Atoq?

Condin Savana's words came back to me, "You are but a leaf between two strong winds. If either feels threatened you will be blown away. Your life depends upon silence."

Fives was Atoq's favorite game, and he was a master at it. He once told me it's like life, part skill and part chance. The board is divided down the middle, either side with five squares through which each player moves twenty colored beans according to the five symbols on a die. The die determines the number of beans that can be advanced in a single move, and provides the opportunity to cross the center line and block an opponent's advance. Plan, gamble, parry, advance - the game of life.

There were hearty greetings when we survivors arrived back at Tipón. I couldn't help noticing that Atoq gave Zapana a warm embrace while Tintaya received a congratulatory nod. The two agents exchanged a cold stare behind their master's back. Atoq spoke at length with the men first. When they summoned me to the private chamber I found Tintaya and Zapana kneeling before Atoq with grim faces. Atoq welcomed me with a broad smile.

"Is it so?" he asked. "Did you really slay Chani unaided?"

"It is so, Lord."

He fixed me with a stare. "How did you feel afterward?"

I summoned the feelings. The men watched my face. If I spoke of my tears Tintaya would sneer. "Weary. Empty. Elated," I said.

Atoq looked surprised. "Elated?"

"Was it not our purpose, Lord? The opportunity came to me, so I acted."

"So you acted. . . " he repeated thoughtfully, nodding to himself. "I heard those of Choqo call you after that great warrior-woman, Chañan Qori Koka. I see now it's well deserved. Tell me how you disposed of Chani."

I lied, telling him that when I saw Chani coming I hid in the bushes with Vinchin's bow and slew him as he walked by, adding made-up details to make it sound convincing. Atoq's eyes never left me. He appeared satisfied. At the end he said, "I'm sorry about your husband."

The words were polite, but spoken as a formality without emotion. Odd, I thought. Atoq was fond of T'ito, or so it seemed. I suppose death is too familiar in his profession, and this is his way of dealing with it.

"It happens," he added, "but I assure you the Emperor will hear of his sacrifice. . . and your bravery."

I lowered my head as if choked by the memory of loss, but secretly delighted that my name would reach the Emperor's ears.

"What's that you're wearing at your breast?"

"This is Eagle Woman, my spirit guardian. Condin Savana made her for me." I slipped Eagle Woman from around my neck and offered her for inspection. He seemed reluctant to touch her at first, but Tintaya gave him a nod. Atoq gingerly turned her until his eyes fastened on the mark of the six-toed jaguar. He quickly handed her back. I knew then that Eagle Woman's deadly secrets were forever safe.

"Tell me everything about Condin Savana, and the message you delivered from Lord Achachi," he said.

Again I elaborated and omitted in the telling, weaving a plausible tale. I told him Condin Savana simply shrugged at Achachi's words and agreed to give us safe passage home. When the Wizard of the East learned of my wish to become a healer he took me to the spirit world, and later taught me the healing plants. Atoq looked impressed.

"Tanta Karwa will be most pleased, as I am," he said at the end of my story. "I'm sure you'll be a great asset to her, and perhaps to the Emperor, too," he added cryptically. "By happy chance Lord Achachi arrived yesterday to examine some of the old Chinchaysuyu khipus. You may deliver Condin Savana's message to him now." Atoq gestured to Tintaya, but before he could move Zapana rose and hurried out. He returned with Lord Achachi. Achachi ignored me completely when he strode into the room. We all stood and bowed.

"What is it now, nephew? I'm busy."

"I'm sorry to trouble you, uncle, but these people have just returned from Antisuyu with a message for you from Condin Savana."

"What?" He looked around as if trying to remember faces. "Oh, yes. These are the ones you sent off on your 'trading' mission," he said looking at Tintaya and Zapana. "Were there not four of them?"

"Yes, and another four as porters. Five of the party did not return."

Achachi's eyes twinkled. "I told you. The great forest is no place to send inexperienced mountain folk. I'm only surprised the Chuncho didn't eat them all. So, you met my old enemy and ally," he said to Tintaya.

Tintaya shook his head and pointed at me. Achachi turned, apparently noticing me for the first time. "Well?"

I repeated Condin Savana's words of greeting, still wondering what the true message was. The others listened intently. When I finished Achachi shrugged and said, "The old bird always did have a flowery way with our language." He turned to Atoq. "Now, if there's nothing else. . . ?"

After Achachi left, Atoq asked me to name my reward. I told him of meeting my brother, and following Qhari's directive, asked that he be transferred closer to Choqo.

Atoq put his hand to his brow. "Ah, yes, I remember now. Tanta Karwa asked me to make inquires about him some time ago. I did, but to no avail. I'm afraid I became too busy to pursue it further. Well, it worked out for the best. You found him. In service with Iñaca Panaqa you say? This may be difficult, but leave it to me."

The game of fives didn't go well for Atoq. Achachi was a shrewd player also, and lucky. Nine of Atoq's counters remained blocked by three of Achachi's, who already had the rest of his beans in his fifth square. Atoq had made no attempt to slow Achachi's progress. It only remained for Achachi to extract his guards and the game was over.

Gloom settled over me. Atoq's imminent loss would cost him all the macaw feathers, and my one chance to be reunited with Qhari. Isn't that what Achachi wants, I wondered, for Qhari to be moved closer? He seems intent on winning the game, and not the least bit interested in me.

One roll, one fateful roll of the die, and Atoq moved a counter into Achachi's fourth square, blocking the retrieval of his guards.

Achachi looked perplexed. "Are you sure you want to make that move, nephew? Shouldn't you be trying to dislodge my guards?"

"You have all of your counters save those three in your fifth square, uncle, and you must move them back over to your side to win. I've blocked them. Now they're your problem."

Achachi huffed and leaned over the board. I peered closer. It was sheer genius! Atoq allowed Achachi to charge ahead, and flushed with pending victory, to over-extend himself, while Atoq's counters remained bunched for the final dash. Now Achachi was trapped by his own moves. At the last moment the balance suddenly shifted in Atoq's favor.

The game soon ended with Achachi jumping to his feet and stomping from the courtyard without a word. Atoq picked up a single bean and smiled at it, turning it slowly between two fingers.

"Let your opponent scheme and enjoy his little victories, Qori," he said. "It's only the final outcome that matters. You see what a difference one well-placed player can make?" His eyes settled on me. "I'll have your brother moved to my father's estate at K'allachaka, across the valley from Choqo. He'll still be a servant, that can't be changed, but to my panaqa. You may visit him as often as you wish."

"My Lord, I'm most grateful, and always your humble servant," I replied in relief.

"Yes. . . " he said, turning an idea over in his mind, "I believe you are. And you may yet be of even greater use in the Emperor's service. I'll contact you after T'ito's mourning rituals end. I have a proposition that may interest you."

XIX

In which Qori performs a Remarkable but Unseemly Feat, and witnesses the Abominable Vice.

"They're upwind from us, Lord, just over this rise," the guide whispered. We huddled in a crouch by the roadside. "A bush-lined stream crosses the field to the left of the road. There are about eighty grazing in the open beyond."

Qhari shared a private grin with Zapana. Zapana flexed his muscles and shook the spears he held in a clenched fist. Qhari bit his lip and nodded. They rolled up their cloaks and tied them around their waists. The two hunters were ready, and the third wasn't about to be left behind.

The guide had roused us at dawn. The herd of guanacos, reported on the back reaches of the estate a few days earlier, was sighted nearby. Though I was twice told to wait at the lodgings I gathered my sling and followed them anyway. Several men from a nearby village waited for us in the road, bundled in their cloaks against the morning chill. We set out immediately with hardly a word. Now, with mist still hugging the ground, excitement hung as heavy as the dew.

I touched Qhari's arm, thanking him again with a look for arranging this. His eyes danced the way they did when we stalked whale bones with our slings on the beaches.

Zapana avoided looking at me, lest his eyes give him away, I assumed. Or is he angry with me? Nothing more than polite formalities passed between us since meeting at K'allachaka the day before. I had spent an entire morning making myself pretty for him. He might at least have admired me.

Tanta Karwa was devastated when I returned from Tipón with the news of T'ito's death.

"It's my fault," she wailed. "I only wanted the two of you to be together. I had no idea Lord Atoq would send you to the jungles of Antisuyu."

I tried to console her. "Mother, it's not your fault, or Lord Atoq's. It was fated to be. The gods decided. Lord Atoq did as you asked - a simple trading expedition to the beautiful forests so T'ito and I could be together. He couldn't have foreseen the outcome."

There was no point in troubling her with the true nature of our mission. She might be proud to know T'ito died in the Emperor's service, but she might also be angry with Atoq for exposing us to such danger. I kept my silence. If Atoq wanted her to know he would tell her. As for the truth about T'ito and me, there was no need to burden her with that either. It was just as well T'ito never managed to build us a house of our own. Tanta Karwa and I were now widows together, and I had long since come to think of her house as my home.

Though we didn't have T'ito's body to wrap, still, his soul had surely found its way back, and we performed the mourning rituals according to custom. Dressing in black, we cut our hair and wore our cloaks over our heads. Many from Ayllu Añawarqe attended the ceremonies, at which we served food and much aqha. They performed slow dances and mourning songs to the measured thud of drums, and gave touching recitals of T'ito's accomplishments, though these were brief and exaggerated. The people really came out of respect for Tanta Karwa. During the rites, which lasted a week, we lit no fires in the house, and burned T'ito's belongings outside along with several new garments sent as offerings. Thereafter we repeated these ceremonies on a lesser scale twice each month, at the time between the old moon and the new when Mama Killa is invisible, and again when She was full. The rites were longer and more elaborate than those for commoners, and less so than those for royalty, as befitted the rank of Ayllu Añawarqe.

Privately, and unexpectedly, I found I enjoyed my short hair. So much lighter, cooler, and easier to wash. If it weren't reserved as a sign of mourning I think I would have always kept it so. After the first week people left us to grieve in peace. Clients stayed away. No one seeks a healer dressed in mourning.

Tanta Karwa was greatly impressed with Eagle Woman, though she respectfully declined to touch her, and with my journey into the spirit world, the lessons in healing I received from Condin Savana, and the various medicines he prepared for me. Although these things were strange to her she declared them powerful beyond measure, and determined to complete my training quickly so I would be a true Inca healer.

I also learned from her the myths and legends of our people, passed down from generation to generation in narrative poems. Some poems, such as those composed for a lover, may consist of no more than a few phrases, while the great epics can take days to recite in their fullness. Runasimi builds new words by inserting parts of several others before and after the stem, so an entire sentence can be expressed in one long word. This makes the heroic poems easier to memorize. I knew in outline the stories of Pachakuti, founder of the Empire, and His son Thupa Inka who expanded our borders to the edges of the world, but Tanta Karwa knew them word for word and tutored me until I, too, could recite them at length. She cautioned me that while the official versions of these stories were preserved by the royal rememberers in Cuzco, they could be rephrased periodically, either ignoring or emphasing certain events to suit a new emperor. The epics were also remembered differently between villages, depending on local allegiances. But, she assured me, the accounts recited in Choqo were the true versions, unaltered through generations.

Thus I passed the time in lessons, and I think she, too, was glad of it, for it helped fill our days. But I often found her staring off, misty eyed, and it broke my heart to watch her mourn T'ito so, because I could not.

The guide pressed his lips, reminding us to move quietly. "I'll take my men ahead," he whispered to Zapana. "We'll stay on the road until we're past the herd. You follow soon, Lord, and take your position along the stream. When you're in place we'll chase them toward you." He moved off, followed by the beaters. The three of us grinned at one another, sharing the excitement.

I tried not to let my gaze linger on Zapana, but it was hopeless. He was so beautiful - piercing eyes, eyelashes a woman would kill for, and long, slender fingers that could . . . . Beside him Qhari was short and slim, as hard and graceful as a cougar to be sure, but lithe and fine-featured. Both wore plain, dark hunting tunics.

Soon after the beaters disappeared over the rise Qhari checked their progress, and then gestured for Zapana to take the place of honor in the lead. Zapana began his crawl forward, followed by Qhari. It was then I discovered a long dress isn't made for stalking animals on your hands and knees. I tried holding up the hem with one hand and dragging myself along with the other, but made little headway and soon fell behind. At last I reached the crest of the hill and saw the herd grazing beyond the stream to the left of the road. The horizon paled yellow, Inti began His ascent, and the morning mist dispersed. Four of the beaters were in place, but the other still worked his way along the roadside in advance of the herd. By this time Zapana and Qhari were well along the bush-lined stream where they blended with the morning shadows, and had I not known where to look I would never have seen them slipping up on their prey. The guanacos kept their heads down, grazing peacefully.

It was a small herd of males, mostly two-year-olds but many yearlings among them. Toward the end of their first year the males are chased away from their family groups, and wander in bachelor herds until each is old enough to gather and defend females of his own. Guanaco families with their many females and young are never hunted, but the bachelor herds are culled at every opportunity. The hair of these small, wild relatives of llamas and alpacas is not fit for yarn, but their hides are used for sandals and bags, and they have excellent meat. My mouth watered at the thought of roast guanaco. With the prey in sight, I tensed.

There was no carefully thought-out plan to what happened next. There was no time for hesitation. Soon the hunters would attack and the herd disperse. It took but a moment to shed my cloak, dress and sandals. I wrapped my sling around my head and tied a bag of stones at my waist. Free of all constricting garments, the cool, wet grass felt clean and alive against my bare skin. My one gesture to modesty was to retie my cloak loosely over my shoulders. Then I set off across the open field on elbows and knees, scurrying to a boulder behind Zapana's position. My complete attention was on reaching that boulder - the men, the guanacos, and everything else out of mind. The others were equally intent on their objectives, and neither the men nor their quarry noticed my wriggling form.

At last I lay curled up behind the boulder, panting quietly. Zapana moved farther along, then gave the 'ready' signal. I drew a deep breath and with one last burst dashed to the stream, arriving on Zapana's left. He still watched the others farther upstream and didn't notice my arrival. I crouched in the position farthest from the road, and peered out from the bushes. The lead guanaco raised its head and sniffed the air. I looked to Zapana. He lifted his arm slowly, preparing to give the signal. Closer to the road Qhari pressed behind a tree, watching Zapana, waiting to relay the signal to the beaters. His arm rose slowly also.

"How did you manage to place me here?" Qhari had asked on my first visit. We walked the K'allachaka terraces, he dressed prosperously in a red tunic and leather sandals. Tiny fish carved of red shell hung from his ears, and his headdress showed a rolled band of red wool with a feather flower at the front, like the native officials at Ica. His hair swept back over his shoulders, and copper bracelets glinted on his wrists. I noticed something new in his eyes, a permanent hint of laughter as if humor readied to leap forth, but stayed constrained in private amusement.

"Lord Atoq made the arrangements," I replied.

"Ah yes, Lord Zapana's father, I've heard of him. You have his ear? You've done well, Qori." So had he, far above my expectations, and his. When Qhari moved to K'allachaka they promoted him to under-steward, where he assisted Zapana, Head Steward, in running the estate. But since Zapana's title was really honorary and he was seldom there, Qhari often dealt directly with the owner - Prince Tupac Amaru, the Emperor's brother and Zapana's grandfather. Qhari's referral to Zapana as 'Lord' was a matter of politeness toward his superior, for Zapana couldn't hold that title until Atoq legally recognized him, which for some unexplained reason he had not. Still, those close to the family readily acknowledged Zapana's parentage, and treated him accordingly.

K'allachaka is an easy walk across the Huatanay Valley from Choqo. The estate is vast, encompassing several villages, but the royal residences are grouped on terraces rippling down an entire side of the Kachimayu ravine outside Cuzco. Like Tipón, the sheltered climate is warmer than in open places, and lush with vegetation. The terraces aren't as high or grand as those of Tipón, but they're far longer and more numerous. Though there are gardens, most terraces support buildings or crops, and springs provide ample water.

Rain pattered softly from a clear sky. A flock of green parrots burst from the bushes in front of us, heading down to the maize terraces closer to the river. I glanced around to make sure we were alone. "Now what is all this about Lord Achachi?" I whispered. "You trust him? Did you know he threatened to harm you?"

Qhari shook his head slowly. "No, Qori, you're wrong about him. He told me about the misunderstanding."

"Misunderstanding?"

"Yes, about the message. 'Your brother is watched over. Stay silent, and stay well.' It was meant to reassure you that I was cared for, and urge you to be patient. What did you think?"

"Well, you said Achachi was the one who murdered those women at Hatunqolla, so I thought. . . ."

"I know. I'm sorry. I guessed wrong. Achachi is one of our friends."

"How can you be sure?"

"Because he told me about the governor at Ica who helped us. He was Achachi's cousin. Remember he died of a mysterious ailment not long after we left Ica? Achachi suspects poison."

I looked away. Qhari asked quietly, "Did you really arrange for Achachi's granddaughter to be sacrificed?"

"No, of course not. That was just an empty threat. For a while I thought he arranged her death to cover himself. Does he think I'm responsible; and he still wants to help us?"

"He's not very pleased with you, but he said there's more at stake than a few lives. 'The Empire needs you.' Those were his words."

"What does that mean?"

"He wouldn't say. Like his cousin, the Ica governor, he said we'd know eventually, but he thought it too dangerous to name names right now."

"But if all this is true, why did he threaten you? He said if I didn't leave him alone he'd find you, and I wouldn't like it."

"Yes, he told me about that. He said it because he thought you were taking risks, and threatening him. You didn't know who your friends and enemies were, and he wanted to keep you quiet."

I sighed with frustration. "Then who are our friends and who are our enemies?"

He shrugged. "Achachi is a friend, for one."

"A fine friend. He doesn't want us near him and he won't tell us anything."

"Patience. That's what he says."

"Qhari, if it wasn't Achachi who murdered those women at the Hatunqolla akllawasi, then who was it?"

He looked at me, and in his face I saw the answer as clearly as if he spoke it. I nodded. It seemed obvious now, but the idea was too incredible to put into words.

Father's captain, Kontor, I thought. Why didn't I think of him before? He entered the akllawasi alone, and returned without the women. After that there is only Kontor's word that he went to Achachi asking rest for his troop. He must have lied, and it was he alone who repeatedly ordered his men into battle hoping all would die.

"Does Lord Achachi suspect Kontor?" I asked quietly.

"I don't know," Qhari said looking away. "It only occurred to me after he left."

"We should go to Achachi and - "

"No! The last time you did that his granddaughter paid for it. Her death wasn't his doing, and if it wasn't yours, then someone is sending him, and us, a message. It's too dangerous, Qori. Let Achachi choose the next meeting."

He was right of course, but the notion of waiting for others to act rankled me. A thought came. The last five-year meeting of the fugitives happened while I was in the akllawasi, but Qhari was free. "Did you attend the festival at the Temple of Wiraqocha in Raqch'i?"

"No, Qori. I tried, but they wouldn't let me go. And you?"

"The same. I was still a chosen woman. It will be years before the next meeting," I said glumly.

"Three years this month," he replied, "but we'll be there, no matter what."

I nodded. "No matter what."

He looked at me quizzically. "Did they come after you again in the akllawasi?"

"Are you jesting? If a man so much as poked his nose in that place he'd lose it. What about you?"

"Once. They came at night. I never saw them. They still think father is alive. They said if I didn't tell them where he and uncle Maita are hiding they'd harm you."

"What did you say?"

"I told them to go ahead."

My hands went to my hips. "Thank you, brother dear."

He shrugged. "What would you have done?"

I let it go. "You've not been troubled since?"

"Well. . . ."

"We must share everything, Qhari."

He sighed and shuffled his feet. "One of the servants forced me to tell him about the messages I delivered between the Iñaca estates." He saw my brows go up and hurried on, "It had nothing to do with us. I think he was a spy for another royal house. Anyway, all he ever got from me were harvest results, orders for more workmen, greetings between nobles, ordinary things of no importance. That's over now. I'm with Lord Zapana and safe under the banner of Capac Panaqa."

"How did this spy 'force' you to tell the business of Iñaca Panaqa?"

"He said he would tell."

"Tell what?"

Qhari stared at me. "Don't press me on this, Qori. It has nothing to do with you."

I stepped back, shaken by his tone. Whatever it is, I decided, he'll tell me when he's ready. Share a confidence to gain a confidence, that's what Tanta Karwa said.

I told him the truth about T'ito.

"Our-our. . . brother?" he sputtered, eyes wide.

"It's true. And Tanta Karwa is our aunt, uncle Maita's wife, though she doesn't know I'm her niece, or T'ito's sister."

"Why was this done to you, Qori? Why were you tricked into marrying our brother?"

I shrugged. "I suppose to have one more thing hanging over my head. It was useless threatening me, but with this they had T'ito, Tanta Karwa, and the honor of our whole ayllu to bargain with."

"But mother and father are dead. They can never prove you're T'ito's sister."

"True, but neither can I accuse anyone of the Hatunqolla murders without declaring who I am. How else could I bear witness and ask that father's name be cleared? How can I, or you, reveal the murderer without revealing the truth about my marriage?

"Clever," he said nodding in resignation. Then, thinking out loud to himself, "And if it becomes known you were married to your brother it will cast doubt on your testimony anyway. Now they've trapped both of us."

"Both of us?"

His eyes came back to me. "Never mind, it's not important now. We'll just have to find a way to avenge father's death ourselves, quietly."

A moment hung, then, misty-eyed, he said, "I didn't even meet my elder brother."

"You didn't miss much."

He looked at me coldly. "How can you say that about our own brother?"

"Don't press me on this, Qhari," I said, imitating his tone. He rubbed his brow and looked away.

Why did I say that? There was no need for it. Sometimes I say cruel things I regret as soon as the words are out of my mouth, but I'm never quick enough to correct it at the time, and I never get around to it later. I imagined Tanta Karwa shaking her finger at me. I tried again, this time telling him about Lord Achachi's secret message to Condin Savana.

"And what did he want this Condin Savana to do for us?"

"The code said the bearer of the message was to be 'prepared.' That should have been T'ito but it turned out to be me. Condin Savana said

Achachi wanted me to succeed. That's all I know."

A boy approached. "Qhari Puma?" Qhari nodded. "The chamberlain wants to see you now about arrangements for Lord Zapana's hunt."

Qhari dismissed him and turned to me with a grin. "My Lord Zapana loves to hunt the hills. Perhaps you'll join us sometime?"

"Is it possible?"

Qhari looked taken aback, as if he hadn't expected me to treat the offer seriously. "Well . . . we've never taken a woman with us before, but Lord Zapana often invites friends. And he listens to me," he added proudly. "Perhaps something can be arranged." I knew that showing-off look.

The prospect of a hunt excited me, but another idea excited me more. Zapana still lingered in my thoughts; indeed, I had to admit that the lover in my fantasies now had a face. Zapana declined once, but I knew he'd been tempted. No, I won't throw myself at him again, I thought, but, if we happen to meet and find ourselves alone . . . .

"Can I join you on this hunt?" I asked.

"This one? You mean in a few days? Well, I . . ."

"Unless, of course, you don't have enough influence to arrange it," I dared him.

He smiled. "You used to trap me like this when we played on the shores. Remember, Qori?"

Caught. I could only chuckle with him, and in my mind's eye again I saw the two of us racing hand in hand along those endless beaches at sunset.

Qhari placed his hand on my shoulder. "I must go now. Leave this to me. I'll show you how to organize a hunt."

Zapana's arm went down, followed by Qhari's. The beaters leapt from cover and ran shouting into the field. The guanacos hesitated but an instant, then all ran, first toward the bush and then parallel to it, as planned. Zapana threw his spears but no animals fell. Qhari stood, whirling bolas above his head, then casting low as the herd rushed by. Much to my surprise, for I'd never seen this weapon in use, the twirling cords with their stone weights entangled the feet of a yearling, which flipped headfirst and landed on its back, both front feet in the air firmly bound by the cords. It lay on its side thrashing when Qhari ran out to finish it with his knife.

I leapt to my feet also, my sling circling. Having broken cover I knew I had one throw. The lead guanaco saw me and veered away. My eyes never left its head. I loosed the stone. Whack! It caught him behind his ear. He collapsed, momentarily stunned. I ran to him and bound his front legs with my sling, but he recovered and kicked his hind legs, raking my thigh and knocking me backwards. I sat up quickly, but a shadow suddenly moved in front of me, and then the guanaco lay twitching on its side, its neck slashed.

With the sun at his back, it took a moment to realize that Zapana stood before me, and a moment longer to remember that I sat on my cloak, naked. I gasped in embarrassment, but remained frozen to the spot, unable to look away from his open-mouth stare. I saw passion in his eyes as they traveled my body, lingering long on my shivering breasts. It wasn't the morning chill that caused me to tremble so. His eyes found mine, a look of bewilderment on his face. He knelt over me. I raised myself, wanting his lips on mine. He covered me with his cloak. Was it pain, or pleading in his eyes? He stood and turned to deal with the guanaco as the beaters hurried over.

I won't claim that my felling of the guanaco was anything more than extreme good luck, for even the most accomplished slinger can't strike a moving target in the one spot that will drop it, at least not with true precision. And I didn't claim otherwise at the time. I simply remained silent and let others boast on my behalf. But Qhari's response was hardly adulation when he arrived with the beaters.

"We left you on the road. How did you get here?" He looked serious.

"I crawled."

He looked at the road and then back at me. "What are you doing here?"

I shrugged. "Hunting."

"With what?"

"My sling." I pointed to where it wrapped the animal's front legs.

"You can't kill a running guanaco with a sling," he insisted, shaking his head.

Zapana interrupted. "But she did, I saw it. I can hardly believe it myself," he said, stooping to retrieve his cloak from where I left it beside the guanaco, "but by the gods I swear it's true. She felled it and I finished it."

All heads turned back to me in curious silence. I stared at my toes and drew my cloak tighter. Although it covered me completely, Qhari suddenly noticed it was the only thing I wore.

"Where are your dress and sandals?" He sounded like father. I allowed him the role, not wanting to embarrass him in front of Zapana.

"At the road," I replied in a small voice, then added in my own defense, "You can't stalk guanacos in a dress, you know."

He gasped and placed an arm around my shoulders, drawing me away from the men and back to the road. The beaters looked everywhere except at me, while Zapana studiously admired my guanaco.

Qhari remained in the role of elder. "A woman doesn't shed her clothes to go running naked through the fields chasing animals. It's not done. And in front of men. You should have stayed at the road. How can you be so shameless? What will Lord Zapana think?" He was truly angry and continued in this vein all the way to the road, where he turned his back and shielded me while I donned my dress.

I held my tongue, afraid he might insist I leave. The first thrill of the day was over, and I didn't want to miss the second.

"I'm sorry, Qhari, forgive me. It won't happen again. Shall we rejoin Lord Zapana?"

"How embarrassing," he muttered.

I looked at him.

"I mean about the clothes, too," he said.

"And?"

"Look, Qori, you don't out-hunt lords, especially if you're a woman."

"You took a guanaco," I pointed out.

"That's different. I'm a man."

I closed my eyes and swallowed hard, then tried another approach. "That was fine handling of the bolas. Where did you learn to use them like that?"

He allowed the deflection. "Oh, a man at Ollantaytampu used to take me hunting. He taught me. Look, Qori, just don't start bragging about that guanaco in front of Lord Zapana. Don't say anything at all. Promise?" He was back to being my brother again.

My celebrity was never really in doubt. That a woman with a sling had out-hunted a man with spears made an excellent tale. The beaters must have told it many times, because in later years I was much gratified to hear travelers tell of a woman named Qori Qoyllur who felled a running guanaco with a single stone. In fact, as some told it, I slew an entire herd.

Zapana politely pretended nothing had happened when we returned, though he was smirking. I glanced at Qhari. Zapana wasn't angry. Qhari sniffed back to show me he was. The beaters slung our kills on poles.

"Take one to my grandfather's house, the yearling will be fine, and the other to your village," Zapana instructed them. They bowed, thanking him, and set off.

The morning sun shone full upon us. Qhari stretched. "It's been an early day," he said through a yawn. "I think I'll rest in that grove." He gestured to a line of trees at the base of the hills in front of us, then turned to Zapana. "Farther along there's a river, my Lord, if you wish to bathe. Come, I'll show you."

I wasn't included in the invitation. Qhari's eyes told me to stay put. I announced I would stay in the shade by the stream. They nodded and walked off, following the creek to the grove at the far side of the field.

I waited patiently until they were out of sight. The excitement of the hunt had heightened my senses. Moving urgently, I made my way to the spot where they had disappeared among the trees.

Sunshine streaked the grove, casting shadows and pools of light amid dense underbrush. Warily I made my way through the foliage, intent on keeping my passage hidden from Qhari, following the sound of rushing water somewhere beyond. I spotted Qhari standing in a clearing. No sign of Zapana. He must be farther ahead to the left, I decided. I crouched behind a fallen tree, preparing to scurry around the clearing. Zapana suddenly stepped into the open and walked up to Qhari. They were unaware of me, preoccupied with. . . I poked my head up and looked again. They were staring into each other's eyes. The trace of a smile settled on Zapana's handsome features. Qhari gazed up at him adoringly, his laughing eyes at last revealing the secret of their amusement.

The kiss was so tender, so gentle, I couldn't tear my eyes away. Men? Two men? My own brother? Qhari was eager but passive in Zapana's arms. When their clothing fluttered to the ground I tried to look away, telling myself I should be ashamed for spying on my brother. But two men? What did they do? The answer soon unfolded - everything the Chimu girl in the akllawasi told us about, except this was between men. Two perfect bodies. Graceful. Sensuous. Unhurried. Qhari knelt facing Zapana. I watched in fascination. So that's how it's done! His pesqo was as stiff as Zapana's when he rose, turning his back in invitation.

A wind came up, mixing the sighs of branches and leaves with Zapana's last shudders. I slipped away, my head spinning with images. Tanta Karwa said it was forbidden under Inca law for two men to lie together. What would happen to Qhari and Zapana if they were found out?

Is Qhari like Sumaq T'ika, only able to love his own kind? I wondered. And Zapana? He's married, but that's expected, indeed, required of men. His interests obviously lie elsewhere. No wonder he declined my offer. It has nothing to do with me - he prefers my brother.

XX

Of how the Deceitful and Deadly Arts were practiced by these Indians.

He came forward slowly, menacing me with his maqana while the others circled around. I knew the tactic, he was the decoy, the attack would come from behind. I watched his eyes. They would reveal the moment to turn and face the others. He blinked. I twirled just as the man at my back lowered his spear and charged. Turning sideways to shrink his target, I caught the shaft with a backward thrust of my forearm. He stumbled into me and I buried my knee in his groin. He went down instantly, but I didn't wait to see him on his knees retching. A quick turn brought me face to face with the maqana wielder. He raised the blade with both hands over his head but the move came too late. I caught his throat in a claw-like vise and the maqana fell from his grip. He clamped both hands on mine, jamming his thumbs into my wrists to break the hold. I spun him around, tripping him into Tintaya's charge. The maqana man stayed on the ground red-faced and coughing, but Tintaya came up in an instant, brandishing his long-handled mace. The six points on the star-shaped bronze head wavered before my eyes.

"Very good, Qori," Tintaya said. "Now it's just you and me."

He backed toward the line drawn in the dirt - the line I had to cross to complete this final test successfully. The advantage was his. Armed and wary, he shifted his weight from foot to foot, ready for any feint, his eyes fixed on mine. Atoq and Zapana stood to the side with their arms folded, watching every move.

"Yes, Tintaya," I said between clenched teeth, "this time it's you or me."

A year and a half had passed since the guanaco hunt. When T'ito's mourning period ended a messenger came with a summons to Tipón. That was in the month of Ayamarka, after the crops were sown and the first rains began. In Choqo, as in towns throughout the land, the mummified ancestors were paraded on litters, feasted, and beseeched to watch over the fields. When these festivals began Tanta Karwa let it be known that I was now a healer, and the people should call upon me when in need. There was no ceremony accompanying this announcement, but word quickly spread and many stopped by to congratulate me. They would be pleased, they said, to have the daughter-in-law of the famous Tanta Karwa tend their families. I was looking forward to my first patient when the messenger arrived.

"There is illness among the servants at Tipón," the messenger said. "Lord Atoq requires your presence immediately."

In the months prior to the summons Qhari and I visited frequently, and twice he came to Choqo to meet Tanta Karwa and the ayllu.

"Lord Achachi came to see Prince Tupac Amaru," he confided during our last visit. Atoq's father, Lord of K'allachaka, was of no special concern to me, but Achachi was.

"Was it about us?"

"No, Qori. I waited on them during the meeting. It seems there is concern about the Emperor's health, and the succession. The Heir, Titu Cusi, is too young to rule, and if Thupa Inka dies before the boy comes of age a regent will have to be named. The Emperor wanted Tupac Amaru for the post but he turned it down, saying he was too old and might be with his ancestors any day himself. I gather there was much discussion among the royal panaqas, but Lord Sapaca, Speaker of Hurincuzco, eventually convinced the Emperor to nominate Lord Wallpaya, the head of Iñaca Panaqa. Achachi was protesting, trying to talk Tupac Amaru into changing his mind and accepting the regent position should it become necessary. Even though Wallpaya is Achachi's brother, and his panaqa leader, Achachi doesn't think much of him."

Qhari was leading up to something and I hurried him to the point. "Did Achachi say anything to you?"

"Not directly. I filled his kero a few times. When he left he looked at me and said, "Thank you for your patience," as if just being uncommonly polite to a retainer, but for an instant he looked me in the eye. I know we can trust him."

I wanted to. But what troubled me was why Condin Savana insisted

I keep Achachi's involvement a secret from Atoq. Why did Achachi hide his intentions from Atoq in the first place? I wondered. What's between them?

Since the guanaco hunt I banished Zapana from my fantasies, yet in a strange way he intrigued me more than ever. Such a complicated man. I felt no anger after my discovery, for with my own eyes I witnessed Qhari's eagerness, and the tender looks that passed between them. I wasn't jealous, although whether because it was something strictly between men and therefore no threat to me, or because it involved Qhari, I couldn't decide. But I often reminded myself, and chuckled, that if I had to compete for a man and lose to another, it was best if the winner was my own brother.

I wasn't supposed to know about Qhari and Zapana, but I did, and with this knowledge came a worry that gnawed me. We were discussing Achachi, but suddenly I had to voice these anxieties. "Are you and Zapana safe?" I asked.

He looked at me suspiciously. "What do you mean?"

"I saw you together in the grove on the guanaco hunt."

"You spied on us?"

"I didn't mean to. I was on my way to the river and . . . ."

Qhari scratched his neck and looked away, reddening. He came up with a challenging look. "He loves me. Does that disgust you? You can't understand. Go ahead, call me a man-woman. It's true. I'm not ashamed of who I am." He glared at me defiantly.

"Qhari," I said softly, "I'm sorry. Maybe I understand more than you think."

"How could you understand?" he demanded.

In my mind I saw Sumaq T'ika's pretty face, and Tanta Karwa nodding encouragement. "Because. . . I just do. I don't care. I mean, I hope you're happy. But what will happen if you're found out?"

He relaxed then. "You're not disgusted? You really don't mind?"

I touched his arm. "You're my brother and I love you."

"I love you too, Qori."

"I know."

"Well," he said, lowering his head, "then you might as well know everything. That man at Ollantaytampu who taught me to hunt with the bolas? He taught me other things, too. I wanted it, Qori. I always knew I was. . . different. I suppose there was gossip. That's what the spy threatened to expose if I didn't tell him the messages I delivered. Then, at K'allachaka, as soon as I saw Zapana, I knew, and he did too. He made me his assistant so we could be together."

"Is it dangerous?"

"I'm a commoner, and because of Zapana's position I'll be executed if found with him. Not even Zapana can change that. He'll lose his title, and be shunned by everyone. That's the law, Qori."

"That's what you meant when you said they'd trapped us both?"

"Yes. I can no more come forward with accusations than you can. If I did, they'd tell, and Zapana would be destroyed too."

I took his hand. "Just because you're . . . different."

He bristled again. "I'm a man-woman. Go ahead, say it, Qori. Say it!"

"My brother is a man-woman," I said proudly, "and I love him." He looked at me fondly. If he could bear this, so could I. "And I committed - "

"No, Qori. Don't say that." He placed a finger on my lips. "It wasn't your fault. You didn't know."

"Maybe not, but it still happened," I said brushing his hand away. "Say it, Qhari. Say it now."

"My sister committed incest, and I love her," he said.

The worst was out now, and somehow saying it aloud took the fear and sting away.

"Man-woman," I mocked.

"Incestuous harlot," he replied accusingly.

We laughed.

"You have the knowledge of a healer, now," Tanta Karwa had said when I left for Tipón, "but you need more practice. When you return we'll tend the sick together, and I'll introduce you to the royal houses of Cuzco. We're widows, you and I, but at least we have each other. We'll make a good team. Give my best wishes to Lord Atoq, and stay safe, Qori. Oh, and stay out of that old fox's bed."

The warning was delivered cheerfully enough, but there was an undertone demanding respect of her territory. I hadn't told her Atoq planned to recall me, or about his vague suggestion I might be of further service to the Emperor - a notion that intrigued me greatly.

On the first day I answered Atoq's summons and sat with him alone in a private room, I learned the seemingly monolithic Empire was full of potentially fatal cracks, and Atoq was the fixer.

"You see, Qori," Atoq explained in his fatherly manner, "there are actually very few of us Incas to rule our many provinces and millions of subjects. There are always revolts on the fringes of the Empire, but our armies deal with those. The greater threat comes from within. To remain strong we must remain united. There are now ten royal households and each has influence at court. Thupa Inka is supreme, but He must strive to keep all the lineages loyal and in harmony. From time to time disputes and greed threaten the peace. Not many years ago one of the Emperor's brothers tried to seize power with the aid of malcontents in the provinces. Had my agents not uncovered the plot they might have succeeded.

"I know," he said answering my raised brows, "few are aware of those events. That's as it should be. Only the nobility knows such matters, lest the commoners lose faith and our enemies think us weak. The culprit, his immediate family, and the main plotters were quietly removed." He put an emphasis on the last word which left no doubt about the finality of the action.

Atoq leaned back with a smirk. "I let my uncle Achachi take all the credit for foiling the plot. Thupa Inka was so pleased he promoted him to Visitor-General. Of course, they both know it was my agents who provided all the essential information."

"I'm sure the Emperor is most grateful," was all I could think to say.

"Yes, He is," Atoq replied. "And He understands the importance of secrecy. Every governor and warlord has his own informants, as do each of the royal houses, but mine is the only officially sanctioned web. I have eyes stationed throughout the Empire, but I also have a small group of special agents who go wherever and whenever I send them, and take whatever action is necessary to preserve the peace. In this the Emperor trusts me completely, as He did my father before me.

"My elite agents are trained in the arts of disguise and removal. Only I know their true identities, although each has a code name by which governors and warlords recognize them. Until now I've never had a female agent. Will you be the first, Qori?"

When we joined Zapana and Tintaya in the courtyard the announcement was not well received.

"She's not even Inca," Tintaya said with a sneer, referring to my Ica origin.

I'm as much Inca as anyone here, I fumed inwardly.

"Her time in the akllawasi and her marriage made her Inca by privilege," Atoq replied. "And her loyalty has been established beyond question."

"But, Lord, she's a woman."

"How observant of you, Tintaya," Atoq said.

Zapana's face held the same skepticism. "You know what is required of us, Lord. Can a woman - "

Atoq cut him off. "She was very effective with Chani, Zapana, and you told me yourself what she can do with a sling," he said, referring to my guanaco.

Zapana glanced at Tintaya. Neither looked convinced.

"She showed the qualities we need," Atoq continued, addressing them as if I wasn't present. "Courage, inventiveness, and the ability to strike quickly. Did she not play her role as the wife of a trader perfectly? Think, Tintaya, she can go places denied men. Every akllawasi in the Empire is open to her, and as a healer she'll be welcome in all royal households. I'll see to it that her fame spreads. Once she's tended the Empress every noble lady in the Empire will seek her advice."

Zapana frowned. "All true, Lord, but she's so small. How can she possibly overpower a man?"

"Have you forgotten your training, Zapana?" Atoq said returning his frown. "The most valuable assets of any agent are wits and words. How many situations have you talked your way into, and out of? You're right, she'll never take a man by strength, but she's quick and cunning. . . and she has other assets."

Tintaya looked askance. "Such as, Lord?"

"As you pointed out, Tintaya, she's a woman." Atoq looked from man to man, daring further rebuttal, but it was evident his mind was made up. Zapana and Tintaya simply shrugged at each other, then bowed to Atoq closing the discussion. Atoq gave me a fatherly smile that made me want to hug him. With the Lord of Tipón as my champion, Tintaya and Zapana had no choice but to accept me.

I might have expected the argument from Tintaya, but Zapana disappointed me. He didn't want me, that was plain, but after Atoq showed his determination and the matter was settled Zapana resigned himself to a welcoming smile. After Atoq and Tintaya left the courtyard Zapana placed his hand on my shoulder. "Don't worry," he said. "I'll train you myself, but Tintaya will test you. You had better be good."

I had no reservations. The invitation to join Atoq's secret force appealed to me immensely, and the preservation of the Emperor's peace was a worthy cause indeed. Condin Savana advised me to bend with the wind and obey my master, and the possibility of winning the Emperor's gratitude shone before me. Qhari and I needed friends in high places, and who better than the Emperor himself? Then too, as an agent I would have complete freedom of movement, and with it the chance to pursue my own inquiries.

The training continued daily without rest. I learned how to enter a room disguised as a maid, and without raising my eyes memorize every face and detail of dress, and later repeat every word spoken. Then there were the names of all the governors, warlords, chief administrators and priests of the Empire to remember, and their wives and children. There were also many code words that could be inserted into innocent-sounding dispatches, and an ingenious method of encoding with knots on a khipu that used numbers and colors to convey secret messages. Fortunately, I have a good memory.

By law all people wore the costume of their province and no other, so their origin could be recognized immediately. Only Atoq's agents were exempt, we being allowed to appear in the dress of any nation for the sake of disguise. I enjoyed assuming identities, and even Tintaya admitted grudgingly that I excelled at it. I could be taller with the aid of special sandals, shorter by hunching my posture, older by painting lines on my face and streaking my hair with ashes, and darker- or lighter-skinned with the help of toning salves. Being naturally youthful of face and lithe of form, it required little costuming for me to appear as a maiden barely entering womanhood. 'Serving girl' and 'crone' were my particular specialties, and I could alter the pitch of my voice accordingly.

Another disguise suggested by Zapana, which I didn't think much of until he reminded me that one day my life might depend on it, was that of a Charka boy. He plastered my hair under a net of colored wool - the headdress of Charka men - and made me don a heavy, quilted man's tunic, such as soldiers wear for protection. This hid my female form. The most disturbing garment was a strategically-padded loincloth. He even made me learn to swagger and sit cross-legged! A few touches of paint hardened my features, but even so he chortled that I made a very pretty boy, and had best stay away from the barracks.

There were many costumed rehearsals. At first these took place only at Tipón, until I became comfortable with my disguises. Atoq was so busy he often spent days secluded in his private chambers, but on one of those occasions when he took his midday refreshments in the warmth of the courtyard Zapana sent me dressed as a maid to do the serving. The test was to be so unobtrusive Atoq wouldn't even notice me, though he would recognize me instantly if he looked. Atoq said nothing more than an absent "Thank you," when I placed the bowl and kero beside him. Then I withdrew and Zapana entered, asking Atoq if he'd seen me recently.

Atoq shrugged. "Not today. I thought she was in your care."

"She is, Lord," Zapana grinned. "Qori," he called, "our Lord wishes his maid to bring more aqha." Atoq's smile was all the praise I needed.

Thereafter I went in various disguises to the neighboring villages, and even into Cuzco where I walked the streets to get the feel of my costumes and perfect the roles. Zapana always lurked nearby in a disguise of his own to judge my performance. On these trips I learned to fall into conversation with strangers and find out as much about them as I could without appearing the least bit interested. That is a talent of immeasurable value, and I became quite good at it. The trick is never to look them in the eye, always agree, and give the impression they are far wiser than you. Once this is established it's amazing how much information people volunteer. During these excursions I also studied people of different classes, their mannerisms, terms of speech, and interests, which helped me blend among them.

Becoming part of where you are is no easy thing. Zapana often corrected me for over-acting and trying to be too invisible. "Sometimes the best place to hide is in plain view," he counseled. "Obscurity is obvious to those who seek you." Then there was learning to become a bush or a stone in a wall, instantly. Perfect stillness and proper silhouette being the answer, with good use of shadow when available.

Self-reliance and improvisation were essential parts of the training. The final test of these came when I was blindfolded and taken far into the hills, tied up, and abandoned. My task was to free myself, determine where I was, pass through the gate guarding the southern entrance to the Huatanay Valley - learning the name of the captain of the guard and how many men were on duty in passing - and return to Tipón along the royal road; this without benefit of any prepared disguise, and with roving patrols searching everywhere, believing me to be a thief. My bindings were difficult, but eventually yielded to determined wiggling, biting and pulling, and then I followed the sun until I reached settled lands. Once on the royal road, I stole clothes from the baggage of a noblewoman's caravan, and, presenting myself as her lady-in-waiting, I reported the theft to the captain of the guard at the Huatanay Gate. While engaging him in friendly conversation I requested an escort back to Cuzco to fetch more clothes for my mistress. He complied most gallantly. The patrols searching for me snapped to attention when I strolled by beneath the banner of my escort. Drawing near to Tipón, I demanded privacy to refresh myself by the river, then slipped away, arriving at Tipón with the required information within the three-day limit allowed for the exercise.

Twice in Cuzco while practicing my disguises I caught sight of the old woman. There was no doubt - she was the same old woman who approached me in the street when Qhari and I first arrived in Cuzco, just before we were attacked. I had no more than fleeting glimpses, but she appeared the same, bent and leaning on her staff, wisps of white hair poking from under the cloak pulled over her head. Each time she vanished the moment I noticed her, and that's what made me certain. She was avoiding me. Why? Who was she?

What lay between Tintaya and Zapana continued to fester, the symptoms flaring each time Tintaya used his rank to goad Zapana in petty ways, which was often. Zapana endured these taunts stoically, outwardly remaining the exemplary second in command, accepting and never questioning, quietly allowing Tintaya's outbursts, insinuations and open contempt, meeting all with veiled eyes that neither acquiesced nor challenged. But all this happened outside Atoq's sight and hearing. In his presence Tintaya treated Zapana decently and Zapana never complained. Atoq was clearly fond of Zapana, showing his affection with gestures and approving smiles whenever they were together, which, I supposed, was the reason Zapana endured. Why won't Atoq openly acknowledge that Zapana is his son? I often wondered.

When I tried to commiserate with Zapana about Tintaya's outrageous treatment of him Zapana simply replied, "Tintaya is Tintaya," and the matter was closed. The only thing the two men had in common was their uncompromising devotion to Atoq, though each for different reasons.

During this time Tintaya made advances, his arrogant eyes suggesting he might condescend to do me a favor. When I ignored him he became more obvious and lewd, until I finally told him I wouldn't let him touch me even if he had golden balls. Thereafter his arrogance turned to open hostility and he sought every opportunity to discredit my training. What had I ever done to him, except refuse to share his blankets? He seemed to forget I'd saved his neck by dispatching Chani. But that is the way of some men; if you don't lie with them they despise you, and if you do they treat you with contempt. Then too, Zapana took such interest in my training that Tintaya was determined I should fail, if only to make Zapana look incompetent.

Zapana was a different sort of man. Sometimes he appeared distant and aloof, and at other times friendly and even charming. He was good at what he did and secure within himself, though never over-confident. He knew Tintaya was hard on me, and why, and did his best to help. Though often away on missions, about which one did not inquire, when at Tipón he spent all his time with me. "You've got to be better than any agent we've ever had," he said, "otherwise you'll never get by Tintaya." Unfair but true, I knew.

Sometimes, upon returning from a long absence, Zapana mentioned that Qhari sent his greetings, casually revealing he had stopped by K'allachaka. I once asked him if Qhari knew what I was doing at Tipón, for during the lengthy period of training I was never granted leave to visit, and Zapana replied, "That you are being trained for the Emperor's service, yes. That he can never tell anyone about this, yes. But the exact nature of your duties, no. And it should remain that way, Qori. You do him no favors leaving him to wonder and worry about you. Leading two lives is the sacrifice we make. What you learn here at Tipón, and the missions Lord Atoq may choose for you, must remain secret even from your family - especially from your family, because enemies may come at you through them. If your loved ones know nothing they're not in danger." He hung his head and said gently, "Qhari understands that I, too, have special duties and must be away often, but we don't discuss it."

And nothing was said between us about him and Qhari, either. It was understood with quiet looks, and he knew I accepted how it was with them. Still, I couldn't help wondering about Zapana's private life with his wife and Qhari. He saw this in my eyes but never volunteered more than an amused smile. Qhari had told me Zapana's wife lived on another of Tupac Amaru's estates by Lake Muyna, and Zapana seldom saw her, or at least that's what Qhari wanted to believe. At times I found Zapana surreptitiously regarding me with masculine appraisal, which was confusing, until I decided it was his way of being friendly. Beautiful male creature that he was, he belonged to Qhari.

Tanta Karwa came to visit Tipón regularly and kept Atoq advised of the Emperor's health. Thupa Inka hadn't left his estate at Chinchero in almost three years, his last appearance in Cuzco having been the day I departed the akllawasi. Her reports were inevitably bad. "He lives only by the will of the gods," she would say, shaking her head.

During these visits I was excused from training to walk with her in the gardens. Atoq must have said something to her, for she never asked about my supposed healing work among the Tipón servants, or when I was coming home to Choqo. What went on at Tipón was not to be questioned. Once, as we strolled arm in arm along the terraces, she remarked that she told people I was tending the sick down valley, but she never mentioned Tipón to them.

"Lord Atoq thinks it wise that no one knows you're here," she said keeping her eyes straight ahead. "People must not associate you with him. It will make your. . . 'service' to the Emperor more effective later." Then she stopped and held her face close to mine, eyes pleading. "But, Qori, please be careful. You're all I have now."

"I will, mother," I promised.

I couldn't help noticing that on most nights she stayed at Tipón she was with Atoq. It pleased me, like seeing my mother and father enjoying each other. Atoq was charming in her presence, even insisting on filling her kero himself, and amused with her constant fussing over his health. Tanta Karwa's tobacco washes cleared his clouded eye, so that both were now equally bright and bottomless, but his stomach still troubled him. Once, during an evening meal I was allowed to share, she snatched a spicy dish away from him, waggling her finger. He laughed, holding up his hands in submission. I wanted to hug them both.

No secrets were kept from me. When Tanta Karwa arrived I attended her meetings with Atoq, and he spoke freely in front of me. Lady Chuqui and her schemes to have her son declared heir remained a concern, and like Achachi, Atoq wasn't pleased that Lord Wallpaya was to be named regent if the Emperor died.

"It's Lord Sapaca," he said spitting the name. "My spies tell me he implies support for Chuqui's son, at least when he talks to her, but publicly he says he'll support the Emperor's choice, which must be Mama Oqllo's son, Titu Cusi. It was also Sapaca who pressured Thupa Inka into naming that greedy Wallpaya future regent. But Wallpaya and

Chuqui are not allied. They hate each other. What is Sapaca playing at? He wants it both ways, and every way, as long as his panaqa and those of Hurincuzco get what they want."

"He is Speaker of Hurincuzco," Tanta Karwa said, "and he must make the best bargains he can on their behalf."

Atoq scowled. "Yes, but he comes dangerously close to driving a wedge between the sayas, setting Hanancuzco against Hurincuzco. That must never happen, at all costs, never!"

My training advanced to the deadly arts. Words and disguises aren't sufficient in all situations, and I had to be prepared to act with force should the need arise. For me, physical strength wasn't even a consideration, but Zapana taught me there are many ways to overcome an opponent of any size with relative ease, surprise and agility being the most important. A simple finger twist - grabbing fingers when the palm faces forward and jerking them back and up - will have a man dancing on his toes, as will jabbing a thumb in under the ear. In more desperate situations fingers rammed up the nostrils and yanked back causes incredible pain, and a claw-like grip on the front of the throat has a similar immobilizing effect. A hard poke just below the ribs leaves an opponent breathless, but a well-placed blow to the groin will have him on his knees in an instant. Although I found the idea of eye gouging repugnant, Zapana assured me that when my life was at stake I would be capable of anything.

Rendering a man unconscious, when I had the element of surprise from behind, turned out to be a simple matter of catching his neck in the crook of my arm and squeezing hard. I practiced this by sneaking up on the Tipón guards, much to their dismay, and found that, if I could hold fast while they thrashed, the struggle soon ended with hardly a sound.

I also increased my skill with the sling until I was able to hit a target the size of my palm from one hundred paces. Zapana presented me with a finely-woven sling of exceptional strength. Because slings are common items, he explained, often carried by men and women for herding or chasing scavengers from the fields, it would appear natural for me to have one about my person. Aside from their ordinary use, they're also effective ligatures. He showed me how to approach a man from behind, and with one deft motion wind the cord around his neck and twist it tight. If I maintained the pressure my victim quickly lost consciousness, and with continued pressure he would die.

Since our duties were accomplished by stealth we couldn't walk about armed with spears, maqanas, or clubs, though Zapana taught me the dodges should I be attacked with such weapons. The only protection allowed was a small obsidian knife, like the one the governor at Ica had given me years before. It rested comfortably beneath my wide belt. It was too small and fragile for stabbing, but effective for cutting throats with a flick.

Eagle Woman's secrets were mine alone, and I was pleased that she, too, fit beneath my belt and out of sight when necessary. There was one other weapon I carried, such an ordinary female thing the men never thought of it, my mantle tupu. Most women's pins have a flattened, half-circle head, but I insisted mine end with two ornate llama heads facing opposite each other. This was thought an eccentricity on my part, but it suited my needs better. The llama heads fit nicely in my clenched fist, while the long pin protruded straight out from my knuckles.

Thus, whether I appeared in my professional role as a healer, or in any of my numerous disguises, I was always armed. Through all this training the most important lesson I learned was confidence - confidence to improvise, confidence to strike in whatever manner required, and confidence to handle any situation under any circumstances. Condin Savana had shown me this, but Atoq's men instilled it in me.

Now I faced the final trial - overcome three armed men intent on stopping me from crossing the line. Two were down. Zapana taught me well, but Tintaya had trained Zapana, and it was Tintaya who now sneered at me. He coiled like a snake ready to strike, fixing me with those cold, piercing eyes. How to best the master?

As with previous tests of all kinds, I wasn't warned in advance of what to expect. I was suddenly called to the training field where Atoq and the others waited, and given my orders - cross the line or die trying. Fortunately when the summons came I wore my native garb of

Kuntisuyu as yet another disguise; not the long dress and mantle of a noble lady, but the short, wrap-around skirt and loose, circular top of a peasant woman. Although not suited to the mountain climate I preferred it when training because it allowed greater freedom, and could be augmented with a long cloak to keep the chill away. When confronted by my three assailants I immediately discarded the cloak to face them unhindered.

I feinted to the left and Tintaya guarded his right, anticipating my moves. None of the usual tricks worked. He knew them all. As long as his eyes remained fixed on mine and alert to my every twitch there was no hope. I had to distract him, but that, too, was a game he knew well. He started to close. My thoughts raced. Think quickly. Something. . . something he has never seen before. But what?

Then it came to me like cool water poured over my head. I allowed him to come within arm's length. He raised his mace and I straightened myself, gave him my winsome girl smile, and pulled up my top exposing my breasts. He faltered, mouth falling open in surprise, eyes on my chest. In that instant I seized his throat in a claw-grip, pulled him toward me and rammed my knee between his legs. He dropped like a stone. I stepped calmly over the line.

Atoq and Zapana roared with laughter. "Well done, Qori!" Zapana exclaimed.

Atoq called to the hapless form curled on the ground, "As you pointed out, Tintaya, she is a woman."

That evening a cool wind rustled the branches along the garden terraces. Atoq walked beside me. The first stars were out and Mama Killa shone full and bright from a cloudless sky.

"You've learned the art well, Qori. Your training is completed, and I'm pleased with you," he said meaning it. He favored me with a proud smile. "Now you're among those chosen few who work quietly to preserve the peace of the Empire. Your praises will never be sung in Cuzco, even your connection with me must remain secret, but be assured the Emperor will know of your service, and one day reward you with whatever you desire."

"What shall I do now, Lord?"

"You know the Emperor has been ill for years, and soon Inti will call Him home. Until a new emperor is named and firmly in power there is danger from within and without. Nothing can be allowed to shatter our unity; without it the Empire is lost. Our duty is to the Heir. No matter from which direction the challenge comes, and no matter what the cost, we must insure a peaceful succession.

"You've heard me speak of the Emperor's sister-consort, Lady Chuqui, and her attempts to have her son declared in place of Titu Cusi. She has the allegiance of some in Cuzco, and also in the provinces. Tintaya will stay close to her Cuzco supporters. They're a tight-lipped bunch accustomed to the ways of intrigue. We still have no idea what their plan is, or when they'll strike, but their provincial confederates are less guarded. A leak at the fringe can reveal the plot at the center. I'm sending agents everywhere. I want you to be my eyes and ears in the lake lands of Qollasuyu."

"Under what guise shall I travel, Lord?"

"You'll be a Qolla servant accompanying Zapana. At his request your brother Qhari will be going also as page. Did you know that Zapana's mother was a Qolla? She was a chosen woman at the Cuzco akllawasi, and later became a lady-in-waiting to my wife."

And your mistress, I thought. Why won't you recognize Zapana?

"Officially, Zapana will be returning to his mother's home province to honor its Hatun Kuraka, who is, in fact, his grandfather. The two of you will learn whether or not the lake peoples have allied themselves with Lady Chuqui, and if so, discover their plan. That's an order. You will succeed. I don't like failure. Zapana will be in charge, of course."

Atoq paused to rub his eyes. "Oh, and one more thing. If you should run across Lord Sapaca stay away from him. He and Lady Sisa left some time ago to tour the shrines of Qollasuyu. I have people watching them. You concentrate on the Qolla and leave Sapaca to others."

Interesting, I thought, that Sapaca should choose this time, with the Emperor's death imminent, to be away from Cuzco.

"Now," Atoq said abruptly, turning his thoughts elsewhere, "two small matters remain for your full induction into the Emperor's service.

First, hide this on your person and carry it with you wherever you go." He handed me a tiny stick banded with colors. "Any official who sees this will know you act with the highest authority, and grant you whatever you need. But don't show it unless absolutely necessary. The fewer people who know about you the better.

"Also, you must have a code name." Atoq stroked his chin thoughtfully and looked up at the night sky. Then a smile came to his lips and he turned to me. "Henceforth, your identity as one of the Emperor's secret agents will be established with the name. . . Inca Moon."

XXI

In which Strange Vessels ply the great inland sea, a Secret Council meets, Death roams the night, and Qori learns a new recipe for peanut sauce.

The sail swelled as the wind shifted to the west, sending the boatmen scurrying to bring the great reed craft back on course. The boat surged over a wave and slid into the hollow leaving a wake. The men grinned. If the wind held we would make the island well before sunset.

Around us the blue-green vastness of Lake Titiqaqa glittered in the afternoon sun. The lake, unpredictable at the best of times, had granted us a fine day. I watched the gulls gliding overhead. As long as the birds stayed with us our passage from the mainland to the big island would be untroubled.

Though I was born on the shores of Mama Qocha, and accustomed to water in all its moods, this was the first time I'd been beyond sight of land, and so entirely at the mercy of the water spirits. Illampu and the Royal Ones floated their snow-capped peaks above the horizon clouds at our backs, but they are the abodes of the ever-watchful mountain spirits, and it was the shores I missed. With fair winds it takes four days to sail the length of Lake Titiqaqa, and a full day to cross. Who would have thought the gods would place such a huge inland sea high in the puna lands of Qollasuyu? For high and cold it is, the air thin and cool, the surface water chilly, and not far below, numbing.

The fishing craft of my youth were merely floats made from netted gourds or inflated sealskins, but those of Titiqaqa are true boats built from the reeds growing abundantly around the lake. They are formed from two large bundles of dried reeds, each tightly stitched, which taper to upturned bow and stern where they are lashed firmly together. On the sides of these rest smaller bundles of equal length to form low gunwales, and the floor is strewn with fresh green stalks. The boats come in many sizes, from small fishing craft holding two people to those that carry ten or twenty. Ours was mid-length, but aside from my three boatmen and myself only four llamas, bound on their sides and looking most unhappy, shared the space.

Most of the vessels we saw that day had sails like ours - a single square of rush matting - but the helmsman excitedly pointed out one swift craft that bore a sail of cloth, a fashion only recently adopted from coastal rafts, which now graced the reed boats of only the wealthiest lords around Lake Titiqaqa.

Soon after casting off we passed a huge reed raft being poled along the shore. It carried a stone column destined for a temple at the south end of the lake, and twenty men worked the poles. My helmsman remarked that without cargo such rafts would carry sixty people.

Throughout the day sails dotted the horizon in all directions, for such is the traffic of Titiqaqa, busy at all times of year. One humble craft passed close and I raised my hand in greeting, but the occupants ignored me.

"Filthy Uru," my helmsman said spitting in their direction.

"From the floating islands?" I asked.

"Floating swamps, more like it," he said turning away in disgust.

"Taquile," the bowman shouted, pointing ahead at the dark outline of the island emerging from the horizon. I returned his smile, feeling more secure with land in sight. But as I watched Taquile rise from the lake my stomach sank. This was no rehearsal at Tipón. Qhari and Zapana waited far behind on the mainland. I am on my own, I thought, and if caught infiltrating the secret council, I will die alone.

"And look at the backside on that one!" the old kuraka had exclaimed when yet another Qolla maiden paraded before Zapana. His grandfather, eyes twinkling, delighted in instructing Zapana and everyone within hearing on selecting potential mistresses. "Hips, boy, hips! That one could give you an army of sons." The girls, all daughters of local chiefs, blushed while they continued serving the meal. I cringed in embarrassment for them, yet any one of them would have gladly taken Zapana in an instant. Little do you know that Zapana prefers your brothers, I thought. The girls smiled shyly at Zapana, pretending not to hear their Hatun Kuraka's assessments of them. I knelt with Qhari behind Zapana and kept my head lowered, reminding myself I was the maidservant Choque, just another of Zapana's retainers.

The journey from K'allachaka to the court of Zapana's grandfather was uneventful, though full of new sights as we traveled the royal road southward into Qollasuyu, passing through provinces with different languages and dress, over high mountain passes, and across the open puna lands where vast herds of llamas and alpacas grazed in the thin air. Though Runasimi is everywhere the language of state, in Qollasuyu the common language is Aymara, of which there are several dialects spoken by various branches of the Qolla, Lupaqa, and Pacaje peoples, some of which I learned in the akllawasi.

Zapana assured me that, though his grandfather had taken part in the great rebellion against Inca rule a generation earlier, he did so reluctantly, and was now a staunch supporter of Thupa Inka, whom the old man repeatedly asked after as if they were long-parted brothers. But other divisions of the Qolla, and the Lupaqa and Pacaje whose lands border the lake, insisted on harkening back to a time when their provinces were independent kingdoms before the Incas came, and these, Zapana reminded me, were the ones to watch.

Since I played the part of Choque, a Qolla serving woman, I wore the garb of that land - a voluminous tent-like dress of heavy black wool that reached to my embroidered slippers. Over the dress I wore an equally large yellow cloak, which comes to the waist in front and hangs to the heels behind. I used a plain, copper tupu pin to fasten it at my breast, as befits a servant, and several smaller tupus adorned my bonnet - a rounded cap like a hood with a wide flap draping halfway down the back to cover my tresses. All women of the lake lands wear versions of this costume, though the dresses of nobles are of much finer cloth and richer colors, and their tupus are silver or gold. I found it a most practical outfit in those cold, rainy puna lands.

Following the imperial manner of showing favor in the provinces, Zapana assumed the men's costume of the lake lands, and had Qhari do the same. They also had slippers, but theirs were of llama hide with the wool turned out, and they wore knee-length tunics with a colored band woven about the middle, and yellow cloaks. Of course, Zapana retained his earspools, and unlike the local men his hair was cropped short in the Inca fashion, but aside from this he pleased his grandfather by donning the high, domed hat worn by lords on the eastern side of the lake, with an upturned crescent ornament on the front, and a pendant with two crossbars at his throat.

The men on the western shores dress similarly, except their tunics are striped, and their hats are conical with a flattened top, and sport a long, jaunty feather at the side. It occurred to me that those conical hats probably fit the shape of their skulls nicely, this being the land of long heads - those who had cloths wrapped about their heads in infancy to make their skulls grow upward.

"Do try the catfish," the old man called out to a Pacaje ambassador, favoring him with a congenial smile. His features hardened when he turned to whisper to Zapana, "Those Pacaje think me a fool, sending that ambassador to keep me busy while the lords of the lake lands hold their meeting without me. Ha! Young pups, all of them. They don't remember the wars that plagued these lands before the Incas brought peace. Oh, I've told them, told them many times that the tribute we send to Cuzco is a guarantee of peace for us all. If it weren't for the Incas, who would settle arguments between the Lupaqa and Pacaje, or between them and ourselves? It would be like it was when my father ruled, nation against nation. But they're too young to remember anything except their fathers dying in the great rebellion, ill-planned venture that it was, and now they think themselves brothers, struggling to throw off Inca bondage. Inca bondage? Ha! It's Inca peace, I tell you. It's peace they grow weary of and - "

"Grandfather," Zapana interrupted, glancing over his shoulder to see if I was listening, "what is this meeting of lords that you've been excluded from?"

The old man turned fox eyes on him. "They think I don't know. Ha! I have my own spies, too, and I can tell you that three days from now all the lords of the lake lands will be meeting on Taquile, in secret, so they think."

"What about?" Zapana asked casually.

The old man frowned. "I don't know exactly. My spies said it has something to do with an emissary from Cuzco, but they must be mistaken. They're planning trouble, that much is certain. But don't worry. I'll have a word with the Inca governor and he'll put a stop to it."

The governor wasn't pleased to see me when I arrived at his quarters in the middle of the night. He handed back my banded stick of authority with a sigh. "Yes, the Hatun Kuraka told me about the meeting," he said, holding his head in his hands and rubbing his eyes. "Now, tell me something I don't know, beginning with who dares to disturb my sleep."

I leaned forward and whispered in his ear, "I am Inca Moon."

He blinked and began twitching his fingers as if fondling the knots on a khipu. Suddenly he froze and looked up, wide-eyed. "But you're a woman."

"My Lord is most observant."

"But. . . but. . . ."

"Perhaps you'd like to verify my identity with my master, the Lord of Tipón?"

This reference to Atoq had immediate effect. The governor swallowed hard, and waved the guards and servants from the room. "No, of course not. . . whatever you need. . . how can I be of service?"

Now our boat sailed into the crescent-shaped harbor of Taquile. Hundreds of stone steps led upward from the pebble beach through long strands of terraces to the summit. My boatmen dropped sail and took up poles, guiding us in among the vessels littering the shore. The llama at my feet raised its head and spat at me, ill-tempered beast.

When the governor said he planned to disrupt the secret meeting on Taquile with a surprise visit of his own, I suggested a different plan. Our mission was, after all, to determine whether Lady Chuqui had enlisted the native lords of Titiqaqa in her scheme to have her son declared emperor. She needed the support of many provinces to force that claim, and with the old Hatun Kuraka's remark that an emissary from Cuzco had secretly contacted the Titiqaqa lords - all except him - it seemed probable that intrigue was indeed in the making.

Rather than simply breaking up the secret council I thought it wiser to let it proceed, and learn precisely what Chuqui had in mind, and what the lords were prepared to do for her. Zapana agreed. He would have gone with me but, being the grandson of the old Inca-loving Hatun Kuraka, the visiting Pacaje ambassador kept a close watch on him. However, it was Zapana who solved the problem of getting me on the island. He suggested I deliver llamas for the chiefs' feast on Taquile; supposedly from a dull-witted cousin of his who lived farther down the lake, and would certainly not be attending the meeting. The governor provided the animals, and Zapana borrowed the vessel and boatmen from his grandfather. Qhari was the only one not in favor of the plan. He wanted to go with me, or take my place, fearing for my safety - brother dear. Zapana assured him that a woman alone would draw less attention, and that I was specially trained for such duties, and Qhari eventually conceded only because he had no say in the matter anyway. Still, Qhari wanted to know what I planned to do upon reaching the island, and with Taquile now looming before me I asked myself the same question.

I humbly introduced myself to the captain of the guard at the landing as the maidservant Choque, and politely insisted I deliver the llamas in person to the Lord of Taquile, so my master would receive due credit. He refused to let me pass until I shyly inquired whether such a handsome man would be kept on duty all evening, for I hoped to stay the night and hated to be alone. The way opened immediately. I glanced back at the boat. The helmsman gave me a nod; he and his men stood by, ready to sail at a moment's notice.

Herding four skittish llamas up five hundred and thirty stone steps proved to be the least difficult part of my stay on the island. The Lord of Taquile came out to nod at the animals, and hear me recite a flowery speech in which Zapana's cousin was credited with the gift, a small token of his everlasting esteem and loyalty to the great Lord of the Island, and requesting that his maidservant Choque, and her boatmen, be allowed to rest before returning to the mainland. He frowned at this last part and looked at the sky. The sun sank low. Boats did not sail at night. "Sleep on the beach," he said turning away. But his steward stepped forward and studied the colored wool tassels dangling from the llamas' ears. The lord paused and questioned him with a look. I kept my eyes straight ahead, but my heart stopped. Had the governor remembered to change the ownership tassels?

"Who did you say sent these animals?" the steward asked suspiciously.

I repeated the cousin's name, adding, "I believe my master took them from some Incas, and thought it would give my Lord pleasure to eat the Incas' meat for a change."

The men exchanged a look and chuckled. "It will indeed," the lord replied. "They've taken enough of ours."

I grinned innocently as they left, then reached up and fingered one of the tassels - red and blue, the colors of the imperial herds. Be this a lesson to you, Inca Moon, I said inwardly. Never let others attend to the details. You should have thought of this yourself.

Pretending to lose my way back to the landing, I wandered the island in the gathering dusk. Inti streaked the clouds red, bathing the peninsulas jutting out from the mainland with His last rays. Around me tidy stone walls enclosed fields and pastures, and lined the paths between villages now falling silent in the evening calm. The island is a model of efficiency, no land wasted, even the steep sides are terraced to the water's edge. An islander hurried by, his long woolen cap folded over one side of his head, earflaps up, hands busy with some small weaving. An odd custom, I was reminded, but here on Taquile the men pride themselves on their weaving more than the women.

Torchlight twinkled far out on the water. Boats still arrived. For an island of three hundred families scattered in several villages, Taquile was unusually busy, and crowded with warriors. I had already spotted Lupaqa and Pacaje attire among the various Qolla costumes; the lords of the lake lands gathered and soon the council would begin. My stomach tightened.

I considered returning to the boat and fleeing back to the mainland. Perhaps they already suspected me because of the tassels on the llamas, I thought. That was the governor's mistake. He should have removed them, but no, instead I was nearly caught because of his incompetence. It's not my fault. I did my part and it didn't work out. The governor can take the blame.

Now then, Inca Moon, take hold, I cautioned myself. She who allows fear to control her loses all. She who rules fear triumphs. You are the maidservant Choque bringing llamas for the chiefs' feast. The Lord of Taquile himself gave you permission to stay the night. What would Choque do? She would go to the kitchens to help prepare the animals, and once there. . . Inca Moon will do what she must.

I watched the ample woman plant her hands on her hips. "You there, guard. Don't give me that insolent look. I'm the Personal Cook of the Lord of Pacaje. That's better. Now, where are the kitchens?"

The guard pointed up the path, and the woman, still red-faced and puffing from climbing those five hundred and thirty stone steps, adjusted the bundle on her back with a heavy sigh and started forward again.

"My Lady," I said, stepping from the shadows, "are you really the famous cook of the Pacaje? Such an honor!" I bowed low. "Please let me take your burden and escort you to the kitchens. I can't believe it's really you. Such an honor."

Finally being treated with the respect she felt her station deserved, she allowed me to shoulder her bundle and babble along at her side. When this chance meeting occurred I was on my way to the kitchens, wondering how I was going to talk my way past the guards. Security tightened noticeably since the afternoon, with sentries now standing in small groups everywhere, and the Island Lord's palace - really just a cluster of small, rough stone buildings with a feasting hall - sprouted an encircling wall of soldiers. But the haughty cook whose vanity I now stoked offered a way through.

Oh, such good fortune, I rattled on. Who would believe that I, the least of women, who always dreamed of cooking for nobility, would actually meet the famous cook of the Pacaje, and even carry her bundle for her. Of course I understood that she couldn't share her secrets, of course not, and I wouldn't dream of asking, but perhaps there was some small tip, a little something she could pass on so I could always say I learned it from her. And oh, I'd give anything just to stand at her side and watch her create her famous fish soup - a safe guess, everyone ate fish soup - and I'd never get in her way, no, never, but I'd be so honored just to fetch anything she needed, instantly. But oh, such a pity the guards will never let me pass, because I could be so useful, and I'd make sure everyone stayed out of her way, and I'd bring her aqha and wait on her, and. . . . Her assistant? She'd do that for me? Yes, yes, just for the night, of course, but, really? Oh, my prayers were answered!

The Personal Cook of the Lord of Pacaje entered the smoky kitchen, her adoring assistant Choque announcing her arrival in a loud, important voice. The other women paused to stare, more surprised than impressed, then turned back to their tasks. The kitchen was an open-fronted shed adjoining the feasting hall. Pots covered three clay ovens, and cauldrons hung over open fires. Roasting spits held haunches of llama and deer, a stack of skinned guinea pigs waited on a mat, catfish hung on a rack, sacks of maize, quinoa, and potatoes stood nearby, and huge urns of aqha crowded a corner. Children scurried about delivering armfuls of precious firewood to their mothers, while others brought shawls full of reeds and dried llama dung to feed the fires. Arguments erupted over the use of some knife, or pot, or space at the hearths. The big grinding stones rocked back and forth, smashing peppers into hot sauce. Women borrowed pinches of herbs from their neighbors, and paused to sniff at their creations. The Personal Cook of the Lord of Pacaje smiled at the confusion, calmly threw back her cloak, rubbed her hands, and with a nod sent her assistant Choque to elbow a place at one of the ovens.

I will say this of her, she was indeed a master, surpassing even my old cooking teacher at the akllawasi, and for as long as I stayed at her side, in truth, I learned a great deal. It turned out to be a precious load of peanuts she carried in her bundle, and from her, the Personal Cook of the Lord of Pacaje, I learned to make the tangy peanut sauce for roast guinea pig which I am famous for today. I know, my mouth waters at the thought of it, too. No, I won't tell you the recipe. Garnish your own guinea pigs.

In the midst of this bustle I watched maids coming and going through a door in the center of the back wall, which opened directly into the feasting hall. Two guards stood with spears crossed at the entrance. Music and laughter filtered back into the hum of the kitchen. The thud of drums and jingle of ankle bells announced a dance troupe performing.

Heaping platters disappeared through the door, to return empty and be refilled. A steward appeared in the entrance and held up three fingers, signaling for three fresh urns of aqha, then hurried back inside to his duties. It required two people to lift one of those urns, and seeing my chance, I slipped away from my mistress and nudged one of the women aside, taking her place across from another as we swung the urn to our shoulders. The crossed spears parted. We entered the feasting hall.

Hundreds crowded that long, narrow room: lords and ladies seated on cushions around the central fires, counselors and officers squatting behind them, and the rest were guards, servants, and performers. Not a trace of Inca presence, I noted from the corner of my eye, neither in dress nor symbol, not even in the pottery vessels they ate from, and only Aymara dialects could be heard above the flutes and drums. We set the urns in a corner, but while the others picked up the empty containers and retreated with heads bowed I lingered, busying myself filling a jug from one of the urns and then moving along the back wall offering aqha to the guards, which, I assured them, their lord wished them to have. I soon became quite popular with them.

Eventually the Lord of Taquile rose and clapped his hands. "Fill the drinking vessels," he ordered his steward, "then clear the hall." The servants and performers filed out. I offered more aqha to those around me, and then faded into a corner. A nearby guard frowned at me. "My lord asked me to stay," I whispered. He pushed up his bottom lip and looked back at the hearth. I exhaled, and pressing my back to the wall slid down slowly until I crouched behind an urn in the shadows.

When the room appeared empty of servants the Island Lord gestured to a man across from him, who stood and addressed the assembly. "My Lords and Ladies," he began, "the tyrant Thupa Inka is dying." He held up his hand to quiet the cheering that followed this announcement. "Two months ago during my residency in Cuzco I was secretly consulted on the matter of the succession."

So, I thought, here we have the emissary. Not an Inca but one of their own, a Lupaqa by dress.

The man swept the room with his eyes, pausing for effect. "If Mama

Oqllo's boy Titu Cusi becomes the next emperor, nothing will change for us here. If, however, Prince Wari, son of Lady Chuqui, is granted the Royal Fringe there will be many changes. The greedy Incas, like those who cling to their estates in our lands, support Titu Cusi, but it's said that Hurincuzco and many in the provinces favor a more enlightened reign by Prince Wari."

"And what does Wari offer?" a woman asked, cutting straight to the point.

"Lady Chuqui herself has promised that if we of Titiqaqa support Wari, many of the Inca estates and some of the imperial lands will be returned to us, along with ten thousand head of llamas and alpacas for each lord. Further, many of our people serving as retainers and colonists in distant parts of their Tawantinsuyu will be returned, and our military levy will be reduced by half."

Silence fell. It was a generous offer indeed.

"And how are we to show our support?" a man asked.

"We'll be notified as soon as Wari is declared crown prince in the great square of Cuzco. On that day each of us will lay siege to the Inca settlements in our lands, and, if there is strife over the succession and their southern army remains loyal to Titu Cusi, we'll crush them. It will be the same in other provinces. Those of Hurincuzco will secure Prince Wari's place in Cuzco, and protect our sons who dwell there as hostages. There will be no army of retribution troubling us as there was in the time of our fathers."

Another woman spoke. "Can we trust this Lady Chuqui to keep the bargain?"

"My Lady, with respect," the speaker replied, "I wouldn't trust an Inca with my shit let alone my life." When the laughter died he continued, "I suggest we accept Lady Chuqui's proposal. . . but, not act until we're sure which way bends the tree. Consider. If the Incas fall out among themselves over who will rule them, might they not recall their southern army to fight in Cuzco? And while they're tearing themselves apart," he raised his voice and his hands, "we will rise and claim the lands of our ancestors!"

In the roar that followed the crowd rose, stamping and cheering, waving spears and maces, women and men shouting in a chorus that trembled the stone walls. And I was with them, blown to my feet as if by a gale. It wasn't the words; it was the emotion of so many hearts beating as one. Had I been born a Qolla or Lupaqa or Pacaje, I would have joined them in an instant. As it was, in the frenzy I hugged the man in front of me - a lord, but neither he nor I cared - and then the lady with him, and then another, and another, and as people stumbled from one embrace to next, cheering as if the lake lands were already free, I found myself standing by the kitchen door.

The night wind chilled my face, bringing reason back. Those outside were unsure what had happened, but the joyous clamor from within reflected on excited faces. Warriors shook their weapons and called lustily to one another. The air came alive. As if hearing their cries to war, Illap'a split the sky with lightning and cracked His sling, sending thunder rolling across the lake. The men cheered and roared back at Him. In response He ripped the horizon with a many-armed bolt, lighting the night. I pulled my hood low and started for the landing.

"Where are you going?" The sentry stood in my path, a youth barely of warrior age.

I tried to smile. "To join one of your comrades down by the water."

"What's going on over there?" He gestured to the shouting at the palace.

I shrugged and tried to pass. "Wait," he said, holding his spear crossways. "My orders are that no one passes without the captain's permission. You'll have to come with me."

There was no time for this. The darkness and coming storm on the lake were nothing compared with the urgency for flight, or with the gravity of the news only I could deliver. Nothing would stop Inca Moon.

I reached beneath my cloak, finding Eagle Woman suspended snug against my side. No, I decided, why waste a stinger on this one? I opened my shoulder bag. "Look," I said, "if you let me go I'll give you this." He bent forward to examine the obsidian knife. I closed my eyes and heard Condin Savana say, "Hesitate and you are lost." Zapana's voice said, "Don't think. Act." Suddenly the boy was on his knees, both hands at his throat. I stared at my knife hand. It was covered in blood. The boy gurgled, his tunic soaked, and collapsed forward, leaving a wide smear of blood on my dress.

I wanted to drop the knife and run. No, I caught myself, think. Get rid of the body. It's dark. They won't find him or see the blood on my dress. Another flash of lightning lit the night, revealing a widening pool of wetness around the boy's head. Be quick, I thought, drag him behind that wall. Now, to the boat.

I flew through the night and, in what seemed no more than a breath, I found myself at the top of the stairway leading down to the landing. Here, two more guards faced me.

"Where are you off to in such a hurry?"

"I'm to meet the Captain of the Guard down there," I said pointing down the steps.

"Old Toothless? You'll do better to stay here with us," one said, leering. In the darkness they didn't notice the blood on my clothes.

"I don't think you know what you're asking. For your sakes you had better let me pass." The menace in my voice was real, but they seemed to think I was threatening them with the wrath of Old Toothless.

"Let him have her," one said with a shrug.

The other stepped forward. "Very well, just as soon as she's been thoroughly searched." His hands darted under my cloak and squeezed my breasts. I should have let him, but my training taught me to respond instantly to sudden moves. In the same moment I rammed my knee into his groin. He fell to his knees, retching.

I looked apologetically at his surprised partner. "Sorry. Would you like to try? I promise not to hurt you quite so badly."

It all happened too fast for him. He shook his head as if to clear it. "Be gone," he said, bending over his comrade.

I reached the bottom step when I felt a tug at my elbow. "Ah, my pretty, you did come back. Come here and let me keep you warm."

I looked up at the Captain of the Guard, Old Toothless, an ugly fellow forty years my senior. Behind him a fire glowed down the beach where the boatmen gathered, except for mine, who waited faithfully nearby.

"Of course I returned, you handsome brute. Now send your men away. I don't like an audience."

He grinned showing vacant gums, wiped the slobber from his chin, and waved the others off toward the fire. "Go and warm yourselves. I have my own warmer here." When their laughter faded I took his gnarled hand and led him behind some bushes.

A moment later I emerged wiping the knife on my cloak. It didn't matter; I was covered in blood anyway. The second kill was easier. My hands no longer shook.

"But it's night and a storm is coming," my helmsman protested. The other two nodded.

"Would you rather chance the waters or die under torture when they catch us? Or perhaps I should just cut your throats for you now?" Fingers of lightning illuminated the night again. The shock of what they saw showed in their faces - a small woman, knife in hand, covered in the blood of two men, eyes burning. They delivered the maidservant Choque that afternoon, but it was Inca Moon they now faced on the night beach.

"Move! Put your backs into it," the helmsman shouted. The three dragged the reed craft over the pebble landing. I bounded through shallow, frigid water, and clambered aboard as the helmsman bellowed, "To the poles. Push off." The boatmen strained, but the big craft seemed hardly to move. Suddenly torches appeared at the top of the stairway and a cry came faintly from above, "There's a spy in our midst. Seal the harbor." They'd found the boy.

Another lightning flash showed men running up the beach toward us. A voice, much closer, shouted, "Where's the Captain of the Guard? Look, there's a boat leaving. Stop them."

Then with a jolt the stern found deep water and we glided out. But one of the guards plunged after us, and, waist deep, grasped the stern. "You there, hold. Drop those poles."

My helmsman glanced over his shoulder at me, and then rammed the butt of his pole into the man's face. "Now raise the sail," he ordered, "and may the gods watch over us."

We needed that invocation. Above, a line of torches raced down the stairway like a fiery serpent. A voice on the beach yelled, "Launch the boats. No, the big ones."

The wind blew in our favor, gusting from the south, and as we cleared the shelter of the island our sail caught full, driving us straight for the north shore. But much water lay between the mainland and us, and with only three boatmen and a reed sail our passage wasn't swift enough. Three boats coasted out from the island in pursuit. The lead craft, already in our wake, was a long, sleek vessel built for speed, with a huge sail of cloth. Warriors crowded its length. When its sail caught it leapt forward like a hound on the scent. The other two, of equal size but with reed sails, flanked the leader, trailing several lengths behind. Shouts echoed across the water. Torches flickered over the swells, marking their advance moment by moment: eight boat lengths, seven, five.

I looked up at my helmsman. His face was hard and fixed straight ahead. His eyes met mine for an instant. Hopeless, they said.

XXII

In which is given a Sordid Narrative detailing the manner in which these misguided Indians Sinned Mightily with their bodies, and reveled in Obscene Acts of Lust which no persons of pure heart should read lest they be infected with vile impulses.

A week had passed since my capture by the Uru. The storm that saved me from the Aymara pursuit boats already seemed like a dream. The Uru kept me bound but treated me well. My 'hostess,' the Uru headman's wife, even appeared friendly, especially when she spoke of the enormous ransom the Aymara lords agreed to pay for my return.

After the first days, when rest and bowls of fish soup restored my spirit, I planned my escape from the floating island. Eagle Woman remained on a cord around my neck, for the Uru feared to touch a spirit guardian. But I didn't want to unleash her deadly secrets unless necessary, and the Uru guards weren't difficult to handle. With my strength replenished I wiggled from my bonds and broke free one night, leaving three of them unconscious in my flight. I slipped into the cold lake once again, intent on swimming to the mainland. But they soon discovered I was missing and their boats caught up with me. They hauled me in, coiled me tight in one long rope from shoulders to feet, and returned me to my hut with guards doubled. And that's how the Qolla found me when they arrived a few days later to pay the ransom - tied stiff as a corpse. I was relieved when the owner of the rope demanded its return before handing me over to the Qolla, who settled for binding my wrists.

"You're early," the Uru headman said. The Qolla porters paid no attention and continued unloading the boats. Mounds of blankets, clothing, and clay pots rose around the landing. The Uru eyed them greedily.

The Qolla leader walked over to us. "So this is the one? Not much to look at. I hope she's worth what we're paying." He spit in my face. I winced. He glared back, fury rising. "Inca bitch!" The slap that followed spun my head.

The headman held up his hand. "Once you've unloaded and departed she's yours to do with as you wish - and good riddance to her for she's caused enough trouble on my island - but until then she's under my care, and far too valuable to be mistreated."

The Qolla gave me an evil look.

"And the sail?" the headman asked.

"Here it is now," the Qolla leader said. He indicated four men struggling with a bundle. "One cotton sail, worth a fortune by itself, and the two hundred blankets, one hundred dresses, cloaks, and tunics, and three hundred pots. All here as agreed, you filthy reed-eating bastard, and now the woman is mine."

The headman beamed pleasantly. "Take her, and may the water spirits prepare a bed for you and your family, so you can feed the fishes we will catch and eat, you stinking, lice-ridden Qolla shit." The headman had a most poetic way with the Qolla language.

But in his excitement at the unheard-of wealth being dumped on his island he failed to notice the Qolla leader, though dressed for the part, wore a long-haired wig. Of course, I recognized Zapana the moment he stepped ashore, but his eyes flashed caution, so I held my tongue and played along. The slap was an unnecessary bit of over-acting, I thought sullenly.

"Sails," one of Zapana's men shouted. We turned to see a flotilla of Lupaqa boats coming into view.

"Well, that concludes our business," Zapana said briskly to the headman. "We'll be off now that our escort is here. And don't ever let me catch you in my lands, you puke-eating Uru."

"May your wife one day find a man to satisfy her," the headman replied amiably.

With the island fading behind us, I held out my bound wrists for Zapana to cut the cords. The Lupaqa vessels neared the Uru landing. They'd soon know their prey had flown, but the wind filled our sail and they'd never catch us.

"I should leave you tied up," Zapana griped. "Do you know what you've cost us?" I shrugged. He cut the cords and stared at me intently. "Tell me you have news. Tell me that enormous ransom is worth it."

"I have all the Aymara plans," I replied calmly.

Zapana exhaled in relief. "Maybe Lord Atoq will let you keep your head. Maybe."

I shrugged again.

After my report detailing everything that happened since leaving his grandfather's court, it was my turn to ask questions. "Where's Qhari? Does he know I'm alive?"

"He didn't know you were dead. I haven't told him anything. Our boat is bound for Puno now. He'll meet us there at the Inca garrison tomorrow."

"What happened to the Pacaje ambassador? I thought he was watching you?"

"He was. He had an accident," Zapana said dryly.

"How did you know the Uru had me?"

"I didn't. At first I thought you dead." There was a hush in his voice when he said this, as if admitting a private weakness. "I heard your boat was over-turned in a storm, and there were no survivors, but then my grandfather's spies reported the Aymara lords were secretly raising a huge ransom to give to the Uru. The spies had no idea who the ransom was for, but I guessed. The Aymara usually take what they want from the Uru, so the ransom had to be for someone extremely important to all of them, someone they couldn't chance losing. The goods were collected on Taquile, so I reasoned you were being held on one of the Uru islands nearby, and since everything had to arrive by today this was obviously the agreed time for the exchange."

"So you pretended to be the ransom party. Clever."

"We were lucky to get you away before the real emissaries arrived. Those were their boats approaching when we left."

"Why didn't you come under Thupa Inka's banner? Why pay the ransom?"

"We couldn't risk running into the Lord of Taquile and his friends. Open fighting between Incas and Aymara could touch off the lake lands, and if you had information we wanted to keep it secret. The governor provided the ransom from the royal stores, and my grandfather lent me these vessels and men. Tomorrow he'll contact the plotters and offer to sell you for twice the Uru ransom. They'll try to steal you back, of course, and this will go easy for them, but in the attempt a young woman who looks very much like you will die. That will satisfy everyone."

"Who is this woman?"

"Does it matter? A peasant, I suppose. She's the price we pay to keep the Empire at peace. . . along with what I gave the Uru today, and the five thousand alpacas and five cloth sails the governor promised to my grandfather for his assistance in this. Also, the Inca garrison in his province is being tripled. Your information comes at a high price, Qori."

Dusk settled over Puno, a gathering dimness hugging the land, but overhead the first stars appeared in a clear night sky. Looking down from the garrison above, the village was a field of thatch roofs sloping toward the lakeshore, lights twinkling here and there where hearths still burned, and occasional torches threading the streets, their bearers masked in shadow. Zapana's summons reached me as I left my bath, my stomach already satisfied with civilized food, and a new dress awaiting me. Now, clean and warm and dry for the first time in a week, I was determined that whatever Zapana had to say wouldn't spoil my mood.

What does he want, I wondered. I completed my mission; it isn't my fault if it didn't go as planned and cost a princely ransom.

Qhari will be joining us in the morning, I thought. Best not to trouble him with the details of my escapades. It already seems like a dream. Did I, Qori Qoyllur, really do all those things? No, it was Inca Moon doing what she had to do. It was Inca Moon who slew those men, and she did it for her emperor. Tonight Inca Moon can rest, and Qori will enjoy some peace for a change.

Outside the garrison I would wear Qolla clothes and be Choque the maidservant again, but here in this island of security I allowed myself the pleasure of dressing like a proper Inca woman. The garrison commander provided me with an outfit of finest alpaca - thin, light cloth that draped beautifully, and clung softly against my skin. I floated gracefully like the lady I knew myself to be.

"Qori, come in," Zapana said waving a hand in greeting. He was alone and lying back against pillows, a kero in hand, and naked but for his loincloth. The guard bowed me past and slid the door closed on his way out. Tiny lamps burned in the wall niches, casting the room in soft light and shadow; and a low brazier glowed in the middle, warming the rush matts and guanaco hides strewn about. "Aqha?" he asked casually. Without rising he held up a jug.

I took a kero and knelt beside him. While he poured he said, "It is well. The commander dispatched a runner with your news while I bathed, and Lord Atoq will hear it in a few days. He already knows about the expense, of course; but hopefully he'll find the result worth the investment."

Whether my life was worth the cost wasn't a question, an agent's life seldom is. I made the finger-dip to Mama Pacha and raised my kero to Zapana. "What do you think?" I asked.

He returned the toast and said, "I don't think. I follow orders."

My eyes drifted over his languid body, a male animal body, golden brown in the lamplight. For an instant I imagined him with Qhari in the glade and thought, What a waste. But Qhari took his pleasure from this body in ways I could only dream of, and I pushed the image aside. I felt uncomfortable. "Why did you summon me?"

He pursed his lips and made a smacking sound. "Just to tell you the report is on its way. Our work is done for now, and I thought we might enjoy a few keros together."

Why doesn't he have the decency to wear a tunic? I wondered. He lies there displaying himself. Is he taunting me?

"Good," I said, downing mine and holding it out to be refilled. "I never thanked you for fetching me from the Uru. You played your part well."

He smiled warmly. "As did you, but if I hadn't come I'm sure you'd have found a way out yourself, eventually. Here's to us. We make a good team."

I followed his toast, both of us emptying our tumblers and laughing as we wiped the aqha from our chins. He lifted a finger to the corner of my mouth to dab at a drop, but his touch lingered. "Qori, you're a remarkable woman." His voice was low, like the purring of a great cat.

His fingertip traced my lips.

"Well. . . and you're a remarkable man. Here, let me fill your kero." I turned away from him and took the jug, replenishing my tumbler at the same time.

Fool, what are you doing? I cursed myself. Don't drink with him, just get up and leave. What's he doing? He's a man-woman isn't he? What about Qhari?

"It's warm in here," I said.

"Remove your shawl." It was a dare.

I lifted my chin and smirked at him. This is a game, I told myself, nothing more. He said 'no' to me before, and he's Qhari's man. I'm safe with him. Very well, Zapana, let's see how far you'll go.

I plucked the tupu from my shawl, never taking my eyes from him. He rolled on his side and leaned on his elbow facing me, gazing steadily at my eyes. Heat rose in my cheeks. I opened the shawl and let it slip behind, puffing out my chest for him. He allowed himself an appraising look. Still expecting him to laugh or turn away any moment, I stretched out, propping myself on my elbow, bringing my face close to his. "Yes, Zapana, this is more comfortable," I said giving him sultry eyes.

Now is when he'll bolt, I thought. What a wicked game to play with Qhari's lover.

He leaned toward me and paused, the warmth of his breath on my lips. I trembled, thinking, He's not going to kiss me?

I still wanted to pretend it was a game, but when his mouth brushed mine it wasn't. Just a momentary, tentative pressing of lips, and then a nuzzle on my neck and his breath coming faster. Motionless, I stared straight ahead, begging him in my mind to stop, because I could not. He brought his moist lips to mine again, searing me, stealing my breath and my will.

I wanted to say, You're a man-woman, what are you doing? but no sound came. Expertly, he slipped a tupu from its shoulder-fastening and pushed back the side-fold of my dress, revealing a naked breast. My eyes must have been wide as an owl's, but my mouth remained silent and frozen in surprise. A look of curiosity came over his face, and with two fingers he stroked my nipple, watching in fascination as it stiffened, then he pinched hard and pulled.

I may have moaned, I can't remember, but I do remember crushing my mouth to his in frenzy - a wet, open-mouthed kiss that ignited him to passion. Pushing him on his back I sucked and bit at his lips and searched his mouth, my hands caressing hard bronze muscle.

T'ito, the only man I'd known before this, was a cold disappointment, but all the lust and pent-up hunger now pulsated through me, and Zapana couldn't have escaped had he wanted. My hunger caught him by surprise - he didn't know what fires he aroused - but he gave back eagerly, my fire stoking his. I hadn't known such abandon since Sumaq T'ika took me in her arms, and the passion isn't so different, the need of one body for another, but now I had a willing male and curiosity inflamed me.

I sat up and threw my dress aside, then tore at his loincloth, whining with urgency. He stopped my shaking hands and calmly undid the knot himself. I yanked the garment aside revealing its treasure, and when I saw it I stopped in wonder, devouring it with my eyes. A sturdy male pole, hairless, smooth and thick-veined, mushrooming at the tip, and its two companions tucked in a sack big enough to fill my hand. T'ito had denied me that which the Chimu girl in the akllawasi spoke of, but I watched Qhari do it to Zapana and knew he wouldn't protest. I lowered my mouth to its craving, licked from base to tip, and parted my lips to savor the pleasures Qhari knew. Zapana relaxed with a deep sigh, surrendering to my whims.

I couldn't get enough of his throbbing maleness, lovingly drawing it over my face and breasts, then licking and kissing and nibbling the beautiful thing before once more returning it to my lips for deeper caresses. Kneeling over his prone body, I felt a hand come around and search between my thighs from behind. My knees sprang apart. His fingers found abundant wetness and began stroking my lips, then one digit coyly circled the entrance until I thought I would die if he didn't delve inward. First one finger, then two more entered causing me to release his pesqo and gasp at this delightful intrusion.

I could not but sit up straight then, rocking back and forth on those devilish fingers, lost to all but their insistent probing. Zapana turned on his side to bring his other hand into play at the front, rubbing his thumb against the place of passion while lifting his hungry lips to my breast. Yes, Zapana knew how to please a woman's body, and his eagerness showed he knew how to derive his pleasure from hers, too.

But it was an awkward position to hold for long, and as much as I wanted his hands to continue I wanted his pesqo more. I lifted myself and fell beside him, grabbing for his manhood. He made as if to resist, pushing me away while a look of wild glee played on his face. With a flare of frustration I lunged at him, rolling him on his back. He laughed and a frantic wrestling match began, which at first I was determined to win, then happily ready to lose. Straining against his strength was strangely exciting, making him prove himself persistent and worthy of the capture.

I became like a wild animal, biting and scratching, wriggling to escape his grasp, but soon found myself forced onto my hands and knees with him kneeling behind, poised. For a heartbeat I thought he might enter me as he did Qhari. But if that is his pleasure, I thought, he can have me anyway he wants.

Then I felt the smooth knob of his pesqo pressing the entrance to my raka, and with no resistance or need for guidance slipping just inside. I couldn't wait. Pushing back against him I impaled myself fully, taking his shaft to the hilt. He growled an animal growl and leaned over me, fists bunched against the pallet on either side, with arms braced straight, and bit the back of my neck with a throaty snarl as if I might try to escape. I responded from some place deep in my woman's soul - a tiny female thing overpowered yet leading her mate with her own desperate need, hissing back encouragement to his growls, motionless and open to his pounding thrusts.

He stopped suddenly and brought his body upright. I rocked against him, urging him on. His hands seized my hips in a metal grip to still me, and the sharp intake of breath between clenched teeth told me he was holding himself back to enjoy his wildcat a little longer. I waited patiently, catching my breath and savoring the feel of him inside me, my raka gripping the welcome intruder in spasms. Then, gently, he withdrew and collapsed on his back, his pesqo pointing straight up his belly.

There was a strange look in his eyes when he lay there panting, a questioning look of wonder and surprise. Had I not known better I might have thought I was the first woman he was ever with, but Zapana was an accomplished lover with either sex, and I was still too much in the throes of passion to pause for conversation. He watched while I pushed his legs apart and knelt between, then fastened my hand around the base of his shaft and brought it upright. His eyes fixed on mine, seeing the hooded, consuming passion simmering there, and when I traced my tongue over my lips to signal my intent he took on a peaceful look of total surrender. I paused in wonder, knowing that face but never having seen it cast in surrender to anything or anyone. I sensed this was a rare moment, that few, if any, had ever seen that look.

When I lowered my mouth to its pleasure I tasted Sumaq T'ika. No, not Sumaq - me, woman - female tang on a decidedly male shape, mingled and teasing my palate. In a moment of abandoned erotica I pretended it was Sumaq's musk, and perhaps the pesqo was hers too. Zapana and Sumaq in one - now there was bliss!

When I sensed Zapana's moment was near I forced myself to stop, for I wasn't done with him yet. He whimpered. I straddled him and guided his shaft, just the tip at first, then deeper, fuller, my raka demanding all of him. Arching back, I placed my hands on his legs and rocked gently at first, then faster, and harder, all thoughts gone and consumed with sensation, my body its own mistress. Forward then, leaning over him, forcing my breasts to his mouth, my hips thrusting violently, frantic, demanding, forcing him, taking him, possessing him until he vanished and there was nothing but wave after wave of shattering cloudbursts lifting me to the gods.

When the world reappeared I found myself curled up with my head on Zapana's shoulder. "I thought you didn't like women," I said lazily.

He smiled through closed eyes and said, "I married one, didn't I?"

"Yes, but I thought. . . I mean. . . you and Qhari?"

He chuckled. "Yes, Qhari told me you knew about us, and you know about my wife. Are you surprised? My wife chooses to live at another of grandfather Tupac Amaru's estates near Lake Muyna, far down-valley from Cuzco. We enjoy each other when I visit. As for Qhari and his kind, well, I'm a man of broad tastes."

Broad tastes? I thought. Evidently. But you said "Qhari and his kind." You don't count yourself one of them? Qhari told me he loves you, and he thinks you love him. Oh Qhari, do you know he's just play-ing with you? It will break your heart to know the truth.

"And me?" I asked. "Am I another exotic dish?"

He yawned and stretched like a cat. "It's been a while since I've been with a woman. I was curious. Don't tell me you didn't enjoy it, too."

There was nothing cruel in his voice, and it was true I knew ecstasy. I was relieved he didn't speak of love, or try to make it more than what it was - a splendid thing shared once, like travelers at a warm hearth. It was real, yes very real - the urgent excitement, the mutual search and dis-covery, the gasps and moans of passion, the shared surrender to sensa-tion - and through it all an undercurrent of feeling, strong, genuine, that connected our souls in harmony; yet that tenderness was now denied by silent agreement.

It's desire that drives us, I told myself, a shared need born of loneli-ness and curiosity and the camaraderie of dangers shared, but not love. It can't be. We're friends, Zapana and I, and he watches over Qhari and me in his own peculiar way. Does it excite him to know he's now had brother and sister? I wondered, amused at the thought.

"No, Zapana, I'll not deny it was good, but why now? We could have done this long ago, that night on the way back from the jungle, or at Tipón."

He sighed at the memory. "Yes, that night you came out to watch the heavens and we stood by the llama corral. I was sorely tempted, Qori," he said. "I knew you wanted me, and I was drawn to your flame. But. . ." he sighed again, "I couldn't risk it."

Risk? Whatever he meant, I knew his words came from the heart. I snuggled closer. "You couldn't risk what?"

"Tintaya finding us. I know he was supposedly sleeping in the cot-tage behind; but I don't trust him awake or asleep. He would have reported me to Atoq."

"Would it have been such a crime?"

Zapana laughed without humor. "Not of itself, but Tintaya would have made the most of it - unbecoming conduct, adultery, abandoning my post, disobeying orders, and anything else he could think of."

"Why does he hate you so?"

Zapana raised himself on his elbow and looked at me with those piercing eyes. "Tintaya wants to succeed Atoq as Lord of Tipón, but if father ever grants me my birthright that title will come to me. Tintaya does all he can to make sure this doesn't happen. Since he's senior in rank I must be careful."

The words fell easily from his lips, a simple statement of fact, but they carried with them years of resentment. Both men were faithful to Atoq - worshipped him, even - that much I'd seen at Tipón, but Tintaya's loyalty was that of an understudy while Zapana's was that of a son. Tintaya wanted Atoq's power. Zapana wanted his father's acceptance, an acceptance that could only come with his legitimization as official son and heir. For him the lordship of Tipón was but a necessary consequence of that recognition.

Zapana lay back with his hands behind his head and stared unblinking at the roof, but I felt his heart was still open to me. Gently I asked, "Why won't your father recognize you?"

"He wants to, I'm sure. When I was growing up at Tipón we were like father and son. He used to lug me around on his back, and take my hand when we walked in the gardens together, just the two of us." A faint smile traced his lips, but his words came as from one in a trance, giving voice to inner thoughts. Then his jaw set. "I was young when they sent me to live with my grandfather at K'allachaka. It wasn't explained to me then, but later I realized my displacement came when my father took a larger role in running the imperial spy web. Grandfather Tupac Amaru had organized and headed it, but gradually he turned it over to his eldest son. Soon Tipón and not K'allachaka was the center of command.

"Of course, I was barely aware of this when I was growing up. I was more concerned with returning to Tipón to be with my father. When I reached manhood my grandfather took me into his service - for Atoq values good agents, and I was determined to be the best - and my training began as did yours, at Tipón. But when I returned to those sunlit terraces I found that Tintaya, a member of another branch of our panaqa, had appeared in my absence and risen to senior command. His ambitions were clear, and he wasn't pleased to see me.

"If you think Tintaya was hard on you, imagine what I went through. I resolved never to give him cause to fault my conduct, though, as you know, he never misses a chance to bait me even now. When my training ended grandfather made me Steward of K'allachaka as a respectable cover for my real duties, but also to give me a place away from Tintaya. I've risen through the ranks on my own in spite of Tintaya," he said proudly, "and earned all that I am due."

While he spoke I glided a fingertip in spirals over his smooth chest, not wanting to interrupt his story, but still perplexed by Atoq's contrary behavior. I often saw Atoq regard him in a fatherly manner. The bond between them was evident to all, but still Atoq held back.

"Why does Lord Atoq favor Tintaya over you?" I wondered aloud. It was the wrong question. Zapana sat straight up and fixed his gaze on me.

"My father loves me," he declared, "and I love him. Never was there a more loyal son than me. I'll do anything for him - anything!" It was almost a plea.

"Please, Zapana, no one doubts your loyalty, or Tintaya's for that matter, but why - "

"Because Tintaya is more ruthless than I; that's what my grandfather says. Tintaya has ice in his veins. It may be so, but if that's what it takes then I'll show them I can be just as ruthless, and far more cunning. But it's not only that. There's a person, Qori, one of immense power who sways my father, who fears me because I can't be swayed, and who champions Tintaya because he is easily managed."

Zapana stopped speaking leaving a huge silence in the room. He looked away from me, aware he'd said more than intended. I sensed I was the first allowed a glimpse beneath his outer shell.

Who holds enough power to influence the great Lord Atoq? I wondered. And who would back Tintaya over Zapana?

The moment was gone between us. Zapana rose and stretched, closing the subject by turning his back to me. "You'll not tell anyone?" he asked hesitantly while poking at a lamp wick.

"Never," I replied. His shoulders relaxed.

I sat up and watched him, knowing when I left his room we'd revert to our customary roles, and he would be closed to me again.

"You didn't come to me at Tipón, either," I said, thinking I was shifting the conversation back to us, "even when Tintaya was away."

He chuckled and turned to face me, arms crossed on his chest, leaning unashamedly naked against the wall in the soft glow of the lamplight. He had nothing to be ashamed of. "I would have been disobeying orders," he said. "Tintaya was the one assigned to seduce you."

"Seduce me?" The thought of coupling with Tintaya nauseated me. "What do you mean 'assigned'? By whom? What for?"

Zapana laughed. "It was a joy watching Tintaya fail."

"Atoq?" I asked.

Zapana nodded. "Think of it as a test, to see if men were a weakness for you. And, as with all other evaluations, you passed brilliantly."

"And now you've succeeded where Tintaya failed," I said, suddenly feeling cold. "You've defeated him again."

Zapana went to his knees in front of me, palms held upward. "It's not so, I swear. No, Qori, tonight wasn't about orders or rivalries. Tonight was for us. It's the first time you and I have ever been truly alone together, and with your brother arriving tomorrow, it may be the last." He sat and placed an arm around me, bringing my head to his shoulder. "I don't know why tonight happened, Qori," he said in a puzzled voice, then, to himself, "Why us? Why you? Perhaps we're more alike than either of us wants to admit."

Another communion settled over us, and I felt as if he were looking into my thoughts. Like you, Zapana, there's room in my heart for men and women, and we both live the double life of danger. To whom else can we show our real selves? Who could possibly understand? Then there are the secret needs that drive us - you committed to your father's acceptance, and I to my father's revenge, and both of us determined to succeed no matter what the cost.

Zapana listened to my silence, then said, "Tomorrow things will be the same between us as they were before. It must be that way. Do you understand?"

I did, but suddenly I was not feeling charitable. "Does Lord Atoq know about you and Qhari?" I asked bluntly. "If Tintaya finds out. . . ."

"Tintaya knows and will do nothing." I looked at him in surprise. He chuckled. "My father understands the world," he explained, "and being able to lie with man or woman is a desirable trait in a good agent. It makes me more valuable. Tintaya doesn't have this ability," he said with a smirk. "My father and I don't discuss it, it's simply understood. Tintaya knows when I'm so engaged it's by the will of Lord Atoq. He wouldn't dare interfere. When Qhari was sent to K'allachaka Atoq made inquires and learned of Qhari's preferences. He asked me to 'watch over' Qhari, so he wouldn't be tempted by men who might force him into spying for other royal houses."

As Qhari did when he served Iñaca Panaqa, I thought. How clever of Atoq. "So while Tintaya was assigned to seduce me, you were assigned to Qhari," I said.

He responded with an open-handed shrug.

"Are you going to tell Qhari about us?" I asked.

"Are you?"

XXIII

**In which a Maiden Foully Murdered is discovered amid the
Towers of the Dead, and the howling Phuku Demon attacks.**

The girl had been dead for two or three days. The condors were
feasting on her, but what remained left no doubt about her fate. She lay
on her back behind a pair of burial towers, dress ripped open, legs
sprawled wide showing where she was brutally violated, a dark bruise
around her neck, cheeks slashed and tongue ripped out. Zapana held his
nose at the stench and turned away. Qhari nudged me. I glanced at him
and nodded. Father said one of the women at the Hatunqolla akllawasi
was raped and mutilated, and Tanta Karwa identified her as the governess Ronto, adding that after the rape she was strangled and her tongue
cut out. I had related these details to Qhari and I knew what he was
thinking. The girl before us, perhaps fifteen or sixteen years of age and
once pretty, met the same fate. Was it coincidence?

"The other murder was twenty years ago," Qhari whispered hearing
my thoughts. "Is Kontor still at work?"

Father's captain, Kontor, never left our thoughts since the day we
realized he had to be the murderer.

"Kontor is still alive, it's true," I replied quietly. "He murdered
Ronto like this, and he sent assassins after father. Now he stalks uncle
Maita, if Maita is still alive. He must have arranged my marriage to
T'ito, and so holds the power of life and death over me. But did he com-
mit this murder?"

"Can there be another so demented?" Qhari asked.

Zapana returned. "I've sent a runner to report this to the governor at
Hatunqolla," he said. "He'll send someone to investigate. It's not our
affair."

Qhari joined us in Puno that morning, arriving from the court of
Zapana's grandfather with various greetings and messages. "The wandering maid Choque," he said facetiously, embracing me. "Where have
you been? If you were going to be away so long you should have told

me," he scolded. "I was getting a little concerned about you."

I thought, If you only knew the truth of it, brother dear.

Qhari exchanged a look with Zapana, then turned to me again. "I know I'm not supposed to ask what you were doing, but tell me about those reed boats. What's it like to sail in one?"

Zapana's manner revealed nothing to Qhari about our night of passion. Indeed, Zapana was his usual aloof self again, and what had been between us was locked away in one of his many compartments. He explained this to me long ago at Tipón, saying, "An agent has many lives. You must learn to be this way with some, that way with others, and keep each separate, including your inner feelings, or your face will betray you. Whatever the role, you can only play it convincingly if you believe it yourself. Thoughts that aren't relevant must be banished." What happened between us was irrelevant to our mission, and would only hurt Qhari if he knew. I tucked it away in a private place, knowing it wasn't likely to happen again, at least not soon. My curiosity was satisfied - abundantly so, and I felt more a woman for it. We agreed not to tell Qhari. Without regret I relinquished Zapana to Qhari once more, thanking him silently for the loan.

We journeyed on to Hatunqolla, with the maidservant Choque following in Zapana's train. The town overlooks a broad plain patterned with maize and potato fields, and behind, marching up the hill of Qollqa Chupa, are row upon row of imperial storehouses, for Hatunqolla is the principal center of the region and gateway to the lake lands. It's laid out on a grid with straight, narrow streets separating the high-walled kanchas - rectangular compounds housing nobles, priests, and administrators. As we walked the streets I imagined father bravely fighting his way down those narrow confines.

At Qhari's urging Zapana allowed a detour past the akllawasi and here we paused, staring at the great door while its elderly guards regarded us quizzically. I took Qhari's hand and envisioned father and uncle Maita waiting outside, while Kontor entered against the protests of the vain and doomed Ronto. "This is where it all began," Qhari muttered, "but where will it end?"

Zapana's grandfather, vastly disappointed that Zapana didn't choose any women from his court, insisted he at least pay homage at the tomb of his ancestors. This was near Hatunqolla at Sillustani, the burial place of Qolla nobility located on a high, wind-swept hill at the end of a peninsula jutting into Lake Umayo. From the hilltop emerge round towers built from smooth, massive blocks of gray or white stone, and increasing in width as they rise upward like giant inverted cones. From these great towers on their dominating hill one looks out over the blue waters of Lake Umayo to a flat-topped island, and beyond to the treeless, rolling green hills of the puna lands. High overhead condors circle on the wind like silent guardians keeping an eternal vigil. This place of the dead holds a power that makes one speak in whispers.

But the condors had landed, and that's what led us to the body behind a pair of identical towers that stand by the cliff edge overlooking Lake Umayo. Sillustani is a sufficiently lonely place for a despicable murder like this, I reflected, for only mourners and pilgrims trek here, and visits are infrequent. Had we not happened along the condors would have removed all but the bones of the girl within a few days. I glanced at the great birds now watching us angrily from atop nearby towers.

Qhari nudged me. "Don't look now, but. . . ." Of course I looked, and then shook my head in surprise. A troop of soldiers arrived to investigate led by Lord Achachi. All wore the blue and purple of Iñaca Panaqa.

"Zapana," Achachi said in curt acknowledgement as the two met. Zapana returned a nod and bowed, as did we all. I hovered behind Zapana, half turned away with my chin on my breast. Achachi ignored Choque the maidservant, but he gave Qhari a gesture of recognition. Qhari smiled.

"The resting place of your ancestors," Achachi said to Zapana, turning to survey the towers.

"It is so, Lord." Zapana said. He kept his eyes lowered.

The old warlord retied the jaguar pelt draped over his shoulders and set his big hands on his hips, continuing to look everywhere except at Zapana. "I have one or two relatives here myself," he said.

"I travel with Lord Atoq's permission," Zapana volunteered, anticipating the inevitable question that accompanies the meeting of unequal ranks.

Achachi sighed heavily at mention of Atoq. "Yes, I'm sure you do." He appeared uninterested. "Well, what's this about a murder? Where's the victim?"

"Ah, yes," Zapana said, "the girl. She's behind those towers."

While Achachi trudged off I exchanged looks with Qhari and Zapana. What's Achachi doing here? I wondered. He's Overlord of Chinchaysuyu, and this is Qollasuyu. How is it he happens to turn up at Sillustani now? He must have been with the Hatunqolla governor when Zapana's messenger arrived. Why did he come up here in person?

Qhari's eyes shared my questions, but Zapana looked unconcerned. He and Achachi sniffed around each other like male dogs, neither showing any surprise at seeing the other, both noncommittal. But then, I reminded myself, Achachi and Atoq don't trust each other, and Zapana is Atoq's loyal son. They're both being cautious. It's just as well Achachi chooses not to recognize me.

Moments later Achachi returned shaking his head. "Strange," he said, "we found a girl like that a few weeks ago near Tiwanaku."

"Mutilated in the same way?" Zapana asked, looking Achachi full in the face with interest.

"Exactly the same," Achachi said. "Raped, strangled, tongue gone. I thought they'd have caught the villain by now. It appears he fled north. Well, I'll tell the local authorities and they can deal with it. I'm leaving in the morning."

Achachi tried to sound disinterested, and Zapana still attempted to appear so, but I caught a flicker between them. These murders mean more to them than either is letting on, I realized.

"You travel to Cuzco?" Zapana asked, the stiffness of their first meeting now evaporating.

"Indeed," Achachi said. "I wanted to make one last pilgrimage to the shrines of Tiwanaku and the Island of the Sun before I'm too old to travel." He slapped his broad belly and chuckled. In spite of his silvery hair he still looked as solid as a timber. The ruins of Tiwanaku where Wiraqocha created the first Incas are to the south of Lake Titiqaqa, while close to the south shore is the island where Father Sun first rose. Both places are sacred destinations. "But I've already been away too long from my duties in Chinchaysuyu," Achachi continued. "I hoped to return home with Lord Sapaca, but some of my men became ill in the south, and Sapaca was eager to proceed, so he and Lady Sisa went on ahead. They left Hatunqolla three days ago."

Atoq told me Sapaca and Sisa were touring in the south, and warned me to stay away from them. Something in Achachi's voice suggested his own journey had motives beyond visiting shrines.

Zapana looked down, idly shifting the dirt at his feet. "You met up with Lord Sapaca?" he asked casually. Anyone watching Zapana would have thought he wasn't at all interested and only making polite conversation, but I knew better.

"Met him in Tiwanaku," Achachi said, turning once more to look at the towers. "Only overlapped a day. That's where my men got sick, and me too. Bad fish, I suppose. Thought I'd catch up with Sapaca and Sisa in Hatunqolla, but, missed them by a few days."

Zapana said, "I'm returning to Cuzco tomorrow, also."

Achachi looked at him, and then said indifferently, "In that case I suppose our caravans might as well travel together. The high passes are dangerous at this time of year, and that old knot counter Tupac Amaru would never forgive me if anything happened to you." Achachi was fond of referring to his esteemed elder half-brother, Zapana's Inca grandfather, as 'that old knot counter,' but he did so with an undertone of respect.

One of Achachi's soldiers approached escorting a tall man in a black, hooded robe, beaded with shells and animal bones. I could smell him coming. The soldier halted before Achachi and pulled back the man's hood, revealing a face and long hair as filthy as his robe.

"I found him lurking behind one of the towers back there," the soldier said.

Achachi eyed the stranger. "What are you doing here?"

"I'm a priest," the man said in broken Aymara.

"That much is evident from your stench. What do you know about the girl?" Achachi asked, switching to Aymara.

"What girl? I only just arrived."

Another soldier spoke up. "It is so, Lord. I saw him following us from Hatunqolla."

Achachi regarded the priest. "How long have you been in these lands?"

"I arrived a few days ago."

"Where are you from, and by whose permission do you travel?"

"I'm from the deserts of Atacama, far to the south. The governor of Catarpe granted me permission to make a pilgrimage to the holy places of the lake lands. I came to see the towers. Tomorrow I'll return home. Is there trouble here?"

"Yes, but it's too late for a priest, unless you're a diviner?"

The man spread his dirty hands and shrugged.

"Then be gone from here, priest. Wait, what is your name?"

The man hesitated, then replied, "I'm called Michimalongo, Lord."

Zapana turned his back on the man and whispered to Achachi in Runasimi, "Pardon, Lord, but shouldn't he be taken back to Hatunqolla for questioning, at least to have his story verified?"

I was thinking the same. There was something about this Michimalongo that drew suspicion, perhaps because he was trying so hard not to appear suspicious. But the decision was Achachi's.

"If he had anything to do with this murder why would he return here today?" Achachi asked. "No, he's but a wandering pilgrim as he says. Besides, it will take days to get a message all the way down to Catarpe to check his story, and my men are eager to return home without further delay. I'll report what we've seen to the authorities at Hatunqolla and leave the matter to them." Achachi paused and regarded Zapana knowingly. "You, no doubt, will give a full account to Lord Atoq." Zapana stared off without answering. Achachi smiled to himself, then turned to the priest, whose dark eyes were anxiously shifting from Zapana to Achachi, and said, "Very well, Priest Michimalongo, be on your way."

The man hurried off and Achachi ordered his men to wrap the dead girl in their cloaks, and follow us back to town. In response to the disgust on their faces he promised to have new cloaks issued from the royal storehouses at Qollqa Chupa. It was a somber group that returned to

Hatunqolla at sunset with the two rear men carrying the bundled remains
of that poor, nameless girl who met such a foul end among the towers of
the dead. Qhari and I exchanged looks several times. It appeared Kontor
was still at work, and nearby.

Ice crystals sparkled in the air. Breath hung in clouds. Immense
frozen mountains brooded over us, demanding awe and silence as we
trudged the highest pass between Hatunqolla and Cuzco. I knew this
place from our journey southward. The narrow valley bottom is a patch-
work of snow and grass, and here one finds strange-smelling pools of
warm water that beckon the weary traveler, gusting clouds of steam in
the thin mountain air. But this time our caravan - two hundred people
and twice that number of pack llamas - didn't stop at the inviting waters.
When we came through earlier the pass was bright and clear, but it was
now the season of storms when, it was said, whole caravans became lost
in blizzards to be found frozen solid months later when the snow melted. The sky sat low now, promising snow. Inti cast a dull beam in the
west. We were still a half-day from the next tampu. Even the llamas
were uneasy. No one had to be told to hurry.

I stayed with the women bunched at the rear; all of us with our cloaks
wrapped tight, heads bowed under the bundles on our backs, intent on
keeping pace with the men. Many were soldiers' wives returning home
now that their husbands' tours had ended. The couples joined Lord
Achachi's entourage as he passed through the southern garrison towns.
When men are called to serve their mit'a tax in the army their wives
often accompany them. But this is a matter of choice between the couple. Like the men, some women look forward to escaping the routine of
village life and seeing new lands, but arrangements must be made with
the ayllu to care for their children. Besides the adventure, I think some
went just to keep an eye on their husbands. Officers often took their
wives, who kept the soldiers' wives in line and insured decorum in camp.
Since all the men serving together in a unit came from the same vicini-
ty, I think even the soldiers who traveled alone watched themselves lest
tales of untoward behavior find their way back home. It always seemed

to me that orderly conduct while on campaign owed much to these courageous women.

Since meeting Achachi I did my best to stay out of sight, though I knew Achachi had the answers to many troubling questions. During the day he usually led anyway while I trailed at the rear, but at night everyone crowded into the open sleeping halls at the tampus, soldiers, and servants and lords together. Achachi never gave the slightest indication he knew who I was, aside from being Choque, just another of Zapana's maids, and I decided it was best to leave it that way. With slippers stuffed to elevate my height, a coating of berry juice to darken my skin, and shadow lines painted on my face he never gave me a second look. Qhari made a point of serving Achachi in the hope Achachi might reveal something to him, but again all Achachi would say was, "Thank you for your patience," as if merely being kind to a page. But Qhari reported the words came with a look of caution. Achachi wasn't yet ready to reveal his secrets.

Achachi and Zapana seemed to get on amiably enough once the journey began, but beyond the immediate responsibilities of the caravan their exchanges were guarded. No doubt Achachi assumed everything he said would be reported to Atoq, which, of course, it would be.

"It's a good opportunity," Zapana said when I asked him why we traveled with Achachi. "Lord Atoq always likes to stay informed of what the various officials are doing, and it's a piece of luck that we met Lord Achachi. I would have insisted on accompanying him whether he offered or not."

"But he knows you," I said, "and he's not likely to say anything to you he wouldn't say to Lord Atoq in person."

"True, Qori, but as Lord Atoq taught us, there is as much to be learned from what's not said as from that which is, and besides, Lord Achachi is an old warrior and fond of his aqha. He may yet let slip some useful tidbit."

"Why are we interested in Lord Achachi?" I asked. "Surely he's not involved with Lady Chuqui?"

"Indeed not. No, never question Achachi's loyalty to the Emperor, Qori. Lord Achachi always does what he thinks best for the Empire, but. . . Lord

Atoq has a larger view of things, and he feels Achachi's concerns are sometimes misguided." Zapana held his hands palms upward and shrugged, "These aren't matters for you to be concerned about. They're between my father and his uncle. As for me, well, had I passed up this opportunity to trail along in Achachi's company Atoq would be angry. Besides, it's safer traveling with a large caravan through the high passes."

Achachi was made for the soldier's life. During the daily march the old warlord seemed to be everywhere at once, shouting orders and tending to myriad details that kept the huge column moving, and all the while pausing for a kind word here, a look of reassurance there, and pelting his men with coarse soldiers' oaths which kept them grinning. Watching him perpetually in motion it was hard to believe he had grandsons old enough to be officers themselves. But he is accustomed to moving armies of forty thousand across the Empire, I reflected, so our caravan, though it seems large to me, is no more than an exercise to keep him occupied.

At first it puzzled me why the Overlord of Chinchaysuyu bothered to take personal command of our train, he could have delegated the task, but then I saw the junior officers following him around and realized that, besides enjoying himself, he taught them by example. For all his lofty titles he was still an old veteran longing for the campaign trails, and eager to pass on his skills.

I also took pleasure in watching Zapana. He, too, was born for his profession, ever the gatherer of information, engaging Achachi's men in seemingly idle conversation, as well as those returning home from the southern garrisons, and I'm sure he managed to speak with every driver and porter as well. He sought nothing in particular. Like Achachi he merely enjoyed keeping his skills honed - skills that I had enough knowledge of to appreciate - and it made my heart swell to watch his expertise. Being privy to the women's gossip I knew Zapana was thought the most desirable of men, and on more than a few occasions I had to chastise my sisters for making lewd speculations concerning his person. The nerve of some women!

Qhari delighted in ordering me about and winking at me after each performance. When no one was looking I stuck my tongue out at him, setting him laughing, and leaving those around us wondering what was so humorous. Ceasing this brotherly teasing was the price he paid when he shyly approached me one evening and asked if I would stand watch while he and Zapana had some time alone in a nearby shed. Oddly enough, thereafter I came to miss his teasing, and a few days later I goaded him back into action. We silently agreed that one sentry watch was worth one day's truce.

Privately I was glad Qhari was with Zapana again. It eased my conscience, and he was always more animated around Zapana. One day he would discover the love he bore for Zapana was returned only by amusement, but it was a discovery he had to make on his own. And I was quietly pleased Zapana seemed to prefer my brother over me again, for it made my life less complicated.

A snowflake stuck to my nose, pulling me back to the high pass. The mountaintops vanished behind a screen of white. The wind bit my cheeks. It's said the wind of the puna, the tutukas wayra, can dislocate your jaw and knock you off your feet, rip the roof from a hut, and smash cliffs into boulders. But it's not as bad as the demon phuku wind that sweeps the high mountain passes. That one brings blizzards and blinding whirlwinds that penetrate the body deeper than the sun can reach. Suddenly a gust hit with such force I was thrown to my knees. Snow driven sideways stung my eyes, and as if having heard my fears someone shouted, "Phuku!"

Struggling to my feet I set my legs against the blast and looked around. White. Those ahead and behind me in the column were faint blurs. Another gust nearly toppled me. Then a voice came from far ahead, "K-e-e-p M-o-v-i-n-g." I turned, and cupping my hands to my mouth repeated the call. The column lurched forward, each of us trying to keep the person in front within sight. We were over midway through the pass when the demon struck, and there was nothing to be done but plod ahead to the next tampu. The wind could be gone in a short while, or blow for days, there was no way of knowing.

Achachi was in the lead, and Qhari was somewhere ahead with Zapana. Though I followed in the trail of those before me the snow deepened from ankle to mid-calf, each step becoming harder, straining my legs. A whirlwind descended on us now - snow blowing from both sides and up from the ground into my face. I covered my head and peered between my fingers, struggling, stumbling, trying to see the dark shape of the person before me. To step from the line meant death.

The wind carried voices: people calling out, trying to stay together. Some cried for help having taken a wrong step and lost the column, though it might be only a few paces away. Such a voice called out piteously on my left, a woman, though I couldn't see her. I turned and reached toward the cry, the snow now up to my knees, but my fingers only grasped wind. She called again, begging someone to find her, and this time I swore she stood beside me. I took a few steps and flailed my arms in all directions. Nothing. The other shouts grew fainter, and no more cries came from her. I turned, and turned again. The column, where is it? I wondered. I can hear voices, but from which direction? This way? No, that way. Or. . . ?

The storm blew at its height, or at least I couldn't imagine how it could get any worse, and though the caravan might be only steps away I could see nothing but blinding, swirling white, and I lost all sense of direction. I called out but only the screech of the wind answered me. How long will this last? I wondered. How long will I last? I can't feel my feet, and my fingers are icicles.

I folded my woolen dress under me and sat in the snow, pulling my cloak tightly over my head. Inside this tent it seemed safer, warmer. In this position the snow was chest high and deepening by the moment, but I tried not to let myself think of what time might bring. I blew on my fingers. Is Qhari safe? I wondered. The tampu can't be far ahead. Has Achachi already reached it? I'll be fine, I told myself, if only the phuku demon passes over soon.

How long I sat like this I can't say, but long enough to lose all feeling in my legs, though I couldn't tell whether this was from cold or sitting on them. I felt myself sliding into a warm, dark sleep. And then something fell on me, or over me, and I heard a curse.

"What the. . . ? Here's another one. Get up, you motherless shit.

Come now, on your feet. Move."

It was Achachi. He grabbed my elbows and picked me out of the snow, but my legs wouldn't unfold. The storm raged. I had been buried to my neck in powdery white.

"Come on, help me. I won't carry you. Do you want to live?" Then in a disappointed tone he said, "Oh, it's a woman."

Before I could reply he shouted to someone nearby, "Give me a hand." I felt a grip on my other arm, and then they dragged me over the snow between them.

They pushed my hands against the shaggy sides of a llama. "Take hold," Achachi shouted over the wind, "and move your legs. You've got to keep moving." And then he left, bellowing for his lost men.

The beast I clung to wasn't pleased with my added weight, but whoever led it soon had it moving again, and gradually some feeling returned to my legs. At least I could stand and stagger along, now clutching the llama's cargo ropes. Step after exhausting step, blinded by swirling snow and wind, we pushed on until I had no strength left. . . and then we went farther.

I don't know who carried me into the tampu hall. I don't even remember being taken inside. One moment I had my face buried in the thick hair of the llama's neck, and the next I stared up at the underside of a thatch roof. The room was packed. Someone nearby coughed gently. A head count began and names were called. I sat up and looked around, starting my own search. A blast of wind hit with such force that for a moment it seemed the roof must be torn away, but it held, and everyone breathed a sigh of relief, returning weary eyes to the floor. Then I heard Zapana's voice calling, "Choque? Qhari?"

I struggled to my feet, keeping my back against the wall for support. "Lord Zapana, over here."

"Ah, Choque, have you seen Qhari? Where is he?" Concern edged his voice, exciting my worst fears.

"I thought he was with you, Lord."

"No, somehow we lost each other. I've already searched the other buildings. He must still be out - " His words were cut short as another howling demon seized the building, shaking the rafters. Eyes raised again, everyone fell silent until it let go.

The door flew open, and amid a blast of swirling powdery white another group stumbled in, looking like snowdrifts. Those already inside tried to back away while the newcomers shook themselves, but now there was only standing room in the tampu hall. The last to enter was Achachi, calling out the names of his missing men. The door closed again.

When we reached Achachi's side he gave Zapana the hollow look of one who has many times gone beyond his limits. His cheeks were white with cold and his eyes red rimmed. He swayed slightly, seemingly on the verge of collapse. "No, I haven't seen Qhari," he replied to Zapana, and then muttered to himself, "Still three of mine missing."

I tried to lead Achachi to the fire but he shrugged off my grip and turned back to the door.

"Lord," one of his men called, "leave them to their fate. You've done all you can. If you go out there again you'll die."

Achachi stared at the man. "I led you south, and I'll lead you home again. Every one of you." He pushed the door aside and stepped out, vanishing in the driven snow and darkness. Zapana followed, leaving me staring blankly after them.

XXIV

**Of those who Survived and those who did not, and of Secrets
hitherto unknown revealed by Lord Atoq, after which
Qori is Punished.**

The tampu hall hung thick with the smell of soaked woolen clothes,
now steaming on those huddled next to the hearths, and a hum of whispers and moans drifted in the close air. Some dozed from sheer exhaustion, crowded shoulder to shoulder and back to back against their fel-
lows; others, like me, were unable to do anything but stare at the coals.
Half the night drifted by while I sat beside a brazier wondering if I'd ever
see Qhari again, or Zapana or Achachi. Gradually, feeling returned to
my hands and feet, though the tips of my fingers remained numb for
some time, and searing pain throbbed in my thawing limbs. The wind
finally died, but as the moments passed it seemed less and less likely the
search party would find anyone alive, or even return itself. One of the
soldiers finally said, "It's been too long. We've lost Lord Achachi."

The words hardly left his mouth when the door burst open and
Zapana stumbled in dragging Qhari. Then came Achachi, supporting
one of his lost men while two more, their arms around each other, hobbled behind. Once through the door all six collapsed on the floor. I knelt
beside Qhari in an instant, cradling his head.

"Qhari, dear Qhari! I thought I'd lost you. Are you all right? Here,
let me warm you. Oh, Qhari, speak to me."

His face was white and cold as snow, but his teeth didn't chatter - he
was beyond that. I clasped him to me and rocked while frantically rubbing his frozen hands. In the relief of the moment no one noticed the
maidservant Choque lost her Aymara accent.

At last a moan came from him. He tried moving his lips. I leaned
closer, pressing my ear to his mouth. His words came haltingly, and in
a bare whisper. "Stop. . . stop. . . squeezing me. . . so hard."

"Well, fine!" I jumped to my feet, hands on my hips. "You just lie
there and freeze, Qhari Puma. You don't need me. Perhaps you'd like

to go out for a walk?"

I saw the trace of a smile, and then he rolled to the side and threw his arms over the prone figure of Zapana. I became aware of the arc of people forming around us. Achachi and the others were carried to the fire. The man who moments earlier announced their certain death now said, "I knew you'd find them, Lord, and get everyone back safely. I never doubted it for a moment." But those around us watched Qhari hugging the half-conscious Zapana, and looked uncomfortable.

"My Lord," I said, now back in the role of Choque as I pushed Qhari aside and shook Zapana's shoulder, "all is well. You have saved your people. Even this humble page owes you his life. Such bravery! Is Lord Zapana not brave?" I asked the crowd. They nodded and backed away when I shooed them with my hands. "Room, give Lord Zapana room. Help him to the fire. Oh, and his unworthy page, too." I said this last part louder for Qhari's benefit, and 'accidentally' kicked him when I leaned over to take his arms. Eyes closed, he winced, then smiled peacefully.

We stayed at the tampu all the next day, thawing and recovering from the rigors of the storm. Four people and thirty-three llamas remained lost, but later that afternoon someone discovered the llamas huddled in two groups near the tampu. Not so the people, a driver and three porters, who would only emerge when the snow melted. Considering the size of our train and the ferocity of the storm we counted ourselves fortunate that losses weren't greater. Had Achachi and Zapana not dared the gods, they would have been. Like me, Qhari stepped from the column answering a cry for help and became lost himself, thinking he knew where the caravan was and walking in the opposite direction before collapsing.

"The phuku demon almost had me, Qori," he whispered as I fussed with his blankets.

I sat back and regarded him solemnly. "I know. It almost had me, too." "Will I die?"

"That burning in your hands and feet means the feeling is coming back. The flesh hasn't blackened. Your limbs will be whole again. I'll bring more of the brewed herbs to help you sleep."

"I thought I wouldn't see you again," he said.

I couldn't swallow the lump in my throat. "Nor I you," I managed, taking his hand.

"Qori, we can die, you know?" The realization seemed new to him.

"No we can't. At least not until father is avenged."

He smiled back.

Zapana bore the pain of thawing with hardly a groan. "How can I thank you for saving Qhari?" I asked. He fixed me with his piercing gaze but remained silent. "You do care for Qhari, don't you?" I said.

"I'm responsible for him," Zapana said without a trace of emotion. I assumed he meant he was responsible for those under him. A cold response, but accurate and typical of Zapana. He meant that he had Qhari and me in our compartments, as was correct, and now he'd rescued us both at tremendous risk to himself, so I didn't push.

"I won't have my strength back for some time," Zapana said. "When we get below the snow line you'd better go on alone and deliver our report to Lord Atoq. That will be faster. Tell him I'll be there as soon as I can. Oh, and I'm sure he'll be interested to hear about the girl we found at Sillustani."

Achachi remained indifferent toward me. When Choque tried to thank him, kneeling before him with head bowed, he looked blank. He pulled a few women from the snow, he replied, was I one of them? His men couldn't do enough for him and were effuse in their acclamation of his bravery, but he took no notice, saying he had only done his duty. To a man they vowed to follow him anywhere. I wanted to add my voice to the chorus.

On the second day, stiff and limping, the caravan continued under a bright sky surrounded by a glittering, snow-clad landscape. Qhari, Zapana, and some of Achachi's men had to be carried on stretchers. Though Achachi protested, his men insisted on carrying him on a lattice of spears, at least for half a day, until they decided his good-natured insults and bellowing returned to normal. Then they allowed him to limp along between two sturdy aides. When one of these aides was overcome with surumpi - the temporary but painful blindness that comes when sun glints off snow - Achachi bandaged his eyes and, tying a rope around his own waist, had the man grasp the other end so he could be led. This,

Achachi declared, was to show everyone what a fool the man had been not to guard his eyes, and he cursed him loudly, but I heard him murmuring encouragement and describing the footing like a concerned father. It was a lesson to the rest of us, and for the remainder of that day we stumbled along peering out from under hats and cloaks, our faces already scorched raw and lips blistered by the unrelenting glare of sun on ice.

It was a bedraggled and grateful column that finally staggered down to lower elevations, where trees and grass and gurgling brooks lined the royal road. That night the howling was terrible, for many had blackened fingers and toes that had to be removed. Much to my relief Zapana cautioned me not to attend, for maids know nothing of healing ways and I had to stay in disguise. Though I have never been much inclined to pray I did that night, thanking the gods for delivering my loved ones whole.

"So, the fiend is at it again," Atoq said furrowing his brows. I had just told him of the murdered girl at Sillustani, and of Achachi's comment that he saw another like her farther south a few weeks earlier. We faced each other alone in his audience chamber at Tipón. While he leaned back on his stool and stroked his chin I tried not to stare at him, but I shook with anger and he knew it.

Qhari and Zapana stayed with Achachi and the caravan at the first tampu below the snow line, while I hurried on to deliver our report to Atoq. When I arrived at Tipón I brushed past the guards. Though they didn't recognize Choque the maidservant they knew my normal speaking voice, especially when I reminded them of how I'd choked them from behind during my training. I wanted to see Atoq's reaction to news of the murdered girls, and I was in no mood to stand about awaiting his pleasure.

I found Atoq in the courtyard - not alone. The woman's laughter reached me even before I entered. From the look on Lady Sisa's face, her tousled hair and disheveled dress, it was clear what they had been doing. Neither seemed perturbed at my sudden appearance. Before greeting me Atoq turned to Sisa and calmly suggested she might like a stroll in the gardens. Sisa regarded me with mild curiosity, and a look that dared. What could I say? Tanta Karwa was Atoq's lover, not Sisa. I felt as if I'd just found my father with another woman, and on Tanta Karwa's behalf I was outraged.

How can Atoq do this to Tanta Karwa? I wondered. How can he do it to me? Yes, Lady Sisa is breath-taking, but she's married, the bitch.

I told myself she must have seduced Atoq, but I knew, just from watching them together, that this wasn't the first time they'd met in this way. And there she sat, one of the most powerful, and certainly the most beautiful woman in the Empire, daring me to say something with those huge doe eyes of hers. She turned to Atoq and laid a hand on his arm.

"A walk in your garden? Nothing would give me greater pleasure. . . well, almost nothing," she said, laughing like music and butting her head against his. He laughed with her, a lovers' joke, his eyes adoring her. "But I'm afraid the time has come for me to continue on to Cuzco. These past days have been so pleasant. . . and exciting. Will you miss me?"

While Atoq helped her rise and stuttered he was already missing her, I tried not to vomit all over her. Surely he knew he was being used, but he obviously enjoyed it. Sisa was the only person I ever knew who could fluster Atoq. She turned back once to smile at him and then floated by me without a glance, as if saying, That's how it's done, little one, but you don't matter a dog turd anyway.

Atoq pointedly ignored my anger as I followed him to his audience chamber, lavishing praise on me for my excellent work in Qollasuyu, and going on as if Sisa had never been there. I wasn't so out of control that I didn't recognize the silent order - Sisa wasn't to be talked about, or her presence at Tipón ever mentioned. In an odd way I felt flattered to be trusted with the secrets of his intimate life, but I remained angry with him for betraying Tanta Karwa.

Now, kneeling before him on the rush matting, he seated on his ornate ceremonial stool, it occurred to me that perhaps Atoq was playing Sisa's game for his own ends. After all, he was suspicious of Sisa's husband, Lord Sapaca. Perhaps she was naught but a gaming piece between them? But the thought of them rolled snugly in his blankets, laughing and sporting while we struggled through the frozen pass, left me as cold as the phuku demon.

Having digested my report on the murdered girl at Sillustani, Atoq sighed and nodded to himself as if reaching a difficult decision. "I had hoped not to burden you with this," he said, "but the time has come for you to know about these murders and the madman who haunts this earth. No, these are not unique occurrences. They've been happening in the same way for over twenty years."

I sat up and listened, my anger on Tanta Karwa's behalf suddenly forgotten.

"It started at the Hatunqolla akllawasi during the Qolla rebellion," he said, folding his arms and stretching his legs in front of him. "That must have been before you were born, but you've heard about those bloody times, yes?" I nodded. He stared at the floor. "I was there when we finally broke their line and swept the city, and I was one of the first to reach the akllawasi - but not the first. The front gate was ajar when I arrived, and I didn't think I'd find anyone alive. I entered anyway, searching for the Inca nobles who were trapped in the city when the rebellion began, or their bodies."

Atoq rose and paced, hands clasped at his back. I waited. The audience chamber, small and windowless, filled with the weight of his hesitation. A wicker door held back the daylight but a few rays penetrated, and small lamps flickering in the wall niches helped dispel the dimness, casting our shadows. He paused in profile and absently poked at a guttering wick, coaxing it to brightness again, setting the flame glinting off his gold earspools. He wore his usual dark red tunic and black cloak, a simple but elegant costume of finest weave. The silence felt crushing. When he spoke again his eyes stayed on the lamp.

"In an anteroom facing the main courtyard, I found them - two women. The younger one, once beautiful, lay on her back, garments ripped aside, raped, strangled, and with her cheeks slashed and tongue gone, just as you described the girl at Sillustani. At first I assumed the Qolla did it, exacting their last revenge. Close by lay a priestess. She wasn't violated or mutilated, but she had been clubbed, and her head rested in a pool of blood. I thought her dead, too, but then she moaned and opened her eyes. I knelt to comfort her, and with her last breaths she told me what happened. It wasn't the Qolla." He paused and swallowed hard at the memory, then in a shaky voice he finished, "It was an Inca captain."

Atoq turned to see my hand at my mouth. "I know," he said, "it's too horrible to contemplate. But, I can only repeat what she told me. Yes, an Inca captain, an officer. He left his men outside the gate and forced his way in, and then he seized the younger woman, one called Ronto, and tried to use her. The priestess attempted to stop him but he silenced her with his mace. That was the last she remembered until she saw me bending over her."

I knelt with my back straight, motionless as stone, devouring his words. Atoq was there; he saw it, I thought. He doesn't know who the Inca captain was, but I do - Kontor. Yes, this confirms it, Kontor, father's trusted captain and supposed confederate in their escape. Father said Kontor entered the akllawasi alone, was gone a long time, and returned without the women they all saw earlier at the gate. Kontor is the Hatunqolla murderer, and from what we saw at Sillustani, he's still at work.

Yet still my head whirled with questions.

Atoq spoke again. "The priestess told me Princess Sisa hid in a brewing urn elsewhere in the complex, where they placed her when the clamor of battle drew near. Those were her last words. She closed her eyes and joined her ancestors. I searched and found the princess. She almost fainted with fright when I lifted the lid. Fortunately for one of her tender disposition she was unaware of what happened in the anteroom, or even that the city was being liberated."

Atoq released a heavy sigh and took his stool. "So there it is. At the fall of Hatunqolla an Inca captain forced his way into the akllawasi and murdered two women - one most foully - and then escaped in the confusion of the rout. Why? I've asked myself that question many times. The women were helpless and alone. Ronto was exceptionally beautiful. The evil inside some men is immeasurable. Perhaps he was seized by a demon.

"I didn't report it at the time because I had no proof. The only witness was dead and there were hundreds of Inca captains at Hatunqolla that day. We won a great victory, Princess Sisa was rescued, and it wasn't the time for a junior officer - which is all I was at the time - to start accusing his fellow officers of murder. Yet the culprit is still alive and committing the same crime again and again," he said pounding his fist on his thigh. "I've been watching for him, but, in truth, I have no idea who I should be watching for, because he leaves no clues, only bodies. The reports that reach me are always the same; some young woman murdered in a distant place, the body always mutilated in the same way."

Atoq folded his legs and planted his hands on his knees, leaning forward to search my face. I held his gaze. Was this the time to tell him what I knew?

"On the long-ago day of those first murders," he said, "I would have gladly - indeed, joyfully - claimed Princess Sisa's hand, which Thupa Inka promised to the man who rescued her. In truth, Qori, I'd been watching over Sisa since we were children at court together. Her mother died when she was young, and old Emperor Pachakuti could hardly remember the names of his first twenty children, let alone those of minor concubines. I wanted to care for her always, but my father forced me into an early marriage for political gain."

Atoq sighed. "Thus, when I found her at Hatunqolla I was already married, and had I claimed her then she would only have had the status of a consort in my household. I couldn't do that to her. She deserved much more, to be full wife and first lady of a noble house at least. I left the akllawasi, and outside in the street the first suitable man of royalty I encountered was Lord Sapaca. You wouldn't believe it to see him now, but in those days he was a fine, courageous man, and most important at the time, he was unmarried. I told him where to find Princess Sisa, and he received the credit for rescuing her. Thupa Inka honored his pledge and they were married soon after. Years later Sapaca became Speaker of Hurincuzco, and turned into the crude drunkard he is today. But Sisa and I always remained close, especially after my wife died. Do you begrudge us our brief times of joy together?"

I felt nothing for Sisa; but I didn't want to be angry with Atoq. I thought, How noble of him to give up Sisa so she could have the high station he felt she deserved. Sisa isn't good enough for him. How dare she steal from Tanta Karwa.

And what of the other matter? I wondered. Shall I tell him father's story of the Hatunqolla murders? What will it add that he doesn't already know? A name, Kontor, and a place, the Temple of Wiraqocha. The five-year meeting of the fugitives is less than a year away. If I reveal myself now Atoq will know I'm the daughter of a deserter, and it will come out that I married my brother. True, none of it is my fault, but Atoq is sworn to uphold the law regardless of circumstance. No, Qhari must help me decide what to do.

"If you so wish it, Lord," I said, "I won't mention Lady Sisa to anyone."

"I knew you'd understand," he said, rising and helping me to my feet.

"But, Lord, what of Lord Sapaca. . . I mean. . . is he not implicated in Lady Chuqui's plot to have her son declared heir?"

Atoq's eyes came back to me. "That matter remains as it was before. Publicly he insists he'll support the Emperor's choice, but privately he appears to favor Lady Chuqui." Atoq paused and arched his brows, suddenly catching my meaning. "You're wondering how Lady Sisa fits into this? She doesn't. She'd tell me if she knew anything, but Sapaca doesn't share his counsel with her. They live in the same kancha, attend public festivals and travel together for appearances sake, but their lives are separate. He has his servants and she hers, he has his lovers and she. . . well, can you blame her? They haven't slept together in years. Imagine, the most beautiful woman in Tawantinsuyu sharing his roof and she won't let him touch her. Sapaca may win at some of his games, but there's one pleasure only I - " Atoq caught himself and looked away, but the triumph in his voice hung in the room.

I caught the whiff of an old rivalry in these words, and for an instant I imagined the three of them - Sapaca, Sisa, and Atoq - as young nobles at court together. Sapaca eventually gained Sisa's hand only because Atoq allowed it. But no one ever really bested Atoq.

I was hearing more than I wanted to and felt uneasy, because he spoke to me like an intimate and I preferred to admire him from afar. He turned back and spread his hands. "You see, I'm human after all," he said.

"My Lord is burdened with many concerns," I said lowering my head in formal posture, "and this foolish woman has already forgotten everything she doesn't need to know."

He sighed, placing his hand on my shoulder. "I know I can trust you," he said giving me the fond smile that made me want to call him father. Then his face set and he returned to being the wise master, the relationship I felt more comfortable with. "Should you ever encounter another murder like that at Sillustani, inform me immediately. I've had agents working on this for years, but still I lack even a single clue to the identity of the culprit. Keep your eyes open, and if you have any suspicions, no matter how slender, share them with me, won't you? For now, I'll have others investigate this most recent episode. Rest assured that our people in Hatunqolla will search diligently. I'd send you but there are more pressing matters here that require your skills.

"I'm grieved to inform you the Emperor will leave us soon. Tanta Karwa tells me it's only a matter of weeks, if not days. He still hasn't proclaimed his heir. Thanks to you we know what Lady Chuqui is plotting, at least in the provinces. Precautions have been taken and the Aymara lords will be watched closely, as will the native rulers in all the provinces. But from what you reported about their duplicity it wouldn't surprise me if the Aymara have gone ahead and pledged support to Lady Chuqui, even though they have no intention of acting. After all, what do they have to lose?

"They think you're dead, by the way. Zapana arranged it." Atoq paused to grin at the thought. "Zapana is a clever man," he said, the fondness in these words lifting the corners of his eyes. "He had his Qolla grandfather offer to sell you to the Lupaqa, and when they tried to steal you without paying, as he knew they would, you - or a woman who had the misfortune to look like you - died in the attempt. The Aymara are satisfied their plans remain secret. The Uru are delighted with their new wealth, and Zapana's grandfather is pleased with his new herd of alpacas.

"As I said, the information you brought us is priceless, but I've decided to reward you as best I can." He then repeated the precise number of blankets, clothes and clay pots paid to the Uru, their cotton sail plus five more for the old Hatun Kuraka, and his five thousand alpacas. "Of course, it was careless of you to let yourself be caught by the Uru. You know the rule - agents are never taken alive. However, it turned out well this time, and I'm sure you'll want to use your new wealth to repay the Emperor's generosity, for He provided the ransom that saved you."

"The Emperor knows of my deeds?"

"Well, not directly. He's too ill to be troubled with details. The stewards of the royal stores acted under my orders. Of course, you'll want to set matters right with them?"

"Of course, Lord."

"Good. I'll make the arrangements for you."

For a heartbeat I was a rich woman, and though my wealth vanished as quickly as it came I couldn't be angry with him. Rules must be observed, and I was wondering how he would punish me for being captured. But he found a way to reward me and chastise me at the same time. That's why he's Atoq, Lord of Tipón, I thought with an inward chuckle.

"Now then," Atoq continued, "you deserve a rest. Stay with Tanta Karwa at Choqo. She'll be summoned the moment the Emperor's condition weakens. When word arrives go with her to Chinchero where He rests, and stay close to Him. It's still unknown when or how Lady Chuqui will put her schemes in motion, but I want you near the Emperor when His time comes. Oh, and stay alert for any news of Lord Wallpaya. He's been meeting lords in secret ever since Sapaca pressured Thupa Inka into nominating him regent until Titu Cusi comes of age. I don't trust him. He's not in this with Lady Chuqui - no, not that sly fox - but I fear he has his own plans."

XXV

In which the consequences of Abhorrent Conduct are visited upon the sinners, Lord Sapaca drinks maize beer with Lord Wallpaya, and these Indians debase themselves further.

The terraces of K'allachaka rippled down the slopes below me, descending on the now stagnant channel of the Kachimayu where shallow pools withered in the sun. It should have run full by now, but the rainy season was late. On my way from Choqo that morning I twice passed black llamas tied to posts, left to perish from hunger and thirst so their cries would bring the pity of the gods. Concern showed on every farmer's face. Why were the rains late? What had we done to bring this on ourselves?

But rain wasn't my concern that morning while I waited for Qhari to appear. Decisions had to be made. Should we tell Atoq about Kontor and the coming meeting at the Temple of Wiraqocha, or should we remain silent and attempt to deal justice ourselves?   •

Then there was my child. No one knew about that yet, not even Tanta Karwa. On the journey back from Hatunqolla my moon time hadn't come. At first I thought this due to the excitement of the previous weeks, but then Mama Killa waxed full again and I did not. Strange are the ways of things. After all those tedious, sticky couplings with T'ito, and nothing, and then one night with Zapana and. . . how potent Zapana!

A fatherless child born to a widow, what will happen? I wondered. Some gossip at first, but that will pass with time. Perhaps Illap'a, God of Thunder, saw fit to impregnate me. And why not? After all, I'm a twin, a child of Thunder, and I have healing powers. It will take no more than a few carefully dropped hints and the villagers will surely construct a legend of their own. Tanta Karwa will be too delighted with a grandchild to stay angry with me. Atoq and Tintaya won't be pleased to lose one of their prized agents for a time, but motherhood won't keep me from serving the Emperor. Tanta Karwa and the ayllu can care for the child when I'm called away on missions, and my daughter will be waiting safely for me when I return to our home in Choqo.

Yes, I had decided I carried a daughter, and her name would be Sumaq T'ika, Beautiful Flower, after my beloved friend in the akllawasi. I imagined how pleased Sumaq would be to have a girl child named after her. Sumaq would be my daughter's aunt, Qhari her uncle, and Tanta Karwa her grandmother, and we'd all be very happy. These thoughts had become too cherished to share with anyone yet. I wanted to savor and elaborate the story of how it would be before making the announcement.

And Zapana? I wondered. I've not seen him since returning from Qollasuyu. He must be told, of course, but he's already married. There's nothing he can do for us, and even if there were, I wouldn't ask. This child is mine.

The real problem is Qhari. How to tell him? And what to say when he asks about the father?

"Daughter!" Tanta Karwa had greeted me at the door of our cottage when I returned from Qollasuyu. It was months since we'd seen each other. So much had happened. She dropped the bowl she carried and seized me in a hug. We wept in each other's arms, and then we sat side by side on a bench beneath the eaves, still embracing, and still I was unable to speak. She wiped the tears from my cheeks, and when I said, "Mother. . . I. . . " and began sobbing on her shoulder again, she held me close and rocked me, whispering, "I know, child, it's been a long time. There now, my dove, you're home. I'll look after you. You need say nothing. I'm happy just to sit with you."

During the months of travel, and so many near-death escapes, Inca Moon hadn't allowed herself the luxury of tears. How could she? She thought she'd left something of herself behind on the island of Taquile with those dead guards. As the life force oozed from them it seemed something had flowed from her too, leaving behind a cold heart and steady hand. Atoq was my confessor for those deaths, though he probably thought I was only delivering a dispassionate account of my mission, which I was, but I felt oddly cleansed afterwards. Not even Qhari knew what I had done; what I had to do. Now, safe in Tanta Karwa's embrace, Inca Moon was put away, and Qori found she had lost nothing of herself.

The little cottage on the edge of Choqo with its tall roof of thatch was still the same; the sheds framing the patio were in good repair, firewood stood neatly stacked by the door, a flock of tame ducks searched the shrubbery for insects, and a new male llama tethered to a tree kept an eye on a nearby female. Tanta Karwa's patients continued to look after her needs, and she continued to prosper. The male llama pulled on his rope trying to get closer to the female. Tanta Karwa smiled at him.

"I received that one last month," she said nodding at the male. "I thought I might offer him to the hanansaya couple who are sponsoring the ancestor-tree celebration this year, but, I've grown rather fond of him. I might keep him." Tanta Karwa never allowed herself to accumulate more than a few animals, "Can't be bothered with them," she would say, and most were soon given to members of Ayllu Añawarqe as wedding gifts or for community feasts. "I call him The-One-Confused-Like-A-Man."

"The-One-Confused-Like-A-Man?"

"Yes, he doesn't know when the females want him. He thinks every day is mating time."

We laughed together until the tears rolled down our cheeks again, far longer and harder than the jest warranted, but I needed it. Tanta Karwa knew that.

Seeing I was now pleasantly drained, Tanta Karwa took my hand and looked into my face. "I've told everyone in Choqo you've been tending the sick down valley, including royalty. When nobles are involved the people know better than to ask questions. You needn't explain your travels to them." She touched the blisters on my lips. "You've been in the high passes. . . and your feet! Poor thing. I'll look after you. Tell me nothing unless you want to, and if you do, you know it's safe with me. Now, I have dresses and shawls enough for five women. Come, take your pick. I'll fetch water from the spring for you to bathe."

That night I slept more soundly than I had in months, and didn't arise next day until midmorning. Tanta Karwa only grinned when I emerged wiping sleep from my eyes. Half the day was already gone. She sat under a shade tree mixing medicines, while The-One-Confused-Like-A-

Man grazed the hillside above her herb garden and eyed the nearby female. Word of my arrival spread quickly, and ayllu sisters, many with babies in arm, began dropping by to visit. Tanta Karwa prepared bowls of boiled potatoes with freshly ground chili pepper sauce, and we all sat in the shade peeling the moist skins with our fingers and dipping the warm potatoes in the tangy concoction, gossiping and sipping aqha. The lacquered kero that marked my adoption into the ayllu stayed safe with Tanta Karwa, and I put it to good use answering the many toasts that came my way. The healer Qori Qoyllur had returned to the bosom of Ayllu Añawarqe.

Qhari came from behind, snatching me from my thoughts with a hug. "You look well, Qori." He took my arm and we strolled the K'allachaka terraces.

"And you also, brother. Let me see those poor hands of yours." He allowed me to study them for any permanent effects of the cold. There were none.

"Whole and fit, as you can see," he said withdrawing his hands. "How is Tanta Karwa?"

I recounted everything of the time I spent with her and the ayllu at Choqo, and when I finished his only remark was, "I didn't know there were so many babies born to Ayllu Añawarqe."

So many? Without realizing it I had dwelled at length on the new mothers with their infants. In truth, there were no more than usual but I never noticed before.

Qhari looked at me quizzically. "Qori, what are you thinking?"

I turned away, fidgeting with the silver tupu Tanta Karwa had given me. I wasn't yet ready to tell him about the child Zapana and I created.

"It's Lord Atoq," I said. "Qhari, he was there at the Hatunqolla akllawasi when the first murders happened."

Qhari's head jerked around. "He was there? He saw something? Does he know who did it?"

"It's as we suspected - Kontor."

I repeated the full story to him as Atoq told it to me. When I finished he said, "So, we were right. It all makes sense. After Kontor murdered those women he lied to father and the others about going to Lord Achachi. It was Kontor who kept them in battle, hoping they'd all be killed to eliminate witnesses. That also explains why Kontor argued against uncle Maita's plan to flee, and when he saw they were resolved to do so anyway, Kontor wanted to know where each would go to hide. Again it was Maita who thought this unsafe and insisted each man keep his destination secret. So Kontor has been hunting them all these years, because they're the only ones who can implicate him. But, Qori, how does he manage to travel and elude Atoq's agents?"

I shrugged. "He must be living under another name, and nowhere near Choqo, otherwise he'd be recognized. Then, too, someone of power must be protecting him and authorizing his travels."

Qhari slapped his forehead. "If he travels! Remember, Kontor didn't come in person for father. He sent assassins. And it must have been Kontor who arranged for the ambush in the desert, and those who attacked us at the bridge, and later in Cuzco. He has others to do his bidding."

"No, he travels, Qhari. Lord Atoq told me that women murdered like his first victim, Ronto, and the poor girl we saw at Sillustani, have been reported all over the Empire. But you're right, he does have the power to command assassins, even whole bands of brigands."

Qhari held up his hand. "But wait. Remember the assassin who came for father? He seemed to believe father was guilty of the crime. So the men Kontor commands don't know his real motive."

"That makes sense," I said, "but what really puzzles me is how Kontor gained all this power. After all, he was only an ayllu war leader from the village of Choqo, hardly royalty."

"True, sister, but here I think you've hit upon it. Only royalty commands the sort of power it takes to reach across the Empire, and avoid Lord Atoq's many eyes all these years. Someone in one of the noble houses must be shielding Kontor, and sending assassins to do his work for him. This must be the same person who arranged your marriage, and threatened to expose me."

"Yes, our silence is sealed on those accounts, it's true. That's why I haven't told Lord Atoq what we know yet. What do you think we should do?"

"If we tell Atoq he'll find Kontor and put an end to all this, but it will be our end, too."

"And Tanta Karwa, and the honor of Ayllu Añawarqe," I said, feeling the weight of it. "Who could be protecting Kontor, and why? What does he have to gain? Or, what is he afraid of?"

Qhari shook his head in reply.

"Then let's make a bargain, Qhari. The five-year meeting at the Temple of Wiraqocha is ten months away. Kontor still thinks father is alive. He'll be there looking for him and uncle Maita. And we'll be there too. . . no matter what." Qhari nodded vigorously at this. "We'll remain silent until then," I said, "but if we don't find Kontor ourselves we'll tell Lord Atoq everything we know and accept the consequences. This must stop, Qhari. Not just for us, but for all those murdered girls and their families, and his future victims."

Qhari met my eyes. "Agreed," he said, his voice firm.

I suddenly realized in ten months' time I'd be a mother.

Qhari cleared his throat. "Qori, there's something you should know," he said, then swallowed and looked at his feet. "The Lord of K'allachaka, old Prince Tupac Amaru, has ordered me to marry."

I could imagine what this meant to him for I'd seen the agony in Sumaq T'ika's eyes when she thought she'd be forced to marry, and the same terrified, pleading look was on my brother's face. I sensed Qhari actually liked women, as friends, but the idea of bedding one repulsed him.

"And what does Zapana say?" I asked.

Qhari gestured the futility with his hands. "He has no authority, certainly not over his grandfather's decrees. If he protested on my behalf it might cast suspicion on him, and besides, he has a wife, though I don't know how he manages it," he said grimacing. "Anyway, it's the law that a man is not an adult until he marries. Tupac Amaru says I'm of age, and it's improper to have a bachelor in his service. He's given me a month to find a bride, and if I don't he'll assign one to me." Qhari looked down and shuffled his feet. "I just thought you should know."

I pressed his arm. "Fear not, brother. I'll look after this for you."

"You? But what can you do?"

"Do you trust me?"

"Yes."

"Then trust me in this."

The sentry peered into the night, straining to hear. He called out a challenge. No answer. With spear leveled he left his post at the gate and walked over to prod the bushes. As soon as he passed the spot where I crouched in the darkness outside the gate, I dashed through the entrance. From there I cast one more stone over his head to keep him moving away.

Inside I slipped behind a bush near the kancha wall and froze in the shadows. The sweet potatoes I carried in my shoulder bag had not been necessary thus far, but I knew my life might yet depend upon them and hoped I'd brought enough. Mama Killa was near full, but the night sky was cloudy. I waited for another drifting bank to obscure Her face. Across the courtyard stood a storage hut. Beside it was an open-fronted building where servants hastily laid out mats and food before a fire - obviously the place where the two lords would meet.

The sentry returned to his post at the gate. Two more guards making their rounds inside the walls paused with him in idle conversation. I stood but twenty paces from them. When the discussion ended they would be headed straight for me. I stopped breathing and braced myself against the wall, ready to dash for the storage hut. Suddenly a low, throaty growl sounded at my side, raising the hairs on my neck.

The dog appeared from nowhere. Sitting on its haunches at my feet, it stared up at me, fangs bared, watching for a twitch to bark at. "Faithful friend," I whispered in a reassuring tone, "good, faithful friend. Good dog. A sweet potato for good dog?" The beast cocked its head and raised its ears, watching my hand slowly descend into the bag hanging at my hip and emerge with a boiled sweet potato. Drooling jaws snapped it up, then turned to devour it on the ground. I threw another a few paces away, and another just beyond that. The cur wagged its tail and followed the trail. Zapana had shown me this trick; mountain dogs can no more resist sweet potatoes than coastal dogs can resist fish. The men exchanged farewells, preparing to continue their patrol. Thick blackness settled on the kancha as the clouds hid the last of Mama Killa. Crouching low I took a deep breath and ran.

Once inside the storage hut I allowed myself to exhale, but held the next breath, listening. No shouting. No barking. I waited motionless while my eyes adjusted to the dark. The interior of the shed was bare except for a few sacks of maize standing upright at the back, and a pile of empty bags beside them. A crack in the wattle-and-daub wall provided a view of the courtyard and open-fronted building on my right. The lords had not yet appeared.

Tanta Karwa had recognized the two men when they arrived at our cottage the day before, and immediately excused herself when they said they came to consult the healer Qori Qoyllur. The message wasn't for her. She went to tend her herb garden. The men entered.

Zapana dropped a bundle against the wall. "Some clothes for you," he said. Tintaya glanced around our cottage with disdain.

Both were in disguise, dressed as commoners and wearing wooden ear-spools, either coming from, or returning to Tipón, I surmised. One didn't ask. Zapana was a handsome man no matter how he dressed. I couldn't help running an appraising eye over him and smiling inwardly. You had this man, I thought, savoring the memory. You know his most intimate secrets, but you still have one surprise for him. How will he take it?

Tintaya's cold, flinty eyes settled on me. "It's about time you were back. Enjoy your little holiday in the lake lands?"

"Tintaya," Zapana said, "you know what she - "

Tintaya cut him off. "I know what she did, nothing more than is expected of any of us. She did her duty, lucky first time out. It's one thing to play with those provincials, but around the capital it's different. Here everyone is an expert." He stood with his toes against mine, glaring down at me.

There was no point in provoking him. He was senior to both of us. Zapana bit his lip and remained silent. I held Tintaya's gaze a moment, then bowed my head submissively. If I'd lain with Tintaya when he wanted me I'd probably be his favorite now, I thought.

"I hope my Lord Tintaya will continue to find my service acceptable," I said.

"So far," he said. Then he turned his back on us and spoke.

"We're busy with Lady Chuqui's people. All our best agents are needed. But a lesser problem has arisen, something even you should be able to handle."

Zapana rolled his eyes at the roof and opened his hands, then glanced sideways at me. I smiled and gave him a little nod. He nodded back. Yes, he knew I could handle Tintaya.

"The man who is to be regent when the Emperor dies has been meeting secretly with the other royal houses. Do you know who this man is?"

Atoq had explained it to me, but Tintaya wasn't to be denied his dramatics. "Lord Wallpaya?" I suggested.

Tintaya spun around as if he hadn't heard me. "No, it's Lord Wallpaya. Don't you know anything?"

I lowered my head, this time to keep from snickering.

"And do you know who arranged for Lord Wallpaya to be named regent? Do you? No, of course you don't," he hurried on without giving me a chance to answer. "It was Lord Sapaca." He let the name dangle. Zapana shuffled his feet and looked away. "You do know who Lord Sapaca is, don't you?" Tintaya asked.

"Speaker of Hurincuzco, Lord," I answered quickly.

"Very good. She does know something after all, Zapana." Zapana gave him a thin smile.

Tintaya said, "Now listen carefully. We've learned that Lord Wallpaya is going into the hills above the city tomorrow. He will worship at the shrine of Q'enko and then go on to pass the night at Pukapukara, his father's hunting lodge. It so happens that Lord Sapaca is currently inspecting the Hurincuzco sections of the new walls at Saqsawaman, an easy distance from Wallpaya's route. You will follow Wallpaya and see whether he meets with Sapaca, and if he does, you will find out what the two of them are planning."

He made it sound as if I were being sent on a minor errand: simply follow two of the most powerful men in the Empire, penetrate their rings of guards, slip into their inner council, and report back on their conversation. Child's play.

Tintaya fixed me with those cold eyes again. "You will not fail. You know how Lord Atoq and I dislike failure." His lips curled in a vicious grin and he added, "Zapana has been out of practice with his maqana lately." I envisioned the execution on the terrace at Tipón years before. "And remember, if anything happens, this time you will not be taken alive. Do you understand? Lord Atoq showed mercy after your first clumsy escapade among the Uru, but here there'll be no second chance. Lord Atoq won't intervene for you again. I am your commander, and my agents are never captured. If you are, then believe me, you'll wish you'd died quickly by your own hand when I'm finished with you."

I believed him.

With that he turned and strode out the door, calling over his shoulder, "Come along, Zapana, there's no use wasting more of the day here."

The instant Tintaya left I said, "Zapana, there's something you must know." Unsure how to begin, I guided his hand to my belly. He hesitated, searching my face. I faltered, "I. . . that is, you and I - "

"Zapana," Tintaya's voice boomed from outside. It was an order.

Zapana gave me a wan smile. "I know; I've been thinking about you, too." It came like a confession torn from him, as if revealing a vulnerability, a depth of feeling I hadn't guessed. It wasn't what I expected.

"No. . . Zapana. . . that's not it. I mean - "

He placed a finger on my lips. "Stay safe, Qori. I'll see you soon. We'll talk then." He vanished through the door.

That night Tanta Karwa awoke to find Inca Moon transforming herself into the 'crone.' A single lamp lit the room. She said nothing after Zapana and Tintaya left. A silence had descended between us. "I must go away for a while," was all I told her. She simply nodded. My duty was to the Empire, and in all matters concerning Atoq and his men no questions were asked. Now she watched me practice hobbling up and down the room, bent over, ashes graying my hair, wearing ragged, discarded clothes from the bundle Zapana brought, and leaning on a staff.

I'm frail, I told myself, frail and helpless - except for Eagle Woman suspended under my dress, two knives beneath my belt, a sling, and the long tupu pin fastening my cloak.

Tanta Karwa watched silently while I added some boiled sweet potatoes to my shoulder bag. Inca Moon was ready.

"May I borrow The-One-Confused-Like-A-Man?" I asked in my
creaking, old-woman voice. "I need to deliver some wood."

She started when she heard my voice, then nodded approvingly,
impressed with my transformation. "Take him," she said, "and all the
wood you need. But Qori, please. . . stay safe, daughter."

Inca Moon slipped into the chill, pre-dawn air.

The hill of Saqsawaman looks down on Cuzco, its lower south slope
crowded with buildings of the city's Qolqampata district, above which the
incline is too steep for dwellings. In later years fine structures crowned the
top of Saqsawaman, and on the north face three enormous walls set one
behind the other overlooked a broad parade ground, but at the time of
which I speak there were only temporary compounds on the summit, and
the second of the three north walls was still under construction.

It's said Emperor Pachakuti began the work, but it was Thupa Inka
who glorified Saqsawaman with the ambitious building campaign that
continued for years after Him, and in the end never was completed. For
tens of years a levy throughout the provinces provided four thousand
men for the quarries, six thousand to haul the massive blocks, and many
others to move earth, lay foundations, and hew logs for the timbers. The
place was an ant hill with swarms of men sweating and grunting from
dawn to dusk, slowly, gradually, fitting one giant block at a time. Once
cut, there is only one place where each stone will fit, and without it, however great or small it is, the wall isn't complete. I could never look at
those salients without thinking of the Empire, carefully built from many
provinces and diverse peoples, each with its own unique place and role
to play, each supporting those around it, safe within the matrix of
Tawantinsuyu - and yet without the least of them the structure would be
weakened, the mosaic incomplete, the harmony shattered.

All day I meandered toward Saqsawaman, skirting the city and the
hauling crews, shuffling along back trails up the Tullumayu ravine on the
east side of the hill. Here the path was a slash of red winding through
dusty glades, where every bush and bird watched the parched clouds.

The few people who passed me hardly gave the old woman and her llama a second glance. Whenever someone approached I maneuvered The-One-Confused-Like-A-Man to the side, letting the swifter traffic pass, and received a grateful, "Good day to you, grandmother."

Where the meeting between Wallpaya and Sapaca would take place, if at all, was uncertain. Wallpaya could go to Sapaca from either Q'enko or Pukapukara; or, Sapaca might meet Wallpaya at either of those places, or elsewhere. Since the cover was best in the ravine below Saqsawaman I decided to station myself there, beside the least used but most direct route, and follow whomever appeared first.

The woods were dry, wanting rain. Branches crackled under my feet. The-One-Confused-Like-A-Man sniffed the air, as thirsty as the forest. I unloaded Tanta Karwa's firewood, tethered him, and removed his ear tassels so he wouldn't be identified. From here on I had to move quickly and alone.

It was Wallpaya and ten of his men who passed my hiding place shortly after sunset. No torches lit their way. The men moved purposefully, casting furtive glances as they went, and followed the trail upward to Saqsawaman. Tintaya was right about a clandestine meeting. Interesting that Wallpaya goes to Sapaca, I thought, for it shows who is the seeker and who is the grantor of favors.

I trailed the party to the parade ground above, or what would become the parade ground - in those days the field was littered with huge stone blocks in various stages of preparation, coils of thick cables, log supports, piles of hammer stones, and earthen ramps providing gentler inclines for positioning the upper courses in the great walls lining one side of the field. The laborers and foremen had long since returned to their villages for the night, and the site lay empty. With no difficulty I followed Wallpaya's men, slipping from cover to cover across the field, and up through the half-finished walls to the broad summit where they disappeared through a gate in a makeshift compound. It was the sentry outside this entrance who left his post to investigate strange noises in the bushes.

Now, crouched in the storage hut, I watched a procession of torches enter the courtyard. The two lords walked side by side in their midst.

Sapaca seemed even larger than at his daughter Q'enti's womanhood celebration a few years earlier. He towered over all around him, a mountain of a man with a girth to match, yet stepped lightly and wore his tunic well, though it must have required twice as much cloth as for a normal man's vestments. His thick lips carried a bemused smile, and his gold earspools, armbands, and bracelets glittered in the torchlight. The feather flower emerging from the gold disc fastened to the front of his headband was small - nothing was required to emphasize his height.

In contrast Lord Wallpaya was a short man, and wore a cluster of beaten gold feathers two hand spans tall on his brow. He, too, was layered in gold jewelry, and a pectoral of sacred shell beads - thousands upon thousands of them depicting the royal puma in red on a white ground - covered the upper part of his tunic like a huge bib. His tiny eyes, set too close together, seemed uneasy. The bump of a coca quid protruded low on his left cheek.

The procession headed to the open-fronted building next to my hiding place, where Sapaca's servants spread a feast and busily fluffed pillows. In a moment the lords would be walking by the open door of the storage hut. I retreated into the shadows and wondered how I could get closer to hear their conversation. As they passed the hut Wallpaya stopped and took Sapaca by the arm. "Step in here with me for a moment," he said gesturing at the darkened doorway, "I want to have a word with you in private."

There was a pause. Then Sapaca shrugged, and stooping low he entered the shed. Wallpaya followed, waving for the others to continue and declining the offer of a torch. Once inside the two men faced each other, filling the small space. Sapaca kept his head bowed because of the low roof. Wallpaya looked up at him.

Wallpaya said, "When we sit with the others, let's talk of nothing but fully supporting Titu Cusi as heir. The night has ears, and I don't trust my men any more than you trust yours."

Sapaca nodded.

Wallpaya cleared his throat. "The arms are being produced and hidden as I told you, and they'll be delivered at the appropriate time. Those preparations progress well. But while we have this moment alone, I want to make sure the rest of our bargain still holds."

"All remains as we agreed," Sapaca said.

"Then I can count on Hurincuzco?"

"If Hurincuzco can count on you."

"You know I'm a man of my word, Sapaca."

Sapaca didn't respond.

"And what of Lady Chuqui?" Wallpaya asked.

"That's up to Lady Chuqui."

"Do you intend to support her son first?"

"I'll support the heir," Sapaca replied.

A pause followed while Wallpaya waited for Sapaca to say more, but he remained silent. Wallpaya sighed heavily. "You should be more open with your friends, Sapaca."

"I am open with my friends," Sapaca said.

Wallpaya sighed again. "Just as long as we understand each other."

"Oh, I think we understand each other very well," Sapaca chuckled. "Now, I have a terrible thirst. Would you be so kind as to sample my aqha? I have an exceptionally strong brew waiting."

When their footsteps retreated I waited a moment longer to make certain I was alone, then pulled the sack down around my shoulders, gasping for air. It was one of the most useful lessons I'd been taught at Tipón - becoming part of your surroundings, instantly. When Wallpaya paused outside and motioned Sapaca to the shed, I didn't think, I moved. The only surroundings inside the hut to become part of were the sacks of maize standing at the back. I grabbed an empty bag and joined them. The hard part was not trembling, and trying to breath quietly while my heart thudded like a drum. But it worked perfectly. The plotters were even considerate enough to stand by me while they spoke. But spoke of what? The two had a plan that evidently did not include Titu Cusi becoming heir. There was vague reference to weapons being secretly hoarded and an unspecified delivery date. How many? Where and when? Little to go on. Still, I wasn't likely to hear anything more of use, given that Wallpaya didn't even trust his own escort. I remembered

Princess Koka saying that her father regarded Sapaca as one of the shrewdest bargainers He'd ever known. Now I understood, and had a new respect for the Speaker of Hurincuzco, however crude his manner.

Escape was all that was required now, but as long as the feasting by torchlight went on only paces away I was trapped. A dog appeared at the door and gave a low growl, its eyes fixed on me. I sighed and tossed it a sweet potato. Soon I had a friend sitting beside me wagging her tail. She kept me company while the night dragged on. Somehow I had to get out of there before dawn.

Sapaca engaged Wallpaya and his men in a drinking bout, but eventually I heard him bid them good night and retire. Not Wallpaya. His words loud and slurred, he insisted on a fresh urn and more wood for the fire. I waited. Eventually Wallpaya's was the only voice droning on, and then silence, broken only by loud snores.

I peered out. The servants had quietly departed, having covered Lord Wallpaya and his men with blankets where they sprawled around the fire. From the look of them Sapaca's aqha was indeed especially powerful. Good. The courtyard was empty, but a new guard stood alert at the gate. It wouldn't have been difficult to 'remove' him, but I learned on Taquile that it's best not to leave bodies behind if you want to make a clean escape. Looking around, I spotted a pile of firewood stacked high against the inside wall on the far side of the compound. If I stood on it I would be able to reach the top of the wall and pull myself over. Mama Killa hid behind the clouds again. I gave the last sweet potato to my new friend and slipped into the night.

I became a shadow flitting from corner to corner, until there was just one building left to pass before reaching the woodpile. It was a long, narrow structure with a series of wicker doors, behind which men snored. As I crept by, one of the doors slid open. I flattened against the wall. A man emerged and groggily stumbled forward, scratching his backside. He belched and wet the ground for an eternity, then expelled gut wind and returned to his pallet, passing me at arm's length. I breathed again and praised Sapaca's aqha.

A lamp glowed behind the last door. Edging by, I heard a heavy, satisfied sigh from within, and paused to peek through a crack, then froze. Sapaca lay on his back, tunic pulled up, loincloth discarded, and eyes closed in a smile. A skinny, naked girl with her back to me stood up from where she had just straddled him. The lamp glowed on smooth, honey-golden skin, and shiny black hair flowing to her waist. Not more than fifteen, I decided disapprovingly. A dry branch cracked under my foot. Startled, the girl looked over her shoulder at the door. For an instant I found myself looking into the eyes of Sapaca's daughter, Q'enti.

XXVI

Of the Heathen Emperor whom these Indians called the Ideal Pattern of All Things, and the Immense Reverence in which he was held, and of how a Great Treachery came to pass.

The courtyard brimmed with loitering nobility, and over the drone of the crowds came the wailing and babbling of seers. A sacrificed llama lay on its side while a priest, arms covered in blood, searched the entrails for signs. Slanting rays of the afternoon sun cast shadows across the intricate stone walls and high, thatch roofs of Chinchero. It wasn't only those gathered at the royal estate who waited; the whole world held its breath.

Tanta Karwa appeared at my side. "They told me you were coming," she said. "What do you want me to do?"

"Just get me into the room with the Emperor," I said, "and I'll do the rest. How long does He have?"

In answer she directed my eyes to the sun, sinking ever lower. Lady Chuqui had to make her move soon.

I would have joined Tanta Karwa and the Cuzco nobility in their dash to Chinchero, but when word came of the impending death I was sequestered in a confessional at the Qorikancha. Still, it's a day's journey from Cuzco to Chinchero, and I made it in half that time, not long behind the others.

I looked over the solemn faces crowding the courtyard. Qhari glanced at me blankly from his position by the gate, and though I wasn't in disguise he turned away without recognition. He had been instructed well. Tintaya, I was amused to see, was presenting himself as a female seer, none too convincingly.

Empress Mama Oqllo and Princess Koka stood in one corner surrounded by the mournful reverence of their ladies-in-waiting, while in the opposite corner the First Consort, Lady Chuqui, whispered behind her hand to some lords who nodded thoughtfully. Her son, Prince Wari, pretender to the Royal Fringe, stood at her side peering nervously through the crowd. A handsome youth, I decided, but thin, and with a permanently furrowed brow, no doubt from carrying the weight of being Chuqui's son. I judged him to be a year senior to Titu Cusi, the Heir Apparent.

Titu Cusi was not present. His father insisted on keeping him sequestered at Qispikancha below Tipón, and even now he remained in seclusion. Also absent was Lord Wallpaya, the regent-to-be, which seemed odd, but then, if there was intrigue in the making he probably thought it wise to be elsewhere.

My gaze settled on the hulking form of Sapaca. Beast! I thought. How could you do that to your own daughter? No, that wasn't in my report to Atoq. How could it be? If I accuse you of incest, who will come forward to accuse me of the same? And who will be believed, the Speaker of Hurincuzco or the second rank noble Qori Qoyllur, demonstrably guilty herself?

Q'enti hadn't seen me that night. In two bounds I made the wood pile and scrambled over the compound wall, fleeing through the night pursued only by my own rage and disgust, my presence undetected and the escape clean. 'Crone' and The-One-Confused-Like-A-Man were on the trail to Tipón by dawn.

Tanta Karwa took my arm. "The Emperor's room is this way," she said.

Making our way from the courtyard to the restricted buildings crowning the hilltop, it still surprised me to find that the private quarters of royalty weren't much larger than our cottage at Choqo. To be sure, the walls are of finely cut stone blocks with double- and triple-jamb doorways, and with splendid wall niches inside, but the floor area of these single-story structures affords little extra room. But then, as I've said, people rise and rest with the sun, and life is lived in the open. It's no different for royalty. Private rooms are used only for sleeping. Of course, there are separate structures for other needs: open-fronted buildings are used as kitchens and for lounging, there are temples and storehouses, and great feasting halls that hold hundreds of guests, so an entire royal complex can be scattered along a hillside as at K'allachaka, or, where constrained by natural bounds, tightly packed as on the hill of

344

Chinchero overlooking the Yucay Valley.

The Emperor had been gravely ill for years, hardly able to move, and his audience hall was converted into a bedroom for his convenience. It was an extended building with four doors spaced down one of its long walls, three of them now closed and the fourth guarded. The crossed spears of the sentries snapped upright when Tanta Karwa approached, but a warlord with a disc of gold on his chest stepped into our path.

"Tanta Karwa," he said, "you may pass, but only you." He eyed me suspiciously.

"This is my assistant, the healer Qori Qoyllur," Tanta Karwa said nodding to me. "I require her help."

"Her name is not among those with permission to enter," the warlord replied, throwing back his shoulders and lifting a stubborn chin.

I stepped forward. "My Lord, if you'll only look at this. . . ." I opened my palm showing him the tiny stick. No more than a sliver of hardwood the length of a finger, it carried the colored bands representing Tipón and Atoq's authority. The warlord peered at it, and then nervously shifted his eyes from side to side, hesitating.

I leaned closer. "A private word, Lord."

He glanced around, then lowered his head to listen.

"I am Inca Moon," I whispered.

He jerked upright and eyed me. "But. . . but you're a - "

"A woman," I finished for him.

He caught himself, masking his surprise. "You shall pass, and it's my duty to provide anything you need," he said, reluctantly stepping aside. Tanta Karwa cast me an admiring glance.

A maid holding a tray piled with fruit appeared in the doorway, bowed, and offered the tray for our selection. We each chose a piece; the necessary token offering, for no one goes before the Emperor with empty hands.

Inside, cloth screens partitioned one end of the hall affording the patient some privacy; guards and servants lined the walls, motionless. We handed our offerings of fruit to an attendant, who accepted them, bowed, and backed away. Though we couldn't see the Emperor a chamberlain indicated the screen behind which He rested, and we performed the much'a to our semi-divinity, bowing low from the waist with arms stretched level with our heads, then bringing our fingertips to our lips and blowing a kiss in His direction. The chamberlain nodded and pushed one end of the screen aside. Following Tanta Karwa's lead I knelt and placed my forehead on the rush matting, then shinnied forward beside her. The screen closed behind us.

We remained on our knees, as all must in the presence of the Emperor, but we were allowed to lift our heads, a singular honor reserved for immediate family and the highest lords of the Empire, and healers in the course of their duties. Thupa Inka lay on a pallet of alpaca blankets, his thin frame covered by more blankets of soft vicuña wool, over which were laid tunics and cloaks rich in color and weave. These were the clothes He would have worn that day. Like the statues of the gods, the Emperor was dressed in new clothes daily, and those of the previous day were either permanently stored or burned. He wore the Royal Fringe, a headband of corded red wool with two tubular gold beads at the front, below which a wide tassel hung to His eyebrows.

Three of His concubines silently attended, one waving a feather fan over his face, another poised to offer him food and drink from golden vessels should he awake, and the third studying the pillow on which His head rested. As I watched she triumphantly picked a silver hair from the pillow and popped it in her mouth - a precaution against sorcery.

The Emperor's audience stool stood before us, a magnificent snarling puma carved from black hardwood with emerald eyes, inlaid with turquoise and sacred red shell, and knee high, the tallest in the land. In wall niches behind leaned the imperial standard, scepter, and war club of gold, the symbols of Thupa Inka's divine royalty, and below these knelt a row of silent priests, wizards, and healers. The healers watched our every move with interest and scorn. Other servitors tended the golden braziers heating the room. A huge disc of gold hung at the head of the Emperor's pallet, and another of silver at the foot. Father Sun and Mother Moon had come from their temples to watch over their beloved Son.

Tanta Karwa nudged me forward, and I trembled to look upon the face of the demigod Son of the Sun, Lord of Tawantinsuyu, Ideal Pattern of All Things, Most Beautiful and Precious Creation - the Emperor Thupa Inka. I pardon myself if my breath caught and I near-fainted in awe. That I, Qori Qoyllur of Choqo, but one in millions of His devoted subjects, should have the privilege of actually looking into the face of the Divine Lord, Shaper of the World, was too much to grasp. In that momentary glance I saw a grandfatherly countenance, thin and drawn, care-worn but calm. Who could not love Him - He who had marched with His armies, hundreds of thousands strong, to bring peace and enlightenment to the far reaches of the world; He whose word was heard at every hearth, however humble, who cared for the least of His people that none went hungry; He who held the savages back from our doors, who was the ultimate mediator between us and the gods, whose every waking thought was for His people? But the years of stewardship were etched on His kindly face, their toll inscribed in creases at forehead, eyes, and mouth. A sob escaped me when I saw how His left eye and the left side of His mouth drooped.

Tanta Karwa took my arm and, still on our knees, we withdrew to a place by the wall.

"He is old, Qori," she whispered. "He can't stay with us forever."

"But, mother, what have we done to bring this illness upon Him?"

Tanta Karwa sighed heavily. "The priests have offered every prayer and sacrifice for Him, and we healers have prescribed every herb known to us. The people have cleansed their hearts; did you not see the lines before the confessionals in Cuzco? Did you not go to confession your-self? We all have. No, it's not our doing; it's just the way of life. He is old, Qori, and His time has come."

As we settled back in silence to keep the death vigil my thoughts strayed back to the Qorikancha that morning. Confession? Yes, I sup-pose it was, although at the time I thought of it as a sharing with my dear friend Sumaq T'ika. I arrived shortly after dawn to find Sumaq busy in her husband's shrine. She had just dressed Him in a splendid new tunic, and was tilting a golden tray containing His breakfast into a brazier. She turned and smiled while I performed the much'a to Him. Illap'a looked down on me impassively, His image that of a man, life size, and wrought of gold, with golden headband and earspools, and in one hand He held His gold war club. God of War, Thunder, Lightning, Rain and Rainbows, after Inti the most powerful male deity. The countryside was still parched. I spoke a prayer for rain while Sumaq watched approvingly, though it was the prayer of the warrior that came to mind - Lord Illap'a, let me die bravely with weapons in hand, serving my Emperor.

"Qori, there's something special about you today," Sumaq said. "What's happened? Tell me your news."

It was several months since I'd seen Sumaq - our last meeting was before I left for Qollasuyu - and indeed, much had happened. She pulled her cloak over her head and assumed the posture of confessor in the temple alcove. I knew what it was she saw in me, and there in the sanctity of the confessional I didn't hesitate. Kneeling before her, I touched her hand. Her fingers eagerly entwined mine.

"Sumaq, heart of my heart, I'm to be a mother."

"Qori, when? Who? This is wonderful!"

I related all, the truth of it, and her eyes shone, especially when I told her my daughter's name would be Sumaq T'ika. Neither of us doubted it would be a daughter, and I think Sumaq was envious that I could have a child without the bothersome interference of a husband. She was excitedly telling me about the baby clothes she was going to make when I reminded her that for now I wanted to keep it a secret. Though I didn't explain to Sumaq - she seemed delighted to have this secret just between us for a little while longer anyway - a voice inside me urged delaying the announcement until after Titu Cusi was safely installed as Crown Prince. If Atoq knew of my pregnancy he might insist I retire to Choqo, and I'd miss my chance to serve Tawantinsuyu in this the most crucial of times.

When I told Sumaq about Qhari and the marriage being forced on him she listened solemnly, her pretty face drawn and clouded as she commiserated with his plight. Yes, she understood all too well, and yes, she would be pleased to help. "Have I not always gone along with your plans?" she said with a wink.

I stuck out my tongue and blew the sound of the farting sorceress.

Sumaq shook with giggles.

Dear, sweet Sumaq. So beautiful. The only real friend of my girl-hood, the only one I had to measure the years with, to share memories and keep secrets with, to count on in ways that Qhari and Tanta Karwa could not fill.

Sumaq had by now suspected the double life I led. How could I tell her about Qollasuyu and Lake Titiqaqa without explaining why I was there?

"Sometimes I serve the Lord of Tipón," I answered her raised brows.

Sumaq understood and nodded thoughtfully. "To be one of those who work quietly to keep peace in the Empire is a high calling," she replied solemnly. "I'm proud of you Qori." I blushed under her praise. "But Qori, isn't it dangerous?"

I shrugged. "No more than raiding the akllawasi storehouses."

"And you were always the best at that," she said chuckling at the memory.

"I had excellent help," I reminded her.

She met my smile, and in her eyes I saw that she would ask no more about my other life, unless I offered. I told her about Sapaca and his daughter Q'enti. It was a rage that burned inside me, though it had noth-ing to do with my life - complicated enough as it was - or with the intrigue now unfolding over the succession. Yet the memory of what I saw still seized my heart in an icy grip. I hated Sapaca for it, but I was beginning to admit to myself that what troubled me more were Q'enti's eyes, which had held no hurt, no fear, no revulsion. True, I looked into her eyes for only an instant, but I couldn't deny what I'd seen there - nothing. There was nothing, only eyes like deep, still pools, devoid of emotion. I saw her standing up from straddling him, but her face showed no more concern than if she had just finished washing her hands, and her mind was already elsewhere. Didn't she understand what he was forc-ing her to do? Didn't she care?

Sumaq cleared her throat and fidgeted. I wondered how many such horrors she had heard in the confessional. How did she carry the weight?

"Mama Killa has heard you, Qori," she said in her formal priestess voice. "We must keep Q'enti in our prayers, and I'll ask my husband to make Lord Sapaca see the filth of his sin."

Is that all? I wanted to shout, but even as the words choked in my throat I knew the answer. What could be done? Sumaq was sworn to the secrecy of the confessional, and I. . . well. . . perhaps that's what troubled me most - I was the only one who knew, yet I was powerless to stop it without sacrificing myself, Qhari, Tanta Karwa, and the honor of my ayllu brothers and sisters. If it were up to me alone, I assured myself, I would do what is right, but is it right to destroy so many innocents in the doing?

Sadly I took my leave of Sumaq T'ika, but when I stepped from the alcove I bumped into old Cormorant. She must have been hovering just outside. Had she heard us? The scowl on her face offered no answer; it was the same disapproving grimace she always gave me when I was an aklla. Well, she too is a priestess, I thought, and sworn to the sanctity of the confessional. Perhaps, having lived shut away from the world for so long, she secretly thrives on the troubles of others. Cormorant shrugged her cloak over her head and scuttled away without a word.

Zapana waited for me a block from the Qorikancha, where worshippers step back into their sandals.

"I thought you'd be in there all morning," he complained. Before I could reply he rushed on, "Now listen carefully. Tanta Karwa has already been summoned to Chinchero. Yes, the Emperor's time has come. You're to go there immediately and stay close to Him. Tintaya is there now. I must stay in the city and keep an eye on Lady Chuqui's confederates. I've sent Qhari to Chinchero in case you need a reliable messenger. He knows where to find me in Cuzco. Now hurry, Qori, hurry!"

While he blurted this at me all I could think was, You're going to be a father, and I must have muttered it for he said, "What? What are you babbling about? Are you in some temple trance? Qori, this is urgent. Move!"

The sound of the room catching its breath brought me back to the Emperor's deathwatch. Hands flew to mouths. The Son of the Sun was stirring. One of his concubines leaned over to catch his whispers, and then dashed for the door. While she was gone the other two placed cushions and helped Him sit up. Tanta Karwa held her arm across my chest, keeping me still, her eyes never leaving the Emperor's face.

"This is the moment," she whispered. "He will name His heir now, or never."

Attendants pulled back the screens, opening the hall. Nobles flooded through the door, each trying to perform the much'a and kneel while others jostled behind. The building filled with prostrate bodies. A space opened for Mama Oqllo and Princess Koka at the front. Lady Chuqui and Prince Wari shouldered in beside them. A Sun Priest and Sun Priestess in temple robes took their places at the head and foot of the royal pallet, standing before the great discs representing Inti and Mama Killa. A murmur arose as more nobles pushed forward, demanding a place closer to the Emperor.

Then Thupa Inka raised His hand, all shuffling ceased, and silence heavy with expectation filled the room.

When the Most Beautiful and Perfect Creation spoke His voice did not carry the weakness of age, though His speech was thick because of the illness that left one side of his mouth drooping.

"My dear family, friends, and relations," He began. "My father Inti wants me to dwell with Him, and I wish to go and rest in His presence. I have summoned you to hear the name of the one whom I desire to succeed me as Lord of Tawantinsuyu, to govern and rule over you."

A buzz swept the assembly, but the Sun Priest held up his hands for silence and answered on behalf of the crowd, "Lord, we are much grieved at your illness, but if Inti has willed it, so must it be. His will be done. Who do you nominate for your successor?"

"I choose Titu Cusi, son of my sister and wife, Mama Oqllo."

I joined the collective sigh of relief that followed. The Emperor had finally named His heir. In truth it wasn't a decree, it was a nomination to be confirmed by the heads of the royal panaqas. The choice wouldn't be finalized for a year. But the Emperor's wishes carried enormous weight, and as long as the Crown Prince had the favor of the majority his place was secure.

My eyes settled on Lady Chuqui. There was no defeat on her face, or acceptance, or defiance. She played her game well. When Atoq plays fives he likes to let his opponents think they're winning, I reminded myself, just before he springs his trap.

The Emperor slumped back on his pallet, closing His eyes again. The priests exchanged a nod and held up their arms, silently shooing the assembly outside. Everyone rose holding a deep bow, careful not to turn their backs on the Emperor, and began shuffling backwards through the door.

My eyes never left Lady Chuqui. Tanta Karwa tugged at my arm but I lingered, gesturing for her to go ahead. Chuqui made all the motions of leaving, but didn't move far. I edged my way to a stack of blankets against the wall and sank down beside it, becoming part of it. No one seemed to notice. From this vantage I had a clear view of the Emperor's face. Prince Wari was the last to leave, raising his head slightly to exchange a look with his mother as he backed through the door. His eyes pleaded, but Chuqui's face was stone.

As the screens were drawn again Chuqui knelt by Thupa Inka's pallet. The three concubines also stayed behind, hovering over the Emperor with large fans, which, I realized later, obscured the view of the others who remained. Several guards and servants stood like statues against the walls, and the Sun Priest and Priestess kept their foreheads pressed to the matting. Chuqui squinted her tiny eyes around the room to make sure no one else was present. She didn't notice the extra 'blanket.'

The hall darkened, and I envisioned Inti like a blazing orb settling behind the western hills. The Emperor's chest barely raised the covers now, his breath but a ragged whisper. Lady Chuqui sat patiently. No one moved. His time was close. Again I was struck with the awe of it, that I, Qori Qoyllur, should witness Thupa Inka's last breath, and with it the passing of a legend.

The Emperor's breathing stopped, and with a deep, audible sigh, that part of the spirit which leaves the body took flight, seeking its home with its celestial parents. Chuqui leaned over the Emperor and put her ear to His lips, while the concubines fluttered their fans and looked nervously over their shoulders. The servitors and priests were unaware that Thupa Inka had breathed his last.

Chuqui stood with a smile. "The Emperor has changed His mind," she announced in a clear voice that almost caused me to fall over. "He wishes

Prince Wari to follow Him. Go forth and make the announcement."

So that was it! With the Emperor dead who could dispute her? The faces of the concubines showed they were part of it, convenient witnesses to back up the claim. "I will summon the people," one replied.

Still crouching against the wall, I watched open-mouthed as the screens moved and the room once more flooded with royalty, this time in a bustle of confusion. Tanta Karwa and the other healers surrounded the Emperor. Chuqui held up her hand for silence.

"My brother and lord, Thupa Inka, has changed his mind," she said. "He spoke to me, saying He was forced into naming Titu Cusi, but He couldn't join His Father with an impure heart. He desires Wari to be His successor. Ask Him. Ask the Lord of the World."

The pandemonium was silenced when Tanta Karwa stood and turned to face the crowd, the other healers solemnly flanking her. "The Lord cannot answer," she said quietly. "He has gone home."

"What?" Chuqui gasped. "How can this be? He spoke with me but a moment ago."

Tanta Karwa lowered her head. "It is so, Lady. The Emperor is with His Father now."

A rush of angry voices rose, but the Sun Priest stepped forward. "Silence! The Son of the Sun is still warm on His deathbed and you stand there haggling? The succession will be discussed in the courtyard. Now, clear the hall and grant our Lord the dignity of His eternal rest."

As the hall emptied again Tanta Karwa came to me, the question in her eyes. I shook my head. "Then what are we to do?" she asked. I had no answer.

The courtyard resounded with wailing, every cloak drawn over its owner's head to mark the mourning, but the death was overshadowed by the concerns of the living. Tight circles whispered as people scurried from one group to the next. The Emperor's death had to be kept secret until the Crown Prince was announced in the great square of Cuzco, and the proper rituals performed. Until then Tawantinsuyu was vulnerable - a body without a head.

A circle formed around Mama Oqllo and Lady Chuqui, who stood glaring at each other. "Oh, sister, I never thought you'd stoop to such treachery," Mama Oqllo said, her eyes casting daggers.

"Treachery? Sister, I speak the truth," Chuqui replied innocently. "Our brother always wanted what's best for the Empire. Is it my fault He chose my son over yours?"

"Did He?" Mama Oqllo asked, the question really an accusation.

Tanta Karwa stepped between them asking for calm. The women fell silent but continued to stick out their chins at each other, each fiercely holding the other's gaze. For an instant I saw two little princesses arguing over a doll with their governess trying to part them. It had undoubtedly been so many times while they grew up together, sisters betrothed to their own brother, vying for his affection, but only one destined to be his wife. But this time no mere doll was at stake. The rivalry of a lifetime had come to a head, and the fate of the Empire hung on the outcome. Chuqui was having her revenge for being relegated to First Consort while her sister ruled as Empress.

"My Ladies, calm yourselves, please," Tanta Karwa said. "We must think of your holy brother now, and do what is right for Him."

Chuqui ignored her. "I have witnesses," she shouted, "ask them." She pointed a finger at the three concubines, all of who nodded.

"It is so," one said. "We heard the Emperor name Prince Wari." All three heads bobbed emphatically.

They were poor liars, but they were royal ladies and senior concubines. What have they been promised for this performance? I wondered. Overlordships for their sons, or merely estates for themselves?

"And, ask the priests," Chuqui said, her eyes glinting triumph.

All heads swung to the priest and priestess who had remained by the Emperor. They looked at each other and, taking a deep breath, the man replied for both, "We can neither confirm nor deny it. We were in the room but our heads were bowed in prayer."

Chuqui shot them a glance that said they hadn't fulfilled their part of a bargain, but they paid no heed, looking instead at Lord Sapaca's bulk looming at the back of the crowd. Sapaca steadily returned their gaze without a twitch. He said nothing, offering neither aid nor hindrance to

Chuqui's claim, waiting for the outcome before choosing sides.

"What about the guards and servants?" someone asked. The Captain of the Guard spoke for all of them. "We hear nothing that is said in the royal presence, but yes, I did see Lady Chuqui place her ear to the Emperor's lips. He may have whispered something but I can't be sure."

Chuqui looked delighted with the answer. She didn't need unanimous support, only doubt, and that began to creep over many faces.

"Consult the diviners," Chuqui suggested. "Ask them if I speak the truth." As if awaiting her call - which they undoubtedly had been - five men pushed through the crowd carrying two braziers. They were fire-diviners from the town of Huaro, respected by all, and equally feared because their word was considered final. They seated themselves around their braziers, and four of them began blowing on the fat-soaked wood through long, silver-tipped tubes while their leader questioned the spirits. When flames shot from one of the many openings cut in the braziers he received his answer. The confidence on Chuqui's face told me the outcome before the ceremony progressed far. I left, curious to know what was happening elsewhere while this performance held everyone's attention.

Torches were lit as I approached Qhari by the gate. "Is it true?" he asked.

"Not a word of it. I was in the room, Qhari. The Emperor died before Chuqui pretended to hear him speak."

"I thought so," he said. "What can we do?"

I had no answer to that yet. "Have you stayed at your post?"

"Yes."

"Have you seen anything?"

"An imperial runner left as soon as Thupa Inka named Titu Cusi. He's probably bound for Qispikancha, where the Heir waits. But another runner, one of Chuqui's men, slipped down the road just moments ago."

Titu Cusi will stay at Qispikancha until Mama Oqllo returns to Cuzco, I reasoned, but She won't set out at night. It will take Her entourage all of tomorrow to reach the city. Titu Cusi won't be confirmed in the great square until noon of the following day. But with

Chuqui's runner already on the way, her people in Cuzco will be notified tonight and have ample time to rally their forces. If Wari arrives in Cuzco before Titu Cusi and is announced in the great square, their coup will be complete before Mama Oqllo even reaches the city.

I grasped my brother's hands. "Qhari, there may be little hope, but we must do what we can. I must stay close to Prince Wari, and you...."

"Yes, go on," he said eagerly.

I hated to involve him, but this wasn't about us, it was about our duty to the Emperor and Tawantinsuyu.

"Remember how you used to run on the beaches?"

Qhari swallowed and looked away. He was thinking of the last time his toes gripped the sand, and he ran and ran and ran, the night father died. Brushing past the memory he replied, "When I came to these mountains they made me a messenger."

"Qhari, I wouldn't ask, but I could never catch Chuqui's runner. Do you still have the wind?"

He smiled and nodded.

"Then you must stop him."

"Stop Chuqui's runner?"

"Yes. Permanently."

"I'll do it," he said with a grin, squeezing my hands, "or forfeit my life trying."

XXVII

In which the Conspirators further ignite their Plot, the drought is ended, maize beer is served, and a Desperate Battle rages with deeds of such Daring and Courage that had it not happened just so it would not be believed.

A hum of excitement rose from the crowd surrounding the Huaro fire-seers. Lady Chuqui's voice proclaimed over the din, "You see, I speak the truth, the Emperor changed His mind. Wari is Crown Prince!" In the ensuing clamor accusations flew and angry fingers wagged, but Lady Chuqui turned her back and defiantly strode away.

Chuqui will have many debts to settle if she succeeds, I thought, but then, she'll have the Empire to give away.

"Don't turn around," a voice behind me said. Over my shoulder I glimpsed a woman with her back to me. I held my eyes forward. Tintaya, still disguised as a female seer, wanted a word. I smiled to myself. He looked foolish in that costume, and not at all convincing.

"What happened in the Emperor's room?" he whispered.

I told him. He said, "We should have expected something like that. Have any of Chuqui's people left yet?"

"A runner. I've seen to it that he won't reach Cuzco." I bit my lip, imagining Qhari racing down the night road, gaining on his target. Qhari has never killed before, I thought, how will he manage? At the very least I hope he's able to defend himself, but. . . Chuqui's men are ruthless.

"Good," Tintaya said, though he sounded hesitant. I knew he fumed inwardly at my efficiency, but his next words surprised me. "Qori, they've spotted me. . . Chuqui's men." There was a resignation in his voice I hadn't heard before. "They're watching now. I can't get near Chuqui so you'll have to be the one to watch her. Chuqui and Wari are preparing to leave for Cuzco tonight. You know what that means. By noon tomorrow they'll be announcing Wari in the great square, and then civil war will surely follow. We can't let that happen, Qori. We can't."

He was pleading, and not for himself. For all his arrogance and meanness he was first of all loyal to the Empire. Civil war meant the end of Tawantinsuyu, because the moment we finished tearing ourselves apart subject peoples like the Chuncho and Lupaqa would be at the throats of the survivors. Chuqui gambled that to avoid such fratricidal weakening the Cuzco nobility would accept her son, the false heir. But Atoq once told me the warlords faithful to Thupa Inka and Mama Oqllo would never allow it. Chuqui and her reluctant son must not reach the great square. The fate of the Empire rested with we few.

"They're watching me again," Tintaya whispered, keeping his head down. "I'll remain here and keep an eye on Lord Sapaca. You must stay close to Lady Chuqui, follow her, find out where she goes and who she meets, and what her plans are. Then find a way to stop her."

"Is that all?"

"No. Zapana waits in Cuzco. Send someone - "

"I already have. Once Qhari finishes with Chuqui's messenger he'll find Zapana and alert him to what's happened here."

"Qhari, your brother?" I felt his resigned shrug. "Very well, but remember, our agents are never taken alive."

I threaded my way into the milling crowd, around me torchlight sparkling on gold and silver baubles like moonlight on water. Coolness descended on the night with a breeze that drew cloaks tighter, and the smell of charred flesh wafted from the sacrificial fires.

A hand gripped my arm.

"I won't marry him, Qori. I won't."

I turned to find Princess Koka staring earnestly at me. She had grown womanly in the years since I sat up all night comforting her in her room, though no taller, being graced with her mother's stature - about my height. I visited her a few times since when Tanta Karwa attended the Empress, and though our meetings were brief Koka still considered me a confidant. But then, I was from outside the circle of palace retainers and therefore a 'safe' friend. Though her father just died and the Empire faced crisis, still her only concern was the threatened marriage to her brother, which would make her Empress of the world. I was probably the only woman in Tawantinsuyu who felt sorry for her.

"You haven't come to see me in so long," she said, keeping her grip on my arm. "He still tries to touch me, Qori. He says when he's Emperor he'll do anything he wants with me. Qori, please. . . ."

She looks like a woman, I thought, but right now she has the eyes of a frightened little girl. Koka, this is not the time.

"Yes, my Lady, I understand. But your poor father has just left us - "

"Yes, and I'm sorry, but I hardly knew Him. Qori, what am I to do about Titu Cusi? No one else cares how I feel. You're the only one I can trust. Listen, there's more," she said lowering her eyes. "I can't stand my brother, that's true; but, Qori, I don't want to be empress. I don't want my mother's life. I can't do it! Don't you see?"

Suddenly I did, and clearly. Mama Oqllo's every waking moment was devoted to the Empire in endless court receptions, temple celebrations, diplomatic negotiations, and a thousand daily details besides. Koka grew up watching Her carry this enormous burden, and it wasn't a life she wanted.

But there was more in Koka's eyes than in her words, and it was there I saw the honesty of her confession. No, it wasn't simply because she loathed a brother she barely knew, or because she didn't want to be troubled with the duties of Empress, or even because she was plagued with self-doubt, it was because she honestly knew within herself that she didn't have the abilities to lead Tawantinsuyu. It was this truth that lay behind her rebellion, a truth she always felt but was unable to express, and had she tried, it would have fallen on the deaf ears of those who had already decided her future. Koka, I suddenly realized, wasn't being a spoiled princess, she was acting in the best interests of the Empire, which was only as strong as its leaders.

From the corner of my eye I saw Chuqui's entourage forming by the gate. Litters were brought for Chuqui and Wari. So, I thought, the bitch intends to have him carried into Cuzco like an emperor.

"My Lady, leave this with me. All will be well," I said, trying to brush her hand from my arm.

"Promise I won't have to marry him," she demanded, still clutching.

"I promise you won't have to marry him," I replied. She was about to say more when Tanta Karwa appeared. "Mother," I said, "you remember my friend, Princess Koka? Yes, of course you do. The poor thing is so distraught over her father's passing."

Tanta Karwa caught my look and immediately took over, gently freeing my arm from Koka's grasp. "You poor thing. I can't tell you how sorry we all are. Please come and take some aqha with the ladies." She gave me a wink over her shoulder as she placed her arm around Koka and led her away.

Chuqui's people formed a column and prepared to depart for Cuzco by torchlight. I needed a disguise to mask my presence among them. A maid with a bundle on her back hurried to the rear of the procession, a Qolla woman wearing the huge dress and cap-hood of her homeland. Ah, yes, I thought, just the outfit for Choque the maidservant. Come here my dear.

"But. . . but. . . ."

"You haven't had your aqha yet? Lady Chuqui insisted all her servants enjoy a kero before setting out, to give you strength for the journey. Come with me behind that shed and I'll get some for you. Hurry."

A few pinches of Condin Savana's sleeping powder in the aqha had the girl unconscious in moments. When she awoke she would find herself dressed in the richer garments of Qori Qoyllur. A shame I wouldn't be there to see the look on her face. I shouldered her bundle, pulled the hood low, and slipped in at the rear as the last torches paraded through the gate.

Mama Killa was in Her uña paqarin phase, the moon just born, and low clouds hid the stars. The air, heavy and cool, gathered now in a steady breeze that hinted change. I kept my head lowered, and though the night chill descended I felt myself sweating. Soldiers armed with maqanas and spears marched on either side, eyes alert. Retainers trudged ahead, and beyond them were the treacherous Huaro fire-seers and the three concubines, Chuqui's 'witnesses,' eager to repeat their lies for her Cuzco confederates. Lady Chuqui and Prince Wari floated on litters at the head of the procession, surrounded by ranks of bodyguards. I clutched Eagle Woman, thinking of using her to end this charade there and then on the road to Cuzco and save the Empire - my own death would follow immediately, but in truth that wasn't a concern - but Chuqui and Wari were royalty, and without Atoq's authorization they were untouchable.

For a royal entourage we moved quickly through the night, four sets of bearers taking turns with the litters, shifting the poles to fresh shoulders without a break in stride. Strutting just short of a run the column pushed on without rest, racing to meet the dawn in Cuzco. Suddenly Illap'a cracked His sling and the cascade began. No gentle drops of warning, it was as if a curtain had dropped transforming the night into a deluge. A sigh swept the ranks and for a moment our steps faltered, smiling faces lifted to the sky. The drought was over. The gods may have been deaf to the temple prayers, but the heavens wept at the passing of our beloved Emperor Thupa Inka. It was He who the people now thanked for their deliverance. I imagined The-One-Confused-Like-A-Man pulling at his tether and kicking his hind legs. In villages throughout the land farmers stirred in their beds, then rushed outside, hugging neighbors and rejoicing that Mama Pacha's thirst was finally quenched. Yet soon the land would be plunged into mourning. I prayed it would only be for the Emperor.

The torchlight sputtered and vanished in smoky wisps. For the remainder of the night the column continued in drenched darkness, silent but grimly determined, slipping and stumbling, but never ceasing the pace. The rain slackened to a drizzle as we approached the outlying districts of Cuzco in the gray, pre-dawn light. Inti began to lighten the eastern sky, but remained dozing behind the hills rimming the Huatanay Valley where slumbered the holy city. I shook myself to readiness.

"You look tired and wet," the voice said.

I didn't allow myself to turn. How had he managed to recognize me and slip past the guards to my side? Perhaps he was more capable than I dared guess.

"And you sound very pleased with yourself," I whispered. "Keep your voice down and eyes straight ahead." I glanced nervously at the escort. Their lines straggled, and they hadn't yet roused themselves from their somnolent walk.

"Why shouldn't I be? It's been an exciting night," Qhari replied.

I wanted to hug him. "You were successful?"

"Of course. Was there ever any doubt?"

I could feel his self-satisfied grin, and had to stop myself from tripping the braggart.

"I caught up with Chuqui's messenger not far from Chinchero," he said, "and stopped him - permanently. That was the easy part."

"The easy part?"

"Yes, there were two or three other brigands who tried to stop me on the road to Cuzco, but I dealt with them, too," he said, making it sound like he merely swatted flies.

I thought, Two or three others indeed, brother. As if you didn't keep count.

"But Qhari, how did you kill - "

"Don't ask, sister. It's better you don't know about such things."

I tripped him.

"I found Zapana, too," he said, recovering with a grin. "He's gone for more men. One of his spies is watching us now - don't look around - and will tell Zapana where we're going. Where are we going?"

"I have no idea."

He shrugged as if it were of no concern. "Zapana says the plotters will probably gather in a kancha to await midday and the public declaration in the great square. He's going to attack, but he doesn't want the city roused, so he's going to break through and surprise them in their stronghold. He wants you on the inside, ready to open the gate when he gives the signal."

"Very well. Now go."

"Go? Go where?"

"Away from here, Qhari. Just slip away. Go. Shoo."

"I'm not leaving you, sister. This is dangerous. I'll protect you."

I rolled my eyes, thinking, He's going to protect me? Just what I need, another hero to look after. True, he stopped Chuqui's runner, and perhaps a few others - if he's not exaggerating, which he surely is - but I can't do what I must and worry about my brother at the same time.

"I said, go. That's an order."

"Stay close to me. That's an order," he replied.

One of the soldiers looked at us curiously. "Nor will I ever marry you," I shouted at Qhari. The man smiled and looked away. We fell silent. I shot Qhari a look, commanding him to leave. He stuck his tongue out at me.

The column paused and the door of a high-walled kancha opened. We were still on the outskirts in a district of provincial lords, but the great plaza was no more than one long run away. The drizzle stopped. A few workers yawned and looked at us sleepily as they strolled past on their way into the city. The litters came down from the bearers' shoulders and the entourage filed through the door. This is it, I thought, once inside there's no escape.

Qhari tried to put his arm around me but I pushed him away. The soldier who had been watching us snickered, then stood aside with some others to guard the street.

Excitement swept the mob gathered inside when Chuqui and Wari were carried to the far end and raised high on their litters. The surrounding walls were new, enclosing an area sufficient for four spacious kanchas, which is the number one would have presumed from outside appearances. But the interior was undivided, and though a few buildings with thatch roofs stood against the inner walls, the open central area provided the perfect setting for a host to gather secretly. Chuqui had planned well. It was now filled to bursting with the hundreds who waited all night for their favorite. Soldiers lined the walls three deep, and lords and ladies from the provinces stood shoulder to shoulder with Cuzco royalty, most from Hurincuzco, but some Hanancuzcos among them.

They don't necessarily represent the wishes of their panaqas, I reflected, but they're showing personal support. It seems Chuqui has made bargains with half of Cuzco. Now, study the faces. Lord Atoq will want a full report.

Qhari nudged me. I followed his nod. Well, well, I thought, Lord Aquixe, Hatun Kuraka of Ica, so you've been drawn into this too. I see you haven't grown a chin yet. Are you wearing every jewel and scrape of gold you own? You've certainly prospered under Lady Chuqui's tute-lage. How convenient that you happen to be taking your annual resi-dency in Cuzco just now. Never one to miss a party, are you?

I watched Aquixe waving his kero, persistently engaging another lord in conversation, who seemed not the least bit interested and looked around for someone more important to talk to. Aquixe's frog-eyes bulged. He tapped a bony finger on the man's chest to get his attention again, squeak-ing about some trivia and unaware that a hush had fallen over the crowd. His companion put a hand on his shoulder to silence him.

Chuqui and Wari stood on their litters looking over the mob. Wari remained silent, shifting uncomfortably while his mother repeated her lies about Thupa Inka's change of mind, and introduced her 'witnesses.' Each spoke, as did several prominent lords and ladies gathered in the front row. Aquixe kept darting his hand up and wiggling it, hoping for a nod to include him among the speakers, but no one paid any attention to him. The morning sun seeped over the courtyard. Qhari measured it and gave me a worried look.

". . . and with your support," Chuqui shouted, "and the support of multitudes who cannot be with us today, we will declare my son Wari the rightful Crown Prince, and present him to the people in the great square at midday." A roar of approval followed.

While the sun rose ever higher and the speeches droned on, Qhari and I edged our way around the courtyard playing the roles of servants offering aqha. Qhari lugged the urn and Choque the Qolla maid poured, while we memorized the faces peering intently at the speakers. The war-riors lining the walls had their heads turned to the raised litters at the far end of the courtyard, too. Three stout poles set crossways barred the only gate from the inside, where ten soldiers armed with spears and maqanas stood guard. Somehow I had to open that gate for Zapana. Qhari followed my gaze and frowned, shaking his head.

I whispered, "You and me against ten. Well, as the old captain in the desert said, not very good odds for them." He gave me a wan smile.

A cane hut filled with building supplies stood in one corner near the gate. I looked at it and then at Qhari. He nodded, this time with a grin.

"Excuse me, Captain," Choque said in her accented Runasimi to a young soldier by the gate. The boy didn't mind being mistaken for a captain. "Lady Chuqui has ordered aqha for your men. Would you please assist me? I'm not strong enough to lift those big urns."

He followed me like a strutting puppy, and when we entered the hut he didn't see Qhari poised with the club, and he didn't see anything afterwards. At decent intervals three more followed, one at a time, and joined their friends trussed on the floor while their comrades at the gate remained intent on the speeches. Qhari was proving useful after all. But when I emerged to select a fifth candidate I glanced at the sun and realized the morning was nearly spent. There wasn't time to dispatch them all in this fashion, and soon someone was bound to notice their numbers diminishing. Then a streak of smoke arched through the sky - a sling stone wrapped in smoldering cloth. It came from outside and passed high overhead, disappearing beyond the opposite wall. Zapana's signal. He must have cleared the street and only waited for the gate to open. I glanced around. The crowd still faced straight ahead. No one noticed the vanishing trail of smoke in the sky.

"Just do it, Qhari. Slip down to the far end and ignite the roof thatch. While they're busy putting it out I'll take care of the rest of the guards at the gate."

"You against six?"

"I know. Not very good odds for them. Now go, Qhari. Go!" For once he obeyed, but I wished he hadn't hugged me first. There was no time to think of ourselves.

Inside the hut I found a tray and filled six keros, but when I turned to leave a soldier appeared in the doorway, as surprised to see me as I was to see him. We froze and stared at each other over the tray I held between us. "Who are you?" he asked, but then his gaze moved behind me to the bound guards. His mouth fell open.

"Here, hold this," I said thrusting the tray toward him. In the shock of the moment he accepted it with both hands, holding it chest high and letting his spear slide back against his shoulder. Before he could blink twice Eagle Woman stung him in the belly. I re-sealed her and tucked her back under my cloak while he stood there with the tray still in hand, mouth working soundlessly, eyelids fluttering, a bluish color spreading over his face. "Thank you," I said, retrieving the tray an instant before his arms went slack. I gave him a kick as I squeezed past through the doorway, and he collapsed into the hut.

On my way to the gate another soldier looked at me questioningly from several paces away. I gave him my most fetching smile, and he nodded me on with a lecherous grin.

"And for you, you handsome creature," Choque said as she offered the last kero from her tray. The first guard had finished downing his in one long gulp. A cry came from the other end of the courtyard, "Fire!" All heads turned to a dense plume of smoke rising from the roof of a shed. Well done, Qhari, I thought. Now, did I get the right measure of Condin Savana's sleeping powder in each kero?

"Who gave you permission to drink on duty? Where are the others?" the captain shouted, turning from the rear of the crowd and striding to the men at the gate.

"May I get you some aqha, Captain," I offered lamely.
He ignored me. "You there, stand up straight. Where's the man I left in charge? Open your eyes, soldier. What's wrong with you all?"

The men, heavy lidded and tottering now, reached out to steady themselves. One tried to speak but his own yawn stopped him, and another collapsed with a thud. The captain's eyes widened. I heard two more thuds behind me. "Guard," he bellowed over his shoulder, and seized me with both hands. My tray clattered to the ground. Eagle Woman was not re-armed; there hadn't been time. I stared into his eyes.

"Please release me, Captain," I said evenly.

"Hold, witch. Guard, hurry!"

"I said release me now, Captain."

He ignored me, and then his eyes bulged and a trickle of blood spilled from the corner of his mouth, but my eyes never left his face. When my blade searched his gut a second time his hands dropped and he tottered on his heels, then fell flat on his back. The four guards arriving behind him paused in mid-step, staring at the tiny woman holding the bloody knife. I glanced over my shoulder. All six of the aqha drinkers were down; their motionless bodies slumped in front of the gate. You're the lucky ones, I thought.

Foolishly they came forward to grab me, as if I wouldn't fight. Better at close quarters where my speed counts, I thought. Come on. . . come on. Now!

The hand that reached for me found its arm slashed from elbow to wrist. The shriek was hardly out of its owner's mouth when I rounded on another, knocking his spear aside with my forearm and leaving a clean, red line across his throat. A third roared and lifted his maqana over his head with both hands. Stupid. I dug my knee into his groin before he started the swing, and before he hit the ground I had the fourth man on his knees gurgling, my left hand fastened on his throat in a claw-grip. Reluctantly I released him, slamming my knee into the side of his head to keep him down, and turned to face the arc of warriors that formed anew in front of me. The element of surprise was lost, the alarm sounded, and I stood alone with my back to the barred gate.

"Get her," an officer shouted, but they had already seen me in action and edged forward warily. Slowly, never taking my eyes from them, I removed my hood and let my cloak fall away. Less encumbered now, I stepped back over crumpled bodies, my heels feeling the way, and heft-ed my dagger. Come on. . . come on, I urged in my mind. Who's next? That's it. Closer. . . closer.

I lashed out at the man edging in on the right, knocking the mace from his hand with a back kick, and then twirled to drive the heel of my palm upward into his nose. That left hardly a gasp to whirl on the war-rior charging with a spear from behind, but I deflected the thrust and buried my dagger in his thigh. It stuck in the bone. Weaponless, I dived and rolled out of the way of the next attacker, then tripped another. But the lout fell on me, leaving me wiggling under his bulk while two others pinned my arms to the ground.

The lout picked up his maqana and heaved himself to his feet, sneer-ing down at me. I stopped struggling and glared back.

"That's it, my pretty, just lie still and old Head-Smasher will put you to sleep," he said stroking the great, two-handed weapon. I spit at him. His sneer faded as he took the handle in both hands and lifted the blade high. Then a look of surprise came over his face, and I followed his eyes downward to his belly. . . where the tip of a spear protruded.

"Q-O-O-O-R-I-I-I!!!"

The lout collapsed sideways and I lifted my head to see Qhari standing twenty paces away, a second spear already in his hands. He charged, screaming "Q-O-O-O-R-I-I-I!" like a battle cry, and my captors fell over themselves trying to get out of the way. I nearly jumped with them, so terrible was the rage on Qhari's face.

In an instant I found my feet and, armed with a spear from one of my victories, I stood back to back with my brother in the sprawl of bodies.

"Hold them, Qhari. Hold them!"

I feinted a lunge at a man by the gate and he jumped aside. The others formed an arc before us again. Qhari crouched, spear leveled. I took a deep breath and leapt for the gate, grabbing the top crossbar. When it crashed to the ground they swarmed again. I forced myself not to turn and see what was happening to Qhari. The second bar fell. One more and Zapana would be through.

Huge sweaty arms grabbed me from behind, lifting me high and squeezing the light from my eyes. I clamped my teeth on his wrist and tasted blood, coming away with a piece of flesh. He cursed and flung me against the wall with such force I fell at his feet, breathless. He picked me up - a giant of a man with arms like bridge cables - and smashed me into the wall again like a cotton doll. I felt myself lifted once more. He gripped me under my arms and held me facing him, my feet dangling off the ground, head lolling on my shoulders, and laughed in my face. He shouldn't have done that. I ripped a tupu from the shoulder of my dress and plunged the long pin into his eye.

Oblivious to the giant's screams, I scrambled over bodies to the gate and slipped the last crossbar to the ground. The big door wavered for a moment, and then slowly fell inward, catching me beneath. I heard new sounds - war cries, and then feet thudding over top of me. Zapana's brigade!

When the feet stopped pounding above I crawled free. A battle raged in the courtyard, but my only thought was for Qhari. I shuffled forward on my knees, turning bodies.

"Why are you worried about them?"

I looked up. Qhari stood over me, one hand covering a gory wound in his thigh, the other trying to staunch the blood oozing from a gash on his forehead. He looked too pleased with himself.

"Well. . . I thought you were dead," I said raising myself. The ground swayed. He placed a bloody hand on my shoulder to steady me.

"Dead? I couldn't afford to die with you hiding under that door. Someone had to do the fighting."

"Oh, and I suppose it was you, Qhari Puma, who opened the gate? Well, was it?"

"Perhaps I had a little help," he conceded.

Two men locked together crashed into us, then like drunken dancers fell nearby. The battle wasn't over. Qhari picked up a mace and limped over to where the two struggled on the ground, one atop the other. He paused to see who was who, then calmly whacked the upper man on the back of the head. The one below heaved the dead weight off of him.

"Thank you," Zapana said sitting up. "I'm pleased to see you're both alive. What took you so long opening the gate?"

I was still trying to form a response when I saw his look, and realized that with one tupu gone my dress hung open. I snatched it closed and turned away.

"Very pretty," he said, standing, "but is this the time and place?"

Qhari chuckled with him. I fumed at them both.

"Lord!" It was a plea to Zapana. We turned to see one of his men take two faltering steps and fall on his face, a dagger planted between his shoulders. Beyond, the tide of battle swept back toward us. A mob of attackers formed on our right, and more on the left. I looked to the gate. Some of Chuqui's men had edged behind us and closed it again. We were surrounded.

"How many men did you bring?" Qhari asked.

Zapana shrugged. "All I could find. It seems Lady Chuqui arranged for the imperial ranks to be stationed elsewhere today. The city is almost defenseless."

"How many did you bring?" Qhari repeated.

"Perhaps fifty."

"Fifty? But Chuqui has hundreds."

"I've noticed," Zapana replied grimly.

XXVIII

Of how the battle concluded, and then of a Strange Wedding where a summons most ominous arrives.

The fight inside the kancha was valiant, but in vain. Most of Zapana's men were lost. We stood surrounded by Chuqui's rebels, who sealed the gate and now crouched in readiness for the final charge. Had there been room for slings and spears they could have finished us with a volley, but the rebels were crowded shoulder to shoulder with only five paces between their ranks and ours. Somewhere beyond the thorny hedge of battle axes, maces, maqanas and thrusting spears, the lords and ladies huddled around Lady Chuqui, waiting for the way to be cleared so they could parade Prince Wari to the great square unhindered.

Qhari picked up a spear and hobbled to Zapana's side.

"You can't do that," I shouted at him, hands on my hips. "Qhari Puma, you come back here. You're wounded. You can hardly stand."

"Better to die on my feet," he said over his shoulder.

The buzzing in my ears from when the giant bounced me off the wall hadn't stopped, and now tiny lights danced before my eyes sending me to my knees. "But you're not a warrior. Stop playing soldier and come back here."

He looked at me. "I seem to have done well so far, wouldn't you agree? Zapana trains daily, and I with him."

It was true, much to my surprise, that under Zapana's tutelage Qhari had become an accomplished fighter.

"Now, you just sit there, sister, and let us - "

The clamor cut off his words as the lines closed, shafts splintered, metal rang against metal, clubs hammered shields, and over it all shrill war cries rent the air. Someone stumbled backwards over me, and then another. My head spun and I held it in both hands, aware of a sickness building in my stomach. My stomach? Baby Sumaq T'ika!

On hands and knees I crawled over bodies, propelled by the backs of legs as our little circle shrank. Then I found my face pressed against the wall, and suddenly the shouting ceased, both sides stepping back to catch their breaths.

My head cleared, and gradually I drew myself up until I stood. Qhari and Zapana hunched protectively in front of me, still facing the rebels, their backs heaving, gulping air. A few men stood on either side of them, bodies tense, none heeding his wounds.

Qhari is right, I thought; better to die on my feet with weapon in hand. For Zapana and me there is no capture. Will I be knocked unconscious and taken away? No, that must not happen. You know the rules by which you live and die, Inca Moon - no surrender, no capture. I picked up a dagger. The man who slays Qhari will taste this, and then . . . one quick thrust under my own chin. Illap'a give me strength.

Qhari reached a hand behind, never taking his eyes from the rebels. I took his hand in mine and kissed it. He squeezed once and then withdrew, gripping his spear.

"Zapana, there's something you should know," I said.

Zapana stiffened but didn't turn, no doubt thinking I was about to make a declaration of love. "Not now, Qori," he said.

"No, what I mean is - "

"Surrender to me now," a rebel commander shouted.

Our men glanced at Zapana from the corners of their eyes, then hardened their faces. No surrender. When the commander raised his mace a crescent wall of spears leveled at us. The only sound in the kancha was dripping sweat.

Thud. . . Thud. . . Thud. All eyes turned to the gate, which shook and strained against the cross-poles. Thud. . . Thud. With a snap the butt of a timber rammed through the door, vanished, thudded again, and broke through in another place. The rebel commander froze with mace raised, the unspoken order to charge still in his open mouth. His men lowered their spears and looked at one another, blinking.

Thud. . . Thud. . . Crack! A cross-pole on the gate shattered. Hands from outside tore at the splintered wood. A soldier squeezed through the jagged hole and tumbled the last restraints while Chuqui's men stood frozen in silence. The great door swayed and fell inward, and over it swarmed the first wave, Achachi in the lead shouting, "Illap'a!"

Our little group was instantly forgotten. Rebel officers roused their men and the charge was joined in an earsplitting clash of arms and war cries. I slumped against the wall, suddenly dizzy again.

Qhari sighed heavily and gave me a weary smile. Zapana looked around with hollow, bloodshot eyes as if he expected to see the three of us lying dead, and this a dream. Then the light came back to his face and his gaze settled on me with warmth. A moment hung in which I thought he was going to embrace me. No, I pleaded inwardly, Qhari first. Qhari turned to Zapana and placed a hand on his shoulder, expecting a gesture in return, but his mouth fell open when he saw Zapana staring at me. Zapana caught himself and gave Qhari a brotherly slap on the back, then, with a backward glance of relief at me, he strode to the fore of the battle. Qhari's shoulders slumped. We couldn't look at each other.

Imperial guards still poured through the shattered gate. Lord Achachi hadn't come with a mere fifty - several companies were already through and more followed. I caught a glimpse of Achachi's squat, muscled frame wielding a huge maqana over his head, cutting a swath through the rebel lines. "Come on, you motherless shit-eaters," the old warlord boomed, "come and get some!"

A warm sun looked down on the K'allachaka terraces. Below, crystals from the morning rain still glistened on stalks emerging from the red earth of the planting terraces. And on the walks above, celebrants in their festive garb were an undulating press of royal blues and reds, bright yellows and oranges, pale greens and purples, sparkling gold and silver. Soon Prince Tupac Amaru would officiate at the offering, and then, as an added feature for the gathering, there would be a wedding.

Such a perfect day for a wedding, I thought. The bride is winsome, the groom bashful and full of smiles. I've never seen you looking so handsome, Qhari, and I never thought I'd live to see you married.

Though it was but a month since the Emperor's death and the land was in mourning, the heads of the panaqas decided the traditional celebrations of the year must continue. It was Kamay, the second month of the rainy season, and thus far the festivals had gone well.

On the day of the new moon the month-long fast from salt and hot peppers ended. The Cuzco youth who recently completed their manhood rites gathered in the great square, where the ranks of Hanancuzco faced those of Hurincuzco in tinku. They hurled hard, unripened fruit with their slings, and tussled in brawls to prove their strength and bravery. Many llamas were sacrificed, and others delivered into the care of representatives from the four suyus, to be returned for offering the following year.

When the full moon appeared, fine garments contributed by the royal households were burned in a public offering to the gods, and the Great Rope was brought out and stretched around the square. It was as thick as a man's arm, and woven from wool cords in red, black, white, and yellow, with red balls at either end. Its length was over a thousand paces, and sewn to it were tiny discs of gold. Men took up one side of the rope and women the other. As the music started they began a winding dance around the ushnu, each dressed in black robes with white fringes, tall white plumes on their heads, and all spiraling inward until the Great Rope lay coiled like a huge serpent. The drums pounded to a halt, and the crowds roared their approval of this faultless performance.

That had been two days ago. To complete the festivities of Kamay a few days hence, all the ashes from sacrifices throughout the year would be brought from the temples and ground with coca leaves, flowers, salt, peppers, and charred peanuts to make a powder, some of which is kept and the remainder taken to the Puma's Tail, where the Tullu and Huatanay rivers tinku at the edge of the city. There at dusk they'd throw the powder into the waters to be carried off to the sea and The Creator, Wiraqocha. It's a gay celebration, with the gods brought from their temples on litters to witness the event, all the nobles present, abundant aqha, and bonfires lighting the river so two hundred men with poles can race along the banks all the way to the next town, making sure the sacred powder stayed in the current on its journey to the Maker of All Things.

But in the interval old Prince Tupac Amaru decided to host a royal gathering at K'allachaka to mark the season, and thought it would add a nice touch to the day if his under-steward Qhari Puma was married as part of the proceedings. The elderly prince felt he would be following his illustrious brother soon, and he wanted to see his terraces alive with revelry one last time. He did, but from sightless eyes, for the heavenly part of his spirit had gone to join Father Inti and his divine brother the night before. His last wish was for the celebration to proceed on the morrow with his blessing and no long faces. He now sat propped on a dais welcoming the guests, and they greeting him as if alive, while four of his concubines kept the flies away with whisks. The mummies of his parents, Emperor Pachakuti and Empress Mama Añawarqe, sat beside him, for he had wanted them to share in the day, too.

As usual Lord Atoq was absent. With his father's death Atoq's power was now supreme in all matters of administration and security, though it had been so in practice for years. All that changed was that now no one, not even in name, stood between him and ultimate command of the Empire's secret forces. And still he chose to remain invisible, even on the day of his father's farewell celebration, for as he explained when I reported to him the Empire does not rest and neither does he. Still, I thought ruefully, he's been so long at Tipón that few would recognize him anyway.

Lord Achachi received official credit for foiling Lady Chuqui's plot. When a messenger reached Qispikancha where Achachi guarded the Heir, and related the events at Chinchero, Achachi rushed Titu Cusi to Cuzco and secured him in the Qorikancha. Then, aided by Zapana's spies, he turned his force on Chuqui's stronghold - and none too soon. The story was put about that he had merely gone to speak with Chuqui when her soldiers attacked him. Lord Wallpaya, now Regent, was only too pleased to give official sanction to this version. Of course the clamor of the battle hadn't escaped the attention of those who lived in the district, but with Chuqui defeated everyone seemed anxious to distance themselves and accept whatever pleased the Regent. Those who dwelled outside Cuzco, especially the commoners, knew nothing, and the Aymara lords remained peaceful. The Empire remained blissfully unaware of how close it came to civil war.

Lady Chuqui and her three concubine 'witnesses' were quietly separated from their heads, but it was said they volunteered to accompany Thupa Inka to the afterlife, as many of His other concubines and servants genuinely had. Prince Wari, always the reluctant center of his mother's schemes, was banished to Chinchero for life. The other plotters were allowed to live, but secretly fined. A mass disappearance of so many nobles would raise questions. Most, like Lord Aquixe, were repentant and pleased just to be alive.

Three days after the Emperor's passing, after His body returned to Cuzco at a stately pace, they announced the death in the great square. The High Priest of the Sun placed the yellow headband of Crown Prince on Titu Cusi's brow. Sapaca and Wallpaya had remained safely out of harm's way until the dust settled and a clear winner emerged. At the crowning ceremony they stood together, neither showing the slightest twitch of anything untoward, and both looking too pleased. Since Sapaca so easily abandoned Chuqui, I wondered if Wallpaya was feeling nervous about his new friend. Wallpaya, too, had waited patiently to see if Chuqui would be successful, and now with her out of the way he was free to pursue his own plans.

Of Titu Cusi himself, I, like all of Cuzco, was most curious to see this youth whom the Emperor had kept secluded at Qispikancha for so many years. Titu Cusi was short and square of stature, with a grave but pleasant face, and though about seventeen at the time he looked fourteen, if that. Well, I thought, if we can keep you alive until the Royal Fringe of emperorship is bestowed a year from now, you'll be the youngest emperor ever to rule Tawantinsuyu.

Once these proceedings ended I expected to find myself sobbing in Tanta Karwa's arms again, as I had after my return from Qollasuyu when all the danger had passed - release, sweet heartfelt release, an emptying of all my fears and worries, and absolution in my mother's arms. I think we were both disappointed when this didn't happen. Whether Inca Moon and all her deeds were now securely locked in their own compartment, or whether Inca Moon had merged with Qori Qoyllur, I cannot say. Tanta Karwa kept looking my way as if expecting me to rush for her embrace at any moment, but it never happened. I simply no longer felt the need. What was done was necessary. Inca Moon performed fault-lessly in the service of Tawantinsuyu, and Qori Qoyllur was content.

Zapana arranged for us to attend Qhari's wedding. Tanta Karwa was up long before dawn, fussing and changing outfits, worrying it might rain, and wondering over and over who would be present. At first I thought this performance was all for my benefit, but no, she loved wed-dings, the dear, and it was as if her own son were being married. It would have increased her joy immeasurably to know that Qhari was real-ly her nephew.

The K'allachaka terraces began to buzz. Tanta Karwa nodded my attention to where a knot of guests stood aside, making room for a new arrival being escorted under a feather parasol.

"Look at that," she said, delight in her voice, "have you ever seen such a dress?"

Every man and woman turned to look at Lady Sisa, gliding elegant-ly as if her feet didn't touch the ground, a maid hurrying behind holding the brilliant parasol of red and blue macaw feathers. Her dress and cloak were silver-white, with bands of green and purple maize stalks, the cloth so fine it draped like a sheath. The wide belt with matching designs cinched a waist as narrow as a girl's, but the firm, full curves above and below were mature woman. She could be a maize goddess incarnate, I thought, the essence of sensuous fecundity. She must be over forty by now, how does she manage? The question was in every woman's mind, and for a moment I, too, fell under her spell.

"It's true, mother," I said to Tanta Karwa, "I've never seen such a garment. Surely the Empress owns one, but. . . ."

"She may, but only our Lady Sisa can do it justice," she said, then her hand went to her mouth. "Oh, forgive me, that was blasphemy. No, the Empress is fairest in whatever she wears, but, after her. . . ."

In truth, each time one saw Lady Sisa it was an occasion to remem-ber. That oval face of smooth, unblemished copper, high cheeks, full lips, and huge liquid eyes like bottomless pools held one's gaze as to a fire. She had the sultry beauty that inspires obsession in men, all the more because she never seemed aware of it. And women flocked to her too, seeking the smiles she was so free with, eager for a friendly word, imitating her every gesture.

I saw the admiration on Tanta Karwa's face, and wondered what she'd think if she knew her lover Atoq bedded Sisa at every opportunity. Poor Tanta Karwa, poor mother, I thought. I could never break your heart by telling you. But, Lady Sisa, for all your charms and graces, I know you detest your husband and your marriage is a sham. Do you know what your husband is doing to your daughter? No, you don't, no mother could bear that. And where is Q'enti today? This is the first time I've known you to appear in public without your daughter at your side.

As if in answer to my thoughts another stir rippled through the crowd, another parasol appeared, and there glided Lady Q'enti in an outfit predictably identical to her mother's. She was now fifteen and being granted her own entrance, though she immediately went and stood beside her mother. Looking from one to the other I saw Sisa as she must have been at fifteen. Breathtaking was the only word to describe Q'enti, her appearance and gestures the mirror image of her mother. Even her voice and bashful, sensuous innocence were studied copies. Around me speculation began immediately on whom Q'enti would marry. Though the talkers had difficulty suggesting deserving candidates of sufficient rank, there was unanimous agreement that young Lady Q'enti was the most marriageable woman in the Empire.

I left Tanta Karwa to speculate on these matters with the women, and strolled up to the next terrace, admiring the finery of the guests. Those from Capac Panaqa, the ayllu of Thupa Inka and Tupac Amaru, wore mourning black, and the women had cut their hair. But guests from other panaqas wore their best to honor Tupac Amaru's last wish for a proper Kamay celebration. On the morrow everyone would return to mourning colors.

A young mother nursing her baby caught my eye, sitting contentedly, perhaps even proudly, while the tiny, fat-cheeked brown face, eyes closed, worked hungrily at her breast. My hand went to my belly.

Over three months now, and still not showing, I thought. You had quite a tumble, Little One, while your mother wrestled with Lady Chuqui's henchmen. You're fine, I know you are, but I'll not put you through that again, poor thing. Your aunt Sumaq T'ika would never forgive me if anything happened to you, and neither would I. We'll look after you, but you'll have to put up with your grandmother Tanta Karwa parading you through every village in the valley, and your uncle Qhari lugging you around on his shoulders. Oh, you're going to make us all so happy.

"Lady Qori Qoyllur, a pleasure," he said with mock gravity and a gracious bow. Only peasants called me 'Lady' Qori, or nobility who wanted something. He was neither. I returned the pleasantry.

"Lord Zapana," I replied with a bow of my own. "Does the Steward of K'allachaka personally greet each guest?"

He smiled. "Only the important ones. Besides, my under-steward is busy today."

Zapana dressed in mourning black for his grandfather. It made him look dignified, and handsome.

"Yes, he seems to be getting himself married," I replied, while the look I gave him asked bluntly, How is it between you and Qhari now? It wasn't the marriage I was concerned about. I'd sensed coolness between the men, and although Qhari acted no differently toward me I knew I was the cause. Qhari and I didn't need words for such things. After Zapana turned to me with relief when Achachi's reinforcements arrived - his look held more than relief, but worse, he thought of me before Qhari - Qhari knew simply by looking in my eyes what happened between Zapana and me, and I knew he had already forgiven my part. But had he forgiven Zapana?

Zapana caught my questioning look and dismissed it with a wave. "I'm sure Qhari will be a happily married man," he said.

"Like you?" I asked pointedly.

Zapana frowned but remained silent. He approached me bearing the gaiety of the day, but I only had sharp words for him. Why? I asked myself. Do I think I'm defending my brother, or perhaps I feel guilty? What is it I feel? Ah, there's the question and the answer, I do feel something for Zapana. I don't know whether to laugh or be angry with him. Things were so simple before Puno. Now he makes me nervous. I like it. How can this be? I've been trying to tell him I carry his child, and now is the time, but. . . I don't trust myself. I'll say things to hurt him. What's happening to me?

"The groom looks happy today," Zapana said lamely, gesturing to Qhari on a terrace below. Qhari still favored his left leg but the wound healed well, as did his other cuts. "A hunting mishap," Qhari told the guests, and they nodded solemnly as if they believed him.

"Should he not be happy?" I replied in a tone I didn't mean.

"No, of course not, I mean. . . it's good to see him . . . well, you know . . . enjoying himself. . . ."

"And the bride is beautiful," I offered, saving him.

"Yes, indeed, she is certainly a beautiful young woman," he said, eager to agree and shifting from foot to foot.

A page came to Zapana's side and whispered to him. Zapana looked at me apologetically and said, "The Steward of K'allachaka is needed. I hope I'll see you again soon." He bowed gallantly and departed, leaving me trying to say a pleasant farewell, but no words left my mouth.

I watched his back retreat through the crowd, and then my blood chilled. Sapaca lurched nearby, kero in hand. Oh, Lord Sapaca, I thought, so you've honored my brother's wedding, too. No, you're here for Tupac Amaru, supposedly, but in truth you're meeting with Wallpaya's supporters, aren't you? Are you still abusing your daughter? Beast! How can I put a stop to it without sacrificing myself and those I love?

Flute and drum music heralded the beginning of the matrimony. I rejoined Tanta Karwa and together we nudged our way through the crowd to Qhari's side. I was, after all, the only known relative he had present. He bit his finger and grinned at me, forcing me to choke back a tear. He looked so handsome, so happy. Surely mother and father were with us now. Tanta Karwa squeezed his elbow and, closing her eyes in a hunched grin, stepped back into the front row.

Servants and lesser retainers gathered around while the royals looked down on the wedding party from above, politely amused at the afternoon spectacle. While I smoothed my dress and tried to look dignified, Qhari faced his bride. Zapana and I had agreed the girl was beautiful mainly to have something to agree upon. Besides, all brides are beautiful, and who at a wedding would say otherwise? But in truth she was a plain creature, not without pleasing features, but not threatening to other women. An interesting, honest face, I decided. I looked forward to meeting my new sister-in-law.

The bride's parents brought her forward, presenting their daughter with a blessing. Qhari stooped to place a woolen sandal on her right foot, the symbol of virginity. Had she not been so she would have received a grass sandal, but as I have said, virginity, except among the Emperor's chosen women, is no special virtue, and a grass sandal at a wedding is more common and of no consequence. The bride responded by presenting Qhari with a new alpaca tunic, headband, and a bronze tumi knife. I helped hold up the blankets while Qhari changed into his new clothes, and then it was time for lectures on the duties of married life. I looked forward to this part, for the pleasure of addressing Qhari was all mine.

"Now you listen to me, Qhari Puma," I began sternly, wagging a finger in his face. He stifled a taunting grin and settled down under my glare. "It's your duty to care for this woman with all your heart, with all your strength, with all your possessions. You belong to her now. Together you are one, equal and in harmony like hanan and hurin, and from this day forth neither of you is complete without the other."

For once Qhari had to stand silently and listen, and though I admit I laid it on extra thick, he took it all with the proper solemnity, at least until I concluded, "And if you ever neglect or mistreat her, you'll have me to deal with, Qhari Puma."

He met this challenge with a cough to cover his mumbled response, "I've been dealing with you all my life."

The mischievous wink that followed made me bite my lip to stop a snicker. Then a pain welled in my throat and my eyes filled. "I'm so happy for you," I exclaimed, flinging my arms around him. Behind us Tanta Karwa sobbed loudly, hugging the person next to her.

When the lectures ended the gift presentations began. Atoq granted me the choice of his storehouses after the Chuqui affair, so I came to my brother's wedding prepared. For my sister-in-law I had an exquisite dress, which she and her family seemed to think I wove myself - and I would have had there been time, but then, my loom was in poor repair - and a large kero, which I told her she would need for comfort being married to my brother. I placed a small oval of turquoise in Qhari's hand. "Its name is Sayri, to remember father by," I whispered.

Qhari poked a knuckle at something in his eye, then tapped the front of his headband, "It will live here," he said, "and be worn with pride for all the world to see."

Then I gave him a tiny silver llama, a male. "It's name is Zapana," I whispered, "and I will give Zapana its mate. A male named Qhari."

Qhari sniffed when I mentioned Zapana, but then he hugged me fiercely. "Thank you, sister. However you arranged this, thank you."

In truth I did little, other than pass on the idea before leaving for Chinchero. It was Sumaq T'ika who made the arrangements. Once I explained Qhari's plight she was only too eager to help. Yes, she knew of a suitable young woman who, in the secrecy of the confessional, had admitted her love of women, and her fear of being forced to marry. She was the daughter of a servant, and Qhari's position as under-steward of K'allachaka meant a great step up in the world for her whole family. Sumaq discreetly spoke with the girl, who was under pressure to marry, and she quickly agreed to the plan. Qhari was also delighted and wasted no time paying suit. Everyone concerned felt relieved to see them finally taking an interest in the opposite sex, and delirious with joy when they sought permission to marry.

I was impatient now for the gift giving to end so the feasting and dancing could begin. Many of the viewing nobles sent their servants down with small gifts, which amounted to a handsome pile, and a line of well-wishers formed. Tanta Karwa was ensconced with an old friend, the two women muttering over the value of the wedding gifts and exchanging gossip about the guests.

An attendant approached me. "Qori Qoyllur, the healer?" he asked stiffly.

He wasn't one of the K'allachaka servitors. The rounded feathers on his necklace identified him with Chima Panaqa, the house of Sapaca and

382

Sisa. "Yes?" I replied, not liking his superior tone.

"Lady Sisa wishes to speak with you. Now."

"With me?" I turned to Tanta Karwa. She stopped her chatter and looked up at the attendant. We exchanged a puzzled glance. "Tanta Karwa and I will be pleased - " I began, but he cut me short.

"No. You alone. Now."

This wasn't right. Tanta Karwa was senior healer. "But surely you mean - "

"Alone. Now."

His expression left no room for discussion. Tanta Karwa furrowed her brows and shrugged, then turned back to her companion.

A summons from royalty always means 'Now,' I thought, but it doesn't have to be delivered so rudely.

"My Lady is strolling over to view the new shrine of Chuquikancha," he said, pointing beyond the gathering to a path winding over a hill. "You will approach her there."

Prince Tupac Amaru always embellished his estate with new shrines, though Chuquikancha - in no way related to Lady Chuqui - would be the last of his design. Having delivered the summons the man spun on his heels and walked off.

Evidently I'm not being granted the courtesy of an escort, I fumed after him. Very well, Lady Sisa, you have me intrigued. What is it that only Qori Qoyllur can do for you?

"Good afternoon, grandmother," I said to the old woman leaning on her staff, bobbing her gray head in a bow as she stood aside to let me pass on the trail. Behind me the banquet began, musicians clamored and dancers whirled, aqha flowed, and the K'allachaka terraces filled with gaiety. The path across the hillside to Chuquikancha was empty except for the old woman. The old woman? I stopped and looked back. She had vanished. So, grandmother, it was you again, I thought. It's been a long time since you let me glimpse you, or do you think I don't notice? I could find you now, except I have more pressing matters.

The grassy hill of Chuquikancha rose before me, the new hall dedicated to the Sun crowning its summit. Cuzco basked in the distance and sunshine bathed the slopes below me. The hall and its outbuildings were still under construction, and though the walls were up, unplastered sections showed the bare stone of the lower course and the mud bricks of the upper, and the roof poles still awaited their thatch cover. Two open doorways in the front wall looked out across the valley. Through one of these the party emerged, maids scurrying to set the feather parasols over Sisa and Q'enti, both of whom were surrounded by their male admirers. Sapaca was not among these.

I waited a few paces away for Sisa to notice me, but she remained focused on the man at her side. With a start I recognized Tintaya. The two were in merry conversation, which I couldn't hear from where I stood, but the looks that passed between them were unmistakable. Sisa's suggestive eyes flashed for Tintaya, who bubbled and grinned and nodded and did everything but get down and lick her feet.

A cold certainty came over me like a wave. Zapana's anguished words returned, "There is a person, Qori, one of immense power who sways my father, who fears me because I cannot be swayed, and who champions Tintaya because he is easily managed." Suddenly it became clear. Sisa. Sisa was the one backing Tintaya and holding Zapana from his birthright. It made sense.

It is impossible to think Lord Atoq could be threatened by raw power, I thought. No, Sisa's power is her beauty, and Atoq is smitten. Look at her leading Tintaya. She doesn't reserve her charms for Atoq alone; she uses them on all men. But to what end?

At least I've identified your true enemy, Zapana, I thought. I admire your resistance to her charms, but what does she hide? What is it she fears you might learn?

With a nod Sisa directed Tintaya's gaze to where Q'enti stood. No, I thought, is she really offering her own daughter? Ah yes, Sisa, with the lovely Q'enti you have another prize to bargain with. You're probably playing Sapaca's game of implying without committing. You're determined to control the Lord of Tipón whether he is Atoq or Tintaya.

Without looking in my direction Sisa motioned a maid to fetch me. Why have you summoned me alone? I wondered as I stepped forward, and why have you called me away from my brother's wedding?

Tintaya gave me a sour look, but he didn't appear surprised to see me. Sisa toyed with the gold rings on her fingers, still not acknowledging my presence. Then she said without turning, "You will attend me at this same time in my kancha tomorrow." She looked up at Tintaya and continued with their conversation.

I froze in confusion. "My Lady. . . tomorrow. . . concerning?"

Tintaya scowled at me. "You heard Lady Sisa. Now be gone." Sisa gave no further indication I existed.

XXIX

In which Qori and Tanta Karwa have audience with the two most Powerful Women in the realm, and Tragedy Descends.

The old herald pouted a disdainful look, and gestured with his nose for us to follow him. He had a silent, practiced way of letting his charges know that in executing his duty he did them an enormous favor. Guards snapped to attention and crossed spears parted. We entered the courtyard.

Mama Oqllo sat on Her dais of blankets and pillows, a maid behind Her with a feather parasol, another at Her side waving a feather fan. An official kneeling before Her stopped in mid-sentence and gave us an irritated look. Mama Oqllo glanced up from Her embroidery. We handed our token flower offerings to an attendant, and performed the much'a to the Daughter of the Moon. I was pleased to see the princesses were not present.

"The healers Tanta Karwa and Qori Qoyllur of Choqo," the herald announced sonorously, then backed away holding a deep bow.

With a regal gesture of Her hand, the Empress allowed us to approach and kiss her feet, then She indicated a place to the side, and nodded for the administrator to continue his report. The man returned to a droning recitation of imperial storehouse contents in a distant province, his fingers gliding over the knots of a colorful, many-corded khipu. We knelt and waited. I cast a sideways glance at Tanta Karwa to reassure her all had gone well at the Qorikancha. I was almost late for our audience with the Empress, and when I arrived Tanta Karwa was pacing nervously, but the herald summoned us before I could speak with her. No matter. She relaxed when she saw my look.

The droning came to an end. "Thank you," the Empress said, dismissing the official with a wave. The man gathered his khipu and backed away bowing. "Aqha," She said in a loud voice, making it a command, and in an instant keros appeared in our hands. We followed Her finger-dip to Mama Pacha and drank after Her. Then She gestured for us to kneel before Her, and sent Her maids and guards away.

"Now then, Tanta Karwa, you've requested this private audience on a matter of urgency. As you can see I'm busy with affairs of state while the Crown Prince is learning his temple duties. However, you have been of service to this house. Speak."

"Highness, I come to tell what has been revealed to me in a dream."

Mama Oqllo cleared her throat impatiently. "I have many dreamers in my court, Tanta Karwa. Shouldn't you be taking this dream of yours to a priestess at the temple?"

"Highness, it is for your ears alone. This dream was sent to me by Mama Killa, and You are Her daughter."

"I see." Mama Oqllo looked at me, wondering why I was there. Atoq must have told Her about my part in stopping Lady Chuqui's coup, but she gave me no special sign of recognition. Today I was simply Tanta Karwa's assistant.

Tanta Karwa took a deep breath. "Highness, one night I dreamed Mama Killa shone silver in a blue sky, and a young bird, a royal falcon, tested its wings and tried to fly with a beautiful parrot. But the female parrot, though regal, would have nothing to do with him. Nearby his true mate, another falcon, flew alone, waiting to be noticed. Mama Killa was saddened - "

"Wait," the Empress commanded. "What is this dream telling you?"

Tanta Karwa lowered her head. "It can only speak of the Crown Prince Titu Cusi and his sister Koka. Surely Mama Killa favors Princess Kusi Rimaq - "

The Empress held up one hand and covered Her eyes with the other, stroking Her brow. "And you, Qori Qoyllur? I suppose you had the same dream." Her voice was toneless.

"No, Highness. But I was there when Tanta Karwa awoke, and she told me the dream exactly as she told You. I am here to witness for her."

It wasn't a lie. Unable to think of a way to help Koka out of her impending marriage - for I hadn't forgotten my promise to her - I finally sought Tanta Karwa's advice. Once she understood the loathing Koka felt for her brother, and her honest apprehensions of being Empress, Tanta Karwa's sympathies reached out to the girl. That, and the fact that an unhappy royal union wasn't in the best interest of the realm, caused her to think mightily on the matter. She had indeed risen one morning and repeated her dream, which was very real to her, resolving that it must be told to the Empress. But it was a women's matter, she cautioned me, and Lord Atoq shouldn't be troubled with it. "Men are useless in such affairs," she said.

Everyone knew, at least all the ladies at court knew, that Koka's younger sister, Princess Kusi Rimaq, better displayed the qualities of a future empress, and she was completely devoted to her brother. But Titu Cusi wanted Koka, and to overrule the Crown Prince required a resounding consensus among the royal houses. Thus far the men weren't even aware a problem existed, while their wives would say nothing unless the Empress encouraged them. Tanta Karwa knew what had to be done.

The Empress shook Her head slowly. "No, such a change of plans is not possible. Of course Koka quarrels with Titu Cusi, she is his elder sister, that's natural, but Koka will grow out of it, and Titu Cusi adores her." She said this with an affected certitude, trying to convince Herself as She spoke. It was clear Tanta Karwa touched a sore place, but the Empress continued, "Besides, the future of Tawantinsuyu depends on this marriage. It must be harmonious." Mama Oqllo paused and looked away for a moment, then studied us. "We are not like you," She said, referring to royalty. "We do not have the luxury of choosing what we want; we must do what is best for our people."

"But surely, Highness, an unhappy marriage - "

"It will not be unhappy," She said making it an order. "Who else have you told about this, no one? Very well, I command you to hold your tongue. This is the sort of rumor that travels fast and pleases our enemies."

Bravely Tanta Karwa persisted, "But the dream, Highness? It came from Mama Killa. I am but Her messenger. Surely it will do no harm to consult the oracles at the Qorikancha?"

The Empress sighed heavily and drummed Her knee, eyes lifted to the heavens. The struggle on Her face showed Tanta Karwa was right, Mama Oqllo was indeed aware of Koka's distress, but She tried to ignore Her own misgivings. Now, Tanta Karwa, like the skilled healer she was, had voiced her patient's concern, helping Her face the reality. Finally the Empress spoke. "Very well, Tanta Karwa. This once, and only this once, I will follow your advice and consult my Celestial Mother at the Qorikancha. The auguries and oracles will speak for Her, but if you are wrong you will never come into my presence again."

"You will wait here," the chamberlain said in a sullen tone, "and Lady Sisa will see you when it pleases her." He turned and brusquely waved the servants through a side door, leaving Tanta Karwa and me alone in the little patio. When we entered two men butchered a deer strung from a tripod in the corner, a girl scattered fresh greens for the guinea pigs squeaking around the walls, and a woman knelt at a mill working the smooth rocker stone over maize flour. Suddenly the enclosure was silent and empty. I exchanged a look with Tanta Karwa. The kitchen annex? I thought. Lady Sisa has us waiting like peasants. This does not bode well.

The day before at K'allachaka, after walking all the way out to the Chuquikancha shrine, Sisa's curt summons left me shaking my head in disbelief.

"That was all she requested?" Tanta Karwa had asked.

"It wasn't a request, it was an order," I replied, "but, yes, 'You will attend me at this same time in my kancha tomorrow,' was all she said."

"And for this she made you leave your brother's wedding and walk all the way out to Chuquikancha?" Tanta Karwa muttered, shaking her head.

It perplexed me, too. Sisa might have just as easily asked her attendant to relay the summons. She did it because she is Sisa, I decided, and because she can. She's flaunting her power and trying to humble me, but why?

"Mother, what do you suppose she wants with me?"

Tanta Karwa exhaled loudly. "Perhaps Q'enti needs tending, though she looked well enough to me, but. . . . The First Ladies know that Mama Oqllo allows you to visit Princess Koka. Maybe Sisa thinks her daughter deserves the same attention."

It sounded plausible, though I had no wish to be Q'enti's confidant, too.

"You've already arranged an audience for us with the Empress tomorrow, Mother. Will there be enough time to visit Lady Sisa, also?"

"Do not be troubled," Tanta Karwa said. "Lady Sisa doesn't want you until midafternoon, and our meeting with Mama Oqllo is midmorning. I'm more concerned that you'll have enough time to consult your friends in the Qorikancha before the Daughter of the Moon shines Her light on us."

That night the thought of a private meeting with Lady Sisa filled me with a mixture of curiosity and dread. Why did she ask for me? I wondered. For whatever reason, this will be the time to tell her what her drunken husband is doing to their daughter, if I dare. And there lies the dread. If I speak up it will be the end of me and those I love, and if I don't seize the opportunity I'll remain a silent accomplice, condemning poor Q'enti to further horrors.

Neither of us could sleep that night. We sat by the hearth in our cottage at Choqo, Tanta Karwa feeding the fire, watching my turmoil, patiently waiting for me to speak the unspeakable. At last I could bear it no longer, the decision too much for me to make on my own. Tanta Karwa listened quietly, watching the flames. I told her what I witnessed between father and daughter at Saqsawaman, and then added I had not told Atoq because it was incidental to the purpose of my mission that night, and if I spoke to Lady Sisa about it now I would reveal myself as an imperial agent. Tanta Karwa accepted this, knowing there was more but not pressing, and when I finished her face set with determination.

"I understand your difficulty," she said adding another branch to the fire, "but you're right, this incest must end. It must! You wonder why you saw no emotion on Q'enti's face? It is so with the innocent who are thus misused. The demon that makes her father do this has stolen her feelings from her. How else could she live with herself? Poor thing. She has to pretend it doesn't happen, and from what you saw on her face this wasn't the first time he used her. She may have been his victim for years."

Tanta Karwa turned and fixed me with intense eyes. "This is what we must do. After our meeting with the Empress I'll go with you to call on Lady Sisa. No, don't protest, I know the summons was for you only, but I'm not without influence. Besides, I have more experience dealing with royal temperaments. This must be revealed to Lady Sisa gently. I'm closer to her age and she'll listen to me. Now, no arguments," she said holding up a hand to silence me. "She'll hear it from me alone, and I'll not mention you. You can be elsewhere tending Q'enti. I'll tell Lady Sisa I divined it. Fear not, your part won't even be mentioned."

Flies rose from the hanging deer carcass, momentarily filling the kitchen annex with their buzz as our hostess and her ladies filed in, the last closing the door behind her. Sisa and Q'enti stood in the center, dressed identically as usual, the semblance of face uncanny. The first ladies from the other four panaqas of Hurincuzco flanked them, including Sumaq's mother, Lady Hilpay. I allowed myself to scowl back at her.

So, Hilpay, I thought, your daughter once described you as a hooknosed old potato, and you haven't changed. You played your part in marrying me to my own brother. On whose orders did you act? Oh, how I yearn for a moment alone with you.

"Would you care for food and drink?" Sisa said to me coldly, ignoring Tanta Karwa. It was a slight. Honored guests are never asked; the refreshments simply appear. But then, honored guests are never met in the kitchen like beggars. I shook my head.

Sisa looked over our attire contemptuously. We wore our best clothes, the finest women of our rank were allowed to wear, but of course the first ladies were more splendidly robed. I shifted uncomfortably. They all enjoyed that.

"Was it a long journey into the city for you?" Sisa asked lifting her nose. Q'enti parroted the gesture. "But oh, I forgot, you're used to walking."

I smiled weakly in reply. She kept staring at me, forcing me to keep my eyes lowered in the presence of royalty.

"I told you to come by yourself," Sisa said, all pretense of civility gone.

"My Lady," Tanta Karwa spoke up, "it was I who assumed you would wish my presence also. Qori will accompany Lady Q'enti to her room, and then you and I can talk. . . alone."

Q'enti edged closer to her mother and entwined her arm, never taking her eyes from us. Her face was not devoid of emotion today. Hatred gushed from her eyes.

"Would that suit you, Tanta Karwa?" Sisa said. "Did I summon you? No! But if you insist on being part of this disgrace then be prepared to share the consequences."

Tanta Karwa glanced at me, willing my silence. I'll handle this, her eyes said.

"My Lady," she tried again, "I know not of what you speak. I ask only a few moments - "

"Silence!" Sisa shrieked. The other women smiled cruelly to see us shrink. "You, Qori Qoyllur of Choqo, have been spreading malicious lies about my family," Sisa said pointing an accusing finger at me. "You've been trying to dishonor this house and all of Hurincuzco." At this the other women hissed and took a menacing step forward, except Hilpay, who stood regarding me stonily.

Tanta Karwa shot me another look. I held up my hands and shook my head numbly to tell her I had no idea how they could know, since the only other person I'd told about the incest was Sumaq T'ika, in the confessional, and Sumaq would never. . . . It came to me suddenly then. Oh yes, now I see. It's on your face Hilpay. No, Sumaq didn't betray me, you did. In my mind's eye I saw myself leaving the confessional and bumping into old Cormorant, wondering if she'd been listening, but assuming the silence of the temple was sacred even to her. How naive, I cursed myself. Cormorant follows Hilpay around like a dog. From Cormorant to Hilpay, and straight to Sisa. Yes, Hilpay, you'll do anything to redeem the disgrace of your panaqa, won't you? Playing spy for the Lady Speaker of Hurincuzco is a small price to stop wagging heads from remembering your mad ancestress. She ate her child, and you spy on yours.

I tried addressing Sisa. "My Lady, these are matters that are best discussed in private."

Sisa balked. "In private? There are no secrets between the houses of Hurincuzco. The First Ladies are here to witness your treachery. How dare you accuse my daughter of incest!"

"My Lady, I do not accuse your daughter of anything. It's your husband's doing. Ask Q'enti."

"Bitch," Q'enti spat. "It's a lie. She's lying!"

Tanta Karwa stepped between us with arms spread. "Now wait, both of you. Q'enti, this isn't your fault," she said evenly. "You're not to blame, child. You're innocent. We're here to care for you."

"It's a lie!" Q'enti screamed again. "How can you believe her," she said pointing a trembling finger at me, "she who carries a bastard child in her belly."

All eyes turned on me. The women sneered. Tanta Karwa studied my face, eyes wide, waiting for me to deny it. I opened my mouth, but words failed. She saw the truth then, but she stood by me.

"These are other matters to be discussed later," Tanta Karwa said quietly, gathering herself. "But first we must speak of the unspeakable. Your daughter has been harmed, Lady Sisa."

"Lies! Lies!" Q'enti wailed. Then to everyone's surprise she let go her mother's arm and slapped me. I simply stood there in shock, my hand to my cheek. Tanta Karwa came to my defense, planting herself between us and turning on Q'enti.

"Child, get a hold of yourself," she ordered taking Q'enti firmly by the shoulders. Sisa lashed out with both hands, shoving Tanta Karwa away from Q'enti with demon force. Tanta Karwa stumbled backwards, falling just beyond my outstretched arms. There came a sickening crack! when her head smashed against the milling stone.

"Mother!" I screamed racing to her side. I knelt over her but Q'enti dashed forward and kicked me in the stomach. Searing pain tore my insides, freezing me in open-mouthed agony.

"Take it," Tanta Karwa said feebly, handing me her necklace with its tiny emerald. "Remember its name is Añawarqe, and it was a gift from the Empress Añawarqe to her sister - your grandmother." We lay side by side on pallets in a darkened room of Sisa's compound, a few wavering lamps casting shadows from their niches. Tanta Karwa saw my eyes widen when she said, "your grandmother," but patted my hand for silence. Too weak for words, she pushed her healing bag toward me; the yellow one with the red llamas I used to carry for her, and with her eyes asked me to accept it.

"It's the first time she's been conscious since the fall," a maid whispered, fussing with Tanta Karwa's blanket and trying to get her to lie still. I'd had my own period of blackness, and only regained my senses moments before, opening my eyes to find Tanta Karwa motionless beside me. I cursed myself. Where was Inca Moon when this happened? I can fight six men, yet I couldn't stop Sisa and her venomous daughter Q'enti. Not long ago I saved the Empire, but I couldn't save you, Tanta Karwa, mother of my heart. Fat tears rolled down my cheeks.

True, I admitted to myself, what happened wasn't planned by anyone, and perhaps that's why I couldn't respond. Sisa and Q'enti acted in the heat of the moment, but they're not displeased with the outcome.

I felt cold and empty. Yes, empty. I didn't need to touch myself or look, I knew the baby was gone.

Oh, little Sumaq, my daughter, I've lost you. I couldn't protect you either.

The maid leaned over me to stop my sobbing. "There, there. The gods have called your child, but you will live and, perhaps, one day you'll have another."

Anger welled within me. Yes, as you say, 'perhaps,' maybe I'll have another, but I know these injuries and it's just as likely I'll never have a child again. Never! But it's not the future that gnaws me, it's my poor baby, her tender life stolen by. . . . Oh, Q'enti, you'll pay for this. I swear on my dead child, you'll pay.

Tanta Karwa moaned. The maid washed away the blood, and used an obsidian blade to shave the side of her shattered head. An angry, concave gash above her left temple showed where the bone was smashed inward. They were going to attempt to remove the skull fragments to relieve the pressure, a dangerous operation under the best of circumstances, which no more than half the patients survive.

Sisa's chamberlain entered and watched for a moment. "We've sent for the surgeon," he said to me. "Lady Sisa wishes you to know she's sorry Tanta Karwa took an accidental fall while visiting, and that you injured yourself trying to help her." He was being brusque and efficient.

"But, she assures you that no one need know about the unborn child of a widow, so no tongues will wag on that account." Then his voice became stone. "She also wanted me to tell you that neither will anyone know who your husband was, providing you don't trouble her and her family again." He departed with a smirk.

There's the official story, I thought. Tanta Karwa and I fell accidentally - such unfortunate accidents at the kancha of Chima Panaqa. Hilpay arranged my marriage to my brother, and she told Sisa about T'ito. Now Sisa uses this to seal my silence - my silence maybe, but not my revenge.

"I'll fetch the surgeon now," the maid said slipping from the room. The moment she left Tanta Karwa reached out and took my hand. "Are we alone?" she asked.

I raised my head. The room was empty. "It is so, mother."

"I must look terrible," she said through closed eyes. "Did they take all my hair?"

"Only what was necessary, mother."

"Don't let anyone see me like this, Qori. . . I mean. . . after."

I squeezed her hand. "No, of course not. I promise."

She knew what was about to happen. The surgeons were always military men because this type of injury is most common among soldiers. Many survive and have a hollow place on their skulls where the bone fragments were removed - some men have two or three such hollows - but just as many die partway through the procedure.

"I don't know where you came from, Qori, or how you came to be among us, but I've always known in my heart who you are, and loved you like my own daughter. And your child . . . yes, I knew about that, too. I felt it."

"Shhh, mother, don't strain yourself."

"You shhh, daughter. These may be my last words and I'll say what I wish. I've always felt you're special, Qori, one with a purpose in this world. I don't know what that is, but I suspect it's greater than you can imagine. It's greater than all of us. For you the events of daily life - yes, even what happened here today - though they seem of such importance in the moment, are really just markers on your journey. Thank you for letting me be a small part of it, and please, Qori, always keep me in your heart, as you are in mine."

I didn't want to hear her talk this way, but all I could do was squeeze her hand. The prophetic moment passed, and then a look of curiosity came over her.

"Is my sister still alive?" she asked.

"She died of an illness nine years ago, mother."

Tanta Karwa nodded to herself. "Then she did live a long life, and you knew her."

"Yes, mother."

"Did she tell you about your father?"

I assumed she meant that he died bravely in battle along with his brother Maita, Tanta Karwa's husband, for that was the only version of the story she knew. "She was very proud of him," I assured her.

Tanta Karwa looked confused. "Proud? Proud?" she repeated again, as if I'd spoken the unbelievable. "What did she tell you?"

For an instant I sensed Tanta Karwa knew something I was unaware of, but before I could reply the surgeon strode briskly into the room and knelt at her side, his attendants hovering behind with basins of water and dressings. One held her head in strong hands, turning it for the surgeon. He gave the wound an efficient glance, then held a cup to her lips. What she had been trying to tell me a moment earlier would have to wait, though I wasn't sure I wanted to hear it.

Tanta Karwa paused, her lips to the rim. "Don't forget me, Qori." She drank, and in moments her body relaxed into sleep. I continued holding her outstretched hand. The surgeon examined her, then nodded to himself and unrolled a cloth containing several fine obsidian blades. An assistant kneeling before a small brazier reached tongs into the coals and held up a glowing metal pin for the surgeon to inspect. I looked away.

I'd seen this operation before. The surgeon now would be praying to his spirit guardian, blade in hand. I clutched the emerald Añawarqe and joined him. Then a half-moon incision is cut around the wound and the scalp peeled back, revealing the broken white bone of the skull. Tweezers hold back the skin flap, and a heated pin is used to seal the edges of the incision. A stouter but equally sharp blade is used to incise lines through the skull around the shattered area. When the lines join the fragments are lifted out, and the skin flap replaced with a smear of resin.

A sharp hiss followed by the stench of burning flesh announced the surgeon's progress.

Mother Moon, I prayed, give her back to me and I'll be your servant for the rest of my life. Never will I sin again. I'll bring aqha to your temple daily, or, if it pleases You, I'll give away all I have and take your cult to the savage women of the jungles. Hear me, Mother. Spare Tanta Karwa! But in all things, your will, not mine, be done.

XXX

Concerning events at the Temple of Wiraqocha where the prospects of Princess Koka worsen, Qori goes about dressed as a boy, Lord Aquixe receives a False Message, and a Mysterious Man attends Lord Sapaca.

The Temple of Wiraqocha throbbed with the colors of Cuzco nobility and every province in the Empire. In the cavernous hall provincial lords and ladies from Quito to Catarpe mingled with the royal panaqas, while courtiers and ladies-in-waiting, priests, seers and servants moved through the jeweled and feathered throng. They all came to this holy place in the Vilcanota Valley to celebrate the annual festival. But Qhari and I were there for our own reasons - it was time for the five-year meeting of the fugitives, and somewhere in the crush the demon Kontor stalked uncle Maita. Qhari caught my eye and shook his head, releasing a heavy sigh. We had names, a time and place, but what did our quarry look like?

Tanta Karwa should be here, I thought, telling myself she would have enjoyed the festival, but also knowing I had wanted her to identify her husband Maita for us. But Mama Killa decided otherwise. As I lay beside Tanta Karwa in that tiny, shadowy room at Sisa's kancha, while the surgeon attempted his miracles, and I held her hand, praying, her life breath ceased and I felt an absence in the room. The surgeon kneeling over her suddenly stopped the operation and pressed his ear to her breast. Moments later he straightened his back, looked at me sadly, and gathered his instruments.

I took Tanta Karwa to Choqo and began the mourning rituals, keeping her partially shaved head covered from prying eyes as she wanted. The entire village took part led by Ayllu Añawarqe. When we placed her with the ancestors in the cave-shrine of Llipiquiliscacho a heart-felt wailing rang over the hills and valleys beyond.

The little cottage on the edge of Choqo was mine now, but it was as empty as my heart. Disbelief and then hatred consumed me. Oh, Lady Sisa, I thought, you and your evil daughter Q'enti will answer for this! But as the days became weeks a hollow numbness settled over me, and even the craving for revenge fell dormant.

I expected a summons from Lord Atoq. Surely Sisa will tell him about T'ito and me to protect herself, I reasoned. But when the messenger appeared at my door he didn't come with a summons.

"Lord Atoq grieves at Tanta Karwa's passing," Zapana said in sympathy. "He wants you to know he's ordered prayers for her in the temples, and his grief matches yours. You'll not be called to duty again until your six months of mourning have passed."

I nodded weakly. Evidently Sisa had decided not to tell Atoq about me, or her part in Tanta Karwa's death. Surely Atoq didn't believe that one of his mistresses had died from an 'accidental' fall while visiting another? No, he knows something is amiss, I decided. Perhaps he doesn't want an inquiry either, lest his dalliance with Sisa become known.

"And you, Zapana, do think Tanta Karwa's death was an accident?"

"No," he replied without hesitation.

This surprised me for Zapana wasn't usually so open. "Qori. . ." he said softly. I looked up at him, suddenly feeling his presence. I hadn't seen the eyes that now regarded me since our night together in Puno, and there was something else, almost a pleading, that he never showed me before. He wrapped his arms around me, pressing me to his breast.

"Qori. . ." he whispered again, resting his chin on my head. We remained in this embrace.

"I know Sisa is the one who keeps you from your birthright," I said without looking up.

He continued to rock me gently from side to side. "Yes," he said, his tone resigned.

"Why does she fear you?"

"Because she can't control me, as she does my father."

"Why does that worry her?"

"Because a future Lord of Tipón may not allow her husband to continue with his intrigues. If Sapaca loses his position, she loses hers."

It was a rare moment. Zapana was entirely open to me. Were we lovers or friends? The question seemed irrelevant just then.

"You want Sisa removed," I said.

"After what she did to Tanta Karwa, don't you?"

"Do you know what happened at Sisa's kancha that day?"

"Only that you visited at her request, and Tanta Karwa didn't leave alive. Also that you were injured somehow. Do you want to tell me about it?"

I did not. It was still too painful. Zapana never knew about our child, and now. . . he had his own reasons for hating Sisa.

"Why do you suppose Sisa attacked Tanta Karwa?" I said.

"Because she was jealous. Tanta Karwa shared my father's bed, too."

So, I thought, he knows about his father's lovers. I let it go. "And you think Lord Atoq allows Sapaca to scheme unhindered because Atoq is protecting Sisa's position?"

Zapana flinched. "My father is loyal to the Empire, Qori, but in some matters I fear Sisa clouds his reason."

He stroked my hair, turning my thoughts back to the two of us. He said, "I know I seldom show it, but I've been thinking of you a great deal. . . even when I don't want to." It was a huge confession for Zapana, a vulnerability placed trustingly in my hands, but it wasn't what I wanted to hear just then. "You and I are the same, Qori. We thrive on danger. We need it as much as we need the air we breathe."

"What about Qhari?" I asked.

Zapana sighed heavily. "Qhari and I have talked. We're not seeing each other in that way anymore. I gave him back the llama figurine named Qhari."

I felt relieved for both of them, but especially for myself. Being part of a triangle with one's own brother was difficult, and confusing. Now Zapana and Qhari were both free, except for their wives.

In the pause that followed I sensed Zapana was about to share more of himself, unbidden, freely. Such a complicated man, I reflected. Often aloof, sometimes friendly but reserved, frequently distant. What is this new side he's showing? I glimpsed it once at Puno, but then he retreated. Now he's back of his own accord but. . . there's no room in my heart for another right now. I'm grieving. Get back in your own compartment, Zapana, and leave me in mine.

I stood away from him. "Thank you for coming, Zapana."

He opened his arms wide, palms up, and begged me with his eyes. I took another step backward and shook my head. His hands fell at his sides. Heavily he turned and left without a word.

Qhari came regularly at first with invitations to visit K'allachaka, but I had no wish to leave Choqo. He now wore the turquoise oval named Sayri on the front of his headband. I mentioned the llama figurine Zapana returned to him. Yes, he said, he now had both silver llamas, Zapana and Qhari, though he was thinking of changing Zapana's name to something else. I shouldn't worry. He was glad it had ended. "Besides," he said with mock dignity, "I'm a married man now." His eyes danced mischievously. We laughed together.

Once, Qhari brought his wife, a shy thing unsure whether to smile or grieve, and we made desultory conversation sitting in the patio. To find common ground she tried leading me into talk of weaving and cooking, and though I could have enlightened her on both, words failed me. The poor thing was as relieved as I was when the visit ended.

"I miss Tanta Karwa, too," Qhari said at the close of this visit, "and I'm sorry about your child. I wish you'd told me before. You know I'll stand by you when you're ready to take revenge on Sisa and Q'enti."

When I told him the story of what happened at Sisa's kancha he went into a rage, but it settled with time and now he waited for a sign from me. I didn't tell him who the father of my child was, yet I know he sensed the truth. "But, Qori," he said, giving me a farewell hug, "if you insist on brooding don't expect others to come around trying to cheer you."

He was right, of course. Those who won't be consoled prolong their grief and try the patience of others, but I couldn't help myself. Often during those days I found myself weeping uncontrollably, for no reason, and some mornings it took more strength than I could muster to lift myself from bed.

Zapana never returned. Qhari told me Zapana took his wife on a pilgrimage to Thupa Inka's shrines in Kuntisuyu, though I knew it was surely a cover for him to gather information. Qhari's visits to Choqo became infrequent, and eventually I was left alone with my melancholy.

The rains fell through the warm, green months of growing, and in

Choqo the harvest was good. Then came the brown months of dry and cold, bringing the Sun festival of Inti Raymi, marking the shortest day of the year. Sacrifices to the spirits of the irrigation canals followed, and then came planting of early potatoes and maize, and the cycle continued.

My mood was that of the Empire's, still mourning the passing of the Emperor. His rituals had to continue for a full year, after which the final ceremony would release Him to the ranks of the honored ancestors, and Crown Prince Titu Cusi would become The Light of the Sun. Soon after Thupa Inka's death many of His favorite servants and some of His women volunteered to join Him. At a public mourning dance they were made drunk and strangled, and at a pre-arranged time hundreds of youths throughout the Empire were sacrificed at holy places to ease His passage. Like Zapana, thousands made pilgrimages to the places Thupa Inka had frequented, and everywhere bales of the finest cloth were burned, animals slaughtered, and all manner of things precious consigned to the gods.

I also made sacrifices, but mine were for Tanta Karwa and my unborn child. Did the gods not weep at their passing, too? Had the world even noticed? I took The-One-Confused-Like-A-Man to the temple and had him sent to join Tanta Karwa, so she could sling my baby on his back and bounce her along to make her laugh. In my mind's eye I saw them together in a sunlit field; Tanta Karwa's lush, glorious black hair falling behind her in a thick braid, her face younger and free of wrinkles, wearing a soft-colored dress, feet and arms bare, and baby Sumaq squealing in delight on the back of The-One-Confused-Like-A-Man. Many times I thought of joining them, but Tanta Karwa did not beckon. They were content together, grandmother and granddaughter, both forever young, and I knew I was not meant to be with them. Not yet.

The villagers nodded respectfully when they saw the emerald named Añawarqe at my throat, and Tanta Karwa's healing bag with the red llamas slung over my shoulder. It was accepted that Choqo had a new chief healer. And thus I passed those days of mourning tending the ailments of the community, while ever closer drew the time of the five-year meeting.

Soon after Tanta Karwa's rituals ended Zapana and Tintaya arrived with news of the Regent, Lord Wallpaya. Zapana held back, but his eyes quietly sought a sign from mine, asking, 'How is it between us now?' Tintaya did the talking. Though he remained out of the way at Chinchero while I single-handedly thwarted Chuqui's coup - well, perhaps I had some help - his natural demeanor was unchanged. Taking a bundle from Zapana's shoulder he dropped it at my feet. Men's clothing spilled on the floor.

"For you," he said. "Now then, it seems your little escapade at Saqsawaman was of some use after all. While you've been lounging my best agents have been busy. You were right, Sapaca and Wallpaya are planning something - treason. Wallpaya intends to depose Titu Cusi before the inauguration and have one of his own sons declared Emperor. Lord Sapaca agreed to support his claim, in exchange for the usual concessions, of course. The regular army remains loyal to Titu Cusi, so Wallpaya must smuggle arms into the city for his men. These are being secretly produced in the provinces as we speak, Kuntisuyu apparently being the main source." He glanced at Zapana when he said this. Zapana examined his sandals with a satisfied grin. His time in Kuntisuyu hadn't all been spent at shrines.

"The weapons will arrive in one large consignment," Tintaya said. "This shipment has to be stopped before it reaches Cuzco, but the timing and route are still a mystery. Lord Atoq suspects Wallpaya will use the annual festival at the Temple of Wiraqocha as an excuse to meet with his provincial supporters, and finalize arrangements. For some reason, and against my advice, he thinks you might be useful. I suppose we need everyone, even you. You will attend."

He said this last as if expecting an argument, little knowing that nothing could keep me from the Temple of Wiraqocha this year. Wallpaya's plot only provided me with an official reason to attend. Titu Cusi's coronation is just three months away, I realized. Wallpaya will have to move soon. My blood quickened, and for the first time in months my thoughts fastened on something other than myself. Father's revenge is at hand, I thought, and the peace of the Empire is threatened. All must be resolved at the Temple of Wiraqocha. Inca Moon will not fail.

The paralyzing grief slipped from me like a burden set down. I thought, I've done all I can for you, Tanta Karwa. Your rituals have ended, and you're now among the honored ancestors. Yes, I can feel you wanting me to do this, to live again. Take care of baby Sumaq. I love you both.

"Well?" Tintaya demanded.

"Of course, Lord," I replied, casting a furtive smile at Zapana. He stifled a grin, knowing I was back. "Your humble servant understands, and will do her part."

"Good. And stay out of my way, unless I need you to run errands."

Now I watched the smoke from sacrificial braziers drift around the huge rafters at the Temple of Wiraqocha. Lord Achachi suddenly appeared. "You there, boy, fetch that basket of coca leaves and follow me."

For a moment I forgot I was disguised as a Charka youth and continued staring at the massive timbers and thatch roof overhead, hoping he wouldn't notice me, but he grabbed my arm impatiently and shoved me toward a basket of leaves by the wall. There was no flicker of recognition. Condin Savana's jaguar pelt still draped his broad shoulders, covering a form as solid as a stump. The memory of him wading into Chuqui's troops with his maqana circling his head caused me to shudder. Not a man to have angry with you, I thought.

"Your first visit here?" he asked. I nodded and picked up the basket. "Well, at least you understand Runasimi, which is more than I can say for your countrymen." I smiled to myself. The disguise worked well. "Now come with me to the front altar, and stop gawking," he commanded in a mock military tone, which made me snap to attention. He chortled happily to himself.

In truth, there was much to gawk at. The Temple of Wiraqocha, a great hall four stories high at its peak, was one of the largest roofed structures in the realm, and on that day crowded with a thousand nobles, if not more. Qhari claimed the interior was one hundred twenty paces in length by thirty wide, and as I looked about I had no reason to doubt him. To support the roof a thick wall pierced by ten doors divides the interior lengthways, and on either side, between the center and outer walls, are spaced eleven pillars to brace the slope of the roof. This awesome structure with its adjoining complexes and gardens was built by Thupa Inka to mark Wiraqocha's miracle of heavenly fire.

It's said that after Wiraqocha made all things He walked the earth to admire His creations and teach people how to live. When He came to this place on the Vilcanota River the people didn't recognize Him, for He appeared as a man with white skin, and they prepared to attack Him. Seeing them approach with stones in their hands, Wiraqocha knelt and raised his hands to beseech the heavens, and there appeared a great fire in the sky, which caused the people to tremble and beg for mercy. At this Wiraqocha commanded the fire to cease, but the heat so scorched the earth that rocks were left porous and light as bundled cloth. All this is true, the Reverend Mothers in the akllawasi said, for if you visit the Temple of Wiraqocha you will see those burned stones covering the hillsides around the temple. I can witness that it is so, for when I arrived I picked up such a stone, the size of a head, with one hand.

"How many people does this temple hold?" I asked idly, still gawking at the cavernous interior.

Achachi looked amused. "That depends on how many are standing outside when it starts to rain. Now, put the basket over there."

Like most nobility Achachi also held priestly office, and today he participated in presentations to Wiraqocha on behalf of Illap'a the war god. When I set the basket on a pile of offerings he grunted approvingly, patted my head, and marched off to other duties leaving me to admire the stone statue of Wiraqocha. It stood in a narrow niche, a solemn-looking man staring back at me with hands on His hips, elbows out. At His temple in Cuzco, Wiraqocha is a statue of solid gold about the height of a ten year old boy, and in the Qorikancha his image is made of fine mantles, but in whatever guise He is First Cause, Divine Origin, Instructor of the World. I performed the much'a, bowing low and kissing my fingertips toward Him, and prayed for His help in locating uncle Maita before Kontor found him.

I loitered near a door in the great dividing wall, a skin of aqha over my shoulder to fill the thirsty keros of nobility, when Qhari appeared behind me and pinched my siki!

"Stop that. Behave yourself."

"Ah, my sapling," he said leering, "you have a beautiful bottom. If only you had the rest of the equipment to go with it."

He'd been carrying on this way ever since he saw me in my Charka boy disguise, and I was not amused. I had piled my hair atop my head under a net of colored wool, the headdress of Charka males, and I wore a quilted tunic that concealed my feminine shape, though Qhari still seemed intrigued with my backside. Berry juice and charcoal darkened my skin and hardened my features. Being naturally youthful of face I suppose I appeared fourteen - too young to have my ears pierced, which explained the absence of earspools. The short cloak tied at my left shoulder draped under my right arm in customary fashion, shielding Eagle Woman where she dangled at my hip, and the press of a blade against the small of my back was reassuringly cool. Strange as it felt to wear a tunic, I had to admit it provided a freedom never allowed by a dress. The most uncomfortable part was the loincloth. Such an odd garment.

I pushed Qhari's hand away from my siki again. "I said stop it. You know what's under my loincloth, is that what you want?"

He paused as if summoning an image, then made a face.

"Fine," I said, "then keep your hands to yourself. Have you spotted anyone suspicious?"

He skimmed the nobles once and returned a blank face. "Several hundred."

"Then look for someone trying to act inconspicuous."

"Several hundred," he muttered again. Then he touched my elbow, directing my eyes with a nod. The royal party arrived led by Titu Cusi escorting his sister Kusi Rimaq, while Mama Oqllo and Princess Koka walked behind. After Koka, Kusi Rimaq was the next eldest, and she was obviously more than pleased to be at her brother's side. Koka walked in a daze.

"Have you heard the gossip?" Qhari asked. "Everyone in Cuzco is talking about it. Princess Koka didn't want to be Empress. Can you imagine? So she won't be marrying Titu Cusi after all."

Oh yes, I thought, that seed sprouted well. It's Tanta Karwa's last gift to the Empire - the healing of an ill before it began. She was the only one who had the courage to confront the Empress. Of course, Sumaq T'ika and the other priestesses at the Qorikancha did their part.

The Qorikancha had been my last stop before joining Tanta Karwa for our audience with Mama Oqllo. Sumaq, also wishing to spare Koka, agreed that Princess Kusi Rimaq would make a better empress. In truth, all the priestesses and royal ladies had been thinking the same, Sumaq told me, but none dared approach Mama Oqllo. When She finally agreed to consult at the Qorikancha, Sumaq and her friends had all the proper responses waiting for Her. It's said She was relieved when the oracles and auguries agreed that Koka's marriage to Titu Cusi was wrong for Tawantinsuyu, hence confirming what She must have felt but was unable to admit.

Armed with the authority of the temple, Mama Oqllo had no difficulty persuading the noblewomen, who in turn enlisted their husbands' support. Titu Cusi, it was said, was furious to find everyone against him in this, and went to his father as final arbitrator. But Sumaq had already spoken with the oracle for Thupa Inka's mummy, who delivered the appropriate answer, and Titu Cusi resigned himself to marrying Kusi Rimaq. All this being so, I wondered why Koka had such a long face today.

"Yes, I know about Princess Koka," I said to Qhari, "so now she can marry whomever she wishes."

Qhari's brows went up. "Haven't you heard? This morning Titu Cusi announced that on the day he becomes emperor Princess Koka must marry that man over there." I followed his finger, at first not sure I saw the one he pointed at, and then afraid I did.

"I know," Qhari answered my look, "and he's just a minor kuraka."

So this is Titu Cusi's revenge for not getting his own way, I thought. The groom-to-be was a scrawny ancient, exceptionally ugly, with a wad of coca bulging his cheek and green slime dribbling from the corner of his mouth. He offered Koka a toothless leer as she passed, spilling more slime on his chin. From bad to worse, I moaned inwardly. Poor Koka. You may be safe from your brother's bed, but as Crown Prince he still has the authority to choose your husband.

The royal entourage paused to exchange pleasantries with the nobles crowding around them. Leaving Qhari to continue the search for Kontor, I drifted to Koka's side and tilted my skin bag to her kero. Of course she took no notice, servants being little more than furnishings, but as I poured I whispered in the deepest male voice I could manage, "My Lady, I bear greetings from your friend, the healer Qori Qoyllur."

Catching my secretive tone she lowered her head and looked away, keeping her voice for my ears alone. "My friend Qori? Where has she been? Has everyone abandoned me?"

"Qori Qoyllur has not abandoned you, Lady. She wants to know how she can help."

"Help? Tell Qori it's too late for help. My mother tried all day to arrange another match, promising anything, but no noble will risk the wrath of the future emperor, and my brother won't be moved. I would forsake men and live my life alone on the farthest mountaintop to escape this marriage, but no mountain is beyond the reach of The Perfect Pattern of All Things," she said, her voice heavy with sarcasm. "My dear brother has me watched day and night. No, there is only one final escape. Many of my father's women joined Him in death, why shouldn't His daughter?"

I glanced at her face expecting to see an idle threat, but she was resolved. "My Lady, you can't mean you that?"

She gazed at the wall, but looked beyond. "If that's the only door left open to me, why shouldn't I go with honor?" Then, collecting herself she said, "Tell no one of this. Why am I talking to a page? Give your mistress my greetings and ask her to come visit me one last time. And tell her she'd better come soon." Koka started off again with the entourage.

The Regent Wallpaya bobbed the golden feathers of his headdress at the hulk before him. Sapaca threw back his head and laughed at something Wallpaya said. I tipped my skin bag above his kero. It was a bottomless crater that any other man would have needed both hands to hold, but he managed it in one paw.

To look at Sapaca you'd think him a generous, friendly giant of a man, quick to laugh, interested in everyone, eager to distribute his wealth, find positions for second sons, arrange promotions, and do what he could for all who approached him. It was said there never was a cel-

408

ebration he didn't attend, and every hostess knew to keep extra drink on hand for his arrival. Had I not known about the incest, and his collusions with every plotter in Cuzco, I might actually have liked the man. True, as Speaker of Hurincuzco it was his duty to promote the interests of his saya, and he might have been forgiven his subterfuge if it didn't imperil the Empire. As for lying with his daughter, well, I no longer cared what happened to Q'enti, but the thought of the incest sickened me, perhaps because in a corner of my mind I still harbored guilt about my own. Anyway, these were good enough reasons to loath Sapaca.

Wallpaya's talk was about a new male llama he'd acquired, and the men were guffawing about the number of females it could breed in a day, while insinuating their own prowess. Undoubtedly Wallpaya and Sapaca know they're being watched, I decided, or they assume it. Nothing of importance will pass their lips in front of an audience. I might as well search the grounds for Maita and Kontor.

At the center of the temple complex is a tranquil pond fed by underground canals, its banks rimmed with rushes and gardens. The great temple frames one end of this long, shallow pool. At the other is a causeway crossing marshy ground, and along the south side are a series of walled compounds where the nobles and priests stay. A low hill borders the north, set with smaller temples and private quarters. I wandered by the pool studying the faces of the pilgrims, thousands of them, and wondered if this or that man might be uncle Maita, or the killer who stalked him. This was the day I waited so long for, and it wouldn't come again for another five years. By then it could be too late, if it wasn't already.

A man tapped my shoulder as he passed, walking on several paces before turning. The eyes beneath the feathered headdress directed me to the temple where Wallpaya and Sapaca now emerged, slapping each other on the back in parting. I looked back at the man and recognized Tintaya. A Pasto chief today, my Lord? You look the part. That long-haired wig suits you. His eyes flickered to the crowd at my side. Zapana? A hunchback Chupaychu woman? Convincing. I haven't seen that one before. Tintaya gestured with twitches of his shoulders that I was to follow Sapaca, while he and Zapana shadowed Wallpaya. I lowered my eyes in understanding and set off with my skin bag. Sapaca was always thirsty.

A foreign priest fell in beside Sapaca while he strolled by the pond, and the two began an animated discussion, broken occasionally by Sapaca's chuckles. They seemed to know each other, and I assumed the priest was trying to ingratiate himself further with the Speaker of Hurincuzco, who let himself be amused. I dawdled a few paces behind, head down, looking everywhere except at the two men. The priest's stench hung like a rotting carcass. How can he live with himself? I wondered. At least our priests bathe. . . well, most of them. Greasy hair dangled over the back of his cowl, and the animal bones sewn to his filth-encrusted robe clattered as he walked along, hem dusting the path. The image of the dead girl behind the burial towers at Sillustani leapt to mind, and then a name to match the smell - Michimalongo, the wandering priest from the Atacama deserts.

I pretended to stumble into Sapaca, a giddy boy so awed by the great temple he didn't look where he was going. It was my way of blending with the surroundings, and being inconspicuous by being obvious. It worked. While I stuttered and bowed, and stuttered and bowed again, the men ignored me, returning to their chatter while accepting aqha from my shaking hands. The talk was of oracles and shrines, but what caught my attention was Michimalongo's accented Runasimi. I know nothing of the language of Atacama, but I know when a native speaker of Runasimi is trying to sound like a foreigner - having had so much practice myself - and that's what struck me like a maul when I heard Michimalongo speak. At Sillustani he was calmer, but today he chattered nervously and bobbed his head.

I let them stroll on while I stood in the path, thunderstruck. Kontor needs a traveling disguise, I reasoned, and he needs a protector, someone of power who can send assassins across the Empire, searching out witnesses to the murders at the Hatunqolla akllawasi. Michimalongo was in the area when the murder occurred at Sillustani. Was he driven to haunt the scene of his crime the day we saw him? Now he appears at the five-year meeting, speaking to Sapaca. Michimalongo - Kontor. Sapaca - Protector. Somehow it makes sense, though the 'why' escapes me.

"You're not jesting?" Qhari said when I shared my suspicions. I gave him a look that left no doubt about levity. "Michimalongo is Kontor," he said to himself, regarding the sky and tapping his finger on his chin. "Let's be certain about this. You said his accent didn't sound right. I don't speak the Atacama tongue either, but I know someone who does, a page, and he's here today. I'll ask him to have a few words with this Michimalongo to see if he's genuine. Keep an eye on him and we'll meet you by the pond."

Michimalongo and Sapaca still strolled together. As I hurried through the crowd toward them I came upon a group of provincial lords wearing the familiar bird and fish designs of my native Kuntisuyu, and solemnly whispering in their midst was the Hatun Kuraka of Ica, frog-eyes bulging while he excitedly poked the man beside him trying to get his attention. Ah yes, I thought, the great Lord Aquixe, spared after Chuqui's coup attempt, and now probably eager to ingratiate yourself with the Regent Wallpaya. Are you one of those sending weapons for this new treachery? Hmmm, a reasonable guess. You like to be on the inside of whatever is going on, and you like to talk. Let's see how talkative you are today.

"Aqha, my Lord?"

He hardly glanced at me, never suspecting the Charka boy at his side was the same girl who stayed a few weeks in his kancha years before. I poured, and leaning closer I whispered in the Ica tongue, "A message from the Regent, Lord, in private please."

His brows went up, and for a moment I feared he might announce the Regent had sent him a secret message, but then he tried to look crafty, making sure everyone saw him do so, and followed me aside.

"You speak my language?"

I sighed to myself, Obviously, you fool. I just did. "Yes, Lord, and I'm really a woman disguised as a boy," I said, returning my voice to its natural tone.

"Say you so?" he replied, regarding me skeptically.

"It is so, Lord. Lord Wallpaya asked me to appear this way because his message comes with utmost secrecy."

Aquixe loved secrets and his eyes lit up, but some hesitation remained.

"A woman? Really?"

I sighed. "If my Lord has doubts he need only place his hand on my chest." We stood off to one side by the causeway at the far end of the pond. He looked around furtively, then placed a hand on my breast, pushing me to the wall.

"Can't tell," he said. "Not much there."

Fool, I thought. If this tunic weren't so thick it would be obvious. "Try my loincloth, Lord."

He glanced over his shoulder again and lifted the front of my tunic, wiggling his fingers into the loincloth. It amused me to think anyone watching would certainly have ideas about Aquixe's preferences.

"A raka!" His face reddened with the discovery.

"Yes, Lord. Does this not prove what I say is true?"

"And the Regent has a secret message for me?" he said drawing himself up. His shoulders were those of a fish, and if he had a chin he would have thrust it out, but he did his best to look impressive.

"A message of utmost importance, Lord, for your ears only. Everything depends on you." Aquixe grinned eagerly. Staring straight ahead I recited formally, "I, Lord Wallpaya, Regent of Tawantinsuyu, send you greetings Lord Aquixe, my trusted friend." Aquixe liked the opening. "The faithful messenger who speaks my words has been entrusted with all confidences, and you may speak with her freely, but only with her." I emphasized the 'her' for Aquixe's benefit. He bobbed his head. "Matters have arisen that require the 'consignment of goods' to be delivered a week earlier than planned."

"Stop. What are the code words?" he asked, narrowing his eyes.

Without pause I replied, "The code words, Lord? Ah yes, you're right of course. I should have given them first. But that is the other part of the message. The code words have been changed. For today only they are. . . Inca Moon." It meant nothing to him, and wouldn't have to any but the highest Inca officials. "But," I rushed on, "I will tell Lord Wallpaya how cautious you are, and rightfully so - there are devious spies everywhere - and his esteem for you will grow even more. Now, my Lord, the Regent wishes you to reply through me whether or not you can meet the new delivery time."

Aquixe frowned and muttered, "But it will take a week to get the message to our people, and even on forced march it will take them another week to reach Limatampu."

Limatampu isn't far from Cuzco, and a perfect place to dispense weapons for an armed rush on the city. No doubt some caravan would arrive with the weapons concealed inside bales, while Wallpaya arranged for the city guard to be elsewhere. All I needed was the schedule.

"Yes, Limatampu," I repeated. "What is the earliest arrival time?"

Aquixe rubbed the place where his chin should have been. "Well, it will be difficult. . . and I'll have to speak with the other lords, but, I suppose we might manage it by next month."

"On the day of the new moon," I suggested. He hesitated, twisting his mouth. "Please, Lord," I pressed, "everything depends on you. Lord Wallpaya must know the exact day."

"Very well, it shall be so," he said nodding like a generous father dispensing favors. "Tell the Regent I'll arrange for his goods to be at Limatampu on the day of the new moon."

"The Empire is grateful to you: You will be justly rewarded, Lord, rest assured of that. Oh, one more thing, Lord Wallpaya suspects there's a spy in our midst. Until we discover who it is, it's better to pretend the original plan is going ahead. Caution your friends not to say anything to anyone about this change. Only the select few of the inner circle know. Also, to maintain security Lord Wallpaya doesn't want you or the others to make any further contact with him." I directed his eyes to the knot of Kuntisuyu nobles.

"I'll handle them," he said slyly. "After all, the orders come from the Regent."

"Indeed, Lord. And remember, tomorrow the pass words will be the same as before. Don't mention 'Inca Moon' to anyone, not even your Kuntisuyu brothers. It's our secret." I winked. In response he blinked both eyes trying to imitate me.

Atoq said a leak at the fringe can reveal the plot at the center, and again he was right. Zapana had traipsed all over Kuntisuyu, and Tintaya had diligently shadowed the tight-lipped Cuzco conspirators. When I provided the details of their plan he would be furious. The profuse thanks I left with Aquixe were genuine.

Michimalongo shifted nervously. Qhari and I watched from a distance while Qhari's friend engaged Michimalongo in polite conversation. Sapaca, not understanding a word, looked bored and made motions to leave. The page backed away from them bowing, and headed over to us. Michimalongo tugged at Sapaca's arm trying to lead him into the hostel complex, but Sapaca brushed off his persistence and left him standing alone.

"Well?" Qhari asked when the page joined us.

The young man shrugged. "Well, he speaks the Atacama tongue, but poorly. He's not one of our people."

I looked at Qhari. No words needed to pass between us. We turned as one and started for Michimalongo.

XXXI

In which the Fated Meeting comes to pass, and what its outcome was.

Michimalongo stood by a door piercing the high wall of the hostel complex, alone and muttering to himself. He didn't notice us approach behind the lines of pilgrims streaming to the temple, where moaning blasts of a conch shell trumpet summoned all to worship. I kept my eyes straight ahead, willing Qhari to do the same, neither of us daring to breathe.

It will be over soon, I told myself, all those years of fear and hiding. You made our father a fugitive, Kontor, and you had him killed to hide your evil. Because of you Qhari and I were terrorized, and I was married to my brother. Then there are the others who died because of you: the governor of Ica, the old captain and his faithful troop in the desert, the micheq at the bridge, even Achachi's granddaughter. And what of all the girls you murdered? Do you hear their screams in your nightmares? Today there will be one more scream, the last you ever hear, and it will be yours.

Michimalongo's stink settled over us like a quilt. Qhari squared his shoulders and worked his fists. Move easy, Qhari, I willed, we've come too far to lose him now, and I want you alive when this is done. He's a demon, but a master demon. He's outwitted everyone for over twenty years, even Lord Atoq, and he's drenched in the blood of countless victims. But today, Kontor, you don't have a helpless girl trembling before you. Today you meet Inca Moon, and she has special plans for you.

The backs of the last pilgrims were ahead of us now, joining the throngs already huddled in prayer against the temple wall. The remaining nobles squeezed into the packed hall. The garden lay vacant in the afternoon sun, a few ducks noisily gliding in to crease the pond leaving spreading fingers of silver in their wake. High above a pair of condors circled. The great birds of death knew what was about to happen. I slid my hand beneath my cloak and caressed Eagle Woman.

When we drew abreast of Michimalongo no signal was needed - our minds were one, wheeling us at the same instant to face the demon. Qhari stepped up to Michimalongo as if to ask a question, then his hand shot out, flipping back Michimalongo's long hair and answering the last question about his identity. His earlobes had been cut away removing his Inca past, but the scars proved he had something to hide. In that moment I saw a face worn thin and lined with years, a mouth that might have been handsome if it ever smiled, and determined eyes now caught in surprise.

"Greetings, Kontor," I said.

He froze against the wall, hands spread, eyes darting, but there was no denial on his face, only the look of a cornered animal. Suddenly he nodded at something behind us and we whirled to meet the attack. Nothing. In a blur Kontor vanished through the door.

Stupid! I howled inwardly as we gave chase. How many times have you used that one yourself, Inca Moon? Fool!

A narrow passageway ran the length of the inside wall, allowing access to five identical courtyards. Each courtyard had two houses on either side and two at the end, with two doors in each facade. A central alley connected the length of the complex, making it a maze. The guards were at the temple with their masters. Only a few bewildered servants remained to watch us dash from corner to corner, searching each room with a sweep of our eyes.

"This way," Qhari shouted.

I turned fast enough to glimpse a flutter disappear down the alley. We rushed through, emerging in another courtyard indistinguishable from the last, its twelve doors staring blindly at us.

"You search these," Qhari said, waving at the houses on either side of me. He ran to their mates across the courtyard. Aside from the clothing and regalia lying about, the rooms were identical with the same seven niches in the back wall and two at either end. Being no more than fifteen paces in length we searched each with a glance. But I didn't need to see Kontor; it was his smell I sought.

"Qori!"

I whirled to see Qhari chasing into the next compound and sped after him, my feet barely touching the ground. As I started down the alley a thought came to me, If I were being pursued in this maze what would I do? Perhaps it was this question or perhaps it was intuition that made me crouch when I sprang into the courtyard. As I did so something whizzed over my head and hit the wall showering me with plaster.

"Bitch," the man with the two-handed axe exclaimed. His outstretched arms still reverberated from having driven the blade into the stonewall a palm-span above me. Qhari sprawled motionless on the ground to one side, the man standing over him lifting his spear with both hands for the plunge.

"Qhari!"

With one bound I hurled myself at his attacker, catching him from the side as he poised to strike. We regained our feet at the same instant and he turned his weapon on me, waving the point back and forth in front of my face. I found myself staring down the shaft at an ugly brute with a flattened nose and one front tooth missing.

"You owe me, you little bitch," he hissed.

The man with the axe circled behind. "Just gore her nicely," he said, "she owes me too."

I looked from face to face. Bitch? I wondered. Obviously they see through my Charka boy disguise, but. . . I owe them?

"You've caused me a lot of trouble, Qori Qoyllur," the axe man said, "but now I can do with you as I please. First, I think I'll have your eyes for a necklace, and then my friend here can do what he wants."

Peering closer I saw a white scar on his neck, but even without this souvenir of our first meeting I recognized the voice - the same one that commanded the brigands in the desert, and in Cuzco threatened to gouge my eyes while Qhari was strangled. Did I not also hear him at Sapaca's kancha during Q'enti's womanhood celebration? Why didn't I see it then - Sapaca's man. He's here to protect Kontor.

The flat-nosed one tensed, preparing a thrust. Now I remember smashing that brick in your face, I thought, admiring the alterations it caused. A nice piece of work for a girl, but it's not a girl you're dealing with now.

Flat-nose made his lunge, a pitifully slow jab as far as I was concerned. Turning sideways I deflected the shaft with a backhand and drove my knee into his groin sending him down, then spun and removed his remaining front tooth with a back kick. Eye-gouger swung. I ducked and rolled to the side, leaving him cursing again.

Qhari moaned and tried raising himself, then collapsed face down. No blood, I noticed.

Eye-gouger regarded me calmly and nodded to himself. "You're too fast for this, aren't you?" he said hefting his axe. "Yes, they trained you to defend yourself, I can see that." His eyes shifted to Flat-nose on his knees, spitting up blood and vomit. "And they trained you well," he said, nodding appreciatively. He dropped the axe and reached down the back of his neck, pulling a long, wicked-looking dagger from its hiding place between his shoulders, his eyes never leaving mine. "Chimu bronze," he announced, twisting the blade at me.

I slipped the tiny stone knife from the small of my back and waved it at him. "Quispisisa obsidian."

He regarded the brownish-red, finger-length blade with a smirk, and held his dagger across his chest, pressing the point to his left palm. It was two hands long.

Qhari moaned again. Eye-gouger glanced at him, and then gave me a cruel smile. So that's your move, I thought. You're not as stupid as you look. You know I can't be taken with something as clumsy as a long-handled axe, so you've gone to the knife. And you know I can defend myself so you're not going to attack me - no, you'll fall on Qhari and force me on the offensive, giving you the advantage.

Before I could think of a countermove he realized this plan in a flicker, dropping on Qhari's prostrate form like a rock. I had no choice but to dive at him in the same instant. Crouched and steadied, he lunged up, grabbing my knife hand and twisting as he flipped me over his head. I landed flat on my back, knife gone, breathless.

Flat-nose fell on me with the shriek of an animal, his huge hands crushing my throat.

"Get out of the way, fool," Eye-gouger shouted at him from behind, but Flat-nose remained intent on his revenge. His bloody face was a mask of quivering rage, and strings of vomit still dangled from his mouth.

I didn't have the strength to break his hold, and pricks of light against a black curtain swarmed before my eyes. I fumbled frantically at my side for Eagle Woman, and pulling her open I released her stinger with an upward stab. Flat-nose hardly blinked when the stinger bit his side, but an instant later, as the black curtain was about to close over me, his grip loosened and his tongue came out in a croaking gasp. The paws at my throat went slack allowing me a blessed gulp of air, and Flat-nose collapsed like an empty sack.

Eye-gouger looked stunned. From where he stood he hadn't seen Eagle Woman do her work, and the result was a mystery. "What?" he asked himself.

It was an unfortunate waste of a stinger as far as I was concerned, and I cursed myself for not having dealt properly with Flat-nose before. There was no time to fit Eagle Woman again, even if I weren't still sputtering and coughing on the ground. Eye-gouger narrowed his eyes at me and set his chin.

I began a roll to the left and then dodged to the right when he sprang, but he anticipated the feint and landed on top of me, pinning my arms. He tried to hold me down with one hand while he raised his dagger to strike but I wiggled an arm free and deflected the blow. The blade hit the ground a finger-breadth from my neck. I sank my teeth into his wrist with all my force. He screeched and pummeled me with his fist. Jerking himself up he straddled my chest, his wrist still clamped in my mouth, and began slapping wildly with his free hand, the dagger momentarily forgotten. I grabbed the front of his loincloth in a claw-grip and squeezed hard, and in the same motion my right hand found the hilt of the dagger.

The claw in his groin set his priorities straight. When I pulled the dagger from the ground his arm flew away from my mouth, leaving me choking on a lump of flesh. He clamped both hands between his legs, jabbing his thumbs into my wrist to break the hold. It worked, and I only managed one wild slash with the dagger before he knocked it from my hand. Still, it removed his nose.

In a blind fury he fell on me again, blood spurting everywhere, our hands slippery with it, grappling and twisting as I tried to break free.

Being no match for brute strength, especially that of a shrieking demon, I became a wiggling eel, wishing I could be water itself. His weight smothered me, but when I grabbed for his crotch again he hunched defensively and I slipped free - almost. A hand like a vise clamped my ankle, drawing me back.

We came up on our knees, he behind me, an arm like stone crushing my throat, squeezing the light from my eyes. His left hand locked the arm in place, and he held me away from him so I couldn't reach behind and trouble his privates. I struggled hopelessly, fighting back the thickening darkness.

There was only one move left. When Zapana taught it to me he said I would use it when my life depended on it, though I hadn't believed him. Thrusting both hands behind my head I grabbed his face. My thumbs became hooks, diving like hawks into yielding sockets and ripping out the orbs they found there.

The scream that followed was so long and piercing that birds must have dropped from the sky, and every head at the great temple must have turned as one. I sat back panting, stroking my neck, and watched as if from a distant place. He remained sitting back on his heels, arms motionless at his sides, noseless face to the sky, mouth open, eyeballs hanging on his cheeks. And then the sound suddenly stopped, and his soul must have fled from the shock alone, for he never twitched again.

Qhari groaned and turned himself over, coming up on one knee and rubbing the back of his head. "What was that terrible sound?" he asked.

I sighed in relief to see he was all right, but I couldn't speak. He heaved himself to his feet and looked around, blinking. "What happened to you?"

I regarded him silently and thought, I've been beaten, crushed, strangled, I'm sitting here covered in blood, and you want to know what happened, brother dear?

He walked over to Eye-gouger and grimaced, casting a disapproving glance my way. "Did you have to do that?"

I said nothing.

He looked at Flat-nose, now a blue-faced log. "What happened to him?"

Not even Qhari knew about Eagle Woman, and I was in no condition to explain.

"Well then," he said putting his hands on his hips, "at least tell me who they were."

"Sapaca's men," I managed weakly.

"Sapaca's men," he repeated, nodding to himself. "What were their names?"

"They didn't introduce themselves, but that one commanded the brigands in the desert. He's the one who threatened to rip out my eyes in Cuzco." Qhari whistled and gave me a respectful look. "The other is one of those who strangled you, remember?"

Qhari shrugged at the memory. "Then you should have left him for me to deal with."

"You? You, Qhari Puma?" I said, pulling myself to my feet. "You were flat on your face having a nap."

He held up his hands, palms outward, but my finger was already pointing. "A lot of help you were. Yes, you, Qhari Puma - he who goes charging around corners without looking. You deserve to get bashed on the head. Just be thankful I arrived before they skewered you."

He grinned. "For a moment I was worried you'd been hurt."

"Well. . . well, maybe not bad, but no thanks to you, Qhari Puma."

"Good. Now, let's go after Kontor. . . that is, if you're able."

"If I'm able? If I'm able! While you lay there snoozing I was - "

"Yes, yes," he cut me short, glancing at the two bodies again, "I can see what you were doing. But there's no time to lose discussing it. Just before they hit me I glimpsed Kontor running that way," he nodded to the far end of the courtyard, "and two others were right behind him. More of Sapaca's men, I suppose. Let's go," he cried, snatching up Eye-gouger's dagger and setting off at a run.

I retrieved my obsidian blade and followed, shouting for him to be careful around corners. He gave me an indignant look over his shoulder. Passing between the two houses at the end of the courtyard we entered another enclosure, vacant save for a foreman's hut. A narrow opening in the rear wall with a few stone stairs led us into the temple's storage complex. Here, rows of huge, round storehouses marched away in long, orderly lines.

Qhari jerked to a stop and looked around. He cast me a questioning look. Right or left?

"If I were being chased in here," I thought aloud, "my pursuers would expect me to dodge and turn, so I'd take the straight course. That's it Qhari, straight ahead. Remember, we don't have to see him, if he's close we'll smell him."

Like hounds we began sniffing our way down a path between two ranks of identical storehouses. Each had a conical thatch roof, coarse stone walls, and a single, narrow door facing its neighbor across the path. Uneasiness built in my stomach as we progressed. The storage area was walled and accessible only through the passages of the hostel compounds. But the enclosed space was vast, presenting numerous possibilities for concealment and ambush. I thought, Kontor and the rest of Sapaca's men could be hiding between the storehouses, or inside them, waiting for us to stumble into their trap. Then again, once we reach the far end they might dash out the way they came and disappear in the crowds outside. Which outcome are you hoping for?

Qhari stopped and wiped his brow. He'd been sharing my thoughts and now replied for both of us, "This is for father." He tapped the turquoise oval on his headband.

"For father," I said.

He forced a smile. "And we are together."

"Together," I repeated.

All of it will stop here today, I resolved anew. Father's dishonor and death will be avenged, and Kontor's savage killing spree ended.

Qhari took a deep breath and started down the path again, sniffing at each door. I followed on the opposite side, tensed for the attack that might come at any moment, my senses reaching out to feel the unseen ahead. The condors continued circling above.

We reached the end and had come partway back on another path when a breeze came up, bringing wood smoke and the smell of burnt offerings from the temple, and, faintly, something else. Qhari stiffened

422

and turned to me. Words didn't have to be exchanged. A rotting carcass, or a filthy priest, hung nearby.

With gestures I sent Qhari between two structures to circle behind, and I did the same on my side moving like a fox on its prey, searching for the men I was sure crouched in waiting for us. But four storehouses ahead I realized the stench was fading. Qhari looked at me from across the path and shrugged. Nothing on his side either. Very well, I decided, they're inside one of these buildings. I imagined Sapaca's men huddled within, breathing Kontor's stink.

We stepped back on the path and crept from door to door with our noses high. Qhari had checked one storehouse and proceeded to the next when a dark head poked from its entrance, and instantly retreated.

"Kontor!" Qhari roared, and before I could stop him he plunged through the doorway.

Stupid brother, I cursed, somersaulting low through the narrow door behind him. Of course he was already knocked senseless when I gained my feet. Kontor leapt back from my tumbling entry and now stood a few steps away with Qhari's dagger in his hand, wild eyes fixed on the door behind me. In a blink I saw he was alone. His animal bone robe lay discarded to the side, and he wore a provincial tunic. Several bales of the same garments lay against the wall, but aside from these the storehouse was empty. Evidently Kontor was searching the buildings for a new disguise, and we caught him in the transformation. A wedge of sunlight from the door pierced the gloom, revealing a circular room ten paces wide. The place hung thick with the stench of his priestly robe.

Close quarters and alone, I thought, this is how I've dreamed of finding you, Kontor.

Kontor went into a fighting crouch, his gaunt form tense, corded muscles twitching his long arms, eyes wavering from me to the door. "You're not going out of here alive," I said producing my knife.

Qhari picked himself up from where he had been smashed against the wall and shook the daze from his head. "You're just in time to help me finish him," he said.

I rolled my eyes at the roof, and Kontor struck like lightning. My knife hand - suddenly empty - went numb from the force of his kick, and in the same motion he had Qhari pinned against the wall, dagger poised. Qhari growled through clenched teeth, clutching the blade in his bare hand and leaving a smear of red on the wall as he forced it down.

Jumping up from behind I landed my knee in Kontor's back, knocking him aside, and followed with a kick to his head. Then I grabbed his long hair in my good hand to deliver a knee in his face, but he rammed his fist into my crotch sending me off balance. The damage wasn't what it might have been had I been a man, but it provided enough of a pause for the two of us to square off again.

"Cover the door, Qhari," I shouted over my shoulder. Kontor eased himself up, eyes fixed on mine with new respect, blade steady and pointed at me. Qhari bundled his injured hand to his chest and took his position.

Kontor eyed me warily, waiting for me to dive for my knife. His eyes narrowed when he saw me hesitate. My right hand was useless, but it was another realization that sent fingers of ice searching my stomach - I hadn't given Eagle Woman a fresh stinger. I was naked.

Kontor edged along the wall to my fallen blade, keeping his point ready, eyes shifting rapidly between Qhari and me. Now the question was, who had who cornered?

"Leave now, Qhari," I commanded.

He baulked. "After you."

Kontor grinned. Slowly he squatted, feeling the floor for my knife with his free hand, watching us. But when he found what he sought he couldn't help glancing down at it. I sprang faster than he could blink knocking both of us off balance. Qhari lunged at the same instant hitting Kontor from the other side, and the two rolled fighting for the dagger. I stumbled up in time to see Kontor raise the obsidian blade and plunge it into Qhari's side. Qhari cried out and went limp. Kontor whirled and came up on his knees, dagger at the ready. I shot my foot to his mouth, toppling him back. I aimed another kick at his knife hand but he dodged and leapt to his feet, lips bloodied, cursing. He faced me.

I looked at Qhari's still form. It doesn't matter anymore, I thought. Qhari has met his end, and I may too, but Kontor is coming with us.

"All right, Kontor," I said heaving for breath, "let's make an end to this. You may get that knife into me, but you won't stop me. . . not until you're dead."

He gave me a puzzled, almost admiring look. I shook my right hand at my side. The tingling stopped and I could move my fingers. Kontor approached cautiously, dagger extended.

I thought, You're right handed, Kontor, so you'll feint to my left and stab to the right when I try to dodge. I'll take my chances and meet your first thrust. Come on. . . that's it. . . closer. . . closer.

His arm flexed and I leaned to my right as if to jump aside, then froze in place. He had already corrected for the anticipated dodge and his blade slashed air where I would have been had I moved. Seizing his throat in a left-handed claw-grip, I slammed my knee into his groin and grabbed his dagger hand at the wrist. I found the strength to twist until he dropped the blade. He fell back coughing and I snatched up the knife. But as I straightened his foot shot out, catching me below the ribs. I landed on my back, breath gone, the dagger flung from my grasp. He scrambled for the knife and was on me before I could lift my head, blade glinting above me while I flailed my arms, gasping for breath.

"Q-O-O-O-R-I-I-I!!!" Qhari suddenly staggered up behind Kontor and leapt as the dagger began its downward plunge, flinging a protective arm in the way and taking the full force of the blow aimed at my heart. The point passed clean through his arm above the elbow. Qhari howled and fainted.

Kontor yanked the blade free with a curse and rolled Qhari aside, lifting the knife high for a final, measured strike at Qhari's chest.

"Not my brother!" I shouted with breath I didn't have, and rising from the waist I buried my fingers in Kontor's neck. I attacked him like a screaming gale, clawing and biting at his face, forcing him on his back, knees hammering his groin.

So surprised was Kontor, and so eager to defend himself against my frenzy, he released the dagger to protect his crotch with both hands and rolled away. I let him, and seizing the fallen knife I readied to meet him when he rose. I caught him in mid-stance and threw him flat against the wall. He only blinked when I rammed the dagger into his belly.

In the next instant the light from the doorway vanished and strong arms grabbed me from behind, flinging me across the room.

XXXII

**In which matters take startling New Turns, the significance of what
has occurred is fully realized, Secrets are Confessed, and previously
obscure incidents explained.**

When my eyes opened I found myself prone on the floor of the storehouse. Gradually I became aware of others in the room. Kontor? Yes,
I drove the dagger in, I remembered, and then I was grabbed from behind
and slammed into the wall.

I tried sitting up, tenderly tracing the lump where my head met
stone. Short, massive legs planted firmly apart came into view. I
looked up at Lord Achachi; his maqana held crossways in his big
hands, face set in a snarl.

Kontor sat slumped against the wall, his hands on his belly where the
hilt of the dagger still protruded. Zapana, now changed from his
Chupaychu woman disguise into male clothes, knelt over him whispering. I blinked, recognizing them, but what were they doing here? Then
events came rushing back.

"Qhari!" I shouted, coming to my knees.

Achachi readied himself, lifting his maqana to his shoulder.

"It's all right," Zapana said from behind.

Achachi exhaled, eyed me warily, and then stepped aside keeping his
maqana at the ready.

Still on my knees I hurried to Qhari's side and raised his blood-
soaked body to my breast. "Qhari, speak to me. Look what the fiend did
to you. Oh, Qhari, my poor sweet brother, you threw yourself in the way
of the dagger for me, you saved me. Now look at you. Don't leave me,
Qhari."

His eyes fluttered, then closed again. "Hold me tighter, sister," he
said in a choked whisper.

I hugged him to me like life itself and began to rock, my tears wet-
ting his cold, pale face. We had come so far together, all the way to the
revenge we pledged as children on that long ago beach. All whom I

might have called family were gone but Qhari. Our hearts had always beat as one.

"You can't leave me now," I wailed. "Not you, Qhari. Not you!"

He moaned.

"Qhari, my own sweet brother, forgive me every harm I've ever done you. Forgive me, Qhari," I pleaded, "I love you."

Slowly he turned his face to mine, a brave but thin smile on his lips. "A little lower," he said.

"What?"

Zapana placed his hand on my shoulder. "He's badly cut," he said, "but he'll live."

"Squeeze my arm a little lower," Qhari repeated, "I think you've almost stopped the bleeding."

"What? Almost stopped the bleeding? Am I your personal tourniquet? Is that it, Qhari Puma? Hold me tight, sister dear, indeed! Well, we'll just have to fix you up, won't we? Here. . ." I ripped a strip from his cloak and tied it above the dagger wound on his arm, cinching it firmly.

"Ouch," he said.

"Tighter, brother dear? Would you like it tighter? Very well, I'll help you."

"Ouch, not so hard," he protested, a dash of color returning to his cheeks.

"Just thought you'd lie there and let sister make a fool of herself, did you? Well, Qhari Puma, if you hadn't come barging in here like some fool recruit - "

"I forgive you," he said holding up a hand.

"Oh, you forgive me. You forgive me, is that it, Qhari Puma?" I tore more strips from his cloak and fashioned a sling for his arm, then turned my attention to the wound in his side. "Here, press down on this. No, harder."

"Ouch!"

"Oh, you're so brave," I said giving him a sour look. "Now sit up so I can wrap this bandage around your waist. Come on, sit up."

"It hurts."

"No more than you deserve, Qhari Puma. You're a stupid, headstrong lump, and dumb as a stone. Do you know that, Qhari Puma? Well, do you?"

Between grimaces he smiled to himself. I tied the last knot and without thinking kissed his forehead. He gave me a shy grin. I scowled back and turned up my nose.

Zapana watched all this with amusement, and sympathy for Qhari. "I sometimes wondered what it would be like to have a sister," he said to Achachi. "If I'm ever wounded, finish me before this one gets her hands on me."

Achachi didn't respond. His gaze stayed on me.

I helped Qhari prop himself against the wall, then stood and faced the men. Zapana knelt by Kontor again, checked his face, and then answered Achachi's look with a shake of his head. Kontor's eyes were like dull obsidian. He breathed no more.

Achachi gestured at the body with his maqana. "Did he tell you anything?" he asked Zapana.

"Enough," Zapana said. "It was as we thought."

Achachi regarded me curiously. "Why did you kill him?"

"Why?" I said in defiance. "Do you know who he was?"

"Of course," Achachi answered. "He was Kontor of Choqo, my subordinate at Hatunqolla during the rebellion, and your father's captain."

Qhari and I exchanged a glance. "What do you know about our father?" Qhari demanded.

"Everything," Achachi said.

"Then you know about us?" I said.

Achachi looked surprised. "We were the ones who brought you here. But before we speak of that, tell me, why did you kill Kontor?"

Qhari nodded his consent, and I repeated what Lord Atoq told me of the long-ago events at the Hatunqolla akllawasi. Atoq arrived to find the murdered governess Ronto, and the old priestess identified Kontor as the killer before she died in Atoq's arms. Kontor ordered his men to certain death to dispose of witnesses. Then he vanished to haunt the land, repeating his fiendish murders again and again, and hunting those few who were wise enough to desert from his doomed troop. While I spoke

Zapana and Achachi shifted uneasily and exchanged glances. When I finished a silence descended on the room.

Zapana made as if to speak, but Achachi stopped him with a look. "I think we had better start at the beginning," Achachi said. "But first, let's get out of this stink."

We stepped into the sunlight, Zapana assisting Qhari and seating him gently against the outside of the storehouse. I blinked at the afternoon clouds drifting in a blue sky overhead, and noticed the circling condors had vanished.

Achachi stared pensively at the ground, and Zapana kept his head turned from me. Achachi heaved a sigh. "That was a well-crafted story Atoq told you," he said, "and there are a few elements of truth in it, but about Kontor - Atoq lied."

"Lied? Lord Atoq?" I looked to Zapana but he bowed his head and turned away. "And what proof have you, Lord?" I asked, my anger rising.

"Proof? The proof of my own eyes," he said fixing me with a sullen stare. "I saw the body of the priestess at the Hatunqolla akllawasi - the one who supposedly identified Kontor as the culprit - and her throat was cut to the bone. She couldn't have uttered a word. Kontor did come to me while the Qolla rebels were driven from the city. He reported two women at the akllawasi one of whom, this Ronto I suppose, demanded rescue by a royal. Does that sound like the act of a murderer trying to hide his deeds? By the time I arrived at the akllawasi Sapaca was already emerging triumphantly with Princess Sisa.

"Atoq was there, too. He arrived before me, and he was there long enough to ascertain the truth and formulate a plan. He knew from the beginning it was Sapaca who murdered those women, but Atoq has a quick mind. Royalty must not be disgraced, and never divided. To avoid a trial in which he, Atoq of hanansaya, would be the only witness against Sapaca of hurinsaya, he agreed to let Sapaca claim Sisa, and blame the deaths on the Qolla." Achachi sighed heavily. "I understand Atoq's reasoning at the time," he said. "Our armies were fighting on two fronts, in Antisuyu and Qollasuyu, and though Hatunqolla had fallen the Aymara rebels were not yet crushed. Many battles lay ahead. Thousands had already died. We could ill afford dissension between the sayas over two unfortunate women."

I must have been standing with my mouth open for he gave an exasperated look and continued, "Don't you see? It was Sapaca who murdered those women. And then he found Sisa, but she was too great a prize to work his twisted passions on. He condemned her to the marriage bed. Sapaca came to me with the order to keep Kontor and his men in battle, until all were dead. I suppose he learned about them from the priestess before he cut her throat. Of course, I didn't understand any of this at the time, and when I protested I was transferred back to the jungle campaign in Antisuyu."

So it was Sapaca, I thought. Father said the one who gave the fatal order to his troop was the murderer. And Achachi has known this all along.

"Wait," I said, the awful truth dawning on me. "Are you saying Kontor was innocent?"

"As innocent as your father. Sapaca wanted Kontor dead, and he knew sooner or later you'd lead his men to him. He was right, and you even did their work for them."

I looked through the storehouse door to the man crumpled against the wall inside, the one who fought like a caged animal and now lay as limp as a doll. "But we saw him with Sapaca," I protested.

Zapana grimaced. "With his dying breath Kontor told me how close he came to finishing Sapaca. He hid in the Atacama desert and emerged from time to time disguised as a priest to search for his comrades. Don't you remember meeting him at Sillustani? I confess I didn't guess who he was either. When he saw the murdered girl in the same condition as others he'd heard about over the years, and learned that Sapaca had recently passed by, he finally guessed the truth. Kontor hadn't seen his friends since the day they parted, and he thought them long dead. He resolved to come here today in disguise and take his revenge. When you spotted Kontor he was trying to lure Sapaca away from the crowds. When you confronted him he thought you were Sapaca's agents and fled."

"But the men who tried to stop us. . ." Qhari said.

Achachi glared at him. "Them? They were Sapaca's men, and were probably watching you all day to see if you'd lead them to Kontor. Once you did your usefulness was at an end, so two executioners remained behind. We, too, were watching you. . . but not closely enough." He gave Zapana a dour look. "We found two bodies in the courtyard back there, and then two more when we started searching this storage compound."

I looked at Qhari. "Didn't you see two men run out of the courtyard with Kontor?"

Qhari frowned. "I said they were right behind him. Now it seems they were chasing him also. He must have dealt with them himself, just before we. . . ."

My eyes strayed to the body in the storehouse again. A horror descended.

"It was Sapaca who ordered my father's troop to certain death?" I said lamely, struggling to grasp the enormity of what I'd done.

"It is so," Achachi said. "He came with the banded stick of imperial authority. How could I refuse? Before I understood what all this was about they transferred me. I'm a soldier, and my first duty was to put down the rebellions threatening the Empire. In later years as Visitor-General I became aware of other young women murdered most foully, all like the governess at the Hatunqolla akllawasi - raped, strangled, and tongue ripped out. Though these deaths happened over many years in distant parts of the Empire, I finally realized one commonalty to them all - Lord Sapaca. Sapaca always traveled in the area when these murders occurred. I bribed one of his servants, and learned Sapaca was away from his bed on the nights of these deeds, supposedly for 'amorous' engagements."

I swallowed hard and looked at Qhari. He nodded, the images coming back to him, too. In my mind I saw the mutilated girl behind the burial towers at Sillustani, and Achachi telling us he'd seen another like her farther south. Achachi had been trailing Sapaca through Qollasuyu after all.

"Naturally, I reported my suspicions to Lord Atoq," Achachi continued, "for I still thought he'd been misled, too. Atoq assured me he'd look into it. Zapana also happened to be at that meeting. . . ."

Zapana nodded and took up the pause. "Lord Atoq told me the same story about Kontor that he told you, Qori, except he said all of Kontor's men, at least those who deserted, were part of the rape and murder. Atoq had us hunting them for years."

My head spun. Again I crouched on the windy ledge clutching my sling, waiting while father kept the assassin talking and Qhari crept closer with his net. "What is my crime supposed to be?" father demanded. "Rape, murder and desertion," the assassin replied.

Zapana saw the faraway look and drew me back. "When Kontor and the others deserted they were clever enough to put their clothes on some headless Qolla bodies, so at first they were believed dead. But, as Lord Atoq related it, the standard-bearer from Kontor's troop was soon captured, and under torture he revealed the plan, though he was brave enough to bite off his own tongue before much was learned."

I remembered father telling us how he once met uncle Maita here at the Temple of Wiraqocha, and Maita reported seeing the standard-bearer captured. He suspected information was wrung from him. They would be gratified to know their old comrade remained true within the limits of human endurance.

Zapana said, "Still, Lord Atoq knew that Kontor and the two brothers were alive and fleeing in different directions. He allowed it to be announced they died heroic deaths to lull them out of hiding."

Tanta Karwa told me how Atoq hosted the young widows, including my mother, at Tipón, where he even bedded some. Now I realized he was only courting them for information about their husbands, though they knew nothing. A bard came to the widows seeking descriptions so the men could be presented in song at court, Tanta Karwa said. Every spy in Tawantinsuyu must have hummed that tune.

"So that's how Atoq learned about them," I said, "but why - "

Zapana motioned for silence. "Qori, please. . . . First I want you to know I had no reason to doubt my father, any more than you did. Atoq never told me the details of how the governess Ronto was murdered, so I had no way of connecting it with the reports of other murdered girls that reached Tipón. And he never let me investigate any of those murders, choosing to leave them to Tintaya. Tintaya refused to see a pattern in the manner of the deaths, claiming them all to be the work of different madmen. But when I heard Lord Achachi make his case against Sapaca, and learned exactly how Ronto died, many things fell into place for me."

Zapana's voice hardened. "Do you know why my father has been protecting Sapaca all these years? It's because of Sisa. You know he's besotted with her?" Zapana arched an eyebrow at me. I nodded. "Well, there it is," Zapana said. "I think Lord Achachi is right about my father's initial motives - preserving peace between the sayas during a critical time of rebellion - but later, when Sapaca became Speaker of Hurincuzco and the murders continued, I think Atoq kept his silence for Sisa's sake. If Sapaca is revealed for the demon he is the shame will descend on his entire panaqa, and Lady Sisa will lose everything. Atoq cares not for Sapaca, but Sisa."

I balked. "And for her Atoq lets Sapaca continue with his murderous ways?"

Zapana shrugged. "My father says the victims are only peasant girls. He probably thinks it's a minor indulgence that can be overlooked to protect Sisa."

"And you, Zapana?" I said meeting his eyes. He blinked and looked away, then flared back at me, "My father's loyalty to the Empire is beyond question!"

"It is so," Achachi added. "Atoq is the faithful guardian of Tawantinsuyu. In all matters concerning the Empire his allegiance is unquestioned. But, in this matter of Sapaca and Sisa. . . ."

"It's that bitch who's clouded his reason," Zapana stormed. "And not only in this." I waited for him to continue, knowing what truly drove him. Zapana bit his lip to hold back the words, but they spilled forth in a torrent. "Long ago you guessed Atoq is my father, and it's true. Is my face not his? Maybe my mother wasn't a legal consort, but I am of his blood. I was raised at Tipón and he treated me like a son, until I came of age and entered service. He has no other children close to him, none like me. I love him! It's Sisa who stops him from declaring me his son and heir. She's afraid she'll lose control over him if I take my rightful place at his side. All I want is justice."

A silence followed his outburst. Achachi looked away uncomfortably while Zapana, still red faced and trembling, cleared his throat and tried to gather himself.

"And so you secretly approached Lord Achachi and offered to help in this matter," I said quietly, "to bring Sapaca down and Sisa with him." Zapana nodded.

I thought, That explains why Achachi avoided meeting your eyes while in Atoq's presence, and why you were eager to fetch Achachi, so you could have a moment to speak privately with him.

Qhari still mulled over Zapana's heartfelt confession, growing angrier by the moment at the ill treatment his lover received. He looked up at Zapana and his thoughts burst forth in a pledge. "You shall have your justice," he declared. He tried to rise, still white-faced and weak, his bandages soaked through.

I went to his side and settled him again. "Gently, brother. I want you with me when that justice is delivered." He pushed me away and growled. A good sign.

"And you, Lord Achachi," I asked, "is it justice you want, too?"

"Of course, but, there are other considerations," he said. "Sapaca is powerful and too eager to advance the wishes of his saya. He's been compliant with every plot in Cuzco for years. True, he never takes an active part, he's too clever for that, but as long as there's something in it for Hurincuzco he doesn't stop the intrigue. He waits to see if it's successful, then claims his prize, or denies complicity depending on the outcome."

Achachi's face clouded. "The peace of the Empire is constantly imperiled. Atoq tolerates Sapaca, but he shouldn't. As Zapana said, it's Atoq's infatuation with Sisa that prevents him from dealing with Sapaca properly. Yet it's true Sapaca can't be destroyed politically. He is Speaker of Hurincuzco, and if he's charged with treason the panaqas of Hurincuzco will close ranks behind him, and holy Cuzco will be split. Peace between hanansaya and hurinsaya must be preserved at all costs, or our enemies will swallow us."

Achachi paused to collect himself before continuing. "But this of the governess Ronto and the other murdered girls is another matter, one of honor not politics, and it's more than enough to seal Sapaca's fate. His kinsmen will scurry to distance themselves from him. If we could get rid of Sapaca Tawantinsuyu would be secure, and that is all I live for."

In the rough features of Achachi's face I saw the truth of his convictions, every battle scar a testament, and I knew in him burned the pure flame of devotion to all that was right and good in Tawantinsuyu. But the Empire was his first concern, the murdered girls were but a convenience for Sapaca's end. And Zapana? Without question Zapana loved Atoq, but he would go behind his father's back to secure his birthright and inherit Tipón.

Perhaps you judge them harshly, I thought. What is it you want - revenge for father's death, a place in this world with honor? Are these selfish desires. I thought of the dead girl behind the burial towers at Sillustani, a gaping hole where her mouth had been. We all want vengeance on Sapaca, I said to that murdered girl, but I will strike the first blow for you.

"I had no witnesses to the other murders," Achachi said, "and so, with the help of Zapana, I've been seeking the fugitives who saw Ronto and the priestess alive at Hatunqolla before Sapaca arrived. When Atoq's spies located your father in Ica, Zapana passed on the news, and I notified my cousin the governor. Atoq's agent arrived first, and then vanished along with your father. But the governor located you in that village at the mouth of the River Ica, had you brought to his court, and arranged to send you on to Cuzco. It cost him his life."

"That must have been Sapaca's doing," Zapana said, a defensive edge to his voice. "I don't think my father ordered it, or the attack in the desert, which, thankfully, you survived," he added, nodding to me.

The image of the kindly governor at Ica came back to me, and of the old captain in the desert valiantly shouting defiance at impossible odds.

"The desert ambush was led by one of Sapaca's men," I said. "I didn't know who he was until today. We left him back there." I gestured to the hostel complex.

Zapana chuckled. "The one with his eyes on his cheeks? We found him. I thought that was your doing." He clicked his tongue and gave his student a look of praise.

"But why didn't you tell us before who you were and what you wanted?" Qhari demanded. "Why did you keep us waiting and guessing all these years?" He gave Zapana a hurt look.

Achachi leaned his maqana against the wall and sighed heavily, spreading his hands. "Looking back on it now perhaps I should have, but you were children then, and if you fell into the wrong hands you might be forced to name us and reveal our plans. I thought it better to proceed quietly.

"Perhaps you remember my granddaughter in the akllawasi?" Achachi said, glowering at me. "She risked her life to tell you Qhari was being watched over. Did you think it a threat? When you confronted me at Tipón we were overheard, as I feared; the stones of that place have ears. I was warned away by having my beautiful granddaughter selected for sacrifice, all because of your rashness. Is it any wonder I hesitated to tell you everything? You would have gone blundering off to seek your own revenge and ruined the plans so many had already died for."

I hung my head, and thinking back to that time I couldn't deny his fears. Yes, Achachi, you're right, I probably would have.

Achachi turned away stiffly, but continued speaking. "That came later. When you first arrived in Cuzco I had no firm evidence against Sapaca without the surviving fugitives to testify, so I decided to tuck you away while we kept looking for them. I thought you'd be safe at that fool Aquixe's kancha - he knew nothing, of course, though his steward was in my pay - but Sapaca traced your path there."

"They attacked us in the street," Qhari said stroking his throat.

"Ah. . . yes," Achachi said slowly, "Aquixe's steward told me you'd been in some trouble. They were looking for your father, I suppose?"

I nodded, remembering Qhari's face turning purple as they cinched the noose tighter and Eye-gouger hissed, "Tell me where your father is or your brother will die."

"Well, at least they didn't kill you," Achachi said trying to make light of it. "As long as Sapaca thought your father might still live he wanted you alive to lure him out, use you to bargain with, and, perhaps, lead him to Kontor and Maita. After Sapaca located you at Aquixe's kancha, I had you both moved to other quarters for your own safety."

I looked at Achachi. "You had me sent to the akllawasi, and Qhari became a retainer to Iñaca Panaqa, your lineage," I said.

Achachi pursed his lips and lifted a shoulder. "It seemed the best asylum at the time. The two officials who came for you are cousins of mine, and as eager as the rest of us to be rid of Sapaca. You were both safe, and conveniently close by if we needed you. We knew your father was dead, as you yourselves verified to the Ica governor and others, but we assumed you knew of his past and would be useful witnesses at Sapaca's trial. Then, too, like Sapaca, we hoped you'd help us identify Maita and Kontor."

Zapana regarded me quietly, struggling with himself, begging me with his eyes to understand his role in all this. "But my father, ever concerned for Sisa," he said her name bitterly, "learned your whereabouts and, I presume, passed on the information to her. It must have been she who arranged your marriage to T'ito, to seal your silence."

"T'ito! You mean Atoq, Sapaca, Sisa, they all knew about that, you knew?"

"We all did, Qori," Achachi said gently. "There was nothing I could do, believe me. None of us have even seen the inside of the akllawasi. Only a woman of Sisa's standing can influence the decisions made within those walls."

They knew. . . they all knew. . . all those years, married to my own brother, my shame an open secret. I saw Sumaq's mother Lady Hilpay flittering around Sisa, and I thought, Oh yes, Hilpay, you're delighted to do Sisa's bidding, aren't you? And you, Lady Sisa, there's no doubt about the ice in your heart, but if you arranged my marriage to protect your husband then you know he is a murderer.

"Sisa is part of this too?" I asked. "She knows about Sapaca's murders?"

"Probably," Achachi replied. "It's no secret at court that Sisa and Sapaca live separate lives at their kancha, it's even said they each have spies to watch the other, but in public their performance is harmonious, and she travels everywhere with him as is only proper for the first couple of Hurincuzco. She must know about Sapaca's demon passion for peasant girls, but she uses Atoq to protect him, and her title."

Oh, Lady Sisa, I thought, it's not only Tanta Karwa you have to answer for.

Qhari gave me a consoling look, but he had questions of his own. "Why was I moved from the estates of Iñaca Panaqa?"

Achachi looked as if he preferred not to answer. He glanced at Zapana. "Lord Atoq was having you watched," Zapana said, "and he knew about your 'preferences' at Ollantaytampu. When you were transferred to Pisaq he sent one of our men to 'persuade' you into revealing the messages you delivered for Iñaca Panaqa." Zapana shrugged. "Of course, the Lord of Tipón must know what all the panaqas are doing."

"I wasn't a spy," Qhari said.

Achachi gave him a look of understanding. "No, of course you weren't, at least not by choice." Qhari hung his head. "Don't worry," Achachi said, "I was having you watched, too, and I also knew about your. . . what word did you use, Zapana. . . preferences? These preferences made you vulnerable. Of course I know Atoq spies on my panaqa, and everyone else for that matter, and I anticipated he'd use you in this way. So I had you assigned to Pisaq where nothing of importance was happening, aside from the ongoing construction of the terraces, and anyone can watch that. The messages you delivered were of minor consequence, and meant for Atoq's ears."

Qhari looked away, flushing in silence. To save him the embarrassment I asked, "You've always known about Qhari?"

Achachi said, "Yes, and his preferences are no concern of mine, but . . . it is against the law, as much as your unfortunate marriage, and these 'circumstances' mean that neither of you can testify before an inquiry."

Qhari and I exchanged a glance. That much we had figured out for ourselves. I wondered if Achachi knew about Zapana's preferences.

The baking sun cast long shadows. Achachi wiped his brow and turned to me. "When you and T'ito were sent to the jungles of Antisuyu I saw an opportunity to have T'ito trained by my old friend Condin

Savana, so he'd be of more active use in the future. That was the message I hid among the gifts and in my greeting. But, as it turned out, T'ito didn't return, and you, Qori, received Condin Savana's knowledge. Zapana told me of your. . . 'remarkable conduct.' You were hardly more than a girl then, and we had no idea that you had such 'abilities' hidden inside you. But Condin Savana knew. Yes, that old fox knows much. I'm still not sure whether he's of this earth. . . ."

In my mind's eye I saw Condin Savana squatting on his haunches by the fire, a tiny, shrunken old man, naked but for his patch of dirty loincloth, licking the juice from a boiled monkey's foot off his forearm. Such an unlikely wrapping for the wisest man I ever met. Is he a man, I wondered, or an ayawaska vision? My hand strayed to Eagle Woman resting at my side. He gave me this, he is real, as real as any spirit of the great forest.

Achachi was conjuring his own memories of Condin Savana, but shook himself and continued. "On your return trip from the jungles Zapana spoke with a man I had waiting at the first garrison, and he sped ahead with news of your mission." I remembered that night. Zapana was telling stories around the fire when I noticed a runner slip away up the road to Cuzco. "When I learned that T'ito was lost I decided to move Qhari closer to you, thinking the two of you might be more useful as a team. But, I didn't want Atoq to be suspicious, so I revealed myself to Qhari and arranged for him to meet you at the gateway shrine of Yuncaycalla. Since you had lost your husband and distinguished yourself on the journey, I assumed Atoq would offer you some reward, and he would consider a simple request to have your brother moved closer a bargain. Naturally I protested when Atoq suggested transferring Qhari from my panaqa to his - that was expected of me - and knowing his penchant for gambling I allowed him to lure me into a game of fives, and promptly lost."

"You mean it was all planned?" I said. "You lost at fives on purpose?"

"The only way to outwit Atoq is to let him outwit himself," Achachi replied.

I nodded respectfully. Achachi may be a gruff old warrior, I thought, but he's no stranger to the subtleties of court intrigue. Outwit Atoq the Master? The old warlord's mind is as sharp as a blade.

"Of course," Achachi continued, "it was also safer having Qhari under Zapana's care at K'allachaka. Atoq evidently thought the same." A self-satisfied smile followed.

Yes, Achachi knows about Zapana's exotic tastes, I realized, and like Atoq he understands the benefits. Both Achachi and Atoq wanted Qhari safe, and who better to look after his needs than Zapana?

Qhari looked from Achachi to Zapana. It began to dawn on him that Zapana was assigned to be his lover. Zapana returned a friendly but unapologetic look. The reaction I feared from Qhari did not come. Instead, he nodded solemnly to himself, appreciating the wisdom of the choice.

Zapana shifted uneasily. "Others will have found the bodies in the courtyard by now, and they'll be searching. We should leave this place."

"What of Tintaya?" I asked Zapana. "Does he know the truth of all this?"

"No more than what Atoq and Sisa tell him. Tintaya is their lap dog. At this moment he'll be recovering from a blow to the back of his thick skull."

I questioned him with raised brows.

"Well, I had to get him out of the way somehow," Zapana said with mock defensiveness. "I'll tell him it was Sapaca's men, and I had to chase after them. There are, after all, a few bodies around to prove it. He'll think it's all part of Wallpaya's schemes."

"Wallpaya," Achachi said, nodding grimly at the name. "He's the most immediate threat to the peace of Tawantinsuyu. I fear some factions will support him if he tries to make his own son Emperor, but many loyal to the rightful heir will oppose him. I can't hold back the warlords. It will be civil war. We can't let it happen."

"Lord," I said calmly, "if you place a detachment in hiding at Limatampu on the new moon next month, you'll find all of Wallpaya's weapons being smuggled in by caravan. I'm sure those you capture can be 'persuaded' to reveal the plot."

Achachi's face lit up. "Limatampu on the new moon? Are you sure?"

Zapana chuckled to himself, shaking his head. "Lord," he said to Achachi, "if Inca Moon says it will be Limatampu, then be assured it will be Limatampu."

"You? You are Inca Moon?" Achachi stared at me in disbelief. Apparently Zapana never told him my code name. "I know the name of course, but I never knew who. You? Really? Inca Moon? Well. . . I. . . . Is it true what they say about you?"

I didn't bother to ask what tales were being told of my exploits, though in truth I was pleased to learn that my name circulated with some awe in the upper echelons. It did no harm for Qhari to see the admiration on Lord Achachi's face.

I thought, Yes, your own sister, you stupid lump. What do you think of me now? Qhari looked suitably impressed. I dismissed Achachi's praise with a modest wave. "Only doing my duty, Lord." I replied.

Achachi's brows furrowed again. "I suppose Sapaca will have to wait until after we've dealt with Wallpaya." He cast a rueful glance at Kontor, still propped up in the storehouse with the dagger hilt protruding from his belly. "And now we've lost our best witness."

I nodded to Qhari. There were no more secrets to hide. It was time to reveal all. Qhari smiled back his agreement. "There is one more," he announced proudly, "one more survivor who can testify against Sapaca - father's brother, our uncle Maita. And he's here at the Temple of Wiraqocha today."

I lifted my head in agreement, buoyed with hope again. Uncle Maita wouldn't let us down.

The men stared at their feet in silence. I looked from face to face, but they avoided me. Finally Achachi cleared his throat and glanced at Zapana. "She must be told," Achachi said to him.

Zapana turned his head this way and that, never meeting my eyes. His mouth worked without sound. Then in a small voice he managed, "Qori, the man Chani whom we hunted in the jungles long ago was no poisoner, he was your uncle Maita."

Agony tore at my vitals like a feral beast and a silent scream rose in my throat, then a black wave descended. If Zapana hadn't caught me in his arms I would have swooned to the ground.

"It's not your fault, you didn't know," Achachi said from far away.

"I tried to save him," Zapana's voice came from a distance. "I should have told you."

I saw the jungle path and Chani walking calmly toward me with that odd smile. Then he paused and looked uncertain. I was sure he returned to kill me. He opened his mouth to speak. I plunged Eagle Woman into his neck.

Maita? My own uncle Maita? "No-No-No!" I shrieked.

Qhari pulled himself up and struggled to my side, grasping my arm. Open-mouthed, he looked from me to Achachi to Zapana. The answers came from Zapana. I listened numbly.

"Maita became the translator Chani among the jungle tribes of Antisuyu. When our spies finally located him I was second in command of the first team sent to. . . to eliminate him. Atoq wanted him dead, and I wanted him alive to testify against Sapaca. Maita didn't know I was there to help him and he fled, but I managed to 'curtail' the expedition, and later was given the duty of beheading its leader for failing."

That had been my first glimpse of Zapana, on the Tipón terraces as he lifted the maqana over the kneeling figure.

"Spies found him again," Zapana continued, head lowered, "but this time they weren't sure Chani of the Chuncho was the man we sought. Lord Atoq decided to send you and T'ito along to see if you'd recognize him. It was Atoq who contrived the story about Chani being a poisoner," he said, chin on his chest, "so the meeting would be a surprise to you, and Tintaya and I could watch for your response to confirm Chani's identity. Along the trail I 'removed' some of the bearers so there would be fewer to deal with later."

I saw one of them lying in his hammock covered with spider bites, another screaming in the viper nest.

"You were clever enough to single out Chani," Zapana said looking up at me, "but not because you recognized him as your uncle. When we went to get the feathers from the storehouse I killed my bearer and told Chani I was there to aid him. He admitted he was Maita, and said he thought you seemed familiar. You reminded him of your mother."

It was my turn to dip my head.

"We arranged to meet later, and then, to make it look convincing, Maita obliged me with a minor wound before he fled. Afterwards I led the others in the wrong direction, we ran into a Chuncho ambush, and all died but Tintaya and me. I'm sorry about T'ito, Qori."

The years had softened me enough to feel sorry for T'ito, but not enough to mourn him. He was proud and arrogant, I reminded myself, and even as a man he was such a pitiful boy. His death gave me new life. I allowed Zapana to interpret my silence as he chose.

"Maita must have returned to the village on his own to meet you. I assume he didn't have a chance to speak?"

I bit my lip at the memory.

"Atoq was genuinely impressed with you," he hurried on, "and wanted you for his first female agent. In that he was not wrong. The Empire owes you much."

Achachi nodded solemnly.

"I didn't know my father's plans for you," Zapana said, "and I was as surprised as Tintaya when Atoq announced you would be joining our secret ranks. It's dangerous work, as you well know, and I feared for your life. But when I saw my father's mind was made up I knew there was no point in arguing with him, so I resolved to make you the best agent in the Empire. And I succeeded." Then his features hardened again. "My father also believed that if anyone could find Kontor, it would be you. He was right again."

Too right, I thought bitterly.

Qhari glanced at me, his thoughts in his eyes. Yes, brother, I thought, we have been used. . . me especially, because I'm too good at what I do. Atoq. I wanted to call you father. You knew that, and you used it, playing me like a fish on the end of your line. Stalwart guardian of the Empire? Perhaps. But you sit at Tipón like a spider in its nest, spinning, ever spinning your web, and sending others to claim your victims.

I don't doubt your loyalty to Tawantinsuyu, Atoq, but you've become a law unto yourself. Does blame lie with the hand that strikes, or the one who orders it? It may have been another's hand that killed my father, but it might as well have been yours. Zapana thinks it was Sapaca who sent the assassin. Maybe. But you've used me with such coldness and deliberation that it wouldn't surprise me if you're behind that, too.

What was my father to you, just another soldier? And all those girls you let Sapaca murder, just peasants? Ask their families what they feel. Is it less than the grief of royalty? You probably think you're still serving the best interests of the Empire by keeping Sapaca in power. Do you lie to yourself about that, too? Have your interests and the Empire's become one? Assuredly so. You're sick and you don't know it. And your disease? Sisa. The beautiful Lady Sisa lies behind all this. How I long for your public humiliation, Lady Sisa, before I take my own revenge.

Lord Sapaca. Lady Sisa. Lord Atoq. You may be three of the most powerful nobles in the Empire, but you have debts to pay, and Inca Moon will extract payment in full!

"The men who could have witnessed against Sapaca are gone," Achachi said. "Now there is only one way to expose Sapaca."

Over Qhari's protests I agreed immediately to his plan.

XXXIII

Of how the matter of Princess Koka came to an end, and what that end was.

"Illness, calamity, and misfortune depart this land!" the Empress shouted from the ushnu, and the multitude assembled in the great square roared back in waves, "Evil be gone. Dangers flee this place." Mimicking Mama Oqllo and the royal party, everyone began slapping their clothes to drive evil away, and squeals and giggles erupted as men and women pretended to help each other by smacking bottoms. The rituals of Sitowa - one of the most important and also light-hearted festivals of the year - were underway.

From where I stood being jostled in the crush, Mama Oqllo's tiny figure high atop the ushnu was visible only in snatches. She shone from head to foot in soft garments of pale silver, her head cloth, dress, and shawl trimmed in black, matched by sandals of pure silver, and a parasol of white feathers shielded her from the morning sun. The two princesses, similarly dressed and wreathed in silver bangles, stood behind Her. Kusi Rimaq laughed as she swatted at her mother, while Koka did her best to produce a wan smile for the crowd. Oh, Princess Koka, I thought, today is your last chance. I hope you're ready.

The noblemen stood to one side on the ushnu and let the women direct the ceremonies. My gaze turned to the Crown Prince Titu Cusi, and to Koka's imminent husband, the drooling old kuraka with his ever-present quid of coca.

It was Qoya Raymi, the second month of planting and a time dedicated to the Moon, for Mama Killa is highest of all female gods and with Her rests the fertility of the growing season.

Throughout the land women led the rituals with sisterhoods vying to outdo other sisterhoods; each woman in her hut especially honored by her husband and male relatives. But within this period of festivals is Sitowa, which begins on the new moon of Qoya Raymi. Wiraqocha is called upon to drive illness and misfortune from Cuzco and the realm, and all pray He will see fit to let the world live to celebrate another Sitowa the following year.

All dogs are removed from the city lest they disturb the proceedings with ill-omened barking, and all those sick or lame or in any way deformed are sent away. Their maladies surely came from their own misdoings, and if present on this first day of Sitowa their misfortune might detract from the good fortune of others. Of course provincials are also sent out of the city to keep the rituals pure. They return for the later festivities and, along with the rest of the populace, eat a lump of the holy maize flour mixed with the blood of sacrificed animals. This remains in the body as a witness should one ever speak evil of the Emperor or the Sun.

"Pardon, grandmother," a youth said, colliding with me as he chased a shrieking girl.

I let him steady me, and with effort lifted my head slightly, one hand on my crooked back, the other gripping my staff. "Misfortune be gone from you," I croaked amiably, making a weak attempt to brush my ash-streaked hair aside. "May Wiraqocha grant us all another Sitowa."

"Thank you, grandmother. Illness be gone from you," he intoned, eyes on the girl who paused to let him catch up. He ran off.

Another time I might have reprimanded the rascal, but during Sitowa no anger is allowed, for whoever becomes upset or quarrels on this day suffers the same throughout the year.

The new moon. Achachi had his men in hiding at Limatampu waiting to ambush the arms caravan. The hopes of those in the square, to have Cuzco and Tawantinsuyu freed of danger, were being fulfilled this day.

My eyes strayed to where the Regent Wallpaya imposed atop the ushnu, the beaten gold feathers of his headdress glinting in the sun. This is your last Sitowa, my Lord, I thought. Sapaca loomed beside him. Lady Sisa and her mirror image Q'enti hovered near the Empress. Their presence at the ceremony was expected, but Achachi had said they were looking forward to his invitation afterwards, as was Inca Moon. But today is for Princess Koka, I reminded myself. When the signal is given you'd better move quick, my Lady.

Silence rushed through the crowd when Mama Oqllo held up her arms. She looked expectantly at the boulder with its gold-sheathed basin beside the ushnu, where libations poured out to Wiraqocha. A priest finished tipping the last urn amid incantations, and the aqha vanished in the drain beneath as the god drank. Four groups of one hundred runners in battle dress waited by the stone, each group facing one of the four royal roads leading out of the great square to the four suyus. The priest set his urn down and the chanting stopped. He nodded up at the Empress; She dropped her arms. The runners brandished their weapons high and in a chorus shouted, "Disease and misfortune depart this land!" then sped down the roads before them, waving their weapons and calling for calamity to be gone. The crowd answered in like manner, and such a roar went up from the city that every lurking demon must have fled in fear as the thunder echoed from stone walls and rooftops. Thus evil was chased from the city for another year.

The runners continued on their course, each group racing down the road of its suyu, until they met others posted along the way who took up the cry and relayed it on to the next station. Eventually, a goodly distance from the city in each direction, the runners would stop at a river and cleanse themselves and their weapons to wash away the last of the evil, consigning it to the swift waters.

Those in the city turned themselves to the next diversion - smearing maize porridge on faces with the same contagious hilarity that accompanied the shaking out of clothes. The younger folk soon turned it into a slinging contest, as is their wont, especially when they know no reprimand will follow.

I accepted a face full gracefully, and then a second coating before I reached the front of the dispersing crowds. They all returned home to splash their door lintels with the porridge, and the places where clothing and food are stored, to keep sickness from entering their belongings. The maize porridge was also dumped into fountains and springs so they wouldn't become sick either.

After these precautions the feasting began, and even in the most humble dwelling only the best food and drink were served, carefully hoarded for this occasion, because anyone who didn't feast lavishly on this day ate poorly for the rest of the year, and had bad luck and hardship.

The nobles banqueted in the great square, everyone arranged according to rank, and the ancestors and gods came forth from their houses to feast with them. While servants laid down matting and blankets and heaping bowls of food, processions of litters arrived from the Qorikancha with the images of the gods, and soon after the panaqas brought in their honored ancestors, the mummies sitting life-like dressed in new clothes. With their litters as daises, the ancestors sat among their descendants again, choice food and drink set around them, and each with servants to whisk away flies and offer the contents of the dishes. The ancestors were happy. The gods were pleased.

I hung back on the fringes of this splendid occasion, waiting for nobility to notice me and send a servant over with another bowl of food, to be accepted with cackling gratitude, all the while watching the royal party. Koka's fate would soon be decided.

"Splendid! Beyond all expectations," Atoq had exclaimed when I reported to him at Tipón. I had come straight from the Temple of Wiraqocha, the revelations of that fateful day burning within me. Zapana and Tintaya had already completed their interviews and were elsewhere. Atoq took my arm and we strolled by the fountains in the garden, the terraces vacant except for guards stationed out of earshot.

Atoq twitched with excitement. "Zapana told me Lord Sapaca's men attacked him when he was chasing Wallpaya's conspirators, but you helped in the fight, and ultimately it was you who discovered the Limatampu shipment. Well done, Qori."

That version will do for now, I thought. "It was as Zapana said, Lord. I was of some assistance in overpowering the conspirators, but it was Lord Aquixe who leaked the information about Limatampu. I suppose Aquixe will lose his head now?"

"Never. A mouth like that is far too valuable. He does us more good left in place."

I nodded, seeing his point.

"And Sapaca," I asked, "surely he'll go down with Wallpaya?"

Atoq pursed his lips and looked at the sky, thinking. "Unfortunately

Sapaca's men were killed, so they can't witness against him. They were his men, true, but he can still claim they were in Wallpaya's pay and had nothing to do with him. We need incontrovertible evidence against one as powerful as Sapaca. Anything less would only raise the ire of Hurincuzco, and that must be avoided. You leave Sapaca to me, Qori." He nodded wisely at me.

Indeed, Lord, I thought, Sapaca will be safe with you. You'll act against Wallpaya - for that I've handed you the evidence - but it's Kontor's death you're really pleased about. Zapana has claimed credit for that, and told you I didn't know who Kontor was. So I'm still your faithful, innocent Qori, and I'll play that role for you one last time today.

It took all my will to force my mind elsewhere, to be the trusting Qori of old. I walked with the master. Atoq knew the language of eyes and tones and gestures, and learned as much from what wasn't said as from that which was. If for one instant I allowed myself to dwell inwardly on the truth he would sense it. At Tipón I was taught not only to act the character of my disguise, but also to think like that person, to convince myself I actually was Choque the maidservant, or 'crone,' or even a Charka boy. Once I believed so I would act so, and be accepted without question. Thus far it had worked well, but the final test was upon me - convince Atoq I was another person, the same trusting soul he duped for so long, and erase the images of father dying by Atoq's orders, and of Maita and Kontor dead by my own hand.

When I arrived at Tipón my first impulse was to kill Atoq with one thrust of Eagle Woman's stinger. But no, I cautioned myself, the Empire needs Atoq until Wallpaya's treachery is settled. If I take my revenge now I'll not live to give Sapaca and Sisa what they deserve. For Tanta Karwa's sake I'll endure a little longer. And so I became the woman I was not, and entered the spider's nest.

I glanced at Atoq. Handsome he was that day on the garden terraces, tall and elegantly dressed in pale red, free of jewelry and garish trappings, fine gold earspools framing his silver head. He's completely gray now, I realized, and it suits him more than ever. Such a refined, stately man. I allowed myself to sink under his spell.

"My Lord, your eye," I exclaimed changing the subject. His left eye had begun to cloud again.

"It's nothing," he said waving my concern aside, "I get along fine without it."

"That may be, Lord, but it's my duty to see to your health. Sit down over there and let me have a look at it." I pointed to a nearby rock and commanded him with a look.

Atoq chuckled. "You and Tanta Karwa," he said complying.

This was the first time I'd seen Atoq since Tanta Karwa's death. He hadn't thought to mention her when I arrived. Already his former mistress was only a fond memory.

"If she were here she would see to it, but now that is my privilege. I'll look after you, Lord."

He sat grinning like a boy enjoying my fussing, but most important he was relaxed.

The eye was long past saving, but I made the appropriate 'hmmmm' and 'uh-huh' noises while I examined him, and eventually he said, "The other healers say it can't be saved."

"Say they so? Had you continued with Tanta Karwa's tobacco wash this wouldn't have happened," I said shaking a finger at him.

He hung his head. "But the others - "

"The others know nothing. I'm your healer now, and I prescribe a strong tobacco wash this very day."

He grimaced but nodded obediently.

A proper cure includes prayers and offerings, preferably at temples, but since Atoq never left Tipón I suggested a gold figurine for the water spirit of the stone reservoir above, where Atoq was also to bathe. He agreed with a shrug. I looked forward to choosing the strongest, harshest tobacco to boil with aqha, salt and sweet root for the eye wash.

Atoq returned to the foiling of Wallpaya's coup. "Name your reward, Qori. The Empire is grateful for your service, as am I, and whatever you wish is yours."

In truth, I had given this some thought. "All I desire, Lord, is a visit to the Empress with my sisters from Ayllu Añawarqe."

Atoq frowned suspiciously. "You seek an audience? For what purpose? You've met Mama Oqllo, haven't you?"

"Twice, Lord, when I accompanied Tanta Karwa on healing missions, but this wouldn't be an audience, only a visit, so my ayllu sisters can meet the Daughter of the Moon."

Atoq closed his eyes and smiled, nodding to himself. "And your village friends can see you drinking with the Empress."

I blushed.

"Don't be embarrassed, Qori," he said patting my cheek. "You deserve the honor of Her presence, and the admiration of your ayllu. I'll send the request to Mama Oqllo, and tell Her how you served Tawantinsuyu. Your ayllu sisters can be told the meeting is a reward for your healing powers. They'll have their kero with the Empress, and afterwards I'm sure you'll be much in demand."

I could have arranged to meet Mama Oqllo through Koka, but palace walls have ears and Atoq would soon learn of it. The prudent course was to have him make the arrangements and let him assume what he wanted. Besides, my ayllu sisters would be busily agog at the occasion, and I'd have an opportunity to speak with the Empress privately.

"Thank you, Lord. And. . . one more thing. . . ."

He smoothed his tunic and looked at me cautiously, evidently thinking his generosity had already been taxed. "Yes?"

"Now that Wallpaya's treason is about to be revealed, I humbly ask to be relieved of my duties for a short time, so I can make a pilgrimage to the Island of the Moon. I'll stay in touch through Zapana, of course, should you need me."

I borrowed the idea from Achachi. The Island of the Moon is at the south end of Lake Titiqaqa, near the Island of the Sun. Like its neighbor it's one of the holiest shrines in the Empire, and a lifetime aspiration of all devout Inca women. No one could fault a visit there. Far from Cuzco, it also meant being absent from Tipón and its master for some months.

Atoq smiled. This request was more in keeping with his anticipations.

"I shall miss you, Qori Qoyllur, but such a journey is the least I can grant. I don't suppose Tawantinsuyu will fall apart before you return, but should I need you. . . you will stay in touch through Zapana?"

I bobbed my head earnestly.

"Very well then, you have my permission. I'll arrange for you and your friends to meet the Empress before you depart. And be sure to have your pick of the storehouses here at Tipón. Some new dresses, perhaps?"

Two nights later Zapana appeared at my door in Choqo.

"Your meeting with Lord Atoq went well," he said. "He believes our version of events at the Temple of Wiraqocha."

I knew it was as difficult for him as it was for me to lie to Atoq, perhaps more so, but in his mind he did it to save his father from himself. "And Tintaya?" I asked.

Zapana smirked. "He remembers nothing after that blow to his head. Someone hit him pretty hard," he said with mock gravity. "I shifted as much of the credit to him as possible, so he's content with our story."

The air in the room suddenly seemed close, sending tendrils of warmth through me. This was the first time I'd been entirely alone with Zapana since our night in Puno. I felt the heat radiating from my cheeks and turned away from him. "Why did you come?" I asked.

He stood behind me, slipping his arms around my waist and leaning me against him. I didn't resist. "Because I had to," he whispered in my ear.

"Why?"

In the pause that followed I knew I wanted him, but on what terms?

"Qori. . . " Zapana began hesitantly, "if Achachi's plan succeeds, have you thought about what will happen after we expose Sapaca?"

I thought about what it meant to Zapana. "Sapaca will be ruined, and Sisa with him. They'll be banished, if not executed, and with Sisa out of the way you'll become Atoq's heir, I'm sure Achachi will see to that, and eventually you'll be Lord of Tipón."

"Then why don't you join me?"

"Where?"

"At Tipón. We'll be a good team, Qori. You'll be the Lady of Tipón. Think of it, Qori, you and me together." He turned me and held my shoulders, grinning at the surprise on my face.

It was closer to an honest proposal of marriage than I had ever come. A good team? As agents we were that already, but that wasn't what he was thinking. No, he wanted me beside him like a wife, except I could never be that because I was a widow, and widows, by law, couldn't marry again.

"What about your wife at Muyna?" I said, my thoughts whirling.

"You know the answer to that," he replied. "The law won't allow me to leave her, but why should I? We're no more than a convenience to each other."

"So I'll not be Lady of Tipón, I'll be your mistress?"

He shrugged. "If you say so. It has a certain ring to it. Mistress of Tipón," he said turning it into a title and raising a hand as if announcing me at court.

He was asking me to join him not as a subordinate but as an equal. He wanted me to live with him, to share his life and the power of Tipón. What more could any man offer? And what other life could there be for me after all I'd been through? Village life provided a quiet respite between missions, but I knew Inca Moon couldn't settle down. The power and danger Zapana offered excited her. And what more perfect man to share such a life with than Zapana? I flushed, thinking of him lying naked in the soft lamp glow.

"You knew my secrets for years, Zapana, but you never let on. If I live with you, will you still keep secrets from me?" Before he could answer I rushed on, "And will you still bed your wife when it suits you, as well as servant boys? You've never had any difficulty betraying your lovers, Zapana. Why should it be any different with me?"

I was being unkind and unfair, and the light vanished from his eyes. I told myself I was pushing him to declare his love, but in truth I wasn't ready to hear it. Too many matters remained unresolved, Atoq being one of them, but I dared not reveal my plans for his beloved father. And after those plans came to pass, would he still want me?

Be careful, Qori Qoyllur, I told myself. End this meeting now and postpone your answer until you're sure of your own heart, and his.

I half expected Zapana to deliver sputtering denials and declare me

the only song of his heart for eternity, but he looked at me without sup-
plication or anger and said, "I offer to share my life with you, and you
demand conditions. So like a woman," he said shaking his head. "I
promise you nothing, except to be who I am. If that isn't enough for you,
then I can offer no more."

Stung by his honesty I hung my head in silence. He turned and
walked to the door. "Zapana. . . ." I said. He paused and looked back at
me, a look of curiosity on his face.

"Why can't women accept men as they are?" he asked. "Why must
you insist on changing us to suit yourselves?" While I searched for an
answer he disappeared.

My visit with Mama Oqllo went as I'd hoped. The women of Ayllu
Añawarqe each had a turn presenting their offerings, performing the
much'a, kissing the demi-god's feet, and having their names whispered
to the Empress for Her to repeat aloud. The village women would be
telling the story of this event for generations. They actually raised a kero
with the Empress of Tawantinsuyu, and their names had passed Her lips.
Mama Oqllo took it all good naturedly, and praised my healing skills
leaving my sisters in open-mouthed awe of me. Koka, upon hearing of
my presence, made an appearance too, and the women were dumb-struck
to see the princess place an arm around my shoulders. It was nothing
really, but they fussed over me so.

Mama Oqllo knew I was there for more than ceremony, and it was
She who motioned me aside.

"Our Lord Atoq speaks well of you, Qori Qoyllur," She said for my
ears with a meaningful look. It was Her tactful way of telling me She
knew of my activities. There was no need to mention details.

"It is my honor to serve, Highness," I replied.

"Is there something I can do for you, Qori Qoyllur?"

"Not for me, Highness, but for a friend of mine, yes."

I stated my wishes.

The Empress looked at me sideways. "You have given your sisters
a day I'm sure they'll remember, but still you think of others? Very well,
I can't promise, but I'll consult with the First Ladies. If they find no fault

the recommendation will go forward."

"Thank you, Highness," I said graciously, "and now there is one more matter. Could Princess Koka join us for a moment?"

"Yes!" Princess Koka exclaimed when my plan unfolded, "Yes, yes, yes!"

Mama Oqllo looked amused. "It's long since I've seen you so pleased, my daughter, but are you sure this is what you want?"

"Yes, mother, this and no more is all I'll ever ask of you."

"Your brother will be furious," the Empress cautioned.

"Won't he though!"

After this meeting Qori Qoyllur made a show of departing the Huatanay Valley on her pilgrimage to Qollasuyu, and for Atoq's benefit she checked at every guard station along the royal road, at least for a distance, but it was Inca Moon who slipped back and joined the throng at Sitowa.

The panpipe music in the great square came to a high-pitched crescendo, and the dancers in their plumed headdresses gave a final twirl and froze. It was a faultless performance, the costumes and intricate steps reserved for this occasion only. Sitowa went well. I watched Koka. Her moment approached. Did she have the resolve to go through with it? I edged into position.

When the drums fell silent Koka rose from her place on the ushnu and said something to her mother. The Empress nodded consent, and Koka left to offer special prayers at the Qorikancha, a fitting gesture for a princess on Sitowa. Kusi Rimaq watched quizzically as she departed, a few ladies-in-waiting and maids trailing behind. Titu Cusi motioned to his soldiers who formed an honor guard around the women at the foot of the ushnu. Koka wasn't allowed to go anywhere without her jailers.

From a corner of the great square a narrow street runs directly to the Qorikancha, and this I took in haste. The gray stone walls of the akllawasi rose above me, coursed lines of smooth blocks shaded by the overhanging eaves of the buildings within. For a moment I allowed my mind to wander back to the years I spent behind those walls, and to the Reverend Mothers going about their duties teaching new generations of akllas, shielded from the world outside. It had become a happy, safe place in my memory. But then I shook myself. More than a wall separated me from the peace within. Some, like Sumaq, strolled with the gods, and others, like me, ran in the world of men. That is your lot in life, I told myself, play it well for Sumaq.

When I left the square Koka and her party started down a parallel street on the other side of the akllawasi. Where the block ends a cross street marks the place where sandals must be removed before approaching the Qorikancha. Here I turned right, walking behind the akllawasi to intercept Koka's party at the opposite corner. Leaning heavily on my staff I slowed to a stooped, tired gait as I passed the old man guarding the rear door of the House of the Chosen Women.

"Illness be gone from you, brother," I greeted him.

"Misfortune be gone from you, sister," he replied, smiling after me.

Koka's group arrived at the corner and paused to remove sandals, maids helping the bearers of Koka's feather parasol and royal banner. The guards wore quilted armor beneath their red and black checkered tunics, and on their heads domed helmets with the standing red fringes. I counted ten guards, and thought, Well, not very good odds for them.

The soldiers lay down their weapons and knelt to untie their lacings. One looked up at the old woman hobbling forward on her staff. "Sickness be gone from you, grandmother," he said pleasantly.

Whack! I smashed my staff into his forehead knocking him flat. Without pause I swung to either side, sending the men to right and left sprawling on the pavement. "Now, Lady, run!" I shouted to Koka. The foolish girl stood there looking around in bewilderment, as if she expected an army to appear for the rescue. I hadn't thought to tell her it would only be me.

"Seize that woman," the captain bellowed, "and hold the Princess."

Grasping my staff crossways, I jabbed the butt into the belly of a man charging on my left, jerked right to catch another likewise, then swung low and up to slam the shaft between the legs of the soldier before me. All three collapsed on their knees. "Run, Princess, run!"

Koka stared blankly at the scene, not comprehending. She had never seen violence before, I realized.

The captain edged forward, mace raised. Two of his men circled around with spears leveled. I allowed my shoulders to droop and let out a great sigh, rolling my eyes at the heavens. "My Lady," I said to Koka, "whenever you're ready . . . ." The maids and ladies-in-waiting crowded around her, hands at their mouths, and a soldier stood before them hefting his maqana. Very well, I thought, I shall have to do it all myself.

The captain was too obvious. He feinted at me but his eyes told the man at my back to charge. I whirled to the lunge and deflected the spear with my staff, cracked its owner across the face, and rounded on the other spearman. I twirled my staff like a whirlwind, catching his weapon and sending it flying. The captain leapt at me from behind but I turned on my heels and came up with a claw-grip on his throat. I pulled him to his knees, keeping my hand fastened. "Stay back," I ordered the others. Several had recovered and were taking up their weapons. My blows were aimed to stun - I wanted no deaths this day. "Stay back or I'll crush his throat," I threatened, tightening my grip to make the captain choke. He shifted on his knees, face turning from red to purple. The soldiers exchanged glances but continued positioning themselves. They were doing their duty, and being imperial guards they would fight to the last breath.

I threw Koka a pleading glance. "Princess?"

Suddenly Koka dashed from the crowd of women past the maqana guard. She reached my side and I turned on the man behind me, throwing myself at him to clear the path for Koka. "Run, Princess, run!" I yelled, hearing her sandals slapping on the pavement as she sped up the street. Three attacked me now and wrenched my staff from my hands, but I wiggled and bit like a serpent, scurrying out on hands and knees from between their legs. Farther ahead I saw a pursuing guard grab the back of Koka's shawl, yanking her down. I rose to my feet but the blunt end of a spear shaft thwacked across my back.

I froze upright. The soldiers backed off. Painfully I worked my shoulders and arched my back, then turned slowly. A young man stood like a statue gripping his spear in both hands above the blade, the butt now resting on the pavement. His eyes darted to his companions. They took another step back. I cleared my throat. He stared at me miserably.

"You shouldn't have done that," I said evenly.

"I know," he sulked.

I made as if to turn away, then somersaulted at him, coming up with a claw-grip on his neck and my knee between his legs. Before he hit the ground I rounded on the others, who leapt aside leaving my path open.

"Spears!" I heard the captain yell, ordering his men to throw at my retreating back.

"But the Princess?" one protested.

It was enough time for me to reach Koka and the guard who held her. He stood pitifully, clutching his prize in one hand, waving his spear at me with the other, and protectively pressing his knees together. I feigned the blow he feared, then rammed my elbow into his throat. Grabbing Koka by the arm I dragged her the last strides to the rear door of the akllawasi.

Throughout the struggle - which in truth lasted only moments - the old akllawasi doorman hopped up and down shouting, "Guard, guard, disturbance, help them!" But he couldn't leave the post he was sworn to defend, and the jubilations in the great square drowned his cries. Having watched my performance he now stood weakly before me, bottom lip up, defying me more with his eyes than with the spear clutched across his chest. I felt sorry for him, and merely slipped a foot behind his toppling him backwards. He fell gratefully and didn't try to rise.

The soldiers caught up. "Get them," the captain shouted.

Arms grabbed from behind, but inside the akllawasi unseen hands slipped the latch, opening the door wide. I shoved Koka through, dropped to my knees leaving the soldiers holding my empty cloak, and somersaulted across the threshold.

The akllawasi door slammed shut on the world of men.

XXXIV

In which is related a tale so evil and foully perverse that it is Beyond Mortal Comprehension, and should not be read by those of tender disposition.

The forest hung heavy and moist along the flagstone road. Off to the right, hidden below bush-choked mountainsides, the sacred Urubamba raced in its narrow channel. Across the valley dark green peaks lurked like giants behind the mists, watching over this dripping land. A short distance ahead lay the estate of Machu Picchu where Lord Achachi waited. The hut Achachi told me about came into view, perched on the verdant slope below the road, a convenience for travelers escaping a downpour, but otherwise empty. An isolated place with plenty of cover, I thought, but close to Machu Picchu, perfect. I scrambled down to the hut and prepared my disguise.

Achachi had gathered descriptions of all the murdered girls, and while none were said to be as beautiful as the first victim Ronto, they all resembled her in some way. So would I. Darkening my skin a shade with toning salves, I outlined my eyes to give them the right shape, stuffed cotton in my cheeks to make my face fuller, padded my breasts and thighs, and added height with special sandals. Then, with Eagle Woman slung on a cord at my back, I donned the cloak and fastened it with a long tupu pin, tied my hair back with a sling, and wedged a small knife under the wide belt. Dressed to kill, I thought, smiling to myself and rumpling the costume so as not to appear too kept.

A runner sped by on the road above, and faintly the rhythm of marching feet reached me. The entourage approached. I took a deep breath and closed my eyes. Father, this is for you, I thought, at last your time has come. Give me strength.

I hurried up to the roadside clutching a jar of aqha and a kero.

A week had passed since Princess Koka became firmly ensconced in the Cuzco akllawasi, beyond even her brother's reach. Though every lady in Cuzco had sympathized with her plight, it was only after the

Empress and Koka herself smiled on my scheme that any action was taken, and even then it was left entirely up to me. But, what other woman in Cuzco could execute such a desperate plan? With the Empress's blessing, Sumaq T'ika and the Most Esteemed Mother waited at the rear door of the akllawasi and pulled it wide when they heard the clamor outside - none too soon - and Koka and I spilled into their waiting arms.

"Welcome to our house, Princess," the Most Esteemed Mother said bowing gracefully. She had been gravely ill for months but insisted on leaving her pallet to welcome Koka.

Sumaq picked me up from where I somersaulted through the door and embraced me, laughing. "Good old Qori. You always knew how to make a dramatic entrance."

"And you're still the prettiest priestess in Cuzco." The words leapt from my mouth, leaving us both blushing. In truth, she was, and I could never look on her beauty without remembering our intimate encounters. These sometimes troubled and sometimes amused me, but always remained my secret. No other woman stirred me in this way, but being near Sumaq always left my cheeks hot. She smiled sweetly at me, the half-lidded look of a lover, flushing me further.

"But. . . my-my brother. . . ." Koka stammered, looking about in a daze while the young akllas gathered around.

"Leave him to us, Princess," the Most Esteemed Mother said. Fifty smiling faces nodded.

I stayed three days with my sisters in the akllawasi, for the doors were watched from without day and night. Those were three of the happiest days I spent in years. The old Most Esteemed Mother gave me free run, asking only that I stay away from the storehouses at night. I pouted for her and promised to do my best to remain out of trouble. She took this with arched brows and a roll of her eyes, delighting me. I attended Sumaq's lessons during the day. The young akllas shyly crowded around me hoping for news of their families, and perhaps the story of how this daring woman came among them, for the gossip lines hummed. I spared them the story of the latter - surely it couldn't be as good as the one they were busily manufacturing for themselves - and related what I could of their relatives, all the while flooded with memories and drinking in the calming routine of this world of women.

The day after Koka's escape Titu Cusi came in person to demand his sister's return. The emperor is the only man allowed inside the walls of the akllawasi, and though Titu Cusi was still only Crown Prince he demanded the right, much to his regret. I watched from a hiding place when he faced the ailing Most Esteemed Mother in the front courtyard. Sumaq T'ika stood defiantly at her side while the other Esteemed Mothers crowded around the arrogant prince. Everyone knew the story, and now that Koka was safe among them all were determined she would stay that way. I kept my hand over my mouth to keep from laughing while I watched the proceedings. The Prince strutted royally through the main gate and - now alone and confronted by the Most Esteemed Mother and her assistants - shifted nervously.

"My sister Princess Koka is here," he said bravely, "return her to me at once."

The most Esteemed Mother sniffed. "She is here, and here she will stay, Lord, until she decides otherwise."

"I am Emperor - "

"You are Crown Prince, and until you become Emperor you have no rights inside this hallowed place. Out, now!" The Most Esteemed Mother stamped her foot, and the women surrounding the Prince leaned forward, hissing.

"Princess Koka was snatched from the streets," he fumed, backing off a few steps. "I demand to know who is responsible for this outrage."

"I am," a chorus boomed around him.

Titu Cusi's eyes shifted from side to side in nervous fury. "On behalf of her husband - "

"Her intended husband, you mean," Sumaq shouted at him. "How could you, Prince, you who will soon rule the world and be Just Father to all, condemn your own sister to such an unhappy marriage? Shame on you!"

I'm not sure whether Sumaq T'ika or the Most Esteemed Mother was more formidable, but once roused Sumaq was ferocious. The Most

Esteemed Mother smiled at her approvingly. Titu Cusi edged back to the gate surrounded by accusing glares.

"On the day of my coronation I shall return," he said.

The Most Esteemed Mother raised a gnarled finger to him. "On that day, Prince, you may remove any woman from this house who is not a priestess, but those married to the gods stay with their husbands. Always."

Titu Cusi slunk away.

Later that day one of the priestesses returned from the Qorikancha with the story that was already making the rounds in the city. Princess Koka's betrothal to the old coca-chewing kuraka was common gossip, and rumor now had it that Titu Cusi's soldiers were overpowered by a mob of angry women who carried Koka off to the akllawasi. I'm sure Koka's imperial guards did nothing to discourage this version; however, I never before heard myself described as a 'mob.'

Old Cormorant stayed out of my way, her usual surliness replaced by nervous cringing at the sight of me. I almost felt sorry for her. Almost. At first opportunity I cornered her in front of others and calmly requested confession. Her jaw dropped but she couldn't refuse, and so with much trepidation she found herself sequestered alone with me. I enjoyed every moment, though it was only a prelude to my final design for her. I was troubled by a dream, I told her, in which a priestess violated the sanctity of the confessional and spent the rest of her life doing terrible penance, which I described for her in vivid detail. Could she interpret this strange dream for me? I wondered.

Throughout the telling I gave no sign that I knew what she had done. But she knew. Had she confessed her wickedness to me, or even stumbled through a standard delivery on the need for forgiveness in this troubled world, I might have softened toward her, pathetic creature that she was, but she didn't. She listened in stony silence, beak held high, and said only that she would think on it for me.

Very well, you old bird, I decided, if you're unrepentant then you deserve what I have planned for you. In the meantime you can brood on your future.

"My mother?" Sumaq looked surprised when I inquired. "I saw her once or twice at the Qorikancha, briefly, but we have nothing to say."

Sumaq seemed to think it an odd question. Her mother, Lady Hilpay, was also in my plans, but for Sumaq's sake I hesitated.

"I thought you two had reconciled."

Sumaq shrugged. "As I told you before, Qori, we're not enemies anymore, but. . . if I had a choice she wouldn't be a friend of mine. I don't care whether I see her or not. Why do you ask?"

"It's just that I've seen her a few times in the city, and I was wondering. . . . "

Sumaq waved her hand carelessly. "I suppose she's still sniveling around Lady Sisa? From what I've heard the Lady Speaker of Hurincuzco has her own problems. They probably deserve each other."

With that the subject was closed, and Lady Hilpay's fate sealed.

Late on the third day I joined the Most Esteemed Mother and Sumaq in a line of priestesses walking to the Qorikancha, a shawl drawn over my head like the others, and once in the confines of Mama Killa's shrine I changed clothes again.

"We're here for you, Qori Qoyllur," the Most Esteemed Mother said, kissing my forehead. "You've delivered Princess Koka, and in so doing granted the Empire a willing empress, her sister Kusi Rimaq. Mama Killa is pleased with you."

"Thank you, Mother," I said, and bowed as she departed. Sumaq T'ika remained with me in Mama Killa's shrine.

The walls of this room were paneled in pure silver, silver figurines adorned the niches, and a massive silver disk with a woman's face covered the back wall. We weren't alone with Mother Moon. The mummies of nine empresses sat arranged below the niches, including my own great aunt, Mama Añawarqe of Choqo.

Sumaq took my hand. "And you know I am always here for you, Qori," she said.

She didn't have to say it in front of Mama Killa and the empresses for me to feel the truth, but in this holy of holies, in front of all that was female and sacred, it came as an honest, unconditional pledge, making me love her more. In reply I lifted her chin and kissed her lips tenderly, my pledge of friendship to her. Then I left her in the care of Mama Killa and slipped back out to the world of men.

Lord Achachi met me at the appointed place, and the final plans were laid.

"It went well at Limatampu, Lord?" I asked.

"It was as you said," Achachi replied. "The caravan walked right into it, and the weapons were hidden in baskets of coca leaves. After some 'persuasion' the smugglers confessed before Titu Cusi and the court. You should have seen Wallpaya's face. Well, no one will be seeing him again," he said drawing a finger across his throat. Achachi seemed younger with the telling, eyes flashing, the muscles of his thick arms flexing.

"And the other plotters?"

"I arranged through Atoq to have Zapana track down and dispose of the few who fled," Achachi said. "Zapana is now on their trail in Antisuyu. The ones who remained saw fit to return their estates and titles to Titu Cusi, and the provincial lords made generous gifts to our temples. It will take generations for their families to recover. But you're wondering about Sapaca? No proof of his involvement." He shook his head sadly. "Never mind. His time is fast coming."

Zapana knew what we planned for Sapaca, but Achachi hadn't told him when the trap would be sprung. Zapana assumed he'd be present to watch Lady Sisa's downfall, but Sisa knew Zapana too well, and I had to agree with Achachi that his presence at Machu Picchu might scare off the quarry, as much as I would have welcomed Zapana's aid. Achachi's suggestion of sending Zapana after the fleeing plotters seemed perfectly reasonable to Atoq - who believed I was far away in Qollasuyu - and Zapana was pleased to undertake the mission because Tintaya was excluded.

I had seen Zapana only once since his visit to Choqo. He said nothing more about his invitation to share Tipón, indeed, he seemed to have me back in my compartment again, and I began to worry his offer wasn't indefinite. Was I going to lose him?

My thoughts turned to Qhari. "Will my brother be joining us, Lord?"

"His wounds heal well, but with Zapana gone it would be awkward to explain the under-steward's absence from K'allachaka." Achachi sighed and looked at me. "In truth, Qori, you know your brother is a little headstrong, and very protective of you. I think you'll agree what lies before us requires the utmost delicacy, and I don't want you distracted. Like Zapana, Qhari knows the plan but not the timing. It's best if things stay that way."

True, I thought, but poor Qhari will be furious, and hurt, when he learns I went ahead without him. Still, there is one more vital role only he can play before our revenge is complete.

"You've been declared Regent, Lord," I remarked, changing subjects.

Achachi pursed his lips and held up his hands with a modest shrug. I gave him a sly smile and a courtly bow. The news had reached me in the akllawasi. To keep the Tipón web secret Atoq once again transferred all credit for foiling the recent coup to Achachi, and Achachi's place at the helm of the Empire could no longer be denied. Tawantinsuyu was at last in safe hands.

"You're now supreme, Lord. Your orders go unquestioned. Command me," I said making further obeisance.

"In other matters I shall," he replied in his deep, gravelly voice, "but in that which lays before us you need no orders from me. . . except, remember that Sapaca must be taken alive. There is to be no killing. Everything depends on this."

I lowered my eyes and bowed again. There was no shadow of doubt concerning Sapaca's guilt, but if he died before confessing to the council of panaqas his Hurincuzco kinsmen would cry foul. His crimes had to be established to everyone's satisfaction, which would be the ultimate humiliation for Lady Sisa.

"It's to be Machu Picchu, then?" I said.

Achachi nodded.

A good choice, I thought, far from Cuzco and surrounded by dense forest - just the sort of place in which Sapaca likes to work his deeds. How can Sapaca and Sisa refuse a gracious invitation from the new Regent to visit his panaqa's estate? Sisa was born to Iñaca Panaqa, and she hasn't yet visited this new jewel of her father's lands. Then, too, with Cuzco still buzzing with rumors of Wallpaya's attempted coup, it's a convenient time for Sapaca to be away from the city.

Achachi looked at me curiously. "Qori, did you have anything to do with that disturbance in Cuzco at Sitowa? It's said Princess Koka fled to the akllawasi and won't come out. Her guards were overpowered. . . ."

"Women's business," I replied curtly.

He chuckled and gave me a knowing smile.

The first banner appeared up the forest road and I fell to my knees, head bowed like an awe-struck peasant girl. Peering expectantly over my brows, I watched the front ranks of Sapaca's honor guard stride into sight.

There are the young nobles of Hurincuzco, I thought, invited along to witness Sapaca's fiendishness so there'll be no arguments later. None of you know it yet, but Achachi will have you present when Sapaca is caught in the act.

Sapaca's litter appeared, the usual number of bearers supplemented to manage his bulk, and behind came another litter carrying Sisa and Q'enti. At the sight of these three a blind fury swelled within me, but I fought it down, becoming the humble peasant girl once again.

What if Sisa and Q'enti recognize me? I wondered. No, they're not expecting me. Atoq told Sisa I'm in Qollasuyu. Today I'm just another peasant, an obedient nothing by the side of the road.

I kept my chin on my breast until Sapaca's litter drew near, and then jumped to my feet in adoration, bowing repeatedly.

"May the Celestial Couple preserve and keep the great Lord Sapaca," I shouted.

Sapaca nodded graciously.

Holding up my jug and kero I pleaded, "Great Lord, I'm all alone here, but I beg you to honor this least of all persons with a drink from my humble kero. Please, Great Lord, that my ayllu may treasure forever that which your lips have touched."

Sapaca looked amused and held up a hand to signal a halt. The procession lurched to a stop. Everyone turned and stared at me.

Sapaca spread his hands magnanimously. "How can I refuse my younger sister? You are also of hurinsaya? Come forward, my dove."

The guards stood back clearing a path to the litter, but an officer stepped in front of me. "Just a precaution, young woman," he said, spreading my arms. I hung my head. He reached under my cloak and patted my sides searching for weapons. "What's this?" he demanded, coming up with Eagle Woman.

"A love charm, Lord," I mumbled. He regarded the solid-looking cylinder and shrugged. Next he sniffed at the aqha, and pouring a little in his hand tasted it. "You may approach Lord Sapaca," he said.

Sapaca accepted the kero and ran an appraising eye over me. I blushed prettily for him. His thick lips parted in a leer, then he downed the kero in a single draught and handed it back to me, wiping his mouth on the back of his hand.

"Where are your husband and children?" he asked my padded breasts. I puffed out my chest for him.

"I have neither, Lord. It's my father's turn to care for this rest station," I said gesturing to the roadside hut, "but he and the family are busy in the fields. I'm here alone, and there's so little traffic on the road. . . ."

"I'm sure you know how to look after travelers' needs," he said leering.

I blushed again. "I always do my best, Lord."

Without another word he turned and waved a hand forward, setting the procession in motion once more. I stepped back and held a bow. During the exchange I dared not look at Sisa's litter, but now it floated by and I couldn't resist a glance. Q'enti held her chin up in a noble pose to the road ahead, but Sisa moved a cold eye over me. There was no spark of recognition.

I thought, Did you enjoy watching me flirt with your husband, Lady Sisa? I hope so, because once I've dealt with him, you and your demon daughter are next.

The light thinned. Birds issued their evening calls and swooped after insects. I kindled a fire in front of the hut and then settled inside to wait, listening to a beetle click its legs together in the thatch overhead. Three cane walls folded me in their shadows, but the front opened to the fire and the fading valley beyond, now tinged red with Inti's last rays. The distant beat of drums echoed from beyond the next ridge, and the high, plaintive strains of panpipe music drifted to my ears. The welcoming feast at Machu Picchu was underway. I turned my attention to dried meat and maize cakes.

The snap of a twig brought me to my knees. An owl hooted nearby - Achachi's signal. I relaxed again. Achachi crept into the firelight. "In here," I told him.

"It's going to be tonight," he said gravely, kneeling beside me.

"Tonight? Sapaca wastes no time."

"None," Achachi said shaking his head. "He's already told his chamberlain he'll be away from his quarters for a while this evening - a girl, he said."

I looked at him.

"I bribed the chamberlain," Achachi explained, "but he doesn't know where the rendezvous will take place. It could be anywhere, depending on Sapaca's whims. If Sapaca doesn't come to this hut then he'll send someone to fetch you. Either way, I'll have to follow him.

"After the feast I'll ask the Hurincuzco lords to help me stop some trouble tonight. They won't know it's Sapaca we're trailing until. . . ." His words faltered.

"I know," I reassured him, "until Sapaca has the cord around my neck and I shout your name, then you'll all come charging in."

"Qori, I don't like this. What if - "

"Don't worry, Lord, I can take care of myself. Since we don't know where the meeting will be, all you need do is let Sapaca lead you there, and I'll be waiting. Fear not. I know how to keep a man busy. I won't let him get close enough to do anything until I hear your owl-hoot. Then, when I know you and the others are in position. . . well, perhaps a few unpleasant moments with the beast, but the instant that cord encircles my neck. . . ."

"Does he use the cord before or after he. . . ."

"Before or after he rapes his victims? I hadn't thought of that. Who knows what goes on in that evil mind of his? Well, I'll do what I must," I said firmly to convince myself. "It will all end tonight. Trust me."

I sat in the shadows and watched the lonely fire sink to embers, the glow barely illuminating the surrounding bushes, reducing my vision to a pale circle.

Look not at the fire, I told myself, let your eyes adjust. What did Condin Savana say? Don't look at the forest, look into it, become one with it. The spirits are loose tonight, I can feel them. This is a time for you and your sorcery, Condin Savana. Are you here with me now? Yes, I believe you are, in one form or another.

I stroked Eagle Woman and repeated the old wizard's words, "If you hesitate you are lost." But then, if I kill Sapaca now, I thought, the truth will never be known. No, Lady, I said to Eagle Woman, you're here for my comfort, but you must stay sheathed.

The night thickened. A world of stars pinpricked the heavenly canopy - sharp, clear, beyond count, making me feel like a spot of insignificance beneath their mystery. Their brightness promised a year of harmony and plenty, and the barely visible outline of the dark cloud Serpent in the Celestial River heralded rain for the fields. The brighter stars, the chasca or shaggy-haired ones, shone down on their earthly charges, one for each type of bird and animal, and sighting the mother llama I offered her a prayer on behalf of herders. A scurrying nearby in the bushes reminded me I was bereft of human company, but not alone. Hastily I sighted the evening star and prayed that pumas, jaguars and bears would leave me be, followed by a similar invocation to the serpent star.

A streak fell through the sky, fading toward the blue-black horizon. Some priest will use that to divine the location of a stolen thing, I mused, or the direction of the thief's house, or maybe the approach of sickness or death. Tanta Karwa never put much faith in those predictions. Perhaps it's a sign for this night's work, but it is favorable?

Footsteps padded softly on the road above. I shrank into the blackness of the hut, knees to my chin. There was a pause, and then rustling on the path leading down to where I waited holding my breath. A cloaked figure stood in front of the glowing embers. "Are you here?" a voice asked.

A woman's voice, I realized. Sapaca has sent his servant to fetch me. "Do you seek shelter?" I replied from the shadows.

"Ah, there you are. Are you alone?"

Where have I heard that voice before? I wondered. "But for the gods and your good company," I said cheerily. "Have you eaten? Shall I rouse the fire?"

No response. I emerged from the hut and stooped to add a few sticks to the coals. Flames kicked up. Sensing movement I looked over my shoulder. The woman lifted her shawl from her head and turned to the fire.

Shock vibrated through me. Q'enti! Sapaca not only uses his daughter, I thought, he sends her to gather his prey. Don't let her see your surprise. Keep your face in the shadows lest she recognizes you.

A second shrouded figure stepped into the fire's glow. Sapaca? I wondered. No, too small.

At a nod from Q'enti the shawl slid back, revealing high cheeks, full lips, a delicate nose, and huge liquid eyes. Sisa!

"Don't be frightened young woman," Sisa cooed, letting her cloak fall. Q'enti also slipped hers from her shoulders, a feral smile playing about her mouth. They were dressed in matching finery, two noblewomen standing in the night forest like apparitions, the fire flickering soft light and shadow on flawless copper skin. Even as I struggled to comprehend I couldn't help seeing their beauty. Two perfect images, identical in face and form like twin sisters, but for a hardness on Sisa's features betraying her years. Neither showed any sign of recognition. They weren't expecting Qori Qoyllur.

"We are goddesses of the night," Q'enti answered my silent stare. She stepped toward me and I backed away. "We saw you offer Lord Sapaca a kero by the roadside today. You're very beautiful. We've come to pass some time with you."

I took another step backwards.

"I command you to stand," Q'enti said. "There, that's better. Don't fear." Her voice came soothingly now. "You're asleep and we've come to you in your dreams. You've drifted into the spirit world. This isn't happening on the earth you know, it's of the other side. Are we not beautiful? Come here and let us get acquainted," she said holding out her hand.

I shrank again, still struggling to grasp what was happening. What did they want from me? Sisa unfastened a leather bag from her waist. My loathing of these two lent an icy calm to my calculations. Whatever it is, I decided, they think me an ignorant peasant. Is Achachi nearby with the others? Time - give Sisa and Q'enti time to expose their game.

Hesitantly I accepted Q'enti's hand. She smiled, drawing me to her. "There, there, pretty one, that's better." She cast a sideways glance at Sisa. Sisa's eyes glowed. "Lift your chin," Q'enti said. "Oh, she's shy. So pretty and shy. We're only here to honor your beauty with our own."

Stunned, I let her lift my chin with a finger. My blood froze when she pressed her lips to mine. Sisa crowded at my side, and when Q'enti released me Sisa placed her arm around my shoulders and turned me to her.

"Yes, my dove," Sisa breathed in my ear, "now you are on the other side with the goddesses of night. In this dream you are the beautiful Ronto. Our own pretty Ronto."

When she said the name of the woman savaged at the Hatunqolla akllawasi - her own governess of long ago years - a thrill of terror raced through me.

"There, there, Ronto," she soothed, "come into my arms and all will be as it was before."

Q'enti pressed against me from behind, hands on my hips. "Ronto, pretty Ronto," she murmured as if in her own dream.

"No!" I screamed, jabbing an elbow into Q'enti. Sisa grabbed my arm but I shoved her away. The leather bag she held fell to the ground spilling its contents - a wooden pestle and a hoop strung with black, shriveled things.

"Wicked Ronto, evil Ronto," Sisa spat.

For an instant her eyes fixed mine, wild, raging, mad eyes - then the cord encircled my neck from behind.

Instantly I threw my weight back against Q'enti and the two of us went down, she on the bottom. The cord fell slack as she gulped for air. I rolled aside. Sisa grabbed my hair before I could rise and pulled savagely, jerking my head this way and that. It wasn't a hold I was trained to break. Men don't fight this way. The shock stopped me from responding. "Wicked Ronto, evil Ronto," Sisa kept muttering while she twisted viciously.

I fumbled beneath my cloak and came up with Eagle Woman. Stinger bared, I thrust blindly over my head at those wrenching hands but missed with each wild stab. Q'enti's weight ploughed into me, pinning me on my side. Sisa filled her clutching fingers with my hair once more and began dragging me while Q'enti, still on top, seized my striking arm and slammed it to the ground knocking Eagle Woman's stinger beyond the fire's glow.

I wiggled onto my back, kicking my heels into the dirt to propel myself forward, trying to ease Sisa's tearing. But Q'enti straddled my chest and once more produced her cord, struggling to wind it around my neck. I shot a claw-grip to her throat, burying my fingers in the soft skin. A wonderful hoarse gurgle rent the night. I toppled her aside, keeping my grip fixed.

"No, stop that. Don't hurt my doll!" Sisa shrieked, releasing my hair and falling on the hold. I rolled away, leaving Q'enti on her side with both hands at her neck and Sisa kneeling over her.

No sooner did I gain my feet than Sisa turned and sprang like a cougar with claws bared. She wasn't a big woman, but her madness gave her the strength of three men. I could handle the cunning moves of trained soldiers, but this wild screaming fury was too much. She descended like a whirlwind, scratching and biting, tumbling me on my back. I responded with nails and teeth, flailing wildly. Down she pushed me, one knee in my stomach, her mad eyes ready to burst from their sockets, foamy spittle on her lips. I plunged my head into her torso and with my entire strength bit at the first place my mouth encountered. It happened to be the tip of one large breast.

The thin, soft fabric of her dress was no protection. Sisa's scream pierced the forest while she frantically beat at my head, but I stayed clamped until cloth and something else came away in my mouth. Tasting blood, I spat the mouthful aside. Sisa sat with her legs outstretched, staring in open-mouthed horror at her breast. Blood oozed from the ragged hole, soaking her dress. I leapt up, spun, and with a back-kick landed a heel in her mouth, knocking her flat.

"Mother!" The cry came from behind. I whirled to find Q'enti back on her feet, eyes bulging. "You bitch," she hissed, pulling a knife from her belt.

"Bitch," I replied, drawing my own.

Q'enti had the fury to be dangerous with a blade, but not the expertise. The other victims, unsuspecting peasant girls awed by the 'goddesses of the night,' probably put up little struggle until it was too late. But though I was a new experience for the mad pair, neither hesitated in the viciousness of her attacks. Q'enti eyed me gloatingly as if her knife were already in my throat. Even with her lips curled she was the essence of flawless beauty. For a breath I almost fell under her spell. The fire's glow played on high, delicate cheeks and smooth, light copper skin. Her huge eyes held mine in the hypnotic trance of a serpent coiled to strike.

The lunge came with a wicked shriek. I caught her descending forearm between crossed wrists, seized her hand and spun her around pinning her arm between her shoulders. Her knife fell, and I pressed mine to her throat. A gasp came from her and she froze. It's too easy, I thought, and too quick. You stole from me, Q'enti. You stole my child and left me barren. Now I'll take that which you treasure most.

"This is for baby Sumaq," I said in Q'enti's ear, slowly moving the blade upward. Her breath caught again, uncertain of my words, but suddenly sure of my intention.

"Please. . . ." she begged.

It was all I wanted to hear. When I pressed the blade into the tender flesh of her cheek she screamed and twisted away. My knife bit deep, laying her face open. She fell to her knees, hands clamped to her gory face, and a long, mournful wail filled the night - the cry of a vanquished she-beast.

"Oh, Q'enti, my poor doll!" Sisa rose behind me like a specter and stood shakily for a moment, sadly watching her crumpled demon-spawn. For an instant I almost felt sympathy for the pity in her voice, but was it pity for her daughter or her toy? Sisa's eyes flared on me. The sound that passed her bloody lips was not of this earth.

Sisa flew at me with arms extended and fingers out like claws, a savage, unstoppable maniacal force swooping like a raptor of death. I stood rooted in terror. Her talons seized my throat, lifting me from the ground as if I were not but a sack of feathers, claws searching the cords of my neck. Thrice I buried my blade in her gut but she took no notice, shaking me like a rag in the wind. As my eyes rolled into my head I managed to press the blade under her ear and rip flesh. She dropped me like a stone.

I lay on my back looking up. Sisa wavered, her talons still extended clutching air, eyes frozen wide and head tilted back, blood spurting from her severed throat. I struggled up, breathless, and plunged my dagger into her breast, leaving it there sunk to the hilt. She stared down at the handle, and then with strength from I know not where she actually took hold and pulled it out, flinging it into the night. And still she wouldn't fall!

With a cry of desperation I threw myself into her. She stumbled back, wavered, and fell spread-eagle on the fire amid a tempest of sparks. On my knees, choking, gasping for air, I watched the first yellow flames lick from her clothes, and then the acrid smell of burning hair caused me to blanche and turn away.

Q'enti remained on her knees, rocking and moaning, oblivious to the scene at her back. It was time to end her life too. She'd had her moment of agony - my revenge, and now the poor sick creature needed to be put out of her misery. I rose heavily, my breast still heaving, and untied the sling from my hair. Q'enti gave no sign of awareness. Without resistance she allowed me to tie the sling noose-like around her neck. I stood behind her, ready to pull it tight.

Suddenly the night flared bright and a horrible gurgle assailed my ears. I spun around. Before my unbelieving eyes Sisa rose, standing straight with hands stretched toward me, wreathed in flames and smoke, and as if in a nightmare I heard myself scream, "N-O-O-O!"

She came at me, not running, but taking one steady step at a time, a hideous bubble escaping the gash at her throat, the stink of burning flesh filling my nostrils. Cold terror turned my limbs to stone. Is she a demon, I wondered in horror, a true spirit of the night, unstoppable?

The smoldering apparition was but a step away when a vision filled my head. Tanta Karwa stood in the sunlit field, her arm around the neck of The-One-Confused-Like-A-Man. One of the paired bags slung over the llama's back held Baby Sumaq. Tanta Karwa looked fearful. "Do it for me," she said.

Without hesitation I jerked the tupu pin from my cloak and drove the long needle into Sisa's left eye, my knuckles slamming into her brow, coming away empty, leaving the tupu head protruding. Sisa made not a sound but stopped, her talons, already curved to the shape of my neck, falling on my shoulders. She wavered, and as if the lights in a house were suddenly extinguished, her right eye, though open, went blank. She collapsed at my feet like a smoldering blanket.

"For you, Tanta Karwa," I breathed again.

Q'enti remained on her knees, back turned, holding her face and whimpering pitifully. The sling was still in place around her neck, waiting for me. I sighed to the stars. The final victory wasn't so sweet, but her miserable existence had to be ended, mercifully, swiftly.

They lose consciousness before they die, I reassured myself, winding the dangling ends around my hands. I set my heels and clenched my teeth, then pulled hard. Every person's body struggles, even when its owner wants death. Q'enti tried to rise, her fingers clawing at the cord. In spite of what she'd done to me tears wet my cheeks, but I held fast, cinching tighter.

"Hold! Stop her!"

The clearing suddenly filled with men and strong hands grabbed me, twisting my arms behind my back and forcing me to my knees.

Shouts burst around me. "Look, it's Lady Q'enti. Hold the assassin!"

XXXV

In which the True Horror is revealed.

"She attacked us," Q'enti wailed. "Mother couldn't sleep so we strolled, and when we came here that woman. . . she. . . she . . . ." Q'enti broke off in another fit of shoulder-heaving sobs. Achachi's eyes pierced me. The Hurincuzco lords looked on with eyes of stone.

"Let her up," Achachi ordered my captors. They obeyed reluctantly.

Achachi took my arm. "What happened? Is that Lady Sisa?" He stared in horror at the crumpled heap of burned cloth.

"What happened?" I repeated incredulously. "That's what I want to know. Where were you?"

"Following Lord Sapaca," he said. "We trailed him to a shed on the other side of the estate where he met a woman, a maid as it turned out, but in the dark I mistook her for you. When I realized the error we rushed here."

"It wasn't Sapaca we wanted," I said, "it was Sisa and Q'enti." I pointed to the leather bag Sisa dropped with its pestle and hoop of trophies. "That's how the women were raped, and that's what became of their tongues."

"They're hers!" Q'enti shrieked. "I've never seen those things before. She. . . that woman," she extended a trembling finger at me, "she had them."

I gave Achachi a skeptical look, but his face remained masked.

"They're not mine," I protested. "Lady Sisa had them."

"Lady Sisa is dead, most horribly," one of the Hurincuzco lords replied coldly. "We have Lady Q'enti's word on what happened here. Are you suggesting Lady Q'enti lies? Who are you, and why did you do this? Who sent you? Speak."

"I am Qori Qoyllur, Healer of Choqo, and Imperial Agent," I said, pulling the cotton from my cheeks and slipping the padding from under my dress. The man stared at me in disbelief, and then his eyes narrowed.

"She is Qori Qoyllur," Achachi confirmed, "and she was engaged on my behalf, but not for this." His eyes settled on Lady Sisa.

I clutched his arm. "But my Lord, you know - "

"Silence!" he roared. "What these good men of Hurincuzco know is only what they have seen with their own eyes. Lady Sisa is dead, and when we arrived you had a noose around Lady Q'enti's neck. Now it's your word against hers. I warned you there was to be no killing tonight."

One look in his eyes convinced me he was serious - deadly serious. Whatever was said or claimed, the Lady Speaker of Hurincuzco was dead, and to preserve the peace someone had to atone for it. Achachi was a man of principal, but he would do anything to prevent a split between the royal houses.

It suddenly occurred to me that Sisa was born into Iñaca Panaqa and was a half-sister of Achachi himself, though the two hardly knew each other. Nonetheless, if Sisa were found to be the culprit her shame would spill onto that royal house, too, and tinge the Regent. I remembered Sumaq T'ika's ancestor, the mad Empress who tried to roast her son, and how that disgrace followed Sumaq's panaqa for generations.

Achachi wanted Sapaca exposed and dishonored, but he hadn't bargained the scandal would touch his own lineage. He knew I spoke the truth about Sisa - I saw it in his face - but now it seemed Sisa's death was convenient, as my own would be.

I protested but Achachi silenced me with a look. While the men finished bandaging Q'enti's face the eastern horizon lightened, but the stars remained bright. I wondered if this would be my last dawn.

"Lord," I said to Achachi, "there's a way to settle this matter." He looked at me as if it was already settled. I explained my plan, my last hope, and concluded, "Surely for all my service to the Empire, Lord, I should be granted this much before sentence is passed."

Achachi looked to the Hurincuzco lords. They had listened carefully, only now aware of the trail of murdered girls. A conference of whispers followed, during which my stomach remained in my throat. Achachi wouldn't meet my eyes. At last their spokesman replied, "So be it. But if this plan of hers doesn't produce the results she claims, then she's ours and justice will be swift."

Dense mist swept up the slopes obscuring the line of men ahead on the narrow flagstone road. Red and purple orchids hung in the dripping greenery, where spider webs glinted their night catch of dew. The road sloped away to a lower ridge, and as the mists parted the men halted for the first view of Machu Picchu. It straddled the spine below us, a cascade of farming terraces marking the entrance. Beyond these lay warrens of stone dwellings. Plazas occupied a broader patch, with temples on one side and more residences on the other. At the end of the ridge, brooding over all, rose the peak of Wayna Picchu, a green-shrouded column like an erect thumb. The Urubamba churned far below, and on every horizon jagged mountains met the eye. I thought, Not by chance did they choose this place to build, for surely here one is close to the gods.

With our descent dawn crept over the thatch roofs of Machu Picchu, turning them gold against the dark green embrace of the forest slopes, and promising a clear morning. The first smoke from cooking fires drifted into the sky, and a barking dog answered the moan of a conch shell trumpet. Burly guards led me forth, while behind me sympathetic lords helped Q'enti along. After her bravado in the clearing she sank into a whimpering silence, allowing herself to be fussed over and gently led. Lord Achachi remained aloof, strutting ahead and leaving the sentries snapped to attention as we passed the checkpoints.

At the first of two lower plazas the party dispersed. The guards led Q'enti away to be attended, and Achachi motioned the men of the Hurincuzco panaqas to follow us. We continued upward to Sapaca's quarters. Achachi walked stiffly behind me. From the uppermost and largest plaza we climbed stone stairs to the level of the royal apartments, then threaded the narrow maze to Sapaca's door.

Sapaca, disheveled and without sleep, stopped pacing when we entered. A look of surprise crossed his face when he saw Achachi and the other men, but my presence didn't register. He locked eyes with Achachi in a long silence.

Achachi produced the hoop of shriveled tongues from behind his back and threw it at Sapaca's feet. Sapaca stared at it wide-eyed, but didn't move.

Achachi shot me a look and sighed heavily, then began as I had instructed him. "Your wife and daughter have been caught murdering a peasant girl. They've confessed everything - this and many other murders. That thing," he pointed at the hoop, "counts their victims. The lords of Hurincuzco are witnesses. Lady Sisa and Lady Q'enti will be executed shortly. Is there any reason why you shouldn't join them?"

Sapaca covered his eyes and slumped against the wall. One of the lords made to speak but caught himself, biting his lower lip. I held my breath. Now was the moment for my fate to be decided.

"I told her," Sapaca moaned. "I begged her to stop, but she laughed at me."

I exhaled audibly.

Achachi cleared his throat. "How long have you known? Since Ronto, the first one?"

"You know it all, then," Sapaca said, dropping his hand and turning to face us with blank, red eyes. "Very well. In truth, I knew nothing at first. I didn't realize it was Sisa who killed those women at the Hatunqolla akllawasi until after we were married. The day of those first deaths it was Atoq who arrived at the akllawasi and found Sisa. He and I were like brothers then, and he gave me the honor of claiming Sisa's hand. Sisa even convinced me an Inca captain had murdered those women, and Atoq gave me the authority to order this captain and his men to certain death in battle. Later, when I became Speaker of Hurincuzco and Sisa traveled the realm with me, I learned of other women murdered in the same way. Each time the victims were found where we had just visited, and eventually I guessed the truth about Sisa's night walks.

"She laughed at me when I confronted her, saying they were only peasant girls, and if I denounced her I would lose my position and shame the panaqa. Besides, she told me the women were violated as if by a man, and on the night of each murder she arranged for a girl to lure me from my quarters."

He looked away sadly. "Sisa was cold to me. From the day we married she refused me, and had I not forced her in drunken frustration we wouldn't even have had Q'enti."

Achachi shifted. "How long has Q'enti been assisting Sisa in these. . .

these crimes?"

"How long? In truth I don't know, I have no control over her either. Q'enti belongs to Sisa, and Sisa raised her to be just like herself." His eyes focused. "I love them both, Achachi. Can you believe that? My wife and my daughter, the two fairest ladies in the Empire, both in my kancha, at my side, around me constantly, yet both detesting me, shunning the love I offered. That's been my life, Achachi, like being condemned to the underworld here on this earth."

I heard the sincerity in his voice, saw it on his face, but it didn't banish the image of him coupling with his own daughter.

"You sent assassins after Kontor and Sayri and Maita," I said coldly. Sapaca cocked his head. "Who?"

"The Inca captain and his men who saw Ronto alive at Hatunqolla," I said.

"Indeed I did not, young woman," he said. "I thought those men died in battle as Atoq planned. They lived? Well, if so I know nothing of them. Sisa has her own spies. She even has me watched."

"But those were your men at the Temple of Wiraqocha chasing Kontor," I insisted.

"Oh, them. Did you have a hand in ending their miserable lives? Yes, they were my men, but years ago I discovered they were really in Sisa's employ. I left them in place and told them only what I wanted Sisa to hear. When I heard they were dead I suspected it was on Sisa's account, but they were no loss to me. Atoq said no inquires would be made, so I assumed it was something between Sisa and him."

"You know about Atoq and Sisa?" I asked, wanting to hurt him.

"You mean that they are lovers? Of course. It's been that way since we were children at court. He's always protected her, even in the matter of these. . . these deaths. Sisa plays him. I know her, and her heart is ice. She can love no man, but she uses us when it suits her. Poor Atoq is beyond infatuation. If there are assassins stalking the land to clean up behind Sisa they must be Atoq's."

Everything leads back to Atoq, I thought.

Achachi appeared to have reached a decision. "Qori, leave us now.

Wait outside. The rest of you stay here," he said to the lords.

In the full light of early morning I stood looking across the plaza to a little temple perched above, yet seeing nothing, my thoughts turned inward. The evil that began with a murder before I was born, that made my father a fugitive and finally took his life, shattered the innocence of our childhood and thrust Qhari and me into a power struggle between the lords of the world, had finally been extinguished. Yet even this triumph wasn't complete, not yet. One conspirator still remained to be dealt with before father's spirit found eternal peace. Then, too, other debts had accumulated along the way, persons who had used and betrayed me. Start with the first, and most difficult, I told myself. The plan had been forming gradually for some time, and now, staring vacantly across the plazas of Machu Picchu, I added the finishing touches. I hoped Qhari was up to it.

So distracted in thought was I that I didn't hear Achachi come to my side. The Hurincuzco lords remained inside with Sapaca. "The bargain is struck with Sapaca," Achachi announced. "He'll trouble us no more."

"Bargain? Is he not to pay for his crimes?"

"His only crime was his silence. Now that he's been subdued he's of no further threat. As soon as we return to the holy city he'll go into honorable retirement, and Hurincuzco will choose a new Speaker."

"Honorable retirement? But the shame - "

"There will be no shame," he cut me off, "at least not publicly. It will be said a madwoman attacked Sisa and Q'enti. This accords with what the lords of Hurincuzco saw. Afterwards the wretch was executed and her body thrown into the Urubamba. In exchange, Sapaca will go into retirement but give unfailing support to Emperor Titu Cusi, and work with me to alleviate any future friction between Hurincuzco and Hanancuzco."

"Then there is to be no confession about the murders before the council of panaqas?"

"None. Only we few know about them, and it will stay that way."

"But what about Q'enti? She helped Sisa. . . ."

"Sapaca will care for her. He insisted she be spared, and she's a small price to pay for peace between the sayas. Don't look so troubled, Qori, this has all worked out well. As long as I have Sapaca in my power the Empire is safe from within, and that's all that matters."

To you, perhaps, I thought. "And you trust Sapaca's word on all this?" I asked skeptically.

"Of course not, but he agreed to these terms in front of his lords and, more important, to seal the bargain he will deliver into my hands ten hairs from the head of his grandfather, ten from his father, and ten of his own."

It was no small pledge. The well being of every lineage depends on its honored ancestors, and powerful sorcery can be worked with a few hairs or any intimate items. Sapaca had placed his own life and his panaqa's prosperity in Achachi's hands.

"So there's to be no justice for the murdered women?"

"Justice? Sisa is dead, what more do you want?"

"She was born into your panaqa, Lord. This hiding of the truth is convenient for you, too, is it not?"

"Now that you point it out, true. Iñaca Panaqa would suffer as much as Chima Panaqa if all was known. Imagine the scandal and finger pointing. The court would break into factions and our enemies would rub their hands in glee. Is that what you want, Qori, to see Tawantinsuyu vulnerable?"

I ignored the question. "And what of those innocent men like my father who died to hide Sisa's evil? We both know who is responsible for that."

"You can't be serious? Atoq is untouchable."

"His reason is clouded, Lord."

Achachi looked thoughtful. "It's true Atoq has become too powerful, and though always loyal he no longer sees the difference between his interests and those of the Empire. Yet, as twice proven in the last year, the Empire needs him, or someone like him." Achachi paused and rubbed his chin, then reached a decision and fixed me with his eyes. "I swore an oath to Zapana long ago; in exchange for his help tracking the fugitives and curbing Sapaca's powers, I promised not to harm Atoq, and one day Zapana would be declared Atoq's legal son and successor."

Yes, everything Zapana ever wanted, I thought.

Achachi shrugged. "But, I said I would never harm Atoq. If someone else wanted to, that would be up to her."

A full moon rose over the broken walls, bathing the ruins in shadow and pale silver light. I coaxed the fire with another handful of twigs and settled down to wait in the collapsed courtyard. The ancient city of Pikillacta, built and abandoned in a time before memory, stood silent and empty in the moonlight. Only lizards and cactus live there. The place is a warren of fallen compounds, some with walls still three stories high, but rubble now blocks the entrances. Fallen sections provide the only passage from one courtyard to the next in a maze of blind turns and dead ends. No one dares walk this emptiness at night for fear of meeting the spirits who inhabit such places. It's a lonely spot a full day's journey down the Huatanay Valley from Cuzco, set high on a plateau overlooking reedy Lake Muyna, but close enough to Tipón.

The click of sliding stones in a rock-strewn passageway jolted my back erect. I wore the head-cloth of a noblewoman and this I pulled farther down on my brow, then lifted the delicate shawl over my head. Such finery I had never worn, but one can become accustomed to anything. Eagle Woman nestled comfortingly at my side. I checked to make sure the skin bag of aqha and two keros were conveniently arranged. The keros rested upside down on their broad rims.

Through a jagged hole in the courtyard wall, framed against the full circle of Mother Moon, a figure appeared, paused, and shuffled toward me. I smiled to myself and thought, It's good to see you, grandmother. You haven't changed since our first meeting in the streets of Cuzco long ago.

The old woman came forward slowly, bent and leaning on her staff, silver hair spilling from beneath the cloak pulled over her head. Without a word I gestured to the stone seat on the other side of the fire. She looked around once, and then sat.

Taking up the bag of aqha I turned the keros over and filled them, then knelt before her offering one. She hesitated, and then reached for the kero held back in my left hand and sniffed the brew. I performed the finger dip to Mama Pacha, then raised my tumbler in a silent toast and drank deeply. She watched me for a moment, and then followed my lead.

I returned to my seat and pulled the shawl from my head. "Thank you for coming, Lord Atoq," I said.

His laughter echoed in the night. "I wondered if it was you," he replied, removing the cloak and wig. He stretched his back, lifting his head to full height. "When your brother brought the message to Tipón saying that Sisa wanted to meet me here alone, urgently, I suspected you might be involved. So, you've finally figured it out, have you? Where is Sisa? You don't fit her clothes very well."

"Dead. Sisa is very dead. Six days ago at Machu Picchu. The news will be made public tomorrow."

That much Achachi had granted me, six days. No one was allowed to leave Machu Picchu until then. The secret of Sisa's death was kept even from Atoq.

He didn't ask how she died or question my words, perhaps he sensed the truth, but as I spoke his head fell forward and a moan of despair escaped him.

"I was in love with her," he said, raising his eyes to the night beyond.

I didn't doubt it. Whatever Atoq had done, he had truly acted from blind love.

"If only she could have returned my love," he said wistfully. "But her heart was cold from the time she was a child. Her mother never hid her disappointment that Sisa was a girl, her only child by the old emperor. And when her mother died Sisa was even more alone at court, shunned by the other princes and princesses at their mothers' urging so she would be less competition for the emperor's favor. But old Pachakuti had so many women and so many children he didn't know who Sisa was anyway. I was her only friend. I knew even then she only used my affections, but I couldn't help myself. Then Ronto arrived to be her governess. Now there was a beautiful schemer! Sisa clung to her, and Ronto used her charms to take control of the orphan princess."

It fit well with what Tanta Karwa told me about Ronto, how she seduced and then abandoned Tanta Karwa for a greater prize, their mistress, whom she thought could arrange a royal marriage for her. I let Atoq continue.

"Ronto's ambition was to marry royalty, and she believed the princess could negotiate this, though Sisa didn't know Ronto's true plans. When they were trapped in the Hatunqolla akllawasi during the rebellion Ronto made her wishes clear for the first time and spoke cruelly, laughing at Sisa's tears and saying their love was nothing, she wanted a man."

The fire popped. I nudged a stick into it with my foot and lifted my kero. Atoq, eyes distant, continued to sip at his. I didn't want to interrupt his story with questions just yet.

"Sisa always felt abandoned by her mother," he explained, saying the words more to himself, to get it right in his own head. "Ronto was the only person she ever allowed herself to love, and now Ronto was being cruel and abandoning her, also. A demon entered Sisa, and she resolved that if she couldn't have Ronto, neither would anyone else.

"Then Kontor and his troop arrived, lifting the siege. But Ronto sent them away, demanding rescue by a man of royalty, someone she could marry, or who might have a marriageable son. Sisa was hiding elsewhere while this happened, and she didn't hear the men come and go. Full of rage, Sisa left her hiding place and strangled Ronto. The old priestess with Ronto tried to stop Sisa, but she couldn't, and afterward Sisa silenced her with a blow to her head. It was the demon who made Sisa cut out Ronto's tongue after she was dead - the tongue that said such hurtful things to her. For some reason Sisa never could part with it," he said shaking his head.

"I arrived to find Sisa sitting beside Ronto's body, the knife in her hand. The priestess still breathed, and from her I learned Kontor and his men were there earlier. Of course, I couldn't leave her alive."

"You cut her throat," I said calmly, remembering Achachi's account of the scene.

Atoq shrugged and waved his hand as if it were nothing. "The deaths could be blamed on the fleeing Qolla. To make it more convincing I used the handle of my mace to make it appear Ronto was raped. Sisa was fascinated with that part. And the rest, Qori, is as I told you before. I was already married and I cared for Sisa too much to have her reduced to a concubine. I found Sapaca, who was unmarried and destined to be Speaker of Hurincuzco, and let him claim the credit for Sisa's rescue. But the matter of Kontor and his men having seen Ronto alive was troublesome, so I told Sapaca it was they who savaged the two women, and I suggested that to save Inca honor we'd say it was the Qolla, and let Kontor and his men perish in battle. Sapaca was most agreeable.

"I thought that was the end of it, but I happened to be present when we captured a deserter some time later, and under torture he revealed he was the Standard Bearer from Kontor's troop. The man bravely bit off his own tongue and bled to death, but before doing so, he confessed Kontor and the brothers Maita and Sayri were still alive and in hiding. Sisa's secret had to remain safe, so I sent agents to hunt down the fugitives."

I shifted where I sat, the fury rising like a wave when Atoq calmly confessed to ordering father's death. But he seemed unaware of me, resigned and far away as if these were inner thoughts, not words.

"But the demon never left Sisa," he continued. "In her travels with Sapaca she sought girls who reminded her of Ronto. She forced them to lie with her first, for she still loved Ronto, but afterwards the evil, hurtful Ronto had to be punished. A pestle became part of the ritual, employed as I used my mace to make it appear the work of a man, though I think in Sisa's mind she was only giving Ronto what she wanted. Sisa told me about each girl afterward so I could protect her, and at these meetings she charmed me again, coaxing me to the blankets. Yes, I knew she was using me, but. . . I couldn't resist her. In truth, I began to look forward to reports of these deaths, knowing she would be coming to me soon. And after all, the demon only directed her to peasant girls."

"How did Q'enti become involved?" I asked.

"Q'enti? She belongs to Sisa, completely. Since she was a child Sisa included her. Q'enti was raised to believe that Ronto must be pleasured and punished over and over again. She knows nothing else." Atoq looked away to his own thoughts. "The beautiful Q'enti. I've lost Sisa, but my daughter will always be there to remind me of her."

"Your daughter?"

"Of course," he said proudly. "You don't think Sisa would ever let Sapaca impregnate her?" He chuckled at the notion. "Sapaca forced himself on her once, and she took her revenge by coming to me," he gloated. "Sapaca still thinks Q'enti is his. That's another little secret Sisa and I enjoyed. No, Q'enti is mine. . . or at least I'm her father," he corrected himself.

"Sapaca used Q'enti," I said flatly, thinking I would shock him.

Atoq laughed. "So you know about that, too. It was a clever ploy of Sisa's to keep Sapaca quiet. When he became suspicious of her she sent Q'enti to seduce him. Q'enti is so exactly the image of Sisa that poor Sapaca couldn't resist. I suppose he was desperate for some form of affection from Q'enti, but he called out Sisa's name in his ecstasy. Once ensnared, if he tried to stop Sisa he would lose his daughter and any vestige of honor left to him. Q'enti insured his silence," he said conversationally, giving no hint of warmth toward his daughter.

"And now the killing will go on," I said. "Q'enti will continue her mother's evil. She knows nothing else but what she was raised to do - scheme and manipulate and kill."

Atoq looked taken aback. "Well, she might; I don't know. But they're only peasant girls. Q'enti never harmed anyone else." He took another sip from his kero. "A sweet brew," he remarked absently.

I struggled to contain myself. Never harmed anyone else? I thought. She stole my child and left me barren. But no, nothing he says is going to rattle Inca Moon. He's toying with Qori Qoyllur. For amusement? Perhaps, but everything Atoq does has a purpose. Why is he telling me all this? Lead him on to buy time, but stay alert, Inca Moon. I shifted the talk away from Q'enti. "You're telling me these things because you know my silence is insured on account of T'ito," I said, staring coldly at him.

A bitter smile came to his lips. "Oh yes, your brother T'ito. Such an obsequious worm, I could hardly stand him. A lot of time invested in that one, and in the end he wasn't much use, except to snare you, of course. Yes, I knew about T'ito since your mother abandoned him. You and your brother Qhari are much more interesting, but I confess I wasn't sure how to deal with you at first. You were most determined children. Not even

Sisa's best man could wrench the truth about Sayri out of you. By the way, is Sayri alive?" I shook my head. "No, I thought not. Well, we weren't sure. Anyway, I learned that you were placed in the akllawasi - Achachi's doing no doubt - but it suited our purposes just as well to have you safe until you could be of use in identifying the fugitives, or so we thought. When the time approached for you to leave the akllawasi Sisa decided to have you married to your brother T'ito. I thought it extremely clever of her," he said fondly. "That insured everyone's silence. She arranged it through that fawning Lady Hilpay."

I nodded to myself, thinking, Sumaq's mother, as I expected, no doubt with old Cormorant's help.

"Sisa and I had some chuckles over that," he said, eyes twinkling as if he expected me to share the joke. "But, when I sent you and T'ito off to identify Chani, who was your uncle Maita, by the way," he added wickedly, "and you not only failed to recognize him but actually killed him, well, I saw other uses for you. And was I wrong about your special skills? Twice you saved Titu Cusi, and the Empire remains whole. Tawantinsuyu is grateful to you, Qori," he said sincerely.

"And Lord Achachi's granddaughter, the aklla who was sacrificed?"

"Oh yes, well, of course everyone visiting Tipón is shadowed. One of my people overheard you approach Achachi about. . . something about a message? Anyway, Sisa made the arrangements through her people in the akllawasi. The girl's death was a warning to Achachi to stay out of this affair."

Yes, and Achachi got your message, I thought. Because of me his granddaughter was selected. No wonder Achachi hesitated to trust me after that.

"Why did Sapaca's men - or, Sisa's men rather - attack us at the Temple of Wiraqocha?"

"They were watching to see if you'd lead them to Kontor. I knew you'd succeed where others failed." He looked at me affectionately. "Kontor was the last witness. Sisa always wanted you and your brother dead, but I made her wait all those years knowing you would yet deliver our quarry, and I was right." Atoq glowed in a self-satisfied grin.

"But, she insisted that once Kontor was spotted her men would take care of him, and you also. Of course I knew they could never harm you, not my Inca Moon, and as I anticipated you took care of everyone, her men and Kontor, leaving no bothersome witnesses."

He gave me that proud, fatherly smile again.

I lifted my kero and took another long draught, regarding him silently. He mocked and praised me in the same breath, admitted his complicity in killing my father, marrying me to my brother, and using me to kill my uncle and everyone else in his way, and through it all he seemed to expect me to appreciate his cleverness. There's more than love-struck devotion driving him, I realized. Atoq has moved beyond reason and decency. Or is he playing me right now for another reason?

Atoq watched my features working with obvious enjoyment. He saluted me with his kero and took a deep drink.

The sound of sliding rocks and a grunt came from the next compound, followed an instant later by metal hitting stone, and something else. I sat rigid, a tingling racing down my spine, my senses probing the night, but my eyes never left Atoq.

He gave me a smile empty of warmth. "I'm afraid that was the sound of your brother being separated from his head. Tintaya is very good with an axe. You didn't think I'd come here alone, did you?"

I stared at the crumbling wall behind which Qhari was stationed. No, I thought, we didn't expect you to come alone.

Atoq continued smugly. "I've only been sitting here passing the time until Tintaya finished. And now, poor Qori, it is your turn to meet your ancestors." He rose and drained his kero in one gulp. "Tintaya," he called.

Qhari stepped through a jagged hole in the wall, an axe in one hand and Tintaya's head in the other. He said not a word but threw the head at Atoq's feet. Then he circled behind him, axe poised. I stood, setting my feet apart, heels dug in.

Atoq leaned his head back and laughed, the sound echoing eerily through the hollow city. "Well done!" he said. "Very well done. I should have expected nothing less of you two. Excellent! I applaud you both." Then his features set. "That leaves you. . . and me," he said menacingly.

"Do you really think you can take me, Atoq, Master of Masters?"

He edged closer to his staff leaning against the stone seat. I knew he was formidable with it, and I knew he had other weapons hidden in his clothes.

He's right, I thought, knowing it. There may be two of us, and he's old and with one eye, but he's still the Master of Masters. Qhari won't last an instant against him, and me not much longer. Achachi once said the only way to outwit Atoq is to let Atoq outwit himself. Stall for time.

I motioned for Qhari to back off a few paces. Atoq held the staff ready.

"Did you ever care for Tanta Karwa, even a little?" I asked.

"Yes, in a way," he said as if the two of us were making friendly conversation. "She was convenient, and willing, and I enjoyed her."

"Convenient?"

"I bound her to me in the hope she might lead me to her husband Maita. Both she and her sister - your mother - were most helpful in providing descriptions of their husbands to the man I sent disguised as a bard. Of course, they thought their husbands were dead heroes whose praise would be sung at court. Such pretty young widows they were, and so eager to be 'hosted' at Tipón."

I remembered Tanta Karwa giggling when she confided how Atoq lured her and others to his bed. But the pillow talk yielded him nothing. Tanta Karwa never knew her husband was alive.

"Tanta Karwa was no help in the matter of her husband's whereabouts," Atoq said. "In time I came to realize she knew nothing. But she was of considerable use in the Emperor's service, bringing me bits of information from all the royal houses I arranged for her to visit. So, you see, my efforts with her weren't wasted."

I thought, Is that what we all were to you Atoq, convenient? You measure everyone by their usefulness to your ends - your ends or the Empire's? They're one in the same to you, aren't they? You've lived too long with guile and deceit. Now they've eaten you.

"As for Qolqe Killa, your mother, she almost led me to Sayri when I gave her leave to undertake her pilgrimage to Pachakamaq. But, the inept spy I sent to follow her lost the trail in Zangalla, and then went north to Pachakamaq never suspecting Sayri had taken her south to Ica. It cost him his head. No matter. It took years, but eventually my agents found Sayri."

Lulled by his words and the memories they called forth Qhari and I stood transfixed, piecing together the last of the mysteries surrounding our parents' flight, or so we thought. It was the effect Atoq sought. With these words, and without a twitch of warning, Atoq suddenly whirled on Qhari swinging his staff at full length. The axe flew from Qhari's grip. I seized Eagle Woman and released her stinger, then stopped in mid stride. Atoq froze in his posture like a statue, eyes staring wide. He tried to cough but it came like a gurgle, and then a gush of blood spewed from his mouth splashing the front of his clothes. His staff clattered to the stones. Qhari, holding his smashed arm, edged around to stand at my side. Atoq turned slowly to stare at us in disbelief.

The poison powder from Eagle Woman's quills had its full effect now. Condin Savana said I'd resort to it when my life depended on it. A smear of honey had glued it to the inside of the overturned kero, and as I anticipated Atoq was too crafty to accept the first kero offered to him. He insisted on taking the one held back, much to my relief, and been caught by his own cleverness.

"You killed my father!" Qhari shouted at him.

Atoq stared in surprise at his blood-soaked front, and then his face twisted in pain as the poison ripped through him again. More blood trickled from his mouth. He fixed us with his one good eye. I slipped my hand into Qhari's.

"You still haven't guessed, have you?" Atoq said, a cruel smile turning the corners of his gory mouth. "Did Sayri tell you that you were born early, about seven months after your mother joined him in exile? Yes, I see by your faces he did. You're wondering how I know this? Because the month after your mother slept with me at Tipón she returned saying she was pregnant, but, I wouldn't take her in." A vat of dark blood gushed from his mouth leaving him dripping in the moonlight. He took one staggering step toward us and drew his last breath. "I didn't kill your father. You have."

XXXVI

Being the concluding part of this Twisted Tale, in which all matters are settled. . . almost.

The High Priest of the Sun lifted the red fringe from the outstretched hand of Inti's golden statue, and settled it on the brow of Titu Cusi, declaring Him Son of the Sun and Emperor of Tawantinsuyu. The throng crowded in the courtyard of the Qorikancha bowed as one and performed the much'a to the new demigod, kissing their fingertips toward the Perfect Pattern of All Things. Titu Cusi looked younger than His eighteen years. Already the eager crowds awaiting His appearance in the great square had begun to call Him Wayna Qhapaq - Resplendent Young Lord, a term of endearment He now adopted for His official name. The year of uncertainty ended. The Empire was whole again.

The funeral rites for Thupa Inka finished on the previous day, one year after His death, with a final round of sacrifices in temples throughout the Empire to ease His way. Thupa Inka now rested firmly with the honored ancestors, one part of His soul with the Celestial Couple, another still residing in His mummified body to watch over His lineage and guide the new emperor. He sat with all the previous emperors watching the proceedings from a place of honor, Mama Oqllo dutifully standing at His side in her silver finery.

Achachi, persistently wearing his mangy jaguar pelt even on this occasion, stood solemnly by like a rock preparing to hand over the golden scepter, the royal war club, and the banner of imperial rule. He would stay on for some years, acting as mentor and chief councilor to Wayna Qhapaq until He was old enough to rule on His own.

While the lords and ladies of the royal panaqas came forward in pairs to swear allegiance to the new emperor, priests and priestesses hurried about preparing the next ceremony - the marriage of Wayna Qhapaq to his sister Kusi Rimaq. I stood on tiptoes beside Qhari and his wife, trying to catch a glimpse over the jeweled and feathered crowd. Achachi finished presenting the royal emblems, and then to everyone's surprise he walked straight over to me.

"It is well, Qori," Achachi said, showing me the broad smile etched on every face that day. "And this blessed event is due in no small part to your efforts."

"I'm pleased to have been of service," I said humbly, while thinking to myself he didn't know the half of it. But the fact that Qhari and I were allowed to attend the coronation was a singular mark of royal favor, which had heads nodding and speculating around us.

"And now, Lord," I said gesturing to the line of bare-footed nobles waiting to offer allegiance, "perhaps you'll be kind enough to present to our new sovereign this least of all nobodies, my unworthy brother Qhari."

Qhari balked at this unexpected honor, then glowed when he saw it wasn't a jest.

"Ah yes," Achachi said, "the new Steward of K'allachaka, Qhari Puma. It will be a pleasure." He turned to Qhari. "The Emperor will announce your title in the great square later today, but he wishes to meet you in person to thank you for your efforts on behalf of Tawantinsuyu. Wait here while I make the arrangements."

"And while you're gone, Lord," I said crisply, "I'll keep this common lout in his place." I gave Qhari a disapproving look. Achachi shook his head and caste a sympathetic glance at Qhari, then pushed his way to the Emperor.

"You never told me how you managed it," Qhari said.

"Managed what? Your promotion? If Lord Zapana is foolish enough to recommend a dog dropping like you, then the responsibility falls on his head. Be assured, brother, I did my best to discourage this nonsense."

"And thank you for doing so, sister dear." Qhari gave me a courtly bow, snickering to himself. I sniffed and turned away.

No one missed Atoq. When Qhari and I dug a hiding place for the bodies in the corner of the ruined courtyard at Pikillacta, we were fortunate to uncover the stone lid of a hollow tomb. Atoq and Tintaya now resided with somebody's ancestors, and the rubble of fallen walls covered all trace of the tomb. Atoq simply vanished, though the story was put out that he was engaged on behalf of the Empire elsewhere. Achachi never asked me about Atoq's disappearance, so neither he nor I had to lie about it, though he gave me a respectful look whenever Atoq's name was mentioned. Qhari and I resolved never to speak of that night's work.

After Atoq uttered his last words and collapsed dead, Qhari and I stood motionless in the moonlight holding hands, our heads bowed, both of us too stunned to speak. I wanted to believe Atoq had lied again - he couldn't be our father - but in my heart I sensed the truth. We always knew we were born just seven months after mother arrived on the shores of Mama Qocha, and Tanta Karwa had said she attended Tipón with her sister, and that she, Tanta Karwa, hadn't been the only one to lie with Atoq. Tanta Karwa knew. That's what she meant when, on her deathbed, she asked if my mother had told me about my father, and when I replied that mother was proud of him, thinking she was referring to Sayri, she looked confused. Atoq had turned my mother away. But before Tanta Karwa could explain the surgeon arrived and sent her off to sleep, forever.

While I reflected on this Qhari had turned to me. His eyes told me he accepted the truth of our parentage also, but stubbornly he raised a finger and tapped the turquoise named Sayri on his headband. "This is father," he said.

I nodded. "Sayri of Choqo was my father," I said. We looked at each other, sealing the bargain with our silence.

Atoq is my birth father, I admitted bitterly to myself, but he isn't the father who loved me, who was there for my first steps and my first words, who swept me up in his arms, who watched over my childhood sicknesses, who taught me honor. Sayri of Choqo is my true father.

But I couldn't help wondering if some of Atoq was in me, too. I was an imperial agent - the best. Where had those talents come from? And other troubling thoughts lingered in the recesses of my mind. Atoq was also Q'enti's father. Q'enti and I were half-sisters, joined by blood.

And Zapana? Yes, my half-brother also. Qhari and I had both lain with our own half-brother. Yet somehow I didn't feel the revulsion that gripped me when I realized T'ito was my brother. Zapana was different, distant to me, and I came to know him as a friend first. I knew Qhari felt the same way about him, and we were the only two who knew the truth. Zapana was unaware of it. With a look we agreed to keep Zapana as we had found him. Did Q'enti know the truth of our shared parentage?

With the deaths of Sisa and Atoq our father Sayri was avenged. Qhari and I fulfilled our promise, and father rested peacefully now. He had wanted us to regain our rightful places in the world. Now I was the respected healer of Choqo, and Qhari steward of a royal estate. Father was proud of us. We could feel it. We had come a long way from the sandy shores of Mama Qocha.

Naturally Zapana was suspicious when he returned from hunting Wallpaya's supporters in Antisuyu. His father had vanished, and his archrival Tintaya with him. But Achachi used his influence to have Zapana declared Atoq's legal heir and successor. Zapana would continue to operate the spy web from Tipón, though it was now reduced in power and answerable to Achachi. I wasn't part of this bargain, though my service to the Empire continued. I was free of the Tipón web but I consented to serve Tawantinsuyu through Achachi as his personal agent, with no others above me or between us. Achachi could then call upon Inca Moon should the need arise, but in the meantime the healer Qori Qoyllur would go quietly about her work.

Zapana wasn't at the coronation. He had already secluded himself at Tipón like his father before him. I visited him there once out of loyalty, perhaps to see what might have been had I accepted his offer. We met as equals.

"You came," he said in a noncommittal voice. We stood in the private courtyard where I had so often taken meals with Atoq and Tanta Karwa.

"I wanted to see you."

"Why?" There was no accusing look, no arrogance, not even curiosity. He is closed to me, I realized sadly.

"I came to congratulate you. You won, Zapana. You have it all now: the title of 'Lord,' the recognition of your birthright, and Tipón. I'm happy for you."

He wore a dark red tunic with a black cloak, headband, and sandals, and his only adornments were exquisite but modest gold earspools. Seeing him thus attired, and with those unmistakable facial features, I could have sworn he was Atoq from twenty years earlier.

"I have it all except my father," he said. A moment hung. He knew, but he would never ask. The fulfillment of his dreams came at a price. Had he known the outcome before, would he have continued? I wondered. What he really wanted was his father's love, but he never knew what Atoq had become.

"Has the new Steward of K'allachaka been chosen yet?" I asked, accepting a kero that appeared from nowhere. A servant glided by and vanished noiselessly.

"You've come on your brother's behalf," he said. "I've already recommended Qhari for the post. In truth, he's been running the estate since he arrived. The leaders of my panaqa have agreed. They're going to ask our new emperor to announce it on the coronation day." Zapana regarded me closely. "You look relieved, Qori. Did you think I'd be angry because I was excluded from the Machu Picchu reckoning? Well, I was, but I assume that was Achachi's decision. They tell me a madwoman attacked poor Lady Sisa. I wonder what madwoman that could be?" For the first time he allowed himself the trace of a smile. I shrugged innocently, which broadened his smile. "Qhari was kept away, too," he continued, "Achachi again, I imagine. Well, Qhari and I were close once, and we're still friends. He fought beside me against Lady Chuqui's forces. Why wouldn't I help him?"

I gestured my understanding, while thinking, If you only knew how much you owe him. It was Qhari who removed Tintaya for you.

I looked up at Zapana's handsome face. Heat flushed my cheeks. "And how is it between us, Zapana?"

His features hardened. "Lord Achachi has explained your new role to me. The Tipón web is at your service should you need us, but Inca Moon comes and goes as she pleases. I have no hold over you."

"I meant, how is it between Zapana and Qori?"

Zapana looked away. For an instant I thought he would open to me, but when he turned back that which was in his eyes didn't find voice. Instead he said, "I'm in mourning for my father now. Please leave me, Qori."

Wayna Qhapaq smiled benevolently as Qhari and his wife performed the much'a and stretched themselves before His dais, while Achachi whispered their names to Him. The Emperor spoke their names aloud, then added quietly, "Lord Achachi says you have done me great service, Qhari Puma, and the heads of Capac Panaqa have asked me to confirm you as Steward of K'allachaka. It will be my pleasure. Rise and continue to serve Tawantinsuyu faithfully." Qhari's eyes danced.

Achachi had wanted to present me, but I insisted Qhari take my place. For Qhari it was the final vindication - the son of Sayri being thanked by the Emperor. Besides, royalty were no longer the mystery to me they once had been. Watching Qhari stroke the oval turquoise on his headband and smiling to himself was all the thanks I needed.

"Qori," a voice came gently from behind. I turned to find Sumaq T'ika smiling at me. "Mother Sumaq," I said extending my hands.

"After today you'll have to call me Most Esteemed Mother Sumaq," she said laughing. I feigned surprise.

"Our old Most Esteemed Mother decided to retire," Sumaq said. "She hasn't been well, and the Empress arranged my appointment. I hope I'm worthy of this trust."

"None more so than you, Most Esteemed Mother Sumaq." With Sumaq as ultimate authority over the Cuzco akllawasi, generations of akllas were assured a firm but compassionate hand. . . and I a safe haven should the need arise. However, henceforth I would have to enter the akllawasi by the front entrance, because the new Emperor had already ordered the rear door walled over.

Sumaq blushed. "Well, I shall do my best. And, today I'm also being declared Principal Wife of Illap'a." She beamed, hunching her shoulders in a gesture of disbelief.

Naturally the Most Esteemed Mother of the akllawasi had to be high priestess of something, and since she was already dedicated to Illap'a . . . . . But this was her moment and I thrilled for her, the tears on my cheeks genuine for her happiness. High Priestess of the God of War, Thunder, Rain, Lightning and all celestial phenomena is a position of immense power. In addition to the image of Illap'a in the Qorikancha, there was another temple in Cuzco dedicated solely to this deity where His life-size statue and the litter on which it stood were of pure gold. Attending to her husband's daily needs there allowed Sumaq more freedom to walk the city, and she would be privy to the concerns of warlords and common soldiers alike.

"As if you didn't know all this," Sumaq said with a meaningful look. "How did you arrange it? It's said Mama Oqllo pressed the First Ladies to appoint me."

"Then you must be Her choice, and you deserve it."

"Qori Qoyllur," Sumaq said sternly, "you may be an accomplished fibber, but you've never fooled me. Is it coincidence that the Empress put my name forward the day after you delivered Princess Koka to safety?"

I thought, Mama Oqllo always fulfills her promises, as does Inca Moon. "Coincidence? It must be, Mother. Perhaps a sorceress farted on Her and clouded Her reason." Sumaq dissolved in laughter.

"Oh, and before I forget," Sumaq said, straightening her vestments and returning a dignified gaze to the shocked stares of nobles around us, "there's someone who wishes to see you, in there." She pointed to the shrine of Mama Killa.

I entered the silver-encrusted room to find Princess Koka awaiting me, resplendent in the robes of High Priestess of the Sun. Fitting, I thought. Koka is, in spite of her youth, the most senior royal lady in temple service. This exalted position is the least they can grant her. Her presence will be required at public and court functions, providing her with more freedom than any other priestess in the land. And, as wife of Inti, she's beyond her brother's reach forever.

On this day of her brother's coronation and marriage Koka stayed discreetly out of sight.

"I wanted to thank you once more, Qori Qoyllur," she said taking my arm in sisterly fashion. She seemed older somehow, or perhaps more poised, the awkwardness of youth having been shed like a skin, so that I scarcely recognized the petulant princess of a year before.

"I hope you'll be happy here, my Lady." I began a bow but she raised me.

"No need to bow in private," she chided. "Happy here? Indeed I am." Her eyes sparkled like the Koka of old. "There's no one telling me what to do all the time and there's so much to learn but Sumaq T'ika is helping me and I have new friends and I can see my family whenever I wish, but, oh, listen to me! Yes, Qori, I'm happy here, and I owe it to you. I can never repay you, but if there is ever anything, no matter how great or small. . . if it's in my power, it's yours."

When I left Koka I spied Sumaq's mother, Lady Hilpay, saying farewell to her daughter. It was a stiff parting. The reconciliation Tanta Karwa brought about didn't mean Sumaq liked her mother, she only accepted her. It troubled Sumaq not in the least to be seeing her for the last time. As usual old Cormorant hovered near Lady Hilpay, the two of them preparing to leave quietly for their banishment after the ceremonies. Sumaq didn't know my part in this, but she would have thanked me.

Hilpay had been Sisa's creature, just as Cormorant had been hers, and both betrayed me. Lord Achachi baulked when I stated my terms for entering his service, but in the end he agreed. Calling in many favors, and using all his influence, he managed to have Lady Hilpay sent away on urgent business to a remote province, permanently, never to see Cuzco again.

As for Cormorant, she was appointed high priestess of a mission to the Chuncho. There, as I warned her in the confessional, she would dine on monkey's paws and roast snake to the end of her days, which, among the Chuncho, could be brief. I thought Condin Savana might be amused with her. Perhaps he would take her to the spirit world and leave her there.

I hurried on, glad to see the last of that pair.

Mama Oqllo fussed over Kusi Rimaq's dress like any mother on her daughter's wedding day, the ladies-in-waiting standing back clicking their tongues and dabbing their eyes. Princess Kusi Rimaq, shortly to be Empress Kusi Rimaq, positively beamed. Mama Oqllo and Kusi exchanged a look when they noticed me passing, and Mama Oqllo nodded to Kusi.

"Lady Qori Qoyllur," Kusi said. It was a command. I halted.

With a reassuring nod from her mother, Kusi came forward and took my arm, leading me aside.

"I remember you from when you came to the palace to cure Koka long ago," she said.

I bowed deeply. "It is kind of your Highness to remember," I said, not sure what this was about, but pleased that she thought to even notice me on this auspicious day.

Kusi glanced around before continuing in a lowered voice. "My mother told me what you did for Koka, and I wanted to thank you for Koka, and for myself. Fear not, my brother will never know about your part, but I wanted you to know that I know, and I'm grateful."

I bowed again.

"My brother can be a bit headstrong," she confided, "and the more Koka pushed him away the more he demanded her. I'm afraid mother always indulged him so. But in truth Koka didn't want to be empress, she often told me so, and I. . . well. . . I was born to it. I've always known that."

It wasn't a boast. Though she was but sixteen she carried herself regally and spoke with understanding and compassion beyond her age. Mama Oqllo would be there to guide her for years to come, and Kusi's calm force of presence left no doubt that was what the Empire, and Wayna Qhapaq, needed.

"Beyond question, your Highness, you are the choice of the people and the gods."

"Yes, well, I wasn't my brother's first choice, but He's done a lot of growing-up recently. Lord Achachi provides a good model, and Titu. . . that is, Wayna Qhapaq, listens to him."

I had heard this from Achachi himself, who claimed Wayna Qhapaq had lost the tempestuous nature of His youth and was fast growing into the role of his exalted office. With Achachi, Mama Oqllo, and Kusi Rimaq to guide Him the future of Tawantinsuyu looked secure.

"But," Kusi said, "if you had not helped Koka things might have been different. You made it possible for me to be Empress, and for that I'm eternally grateful."

In truth it hadn't occurred to me that my compassion for Princess

Koka had cleared the way for her sister to realize her aspirations, and the Empire benefited as a result. But, I decided, if the new Empress chooses to be eternally grateful to me, who am I to quibble?

"Your Highness is most kind," I said humbly.

"Not at all. And now I have one more favor to ask of you."

My stomach tightened. More intrigue? I wondered.

"I would like you to join my court as my personal physician." I must have stared at her blankly for she hurried on, "Of course you'll also attend my ladies and their families, and consult on the Emperor's health, and you'll be Lady Qori, and accorded all due respect, I'll see to that."

My mouth tried to work, and as if anticipating objections she said, "My mother thinks this a fine idea, and so does Lord Achachi. In truth, it was Lord Achachi who suggested it, but had I known about you before I would have thought of it myself. Please say yes."

She could have commanded me but she was asking, and offering friendship. It boded well for her rule as Empress.

Achachi suggested this? I thought. That old fox! He just wants me conveniently ensconced at court to spy for him. Well, if I'm going to remain on guard for the Empire there are worse places to practice my craft. Lady Qori? I suppose I can get used to it.

"Your Highness does me great honor. I will be pleased to offer my poor services as your Highness chooses."

"Wonderful! Mother will be so pleased. Lord Achachi tells me you've been much preoccupied with matters vital to the Empire - whatever he means by that - but I'm sure you're tired, so take as much time as you like and join me when you wish. I'll leave instructions for the royal storehouses to be opened for you. Don't be shy in your choices."

She left me muttering my gratitude, and stunned with my good fortune. I was looking to rejoin Qhari and his wife for the wedding ceremony when I saw Lord Sapaca's thick head towering over the crowd, and Q'enti at his side. Both were dressed in mourning. Sapaca looked gravely dignified, and for once didn't have a kero in hand. Q'enti's cheek was masterfully touched with make-up and hardly noticeable at a glance, but the scar would be with her for the rest of her life - the only imperfection on an otherwise flawless face - and the first thing she saw each time she looked in her bronze mirror.

A change had come over Q'enti, too. Exquisite in manners and dress as always, she now affected an innocent, fawn look - an appealing vulnerability, devastatingly charming, as it was meant to be. Whatever dark forces created Q'enti, I knew she was twisted beyond salvation and the calm, innocent exterior she now cultivated only hid her evil depths. But still I was the only one who knew her true nature. To others she was a tragic figure, a young woman marred trying to save her mother, but still beautiful, oh yes, breathtakingly beautiful. The one blemish on otherwise exquisite perfection being the scar I placed for the world to see - my revenge. But men overlooked that, there was so much else to fill the senses, and every man was keenly aware of her presence. None could resist her. How long would it be before she sought her revenge on me for taking her precious mother?

Suddenly, as if hearing my thoughts across the courtyard, Q'enti looked at me with eyes of ice. A mocking grin wavered on her lips. Absently she traced the scar across her cheek. . . .

THE END

SOURCES

INCA MOON was inspired by the
16th and 17th century chronicles of:

Juan de Betánzos   Christoval de Molina
Pedro de Cieza de León   Pedro Pizarro
Bernabè Cobo   Juan Polo de Ondegardo
Garcilaso de la Vega   Pedro Sarmiento de Gamboa
Felipe Guamán Poma de Ayala   Francisco de Xeres
Juan de Santa Cruz Pachacuti-Yamqui Salcamayhua

and the modern works of:

Catherine Allen	Dorothy Menzel
Brian Bauer	Julia Meyerson
Sergio Chávez	Craig Morris
David Dearborn	John Murra
Marlene Dobkin de Rios	Susan Niles
Jorge Flores-Ochoa	Jean-Pierre Protzen
G. Gasparini & L. Margolies	María Rostworoski de Diez Canseco
Regina Harrison	Ann Rowe
John Hemming	John Rowe
John Hyslop	Irene Silverblatt
Catherine Julien	Donald Thompson
Vincent Lee	Margaret Towle
James Lockhart	Gary Urton
Bruce Mannheim	Thomas Zuidema

Author's Note
Fact and Fiction in Inca Moon

*For things that are not known - at least not anymore - and that there is
now no way of finding out about, one has to fall back on imagination.
This is not the same as truth, but neither is it necessarily a falsehood.*
- William Maxwell

The Inca Empire covered all of what today is highland Ecuador, Peru,
Bolivia, northwestern Argentina, and the northern half of Chile. Millions of
subject people lived within this vast domain of deserts, mountains, and jungles connected by over 20,000 kilometers of excellent roads replete with
bridges, rest stations, and an efficient messenger service. Such a remarkable
level of organization has never since been equaled in the Andean world.

Even at the height of empire there were probably no more than a few
hundred thousand Incas, including tribes near Cuzco who became 'Incas by
privilege.' The millions they ruled kept their own customs, religions, dress,
and languages. If this was an enlightened policy it was also enlightened self-
interest, for keeping the subjugated apart made them easier to govern. It also
helped propagate the myth that the Incas alone were divinely chosen to civ-
ilize and rule the Andean world, a notion that justified the conquest of their
neighbors. While Qori Qoyllur was skeptical of revealed religion, she was
enthralled with her people's accomplishments and as guilty as any of Inca
snobbery.

Through archaeology, ethnography, and ethnohistory we are learning
more about the Incas, but the standard sources are still the chroniclers - pri-
marily those Spaniards who wrote during the century following the
European invasion of 1532. They are an odd assortment of priests, bureau-
crats, and soldier-adventurers, each with an agenda and biases. It is not surprising that their accounts often conflict for information was gathered in different places and times, and it is fair to assume that the Incas, being an oral
society, remembered things differently in Cuzco than in the provinces. The
aspirations and prejudices of the Inca informants must also be considered.
Nonetheless, the broad outlines of Inca culture and its major events are rel-

atively secure. Inconsistencies and details will keep scholars arguing for generations, but ambiguities provide fertile ground for the storyteller.

The voices of women are conspicuously absent in the records of the chroniclers, whose accounts derive from Spanish men talking to Inca men. This is not surprising given sixteenth-century European attitudes, but a close reading reveals Inca women were more powerful and independent than the Spaniards cared to recognize. This disparity inspired the creation of our heroine Qori Qoyllur, whose voice finally breaks the silence of centuries.

The Inca language is still spoken by millions today. Foreigners call it Quechua, a term first used twenty-five years after the Spanish arrived. Whether 'Quechua' refers to an ethnic group who lived northwest of Cuzco, or is derived from a term referring to those who dwell in warm valleys is unknown. Today its speakers call it Runasimi - Human Speech, and if the Incas had a word for their language it may well have been this one. The Incas ruled a polyglot empire in which the nobles spoke several languages, but Runasimi was the language of government. Ironically, it is the Spanish who fostered today's widespread use of Runasimi. Confused by the welter of local languages in their new domain, the Spanish declared Runasimi in the north and Aymara in the south as the official native tongues for commerce and Christian instruction. Local languages eventually disappeared in favor of these lingua francas, and today village folk from northern Ecuador to southern Peru speak Runasimi, and Aymara in Bolivia and northern Chile.

The Runasimi of today is not standard. It is a living language, and in the centuries since the Spanish conquest it has developed several dialects with distinct pronunciations and word meanings. Since the Incas did not have a written language the European conquerors did their best to render it in the Spanish of the day, but sixteenth century Spanish was fluid, and scribes were coping with foreign sounds. Today, Runasimi has adopted an alphabet, but the dialect spoken in Cuzco is different from that used a few hundred kilometers away at Ayacucho. This raises the question of which spellings to follow for Inca names and places; sixteenth century Spanish or one of the modern native dialects? In this work of fiction I have placed my readers first, choosing spellings with flavor that are most pronounceable in English regardless of their source.

The most contentious issue in Inca studies is the proper use and interpretation of the chroniclers. Historicists maintain that in spite of inconsistencies and legendary content, a valid history of the Incas can be drawn from early Spanish writers. But structuralists are adamant that Inca oral traditions are not histories in the European sense, rather, they reflect Andean aspirations within a system so alien to Europeans that it was completely misinterpreted. The debate over whether there was one emperor or two ruling at any given time illustrates these positions. Historicists point out that no chronicler, whether Spanish or Mestizo, ever stated there were two concurrent emperors. Structuralists argue that given the Andean propensity for complimentary dualism, which among the Incas even divided society into the sayas of hanan and hurin, there must have been two emperors to maintain balance, but the concept of dual rulers was too foreign to the chroniclers who wrote for European audiences.

In Inca Moon I have tried to reconcile these positions by suggesting the royal lineages of Hurincuzco elected a couple as 'Speakers' (the fictional Lord Sapaca and Lady Sisa) who were consulted by the emperor and empress (the historical Thupa Inka and Mama Oqllo of Hanancuzco). Historicists and structuralists will find a glimmer of plausibility in this speculation, though it is entirely a fiction of this book.

Another fiction is the imperial spy network of Lord Atoq at Tipón. The Incas used spies frequently - indeed, a state as vast and complex as theirs demanded it - and there are many accounts of spies disguised as traders, military spies, double agents, civilian spies among colonists, and even certain ethnic groups who supplied spies to the Incas. Special inspectors called 'tokoyrikoq' (literally, 'he who sees all') who turned up unannounced in far flung places could be considered another form of spy. Yet for all this spying there is no evidence of a formalized 'secret service' using code names or specializing in disguise and unorthodox fighting methods. But it was fun to write.

References in this novel to people's ages are for convenience. The Incas did not count a person's age in years, but in grades of five to ten year durations. Also for simplicity, I have referred to the cardinal directions as we know them. The Incas did not have words for north, south, east, or west.

They referred to where the sun rose and set, or to a named place on the landscape. Thus, if one stood in Cuzco, north was in the direction of Quito and south lay toward Lake Titiqaqa.

The precise boundaries of the four suyus are not known. Some scholars envision Antisuyu as a tiny area immediately east of Cuzco inhabited by ancestors of the historic Campa, Wachipaeri, and Caravaya. This was certainly true in the early years of the empire. But Antisuyu may have become a generic term for all lands east of the mountains stretching far to the north and south of Cuzco. We are told the Paytiti River marked the eastern boundary of Antisuyu, but where is the Paytiti? Some guess it is the Río Madre de Dios, or another large river due east of Cuzco. However, the only river bearing this name today is in northeastern Bolivia. The tribal name 'Chuncho' appears to be a general term for 'wild people of the jungle.' Qori's path in Antisuyu is left intentionally vague, and the Chuncho she encountered are not based on a historic tribe but represent a widespread life-way in the Amazonian lowlands.

What is real in Inca Moon? Religious beliefs and ceremonies, laws, customs, marriage traditions, dress, and the organization of Tawantinsuyu are as described by the chroniclers. The burial towers of Sillustani, the Temple of Wiraqocha at Raqch'i, the ruins of Pikillacta, the terraces of Tipòn, and all places mentioned are real and may be visited today. According to the chroniclers Thupa Inka died at Chinchero, and the subsequent coups against his heir took place much as described in Inca Moon. What the chroniclers didn't know is that Qori Qoyllur always saved the day.

The principal characters in this book, including Qhari Puma, Tanta Karwa, Sumaq T'ika, Zapana, Atoq, Tintaya, Sisa, and Q'enti are entirely imagined. The emperors and empresses, princes and princesses, together with such figures as Achachi, Condin Savana, Tupac Amaru, and Wallpaya are drawn from the chroniclers.

The story of the mad queen, Chinbo Mama Caua, who suffered from seizures and tried to roast her child, and the tale of Princess Koka escaping to the akllawasi to avoid marrying her brother, were borrowed from the Native chroniclers Guaman Poma and Pachacuti-Yamqui. Scholars may challenge the historical accuracy or structural meaning of such accounts, but to the storyteller they are products of Andean minds and as such allow possibility.

In other instances I have combined stories from different sources. There are several versions of the Inca origin myth, elements of which appear together in the rendition told to Qori in the akllawasi. In such cases my intent has been to capture flavor rather than list ingredients.

For all that is known about the Incas much continues to elude us. The introductory quote from William Maxwell reminds the reader that gaps in knowledge must be filled by imagination, and though this is not the same as truth, informed imagination (imagination operating within the bounds of a given context) is not necessarily false. Thus, vacancies in the record are filled with reasonable possibilities. An example in Inca Moon is the akllawasi, that most Inca of institutions. They did exist and, according to the chroniclers, the selection process and eventual fates of the girls were much as Qori described them (though no akllawasi ever had a back door - a fiction introduced here for the sake of plot). But an akllawasi, which the Spanish quite naturally called a convent, was a world of women forbidden to men. Since our information derives from Spanish men talking to Inca men, how can we know precisely what went on inside? We cannot, and this is where informed imagination comes into play. Qori's adoption into Ayllu Añawarqe, and the use of cotton sails on Lake Titiqaqa, are other examples of 'reasonable possibility' in Inca Moon.

The tinku, or ritual battle, is still practiced in various forms by Andean villagers. We know that the Incas in Cuzco also held an annual tinku, but reports are sketchy. The tinku that Qori participated in, and the mallki or ancestor tree celebrations, were inspired by ethnographic accounts. The Incas would instantly recognize the significance of these events even if they did not perform them in exactly the same way.

There is a covenant between readers and writers of historical fiction. The reader trusts the author to convey the flavor of time and place within a plausible story, and the author trusts the reader not to confuse novels with history books.

Patrick Carmichael